The
LAST THING
YOU
SURRENDER

ALSO BY LEONARD PITTS, JR.

Grant Park
Freeman
Before I Forget
Forward from This Moment
Becoming Dad

The
LAST THING
YOU
SURRENDER

Leonard Pitts, Jr.

BOLDEN

AN **AGATE** IMPRINT

CHICAGO

First printing: February 2019

Printed in the United States of America

10 9 8 7 6 5 4 3 2 1   19 20 21 22 23 24

ISBN-13: 978-1-57284-245-8
ISBN-10: 1-57284-245-8
eISBN-13: 978-1-57284-824-5
eISBN-10: 1-57284-824-3

Bolden Books is an imprint of Agate Publishing. Agate books are available in bulk at discount prices. Single copies are available prepaid direct from the publisher. To learn more, visit agatepublishing.com.

In loving memory of Dad and Mom,
Corporal Leonard G. Pitts, United States Army (1924–1975)
and Mrs. Agnes R. Pitts (1926–1988)

Though he slay me, yet will I trust in him
—Job 13:15

I'm lookin' funny in my eyes and I believe I'm fixin' to die
I know I was born to die but I hate to leave my children cryin'
—from "Fixin' to Die" by Bukka White

one

HE WAS DREAMING OF HOME WHEN THE EXPLOSION CAME.

He came awake in midair, flailing about as the blast, solid as a fist, reverberated around him. He just had time to register what had shoved him off his rack before he landed like a cinder block six feet below, his hip taking the blow, his head cracking against the steel deck.

For a very long moment, Marine Private George Simon could do nothing but lie there, hands cradling his skull. Was he awake? Or was he still curled up on his rack sound asleep and all of this just a very bad dream?

His answer was a bugle call that erupted from the loudspeaker overhead, sharp notes clanging off the bulkhead. This was real. All hell was breaking loose.

"General quarters! General quarters! This is not a drill! Man your battle stations!"

It blared from the same loudspeaker, the voice taut and anxious. Both hatches of the berthing compartment housing the marine guard were closed, but from the other side of the bulkhead, George heard feet rushing by, men shouting, feet clambering up the ladder that connected the third deck to the second and on up to the antiaircraft guns topside, others scrambling down the passageway toward the barbette shielding the number four turret, where they would make their way to the powder handling room and up through the turret to man the big 14-inch guns.

His head chiming like a bell, George tried to push up off the deck and spring to his feet. A bolt of pain lanced through his right hip, and he went right back down, screaming.

Oh God, oh God, oh God. It *hurt.* Something was wrong. His leg would not support his weight. He was helpless, lying on the deck of an

1

otherwise empty compartment in the stern of the ship. Did anyone even know he was here?

Stop it, George! Get moving!

He got his arms beneath him again and pushed up. Bracing himself with his left arm, he hooked his right over the railing of a bottom bunk. He levered himself up, swung his left arm onto the railing, and pulled himself up, his good leg pushing against the deck. The other leg scraped along after him, his pelvis sending up new signal flares of pain with each inch gained.

George ignored it. He sucked in a deep breath, gritted his teeth, and hauled himself up into the bottom rack. There he lay on his side, facing the bulkhead, trying not to lose consciousness. The compartment swam. His stomach was in his throat, and he felt darkness sinking down upon him. He blinked his eyes and wiped at something trickling on his temple. His fingers came away shining red.

Before he could process this, the loudspeaker screamed again. "General quarters! General quarters! This is no drill, goddamn it! This is the real thing!"

The words galvanized him. It was not just the urgency of the message but also the use of such unprofessional language over the ship's PA. That, more than anything, told him how serious the situation topside must be.

Were there bombers? An enemy fleet? One thing was for sure, though. It had to be the Japs. It could only be the Japs.

From the passageway on the other side of the bulkhead, George heard a fresh scuffling of feet rushing by. He called out to them, but his cry was lost in another detonation, an explosion so vast the great ship seemed to shudder.

"Help me!" he cried. "Somebody help me!"

George listened for a response without much hope of actually receiving one. Even if the hatch had been open, he doubted anyone could have heard him through the cacophony that had abruptly shredded the quiet Sunday morning. And now there didn't even seem to be anyone out there. The passageway had gone silent.

All at once, George felt the deck turning beneath him. At first he didn't believe it, refused to believe it. He told himself it was just the nausea, just the vertigo that kept trying to sweep him into darkness, and he waited for it to pass. It didn't. The ship rolled again until he felt gravity tugging him, gently but unmistakably, toward the bulkhead. There came a ghostly sound of metal groaning.

It was not his imagination. The ship was listing hard to port. He was still registering this when another explosion lifted him off his rack. Yet another followed hard after that. George hooked his arm through the railing of the rack to keep from being pulled toward the bulkhead. Bad leg or not, he had to get out of here.

The racks were in stacks of three and rows of two throughout the compartment. George reached out and caught the railing of the rack across from him and two levels up. He gripped it firmly with one hand, then the other, and used the railing like a chin-up bar to pull himself out of the lower bunk and climb up. George got his left leg beneath him, reached back and, with his hand, lifted his useless right leg until it was clear of the bottom bunk. The limb was a dead thing hanging off him, and there was no chance of putting weight on it. George would have to hop, leaning on bulkheads and lockers for support, dragging the leg painfully behind, hoping he ran into someone who could help. Most of the men would be at their stations by now, minus those who had spent the night ashore and were at this moment waking up with throbbing hangovers to find themselves behind bars for some half-remembered revelry, or in the warm beds of Hotel Street prostitutes, or otherwise blissfully unaware of what was transpiring at Pearl just a few miles away.

"Man your battle stations!" cried the loudspeaker again. "This is no shit! This is the real thing!"

No kidding, thought George as he hopped toward the hatch on his good foot. The progress he made was barely worth the name. Each hop cost him pain, forced him to pause and breathe through gritted teeth. It took him an hour to reach the hatch. Or at least, that was how it felt. The hatch had not been dogged—the door had not been sealed to hold it in place—so bracing himself, he was able to pull it open with one hand. The passageway was as empty as he had feared. The ladder was just around the corner, just a few feet away. It was then that George realized a new problem. How could he get over the coaming—the raised section at the bottom of the hatch opening—without putting weight on his dead leg? Obviously, he couldn't just step over it as he had done a thousand times without thinking. Nor could he hop over it; the coaming was too high, the top of the opening too low.

George was pondering this when he felt the ship turn again beneath him. And from somewhere not far distant, he heard a sound that filled his mouth with ashes. It was the rush of water.

"N-Need some help here!" he cried, with more hope than expectation. "Anybody here?"

There came no reply. How many men had even returned to the ship last night? They'd been at sea on maneuvers until Friday, and the men who had liberty had greeted the return to Honolulu eagerly, looking forward to getting laid, getting drunk, or, in the case of a few, spending the evening smiling dopily into the eyes of local girls who had stolen their hearts. George himself had gone ashore but only for a few hours. He'd had beers with a couple fellows he was friendly with. On the street outside the bar, they had tried to cajole him into joining them in a cab ride down to Hotel Street and had laughed when he declined, even though they had known he would.

"Can you imagine Reverend George here with some pretty blonde whore?" crowed Swifty. His Brooklyn accent rendered "whore" with two syllables—"whoo-er."

"Nah," agreed Babe, as he flipped open his Ronson to light the cigarette bobbing in his lips. "Definitely not the Reverend's style," he added, blowing out smoke.

George had laughed, but laughing felt like duty, like something he had to do so the fellas would think he was a good sport. Truth to tell, he hated it when they called him "Reverend" or "Saint," which they did often. It was a strange thing, he thought: if you asked them, probably the vast majority of the men on the ship would have told you they believed in God. Most even went to services, if only occasionally. But if you acted like that belief really meant anything, they treated you like you were not quite right, like some nancy boy with a screw loose.

And Lord help you if you made the mistake of admitting that you were a virgin, that you were saving yourself. They snickered or made jokes, guffawed at you while your cheeks burned and you tried to smile, grateful when they finally changed the subject. What could you do but take it? So he had made himself grin as Swifty widened his eyes, let his face go slack, and spoke in a rube's voice that was meant to be George. "Duh . . . I-I-I don't kn-kn-know, Miss. I d-d-don't think what you're d-d-doing is allowed in the B-B-B-Bible."

George had a stammer when he was excited. He'd had it since he was a kid. "All right, you guys," he'd said through the same tolerant smile. "Cut it out."

Babe had clapped him on the back. "Ah, you know we're just kiddin' with you, Rev."

"Yeah, Rev," said Swifty, lighting up a smoke and shaking out the match. "You go on and catch yourself a movie. Us sinners are going to see what we can do about finding something to dip our wicks into. Pray for us, why don't ya?" He made the sign of the cross with the hand holding the burned-out match, then flipped it into the gutter and burst out laughing. They had parted company there. Babe and Swifty had hailed a cab, and he had walked a couple blocks to a movie house that was showing Abbott and Costello in *Keep 'Em Flying*. It had been a warm evening—all the evenings here were warm—and the streets were crowded with swabbies and marines on shore leave walking in boisterous groups, Christmas shoppers balancing their bags and leading their children. Bright blinking lights in primary colors were strung around windows and doorways. A light breeze had rustled the palm fronds high above.

Had they made it back to the ship? And if so, had they managed to escape when the attack came? Or were they trapped down here just like him? George shook the thought off. What was the sense of wondering? If they were trapped, there was nothing he could do about it. Remembering Babe and Swifty, George found himself thinking idly (and not for the first time) how much Father would hate it if he knew George's pals in Honolulu were a Polack and a dago. This, even though Father himself had come over as a boy. *Stick to the white guys*, Father would have advised—meaning the guys without funny-sounding names and the stink of greenhorn all over them.

Of course, Father hated that he was in Honolulu as a marine in the first place and, worse, that he had enlisted as a lowly grunt. "Allow me to at least arrange a berth for you in Officer Candidate School," John Simon had said once he finally, reluctantly, accepted that George would not be shaken from his determination to join the Corps right out of high school. It had been a tempting offer. George knew it would be easier to spend his hitch giving orders than taking them. But how would that look? He had already been raised with every privilege that wealth and station could bestow. But he was a man now, and he was striving to be a *moral* man. Otherwise, he might as well have gone to college and then applied to law school as Father had planned. He could join Father's firm, take it over when Father retired, amass a fortune, enjoy the admiration of lesser men and women, live a comfortable life. But the problem was, it was more important to George to be the sort of man who did the right thing, not for honor or gain, but simply because it was the right thing. And joining the Corps as an enlisted man, among other common men—he had felt in the pit of his stomach that this was the right thing. A war was coming. He had known that, too, in the pit of his stomach. People told him he was wrong. "We'll stay out of this one," Father had intoned sagely. "We got our fill of helping Europe last time. This time, we'll let them figure it out for themselves. You'll see."

George didn't buy it. Nor did he buy Lindbergh's "America First" isolationism or Roosevelt's promises that American boys would not be fighting in "foreign wars." How could America stand to the side with Hitler gobbling up Europe and the Japanese rampaging in China? Sooner or later, his country would have to take a stand. And when the fighting started, when they came to pull poor boys out of tenements and farms and sent them out to hazard their lives in defense of their country, why should he be excused—or given some cushy job—just because he was a rich man's son? What kind of Christian would that make him? What kind of man? No, George Simon was a *moral* man. And he needed very much to prove himself to himself.

So this time, he had not bent to Father's will. He would not wait, and he would not hide behind some officer's desk, either. George Simon would ante up. He would sign up to be a marine—yes, Father, a lowly grunt, no better or worse than any other lowly grunt. It was, he had realized with a start, the first time he had made an important decision about his own life and stuck to it. It had felt good.

And perhaps God had heard that thought and decided to underscore it. Because it was in that instant that George saw seawater rising toward him from the port side of the ship. His heart took a painful leap in his chest. He was running out of time.

With that realization fueling him, he reached through the opening, grabbed the piping that ran along the overhead, and pulled. Thus braced, he was able to lift his good leg clear of the coaming—like chinups again—and set it down in the passageway. Still holding the piping with his left hand, he reached back with his right and drew the injured leg through the hatch, snarling from the pain and trying not to think how much additional damage he was doing to himself.

"Piece of cake," he told himself, aloud. His voice sounded strained in his own ears. Bracing himself against the passageway, George paused to catch his breath before hopping to the ladder. He tried not to think of how he would haul himself up to the next deck. *One problem at a time*, he told himself.

And then the world exploded. The ship was hit again—and then yet again, two cataclysmic blasts that lifted the vessel and George with it, tossing him back through the hatch into the compartment he had just escaped. And there it was again, that sensation of flying helplessly through the air. But this time, his flailing hand managed to snag something—the rim of the hatch—and this kept him from falling completely ass over tea-kettle to the deck.

George was thanking God for this gift of good fortune when he felt the ship lurch hard toward port. As the deck tilted, gravity seized the hatch door and flung it shut—right on the fingers of George's left hand.

They snapped like pencils. He heard the sound. And he would have reflexively yanked his hand away, except that the closed door prevented this and besides, the same gravity that had closed the door was pushing him against it and he was powerless to resist, to even find enough leverage to pull the hatch off his fingers. Worse, chairs, footlockers, tables—everything that was not secured—were beginning to slide in the same direction. Most of them came to rest against the bulkhead. One of the chairs rolled up against George's feet.

The ship was dying. And he would die with it.

George was embarrassed. What a stupid way to go. Lying there in his skivvies, pinned by his own broken hand inside his own sleeping compartment as his ship keeled over and slipped into the mud at the bottom of the harbor. George told himself he didn't mind dying. When you put on that uniform and took that oath promising to support the Constitution, you accepted dying, at least in the abstract. At least as a distant possibility.

But to die like this, helpless, without even having a chance to fight back, was more than he could stand. He would never see Father or Mother again. Would Father be all the angrier with him, for joining the Corps and then dying there? Would Mother keep a picture of him in uniform up on the mantel? Would they maintain his room as some kind of shrine to the son who never came home? He had a brother, Nick, who was 15 and a sister, Cora, 14. What would they think of him? How would they remember him?

And then there was his fiancée, Sylvia Osborn.

George and Sylvia had practically grown up together, their families living next door to each other for as long as George could remember. Everyone always said they made a gorgeous couple. He was a shade less than six feet, with blonde hair, blue eyes, and a dimpled smile for which he was complimented regularly, but which George thought made him look perpetually 15. And Sylvia was simply a knockout, with a movie-star figure and bright hair that fell in glossy waves to her shoulders.

According to the letters she sent him two or three times a week, she and his mother were even now busy planning the wedding, fine-tuning the menu with the caterer, compiling the guest list, auditioning the band, having the dress made. He was supposed to return home on leave in June. They had planned to be married then.

Sylvia, George was painfully aware, could have had her pick of eligible young men from all the right families. Her family, it was said, traced to the *Mayflower* itself—no vestige of greenhorn tainted *her* blood. She was all American, pure as snow. Mother and Father—especially Father—had always counted it something of a miracle that such a girl would want to marry George. After all, Johan Simek—Father had changed it to the more American-sounding John Simon as soon as he could—had arrived in this country from the Austro-Hungarian Empire only in 1895, a penniless boy with nothing but his smarts and his willingness to work hard, and those things had made him wealthy. As Father saw it, for his oldest child to marry someone like Sylvia was to place a capstone on his own achievement. It meant they were officially no longer a family of immigrants, but full-fledged Americans. Marrying Sylvia was like marrying respectability.

"Only in America is such a thing possible," Father was fond of saying, his voice colored by wonder. But to George, it felt like duty. Not that this was something he could ever have told his father. Joining the Marines without Father's blessing was one thing. Refusing to marry Sylvia Osborn would have been quite another. It would not have made a difference to Father—indeed, it would never have occurred to him to care—that George wasn't at all sure that he loved her. Indeed, he found the idea of spending the rest of his life talking about galas, cotillions, and Paris fashions (the only subjects, a far as he could tell, about which Sylvia had either interest or knowledge) to be a fate, if not worse than death, then perilously close. But that no longer mattered. The marriage would not happen now. George lay helplessly on the deck, the gravity of the listing ship pushing him absurdly against the hatch of his sleeping quarters. He would die here. They wouldn't even be able to retrieve his body.

Sorry, Father. Sorry to let you down.

George was conscious of feeling sorry for himself, but he couldn't help it. It was all so terribly unfair. Ten minutes ago, he had been in his rack, drifting in the blissful unaware. And in moments, without warning, he had been yanked from that to this. As if to emphasize his miserable condition, water began trickling over the coaming, entering the compartment through the gap made by George's broken fingers. He had to close his eyes and purse his lips against the saltwater tang.

He decided to pray. What else was left? He was at the end, wasn't he? Time to accept that. Time to make his peace with God. George closed his eyes. He tried to think past the agony in his hand, the pain in his hip, tried to center himself and think of the right words, words appropriate for a final plea to God, a fitting summation of his 19 years. He wanted large, selfless words that encompassed his imperfections and his love, words that expressed his hopes for his family, words wise and brave enough for a moment such as this. But all he came up with was, *I don't want to die. Help me, God. Help me, God.*

The saltwater across his face was now a steady flow.

"Is it somebody in there?"

George didn't answer. Why bother? Why give cruel fate that final satisfaction? He hadn't heard anything. Obviously, desperation and wishful thinking had combined to put a voice where there was none. But then the voice that wasn't there spoke again.

"Who in there? You all right? Need to get off the ship!"

Something vibrated in George's chest. He lifted his head above the splash of water.

"I-I . . ."

George had occasionally been frustrated by his stammer, but he had never hated it until this very moment. The words needed yelling, needed outcry. Instead, they were sealed in the vault of his thoughts, and he could not pick the lock.

"I-I n-n-n . . . "

"You in there? You need to get out of here!"

"*I need help!*"

Finally the vault came open and the words broke free. Then he couldn't stop the flow. "B-broke something when I fell out of my rack. Then the hatch slammed on my fingers and the ship listed and jammed me up against the door and I can't get myself free. Stupid mistake. I've been lying here . . . "

"Okay, okay," said the voice on the other side. "I'm going to get you out of there."

"Yes!" cried George. "Yes! Thank God you showed up! Thank God!"

"Don't thank him yet," said the voice on the other side. "This might hurt some."

Before George could ask what "this" was, he felt the hatch pushing against him. The man on the other side had put his shoulder to it. It wasn't easy. The listing of the ship meant that he had to push uphill, and the man's feet kept slipping in the rising water. But slowly the hatch came open until George was able to pull his hand free.

Paradoxically, once it was no longer pinned by the hatch, his hand hurt worse, pulsing with an insistent throb that made George growl low in his throat. His hand was a mess. His fingers were crooked, his skin had turned a ghastly white, and the palm had swollen till it resembled a child's catcher's mitt.

But George had no time to lament his injury. The hatch was still pushing, driving him back, his busted hip sending up new bulletins of pain. And as the door came open, the seawater rose, drifting lazily into the compartment under a film the color of rainbows. There was oil and hydraulic fluid in the water. The ship was bleeding. George was processing this when the lights gave a zapping sound, flickered a couple times, and then went out. The emergency auxiliary lights came on, painting the compartment in an eerie pallor.

"Oh shit," said the man on the other side of the hatch. "Got to get out of here."

For a crazy moment, George thought the man was about to abandon him, save his own skin. And who could blame him if he did? Instead, the man wedged himself into the frame of the hatch, got his foot up against it, and pushed, grunting with the exertion of moving George's weight uphill, until he was able to step through. Gravity closed the hatch again. The man knelt and George got his first good look at him.

To George's surprise, he was a hulking colored guy, one of the boys who served up chow and swabbed the enlisted men's mess. George's mind fumbled for his name.

"Gordy?" he said. He made it a question because he wasn't sure. He'd always had trouble telling the colored messboys apart, and truthfully, there'd never been much need to worry about it. One was as good as another when all you needed them for was another scoop of scrambled eggs or a refill on the coffee.

The dark face above him split into a grin of recognition that told George he'd gotten the name right. "Mr. George? How you get yourself in this kind of predicament?"

"Busted my hip real good when I fell out of my rack. Broke my hand in that door when the ship started listing. Truth to t-tell, I thought I was done for. I'm darn lucky you came along."

The Negro put a hand under George's left armpit, another under his right elbow, and helped him lift himself upright.

"Ship's keeling over to port," he explained. "Got to get you up the ladder quick. Ain't got much time." He draped George's right arm over his own neck and braced George around the waist.

Then Gordy pulled the hatch open. More water came in, covering George's bare feet. Gordy helped him get his leg over the coaming. The ladder was to the right, down a passageway too narrow for two men, side by side. They turned sideways, Gordy leading and George following as best he could with his cripple's hop and skip. Their progress was torturous.

"I'm s-s-slowing you down," said George. He felt guilty.

Gordy stopped and turned toward him, though George could not see his face in the shadows. "Yeah, that's right," he said. "You think maybe I ought to leave you here and just go on by myself?"

George was stunned at first. Then he felt himself smiling. He had been ready to belly flop into his own self-pity and this Negro he barely knew had called him on it. George was amused despite himself. "Okay," he said, "I can take a hint."

"All right then," said Gordy in a voice that seemed to hide a chuckle of satisfaction. "Let's go."

The ladder was around a corner only a few feet away, but it was slow going. Water sloshed about their calves. It was hard to keep balanced, braced against one another as they were, the deck tilting crazily, turning the journey toward the ladder on the starboard side into an uphill climb. Gordy was huffing with the exertion. He was virtually dragging George, and with his right leg useless and left hand mangled, George could do precious little to help.

He renewed the prayer.

Help us, Lord. Please.

The ship moaned as it died, a soft keening that seemed to come from all directions at once. George knew it was only metal creaking as pressure changed, as bolts snapped, as things came apart, but there was something about it that made him sad for the old ship. Her dying moans were like the sound of lonely ghosts at midnight.

"Hate that sound," said Gordy as if reading his mind.

"You and me b-b-both," said George.

Finally, they reached the ladder, and Gordy paused there a moment, contemplating it. George saw what he saw. It was too narrow. There was no way Gordy could help him up to the next deck. The Negro turned toward George, his face a blue half-moon, bathed in the emergency lights. "I'm gon' have to carry you," he said.

"I'm sorry," said George, knowing it was a stupid thing to say, unable to help himself.

Gordy shrugged. "What else we gon' do?"

He released George's waist and reached to lift him. Right at that instant, with a sudden heaving motion, the ship turned fully on its side. Unbraced, unbalanced, unable to stop themselves, both men went sliding helplessly down the suddenly vertical corridor, dropping back through the passageway, dropping through where it widened into an open area, dropping along with tables, chairs, desks, and all manner of smaller detritus, toward the port side of the ship. George's head smacked into a bulkhead as he fell, and he splashed into a pool of water that had been a compartment just minutes before. It was not unlike a basketball hitting the rim and dropping neatly through the hoop. The world went away.

He awoke some unknown fragment of time later in a darkness studded with flashing stars. A foulness of oil and hydraulic fluid filled his mouth, and he heard a bowling ball grumbling down the middle of his skull. George felt himself turning without direction in that liquid abyss, too injured and spent to command what was left of his own body. But that didn't bother him. Nothing did anymore. In spite of the pain, in spite of the helplessness, he felt a warmth. He was almost content.

Then, from the darkness above, a hand grabbed his arm. Or at least, it tried. George was so slimy with engine fluids his arm just slipped out of the hand's grip. But the hand in the darkness was insistent. It tried again, this time grabbing the neck of his t-shirt and pulling until George's head was clear of the water.

"Come on, goddamn it!" Gordy's voice snarled out of the darkness. "You got one good leg and one good hand, ain't you? You gon' make me do all the fuckin' work? Help me here!"

The venom of the tirade brought George's eyes open. In the gloom, he saw a figure perched on the bulkhead above the water. "That's better," said Gordy. "Now come on, I can't hold you all day!"

George didn't want to. He wanted to lie there in the warmth and contentment of the abyss. He would have been perfectly happy to do so. But he knew that would disappoint Gordy. And somehow, after all they had gone through in the few short minutes of their acquaintance, it was important to him not to let the Negro down.

So George made himself move. As Gordy pulled at him, he reached with his good hand, grabbed the bulkhead, and hauled himself up out of the water. The metal was slippery in his grip and he felt his hand sliding free, but he caught something protruding from the wall—a mailbox, a pipe, a faucet, he would never know—and crooked his arm around it, drawing himself further up. His good leg scrabbled for purchase in the murk below. It found something solid—he would never know what this was, either—and he pushed against it. The water was rising almost as fast as he was. Within moments, it would engulf their position. Then he was up, and Gordy was hauling him out of the water, and he was lying on a floor that had been a bulkhead not even 10 minutes ago, gagging up foul seawater.

"We got to hurry," said Gordy, drawing George upright. "She ain't done with us yet. She gon' turn turtle, I think."

With a dawning horror, George realized the messboy was right. He could feel the ship still moving, turning beneath him as she sought her final resting place at the bottom of the harbor. She would not stop until she was completely upside down. Worse, the deck they'd had to struggle to walk across was now a sheer, featureless cliff towering over them. It would have been impossible for two uninjured men to climb.

"What are we going to do?" George asked. "How are we going to get up there?"

The Negro was silent for a very long moment. George waited for him to admit their helplessness, to concede the fact of their defeat. For some perverse reason he couldn't name, he was looking forward to hearing the other man say there was nothing they could do but await the inevitable.

Gordy said, "Can't climb the deck."

George said, "Nope."

"But I could probably climb the overhead."

And this, George realized, was right. What had been the ceiling was a tangle of pipes, girders, and braces. It offered plenty of handholds.

"What about me?" said George. "I c-can't c-climb."

"I can carry you."

"That's c-c-crazy. You n-n-need to just go on without me."

Gordy sighed in frustration. "Okay, I will," he said.

George knew the colored man was challenging him again, daring him again to give up. And Lord, he wanted to. He was exhausted, he was nauseous, and he felt tectonic plates grinding together in his skull. Worse, his injured body felt as if it would never be right again. He began to hate the Negro for not understanding this and leaving him be. But George knew he could not honorably give up hope while another man was fighting to save both their lives. And he knew Gordy knew it, too.

George sighed. "So, we're going to climb the overhead."

"Yeah. We can climb back to the ladder, take that up to the top deck."

"No," said George. "The ship is on its s-side, remember? That deck you're talking about is underwater now. We've g-got to go down a level. Harbor ain't that deep. Bottom of the ship might still have air. In any case, it's going to be the last part to flood. Maybe a rescue crew will cut through the hull. We get down there, maybe we can signal them, let them know we're there."

"Then that's what we do," said Gordy.

"Yes," said George. "That's what we do." He forced himself upright. The water was to his shins.

Gordy knelt and George lifted his bad leg until he was straddling

Gordy's broad, powerful back. He wrapped his arms around Gordy's neck, piggyback style, locking one slippery, oil-slicked hand as best he could around one slippery, oil-slicked wrist. The Negro braced his hands under George's thighs, and George almost screamed from the pain in his hip.

"You okay?" asked Gordy.

"Yeah," said George, lying. Then, to change the subject, he said, "A-a-are you sure you c-c-can handle my weight?"

Gordy said, "I don't know. Why don't you climb on and we find out?"

George said, "But I'm already—" Then he got it. "Oh," he said.

Laughing, Gordy straightened up. "How much you figure you weigh, Mr. George? Hundred fifty, maybe?"

"A little more," said George.

"No problem," said Gordy. He found a foothold, a beam that had stretched across the overhead. He found a handhold, a bracket holding a sheaf of pipes. He put a foot on the one, gripped the other, and pushed and pulled the weight of two men up the overhead of the passageway. He reached behind, braced his burden, searched out another handhold, pushed and pulled again. Gordy snarled with each exertion, as if locked in some private battle with the wall that had been a ceiling, as if one or the other would be defeated here and Gordy had determined it would not be him. George concentrated on the task of keeping his hand from sliding off his wrist while also not choking his benefactor. He didn't speak to the other man. All the breath Gordy had, he needed for climbing. But George found himself wondering how much of the Negro's bravado had been for his, George's, benefit. This was useless, wasn't it? Surely, he didn't really think he could climb, with George on his back, all the way up to the starboard side of the ship.

The ship had a beam—a width at its widest point—of more than 95 feet. Thankfully, they were not at its widest point. Rather, they were astern of the number four turret, where the ship tapered. And while the beam measurement was from hull to hull, port to starboard, they were only going from a compartment at one end of a passageway to the ladder at the other end. So with all of that in mind, the distance they were climbing was maybe only . . . what? Forty-five feet? Fifty at the most?

Still too far.

One man climbing through the half-lit darkness using makeshift footholds and handholds with another man's deadweight carcass on his back? George was seized by a sudden certainty: they were not going to make it.

As if to prove the point, Gordy grunted heavily and then stopped. He lowered his head. His breathing was labored.

"Are you all right?" asked George.

"Just need to rest a sec," said Gordy.

They were, George saw, barely a quarter of the way up the wall.

No, they were never going to make it.

And this wasn't right.

That certainty seized George, too. How could he allow this boy to give up his life this way? Without George's weight, he'd at least have a chance. Not a good chance, but a chance. How could George be so selfish as to doom them both? He didn't want to die. Heck, he was only 19. He had barely begun to live. But neither did he want to be responsible for getting another man killed because he, George, didn't have the guts to make the necessary sacrifice. It wouldn't be difficult. Already, he was having trouble keeping his grip. How hard would it be to simply allow his right hand to slide from his left wrist, to just let go and fall back into the water from which Gordy had plucked him? The boy probably wouldn't even know it was suicide; he would probably think George had only lost his hold. And yes, the Lord frowned on taking your own life. But surely, he would forgive if it were done for a noble cause, done as a way to save the life of someone else.

Besides, George was so tired.

His hand slipped. Just an infinitesimal fraction, really, skin sliding against skin, his body finalizing the decision his mind had all but made.

It was in that pregnant instant that the ship turned yet again, turned one final time. Loose furniture clattered about them, seawater came churning toward them.

George heard Gordy yell, "Hold on!"

And then, with a lurch, they were fully over. What had been a ceiling and become a wall was now a floor, and both men were underwater, the sea rushing over them. Sputtering and gasping, George reached up with his right hand and caught the ring of metal in the center of an open hatch door. With an angry roar of effort, he pulled himself upright. Seawater came to his waist.

"Mr. George, is that you?" This cry came from a dark shape ahead of him.

"Yeah," he said, breathlessly.

"Thought I lost you!"

"No such luck! But at least the climbing is over!"

"Yeah, but the drowning gon' begin real soon, we don't get to that ladder."

They grabbed each other by the forearm. Gordy pulled. Both men's hands were slick, and they had to dig into each other's skin to keep a hold. Even then, they had to constantly readjust their grips. But at least it was easier than climbing. Gordy trudged with single-mindedness toward the ladder, and George allowed himself to float along behind him in the water like a balloon after a child some sunny day in Bienville Square back home.

What good times he'd had there. His father's office was on the second floor of a building overlooking the square. As a child, he had spent many happy moments standing on a balcony encircled by lacy curlicues of metal railing, watching people move back and forth across that block of city greenery. All kinds of people, doing all kinds of things—sailors, businessmen, secretaries having lunch, shoppers leading their children, young couples stealing secret kisses in the shadow of the stone cross erected in honor of the city's founder.

Escaping into the sanctuary of memory, George pushed automatically against the bulkheads with his good leg to propel himself through the water. It wasn't until he bumped his head on the deck above him that he realized how high the water had become. The passageway was almost completely flooded. With a sudden stab of fear, George realized he could no longer see the shadow ahead of him.

Where was Gordy? Was Gordy even alive? He felt a forearm still clasped in his greasy hand, but there seemed to be no strength in the other man's grip. George lifted his head above the water, spluttering. "G-Gordy?" he called.

Then, he felt himself yanked forward, hard. The bulkhead on his left turned, and he knew they had reached a corner. And then, they were on the ladder. Gordy was two steps above him, George still lying in the water that lapped around his waist.

"Goddamn," wheezed Gordy. And George, who ordinarily didn't like people taking the Lord's name in vain, could only nod, wearily. As exhausted as he was, he knew Gordy must be even more so. For a few minutes, they sat there in silence, just breathing. Just breathing was enough.

How close George had come to giving up. For the most noble of reasons, yes, but giving up all the same. Now, sitting here on the ladder, the immediate crisis having passed, but relatively safe if not at all out of danger, he felt the memory of that near surrender, that fractional slippage of his right hand from his left wrist, shamed him. He was a white man, yet a humble messboy, black as the ace of spades, had taught him a lesson in courage and resourcefulness.

"What you laughing at, Mr. George?"

And George realized the thought had caused him to chuckle aloud.

"Nothing," he said. The seawater was just below his breastbone.

"You figure it's the Japs done this?" asked Gordy.

"Yeah," said George. "Who else?"

Gordy spat. "Slanty-eyed bastards," he said. "They gon' be singin' a different tune when we get our licks in." His voice brimmed with righteous heat.

George shrugged without much enthusiasm. "Yeah," he said. "I guess they will." He was surprised by his own lack of anger toward the Japs. He knew what he should feel, but he didn't feel it. He had no rage. He had no thought of future retribution. Maybe those would come later. But for now, everything he had, all the presence he could muster, was concentrated in this moment on this ladder of this upturned ship.

Gordy spat again, as if in comment on George's lack of venom. He stood. "Come on, Mr. George," he said. "Got to get movin'. Water comin' up."

Gordy took George on his back again and climbed the ladder up to the bottom of the ship. There, they wandered for long moments through the gloam of empty compartments, past upturned lockers and overturned desks, past abandoned shoes and copies of *Life* magazine. George was stunned. In less than 20 minutes, a vessel of the US Navy, a warship thrumming with power, purpose, and life, had been reduced to this dead thing, this twilight world of half-light and shadows where everything you once knew, the world you had worked and lived and moved through without a second thought had become . . . unknown, a maze of passageways and dark shapes suddenly unrecognizable and foreboding.

He didn't know where he was. He didn't know which way to go.

Gordy lowered George slowly, till he was standing on the tangle of pipes that had once run overhead. Water was already lapping at their shoes. Like George, Gordy seemed afflicted with a sudden sense of dislocation. Like George, he scanned the darkness with a kind of ominous wonder.

The realization descended upon George like a shroud even as he spoke it. "We're trapped," he said.

"Yeah," said Gordy. "I expect we are."

Then there was light in their eyes. "Where did you guys come from?" demanded a voice from the shadows beyond.

It made George jump, startled to find life in this dead place. "Marine guard," he said, squinting against the light. "Third deck."

The other man chuckled. "Damn if you gyrenes don't look almost human in your underwear," he said.

"Yeah," said George, glad for the familiar rhythms of interservice rivalry. "And trust a swabbie not to have enough sense to get the light out of a man's eyes."

"Oh," said the other man, belatedly lowering the battle lantern. "Sorry about that."

The beam fell on George's hip and the man gasped. George followed the man's gaze. The water had rendered George's skivvies nearly translucent, so it was easy to see what the other man saw—that George's hip had become a lump the color of sunset. "What happened to him?" he asked, turning the light toward Gordy. This was the first time he had acknowledged Gordy's presence, but he didn't wait for an answer, turning the light back to George. "What happened to you?"

"Fell off my rack," said George.

"Must have been one hell of a fall."

George shrugged. "Have you seen anyone else?"

"There's a few of us down here," he said, "some in the lucky bag." This was the ship's lost and found. "Some more in the radio room. And then there's a group of us in steering aft. I'm headed back there now. Why don't you follow me?"

"Lead on," said George.

It took them just a few moments, wending their way through the passageways of the stricken ship. At the hatch to the steering aft section, the man paused. He lifted a wrench that had been braced against the hatch and used it to clang three times hard on the metal. After a moment, there was a sloshing of water on the other side, and the hatch opened to admit them.

"Who's this?" asked the face on the other side.

The sailor with the battle lantern shrugged. "Found them wandering around out there. They come from third deck."

As he helped lift George over the coaming and into water almost waist-high, the second man spoke to his friend. "You find any food wandering out there? Maybe some drinkable water? Or beer? Beer would be even better."

"Afraid not," the man with the battle lantern said.

Braced by Gordy, George shuffled forward. He felt 95 years old.

The steering aft compartment was broad at the forward bulkhead, tapering as you went aft. Spilled across what had been its overhead and sticking up out of the water was an assortment of gear bins, bunks, and weight-lifting equipment. Running the length of the compartment was the ship's primary steering shaft. A secondary, nonelectric shaft, operated by four wooden steering wheels, was just starboard of the main shaft. It depended from what was now the ceiling.

It took them a few minutes to get George over the primary shaft. Gordy clambered atop a set of lockers leaning precariously against the structure. The man with the battle lantern and the one who had opened the hatch lifted George up to him. Gordy slipped him over the massive shaft and down to the men on the other side. George concentrated on not screaming. He no longer felt 95. He felt like a sack of potatoes. He felt useless.

Gordy lowered himself from the shaft. The water he dropped into was only ankle-deep. The ship had come to rest at an angle. The three men had entered on the low end where the water was deepest. "You had flooding?" asked George as a couple of men lowered him gently to a makeshift bed—a mattress from one of the bunks laid across an overturned bank of lockers.

"Came in through a vent," one of them explained. "But we got it fixed now."

As his eyes adjusted to the gloom, George realized that there were seven men trapped in there—10 now, as he, Gordy, and the sailor with the battle lantern came among them. The other men watched the two newcomers with neither welcome nor hostility, but rather with a grim neutrality, based, George instinctively realized, on a mathematical equation both obvious and ominous: more bodies equals less air.

"What happened to him?" one of the other sailors asked as the sailor with the battle lantern clambered over the shaft and joined them.

The man with the battle lantern said, "Seems he fell out of bed when the shit hit the fan."

"Broke something," said George. "Got trapped in my compartment. I'm George, by the way." He nodded toward the messboy. "This here is Gordy. He found me. He saved my life."

Another sailor said, "What's it like down there, George?"

"Flooded," said George. "Completely. Anybody else make it out from there?"

The other man shook his head. "You're the first I've seen," he said. Then he looked at the man who had brought George among them. "Better turn that light off," he said. "Save the batteries."

George said, "What do we do now?"

The man said, "We wait."

And the light went out.

Time passed with a sluggishness that felt almost willful.

There were men still trapped in the adjacent sections. Every now and again, you heard them yelling over to assure you they were still there, wanting to know if you were still there too, still waiting just like them. At one point, one of the sailors went to the booth containing a sound-powered phone—similar booths were dispersed throughout the ship—and reported that he heard the voices of other trapped men. Some were in the radio room, some were in the turret. You could hear them yelling all over the ship, trying to locate one another.

After a while, the voices died away.

There was nothing for the men to do but talk, which they did softly, together, in twos and threes. They talked about what they would do when they got out of here. They talked about what they would do to the first Jap they got their hands on. After the first few hours, they began to talk about drinkable water. They pictured it clear and cool and clean, unlike the polluted sludge of seawater and motor fluids that pooled at their ankles. George's throat felt stiff and dry as parchment. He and the man with the light talked off and on as the minutes piled up. George learned his girl's name, his baseball team, his favorite food.

About the man who had saved his life, George learned nothing. Gordy sat there, a shadow among the shadows. He didn't speak. He barely moved. As the other man talked, George found his attention pulled away, found himself glancing at the shape that sat there above him, near enough to touch, yet remote as the moon. He wondered what might be going on inside that woolly head. Such things, he supposed, were not for white men to ever know. What white man could ever hope to pierce the veil that separated the sons of Europe from those of Africa? The very idea that it could be pierced was too foolish for thinking.

And yet, this boy had saved him from a watery grave, carried him on his back while scaling a sheer wall. When George had been ready to give up, the boy had rebuked him, mocked him, made him climb out of the wallow of his own self-pity, stand up, and strive like a man is supposed to do.

So it seemed a shame, seemed fundamentally . . . unfair somehow that, having done all this, Gordy should be relegated to this non-status. George didn't even know the boy's full name. How could someone save your life and you didn't even know who he was?

George spoke without knowing he was going to, cutting off the sailor sitting on his right, who had been making an impassioned case for chicken chow mein. "What do you think, Gordy?" he asked. The Negro looked over. "What do you think?" repeated George. "What's your favorite food? You like chow mein? I'm a steak man myself."

Gordy appeared to give this some thought. Then he shrugged and spoke without inflection. "They both all right by me, I suppose." And he turned back to contemplating whatever it was he had been contemplating before. The reply was not curt, not precisely. Nor was it exactly impolite. Yet, George was still left with an unmistakable sense that it drew closed a curtain he had been caught trying to peer through. He did not have to see the man on his right to know he was staring at George with incredulity. And the conversation about food stuttered into silence.

Time crawled like a snail on a garden path.

Occasionally, a man hammered a wrench against a bulkhead, a signal to any rescuers who might be searching for them. No answer came.

Was anybody looking? Did anyone even know they were there?

A sudden thought struck George like a fist. Perhaps the Japanese, having attacked the fleet, had destroyed all the air cover and landed ground forces. Perhaps columns of the emperor's troops were even now fighting their way up Waiauau Avenue, house by house, setting up machine gun emplacements in backyards, kicking in the front doors of helpless women and children. Though he was lying there in hot, moist darkness, the thought made him shiver as if someone had dumped snow down his collar. He reproached himself for thinking it. He promised himself he wouldn't think it again. But he couldn't stop.

Finally, he had no choice. He had to share the fear. He tried to do it obliquely. "What do you think is going on out there?" he asked the darkness.

"Best not to think about it," said a voice.

"I'll tell you what's going on," said another voice. "Bet our guys are giving the Japs what for, that's what's going on."

"Best not to think about it," said the first voice again, harder. And George knew the owner of that voice shared his own fear.

Time creaked along like an old man with a cane.

George tried to estimate how long they had been there. He lay in a world bereft of visual cues, with no sense of darkness or light, movement or sound, no sign of what was going on out in the real world, just a few feet away, just on the other side of a sheet of armored steel. Might as well have been on the moon.

The attack had come . . . when? About 0800, he supposed. It had taken maybe half an hour for him and Gordy to make their way here. And he had been lying here . . . what? Two hours? Four? Six?

No, he had been lying here forever. He had always lain here. He always would.

George gave up. He closed his eyes into a fitful sleep.

He awoke to the dull clank of metal on metal. "What's that?" he asked.

"The man just bangin' on the bulkhead with that there wrench," said Gordy's voice above him. "Hopin' they somebody out there to hear him. Same as it's been." The Negro's voice was raspy with fatigue.

"Oh," said George.

"Go back to sleep, Mr. George. Rest that hip."

George had almost forgotten his hip. The shattered joint had settled into a dull, thudding ache so familiar that it required an effort of will to remember he had not always hurt like this. His hand throbbed like a tooth. It felt heavy and large.

Obediently, George closed his eyes.

"How you guys doing in there?"

Again his eyes came open—he had no idea how much later it was—but this was not the voice of salvation.

"We're okay," someone called.

"Where are you?"

"We're in steering aft. How about you?"

"Lucky bag," the voice said.

"They'll be coming for us soon."

"Any minute now."

The voices fell silent.

Time stopped moving.

It froze like a lake in winter.

It stood motionless like a statue.

It sat still as midnight.

Time stopped moving and the very idea that it had ever moved came to seem like fiction, a fairy tale, a lie you told children, like Santa Claus and the Tooth Fairy, a thing you said to keep them from knowing the true nature of life, the essential cruelty and hardness of it. Time stopped moving. The minute was, the minute was, the minute was. Unending.

George's stomach gnawed at itself, hunger grinding in his gut like a living thing. And the thirst was even worse. George felt as if he were made of sand. His tongue was a foreign body, a strange thing so swollen he could not close his lips over it. As a result, his mouth hung open, tongue poking through like a turtle peeking out of its shell. He would never be able to drink enough water to quench this. There was not enough water in all the world to make him feel like himself again.

The air was stale and close, smelling of sweat and armpits and piss, of desperation and fear, and it went in and out of you without enriching or renewing. It was just something to breathe, something you took in because you had no choice—you had to breathe something. But this was a useless something, a rank, musty something that made your lungs ache. It was like trying to breathe a blanket.

George closed his eyes. Some amount of frozen time intervened. He opened them. And he wondered where he was and why he was suffering like this.

He remembered after a moment, but his thoughts were slow. They seemed to drop from his mind like water from a leaky faucet. That is, they didn't flow as thoughts and water usually do. Rather, with a maddening, unconnected individuality, they gathered themselves at the rim of thereness and awareness, swelled heavily, then fell and broke.

I'm still here.

I think I'm still here.

So hungry I could eat . . . anything.

Thirsty. God.

How long has it been?

Gordy saved my life. A Negro. A Negro saved my life . . .

Father, I'm sorry. Mother, I'm sorry. Sylvia . . .

Am I dying?

That one stopped him. It shook him. He went back to contemplate it.

Am I dying?

He thought maybe he was.

And he thought of home. Bienville Square would be girdled with lights now, toy trains circling their tracks in department-store windows, baby dolls with blonde curls watching with unseeing eyes, a Norman Rockwell Santa Claus with cheeks like apples beaming from a sign above as he hoisted a bottle of Coca-Cola to his lips, people below singing "Joy to the World" with a lustiness that made you believe it, made you think it a real and immediate thing, if only for the few moments they were singing the song. Joy to the world. And Heaven and nature sing.

When he was a child, how little George Simon had loved coming down to Bienville Square at Christmas. How he wished he were there right now.

"We've got to get out of here."

George opened his eyes (he hadn't realized he had closed them) upon a different kind of darkness, the waking darkness that had become his world. He wasn't sure he had heard the voice at first, but then it spoke again. "We're going to suffocate if we stay in here. We're running out of air."

"But where can we go?" Another voice.

"We can get to the tiller room from here. That hatch there."

The light came on, playing across a hatch on the aft end of the compartment. Now the darkness was alive with the cross talk.

"What if it's flooded?"

"It's probably not flooded. No reason to believe it is."

"But what if it is?"

Silence.

"If it is, we let the water in here. There's a good chance we drown."

"But if we stay here, we're guaranteed to suffocate."

Silence.

"Hell of a choice."

"Yeah."

"Me, I figure if I'm going to die anyway, might as well get it over with."

"Yeah."

"What do you guys want to do?"

"Me? I want to wake up between Rita Hayworth's tits and hear her tell me, 'Shush, baby. You're just having a bad dream.'"

There was laughter. Somebody said, "Yeah, you and me both, buddy."

"Yeah, but really: What do you guys want to do?"

"Let's put it to a vote."

They voted to open the hatch. The light beam followed as two of them moved aft on the canted overhead to the hatch. George watched with bleary eyes and morbid fascination, bracing himself to be swept away in a sudden rush of seawater, helpless to save himself, his life given to the surging ocean. He tried again to pray, failed again to pray anything equal to the moment.

God, I don't want to die.

They got the hatch open. Water did not rush through.

"Air," someone said.

And the compartment rang with weak and relieved laughter.

Most of the men rushed into the new compartment.

Gordy and another man stayed behind to help George. With the light from the tiller room shining on them, the sailor on the high side of the deck draped George's left arm around his neck, while Gordy, on the low side, did the same with George's right arm. Together, they lifted him and began the journey across the compartment.

"I appreciate this, fellas," said George.

"Well, you know how it is," said the man on George's left. "One way or another, Navy's always got to bail the jarheads out."

They laughed. "Guess I'm about as useless as tits on a bull," said George.

"No, sir," said Gordy, deadpan. "Tits on a bull at least be interesting to look at."

There was a surprised beat of silence. Then laughter rang again.

No one would ever know what it was that caused Gordy to lose his footing. It might have been a loose barbell. It might have been an abandoned peacoat. It might have been the oily water they were slogging through. It might have been anything.

All they knew was that one instant, they were laughing and the next, Gordy was gone, sliding sideways down the overhead, his arms flailing, his hands gripping only air. He struck the steering shaft headfirst with a sickening crunch, then dropped into the water below. He didn't even have time to scream.

An open-mouthed moment. A moment when no one breathed.

Then someone said, "Oh, shit!" and two men scrambled from the tiller room. They picked their way carefully down the incline, the light beam playing over the black water under the shaft. George watched, his mouth still open, his breathing stilled, his thoughts blasted, atomized, down to a single word.

No.

No no no no.

It couldn't be. It wasn't.

The Negro had saved George's life. He had done the impossible and made George do it, too. They had overcome everything the ship could throw at them. How could he just slip and fall? How could that be?

The men searched the water for long moments, shoving aside a desk, a mattress, a filing cabinet. Finally, one of them yelled, "Here he is!" And they hauled Gordy's limp form by his dirty apron up the incline to where the water was shallow. His head hung crookedly from his neck. Blood and oil smeared his face.

"Is he all right?" When nobody answered him, George yelled it. "Is he all right?"

One of the men had his fingers on Gordy's neck. With a grimace, he put an ear to Gordy's chest. He lay there a long moment, listening. When he lifted his head, he shook it once, slowly. The sailor was looking directly at George when he spoke.

"He's dead," he said.

two

WHEN GEORGE'S EYES CAME OPEN, A LITTLE BOY WAS STARING at him over the back of the train seat in front of him, brown eyes wide, tousled brown forelock falling haphazardly over his forehead. The child— probably not five years old yet—said nothing, just watched George with an unblinking intensity accessible only to the very young.

In the five days of travel that had taken him from Oahu to San Francisco to this railroad bridge on the Gulf Coast east of New Orleans, George had become used to being stared at. In his new service uniform, he supposed it was something he ought to expect. He wished he'd had a chance to buy some civvies—all his clothing, not to mention his other belongings, now resided at the bottom of Pearl Harbor—before they piled him into that transport headed for the mainland. But things had happened too fast.

As a result, here he was in uniform, enduring yet another pair of staring eyes. But being gawked at wasn't the worst of it. No, the worst of it was that when they saw George coming, hobbling on crutches, his right leg and left hand encased in casts, people stumbled over themselves to hail cabs for him, buy meals for him. Two men even got into an argument over who would carry his bags even though the only bag he had was the small shaving kit he'd managed to pick up before he left Hawaii, and it fit quite easily under his arm.

"Were you at Pearl?" they would ask. And when he couldn't lie, when he had to admit that he had, indeed, been there, their eyes would soften.

"God bless you, son," a woman with snowy hair said, touching his forearm.

"We're going to get those Jap bastards aren't we?" asked a boy with freckles.

"I bet it was hell out there," said a man, lifting a cigar from his mouth. It was as if they needed something from him, something they didn't even know how to voice. Reassurance, perhaps. The promise of a happy ending. The world had shifted around them, the comforting and familiar certainties of their lives had come crashing down like a chandelier from a high ceiling and then, here he came, a US marine in a crisp new uniform, and whatever it was they needed, they seemed to take just from the sight of him—indeed, the very fact of him.

George tried to be patient with this, but it still made him uncomfortable, like he was some kind of fraud putting one over on those who didn't know any better. Their admiring eyes trailed him through crowded train stations like he was Sergeant York and Captain America put together, but he wasn't. He was only a guy who had injured himself falling out of bed and was now traveling in the name of a silly publicity stunt. Of course, he couldn't explain that to people; he had learned to just ignore it as best he could.

So George tried to buy the little boy off with a smile. When the child's expression didn't change, George sighed and escaped by closing his eyes again. He listened to metal singing against metal, giving himself to the gently rocking motion of the train car as it thundered across Louisiana toward the morning sun. Something about it all seemed ludicrous. Two weeks ago, when he was trapped in that drowning ship trying to breathe that unbreathable air, if you had told him he would be here two weeks later, he would have laughed and waved you off like some phantasm of a dying mind.

And yet, here he was.

They had emerged from the tiller room at 1600 Monday afternoon, rescued by a crew of men who literally had cut a path to them through the hull, through an emergency fuel oil tank, through a void space, through steering aft (which had to be pumped out because by then it was full of water), and finally into the tiller room where George and the eight other survivors were huddled.

Thirty-two hours they had been trapped in the ship. Almost a day and a half. When they lifted George up onto the upturned hull through the rectangular hole with blankets draped over its rough edges, he could not help gasping at what he saw. The water was still burning. Dirty, oil-smudged men wandered about the dock. The great ships canted at obscene angles, towers of black smoke rising from mangled superstructures. The air reeked of burning oil and rubber, of blood and death.

"My God," he whispered. He looked to the sailor who was bracing him. "How bad did we get hit?" he asked.

The man told him *Nevada* was beached.

And *California* was sinking.

And *West Virginia* was sunk.

And *Utah* was sunk.

And *Arizona* was gone.

Each name was like a nail pounded into his chest. "How many men?" asked George.

The sailor shrugged. "Hundreds, maybe. Maybe thousands."

"My God," George said again.

"Yeah," said the sailor. "Agree with you there." And he handed George off to two other men, who helped lower him into the waiting barge.

It was six days later that George abruptly awoke staring up at the netless orange rim of a basketball hoop. This had been his waking view ever since he got out of surgery. Overrun with casualties, the hospital at Hospital Point had sent him and dozens of other wounded here to this row of beds set up in a high school gym to recover.

At first, he didn't know what had sundered his nap. He hoped it wasn't the nurse—"the USS Hortense," they called her behind her back, because she had the build and all the warmth of a battleship. Barely 24 hours after surgery, that evil woman had forced him to get out of bed and start walking on crutches. He couldn't even hold the left crutch; he'd had to figure out a way to brace it with his bad hand. But the USS Hortense had been about as moved by his difficulties as a real battleship might have been, and he had shuffled gamely down the row of beds and back. They had done this every day since. His body ached from the ordeal.

"Glad to see you're awake, marine."

The voice brought George's head up sharply from the pillow. What he saw jolted him. Sitting in a chair at his bedside, the silver oak leaf insignias winking on his shoulders, was a lieutenant colonel he didn't know. Standing behind him, hands crossed behind his back, was a man wearing the stripes of a sergeant major. George could not begin to guess what had brought so much rank to his bedside. He could not decide whether to be alarmed or terrified.

"Sir," he said. "Yes, sir."

"I'm Lieutenant Colonel Reeves," said the seated man. He jabbed a thumb toward the other man. "This here is Sergeant Major Stevens."

"Sir, yes sir."

"They treating you okay?" Reeves's hair was a bristly wedge the color of rain clouds. "You getting enough chow?"

"Sir, yes sir."

"I understand you're going to be all right?"

"Yes, sir. They say I can expect a full recovery."

"Kind of an odd thing, isn't it, for a boy your age to break his hip? That's usually something that happens to folks a little older, isn't it?"

"Yes, sir. Doctor said it was a freak thing. He called it a pathological fracture, said I had a cyst on the bone. Apparently, it had been there a long time. I guess the bone was already weak."

"So how long do they figure before you're back at full strength?"

"Four to six months, sir."

Reeves glanced meaningfully at Stevens. Then Reeves said, "Tell us about your escape from the ship."

"Sir?"

"I hear there was a Negro boy, carried you out of a flooded deck on his back? Didn't make it out himself?"

"Yes, sir. I only knew his last name. Gordy."

"Eric Gordy," said Reeves. "Messman 3rd Class Eric Lamont Gordy, to be exact. I hear you think he's some kind of hero."

"Yes, sir, I guess I do." George had told the story of Gordy's heroism to a number of men on the ward. He'd kept a colored orderly from his rounds for almost an hour talking about what Gordy had done.

"Why?" asked Reeves.

So George told it all again, how Gordy wouldn't let him give up, how the Negro rescued him from the flooded compartment when George fell in and climbed the vertical deck with George on his back. The two men let him talk without interruption, their eyes never leaving his. When George was finished, Reeves leaned back. "That's a hell of a story, marine."

"Yes, sir."

"You're grateful to this man, I suppose."

"Yes, sir."

"So here's the thing," said Reeves. He was lighting up a Lucky Strike.

"You're not going to be able to do any fighting anytime soon, but what if there were a way you could still serve your country? Would you be interested in hearing about that?"

"Sir, I'm not sure what you mean, sir."

Reeves squinted through cigarette smoke, appraising George. Finally he said, "Morale is a weapon in war, marine. Especially in a free society. Keeping the public's spirits up is just as important as making sure our fighting men have enough bullets and planes. Do you believe that?"

"I suppose so, sir."

George wasn't sure he believed it at all. He wasn't even sure he understood it.

"You suppose so." Reeves smirked behind the mask of blue smoke. Apparently, this was not the answer he had been looking for. "Tell you what," he said, "how about you take my word for it, son? How about that?"

"Sir, yes sir."

Reeves nodded. "Now, given that morale is so important, I'm sure you would be eager to do your part to protect it."

"Sir, yes sir."

"So here's what we want you to do, private. We want you to pay a courtesy call on Gordy's wife—his widow now, I suppose. And afterward, we want you to do an interview together with her for the local paper. If that works the way we think it might, the next step will be to send the two of you on a tour around the country to a few key cities to do interviews with other papers, maybe a few radio stations, maybe give talks at some colored churches. We want you to tell your story to every colored face you can. And when you do it, really play up the part about this boy saving your life."

"And losing his own in the process," added Stevens, speaking up for the first time.

"Exactly," said Reeves, whirling around to point the two fingers with the cigarette at the sergeant.

George was confused. "But why, sir?"

Reeves blew out a frustrated jet of smoke. "Did you hear what I just said about morale, marine? It's a heartwarming story, this darky saving some Southern white boy's ass. Might even make a few white people shed a tear or two."

The sergeant spoke up again. "Colored newspapers have been playing this story up real big. This Gordy fellow is almost as big a hero for them as Dorie Miller. You probably haven't heard about him; he was a messman on the *West Virginia*, hauled the wounded captain out of harm's way, then grabbed a .50-cal. machine gun and knocked down at least one of those Jap sonsabitches. The Negroes seem to think these two boys are the biggest heroes since Joe Louis. Makes them feel good about themselves, I guess."

"Don't you get it?" asked Reeves, through another jet of smoke. "The picture of you going to Gordy's widow, having a few words with her, thanking her for her husband's sacrifice, it could be very valuable for morale, excite the Negroes, make them feel like part of the war effort. Make them rush to the recruiting office."

"Yes, sir."

"This comes straight from the War Department," said Reeves. "You see, we're trying to head off some of the radical-type Negroes who will try to convince the others that this is a white man's war and they have no reason to fight in it. Had that problem in the last war and we don't want to have it again. I mean, let's face it, the Negroes feel like they get a raw deal here. And hell, maybe they got a point, who knows? What I'm telling you is, we need something to overcome that kind of thinking. And we think the story of you and this Gordy fellow could be just the ticket. Hell, they're already getting up a poster of you and him to send out to colored schools and social clubs. They've even got a slogan for this thing." He turned. "What was it again, sergeant?"

"'All Together Now,'" said Stevens.

"Yeah, that's it," said Reeves. "'All Together Now.' We're going to need you to say that as much as you can. Work it into every conversation."

"So when does this all start, sir?"

"Just as soon as we can line up travel to get you back to the States—easier said than done these days, as I'm sure you can imagine."

"I see, sir. And where will I be going?"

Reeves grinned as he stubbed out his cigarette. "Oh, didn't I mention that? That's the best part. Turns out you and this guy were practically neighbors. You're from the same hometown."

"*Mobile?*"

Reeves looked at him. "You got another hometown?" he said.

And so it was, seven days later, that George Simon's train gave a last exhausted sigh of steam as it rolled to a stop at a platform in the Gulf,

Mobile, and Ohio depot on Beauregard Street. George opened his eyes. The little boy was still staring.

With a private shake of his head, George gathered his shaving kit, braced himself with his crutches, and climbed to his feet as best he could. Inevitably, people reached to help. George fended them off as politely as he could, ignored the motherly gazes of compassion, and edged his way down the aisle. The other passengers kept back to allow him to reach the door first. George accepted assistance from a pair of Negro porters who let him lean on them as he swung carefully down from the train. They would not accept his tip.

Moments later, having waved off still more offers of help from other travelers, he bought a copy of the *Mobile Register* at a newsstand, then hobbled through the ornate station, stood beneath the archways out front, and hailed a cab. He gave the driver his address. The man took his crutches, and he climbed awkwardly into the back seat and lifted the paper. The news was the same as it had been ever since Pearl was struck—a litany of the disheartening. The Japs were running wild all over the South Pacific; Wake Island would fall any minute. So would the Philippines. So would Hong Kong. Given how aggressive they were, George still couldn't figure out why the Japs hadn't come ashore at Oahu after devastating the Pacific fleet. Whatever their reason, he considered it a blessing.

After a moment, the paper became depressing and George stopped reading, but he did not put it down. To do that would have invited conversation with the cabbie. George had had his fill of solicitous questions from strangers who had never felt a ship capsizing beneath them or tasted seawater tainted by hydraulic fluid and oil. He had put up with it for almost six thousand miles, and he was exhausted. So he kept the paper up, using it as a shield against unwanted chitchat from the driver. Holding the paper with his right hand, he turned the pages with the exposed fingertips of his left. As he leafed past the national news, he found that Santa Claus seemed to beam from every other page, smiling in cherubic obliviousness as he offered unbeatable prices on enamelware, shoes, and Philco radios. George found it hard to credit the idea that in a nation at war, Santa Claus was still coming to town.

The cab proceeded west from downtown, down broad avenues canopied by trees, past dignified old homes with arched windows, walls dappled by the weak sun of early winter. After 20 minutes, the cab pulled onto a short street just east of the Country Club of Mobile. Mansions ringed by spacious lawns gazed down with quiet indifference. The Simon home was the last one on the street; it sat at the top of a low hill at the end of a driveway that wound up from the road, through a copse of trees where George had played cowboys and Indians as a child, and on up to the portico where the houseman now stood, waiting. He was a trim, gray-haired old Negro named Benjamin Johnston, who, with his wife, Alice, a cook, had been with the Simon family for almost 30 years. The car came to a stop before him, and Benjamin had pulled open the door and was bracing George up out of the seat before the driver could even come around.

"Hi, Benjy," said George. Since he was a child, he had used the nickname to get a rise out of the Negro. The old man always fussed at him for it, always drew himself up stiffly and said with wounded dignity, "You know I prefer Benjamin, Master George."

But this time, Benjamin Johnston seemed not to have even heard him. Indeed, to George's embarrassment, his eyes were welling pools of sorrow as the two men faced one another. "Master George," he said, "Lord have mercy, look at you."

There was something irksome about it. "I'm fine," said George, more sharply than he'd intended. "No need to make a fuss."

"Yes, sir," said Benjamin, taking George's shaving kit from under his arm. "I guess we was all just worried about you."

"I'm fine," repeated George, ready for the subject to be changed. He paid the cabbie.

"George? Is that really you?"

He looked up and saw that his mother had come through the door and was standing under the portico, hands clasped beneath an expression that couldn't quite decide whether George was real or not. Behind her stood Nick and Cora, watching him with unabashed awe. Behind them stood Sylvia. His father was absent, as George had known he would be. It was a Monday. Homecoming or no homecoming, Father would be working at his office on the Square.

"Yes, Mother," he said, "it's me." And he realized only in that instant that he had been dreading this moment, this return to the embrace of family. He had no idea why. How many other men, after enduring what he had, would have turned cartwheels for the chance to be back at home with his family and his girl—and three days before Christmas, yet? But George was suddenly uncomfortably aware that he was not one of them, that he would have been much happier had he been left in peace on that bed on Oahu, waiting for the USS Hortense to sail in and torture him again.

His mother hugged him, pressing her cheek into his chest. He returned the embrace awkwardly. His sister and brother gabbled excitedly and patted his back. He nodded without really hearing them. Sylvia stood slightly apart from them, and seeing the soft uncertainty in her eyes was like a glimpse into his own heart. George was dimly aware of the sound of the taxicab pulling away. He wished he were still in it. Then he rebuked himself for the wish.

Crutching toward the door, he paused in front of Sylvia and, for a moment, didn't know what to say. Then, he swept his lid off his head, bent forward, and kissed her.

"Hey, kiddo," he said.

She took his forearm and gave him a smile in return. "George," she said, "it's so good to have you home."

She looked as if she might say more, but then tears were tumbling from her eyes. They melted George Simon like steam on ice. They left him feeling three feet tall. How could he have wished he wasn't here? What was wrong with him? "Don't cry," he said, feeling helpless.

"Yes, we'll have none of that," agreed Mother. Her own voice was brittle.

George allowed her to lead him inside, through the front hall. The bigness of the house seemed to swallow him after living in the cramped passageways of a battleship. The entrance hall towered over him, the ornate chandelier breaking the sunlight into rainbows that spilled across the portrait of Zachariah Deas, a Mobile cotton broker turned brigadier general in the army of the Confederacy, glaring down from the wall. It was all familiar and yet all unknown, and all too much. George marveled again at the miracle of finding himself here, two weeks after he had found himself lying in rising water at the bottom of a dying ship, trying to compose his final prayer.

In the west parlor to his right, a Christmas tree stood 10 feet tall, with boxes of ornaments and lights scattered about, waiting to be placed. Mother led him into the east parlor. Here, there were no displays of yuletide, but the vast windows offered a dramatic view of the city below. On a clear day, you could see the ships in the bay.

George lowered himself carefully onto the seat of an overstuffed yellow couch, leaning his crutches against it. His family stood around him as if unsure what to say or do next. Then his mother sat and the others followed suit. Benjamin had quietly disappeared, taking George's small bag to his room upstairs. George wondered idly how the old man expected him to get there.

"So, George," said his mother and it was as if she were talking to a new acquaintance, "you have to tell us again what happened. We were all so frightened when we heard the news on the radio. And I'm afraid your wire didn't tell us much beyond, of course, the welcome news that you were alive and coming home."

At their mother's question, Nick, who was sitting across from George, leaned forward, his chin propped in both hands, as if anticipating some great adventure story such as he had read in books. George was irritated. But then, he reminded himself, he probably would have felt the same if he were 15 and had not lived through it. He kept the story as concise, as plain and businesslike, as possible. No sense talking about the fear. Or the smell. Or the ungodly thirst. Or how it felt when time stopped and he and the other men simply existed in the anteroom of death. And certainly no sense telling them about that moment when his hand slid fractionally across his wrist, his body coming to a decision his mind had not yet reached. That was something they didn't need to know. Even he didn't need to know it. Except, of course, he had no choice.

They interrupted him only with the occasional gasp of amazement or to ask him to explain some bit of military jargon. For the most part, they just listened as George plowed through his account, telling himself as he did that it was just another thing he had to get through. He had the unsettling sense that he was a telling a story he was doomed to repeat for the rest of his life.

When he was through, nobody spoke immediately. In the silence, George was surprised to see that a plate of finger sandwiches and a tray with a teapot and cups had appeared on the table in front of him. Alice had delivered them and he hadn't even seen her. It made him think of Eric. He wondered how it was that Negroes learned to be invisible like that.

"My goodness, George," said Mother finally. "It's a miracle you made it back to us."

"Yes, it is," said George.

"I hope you remembered to thank God for it. I certainly did."

"First thing I did when they hauled me out of the ship," said George. "And probably half a dozen times a day since then."

"So tell us again what they want you to do now?"

"It's a morale campaign," said George.

"That's the part I don't understand," said Sylvia. "The military sent you all the way back here just to speak with the widow of this boy that saved your life? This Gordy woman?"

"Yes," he said.

"And they want the two of you to tour the country talking about this?"

"Like I said, it's a morale campaign," said George. "They think it will get the Negroes excited about participating in the war."

"Seems a lot of needless fuss and bother, if you ask me," said Sylvia with an airy laugh. "You would think seeing their country attacked by the godless Japs would be all the motivation the niggers need."

Niggers.

The word stopped him, and at first, he wasn't sure why. How many times had he heard her use it in all the years he had known her? Hundreds? A thousand? And always, she used it just like that, used it the same way his father did, the same way he had used it himself: casually, no heat behind it, no hatred caged up in it, just a simple acknowledgment of self-evident truth.

How many times? Yet he had never heard it. Not once. Just as he had never once seen Eric Gordy when he had been heaping eggs on his tray or offering a refill of his coffee. Just as he hadn't even seen Alice delivering finger sandwiches just now.

The realization wounded him.

He was striving to be a moral man, was he not? Wasn't that what he always said? But what kind of moral man didn't see people when they were right in front of him? What kind of moral man used that word?

The smile on Sylvia's face congealed, and he realized he was staring at her as if she were a stranger. And in some sense, he thought, maybe she was.

"What?" she asked, confused.

"The man saved my life," he heard himself say. "I wouldn't be here if it wasn't for him."

She laughed her breezy laugh again. "I understand that," she said. "And I understand why you're grateful to him. We all are." She looked to

George's mother, who nodded agreement. "All I'm saying," Sylvia continued, "is that it seems a lot for them to ask you to travel the country because of it, trying to convince the niggers to do what they should be happy to do—fight for their country."

Niggers.

There it was again. How, he wondered, had he never heard that before?

Then it struck him. How many times, in the nearly 30 years that Benjy had been part of their household, had he been passing in a hallway or lingering invisibly in a corner and heard one of them—Sylvia, Mother, Father, even George himself—say that word? Say it laughingly. Say it matter-of-factly. Say it with less thought than you'd give to waving at a fly. Surely, Alice had heard it, too. And if George had never quite heard the word being spoken, Alice and Benjy—*Benjamin*, he corrected himself—could hardly have helped hearing it. God, what must they have thought?

George swallowed. "Maybe they don't think it's their country," he told Sylvia.

She laughed yet again. "Of course it's their country, George. What other country could they have? What do you mean?"

He didn't know what he meant. But he meant *something*. Of that much, he was certain. George shook his head vaguely, not sure what to say. He was suddenly uncomfortably aware that something fundamental had changed in him. He didn't quite know what it was. He only knew that he was not the same man he had been when he climbed into his rack on December 6.

Sylvia was still waiting for his reply. George gave a helpless little shrug. Then Mother rescued him.

"Well, Sylvia, you and I may think it's twaddle, but that doesn't really matter. It's what the military wants and we have to believe the military knows best."

"I suppose you're right," said Sylvia, giving George an uncertain look. Then she brightened. "Anyway," she added, touching his knee, "it means we get to see George again, so I, for one, shan't complain."

"Nor shall I," said Mother.

"So," said Sylvia, "when do you plan to go to that woman's house?"

"Her name is Thelma," said George. "Thelma Gordy."

Sylvia regarded him strangely. "Very well," she said. "When are you going to her house?"

"This afternoon," said George. "After I rest up a bit. A photographer and a reporter are meeting me there."

"So soon? You just got here."

George nodded. "No reason to procrastinate," he said.

Mother said, "Would you like me to go with you? Benjamin could take us in the car. I could ask Alice to whip up a cake."

George tried to imagine his mother pulling up before some Negro woman's house on a dirt street in a chauffeured Packard and stepping out bearing cake. His mind could not conjure up the picture.

"That's all right," he said.

"Are you certain?"

"Yes, Mother, I am."

"Besides," said Sylvia, "that's an awful lot of trouble to go through for this woman, don't you think?"

She didn't say "nigger" that time. But then, thought George, she didn't really need to. It was always there whether she spoke it or not.

"Very well," Mother was saying uncertainly. "I'm sure you know what's best."

"But you know what?" said Sylvia brightly. "All this talk of cake gives me a wonderful idea. Why don't we take George to the bakery so he can see the cake we've chosen for the wedding?" She patted his knee again. "It's hideously expensive, darling, but Father is determined to spare no cost. And speaking of expense, I do wish you could see my wedding gown. Main Bocher himself is designing it. You won't know the name, dear, but he designed Wallis Simpson's wedding dress. It was really a coup to get him to accept the commission. I'm supposed to travel to New York for a fitting next month, but with this dratted war, I'm not sure if—" She stopped. "Darling, why are you staring at me so?"

And it was right in that moment that he suddenly knew what was wrong with him, what had been wrong with him ever since they hauled him up out of the carcass of that ship and had only grown worse with each step closer to home. He knew what was wrong, and he suspected that subconsciously, he had known all along.

He was alive. That's what was wrong.

He was alive, he was home, it was Christmas, he was with his family. And Eric Gordy was a waterlogged corpse that would never see burial.

How, he wondered, did God decide such things? How did God say,

You shall live. You whose courage faltered in the moment of test, you who were worthless and scared shall miraculously survive through no virtue of your own. But you who gave the other man the courage he lacked, who carried him on your back when he could not carry himself will come to the very edge of survival and then be snatched from life by a meaningless, freakish accident.

The man had slipped. *Slipped.* And cracked his head. And drowned in water he could have escaped just by standing.

Where was the fairness in that? Where was the righteousness? And where was God? The question flayed his heart.

That God had to be somewhere George Simon did not doubt, even for a second. His faith was strong. But his understanding failed him entirely.

And his guilt chewed at him from the inside, ate through his vitals like some burrowing beast. George realized that he hated his own survival, hated the breaths that swelled his chest, hated the fact that he would enjoy sunrises and kisses, but Eric Gordy never would. Eric Gordy was dead forever.

Eric Lamont Gordy, Messman 3rd Class.

And how fitting was it that until six days after the attack, George had not even known his full name? Indeed, the very morning of the attack, he'd had to guess at the fragment of name that he did know. And yet, he and Gordy had served on the same ship. Worse, they were also from the same *place*. He had felt a sickness when Reeves told him that, had felt the bottom fall out of his gut.

Eric Lamont Gordy had been just another invisible Negro in a world full of invisible Negroes, a world where they lived their lives and you lived yours and you never even saw them unless you needed an ashtray to be emptied, a shoe to be shined, a cup of coffee to be refilled. They had walked the same streets, he and Eric Lamont Gordy, had gazed up at the same sky, shopped in the same stores, been shaped by the same slow, genteel elegance that sometimes made Mobile feel as if it belonged to the last century, as if it had no place in the restless bustle of modern days.

And yet, though they had come from the same place and served on the same ship, they were strangers, strangers even after Gordy rescued him, strangers right up until the instant of Gordy's death. Strangers, even now.

And here, after all of that, was Sylvia Osborn, proud white daughter of the *Mayflower*, calling Eric "nigger" and prattling on about a wedding dress.

George studied his fiancée. She was a vision, red lipstick framing a glorious smile. So blonde it was almost like staring into the sun. And he knew something then, knew it for the first time, wondered how he could not have known it all along. He knew what he was going to have to do and how she was going to respond, as surely as if it had already happened and he was only remembering the act. He knew all this and he hated himself for it.

"George?" She made his name a question.

He sighed. "Sylvia," he said. He spoke her name like an apology.

Sylvia shot his mother a look of confusion, then looked back at George. "What's wrong, George?" she asked.

"I . . . we need to talk."

Mother took the hint, coming to her feet. "Well," she told her younger children, "why don't we return to trimming the tree and allow Sylvia and your brother some privacy?"

Nick groaned, "Awww," but did as his mother said. Cora kissed her oldest brother on the temple as she passed him. "I'm glad you're back home, Georgie," she said. Her voice was a shy whisper.

"Me too, sis," he said, lying.

And then he was alone in the room with Sylvia. For a moment, neither of them spoke.

"You sound so mysterious," she said, a teasing lilt lifting her voice.

"It's not mysterious," he said.

"Well, what is it?" she said.

George drew a steadying breath and wished there was some other way. He was aware that he was living in the last moments of his old life, before he tore everything asunder, shattered Sylvia's heart, and made a lying heel of himself. There was, he reminded himself, still time to turn back from the cliff, to make a joke, make an excuse, tell her it was nothing, preserve everything the way it was. But that was part of the problem, wasn't it? How could he preserve everything the way it was? It had all already changed—himself, most of all. And it wouldn't be fair to pretend otherwise.

He didn't want to hurt her.

Sylvia smiled encouragement. "What's wrong, George?"

He took another deep breath and made himself say it. "I don't think we should get married."

For a long, unnerving moment, she continued to smile, the words having been heard but not quite processed. Then, slowly, the smile shrank, and her face congealed into a mask of dull confusion. "What?" she asked. And again, in a voice rimmed with disbelief, "*What?*"

Then confusion shattered into pain, her beautiful face contorting itself now into an ugliness of sudden, brutal grief. George lowered his eyes so he would not have to see. He had done this to her. Him. The shame of it was like water. He felt himself drowning.

"What?" she asked yet again, and this time, tears came with it.

"I'm sorry," George said. It was just words. But he didn't know what else to say. Didn't know what else to do. This was as awful as he had known it would be.

"Sorry?" As if he were speaking to her in some dead tongue.

Then Sylvia's crying grew worse. George reached to pat her heaving shoulder. His hand stopped midflight when she swung a stiff index finger beneath his nose. "Don't," she hissed.

George lowered his hand. "I'm sorry," he said.

"For God's sake, would you *please* stop saying that!"

"Sylvia . . . "

"Why?" she demanded.

"What do you . . . ?"

"Why don't you want to *marry* me?" She screamed it, and there was something naked and helpless in her voice. George's mother and the kids had been singing "Joy to the World" in the other parlor. He heard the singing stop. He heard the house go still.

And George knew he had been wrong. This was not as awful as he had feared. This was far worse. He took a deep breath. "I don't know, Sylvia," he said. "It's just . . . things are different now."

"Different? What things? What do you mean?"

"The attack, the war . . . " His voice trailed off. He was conscious of how he was flailing for words to explain a sudden certainty he barely understood himself.

There was something harsh about her laughter. "For goodness' sake, George! You're not making any sense!"

"I know," he said, guiltily.

"Well, don't you think I deserve an explanation?" The words rose on wings of shrill indignation.

"Yes you do," he said. "It's just . . . " His voice waned into silence again.

"Just what?" she demanded.

"It's different now," he insisted, repeating himself with a shrug.

"For God's sake, George, would you please make sense? *What* is 'different?'"

"Me," he said. He felt useless and miserable. "The world."

"I see," she said, though it was obvious she didn't. "Well, here is what I don't understand, George Simon. If you didn't want to marry me, why on earth did you ask me in the first place? Why did you ask me to wait for you while you ran off to play marine?"

Why, indeed? He'd done it because they'd all expected it. She'd expected it, her parents had expected it, and his parents, too. He had done it because they had once played in the same sandbox together and had dated all through high school. What else was left to do?

But George couldn't say those things. He shrugged. "I don't know," he said.

"Don't you love me?" she asked.

And the need in the question was so naked George almost flinched.

He swallowed hard, shook his head slowly. "Not like I'm supposed to," he said.

Sylvia Osborn laughed again. It sounded forced. It sounded wild. "Darling, I think I understand. This is just cold feet. You're just nervous, is all. You *do* love me."

"No," he said. "I don't. Not like I want to."

"Don't say that! You don't know what you're saying."

"Yes, I do," he said. "Maybe for the first time."

"No, you don't!" she cried.

"Sylvia, I'm sorry."

Sylvia slapped him. She stared at him. Then she slapped him again. Hurt boiled in her eyes. She wrenched the engagement ring Father had helped him pick out, helped him pay for, from her ring finger and flung it at him. It struck his chest hard.

"Sylvia," he said.

But she bolted to her feet and fled. She had to shoulder through Mother, Nicky, and Cora, who had gathered, wide-eyed and oval-mouthed, at the door. A moment later, the front door slammed with a righteousness that rattled the windows in the parlor.

Mother regarded him sorrowfully. "Oh, George," she said, "what have you done?"

It was just after four in the afternoon when George's cab pulled up on a dirt road across from a small shotgun house with a front door recessed beneath the overhang of the porch. The reporter and the photographer were already there, smoking cigarettes and leaning against the hood of an old Ford. When they saw George, they ditched the cigarettes and straightened.

"Wait for me," he told the cabbie.

The cabbie did not look pleased. "Don't be too long now," he drawled from a nearly toothless mouth where the few remaining teeth were stained tobacco brown. "I don't like being down here after dark. All these niggers."

"Look," George told him in a voice he hoped was authoritative, "this is a government matter. So you will wait for as long as I need you to wait." It felt foolish to say, but it was, after all, the truth, and he thought it might silence the cabbie. It did.

George was gladder for this mission than he would have thought possible two days ago. It had, after all, gotten him out of the house, provided an escape from Mother's tears and Father's rage. Most of all, it gave him a respite from that question they kept asking and he could not fully answer.

"Why?"

What could he say? He didn't want to marry Sylvia Osborn because she said a word everybody said? Because she was excited about her wedding dress? How foolish did that sound? Even to his ears, it made no sense.

"Is it some other girl, is that it?" demanded Father. John Simon, who had originally seen fit to work his regular schedule even on the day his wounded son returned, had rushed home as soon as Mother called him with the unbelievable news. John Simon, who prided himself on keeping his emotions to himself, spoke in a voice that trembled gravely. "You've met some chippy in Honolulu and she has turned your head?"

George shook his head, miserably. "No," he said, "that's not it."

"*Then what is it?*"

George flinched from the sudden thunderclap. He hunched his shoulders. "I don't love her."

"Love," said Father. He made a dismissive sound.

Mother said, "Are you sure it's not just cold feet, George? That's very common, after all."

Again George shook his head. "No, Mother," he said, "it's not cold feet."

"I hope you're happy with yourself," Father said. His voice simmered. "You have ruined everything," he said. "*Everything*. Bad enough you choose not to go to college. Bad enough you run halfway across the world and nearly get yourself killed. But now you come home and do this? For no reason? No reason at all? I am ashamed of you, George. I am *embarrassed* that you are my son."

He regarded George with hot eyes for a long, meaningful moment. Finally he said, "Well? What do you have to say for yourself?"

George shrugged. "I d-don't know," he answered honestly. "I just . . . I feel different now."

Which explained nothing, he knew. But it was, in its own way, the truth just the same.

Father shook his head, dismissed the words with a wave. "You feel 'different' now," he said in a mocking voice. "Well, by all means, if you feel 'different' now, you can't go through with your obligation, can you? No one could expect you to do something just because you promised to do it, could they?"

George didn't respond. What was there to say? Father was right. What he was doing—jilting Sylvia for no good reason—was dishonorable. He was a cad. He was a heel.

But, he consoled himself, it would also be dishonorable to marry her knowing his feelings had changed. So there was no honor to be found in this, was there? No path for a moral man to take. To take either course was to make himself a liar. To take either course was to be in pain.

There was a long moment. Then Father said, "I can't believe you've done this to me."

They had heard his taxi pull up just then, the driver honking his horn, and George had moved as fast as he could to the driveway, grateful for the escape. Now, as he slammed the cabbie's door and crutched over to the two men, he shook the angry scene from his thoughts. He had a mission. It was time to concentrate on that.

Four little colored girls jumping rope on a dirt patch in front of the house across the street paused to watch as the three white men came together. From someone's yard, George heard the grunt of a pig. From somewhere else, chickens clucked about. The other two men introduced themselves. The photographer was Phil Laney. The reporter was Hank Boggs, who glanced around him, nose wrinkled in distaste. "I don't know how they can live like this," he said.

"You been waiting long?" asked George.

"Not too long," said Boggs. "She know you're coming?"

"She knows she's getting a visit from somebody in the military and that it relates to her husband's death. She doesn't know anything more than that. They wanted her to be surprised."

Boggs scratched this down in a notepad. Laney nodded toward the house. "Need to see if you can get her to come off the porch," he told George. "The way it's built, the front door is all in shadow. Even with a flash, there's a good chance the picture might not come out too good. Especially if she's a dark one. Colored are hard to photograph sometimes. You want to be able to see more than just her smile, get her down into the light."

George nodded. He turned and regarded the house but did not move toward it. Laney and Boggs watched him expectantly. George shook his head. Now he was supposed to go knock on this door, speak to this man's widow and say . . . what, exactly?

I'm sorry for your loss?

Eric died a hero?

He was a good man?

What words were big enough to encompass what she must be going through? What words were soothing enough to douse this thing that burned like acid in his stomach, this guilt at the fact of his own life?

And the worst thing of all was the knowledge, unspeakable to anyone, that no one really cared about her grief, that they were using the man's death and his widow's mourning for some publicity stunt, some scheme to gin up Negro enthusiasm for the war. Invisible in life, Gordy would be manipulated in death, made an image on a poster, a slogan some whiz kid dreamed up, a story George was now obliged to tell as many times as he was asked, about the heroic colored messboy who saved a Southern white boy's white ass.

As if Gordy had never had a life, never existed before what happened. As if his only value was reflected in the fact that George Simon was still drawing air.

"What in the world am I going to say to this woman?" he asked. He was talking to the two journalists. He was talking to the late afternoon sun. "I don't know, marine," said Boggs. "That's up to you." And he scratched something more into his notepad. George grimaced. He had forgotten this wasn't a regular fellow he was talking to. This was a reporter, making note of everything George said or did.

So without further delay, George started toward the house, crossing over a board that bridged an open ditch. Best to just get it over with. He crutched up the one step, made himself rap on the door with two sharp hits. It opened a moment later. But the person at the door was not Thelma Gordy. He was a man, dark-skinned and wiry, who looked to be a few years older than George. His face was a collection of hard angles, his mouth a broad slash between thick lips, his eyes flinty and suspicious.

"Yes?" he said. And that was all he said, spoken with a brusqueness you could not call rude but that certainly wasn't welcoming either. And the man didn't smile. George didn't realize it until that instant, but his whole life, he had been used to Negroes always smiling. Had he ever approached a Negro who didn't smile to see him coming?

George was so taken aback that he almost felt a stammer coming. He swallowed it down. "I am here to see Thelma Gordy," he said.

"I'm Mrs. Gordy's brother," said the man and that was all he said. The implication was clear. He expected George to explain himself. And, noted George, he had made a point of calling his sister "Mrs." A subtle but definite rebuke.

"My name is George Simon. I was with her husband at Pearl Harbor. That is, he saved my life. I came to tell her that."

Something George could not define came into the man's eyes. "You the one?" he said.

George nodded. The man pursed his lips and seemed about to say something. Then a woman's voice called, "Luther?"

He looked back over his shoulder. "Man from the Marines is here. Say he want to talk to you."

The man, Luther, regarded George again out of that closed face. Then a woman's hand nudged him back from the door and Thelma Gordy appeared. She was wearing an apron over a faded housedress and was wiping her hands on a rag. Thelma was dark-skinned like her brother, her lips full like his, but her face was not composed of hard angles. Rather, it had a soft and appealing roundness, dimples framing a mouth that looked as if it smiled a lot and enjoyed doing so, cheeks curving to a strong chin. There was something of her brother in the eyes, though, but where his challenged you, hers were only wary and interested, filled with judgments held in abeyance.

George was surprised to find himself thinking that she was beautiful for a Negress. Indeed, she was beautiful, regardless.

"Yes?" she said. One word, like her brother. But not harsh like her brother. Interested, perhaps. Curious. Waiting.

All at once, George remembered his mission. He took off his lid. "Thelma Gordy?" he said. "My name is Private George Simon. I served with your husband at Pearl."

Some new interest came into her expression, some willingness to listen that made George think perhaps this wouldn't be so bad after all. And it was right as he was thinking this that the flashbulb went off with a crunch and a strobe of pure white light that left George blinking ghosts from his eyes. Thelma Gordy did the same.

"What is this about?" she asked, still wincing. A hardness had crept into her voice.

George glared back at the photographer, who was busy ejecting the spent bulb and going into his pocket for its replacement. Laney didn't even notice George's disapproval. George faced Thelma Gordy. "I'm sorry," he said. "I didn't know he was going to do that."

"What is this about?" she repeated. "And who are these people?"

"They're reporters," said George. "They're here from the paper."

"The paper? But . . . why? They told me somebody from the military was coming. I thought it had something to do with Eric's insurance or something." She paused, her confused gaze lingering on George. "But Eric was in the Navy," she said slowly, the words and the realization coming at the same time, "and you, you a marine."

George swallowed. "No," he said, "this is not about his insurance or anything like that. I just wanted to pay a courtesy call. You see, Gordy—Eric—saved my life. If it wasn't for him, I wouldn't have made it out of that ship. He died saving me."

Her gaze fell inward then, fell upon something George could not see. "A courtesy call," she repeated. And George knew with a sinking certainty that she smelled his treachery. She couldn't place it, but she knew it was there.

Then the reporter helped her. "Your husband's a hero," he shouted from behind George. "The War Department is going to use him for a big publicity push. You and this guy are going to tour the country, talking about what your husband did. How's that feel? Does it make you proud?"

"I . . . don't know what you talking about," she said.

George's cheeks flamed. He felt as if he could gladly have beaten Boggs and Laney to death with his crutches. Oblivious (or perhaps just uncaring), Boggs stepped forward, reaching as he did into the breast pocket of his jacket. He produced a photostat, unfolded it, and handed it to Thelma. She studied it for a moment, then looked up. "This is what you came to talk to me about?" she asked.

"Just a few comments," said Boggs.

"Yeah, and a couple pictures," added Laney. "Like he said, your husband is a hero."

"Let me see that," said George. Thelma handed him the photostat. She seemed dazed.

George studied the image. It was a drawing of something that never happened.

In the background, Japanese planes were dropping bombs, distant ships were erupting in flames. In the foreground, a colored man and a white man faced one another on the canting main deck of their ship as it slipped into the sea. The white man had fallen in water up to his knees, but the colored man, standing with legs straddled on the high side of the deck, had the white man's hand in an iron grip. That grip, black hand locked hard upon white hand, forearms sinewy and strong, was the focal point of the picture, the thing your eyes traveled to first. The two men stared at each other, both with clenched teeth and angry determination. There was, on the white man's face, a bare hint of manly gratitude. Below them, in a dramatic typeface, it said, "We're All Together Now!"

"This what the War Department is putting out?" Thelma Gordy sounded hopelessly confused. "That's supposed to be Eric? It don't even look like him."

"Don't look like me, either," muttered George.

"Your husband's a hero," repeated Boggs—the third time they had told her this. "They're going to put these up in every colored church and schoolhouse, every store and restaurant in the country."

"But why?" she asked.

"They want to use him." Luther was back. He pushed through the door, stood in front of his sister as if to defend her from physical attack. "Don't you get it, Thel?" he asked, glaring with stark hostility at the three white men. "This ain't about paying no respects to Eric. This about using Eric to get more niggers to sign up for the military, that's all."

"Hey," said Laney in a sharp voice, "there's a war on, pal. Or hadn't you heard?"

"Oh, I heard," said Luther. "They's a war on, an' now you all need niggers to be cannon fodder, so you make up this poster, don't look nothin' like my brother-in-law, and you think people gon' see that and run to the recruitin' office."

"Luther," said Thelma, "hush, now." And then, to the white men: "He don't mean no harm."

"You got a smart mouth, don't you?" said Laney, ignoring her.

"So you say," said Luther. "But my smart mouth ain't wrong, is it?"

George was stunned. How quickly this had all gone wrong. In his most pessimistic imaginings, he had never thought anything like this might happen. He'd anticipated his own discomfort with this misbegotten publicity stunt, but it hadn't even occurred to him that Gordy's family might have their own reasons for objecting to it. Now George stood helpless. He had no idea what to do.

"But I still don't understand," Thelma Gordy was saying. She had nudged her brother aside. "Even if that's what you wanted to do, use Eric, why come here? It ain't like you need my permission." She was looking directly at George as she spoke.

George stared back. His mind was white paper. His mouth moved, waiting for words that would not come. Luther answered for him.

"Because they want to use you, too," he said. "Ain't you heard what they said? Take a few pictures of the grieving widow, send you round the country to talk about what a hero Eric was and how proud you are he saved this white guy's ass. They send him over here to pay his respects, so he say, but respect ain't got shit to do with it. He don't care about Eric and he don't care about you. He just tryin' to use you like they usin' Eric."

She looked at George. Disbelief gathered in her eyes. "Is that true?" she asked.

George wanted to lie. It occurred to him that maybe his mission even called for him to lie. Certainly Colonel Reeves would have told him to say whatever was necessary to secure her cooperation. But Colonel Reeves was not standing here on this porch, being searched by those eyes.

"Yes," he said. "It's true. But—"

"Don't need to hear no 'but.'" Luther had a protective arm around his sister and was pulling her back toward the door. She did not resist. Her eyes never left George.

"You all do what you want to do with your poster," said Luther. "Ain't nothin' we can do to stop you. But we ain't gon' have nothin' to do with it."

And the door closed behind them.

For a moment, the three white men were too shocked to speak. Finally, Laney said, "Wow. I've seen 'em uppity before, but that one takes the cake."

Boggs glanced at George. "So what are you going to do now, marine?"

George didn't answer. Laney was still going on. "Don't you think he was uppity?" he demanded.

George spoke in a distant voice. "I think he was right," he said.

He turned on his crutches, ignoring the way Laney's eyes widened. As he did, he was surprised to realize he had something in his hands. It was the photostat of the War Department poster showing two men who did not look like George or Gordy doing something George and Gordy had never done. George let the image fall. It came to rest against the front door as he crutched down from the porch and made his way back to the waiting cab.

"Take me to Bienville Square," he said.

three

Thirty minutes later, Luther was still seething.

He sat at the tiny table in the kitchen, sucking hard at a cigarette, going on and on about the nerve of white people. Thelma, standing at the kerosene stove stirring a pot of red beans, had heard it all before. Being around white people always did this to him, always coiled him tight as a mainspring. She was convinced he was going to get himself killed one day if he didn't learn to control himself, didn't stop talking to white men any old kind of way. It was her deepest fear.

"Think they run the whole damn world," hissed Luther. "That's the problem with 'em. Think we s'pose to jump 'cause they come round and say jump. Hell with 'em. Who they think they are?" The tip of the cigarette glowed orange with another fierce inhalation.

She might have told him to hush up, but she knew her brother well enough to know there was no hushing him until he worked this rage out of his system. Gramp seemed to have reached the same conclusion. He sat at the yellow linoleum table where they took their meals, catacorner from Luther, both hands resting on the head of his gnarled walking stick. His nearly sightless eyes flickered in his placid face.

Roebuck Hayes was Thelma and Luther's paternal grandfather, the only family they had beyond one another. They did not know how old he was—no one did—but he claimed he had been a full-grown man the day emancipation came to the cotton plantation 50 miles north of here where he had been owned, so they figured he had to be nearly one hundred, maybe more.

Ordinarily, Gramp was the one who talked Luther down from his rages, who told him to be calm if only because no good ever came of letting white folks know what you were really thinking. But this time Gramp kept his silence and Thelma fumed.

Why hadn't her brother learned how to behave after living in Alabama his entire life? After 27 years, why couldn't he just keep his mouth shut and leave white folks alone?

But of course, she knew. When Luther had seen their parents—Roebuck's only son and his wife—dragged from their home and lynched together in a little country town not a hundred miles from here, it had driven all capacity for silence from him for good. Thelma was barely out of diapers when it happened. She had seen it too, or so they told her, but she remembered none of it. Poor Luther had been nine, though, and he could *forget* none of it. Not a single second.

This inability to forget lit his eyes like fire when white people came calling. It lubricated his mouth like oil and made him say things colored people usually knew better than to say. This was why he didn't go to white people's places and hated when they came to his.

"Did you hear that one they called George?" Luther spoke behind a cloud of blue smoke. "The marine? He said it plain. They tryin' to use you, Thel. Did you hear it?"

"I heard," she said. There had been, she thought, something of distaste and even pain in the white man's face when he said it, as if he didn't want to tell her the truth but couldn't help himself. "At least he ain't lied about it," she added. "That was something."

Luther snorted. "Ain't had no choice but to tell the truth, knowin' we done seen through they bullshit."

"Luther, watch your language." Thelma was lighting a cigarette from a burner on the stove. "And put some plates on the table."

"I'm just sayin'," he said, getting up and opening the cabinet.

Behind her brother's back, Thelma implored Gramp with her eyes. *Say something. Help me calm him down.*

The old man's face reflected nothing of her unspoken plea. He seemed not to have seen it, and maybe he hadn't. But sometimes, Thelma suspected Gramp saw more than he let on. "Every shut eye ain't sleep," he used to say.

Luther turned around, plates and forks in hand. "They just got a lot of nerve, Thel. That's all I'm sayin'." Each plate landed on the table with a hard clatter, silverware following.

"Luther Hayes, you break my plates, I'm gon' break your neck."

He ignored her. "Ain't enough for 'em Eric died in they damn Navy. Now they want to use him after death." The cigarette in his lips had burned down to a bare stub. He crushed it out in an ashtray. "I swear, this country don't give a nigger a break for nothin'."

"Luther, I ain't gon' ask you again to watch your language," said Thelma, breathing out smoke.

He looked at her. After a moment, he said, "I'm sorry, Thel. I just get sick of it. Why they can't just leave us alone?"

His eyes were wide—angry, but somehow also helpless. A vein in his temple writhed like a worm that had burrowed just beneath the skin. How many times had she heard him go on like this? "I know, sweetie," she said, trying to cool him with her voice.

"I don't see why we got to fight they wars," he said. "How I look riskin' my life to make some other people free, and ain't free my damn self?"

"I know," she said again. "Come on, let's eat."

She got a bottle of buttermilk from the icebox, poured three glasses, and set them on the table. A bowl full of steaming red beans, another bowl of rice, and a pan of fresh cornbread followed. Thelma stubbed out her cigarette and sat down across from her brother.

"Let's bless the meal," she said.

Luther rolled his eyes but did not make the snide remark he ordinarily might have made. Thelma allowed herself to hope his anger had finally spent itself. They all linked hands, and she offered a brief grace. Thelma served the old man first, then she and her brother served themselves.

Gramp felt around for his utensils and found them. They all ate in silence for a moment. Finally the old man spoke around a mouth full of beans. "You know," he said, "your father was in the first one."

Luther looked up. "First what?" he asked.

"First war," said the old man. "Back in '17 and '18. 'War to end all wars,' they called it." He chased this with a snort of derision. "Ain't ended nothin' but a whole bunch of men's lives, you ask me. But reason I mention it, your father asked the same question you asked: 'Why should I fight white men's wars? They ain't done shit-all for us.' And Lord know he had a point."

"But he went anyway," said Luther. It was not a question.

"Yeah, he did," said the old man, after a deep drink of buttermilk. "Fought with the 369th Infantry, your daddy did. All colored. Huns called 'em the Hellfighters 'cause they was so tough. Spent six months on the front line, ain't never lost no ground, nor had a man captured. The French give 'em that French medal. *Croix de Guerre*, they call it. Mean 'cross of war,' your daddy told me."

The old man used a piece of cornbread to nudge some beans onto his fork. He chewed thoughtfully for a moment. "You know why he done it?" he said finally. "You know why he went? Why all the colored men went, I expect."

Luther studied his plate and did not speak. The old man said, "I'll tell you what he told me. He said, 'Pappy, I ain't fightin' for this country. I'm fightin' for what this country s'pose to be. What it ought to be.' That's what he said."

"Yeah," said Luther. "And then, five years later . . . "

He didn't finish the thought. He didn't need to. They all knew the rest of it.

" . . . August 28, 1923," said the old man. "I remember. How I'm gon' forget? He my son, flesh of my flesh. But I'm just tellin' you what he said. Said he was fightin' for the way the country could be in the future." He turned his blind eyes toward Luther and added, "*Your* future."

Luther looked up, a cruel little smile playing at the edges of his mouth. "I wonder if he still felt that way when them crackers set him on fire."

"Luther!" Thelma was scandalized.

He regarded her for a moment. There was a stony defiance in his eyes. Then, almost imperceptibly, something sad drifted into its place. "I'm sorry, Thel," he said in a soft voice. "I'm sorry."

He pushed back from the table, his meal only half-eaten. "I'm goin' out," he said, standing. "I'll be back."

Luther touched his hand to her shoulder as he passed. A moment later, she heard the door close behind him. The old man stared ahead with those sightless eyes, chewing his beans.

She wasn't even surprised. So many of their evenings ended like this. Even when some particular white man hadn't made Luther angry, even when everything seemed peaceful, there was still likely to come a moment when he pushed back from the table or stood up from his chair and declared that he was going out. He would sit for hours at a plank board bar in some neighborhood juke—Sneaky Pete's, Romeo Jones, Mae's Place—and down endless beers.

Her brother was a drunk. He was not a belligerent drunk, did not become contentious or aggressive when he had a bellyfull. And he was not one of those men who drank a job away, either. No, Luther would stagger home tonight as he did so many nights, then get up in the morning, same as always, and get to work right on time at Youngblood's Barber Shop.

But that didn't make him any less a drunk. She knew it and he did, too. Luther told her he drank because it dulled the razor's edge of the memory, made it easier to sleep nights, easier to simply be. He drank because it hurt too much not to.

Thelma looked at her grandfather, feeling with his fork to make sure there was no more food left on his plate. She said, "He never going to get over it, is he?"

Gramp shook his head. "Ain't none of us never gon' get over it, I expect. I sure ain't."

She thought this over and decided it was probably true. What had happened on that August night 18 years ago would haunt all their lives from here to the grave. Thelma was just 21. How odd to feel herself doomed by something she could not even recall.

She finished her dinner, then cleaned up the kitchen, drawing water from the well outside, washing the plates, wiping down the table, and taking the trash to the cans in the backyard. Her chores completed, her day finally done, she settled into the front room and knitted as she tried to listen to *Fibber McGee and Molly*. Gramp snored softly in the chair on the other side of the radio.

The program had only been on for a few minutes when Thelma lowered her knitting. She reached over and turned the radio off in the middle of a commercial extolling the virtues of Johnson Wax. Her heart wasn't in the knitting, nor was it in the radio show. Thelma woke her grandfather and shooed him off to bed. He hobbled on his walking stick toward the room in back that he shared with Luther, grumbling about being a grown man and able to decide for himself when to go to bed. Thelma barely heard. He said the same thing every night.

She took a lamp out to the privy and sat there for a few minutes, smoking a cigarette and listening to cricket songs. When she was done, she came back inside, drew the curtain that hung from a rope between kitchen and front room, pulled her thin old mattress and bedding from a closet in the corner, pushed the chairs to one side, and made up her pallet on the floor. She lit the paraffin heater in the corner and raised the window an inch to vent the smelly oil smoke. Then she changed into her nightdress and crawled on top of her makeshift bed.

She couldn't sleep. She didn't even try. She just lay there on top of the covers, too many questions, too many worries crawling in her mind. She wondered about the marine who had come to her door that day, about that lie he had so obviously wanted to tell and didn't. She thought about Eric and the great thing he had done that the War Department wanted her to talk about so that more Negroes would join the war. And she worried about her brother, about the anger that had burned inside of him for as long as she could remember. How much longer could it burn before it had to explode? Thelma lay there, smoking, watching the shadows of the occasional passing car crawl along her ceiling.

It was after midnight when she heard the kitchen door open and her brother enter, humming "Tuxedo Junction" softly to himself. And that was when her eyes finally closed.

The morning came too soon. It always did.

Thelma rose in the dawn chill. She stowed her bedding, opened the makeshift partition, lit the stove, woke Gramp and Luther, and had scrambled eggs on the table by the time they came staggering in from their room. She ate quickly, dressed quickly, and walked quickly the mile and a half to where her bus would pick her up.

At work, she did the same thing she did every day, eight and a half hours a day, five days a week. She cleaned the home of a white lady who lived west on Government Street, made lunch, got dinner on, and looked after the white lady's three spoiled children as the white lady played bridge with her white friends and later met with the white members of her club. Invisible as a wraith, Thelma brought the ladies refreshments and emptied their ashtrays as they discussed joining a program of Mobile women knitting watch caps for the poor, beleaguered people of England.

"Knittin' for Britain," one of the women said. "What a clever name." And they all laughed.

It was shortly after five that Thelma stepped down from her bus and began the long walk home. She was tired, and her calves were aching. Bad enough she had spent all day on her feet, but the bus had been so crowded she hadn't been able to get a seat. Even the white section was full. When had that ever happened before?

Thelma was wondering if she had time to sit down for a few minutes before getting dinner on. She was wondering what she might fix. She was wondering if there were enough red beans and cornbread for leftovers.

Her mind was running in these prosaic circles, and her eyes were not really seeing. So it wasn't until she was at her front walk that she realized a man was waiting on her porch. Thelma started. It was that marine—George Simon, he had said his name was—and he was sitting there, waiting for her, dressed now in civilian slacks and a sport coat, pants slit over the injured leg that was stretched out in front of him.

Dear Lord, she thought, was he going to try again to talk her into that publicity stunt foolishness? Did he have any idea what Luther might do if he came home and found him here? Hell, Luther might break his other leg for him. And then where would her poor brother be?

The white man struggled to his feet. "What are you doing here?" she demanded, coming up the walk.

He brought his good hand out from behind his back bearing a square box that was wrapped in paper and tied with a red ribbon. Thelma stopped. "What is this?" she asked.

"It's for you," he said. "Merry Christmas."

She was confused. Then she remembered. Today was December 23. She had forgotten Christmas. Lord, where was her mind?

The white man pushed the box toward her. "Merry Christmas," he said again, more insistently. Thelma accepted the box. She didn't know what else to do. "It's a can opener," he told her. "It's electric."

Thelma looked down at the gaily wrapped package, then back up at the white man's hopeful smile. Obviously, she had missed something. But she could not for the life of her say what it was. "A can opener?" she said. She felt slow.

He nodded. "Electric," he said again. "I went shopping yesterday around Bienville Square. I needed to pick up some things—Christmas gifts—for my family. And I saw this and I thought about you."

"A can opener," she said. "But why . . . ?"

At that, a grimace appeared on his face. He ran his good hand through his short-cropped hair. "Look, I wanted to apologize," he said. "For yesterday, I mean. The whole thing."

"I see," she said. But she didn't.

"I didn't mean for it to go like that," he told her.

She nodded toward the door. "Have you been waiting long?"

"Half hour. The old fellow inside wouldn't let me in, told me I should just go away. I told him I would wait here on the porch."

"You shouldn't have come," she said. "My brother . . . "

"Yeah, he was really angry, wasn't he?"

"He don't like white people," she said.

The white man looked surprised, as if it had never occurred to him someone might dislike him. "Oh," he said. And then again, as if the novelty of being disliked had just struck him anew: "Oh."

Thelma's legs were killing her. Her bra strap was cutting into her shoulder. She sat down on the step, putting the box and her purse down next to her. "What is this about?" she asked.

"You and your brother were right," the white man said. "It was a publicity stunt. They want to use Eric and you for a recruitment drive. I didn't think it was a good idea, but nobody asked my opinion. I'm sure Eric told you how it is. When you're in the military, you don't ask questions. You follow orders."

"So now you here to ask me to change my mind?"

"No," he said quickly. "I mean, yes, I'm sure they're going to want me to try and if anybody ever asks, I hope you'll tell them I threw myself at your feet and begged you. But no, I'm not going to ask you to change your mind. Your husband died two weeks ago and here I am, asking you to tour the country for some publicity stunt? And then they show you some stupid poster and the guy on it doesn't even look like Gordy? I don't blame you for being upset. I don't blame your brother, either."

A woman who lived down the street passed by at that moment, hugging a paper bag full of groceries. She stared in confusion, lifted a hand in greeting, and Thelma knew it would soon be all over the neighborhood—probably already was—that she was entertaining some white man. Thelma waved back absently. Luther was going to be furious when he found out about this. But she would deal with that later. Right now, she was curious.

"So if you're not here to get me to change my mind," she said, "why are you here?"

"I told you," he said. "I wanted to apologize. And even though I had to follow orders, and even though it was a terrible idea, I wanted you to know: I *did* care about Eric. I mean, I didn't know him, so I guess that's not it exactly. But he did save my life. And he did die in the process." He gazed down at Thelma, blue eyes wide. "Obviously, that means something to me. Especially since . . . "

He stopped abruptly, as if he had reached a bridge he didn't dare to cross. He looked away. "Especially since what?" asked Thelma.

He still didn't look at her. His voice was raw. "Especially since maybe I didn't deserve it," he said.

"What do you mean?"

He didn't answer all at once. Thelma waited for him, wondering what it was he didn't want to say, wondering if he ever would.

Finally, he did. "I hate that he gave his life for me, okay?" He was looking at her, hard. "I *hate* it. I've been asking myself every day since then: why not me? Why did I survive and he didn't? Your husband was the brave one, Thelma. He was this messboy and I'm a marine, but when the chips were down and it looked really bad, he was the one who kept his head and kept his courage. I was the one . . . "

Again, he stopped. On a porch across the street, four little girls were playing patty-cake to the tune of "Oh Mary Mack," their voices thin and sweet and somehow distant.

"Mr. Simon," she said. It was the first time she had used his name.

He gave a deep sigh. He looked away from her. "I was the one who wanted to give up," he said. "I was ready to just let the water drown me. He was the one who made me keep going."

He turned back to her. "Has anyone told you what happened?" he asked.

Thelma shook her head. "No," she said, "not really. All they told us was that he died saving somebody."

Simon nodded, seemed thoughtful. Then he said, "Would you like me to tell you?"

At first, Thelma wasn't at all sure she could handle it. Besides, it was getting late. But, Thelma thought, maybe she had an obligation to know what had happened. They had not had much of a marriage, but he was still her husband and she was still his wife. Maybe she owed it to him to hear this.

"All right," she said. "Tell me."

She sat still as George Simon spoke. He told her how he broke his hip falling out of bed—off his "rack," as he put it. He told her about the hatch door swinging back on his hand, breaking the bones, and then gravity trapping him there. He told her about Eric coming along, forcing the hatch open, helping him out into the passageway. He told her about the ship turning, about falling down the suddenly vertical deck into the water and thinking maybe this was the end of him and maybe that was all right. He told her about the hand that reached into the water and pulled him up. He told her about Eric hoisting him onto his own back.

"I asked him if my weight was too much and he said, 'I don't know. Why don't you get on and we'll find out?'" The memory wrung a sad laugh from Simon. It made Thelma smile. That sounded like Eric. It really did.

He told her more. He told her about the impossible climb Eric made, the weight of another man clinging to his back. He told her how he began to feel like such a burden that he thought of letting go and how he even let his hand begin to slip. But then the ship turned again and the thought of ending it all was washed away in a torrent of seawater. He told her about waiting for rescue or death in the stench and heat of the steering aft compartment and not caring very much which one it was. He told her how it was when time came to a standstill. And he told about the stupid, stupid, *stupid* way her husband died—how, after everything he had endured and escaped and overcome, he slipped on something and clanged his head on a piece of metal, fell senseless, and drowned in shallow water.

"When I was lying there in steering aft, when I thought I was going to die, I thought about home, you know? I thought about my mom and dad. I thought about Mardi Gras and I thought about Bienville Square and how I used to like going over there this time of year, when it's all lit up for Christmas. You ever do that? Go over and see the lights?"

She looked at him, embarrassed. "I don't go up there," she said. Meaning that she was not allowed to go up there.

It took him a moment. "Oh," he said, and now he seemed embarrassed, too. "I forgot."

They were silent for a moment. Then Thelma said, "I can't imagine what it must have been like."

The sun had fallen nearly to the horizon, trailing streamers of gold, purple, and red. The air had taken on a noticeable bite. Simon looked down at her with naked eyes, his face in shadow. "I've never told anyone any of that," he said. His Adam's apple bobbed in his neck. "Never told my buddies, never told my family, never even told my fiancée."

"Then why are you telling me?" asked Thelma in a soft voice. The porch light came on behind her, and she wondered if Gramp was listening.

"Because you deserve to know," he said. "I mean, he was your husband."

He said it as if it were the simplest thing in the world. But the word forced Thelma to close her eyes against all that it brought back to life. She concentrated for a long moment on just breathing. She did not want to cry. Did *not* want to cry. Partly to distract herself, she went into her purse and rummaged up a cigarette. She struck a match and tried to light it, but her hand couldn't seem to find its way. It was shaking too badly.

Finally, Simon took the match from her and lit the cigarette. "Thank you," she said. A plume of smoke rose slowly on the still air.

"I'm sorry," he said, "I didn't mean to make you—"

She cut him off. "It's not what you think," she said. "Eric and I, we weren't close."

His brow creased. "I don't understand," he said. "You were married, right? He was your husband."

Thelma had a moment then where she marveled at what she was about to tell this white man she didn't even know, this white man—*white* man!—she had never even laid eyes on before yesterday. Luther would think she was crazy if he ever heard. And maybe she was, because she could not, for the life of her, say why she was going to do this. Maybe it was because George Simon had shared his confidences with her, told her something that had obviously cost him to tell, and she felt she owed him the same in return. Or maybe it was because the thing just needed saying, if only to free this earnest white man from the misapprehension that she was a grieving widow mourning the loss of her loving man. It made her feel guilty that he felt that way.

Not that she hadn't liked Eric. She had liked him just fine, but . . .

"Eric and I went to school together," she heard herself say. "I guess we were what you would call sweethearts. It was just one of those things, I suppose. I liked him a lot. I thought I was in love. I guess he thought he was, too."

She could see the discomfort on Simon's face. "Thelma," he began, "you don't have to . . . "

Thelma made herself look elsewhere, concentrated on a tangle of Spanish moss dripping from an oak tree across the street onto the roof of the widow Foster's house. She sighed out smoke.

"This one night, he came over and I knew I shouldn't have let him in because I was all alone. Luther was at the hospital with Gramp—that's what we call my grandfather; you met him at the door. Gramp was real sick—had to be, to get that old man to see a doctor—and we was scared he might die. It's been just the three of us since my Aunt Hattie passed in '32. So anyway, I was alone at the house when Eric came calling. I was barely 15, he was a few years older."

"Thelma," Simon said again.

She kept her gaze on the tangle of moss, growing invisible as light seeped out of the world.

"I was really upset about my grandfather and Eric said he would just sit with me to wait and, you know, comfort me. I don't know, maybe he even meant it when he said it. Or at least, maybe he thought he did. But we were sitting on the couch and one thing led to another, and then things went too far. It . . . it just happened. And next thing I knew, I was going to have a baby."

She looked up at Simon now. His eyes were on her, steady. He had stopped protesting. Maybe he knew it would do no good.

Thelma sighed. "So Eric did the right thing," she said. "He married me. He got a job pumping gas at this garage and I started working for this white lady on Government Street. We realized soon enough that we didn't love each other. Not like you see in the movies, you know?" She smiled. "But we liked each other well enough and we got along well enough.

"Then my time came. I went into labor. And the baby . . . "

She closed her eyes and pinched her brow. She felt tears stinging the corners of her eyes and tried to blink them back.

" . . . the baby . . . "

She couldn't help it. Just saying the words brought it all back . . .

The view, lit by lamplight, framed by her own blood-slick thighs . . .

The midwife looking at her helper, the helper looking at the midwife . . .

Both of them looking at Thelma. Both of them looking helpless.

"I'm sorry," one of them said.

"Sorry?" she said. Not wanting to understand.

"The baby," one of them said.

And when Thelma's expression apparently showed she still didn't under-stand, the midwife holding the baby up . . .

He was so small. Tiny. Everything on him there, everything on him

perfect, like a little doll. Head full of dark, wavy hair, matted to his scalp by
blood and birth fluids. Eyes pinched tight as if in pain.
And not moving.
Still.
Still, like an empty house.
Still, like moonlight.
Still, like the . . .

"My baby died," she told this white man who had shown up on her porch and somehow, in the innocence of his ignorance, required her to relive the worst moment she had ever lived or ever would.

She opened her eyes, hating him for it and knowing she had no reason. His face was stricken.

"I'm so sorry," he said.

She didn't answer.

"Why did you tell me this?"

"I don't know," said Thelma, taking a drag from a cigarette that suddenly tasted like dirty straw. "I suppose I just didn't want you to continue thinking you had to console the grieving widow who had lost her beloved husband. I ain't grieving, not like you think. I liked Eric, he was a good man, but that was all there was to it. Wasn't really nothing more between us."

"I see," said Simon.

"Poor man," she said. "He was really looking forward to being a father, really hoped he was going to have a son. I felt like . . . I let him down somehow. When it happened, he just about lost his mind. Signed up for the Navy two weeks later and I think the main reason he did was that he wanted to get as far away from Mobile as he could. He would send me money. He was real good about that, real dutiful. But I ain't seen him or even talked to him since . . . since it happened, and that's been six years."

She looked at Simon. "Now do you understand?"

"Yes," he said, "I guess so."

"Good," said Thelma. She came to her feet, spoke briskly. "Then it's time for you to leave. My brother be home any minute."

"Okay," said Simon. "I just need to call a cab. Can I use your phone?"

Thelma heard meanness in her own laughter. "Phone? We ain't got no phone, Mr. Simon. Probably no cab'll come down here anyway."

"Oh." The expression on his face was the same as when she had told him Luther didn't like white people, like this was a novelty he had never considered.

With a sigh, Thelma crushed out her cigarette. "Come with me," she said.

Thelma walked with a quick step. She knew he would have trouble following. But she could not make herself care.

Without once looking back for him, she marched to a house two doors down, stood in a pool of yellow light on her neighbor's porch, and knocked. After a moment, a thickly built man opened the door, his bulk straining against a sober black suit. "Rafe," she said without preamble, "I need a favor."

By the time Simon caught up with her a few moments later, it had all been arranged. She nodded her head at the white man. "That's him," she said.

Then she spoke to Simon. "This here is Rafe Plunkett," she said. "He's a driver for a colored funeral home. He can give you a ride. Tell him where you want to go. Give him what you were going to give the taxi man."

"Okay," said Simon, and he mumbled his address. He looked chastised, as though he knew he had offended her and could not figure out how.

But of course, it wasn't his fault. None of it was. He was an earnest man, trying to do the right thing, and who could blame him for that? Everything else was just . . . life, she supposed, just the things you learned to live with after you learned there is no happily ever after. Just life and all the ways it disappointed you, all the ways you disappointed yourself. This is what you learned, growing up. This was what made the difference between grown people and children.

Even he had learned that lesson, hadn't he, hand slipping off wrist, ready for it all to end, riding Eric's back as the "messboy" climbed up through that dying ship?

It was just life, stripping illusions away, like turpentine stripping varnish from old wood.

She wanted to say all this but didn't know how. And there he stood, regarding her with that chastened little boy face that seemed to need her to say *something*. Thelma touched his arm. Her eyes sought his. "Thank you for the can opener," she said in a soft voice. She gave his arm a little squeeze and then hurried home.

four

THE BUS WHEEZED TO A STOP, THE DOOR SIGHED OPEN, AND Thelma exhaled, releasing tension she had not even known she held. She was first in line and, hefting her grocery bag, she climbed on and dropped her fare into the coin box. Then she climbed back down and hurried to the rear door, which stood open to admit her to the colored section.

Thelma had feared the bus might not stop at all. The last two had rolled past without even slowing, too crammed to take on even one more passenger. She'd been waiting over an hour on that Davis Avenue corner, cars trundling by in great clouds of exhaust, chickens clucking and stinking in their coops out front of the grocery store, Lucky Millinder and Fatha Hines blaring into the street from the record store, people shouldering past one another on sidewalks that seemed to have suddenly grown narrow.

This bus, she saw as she climbed on in the rear, was nearly as full as the others. Every seat, colored and white, was taken and by the time five others had squeezed in behind her, Thelma found herself standing wedged in the front of the colored section, just back of the rear door. There was not even space to put her bag down. She tried to balance it in the crook of her right arm while holding on to the metal safety bar with her left hand. The bus took off with a lurch that caused Thelma to take an involuntary step back, right onto the foot of the man behind her.

"I'm sorry," she told him.

"No need to apologize, Miss," he said, smiling. "Just the way the city is, nowadays. Crowded everywhere you go."

And surely that was the truth. All the years Thelma had lived here, Mobile had been a sleepy little town pretending to be a city. But things had changed dramatically since the war began. Thelma had never been to New York City or Chicago. Except for a trip over to Pensacola when she was 12, she had never even been out of Alabama. But she could not imagine those big, bustling Northern metropolises everyone spoke of with such awe could be any louder, busier, or more crowded than Mobile was now.

As if to prove the point, the bus rolled past its next stop without stopping. Thelma watched the disappointed and disbelieving eyes of a large mob of colored and white, heads turning to follow the vehicle as it flew past them. She gave thanks she was not among them.

The word was out. War meant industry—a need to build ships, tanks, guns, and planes, a need for restaurants to feed, stores to clothe, and rooms to house the workers. So there was plenty of work. And with so many men going off to fight, the companies could no longer afford to be choosey about who they hired to fill their spots. They were said to be hiring women and Negroes, even in the all-white, all-male preserve of the shipyards over on Pinto Island.

This thought was good for a private smile of amazement. *What must that be like?* she thought. She tried to imagine herself wearing men's overalls and working in a plant, welding metal or tightening bolts. She tried to imagine the conversation where she explained to her white lady that she wouldn't be coming in anymore, wouldn't be watching the white lady's spoiled children anymore because she, Thelma Gordy, was going to be building warships from now on.

Thelma was trying—and failing—to conjure up this picture when the woman fell against her.

She did not stagger with the motion of the bus. She fell. And even as Thelma cried out in surprise, the woman continued falling, sliding heavily to the floor, where she sat as if stunned, legs drawn up beneath her, hemmed in by bodies all around. People gasped and cried out in alarm.

The driver called out, "What's going on back there? What's that commotion?"

"This white lady done fell out," yelled the Negro man behind Thelma.

"Christ Almighty," sputtered the driver. "That's just what the hell I need."

Thelma crouched until she was face-to-face with the white woman. It was not easy to do with the grocery bag in arm and the bus so crowded and the floor beneath her rocking. The woman wore a faded flower-print dress that had probably been new when Hoover was president. A straw hat sat askew on dark, thin hair that drooped from her scalp as if in surrender.

"I'm all right," she was saying in a little voice that seemed unsure if it even had a right to be heard. She repeated it. "I'm all right, I'm all right."

"Can you stand up?" asked Thelma. She handed her grocery bag up to the Negro man behind her.

"I think so," said the white woman. She rose doubtfully, holding on to Thelma's arm.

"She can have my seat," announced a heavyset woman in the back. And even though it was the colored section, and even though it was against the law, Thelma braced the little white woman as she made her way gingerly back to the open seat, riders squeezing themselves small to make space for them to pass.

The thin woman dropped gratefully into the seat. "Thank you," she said in her feeble voice. Her accent was acrid as woodsmoke, a white trash accent if Thelma had ever heard one.

"Is everything all right back there?" the bus driver called out. "Do I need to stop and get the police?"

Thelma repeated the question with her eyes. The white woman shook her head. "I'm fine," she whispered.

Thelma regarded her for a skeptical beat. Then she called out, "She say she fine." It was not Thelma's job to correct her.

"Glory hallelujah," sang the driver with heavy sarcasm.

"Why you fall out like that?" asked Thelma. "You feelin' poorly?"

"It ain't nothin'," said the woman. "Just ain't et. Just hungry is all."

"You mean, you didn't get breakfast?"

The woman looked up. "No, I mean I ain't been eatin' regular. Not since we come to town. Wasn't eatin' so good before, tell you the truth."

Thelma felt like a fool.

She couldn't believe she had asked about breakfast of a woman whose problems so obviously went deeper than a single missed meal. Her eyes met those of the heavyset woman who had surrendered her seat. That woman shook her head once, sadly. As bad as times had been, somehow you never thought you might meet someone who was actually starving.

The little white woman was oblivious to the exchange. She said, "Earl—that's my husband—he thought maybe things be better here, what with the war and all. So we come here, lookin' for work."

Thelma looked behind her. "Can I have my bag, please?" she asked.

The man who had been holding it passed it to her on the outstretched hands of other riders. As the bag came into Thelma's hands, she asked the white woman, "Would you like some crackers?"

The woman smiled a heartbreaking little smile, and Thelma saw a gap where one of her canine teeth had been. "Oh, I can't do that," she said. "Earl say we don't accept no charity."

It made Thelma impatient. "For goodness' sake," she snapped, "it ain't charity. It's just crackers."

She balanced the shopping bag on the woman's lap without waiting for an answer, pulled out a red and yellow box of Cheez-Its, ran a fingernail under the flap, slit open the bag inside, and presented the box. The little white woman looked up at her, and her expression reminded Thelma for all the world of some mistreated dog that has become wary of taking treats from unfamiliar hands.

"Are you sure?" the woman asked. "I bet your children just love these."

"Ain't got no children," said Thelma, shaking the box.

"Well then," said the woman in a grave voice, "I thank you . . . " She stopped. "I don't even know your name," she said.

"Thelma."

"Flora," said the woman. "Flora Lee Hodges." She extended a bony, solemn hand and Thelma shook it.

Then that hand dove into the box like a swimmer into a pool and came up with a fistfull of orange squares, which she seemed determined to stuff into her mouth all at once. Thelma watched with concerned amusement. She had bought the crackers for Luther—he enjoyed snacking on them with a beer—and she could imagine what he might say if he knew she had given them to some white woman instead. Especially some poor white trash just in from the country. Best to let him think she had just forgotten to buy them.

"Easy," she told the woman. "Don't choke yourself. You can have the box. Really, it's okay."

"Thank you," said Flora Lee. "You very kind. I'm sure I ain't makin' the best impression. It's just, it's been a while since we et."

"Your husband is having trouble finding work?"

Flora Lee nodded, wiping with the back of her hand at the orange cracker dust on her mouth. "Both of us is, but I think it's harder on Earl.

You know, bein' the man and all. Hard on his pride. First the farm failed. Then when the war come, he tried to enlist, but wouldn't none of them take him. They said he was a 4-F. That mean he can't enlist."

"Why they say that?"

"Oh, Earl, he can't read too good. I mean, I ain't no great shakes myself, but I can read some. Poor Earl, he can't read a lick. He say his pappy used to take him out of school for the pickin' and the plantin' seasons and pretty soon, they just figured he might as well stay out. And he also got a problem with his leg. Somethin' he was born with, one shorter'n t'other so he walks with a hitch. One thing after another, poor Earl."

"What about you?" asked Thelma.

"Me?" The hand that had been diving back into the red and yellow box paused.

"Have you tried the shipyards?"

Flora Lee shook her head, mutely.

"They're hiring over there, from what I hear."

"They lookin' for men?"

"They lookin' for women *and* men, so I hear."

"Really?" The hand had resumed digging in the box and Flora Lee was chewing thoughtfully. "But like I say, Earl, he can't read none. And he got that bad leg."

Thelma shrugged. "They may still have some work for him. They can't get enough bodies over there, way I hear."

"Is that right?" said Flora Lee, still chewing meditatively. "I guess this war done really changed everything, ain't it?"

Thelma's eyes fell on an advertising banner above and behind Flora Lee's head. On it, Snap, Crackle, and Pop were flying fighter planes with American stars on the wings while extolling the virtues of Rice Krispies cereal.

"Yeah," said Thelma, "I guess it has."

Flora Lee regarded Thelma with eyes empty of guile. "You really think they might hire me at one of them ship places?"

Thelma shrugged. "Why not?" she said.

Flora Lee seemed to consider it for a moment. She popped two or three of the little crackers into her mouth, then nodded, her decision made. "All right, then," she said, "I'm going to do it."

"Good for you," said Thelma.

All at once, Flora Lee bolted to her feet in alarm, pressing the shopping bag into Thelma's arms. "Oh, goodness," she said, "this here is my stop. And look! There's Earl, waitin' for me." She waved happily.

Thelma followed Flora Lee's gaze. Earl Ray Hodges was not much taller than his wife. His face was acne-pitted, and he wore his dark hair slicked back and piled high on the crown of his head in a pompadour. He had been scowling as the bus pulled up, but when he caught sight of Flora Lee, his eyes sparked in a way that awakened some nameless dread in Thelma's soul.

The bus was idling at the curb, still disgorging passengers. The window was open. So Thelma saw and heard what followed quite clearly.

"Earl!" cried Flora Lee, stepping off the bus, arms open to receive him.

He shoved her arms down. "Flora Lee," he said, and his voice was a razor strop, "tell me I didn't just see what I thought I saw. Tell me I didn't see you comin' out the nigger section, big as day." And Thelma felt her jaw stiffen.

"Earl"—Flora Lee's voice was plaintive and whining—"it weren't like that. Weren't no place for me to sit down and I was feelin' poorly, so one of them offered me a seat, that's all."

"Uh huh. And I suppose you ain't had sense enough to know that's against the law. It's against *state law*, Flora Lee. Not to mention God and nature."

"I'm *sorry*, Earl."

"Uh huh." He pointed to the red and yellow box in her hand. "And where'd that come from?"

Flora Lee lowered her eyes. "One of them women give it to me," she said, "on account I was hungry."

"Uh huh. So I guess you sayin' I don't provide well enough for you. You got to go beggin' niggers, now. Is that what you sayin' Flora Lee?"

"Earl, no, I just . . . "

"You shut your lyin' mouth, Flora Lee," he snarled.

And he hit her.

It seemed louder than just a slap, somehow. In some way Thelma could not explain, the flat bang of it seemed to fill more space than you would expect from just the sound of skin striking skin.

Earl Ray and Flora Lee Hodges were in a crowd, with people watching on the sidewalk and from the bus. Women gasped. Colored men lowered their eyes away from white folks' affairs. White men's eyes narrowed, their lips compressed, and you could see the wheels turning, see them weighing the need to get involved against the need to mind their own business.

Flora Lee touched her hand to the palm-shaped redness on her cheek. "Earl," she hissed, "you ain't had no call to hit me!"

A middle-aged white man wearing glasses and a fuzzy caterpillar of a moustache made his decision then. He drew himself up in indignation. "Now see here, fellow," he began.

That was as far as he got. Earl Ray whirled on him, that spark in his eyes dancing now to some jitterbug beat. He leveled his index finger like a gun and spoke in a low growl. "You stay out of it, you know what's good for you. This here is between her and me."

The other man swallowed. He stared at Earl Ray's crazy, jitterbugging eyes. Then he walked away without saying anything else, the tatters of his dignity trailing behind.

Thelma caught the eye of the heavyset colored woman. The sorrow that passed between them then was bottomless and eternal.

The bus pulled away from the curb in that moment, and Thelma was glad to leave Flora Lee Hodges and her husband behind.

Fifteen minutes later, the bus reached her stop. The door whisked open, and Thelma climbed off as gratefully as she had climbed on. She repositioned the grocery bag onto her hip for the walk home. Her thoughts turned to what she would fix for dinner. It was the first thing that always came to mind when she got off the bus.

And all at once, Thelma was struck by the mechanical sameness of her own days. It was a thought so jolting she actually stopped there on the dirt road to think it. Her life was the same thing every day. She got up, she made breakfast, she rode the bus to work. She cleaned the same furniture, mopped the same floor. On Saturdays, she rode the same bus to the same store, bought the same things, got back on the same bus, walked half an hour on exhausted legs, thinking of what she would make for dinner for her brother and grandfather. She got home, she made the same meals, she listened to her brother rant the same rants, she cleaned up the same kitchen, she fell asleep next to the same radio, half-listening to the same programs.

It was as if her life were so automatic, so defined by all these things she always did, that it hardly needed her to live it. Hire some other woman—any other woman, really—to do the cooking and the cleaning and the going to market, and what need was there for Thelma Mae Gordy?

Maybe she should take the advice she had given that poor little white woman. Maybe *she* was the one who should go over to Pinto Island and apply for a job.

The thought made Thelma laugh. She shook her head and made herself move forward, still chuckling.

Lord, where did that come from?

Probably, it was just that she was tired. Probably, that was it.

When she got to the house she stopped at the mailbox, but it was empty. Apparently, Luther had already retrieved the mail.

Thelma hoped there wasn't another letter in it like the one from the white marine that had arrived like June snow a few weeks ago. With his odd Christmastime visits already a month past by then, Thelma had been shocked to find an envelope bearing George Simon's name in her mailbox. And she had given silent thanks Luther had not been the one to bring the postman's offerings in that day. Heaven only knew what he might have done if he had seen it.

But the fact of the letter hadn't been the only surprising thing. She had been equally surprised—maybe even *more* surprised—by the chatty earnestness of it. No, it was more than that. It was the strange, undue . . . *familiarity* of it.

He had written from Cleveland where, he said, he was still on tour for the War Department talking about what Gordy did for him at Pearl. He said he wanted to apologize—Lord, this boy did more apologizing!—for making her discuss a painful subject. He didn't realize it was something she had made a conscious decision to do.

(Though she still didn't know why.)

He had even prayed for her and sent her a Bible verse—"'For I know the thoughts that I think toward you, saith the Lord, thoughts of peace, and not of evil, to give you an expected end.'—Jeremiah 29:11"—and told her to trust in the Lord.

The tenderness of it made no sense from some white man she hardly knew.

Perhaps most amazing, he had told her he felt indebted to her because of what Eric had done. "I can't imagine there would ever be anything I could do for you," he had insisted, "but if there is, I want you to please ask. I'll do whatever I can. Thelma, I can't stress it enough: I'm *serious* about that. I owe him that much."

She had written back, promising she would trust in the Lord, thanking him for being so kind but assuring him that he owed her nothing. But the whole thing made no sense. What were they doing, exchanging letters? George Simon was a white man who lived somewhere over on the west side out by the country club, and she was a black woman who lived . . . here.

The thought made her pause again, and this time, she looked around.

Water from a recent rain moved sluggishly in the open ditch. From someone's backyard, she heard the alarmed cackle of a chicken, perhaps about to have its neck wrung. And the dirt road, still squishy from that selfsame rain, had deposited mud that climbed halfway up her work shoes, which meant she would spend half an hour after dinner cleaning them with a brush and some Rinso to ensure the blinding whiteness her white lady demanded. She would have to wrap them in bread sacks Monday morning to keep them clean on the way to work if it rained again tomorrow.

The realization reinforced the reality: she was a black woman who lived *here*. So why would he write her a letter like that? And why would she have spoken to him—and written back to him—as she had?

It made no sense. She hoped he wouldn't write her again. And she also hoped he would.

It was as she was trying to sort out this contradiction that she noticed Luther. Apparently, he had been sitting on the porch all along, but she had not seen him. Seeing him now, she knew at once that something was wrong. A cigarette drooped from his lips. His expression was that of a man who has been hit in the face with a rock he never saw coming.

Her first thought was Gramp. Had the old man taken sick? Or worse?

"Luther?" she asked, stepping quickly across the piece of plywood that served as a bridge over the ditch, "what's wrong?"

He looked up. It was a moment before his eyes actually found her. When they did, Luther reached into his shirt pocket without a word, produced an envelope, and handed it to her.

The envelope was cream-colored. It said "Selective Service" in the left-hand corner, and in a box below that, it had been stamped with a local return address. Her brother's name and their address were written haphazardly across the front.

Foreboding squeezed Thelma's heart in a frozen vise. She opened the envelope and pulled from it a piece of paper, cream-colored like the envelope. At the top it said, "ORDER TO REPORT FOR INDUCTION." It was addressed from the president of the United States to Luther.

"Greetings," it began.

Luther had not wanted to register with the Selective Service when the peacetime draft went into effect. It had taken all of Thelma's and Gramp's doing to cajole him into going down and putting his name on the roll, mainly by promising that it was just to keep him from getting in trouble with the law. Somehow, it had never occurred to either one of them that the military might actually want him.

She looked at her brother, touched his shoulder with the caution you might reserve for an unfamiliar dog, and called his name. He didn't answer. She tried again, "Luther, honey . . . ?"

He looked up at her. She braced herself for an epic rant that would blow hard and fierce as the storms that sometimes came in off the Gulf, tearing down trees, turning the ground sodden and useless. But her brother did not raise his voice. Rather, he spoke in a deadly calm that was somehow all the more frightening.

"They killed my mama and my papa," he said.

"I know, honey."

Tears shone, unshed, in his eyes. "I saw all of it," he said. "I remember all of it. And now they want me to go and fight, maybe die for them, in *their* war?"

He shook his head, laughed a joyless laugh. "White folks must be out they goddamn minds," he said softly. "I ain't goin'. I can promise you that."

Thelma was alarmed. "Honey, you got to go. If they call you, you *got* to go."

He lowered his eyes, appeared to study his shoes. "I ain't goin'," he repeated in a dull, soft monotone. "I will not go to war for this country, Thel," he said. "I will *not*."

Thelma felt panic surging in her like water. "Luther, if you don't go, they'll come after you. Maybe arrest you. Maybe throw you in jail."

Now he brought his head up, and something fierce had entered his gaze. Still, he did not raise his voice. "They not gon' get me, Thel. Promise you that."

five

THE FERRY CHUGGED ACROSS THE MOBILE RIVER, JUST ABOVE where it opened into the bay. Colored kept to one side, white to the other, working men and women carrying their lunch pails, chatting softly together as Pinto Island grew closer. Thelma stood a little apart from them all, nervously dragging on a cigarette.

It was a sparkling Saturday morning in April, and she was dressed all wrong. In her flower-print dress with white flats and gloves and a hat pinned just so on the crown of her head, she looked ready for church. But these other women, in their mannish slacks and headscarves, looked ready for *work*. She should have thought about it, she told herself reproachfully, should have dressed like she was ready to pitch right in. But then, she had been so anxious the last few days, she hadn't really thought of very much at all.

And now, here she was, overdressed and fretful, on her way over to apply for a job.

Thelma had laughed the idea off the moment she had it, walking home that day with her arms full of groceries. But the idea had refused to be so easily dismissed. On the contrary, it had only grown as the days became weeks. It had shaken her awake at odd hours, stolen over her as she stood waiting for the bus, slipped up behind her as she was fixing after-school snacks for her white lady's children. "They can't get enough bodies over there," she had told Flora Lee Hodges, and the little white woman's dull eyes had sparkled, lit by the sudden, alien idea that she might take a job.

So why not Thelma? If she thought Flora Lee Hodges was good enough to get work over there, how could she think less of herself? Flora Lee had probably never even graduated high school. Hadn't she confessed that she was "no great shakes" at reading?

But despite her pregnancy, Thelma had managed to graduate Mobile County Training School on time and with honors. Luther had dropped out in 10th grade, saying he didn't need to know nothing about no Shakespeare or algebra in order to cut hair. But Thelma had enjoyed Shakespeare—also Langston Hughes, Countee Cullen, and James Weldon Johnson—and had excelled in algebra. She had gone all the way through and after graduation had even briefly entertained the notion of going to a Negro college and studying to be . . . a teacher, maybe. Or a nurse. She was a smart girl—everybody said so. But then reality had asserted itself—where was she supposed to get money for tuition?—and she had quietly put her daydreams aside and found herself a white lady to work for.

How many times had reality intruded upon something she wanted? How many times had she had that thing snatched away from her? She told herself she'd made peace with her homely, childish dreams being pushed aside in the face of adult concerns. This was what being a grown-up meant, after all. She told herself it was okay.

But it wasn't, really. It never was.

Thelma Mae Gordy was 21 years old, but she felt twice that. She felt as if her life was a script someone else had already written out, and all she had left to do was go through the motions. This was the realization that had stopped her, walking home from the bus that day. In the end, she faced a very simple question, really: Didn't *she* have a right to her own life?

And the answer had to be yes, didn't it? Otherwise, what was the point?

So without telling her brother, without telling their grandfather, she had gotten up this morning and caught the bus to the pier. They would assume she was going to the market up on Davis as she always did on Saturday, and later on, she would. But right now, Thelma had something very different in mind.

She was the last one to step off the ferry. She found herself trickling along at the tail end of a stream that melded into a tributary that melded into a river of people surging through a gate beneath a metal archway that read "Alabama Dry Dock and Shipbuilding Company." For a few moments, Thelma allowed herself to be carried along in the tide of people walking purposefully across the vast plant. Her head turned as if on a swivel. There was so much to take in: the women chattering together as they came out of a building; the men with clipboards, making marks and looking over shoulders as other men turned wrenches; the air loud with the clanging of hammers; the crack and sizzle and flying sparks of metal being joined to metal. Cranes as tall as skyscrapers lifted walls of metal like a toddler lifts building blocks. On the side of a one-story wooden building, mounted and framed, were posters bearing war slogans:

Loose Lips Might Sink Ships!

I Want You for the US Army

Buy War Bonds

And, sure enough: *We're All Together Now.*

Thelma shook her head, amused at the image that was supposed to represent Eric and the white marine. What it depicted was not what had happened, not remotely, but after she got used to the idea, she had decided that that was all right with her, so long as it encouraged people to pull together to win this war. Luther, she knew, wouldn't have shed a tear if the Japanese and the Nazis took over the whole damn country. She tried to tell him the Nazis would be happy to put him and her and all Negroes into one of their camps, maybe even return them to slavery, but Luther just shrugged.

They could march right through Bienville Square for all he cared. Luther was indifferent, not just to the outcome of the war but to the fact of it. He never talked about it, did not read the accounts in the newspaper, had not followed along on a world map as the president spoke on the radio and explained where the troops were fighting and how they were progressing.

For her part, Thelma could not understand how anyone could be apathetic about this war. The Nazis hated everyone who was not like them. And the Japs had attacked her country—yes, *her country,* hateful and mean as it so often was—and she took that personally. She wanted revenge. She wanted to see the enemy crushed. And if a silly poster helped bring that about, it was fine with her.

Thelma turned from the posters—and stopped.

She found herself staring across at a shipway where a battleship was under construction, and the sight stunned her. She realized in that moment that she'd had no idea what a warship really was. She had thought she knew, but nothing she could have pictured would have prepared her for this.

The thing taking shape above her was a behemoth so far out of human proportion as to render human proportion itself insignificant and absurd. Indeed, the people working to put the vessel together, the ones climbing the scaffolding and walking across the footbridges, the ones operating the cranes that delivered building materials to half-formed decks, the ones welding and hammering and pushing levers on heavy machines whose purposes Thelma could not begin to guess, seemed like nothing so much as ants.

Thelma wondered what in the world she could have been thinking to board that ferry and come over here seeking a job building something like that. There was no way in the world she could have a part of anything so . . . astounding.

"It's your first time?"

Thelma was startled by the voice at her elbow. When she turned, she found herself facing the easy smile of a colored man in denim overalls. He appeared to be in his forties, a wiry man with a long, thin face and lively eyes that, just now, watched her with frank interest. "I beg your pardon?" she said.

"I asked if it was your first time over here," said the man. He positioned himself shoulder to shoulder with her so that they were both gazing up at the behemoth. "I asked because first time I come over, I done the same thing you doin'. Stood and looked up at the ships on the shipways. Couldn't make myself understand how big they really was. When I seen you frozen there, lookin' up with that look on your face, it reminded me of my own self, not too long ago."

Thelma nodded. "It is big," she said.

"It is that, indeed," he said. "But you get used to it." After a moment, the man faced her and held out a hand. "Oliver Grimes," he said. "Most folks just call me Ollie."

Thelma spoke her own name as she allowed her hand to be swallowed in his. "Well, Miss Thelma," said Grimes, "I am pleased to make your acquaintance. Hope to see you around here if you get the job. Pretty gal like you would class up the place, I'll say that much. More'n some of these other booger bears we got runnin' round here now, an' that's the truth."

Thelma didn't know how to take that. She lowered her eyes, blushing. It made the man smile. "Oh, I'm just foolin' with you, honey," he said in a gently amused voice. "Don't pay me no never mind."

He touched her elbow and she lifted her eyes. "Look," he said, pointing toward the wood-frame building, "you want a job, that's where you go. Talk to the man in there. Good luck now, you hear?"

Thelma nodded. Grimes flashed her that easy grin and sauntered away, turning back once to lift a farewell salute. Thelma watched until he disappeared into a crowd of men going to work. She took one last eyeful of the skeleton of the mighty, towering ship. Then she steeled herself and walked to the employment office.

She climbed two steps to the door and walked in. A white secretary sat at a desk at the door. She had her head down, scribbling furiously on some piece of paper. Thelma stood there a full five minutes, her purse held before her in two hands, before the woman finally looked up at her without interest. "Yes?" she said.

Thelma cleared her throat. "I'm here to get a job," she said.

Where in the hell was Thelma?

On Saturdays, Luther cut hair for a half a day. Then he went home to spend the afternoon drinking beer, maybe listening to a ball game on the radio. Usually, Thelma was home from the market by now and she had a box of those cheese crackers he liked.

But lately, she had been getting home later and later. She said the buses were crowded, that sometimes, they passed you right by without even stopping. He knew this was true. He had seen it for himself. But even so, it wasn't like her to be this late. The man on the radio said it was after four. She had never gotten home after two on a Saturday. And besides, now that he thought about it, she had left earlier than usual. So what could be taking her so long?

He missed his crackers.

A commercial came on the radio and Luther took the opportunity to get up from the chair in the front room and get another beer from the icebox. The floor seemed to move beneath him, which was no surprise, he supposed, given that he had been sitting here drinking for the better part of three hours. Luther placed his steps carefully, planting one foot, pausing to see what the floor would do, then planting the other.

It took him a moment—the floor slid hard to the left on him at one point, and he almost stumbled but was able to compensate. Eventually, Luther made it to the kitchen, where he picked the last bottle of beer from the icebox. He plucked the cap off with the bottle opener and took a long pull. He sighed with contentment.

Luther was in a good mood today. Even though he didn't have his crackers, he felt good.

It wasn't often that he did.

Usually, he faced the day the way you faced some nigger with a knife in an alley. You braced yourself for what was to come, and you tried to make it through in one piece. Wasn't no feeling good in that. Wasn't no triumph or sense of accomplishment. Because you knew it was just bare luck got you through without injury. And besides, you were just going to have to do it again the next day.

But today was different. Today, he felt good.

He didn't even know why. Maybe it was the beer, but he always had beer. Probably it was that he had collected on a bet from a guy at the shop who had been fool enough to think that white boy Tony Musto had a prayer of upsetting the Brown Bomber. Plus, Gramp was asleep in the back room, so for a change, Luther could enjoy his Saturday without having to listen to the old man picking at him about his drinking. Of course, it didn't really matter why he felt good. What mattered was that he did, and it was a thing so rare that he was determined to savor it, even without his crackers.

The ball game had just come back from commercial, and Luther was entering the front room with the same careful, weaving steps, congratulating himself for not letting the floor trip him up, when he heard a brisk knocking at the front door. At first he thought it was Thelma, and he was glad she was finally home with his crackers. But Thelma wouldn't be knocking, would she? She had her key, didn't she?

The knocking came again, harder this time and filled with authority. And that told Luther that whoever it was, it was a white man. Nobody else knocked at your door like that, like they were offended to find it closed.

Still watching where he placed his feet on the moving floor, Luther made his way to the door. He pulled it open. Two cops were standing on his porch. With them stood another man in an unfamiliar uniform. The gold badge on his chest read—Luther had to squint to see this—Deputy Marshal. White men watching him with white men's contempt.

"Yeah?" he said.

"Luther Hayes?" said the man with the gold star.

"Yeah."

"You're under arrest for violation of the Selective Training and Service Act."

"Select the what?" Luther's mind was whirring like a tire stuck in mud.

"Selective Training and Service Act," said one of the cops, lips puckered in contempt. "The draft, boy. You got two notices for induction, and you missed them both."

"What?" Luther's thoughts were still churning uselessly.

The other cop closed a hard hand on his left forearm. "You need to come with us," he said.

Luther wrenched his arm free. "Fuck you. Ain't goin' nowhere with you. Goin' to sit down and drink my beer is what I'm gon' do."

He tried to turn away, but the second cop caught his forearm again and pulled. Luther had had enough. White men coming to his door pestering him on a Saturday when he was in a good mood, when he was just drinking his beer and not bothering nobody? Uh uh.

He made a fist of the right hand, still holding the half-full bottle, and brought it looping around. The punch was slow and clumsy, but it still managed to clip the first cop on the point of his chin. It was a harmless blow, except that it slung beer all over the front of the white man's shirt.

There was a moment, the cop looking down at his uniform in disbelief. Then his face closed in fury.

The next thing Luther knew, he was landing in a heap on the front walk, skin tearing against the concrete. "Hey, man, hey," he protested, uselessly. Luther rolled over onto his back, trying to figure out what was going on and how he'd ended up here.

Then the cop started kicking him.

The angry voice came from somewhere far above. "Goddamn nigger! Look what you did! Got beer all over me!"

"Fuck you!" cried Luther. "Fuck you! Fuck you!" Tears leaked from his eyes and shredded his voice.

"Fuck me? No, nigger, fuck *you*!"

"He's had enough," said another voice.

But in the same instant, a heavy foot stomped Luther's side. He curled himself tight around the pain. His feet bicycled uselessly against the air. And still feet came slamming down. He lost track of how many times he was kicked before the cop was pulled away.

six

GEORGE'S TRAIN PULLED INTO THE DEPOT ON BEAUREGARD ON a Sunday morning in April. He put aside his Bible and began climbing to his feet. It had been four months since he left Mobile on a tour the War Department had said might last for a month, tops. But each time his minder had told him the next city would be the last, the government had cabled new instructions. And George had seen his life become one unending railroad track until he began to despair of ever again sleeping in anything but a hotel bed.

This was a good thing, he supposed. It meant he was having an effect.

And besides that, every hour that he spent in some Memphis church or Los Angeles radio studio was an hour not spent being reminded what a disappointment he was to his mother and father, how profoundly he had embarrassed them. He had tried writing Mother once. The letter had been chatty, brimming with anecdotes about where he was and what he was doing.

She had responded with a long recitation of the pain poor Sylvia was in, how she had not dared even show her face at the club since Christmas, and how Father was so humiliated that he had taken to avoiding the golf course for fear he might encounter Sylvia's father. George had not answered. He had not heard from his parents, nor they from him, since then, though he had exchanged letters with both his siblings and had written Nick he was coming home today.

George was not proud of himself. The truth was, he felt like a first-class heel. The worst part was, four months later, he still couldn't say exactly why he had jilted a woman any other man would have gladly opened an artery for. All he knew was that as he had sat there on that couch, he had been seized by a certainty: he could not marry that woman. And as awful as he felt about himself, that certainty had never left him.

Tucking the Bible under his arm, George climbed down from the rail-car aided by two porters and the crutches he had by now been using for so long he had all but forgotten what it was like to walk without them. He tipped the porters, took half a step, then stopped, gaping in surprise. His father was waiting on the platform. "Father," he said. "I didn't expect to see you here."

Even when he was not angry, Father was not one for public demonstrations of affection. Or for that matter, private ones. He simply nodded.

"Good to have you back," he said.

There was no welcoming clap on the back, not even a smile of greeting. His tie was perfectly knotted, his glasses wire-framed, his hat a gray homburg, his suit the usual sober black. He did everything in a suit, George knew, except take out the trash.

Father whistled for a porter. "Boy," he said, "come here."

Instantly, a porter appeared, smiling. George handed him his claim check, and the Negro touched his cap and went forward at a trot to the baggage car.

"You had a good trip?" asked Father, watching the Negro hustle off.

"I had an exhausting trip," George replied. He was wary.

"Well, the government seems to have thought it was of some value," said Father. "That's the most important thing."

George waited for more, but that seemed to have depleted his father's capacity for small talk. They waited in silence until the porter returned. The Negro was sweating under the burden of George's bags, but his smile had grown broader, as if the very weight gave him joy. "Got ya bags right here, boss," he said.

George and his father moved away from the train and through the ornate rotunda of the depot without responding. The Negro followed them. "Do you have any idea what they will have you do next?" asked Father.

"I don't know," said George. "I should get off these crutches soon. I suppose my new orders will come through then. Maybe they'll send me back to the Pacific."

"It's a hard thing, war," said his father, who George knew had seen action in the Meuse–Argonne Offensive during the Great War.

"Yes. I know," said George. He tried to tamp down his impatience. Father would get to the point in his own time.

"But this is our country," he was saying, "and we have to defend her."

"I know," said George.

They walked together in silence out the front door and onto Beauregard Street. George was scanning the street for the big Packard—his father usually preferred to drive himself rather than have Benjamin do it—and was surprised when Father moved instead toward a long taxi line. Then he remembered that gasoline rationing was expected to begin soon. It would be just like Father to observe the cutback before it was even in effect.

He would see it as his patriotic duty, indeed, as his family's responsibility as pillars of the community. Father believed in setting an example. He took it with utmost seriousness.

Fifteen minutes crawled by before George and his father worked their way to the front of the taxi line. George had never seen the station so crowded. He mentioned this to Father, who shrugged.

"The whole city is like this now," he said. "They're building new housing as fast as they can to accommodate all the people coming here looking for work."

The cab driver loaded his bags into the trunk. Handing his Bible to his father, George backed into the open rear door of the Buick, then slid across the seat. He drew his crutches in behind him and then Father climbed in. The cab pulled away from the curb and within minutes was frozen in traffic.

Father is right, thought George, gazing at the line of red brake lights stretching ahead of him, *Mobile has changed*. He had never seen it like this.

"So," said Father, "I'm glad we have this time together. I have been wanting to talk with you."

"Yes, I figured," said George. "You want to kick me in the butt again."

"Don't be vulgar," said Father.

George would have slumped in the seat, but the cast on his leg would not permit it. He settled for a sigh of resignation instead.

"Peter Osborn is one of my oldest and dearest friends," said Father, not even bothering to glance over. "The way you have treated his daughter is, frankly, shabby and abominable."

George said, "Father, with all due respect, I don't know that my relationship with Sylvia is any of your business. Or her father's."

Now Father did look at him. His eyes, gray as the homburg on his head, had gone cold, but his voice remained soft and eminently reasonable. "It becomes my business," he said, "when your behavior embarrasses the family."

If it had been a knife, it would have gone into the soft flesh between George's ribs. About the worst sin you could ever commit, as far as Father was concerned, was to embarrass the family. The words hurt all the more because George knew them to be true.

"I'm sorry," he said. His voice was small.

Father didn't respond right away. He produced a pipe and began stuffing it with tobacco from a leather pouch with his initials on it. After a moment, he said, "You are not yet 20 years old, George. For the entirety of your life, we have lived here in Mobile in a very nice house in a very nice part of town. This is all you have ever known. It is all I ever wanted you to know. But it strikes me now that perhaps I should have shielded you less."

"What do you mean?"

Father regarded him. Then he said, "Do you know what a hunky is, George?"

George shrugged.

"Speak up, George."

"No, Father," said George. "What is a hunky?"

"It's me," said Father. "It's a word for any man who comes here from Hungary or, really, anywhere in central Europe, seeking his piece of this American Dream. I can't blame you for not knowing. As I said, I never wanted you to know. I wanted you to be an American. Of course, the first time I myself heard the word, I didn't know that it applied to me. I was working on the line in Mr. Ford's auto plant and I used to hear all the time, 'Hey, you hunkies get back to work! Hey you, hunky, bring me that wrench.' Finally, I asked another man what it meant. I'll never forget what he said. He said, 'It means you and me are one step below the micks and one step above the niggers.'"

A match flared, and Father applied the flame to the bowl of his pipe. He kept the fire there until the tobacco was evenly lit, sucked until he got the pipe going to his satisfaction, then shook out the match. "I was still a greenhorn then," he said, "still speaking with a heavy accent, still cooking the goulash and the cabbage rolls I had learned at my mother's elbow. But I had taken for granted that I was white, according to

America's peculiar racial calculations. What I soon learned was that I was not the right kind of white."

He was looking out the window, watching the crowds passing in the street. "That is why I worked as I did, George. Twelve or 13 hours a day putting together Mr. Ford's cars, then another three hours of schooling every night. But I was determined that I would make something of myself, you see? I was determined that no one else would ever again be able to tell me I was not the right kind of white."

Now he turned to look at George. "Sylvia Osborn," he said, "was born the right kind of white. And for some reason, she is absolutely besotted with you. Marry her and no one will ever dare to call your children—my grandchildren—'hunky.'"

"Father . . ."

"No one will ever be able to say they are just a step above the niggers. No one will ever question whether they are American—and white."

"But Father, don't you see? It doesn't matter what those people said about you. Who cares about some men you worked with 40 years ago? You already proved your point. You worked hard. You got your law degree. You rose to the top of your profession. And you gave your family a good life, a life you couldn't even have dreamed about when you stepped off that ship in Manhattan. We have three cars. We have a nice house. We travel. What else could you want?"

"Money is not the point!" Father cried. George was shocked. Father hardly ever raised his voice. The two men stared at each other. When Father spoke, his voice was soft again.

"Money is not the point," he repeated. "Respectability is."

"And you think that comes from me marrying Sylvia?"

"I do."

"And you think I should go through with that, even if I don't love her?"

Father made a dismissive sound. "What you young people call love is overrated," he said.

The words alarmed George at some primal level. "How do you mean?"

Father took his time answering. He sucked at the stem of his pipe, letting smoke leak from the corner of his mouth. "Young people," he finally said, "always think love is a bolt of lightning from the sky and angel choirs singing your woman's name every time she comes into view. You all watch too many romantic movies and sing too many love songs and they fill your heads with all sorts of cockamamy ideas."

Father laughed softly. "Love is not lightning and angel choirs, my son. Love is something you grow into. You find the right person, someone you understand and who understands you, someone you enjoy being around, someone you don't mind looking at, someone who shares the same fundamental beliefs. And you come together and over the years, she bears your children and takes care of your house and comes to know your moods, as you learn hers, and time passes by and you are comfortable together. That's love, my son."

George didn't know what to think. He was acutely conscious of his own callowness. Maybe he was naïve. But there seemed something shrunken and cold in what his father had said. Was that really all there was to love? Where was passion? Where was joy? Was this dull and dutiful pragmatism that Father described all he had ever felt for Mother? The question made George shift in his seat, and he found that he did not want to think it.

Father was watching him. "So," he said, "did I shatter your illusions?"

"You gave me something to think about," said George, as diplomatically as he could.

"Well, here is something else you should think about," said Father. "You need to go to that girl and beg her forgiveness. She will give it to you; I've been assured of that. As I said, she is besotted with you. And then the two of you need to get married—now, before the military comes up with new orders for you. You can have the big wedding later if you still want. But get married *now*."

"Father, it's still my life. It's still my decision. I have to do what's right for me."

Father's gaze turned searching. "Don't you think you could be happy with Sylvia Osborn?"

George shrugged. "I don't know," he said. "I guess."

Father shook his head. "You guess," he said. He made a sound of disgust. George felt small. He glanced forward to see if the cab driver was paying attention to this exchange. The eyes George saw reflected in the rearview mirror were focused on the road. The cabbie gave a credible imitation of a man interested only in his driving. George did not believe it for a minute. All at once he felt defeated.

George turned to his father as the cab pulled into the long driveway leading up to the house. "Okay, Father," he said, "you've made your point. I will think about it."

Father looked at him. He seemed to be weighing the idea of saying more. Then he decided against it. "Very well, George. Let me know what you conclude."

George blew out a sigh and turned his gaze to the window on his side of the car. He told himself he had no reason to feel guilty. He told himself he had done the right thing—both for himself and for Sylvia. It made no sense to marry some girl he didn't love just to salve Father's feelings about some insulting name he had been called four decades ago. There was absolutely nothing for him to feel guilty about.

But he felt guilty just the same. Indeed, guilt sat in his chest, a heavy, tumorous mass that made him want to beg forgiveness, made him want to run to Sylvia and throw himself on his knees, do anything to make it right. It made no logical sense, he knew. But it was all he could do to resist the urge to fling up his hands and pledge to do whatever Father said so long as it lifted that weight.

The cab pulled beneath the portico and came to a stop. Father leaned forward and handed a sheaf of bills to the cabbie. The driver went around to the trunk and lifted the bags out as George worked his way out of the car. He braced himself on his Father's hand as he climbed to his feet.

"Where the devil is Benjamin?" asked Father as the cab pulled away. "He usually has the hearing of a bat when a car pulls up in front of the house. He's usually out here before you even open the door."

Before George could respond, the front door came open and there was Benjamin Johnston, rushing down the steps toward the two heavy bags.

"Benjamin? I was just telling George, it's not like you not to be out here when a car pulls up. Rarely have I known you to miss one."

"Yes, sir," said Benjamin. "Guess maybe I am slipping at that. I'm sorry, sir."

Father's smile was indulgent. "Not to worry," he said. "I was just giving you a hard time. None of us is perfect."

As he reached for the bags, Benjamin did an odd thing. He shot George an imploring look. Father, standing behind Benjamin, did not see.

George was confused. And now that he was paying attention, he realized Benjamin was sweating. "Benjy," he said, "what's—"

Benjamin ignored him. "Mr. John," he said, lifting one of George's bags in each hand, "Missus called to say she be home from her church meeting just as soon as she can. Say she gettin' a ride from Miz Eldridge. Say she can't wait to see Master George here."

"Very well," said Father. "I will be in my office working if you need me."

The pleading look became one of alarm, though Father still didn't see. "Now, Mr. John, you know Missus frown on you workin' on the Sabbath."

Father smiled. "And who's going to tell her, Benjamin?"

"Well, Mr. John, you know if she ask me I'll have to tell her the truth. Can't be lying to Missus."

Father shook his head. "I don't know what the world is coming to when a man's servants conspire with his wife against him."

Benjamin shot George another meaningful look. "Actually, Mr. John, if you don't mind, could you go upstairs and have a talk with Master Nick? He was mistreating his sister earlier and Missus made him go to his room. She do her best with him, but if you don't mind my saying so, I think he respond better with a good talking to from his daddy."

"They all mistreat their sisters at that age," said Father, puffing on his pipe. "But very well, I'll speak to him." A glance back at George, who stood there, marveling at how deftly the old Negro had manipulated Father. "I'll see you at dinner, son."

George nodded, and his father went through the front door. As soon as he was out of earshot, Benjamin leaned close to George.

"Someone here to see you, Master George."

George was confused. "Someone's in the parlor? Who?"

"She in the back," said Benjamin. "In the kitchen. Ain't got here three minutes before you did. She say she know you."

George pondered this, but he couldn't make it make sense. Who could be there to see him? Why would that person be waiting in the kitchen instead of in one of the parlors? And why was Benjy acting so secretively?

With a sigh of resignation, George followed the old Negro into the house. Benjamin went to the stairs with George's bags, but he nodded down the hallway toward the kitchen, as if George might have forgotten the way. Mystified, George crutched his way down the hall. In the kitchen, he found Alice at her stove, where she had apparently been stirring something in a stewpot. The pot was bubbling, but the ladle was not moving. She was staring toward the door leading to the backyard.

It stood open and a woman—a *Negro* woman, he realized with some surprise—waited on the steps, hands clasped in front of her, silhouetted against the sunshine at her back. George took a step forward. Then he recognized her.

It was Thelma Gordy.

"Hello," she greeted him. "I need your help."

seven

GEORGE LED HER OUT TO THE GARAGE. IT WAS THE ONLY PLACE he could think of.

He certainly could not talk with her in the house, what with her being colored—and a woman. For the same reason, he didn't want to sit with her in the gazebo down near the garden, which was too easily visible from his parents' bedroom upstairs.

The garage, which was accessible from the kitchen, seemed the only practical solution. So Thelma followed him as George crutched his way carefully through the dim half-light past the family cars. His car was the third of three, after the big black Packard Father drove and the creamy tan one Benjy used to take Mother on her shopping trips and to the club. They were a Packard family—George's car was a red One Twenty Victoria convertible. Father had given it to him as a graduation present, though George had hardly ever driven it because he had enlisted in the Marines immediately after high school.

Now he tried the passenger side door and was thankful it opened. He didn't carry a key.

"Sit in the driver's seat," he told her. "I can't because . . . " And he pointed to his right leg. There was no way he could get it behind the steering wheel.

Wordlessly, Thelma nodded and did as she was told. George settled himself into the car, the leg hanging out the open door, crutches leaning against the hood. He looked over at her. "So," he said, "what is it?"

She lowered her head, but she did not speak. Then, all of a sudden, silent tears began to flow from her eyes. George was alarmed. "Hey," he said, "none of that."

"I'm sorry," she told him.

"Just tell me what's wrong."

"Remember you said you'd help me if I needed it? Because of . . . you know . . . Eric?"

"Of course I do."

"I never expected to take you up on it. I mean, I wouldn't ask you now if I had any choice."

"Thelma, what is it?"

She sighed. "It's my brother," she said.

"Luther?"

A nod. "Yes."

"What's wrong with him?"

"He's in jail."

"What? Why?"

"These two policemen and a US marshal came to the house yesterday to get him. He got in a fight with 'em."

George was stunned. "*What?*"

She nodded. "He's lucky he didn't get his fool self killed."

"But why were they coming to get him?"

She dabbed at her eyes. "Luther got his draft notice few months ago. But he said he wasn't going to show up for no induction. And he didn't. He threw the paper in the trash. They sent him another notice and he threw that one away, too. So they sent the police and the marshal to get him and he had been drinking, and well . . . you met Luther. Don't know when to shut his mouth."

She beseeched him with her eyes. "He didn't mean any harm," she said. "Like I say, he could have gotten killed. But thank the Lord, all they did was beat him up something awful and then haul him away. I wasn't home. This wouldn't have ever happened if I was there."

She felt guilty. She thought somehow it was her fault. George heard these things in her voice, but it was like some thin whisper from the bottom of a deep well, a sound barely there. He was too busy grappling with the incredible thing she had said to him, said to a man who had survived Pearl Harbor, said to a *marine* who would probably soon receive orders to the Pacific.

He said he wasn't going to show up for no induction.

"He's a draft evader," George said.

Apparently, Thelma heard the disgust in his voice. She gave him a look as if she thought perhaps she had made a mistake in coming here. And she certainly had if she expected George Simon to have sympathy for *any* man, colored or white, who refused to answer when his country called—especially after Pearl Harbor.

"Yes," she said, "he's a draft evader."

"I don't know that I can do anything to help your brother," said George, his voice stiff like a freshly starched collar. "To be perfectly honest, I don't know that I'd even want to."

She flicked a lingering tear from her cheek as she regarded him. Finally she said, "You haven't asked me why he doesn't want to serve."

"Let me guess," said George. "It's because he hates white people." What was it Reeves had said about the need to boost morale among the Negroes, to make sure the radicals among them did not infect the rest with anti-war sentiment? At the time, George had taken it for just so much soft soap, something they were telling him to make him more eager to participate in their publicity stunt. But maybe, he thought now, they had known what they were talking about after all.

"Yes, he hates white people," said Thelma, and was that actually impatience he heard now at the edge of her voice? *Impatience*? With *him*?

"That's no reason for refusing service," he informed her.

"But that's not all of it," she said.

"What do you mean?"

"You want to know why he hates white people?"

"I don't see what that has to do with—"

"White people killed our parents," she said.

He looked at her. She met his gaze, her eyes glittering but clear, even defiant, in the hazy light. There was a beat. He said, "What do you mean?"

"You know what I mean," she said. Her voice was soft, but challenge ran like an electric current through it. "They lynched them," she said.

"But why?"

Her smile was humorless and tight. "There was some white man who was mad Daddy wouldn't sell him a hog at a cheap price. But of course, white people don't really need a reason."

She said it as though it were obvious, a self-evident truth. George didn't know how to respond. He said nothing.

Thelma fumbled in her pocketbook, found a cigarette, and lit it with unsteady hands. She shook out the match, blew a gray jet of smoke up through the shadow and light toward the ceiling.

"They tell me I saw it," she said, "but I was just out of diapers, don't remember none of it. But Luther . . ." A pause. A silence. A deep drag from the cigarette. "Luther, he was nine. He saw. And he remembers."

She stared at him as if daring him to say anything. Finally, she said, "They dragged 'em out of the house, my mama and papa. They beat 'em. Then they hanged 'em, but they wouldn't let 'em die. Then they set 'em on fire. What you think that would be like, seeing that happen to your parents and you're just a boy? How you think you'd feel about the people who done it?" She sucked hard on the cigarette. Smoke filled the space between them. "Can you imagine how much you'd hate 'em?"

She stared at him again, waiting for him, making it clear the question was not rhetorical, that she required an answer. He had the sense she was challenging him, daring him to . . . *what*? He had no idea. But he could not shake the feeling.

"No," he said, "I can't imagine."

"No," she agreed, nodding. "Me neither. What he saw, it messed his head up. He can't get it out of his thoughts. That's why he drinks so much. And that's why he can't stand white people. I ain't saying he's right. I'm saying he's got a reason. Do you blame him?"

Again, her eyes challenged him. George wanted to pull away from them, but that felt cowardly. So he forced himself to meet the almost physical weight of Thelma Gordy's gaze. Her eyes seemed to know him with a frightening totality. It reminded him of the way her husband, this man he had never really noticed, had snarled and cursed and joshed at him to help him overcome his own fear, had given him what he needed when he needed it—then disappeared into a sphinxlike silence once the danger was gone and his help was no longer required. Lying there in the stench and darkness of waiting, George had come to the conclusion that you never really knew Negroes. But somehow, Negroes seemed to always know you.

"No," he admitted. "I guess I can't blame him."

She sat back in her seat as if satisfied by the admission. She smoked without saying anything else, staring at the blank wall ahead. After a while she said, "You got a nice house here, Mr. George."

"Thank you," he said.

A rueful smile lifted one corner of her mouth. "I see why you think everybody has a telephone. I lived in a house like this, I might think so, too."

"So," said George, and she looked over at him, "what is it you need from me, Thelma? Is it money for bail, is that it?"

She shook her head. "Don't want bail money," she said. "He needs a lawyer."

This surprised him. "What do you mean?" he asked, stupidly.

She arched an eyebrow. "I mean he needs a *lawyer*," she said again, as if he needed her to speak more clearly in order to understand. "Ain't your daddy John Simon? That's what Rafe told me that night he brought you back here. He says your daddy the biggest lawyer in town."

"My . . . father?" George felt slow.

"Your father," she said. Her brow pinched in concern. "Was Rafe wrong? Your father is John Simon, ain't he?"

"Yes, but . . ." George paused, trying to imagine how that conversation might go.

Father, would you be willing to represent a colored draft evader?

How to ask that of his father? Who had fought in the Ardennes. Who had changed his name from Johan to John because he wanted something "more American." Who had said, just today, "This is our country and we have to defend her." His father.

"I don't think that's a very good idea," he told her.

"Why not?"

"You don't know my father," he said.

"What you mean?"

"My father, he . . . well, he isn't likely to have much sympathy for Luther."

"Because Luther don't want to be drafted."

"Yes. You have to understand. Father fought in the first war. Plus, well . . . he really loves this country. He came here from Hungary, you see. He started with nothing, but he worked hard to make his way up. Father always says that no other country in the world would have given that kind of opportunity to a penniless immigrant."

"Sound like my father," she said. "What they've told me about him, at least."

"How do you mean?"

"Hard worker. Determined to pull himself up, make something of himself. And he did. Worked hard, had his own farm, had a Model T back when most people were still riding horses and walking. He was doing good."

George spoke the next words because they seemed to need speaking, because they hung over the silence like a smell. "And then they killed him," he said.

"And then they killed him," she agreed with a nod.

There was a silence. Then Thelma said, "You don't think your father might change his mind because of, you know, what happened to make Luther the way he is?"

George considered this. Father actually tended to be rather sympathetic toward colored people, especially as compared with other white men. He gave to charities that supported them and to book drives that provided for their schools. And he absolutely loathed the types of people who would do what had been done to Thelma's parents. He considered them low-down, contemptible, trash.

"He might," George said. He could, in fact, see his father having compassion for Luther's plight. "But there's another problem," he told her.

"What's that?" she asked, crushing out her cigarette in the ashtray in the dash.

"Me," said George. "It's precisely the wrong time to ask—or at least, for me to ask on your behalf."

She looked startled. "Why?"

He didn't want to say, but for some reason, he said it anyway. "There's a girl they want me to marry," he said. "Our family has known their family for years and we were engaged. And then I sort of, well, backed out."

"Why?"

George looked over at the woman next to him. "I don't love her," he said.

"You didn't know this before you got engaged?"

"No," he said. "Foolish as it sounds, I guess I didn't. I didn't realize until . . . well, we were talking about Eric, in fact, and about the publicity stunt the military wanted me to do, how they wanted to excite Negroes and get them behind this war. And she said she couldn't see why the military would bother. She said something like—excuse my language, but this is what she said—the 'niggers' should be happy to fight for their country. She said that, and I just knew right in that moment that I couldn't marry her."

Thelma didn't bother to hide the skepticism in her eyes. "That's when you knew it? When she said 'niggers?'"

"Yes."

"And she hadn't ever said that before?"

George felt color rushing into his cheeks. "I guess she had," he admitted. "I suppose I hadn't really noticed it before."

"But you notice it now?"

"I guess I do, yeah. Because of Eric."

She considered this for a moment. Then she shrugged. "Nobody can make you marry somebody you don't want to marry," she said.

"That's how I feel," he said and was surprised how pleased he was to have someone take his side. "But apparently, I'm in the minority around here."

"So you think that, because of this girl you won't marry, your father won't help my brother?"

"I think it's very unlikely, yes. It's a bad time for me to go asking favors. And that's what this would be, right? I assume you don't have the money to hire him."

She shook her head. "White lady I work for don't pay me but six dollars a week plus bus fare," she said. "Course, I just got a new job pay a lot more, but I ain't even started that yet."

"I don't know what to tell you," he said.

Disappointment softened her eyes. For a moment, he thought she might cry again, and selfishly, George prayed she wouldn't. He didn't know what he would do if she did.

There was a moment. When Thelma regarded him again, her eyes were dry, but there was a sorrow in them that seemed to go down for miles. "Mr. George," she said, "I know you don't like my brother and I can't blame you for that. Luther don't make it easy for nobody to like him, not even me. But it's not his fault he's the way he is. They say he could get five years for draft evasion, and maybe more time for fighting with the police. And it just don't seem to me he deserve all that. Seem to me that would be like punishing him all over again when he's already punished every day of his life."

"Whatever happened to those men?" asked George.

"What men?"

"The white men who lynched your parents. What did the law do to them?"

"You know the answer to that, Mr. George. The law didn't do nothing to them. The law never does."

And she was right. George had known the answer. But for some reason, he had needed to hear it spoken.

Thelma watched him closely. "I know you say it's a long shot," she said, "but would you at least try? Would you at least ask your daddy?"

George met her eyes. Still that bottomless sorrow. It tore at him. After a moment, he nodded. "Yes," he heard himself say. "I'll talk to him."

She smiled. The relief her eyes reflected all but broke his heart.

George approached his father that evening after dinner. It had been a stilted meal, his parents saying little, Nicky and Cora chattering nervously in hopes of filling the great yawning silence. His brother asked George to describe for the umpteenth time what it was like to be at sea, to feel a great ship moving beneath him and hear the booming of her guns, even if just fired in maneuvers. George obliged Nicky as best he could. He felt sorry for his kid brother and sister; they could sense the tension but couldn't do anything about it. They couldn't even ask about it.

Finally, dinner was done and Alice began clearing away the plates. George cleared his throat as his father rose to go to his study, where he often spent the better part of Sunday evenings reading alone and puffing contemplatively on his pipe. "Father, may I speak with you?" he said.

He saw Father and Mother exchange a glance and knew they were thinking—*hoping*—he was about to change his mind and tell them he would marry Sylvia Osborn after all. Father would be irked when he found out what George really wanted. It would make it that much more unlikely that he would agree to represent Thelma's luckless brother. But George had to at least ask. He owed that much to Eric—and to Thelma.

Father waved a brusque hand. "Join me," he said.

George followed his father to the spacious room off the west parlor. It was still light outside, and the late-day sun cast a mellow gleam on the room, wedges of buttery light falling on the dark, overstuffed leather couch, the massive desk with its leather chair, the towering wooden shelves uniformly stacked with gold-trimmed books of law.

Father closed the door and then closed the blinds, plunging the room into near darkness. A moment later, the light on the desk came on, casting a circle of light that did not reach the corners of the room. Father took a seat in the leather chair, leaned back. "Sit down," he said, waving George to the visitor's chair in front of the desk.

Father produced his pipe and tobacco pouch from the vest pocket of his suit. "So," he said mildly as he unzipped the pouch, "what was it you wanted to talk with me about?"

"It's not what you think," said George.

"Oh?"

"No. I mean, it's not about Sylvia Osborn."

"I see. Then what is it about?"

George steeled himself. "Eric Gordy's widow came here earlier today to speak with me. She needs a lawyer. That is, her brother—his name is Luther Hayes—he needs a lawyer."

"I see," said Father, striking a match and applying the flame to the bowl of his pipe. "And why does this Luther Hayes need a lawyer?"

George told him briefly of Luther's refusal to report for induction and his fight with two city police officers and a US marshal who came to take him into custody. As he had expected, his father's gaze grew sterner with each word. When George finished, his father said, "Have you lost your mind? I cannot believe you would ask me to defend some black draft evader. Especially you, as a military man yourself. And at a time of war?"

George had anticipated this response. "Well," he said in a careful, even voice, "I certainly don't condone his draft evasion, Father. But I can understand why he doesn't want to serve this country. I think you will, too."

"Oh? And why is that?" Father was curious despite himself.

"His parents were lynched, Father."

Father stopped. The angle of his gaze shifted. "Lynched?"

George nodded. "Apparently, it happened when he was a young boy, not yet 10. And he saw it all. First the white men beat them, then they hanged them, then they burned them alive. His sister says it unhinged him. She says it turned him into what he is now, a drunkard who hates whites, hates this whole country. You have to understand: she doesn't condone what he did. As she put it to me, 'I'm not saying he's right. I'm saying he has a reason.' She asked me if I could blame him for feeling the way he does. And Father, I couldn't. I just couldn't."

"*Istenem*," said Father. Roughly translated, it meant, "My God." Father only lapsed into his native tongue when he was particularly disturbed.

"That's how I felt when she told me," said George.

Father regarded him. "As you know, George, I've said for years that the white trash filth who do this sort of thing need to be rounded up and shot."

"I know."

Father didn't speak for a moment. He clamped his teeth on the stem of his pipe and stared into space. George waited.

Finally, Father said, "Tell me about this woman, George. Why are you asking this favor for her?"

"Well, Father, as I've told you, her husband saved my life. I feel I owe a debt because of that, if not to him, then to his widow. I told her that if there was anything I could do for her, I would." George shrugged.

"A very open-ended promise."

"I suppose," said George.

Father gave him a look. "Tell me, George: Are you smitten with this woman? This Negress?"

It stopped him. Not just the absurdity of the idea but the suggestion that slept unspoken just beneath it, the whisper that said if he were, indeed, "smitten," there were things that could be done, arrangements that could be made as white men had done for decades. They had a word for the women in those "arrangements:" concubines. There was no word for the men.

George told himself that this was not what Father had meant. He looked into the older man's face for confirmation, but as usual, John Simon's expression said nothing.

Smitten.

As if he was doing this because he wanted to have sex with Eric Gordy's widow. As if he was doing it from some silly infatuation—which would be impossible anyway, given that she was a Negro. As if he would do it, *could* do it, for any other reason than that it was the honorable thing.

George spoke stiffly. "No. As I said, I simply feel indebted to her husband."

Father's nod was almost imperceptible. "And this favor you ask of me, this would balance the scales?"

George shook his head. "I don't know that anything could ever balance the scales, Father. I wouldn't be here if it weren't for her husband. But, yes, it would make me feel a lot better if I were able to do this favor for her."

"You're an honorable man, George," said Father.

"Thank you," said George.

"About most things," he added.

George winced. "Father . . . ," he said.

His father lifted his hand. Obediently, George fell silent. "Hear me out. I understand why you want to help this woman. I respect that you feel a debt of honor toward the widow of the man who saved your life. As I said, you have a sense of honor, and it pushes you to go beyond what many men in your situation would feel it necessary to do. That's an admirable thing, George. And you follow this sense of honor even though it requires you to importune me for a favor at a time that is most inconvenient for you, given our conversation of this morning."

"It's not just honor," admitted George. "It's also guilt. A man I didn't really even know sacrificed his life for me. To tell you the truth, I don't think I'd ever really even seen him before. I mean, *really* seen him."

Father waved the distinction away. "It doesn't matter," he said. "Whether from honor or from guilt, my point is that you have a sense of responsibility to this woman. Many people in your situation would have paid the courtesy call the government asked of them and that would have been it. Your sense of obligation, your need to do what's right, demands more than that of you, even at the price of your own personal comfort. Am I right?"

George gave a miserable nod. He could see where this was going.

Father smiled a tight smile. "That is why this situation today is so perplexing to me. I fail to understand how you can feel such responsibility to this woman—Thelma, I believe you said her name is—and yet feel so little responsibility toward Sylvia, whom you have known your entire life."

"It's not that I feel nothing toward Sylvia," protested George. "It's just that I don't feel enough for her to sustain a marriage."

"Nonsense," said Father. "I told you earlier and I will tell you again: the idea that you will see a woman and be struck by a lightning bolt is a childish fantasy, a line from a Frank Sinatra record. In reality, you and Sylvia already have everything you need to make a marriage work: mutual affection and mutual respect. The rest comes in time. Trust me, son. Have I ever steered you wrong?"

"No, sir," he said. He felt heavy with resignation.

"Then I beg you to listen to me now."

Father sighed, as if exhausted by the unaccustomed emotionalism. He puffed on his pipe. "Look at it this way," he said behind a cloud of aromatic smoke. "You are trying to fulfill an obligation you feel you owe this woman you don't even know because of something her husband did. Where, then, is your sense of obligation to Sylvia Osborn? You led her to believe you were going to do something you now say you do not want to do. You allowed her to make plans based on what she had believed. And then you utterly humiliated her before all your friends, all of Mobile society. So tell me, George, where is this advanced sense of honor of yours where Sylvia is concerned?"

And even though he had known it was coming, George still felt hammered by shame. Because Father had a point, didn't he? "I don't know," he conceded in a voice shriveled with defeat. Father regarded him, said nothing. George closed his eyes, shook his head. He felt 10 years old. Father was very good at what he did.

"So what are you saying, Father?" he asked in the darkness of lowered lids. "Are you saying you won't help Thelma?"

"That is not what I'm saying at all," said Father.

George opened his eyes. Suddenly, he knew. It had been right in front of him all along. What an idiot he was. What a fool. Father knew that, whatever the reason, it was important to him that Thelma not be hurt. And though George was his son, the lawyer John Simon—always *the lawyer*, was John Simon—had no qualms about using that knowledge, cruelly, ruthlessly . . .

George sighed.

. . . *effectively*.

"You're saying you'll help her if I agree to marry Sylvia Osborn."

Father made a face. His hands had been pressed together. Now, with a little shrug, he held them apart as if to say, What else can I do? As if to suggest that he was reluctant, but this act of emotional blackmail was the only option left to him by his wayward son.

George felt the ground sliding away like sand beneath his feet, carried out to sea by an outrushing wave. He could not believe. He simply could not believe.

But in the end, the guilt was just too much. He *had* led Sylvia Osborn on. He *had* humiliated her. He *had* behaved as an absolute cad.

When George finally spoke, though, it wasn't Sylvia's hurt expression that hovered before him. No, he was seeing Thelma Gordy's eyes.

"Very well," he said. "You win. I'll marry Sylvia."

eight

"HAYES! SOMEONE TO SEE YOU."

Luther had been dozing on the bottom bunk, his right arm pressed against the rib cage those damn cops had kicked in like a flophouse door. He had a bet with himself over how many of his ribs were broken. No fewer than three, he was sure. He was purple with bruises, and his mouth seemed to hang crookedly off his face.

At the sound of the jailer's voice, he managed to wedge open the one eye that still worked and roll it around to the door of the cell. A young police officer was standing there, handcuffs dangling from his right hand.

Luther groaned. Moving was torture. And he had only managed to claim this bunk just a few hours ago when its previous occupant was hauled off to court. The cell, jammed as it had been all weekend with Friday night drunks and Saturday night brawlers, had far more men—all colored—than bunks, and he had been obliged to spend the better part of the last two days sitting on the floor, his back against the wall. Compared to that, this mattress, thin as a banker's smile and reeking of piss though it was, was a little foretaste of Heaven. Luther was loath to give it up.

But the visitor could only be Thelma, taking a day off from work that she could not afford to come down here and make sure her brother was all right. He could not just lie here and ignore her, much as he wanted to, much as it would shame him for her to see him like this.

Luther knew what he was—a drunk burning with an anger that never seemed to exhaust itself. He knew he was hard to live with but his sister and grandfather felt compelled to do so anyway, to endure his rants and rages and inability to be at peace. He was humiliated, knowing he had become something they felt obliged to put up with out of kinship and duty, a disappointment—to Thelma in particular. He knew this, though she did all she could to hide it from him.

Every day, he promised himself he would change. Every day, he told himself he would get himself together, make himself a man no one had to pretend not to be disappointed with.

But then he closed his eyes and saw orange firelight reflected on a white man's sweaty jowls, smelled flesh cooking, and he couldn't help himself. He had to rage, he had to drink, he had to do whatever it took to blur the smells and the sights, to make them something he could at least endure. Not overcome, but endure.

Sometimes, Luther fantasized about making it all go away forever, about taking a rifle, wedging the barrel against the soft flesh under his jaw, reaching down, and pushing the trigger—about going to a place of darkness, nothingness, and peace where he would no longer see, smell, remember.

"Hayes!"

The white cop was growing impatient. With another groan, Luther forced himself to a sitting position, then pushed himself up through pain to his feet. He was hardly upright before two men were arguing over the vacant bed.

Luther didn't even bother to look behind him. The two men were still muttering curses at each other as he shuffled forward and, without a word, reached his hands through the bars. When the cuffs had clicked into place, he withdrew his hands and the officer opened the door. As Luther came through, the door closed behind him, sounding heavy and final. The police officer grabbed Luther's bicep and led him to the visitation room. He walked with a brisk, impatient step, and Luther's agony-racked body was hard put to keep up.

The cop, of course, knew this. He just didn't care.

Luther was thinking to himself how much he hated white people when the door to the visitation room opened. Luther stopped. It was not Thelma who sat at the wooden table, hands clasped, watching him be led in. Rather, it was some old white man in a funeral director's suit, who gazed at him with mild curiosity.

"Who are you?" demanded Luther. His own words made him wince. It hurt to speak.

The man did not stand. He did not proffer the hand that Luther would not have accepted. "Sit down," he said, nodding to the chair across from him.

"I said, who are you?"

This earned Luther a shove in the back from the policeman. "Look like you still need to learn some manners, boy," he said.

The white man lifted his hand. "That won't be necessary," he told the police officer. Then he addressed himself to Luther. "My name is John Simon. I am your lawyer. Come in and sit down so that we may talk."

The door closed behind him. Luther crossed the room warily, as if each panel of the cracked linoleum might conceal a trapdoor. "Ain't got no lawyer," he said as he reached the table and took a seat.

"Yes, you do," the man told him. "And I am he."

"I don't get it."

"Let's just say your sister engaged my services."

"My sister ain't got no money."

"I didn't say she paid me. I said she engaged me."

Luther got the feeling the white man was enjoying this. Maybe he thought it was some kind of game. "You don't start talkin' sense," Luther told him, teeth clenched against the pain of speaking, "I'm gon' get up and get my black ass out of here. Ain't got time to waste fuckin' round with you."

"I'm telling you the truth," said the man. "And as to your freedom, that has already been arranged."

Now Luther knew this white man was just fucking with him. "What are you talkin' about? Who the hell are you?"

"I already told you," said the white man, adjusting his glasses. "My name is John Simon. I am your attorney."

"Simon . . . " Luther repeated the name, hoping that doing so would help him to understand why it sounded so familiar. He had heard this name before, that much he knew. Then it came to him. With his manacled hands, he pointed twin index fingers across the table. "That marine came to the house last Christmas, his name was Simon."

"His name was George Simon," said the lawyer. "He's my oldest son."

"And Thelma's husband saved his life."

"Yes, he did. And for that we are all very grateful."

"So you doin' this for payback, huh?"

"I beg your pardon?"

"This," said Luther, pointing at the table. "You come here to be my lawyer 'cause you feel like you got a debt to Thelma and this how you gon' pay it."

"Something like that," said Simon.

Luther could not read the lawyer's smile, but something about it increased his wariness. "So what you gon' do?" he asked. "You gon' talk for me when we go to court?"

"It's already done," said the lawyer.

"What you mean?"

"I mean that I have talked with the prosecutor and I've gotten him to see that you didn't really mean any harm. I've explained your . . . situation to him, the awful story of what happened to your parents, and he is prepared to be most lenient. You will be able to go home today." He glanced at his watch and added, "You might even be able to be there for dinner depending on how the buses are running. You just need to sign some papers and take care of some formalities."

Simon's smile opened. He was pleased with himself. He was expecting wonderment and gratitude.

"Uh huh," said Luther. "What formalities you talkin' about? What I got to do?"

The lawyer's expression soured, as if he were surprised and displeased by Luther's response. "Well," he said, "you will be on probation for a year. You will also have to apologize to the police officer you hit."

A year of probation wasn't so bad. It was crazy, though, to think he would have to apologize to the bastard who had kicked his ribs in. If anybody owed anybody an apology, the cops owed one to him. But, thought Luther with an inward sigh, he could probably swallow that, too, if it meant he would be sprung from that cell with the bony mattress that reeked of piss.

"Oh," said Simon, "and of course you will have to report for induction."

Luther stared at him. The lawyer had his head down, consulting some piece of paper, so he didn't immediately notice. When he realized Luther had not spoken, he looked up and met his client's eyes. Whatever he saw there made his own eyes widen.

"What's wrong?" he asked.

"What's wrong is, I ain't reportin' for no induction," said Luther. It still hurt to speak, but he was barely aware of it.

"But you have to."

"I won't."

"Luther, listen to me: the whole arrangement falls apart if you don't agree to report. It's all predicated on that. That was the only way I could get them to forgive you."

"Fuck they forgiveness. Don't need they forgiveness."

"Luther, please . . ." The white man was becoming flustered.

"Look," said Luther, "you my lawyer, right?" Simon nodded. "That mean you supposed to represent my interest, right?"

The lawyer sank into the chair, looking like his stomach hurt. He didn't bother to answer the question, just lifted his eyebrows by way of acknowledgment.

"Well, I'm tryin' to tell you," said Luther, "reportin' for induction ain't in my interest."

"But you won't get out of here if you don't agree. Don't you understand? You hit a police officer. You are lucky to be alive. If you do not agree to this arrangement, you will spend the next five years in prison, plus whatever they give you for assaulting the officer, and be liable for a $10,000 fine on top of it."

Luther slammed the table. "I don't give a fuck!" he roared. "I will *not* fight for this fuckin' country."

To Luther's surprise, the white man leaned forward, into Luther's rage. "But it is *your* country," he insisted in a quiet voice. "It is your country as well as it is mine. Why would you not fight to defend your country? You are an American, aren't you?"

And that question was so ridiculous that right in the middle of his fury, Luther erupted in laughter. Earnest confusion shone from Simon's eyes, and Luther realized the lawyer had not the faintest clue what was so funny, could not fathom the idea that a man would not be willing to fight for America. Luther wiped tears from his eyes. "When you get here, man?" he finally asked. "Your family, I mean. When they come to this country?"

Simon stiffened. "I came here from Hungary in 1895, when I was a boy. Twelve years old. My whole family came over."

"My old grandpapa was born here, about 50 years before you got here. He was born up in Mississippi, plantation near Buford. His folks was born in this country, too, and probably they folks before them. Just like me. But wasn't none of them no damn American. And I ain't no American neither."

For a fraction of time, the two men simply sat, hands clasped before them, and stared at one another across the expanse of the wooden table. Luther felt a giddy satisfaction nearly as intoxicating as beer. When had he ever been able to tell a white man just how he felt? When had he ever?

At length, Simon said, "This is about what happened to you? To your parents?"

"This a white man's country," said Luther. "Wasn't made for my mama and my papa. Sure as hell wasn't made for me."

"I am sorry you feel that way."

"You feel that way, too, you was me."

The white man regarded him for a moment. Then he said, "Tell me about it. Tell me about what happened."

"You already know what happened."

"I would prefer to hear it from you."

Now Luther's eyes searched the white man hard, looking for some slightest sign this bastard was playing him. But the white man only stared back, his placid gaze meeting Luther's probing one head-on.

Finally, Luther sighed. He sat back. "I knew somethin' was wrong, days before," he said. "When you a kid, you don't know all that's goin' on, and the grown-ups, they don't talk to you or tell you nothin'. Tryin' to protect you, I guess. But you ain't stupid just 'cause you young, you know? You can smell the tension, even if you don't know what it's all about.

"My grandpapa, Gramp, we call him, he explained a lot of it to me afterward. You know, how them crackers, they ain't never liked my daddy none to begin with. Rest of the colored folks croppin', just strugglin' to make a livin', and here Papa is, done worked Lord know how many jobs—he was a porter, a barber, a mechanic, a handyman; hardest workin' man I ever seen, colored or white. But he done saved money off that, so he done bought his own place while all the other colored folks croppin'. Wasn't a big place—some milk cows, some pigs, some hens, raised a little cotton and corn. But it was all his, you know? That's the first thing they hated him for, that he got somethin' of his own and ain't workin' for none of them."

Luther paused, shook his head in remembrance. "Then there was the car," he said. "One year—long about '21 or '22, I guess it was—Papa bought hisself an old used Model T. This back when even most of the white people in these parts still usin' horse and buggy to go to town. And here come my papa, trundling all over the countryside in that tin lizzie of his. So they hated him for that, too. Said he was gettin' too big for his britches. Said somebody need to knock him down a peg, remind him he still a nigger, 'cause he seem like he done forgot. Then come that business about the hog, and that's what done it."

"Hog?" The lawyer arched an eyebrow.

"Papa bought this hog. I don't remember it, but Gramp say it was the biggest hog anybody in them parts ever seen. He say it weigh seven hundred pounds if it weighed one. Blacker than a crow at midnight. S'pose to been a real sight to behold.

"And all them white mens, they wanted it. Offered him all kind of money for it, but Papa wouldn't sell. He was gon' butcher it that September, keep us in meat through the winter. But the white mens, they wouldn't give up. One in particular. His name Floyd Bitters—'Big Floyd,' they called him, on account he real big and also, he some kind of county commissioner or something. He come out to the house two, three times and each time, he raised his offer. Each time, my papa say no, polite as he can.

"Man say, 'Mason'—that's my papa's name, Mason Hayes—'Mason, I just got to have that hog. You name your price and I'll meet it.'

"And Papa, he always say, 'No, thank you, Mr. Bitters. I appreciate the offer, but I think I'm just gon' hold on to him. Be some good eatin' for my family.'"

"But this man would not give up," said Simon. It was not a question.

Luther shook his head. "No. And one day, he catch Papa in town and he ask him again: 'Now, Mason, what it gon' take for you to sell me that hog of yours?' And Papa, he said no again, but maybe this time, he ain't quite as polite as he been before."

Luther stared at the lawyer to make sure he understood. "Don't get the wrong idea," he said. "He ain't called the white man no name, ain't cussed him out or nothin'. Way I hear it, he just got a little edge in his voice, a little sharpness like he tired of them askin' him the same question all the time. He say, 'I done already told you, Mr. Bitters, he ain't for sale. I'm gon' hold on to him. Butcher him for my family.' Like that. Not nasty. Just impatient, you know?"

Simon nodded.

"But Papa, he know right off he done made a mistake, speakin' to this white man like that, like maybe he think *he* a man, too. Even worse, he done spoke like this to him in front of a bunch of other white men, and now they starin' holes right through him. Papa, he start grinnin', duckin' his head like a little boy, tryin' to make a joke out of it. 'Oh, Big Floyd, I sorry, ain't meant to be so peckish. Ha ha. Got this corn on my foot been givin' me the devil all week, put me in a right sour mood. You know how it is, sir. Ha ha ha. Nigger can't take no pain. We ain't built for it. Ha ha.'

"But he can see in they faces that this ain't workin'. It's like he been wearin' a mask all this time and all of a sudden, they can see him like he really is, so the mask don't work no more. They faces was like stone, that's what Gramp said. They mad enough to cuss. Papa see ain't nothin' he can do. He touch his hat, still grinnin', and walk away to his car, that old Model T they hated so bad. And all the way, he can hear 'em talkin' behind him, loud, like they *wanted* him to hear.

"'They get more uppity every day.'

"'Somebody need to teach that nigger a lesson.'

"From then on," said Luther, "wasn't nothin' but a matter of time. One day, two days, three days, my mama an' papa walkin' round the place on eggshells, snappin' at me and Thelma for little things they wouldn't never have cared about before, cuttin' eyes at each other like they scared of somethin' but too scared to even speak its name. Then one night, I'm lyin' there, just listenin' to the night. Me and Thelma and Gramp all shared a room, and me an' her slept in the same bed and she kickin' my ribs in her sleep like she do every night, so I have to keep pushin' her feet away. And all of a sudden, I hear this loud knocking—bam! bam! bam!—at the door. And somehow I knew, whatever they was worried about, it done finally come."

The boy sat up in the darkness, panting. It had been a steamy day and that had given way to a night that sweltered, the air thick and soupy, the sweat trickling down in large drops upon his brow.

The heavy fist came again against the door. It seemed to shake the tiny house. "Come on out here, Mason. We know you in there, boy."

Now Thelma sat up too, sucking at her thumb, her eyes wide and white in the darkness.

"What's that? Who there?" Gramp was a dark shape on the bed near the wall, fumbling for his glasses.

"It's nothin', Papa." Luther's father was passing in the hallway, guided by the light of an oil lamp he held before him. "Y'all go back to sleep."

But his voice, thin and trembly, made a liar out of him. He sounded scared. This was what Luther would always remember, because it seemed so incredible. His father . . . *scared*.

"Mason, you don't need to be goin' out there." This was Annie, their mother. Her voice was full and urgent.

"What else I'm gon' do? I don't go out there, they gon' come in here."

As if to prove the point, the white man's fist landed again against the door. The blows were so heavy Luther would not have been surprised if his fist had come right through the thin wood.

"Hurry up, Mason! Get your black ass out here!" The voice was rough and slurry.

"Don't go out there, Mason, please." Mama was pleading.

"Hush up, Annie." Papa's voice was harsh.

"At least take your gun."

"No, that just bound to make it worse."

Luther hopped down from the bed. Thelma climbed down and toddled after him. She was at an age where she followed him everywhere. "Y'all come back here," cried Gramp. Luther didn't even think about obeying. He loved his grandfather, but this was obviously trouble and his father needed him.

Even as Luther came into the front room, Papa pulled the door open upon a scene that made the boy's heart grind painfully in his chest. Big Floyd stood there on the porch, grinning stupidly, well above six feet in height with a massive gut that slopped over his belt. In his fist, he gripped a bottle with a black label, half full of some amber liquid. He was so drunk that he seemed to weave in his boots. Behind him were at least a dozen other white men, some bearing pine-tar torches that cast weird, flickering shadows. There was also a smattering of women and even some children, including one little blonde girl not much older than Thelma, who rode her father's shoulders for a better view.

"There he is!" cried Bitters in triumph. "There's the nigger thinks he's just as good as a white man!"

Luther was behind his father, but he could hear in his father's oddly thin voice the tremulous smile that sat uneasily on his face as he spoke. "Mr. Bitters? What this all about, sir? What y'all doin' out here this time of night?"

Bitters ignored him, playing to his jury. "Offered this nigger good money for that there hog," he said, pointing vaguely in the direction of the hog pen. "But he's too good to accept a fair offer. And he talked to me like *I* was the nigger. He as much as said, 'You gettin' on my nerves, Floyd. Shut up and leave me alone.' This *nigger* as much as said that to me, to a *white* man. Are we suppose ta stand still for that? Is that what we're lettin' this country come to? Are we gon' be the niggers now and let the niggers act like they white?"

The crowd howled at the thought of such an outrage.

"Mr. Bitters," said Papa, and the sound of that queasy grin terrified Luther more than all the white men's yelling and all their torches, "ain't like that, sir. Ain't like that at all. Ain't meant to disrespect you none, sir. Just plain wasn't thinkin' is all."

Luther crept closer, pressing against his father from behind, peering cautiously around his hip. He recognized a little boy in the crowd—Jeff Orange—with whom he sometimes went to catch mudbugs in the bayou. Jeff's face was twisted around by a snarl that rendered him all but unrecognizable. Luther could not imagine what his father could have done to make Jeff Orange look at him that way.

"Oh, well you gon' think from now on!" roared Big Floyd. "Gon' teach you how to talk to a white man!"

And, so saying, he reached through the door and grabbed Papa by the upper arm. Papa pulled away. It was a reflex. It was what anyone would have done. But it was the worst thing he could have done. Now Big Floyd seized him with both his massive hands, yanking Mason Hayes forward, and the other white men came onto the porch and swarmed over him, grabbing legs and arms and head and hair, and lifting till he was out the door and his feet did not touch the ground.

"Oh, my God," breathed Gramp. Thelma was staring up at her brother, her eyes large and uncomprehending. And Luther was simply nailed down by terror.

Then Mama screamed. She screamed words that seemed to have no meaning but fury and pain as her husband was borne away, hands reaching and pulling at him. Luther spotted Jeff Orange, trying to tiptoe himself tall enough to spit on the flailing black man.

"Teach the nigger a lesson, boys!" Big Floyd's voice rose above the tumult. He lifted the bottle of brown liquid in a perverse salute. "Teach him how to talk to a white man!"

And now Mama found her words.

"You're doing this over a hog, Floyd Bitters? You're doing this over a goddamn *hog*?"

Her words seemed to pierce something, seemed to pull the men back from the brink of their fever. They paused.

"Annie, get inside!" Papa's voice was stark and clear in the sudden silence.

But she didn't budge. "You want the hog that bad?" She swept her arm toward the pen. "Take it! It's all yours! But you leave my husband alone, you hear me? You bring him back to my children and me."

"Annie . . . " Gramp had his hand on his daughter-in-law's shoulder. She flung it off.

"You hear me? Take it and go, if it means that much to you. Just leave us alone!"

"Mama," said Luther. He pulled at her nightdress. It was like trying to pull at a tree. She didn't even know he was there.

"You better go inside like he say," warned Bitters. "Don't want you, and I don't want your damn hog, neither. Just want him."

"Annie!" Draped with men, unable to reach her, Papa pleaded desperately with his wife. "Get back in the house. Listen to me, now."

"You're a coward, Floyd Bitters! You hear that? Nothing but a coward!"

Bitters's voice was a guttural whisper of menace. "Last time I'm gon' tell you, bitch. Listen to your old man. Go on. Get back inside, 'fore you get yourself hurt."

The whisper of menace in her voice matched that in his. "I will haunt you the rest of your life for this," she told him. "Do you hear me? *The rest of your miserable damn life.* I don't care what I have to do or how far I have to go. I swear before God, you will never know a second of peace."

His eyes, which had been glazed with drink, suddenly cleared. He looked surprised. He swallowed hard. Then Floyd Bitters seemed to gather himself. He laughed. "Don't blame me," he yelled in a voice loud enough for the men behind him to hear. "Blame your old man. Niggers should learn to stay in their places."

Someone yelled. "That's tellin' her, Floyd!"

Bitters allowed himself a tiny smirk of triumph. He was turning away from her when Annie hawked and spat. With a great wet splat, the gob struck his cheek, just in front of his left ear. He turned back toward her, lifting a disbelieving hand to wipe at the wad of spittle dripping off his face.

Annie Hayes was more than a full foot shorter than Floyd Bitters. She had to strain on tiptoe to land the punch. But she did. Her fist caught him cleanly on the nose.

It did not stagger him. He was far too big for that, far too strong. But blood erupted in a geyser from his nose. Stunned, he brought his hands up beneath the flow and watched in wonder as they stained crimson.

Then his eyes came up and they were terrible to behold.

"No, Mr. Floyd," pleaded Gramp. "She ain't meant to do it, sir."

"No!" cried Papa in a long, anguished scream, kicking uselessly against the many hands that held him.

Bitters reached one bloody hand out, palmed Mama's head, and yanked her forward. She flew off the porch and landed in a heap in the yard. "Take her, too!" he snarled.

Luther had been holding on to his mother's nightdress. When she became airborne, he was pulled forward, landing on the porch at the feet of the mountainous white man. He froze there. He didn't dare to breathe. Then Bitters bent down, way down from the sky, it seemed, and with one hand, lifted Luther by the arm. He held him up, and for a moment, man and boy were eye to eye. The sweat on the white man's face reflected the flickering orange glow of the torch flames. His breath smelled like whiskey and onions. Blood dripped on his lips, staining his teeth black in the uncertain light.

Luther peed on himself. He wasn't even aware of it, did not even feel the warm trickle slide down his leg to puddle on the porch.

Mama shrieked. "Leave him alone! Leave him alone!"

Bitters regarded the boy. "Look here," he yelled. "I done caught me a pissy little nigger cub."

"You call that a niglet," yelled one of the men in the yard.

Bitters laughed, flinging Luther away like soiled tissue paper. The boy landed on the floor at his grandfather's feet, bawling like a baby. Thelma was crying, too, her eyes glittering with tears, her mouth gaped with wailing.

"Ma-ma," she cried, reaching chubby arms forward.

Gramp held them back from running to their parents. "Please, sir," he said, "please, sir, please, sir." Like an incantation of some useless, impotent magic. "Please, sir. Please, sir. Please, sir. She got the little ones. He my only son. They ain't meant no harm. Please, sir, don't. Have mercy on them. Please, sir."

Bitters didn't even bother to answer. He had his back to the door, lifting high the hand with the square bottle in it. "Let's get on with it!" he roared.

And they did.

The killing of Mason and Annie Hayes lasted for over two hours, though perhaps it would be more accurate to say that it was *made* to last for over two hours.

First came the beating and the kicking, men, women, and children hammering the prostrate forms at their feet, blows landing with the heavy *chunk* an axe blade makes biting into wood. Mama and Papa curled up against the punches and the kicks, whimpering and crying with the pain. Their faces were dark and ghastly with blood.

Did it go on for a minute? For five minutes? For 10?

"Don't kill 'em yet!" At some point, a man cried this out, and at once, the mob stopped its ceaseless pounding.

Deep in his heart, Luther allowed himself to hope maybe this meant the mob had spent its fury and was done with the two bedraggled heaps, barely still recognizable as human, lying in the yard. But it was a foolish hope. With a wicked gleam in his eye, the man produced a small machete. "Who wants some souvenirs?" he asked.

At that, Gramp closed the door. "Y'all don't need to see this," he said. Even as he herded the two children away, a shriek that did not sound remotely human rose over the yard.

Their grandfather took the two children back to the bedroom. He seemed barely aware, barely there. His eyes saw without seeing. "Lord, Lord, Lord," said the old man. He pressed his hands together as if in prayer. "Lord, Lord, Lord." He closed his weeping eyes. He rocked back and forth. "Lord, Lord, Lord. Jesus, Jesus, Jesus."

From out in the yard, there arose another shriek, a shrill cry of unutterable suffering.

And Luther Hayes, whose parents drove him three miles to Sunday school every week at the clapboard church in the clearing, who knew Psalm 23 by heart and could name all 12 disciples, Luther, whose mother knelt with him by the side of the bed every night to listen to his prayers, lost Jesus in that moment, forever.

He watched the old man without interest. "Lord, Lord, Lord . . . "

"Come on," Luther told his sister.

She followed him obediently, toddling after him, her thumb in her mouth, and they went into his parents' room and climbed on the bed and looked out through their window. Gramp didn't even notice. Somehow, Luther knew even then that he should not do this. But he had no choice. He couldn't not look.

So he did.

And he saw.

Their father was writhing on his back, holding up a hand shorn of fingers and thumb. Only a palm remained, surrounded by five bloody, un-articulated stumps. His fingers and thumb were in other people's hands.

Jeff Orange held up Papa's little finger and laughed.

Mama was on all fours, her nightdress mostly stripped off. She was crawling. There did not seem to be any direction to it, any place she was trying to go except, perhaps, away. She just crawled. Men gathered around her.

"Where you goin', honey? Where you think you're goin'?"

"Ain't so feisty no more, huh?"

"Whoo-wee, look'a them tits!"

A woman kicked her in the jaw then, and the force of it lifted her and dropped her on her back so that she lay with her head facing the house. Mama's dazed and watery eyes caught Luther's then. And even in the very bowels of her agony, the sight of him, of her child, safe behind walls, whole and unmolested, made her smile. With broken teeth and a bloody face, she smiled.

His mother's smile was not at him. Rather, it was *for* him, a lie of reassurance—*It's okay, baby. Don't worry. Mama will be okay. Don't cry.* And that lie was love, a final gift from mother to son. Somehow, he knew all of that, even then—and for it, he loved her back. Though it was the last thing he felt like doing, Luther smiled in return, so that she would know he understood. His smile felt weak and broken. It dripped with tears.

"Somebody get the rope!" a white man yelled.

Then they looped the hangman's nooses around Mama's and Papa's necks, tied their hands behind their backs, and hauled them, stumbling and blind, to the oak tree in the yard. Some woman with a whiny drawl complained then that she hadn't yet gotten a souvenir, so they cut off Papa's right ear and handed it to her. She held it proudly.

The men hauled the rope up over a tree branch, and a team of them pulled, and Mama and Papa were lifted off the ground, feet struggling weakly for purchase in midair. The mob let them hang like that for a few seconds. And then, they brought them down, choking and gasping and just barely this side of life.

Again, Luther allowed himself to hope. Again, hope made him a fool.

The men hauled his parents up again.

After a few moments, they brought them down, let them rest.

Then they hauled them up again.

Then they brought them down again, let them rest.

Then they hauled them up again.

Then they brought them down. Again.

Luther, watching, struggled to understand. What was it about the suffering that made these white people laugh and cheer and slap each other on the back? What was it about Mama's and Papa's legs kicking ever more feebly at the air that made these people pass the bottle like you would at a picnic or a fair? Why did they bring Mama and Papa right to the edge of death, then draw them back again and again? How was this fun to them?

Years later, when he had grown into manhood, Luther would marvel at how much like sex it was, the gratification delayed, the release denied, the tiptoeing right up to the moment of climax, then pulling back, changing the rhythm to prolong the pleasure. But as a boy, all he knew was that the white people seemed to kill his parents forever.

Jeff Orange raised Papa's little finger before Papa's swollen and grotesque face. Luther wanted to scream. He bit his lip hard, felt tears stinging the corners of his eyes, tried to find the reassurance his mother's smile had intended, tried to hold on to that. Failed.

Then a white man yelled, "Who's got the kerosene?"

The can was brought forward. The two bodies were liberally splashed. The smell of it was strong.

Someone lifted a torch, arm extended to give him the maximum distance from the two bodies soaked with accelerant, hanging from the tree.

Mama's head hung to her chest, and Luther was not even sure she was alive. But Papa's head shook dazedly from side to side, so Luther knew he was alive when the fire touched his chest and both of them went up in a great whoosh of sound while the heat carried even through the window and into the house. Papa may have screamed. He threw his head back and his mouth came open, but any sound he made was lost in the roar of the fire and the cackles, hoots, and screams of the crowd. Then the fire took Mama and Papa, and they became something no longer distinguishable as human. They became flame itself. The ropes burned through and the flaming sacks of meat and bone that had been human just minutes before fell in a scatter of sparks and cinders that had the white people scampering back and fanning at their clothes. Jeff Orange yelped and grabbed at his arm as a spark caught him there.

Finally, Luther closed the curtain and slipped down from the window.

He put an arm around his sister, and they sat there together, crying, as they smelled their parents burning. It was a stench so overpowering that it somehow became more than a smell, somehow became a taste, a state of being. It coated the back of the throat. It filled the nostrils. It sank into the pores. It sank into the memory.

And it stayed. It never went away.

From the other room, the old man raised his voice in an anguished cry. "Lord, Lord, Lord."

But they were just words to say. He had lost Jesus, too.

"I don't know how long them people stayed in that yard," Luther told the white lawyer. "Hours, I expect. Me and Thelma sittin' on that bed huggin' each other, smellin' that awful smell, Gramp callin' on the Lord. And they out there whoopin' and hollerin' and shootin', till finally the fire died down.

"A bunch of the men, they turned that old Model T over and shot her full of holes. It ain't never run again. And then, last thing they done, they went over to the side yard. I heard a bang, real close. And then a squeal. They shot the pig and left it there."

Luther fell silent. The white man looked stricken. And he looked . . . *white*, drained of blood. His mouth moved, but no sound came out. He coughed and tried again.

"So this happened when you were a child?" he finally managed to say. His voice was ashen.

"Nine," said Luther.

"And what happened afterward?"

Luther shrugged. "Some colored folks came and they buried the bodies. Gramp wouldn't let us see 'em. I ain't really wanted to. Then colored folks started movin' out that area. We was some of the first. Gramp brung us down here. We been here ever since."

"No," said the lawyer, clearing his throat again. "What I mean is . . . how did the law respond?"

Luther laughed. "*Law?* Ain't you heard a word I said? Ain't no law for colored people. Law ain't done nothin'."

"Well, if your grandfather didn't inform him, perhaps the sheriff was not aware . . . "

Luther snorted, unable to believe how naïve this man was. "Aware? Of course he 'aware.' Them people took pictures of what happened. They had postcards made and sent 'em all over the state, all over the country! Called it a nigger barbecue. Hell, the man who run the grocery kept my father's index finger in a jar on the counter. Wasn't no secret what them people done. The sheriff knew. Every damn body knew."

"I am not naïve," the lawyer said, as though he had heard Luther's thoughts. "I realize things like this happened. But for the law to *know* it happened and do nothing, when it is the law that makes us civilized . . . " He made a helpless, imploring gesture, fell silent.

After a moment, he tried again. "I mean, you read about such things, yes, but . . . " Another gesture. Another silence.

Luther regarded him for a time without speaking. Then he said, "That's why I told you I ain't no damn American. That's why I refuse to fight for this fuckin' country. Now do you understand?"

It took him a moment. Finally, the lawyer said, "Yes. Yes, I do understand."

"So you go back," said Luther, "and you tell them I said no dice. You tell them they can stick they induction notice up they ass."

"But still, that is such a waste," said Simon.

"I will not fight for this country!" cried Luther. "Don't you get that?"

"I understand," the lawyer said. "What I am saying is that you and your family have already been treated so horribly that it just seems to compound the injustice for you to end up spending 10 years breaking rocks on some chain gang. There has to be another way."

Simon steepled his hands, closed his eyes. Luther started to say something, bit it back instead, and waited. At length, the lawyer said, "Suppose I could help you achieve—or at least, *try* to achieve—some rough form of justice, Luther? Would that satisfy you?"

"What you mean?"

"There is no statute of limitations on murder. Suppose I can find a way to have this Floyd Bitters prosecuted for what he did?"

"How you gon' do that?"

The lawyer shrugged. "I have no earthly idea," he admitted.

"Then why should I trust you?"

"Luther, I am one of the top lawyers in this town," he began, then he had to lift his hand like a traffic cop to cut off Luther's retort.

"What I mean is, even though I am a lawyer, most of my work is not in litigation. In fact, I've spent very little time in the courtroom. No, Luther, what I do is, I persuade people to do things, sometimes things they very much don't want to do. That's my real talent, and I am very good at it."

Luther didn't bother hiding his skepticism. "And you think you could 'persuade' somebody to put Floyd Bitters on trial for murder?"

"I do, yes."

"And I'm supposed to believe you even though you say you ain't got no idea how you gon' do it."

"As I said, Luther, this is what I do for a living. I will find a way."

Luther considered this for a moment. Then he said, "Don't make no difference, even if you do. Ain't no jury of white men ever gon' convict one of their own. Not in Alabama, they ain't."

"You're probably right," said the lawyer.

"Then what's the point?"

"The point is, you get your day in court. You get to see this man confronted with what he did."

Luther leaned back in the chair. "And what you get out of this, man?"

"I am doing this as a favor for your sister," said Simon. "In return, my son will do something for me. He feels indebted to your sister because of what her husband did at Pearl."

"What your son gon' do for you?" asked Luther.

"That is my affair," said the lawyer. "It's a family matter with no bearing on this case."

"So we all just tradin' favors, is that it?"

"I suppose you could say that. But it all hinges on your willingness to report for induction. And you must stay out of trouble, complete your training, and do your service."

"Why you care, man? Why you care if I get inducted or end up bustin' rocks like you say on some chain gang?"

"As I said, if I do this for your sister, my son will do something for me. But also, now that I have met you . . . " The lawyer sighed. He glanced away for a moment, then turned back to Luther with a frank gaze. "I would hate to see you do 10 years for this. People like Floyd Bitters are a disgrace to the white race. If you were convicted, it would be as if he were victimizing you all over again. This way, you have at least a chance, albeit a slim one, of turning the tables. So, do we have an agreement? My services free of charge, in exchange for your agreement to report for induction?"

Again, Luther searched the white man closely for signs of duplicity. Again, he came up empty. It unnerved him. Something told him he was a fool to believe anything this white bastard said. "Why should I trust you, man?" he demanded again.

The lawyer shrugged as if the answer was obvious beyond words. "Because I give you my word," he said. He reached a hand across the table. "Now, do we have an agreement, or do we not?"

The hand hung for a long moment, Luther wrestling with the insane idea of trusting some old white man in a mortuary suit whom he'd never seen till an hour ago. His cuffs rattled softly as he reached across and took the plump white hand in his hard brown one.

"Okay, man," he said. "I guess we do."

nine

THE STORY WAS THAT THE NEGRO HAD BOARDED THE BUS AND politely greeted the driver. The driver, a white man, ignored the courtesy. The Negro shrugged and took his seat.

Private Henry Williams, US Army, was just trying to get back to Brookley Army Airfield, where he was stationed. But Grover Chandler, the 29-year-old white man behind the wheel, was in no particular hurry. When he came upon another bus, he and that driver stopped to talk. As they were chattering back and forth about whatever it is that white bus drivers talk about, Henry Williams interrupted them. He had to make a curfew. Could the bus driver please drive the bus?

Chandler became furious. He yelled and cursed at Williams for this effrontery. Williams tried to wave him off. He said, "Man, you better go on and drive your bus and leave me alone."

This only made the driver angrier. He took out a pistol—like other drivers, he was licensed by the police department to carry arms—and stalked to the rear of the bus. There, he pistol-whipped the soldier, three good blows.

Henry Williams had had enough. He got up, picked up his bag, and pushed through the bus door. But his bag fell as he was getting off the bus. They said he asked the driver to hand it down to him.

"And that," said Laverne Rawls, a knowing expression creasing her brown, homely face, "is when that white so-and-so shot him." She pointed her index finger across the table like a gun. "Bang, bang, bang," she said. "One of them bullets hit him right in the head. Killed him on the spot."

Like every other Negro in Mobile, Thelma already knew the story of what had happened to Henry Williams a few nights before. Like every other Negro in Mobile, she couldn't stop talking about it, reliving it, shaking her head over it.

"Damn shame," she said now, behind an exhalation of smoke. She knocked the ash from her cigarette into an ashtray at the center of the table. "Damn shame."

"Ain't that the truth," said Laverne.

They were sitting with Betty Green and Helen Abbott at a table in the lunchroom, the remnants of their meals lying on trays in front of them, still a few minutes to go before their break was done and it would be time to return to work.

Like Thelma, the other three women had never set foot on Pinto Island until just a couple months before. Laverne had been a waitress; Betty and Helen had been housekeepers for white ladies. Like Thelma, they had been seized by the electric idea that even they, Negro and female though they were, might be able to find work in this upside-down new world that had exploded into existence on December 7, creating opportunities that would have seemed ridiculous not so very long ago.

It amazed Thelma how completely her life had changed since the first day she caught the ferry over here. She was a ship painter now. When the champagne bottle was smashed against a ship's bow and the ship slid down the shipway into the water, mostly completed, needing just a few final touches before it could be sent to war, she was part of a crew—mostly women, a few men, all white—that was taken out to it on a ferry. Dressed in bulky protective gear, she used a pressure sprayer to apply zinc chromate and then, over that, gray paint to the decks and bulkheads of the new ship as it bobbed on the gentle chop of Mobile Bay.

And when she got off the bus to walk home now, she wasn't automatically thinking of what she would make for dinner—she had contracted with the widow Izola Foster, who lived across the street, for that. No, when she walked home now, Thelma was thinking of no one thing in particular, except how blissfully tired she was. It was a kind of fatigue she had never felt before, nor even known was possible, a fatigue filled with the sense of satisfaction and accomplishment that come with a good day's work at some important task.

She was classified as an unskilled worker—Negroes were not allowed to do skilled labor—but Thelma loved her job just the same. It made her feel as if she were really contributing to the war. She could not imagine making peanut butter sandwiches for her white lady's children while men like Luther and George were going into harm's way for their country and other women were building ships and planes to arm them.

Let the white lady take care of her own damn children. There was a war on.

Betty, Helen, and Laverne all felt the same. Betty was an apprentice on a burner machine, cutting portholes in hulls, while Helen and Laverne were apprentices in the carpenter shop. It was hard, dirty work. But it was worth it, they all thought, when you saw some ship carrying your sweat and toil sail off to war.

This was why it hurt more when a Negro soldier in uniform was shot and killed over nothing by some hot-tempered white man with a gun. It forced you to question whether you were really part of some larger cause after all or if you were just fooling yourself, just being used because it was an emergency and everybody was needed.

Thelma blew out a jet of angry smoke at the thought of it as she crushed the butt of her cigarette in the ashtray.

"Way I heard it," said Betty, shaking a fresh cigarette from her pack, "is that they got this driver in custody down to the jail, but the police chief done said he won't ever spend a night in a cell. They got this white boy sleepin' on the chief's own cot that he use when he got to stay late at work."

Thelma felt her jaw drop. "What?"

Betty, lighting her cigarette from a match, nodded. "That's what I hear," she said.

"I heard the same thing," said Helen. "That tell you what a colored boy's life worth right there, don't it? Man shoot him on a public bus and white folks don't even pretend to care."

"Y'all seen this?" From the breast pocket of her overalls, Laverne pulled out a flyer. "They's a colored citizens committee sendin' these all round," she said. "I hear the NAACP gon' be in it, too."

Thelma took the paper and read it as Helen and Betty leaned over her shoulder.

Thelma glanced up in surprise. "They gon' boycott the buses?"

"What we gon' do if that happen?" asked Helen. "Lord know I want to support this, but I live a long way out from here. How I'm gon' make it to work if I don't use the bus? What about you, Betty?"

Betty shrugged. "I don't know. I'm in the same boat as you."

Thelma's next words surprised her. "Maybe we could buy a car," she said.

The three of them stared at her as though she had suggested they could flap their arms and fly to work. "Why not?" asked Thelma, feeling swept up in her own out-of-nowhere idea. "Between the four of us, we makin' enough money. Qualify for ration coupons, seem to me we be able to get enough gas to go back and forth to work. Maybe even go to the market once a week if we work it right."

Thelma had suggested it only to be saying something. But the other women seemed to like it, too. Laverne poked her bottom lip out thoughtfully. "That might could work," she said. "Help the boycott and help ourselves at the same time."

"But wait a minute," said Betty. "I can't drive. Can any of you all drive?"

The other three women looked from one to the other with sheepish expressions. After a moment, Thelma raised her hand. Laverne's eyes narrowed. "*You* can drive?"

Thelma nodded.

"How you learn to drive?" Betty was dubious, too. Thelma was the youngest of them all by a few years.

"My brother, Luther," said Thelma. "He had an old piece of car a few years ago. Seem like it spent half the time out front of the house with the hood up 'cause somethin' always wrong with it. But it run long enough for him to teach me. I wasn't no more'n 14 years old, but I still remember."

Again the women's eyes traveled over one another. But sheepishness had faded into a dawning sense that the unlikely thing was, if just barely, possible.

"How much you think it cost to get us a car?" asked Helen.

"I ain't got no idea," admitted Thelma.

"And how we gon' be sure we get a good one?" asked Betty. "I don't know nothin' 'bout cars. Somebody see a bunch of women comin', they try to take advantage for sure."

"Well," said Thelma after a thoughtful moment, "I suppose I could ask Ollie Grimes to come with us."

This brought shrill peals of laughter from the older women. Thelma lowered her eyes in embarrassment.

"I bet he don't mind that *at all*," said Helen.

"I bet he be right glad for it," said Betty. "Be a good chance to spend a little mo' time with Miss Thelma here."

"Y'all shush," said Thelma. "It ain't like that at all."

"Oh, I don't know," said Laverne, her voice juicy with insinuation. "Seem to me I done seen y'all keepin' company quite a bit."

"How you talk!" Thelma was scandalized. "That man old enough to be my daddy. And besides, ain't no keepin' company. We done just took breaks together couple times is all. I ain't never seen him away from this place. Get your minds out the gutter."

"Mmm hmm," said Laverne, lips crimped with knowing skepticism. "That's what she say, y'all. Ain't no tellin' if that's the true story or not."

"Y'all need to quit," protested Thelma as the laughter once again rose like a wall around her.

"What's so funny? What y'all talkin' 'bout?"

The question made Thelma glance around. She was shocked. Flora Lee Hodges was standing there, a grocery bag clenched in one fist, grinning an uncertain grin.

The Negro women's laughter rattled to an awkward end as they took the little white woman in and then looked from one to another, brows wrinkled in consternation. Their expressions all asked the same question. Laverne put it into words.

"Who's this? What she want?" She asked of the other three women in a loud whisper meant for Flora Lee to hear.

"She all right," said Thelma softly. She felt an uneasy smile seesawing on her face. "She don't mean no harm."

"You know this woman, Thelma?" Betty, too, spoke in a whisper meant for the white woman to hear.

"I'm Flora Lee Hodges," Flora announced in her sharp, backcountry twang. She extended her hand, smiling. "Pleased to meet y'all."

Laverne regarded the outstretched hand as if it might have been pulled just that moment from the pit beneath an outhouse. Then she turned to the other women. "I got to get back to work," she told them. "We'll talk later." And she stood and shouldered her way past the little white woman, who only then allowed her hand to drop.

Flora Lee watched Laverne go, puzzlement pinching her face. The other two Negro women glared at Thelma as if Flora Lee were somehow her fault. Thelma made faces in protest. Why was this her fault? She hadn't invited the woman over, had she?

She stood, feeling caught between opposing forces she could not name, guilty for things she hadn't even done. Thelma had seen Flora Lee around the yard a few times—she had even seen that miserable husband of hers, walking in his odd, half-crippled gait, pushing a big metal garbage can with a broom sticking up out of it, so she knew the two of them had found work here. She was pleased—for Flora Lee at least—but it would never have occurred to her to approach Flora Lee at a table full of white women and tell her that. Apparently, Flora Lee suffered under no such constraint.

Thelma took her by the elbow now, led her away from the table where Betty and Helen stared with some mix of frank fascination and flat indignation. "Oh, I didn't mean to take you away from your friends," said Flora Lee. She smiled over her shoulder and waggled her fingers in a friendly wave.

Thelma steered the little woman outside. "What you want, Flora Lee?" She spoke in a harsher tone than she'd meant to.

"Ain't your friends gon' be mad, me takin' you away from them like this?"

"They be all right."

"Are you sure?"

Thelma sighed. "I don't think they too"—she searched for the word—"*comfortable* around you, Flora Lee."

Flora Lee's eyebrows went up. "Why? What I ever done to them? Land sakes, I just met 'em!"

Thelma had to wrestle the smile that tried to surface then. God, but this woman was dumb.

No, not dumb. Thelma's thought corrected itself almost at once. Not dumb at all. *Naïve*, maybe. And Lord, how did she manage that?

Thelma softened her voice. "You ain't done nothin' to them. It ain't about you, exactly. Not you personally. It's more because you, well . . . you know, *white*."

"Well, I can't help that!" protested Flora Lee.

And there was something so perfect in that response that Thelma could only smile. "Flora Lee, I don't know about you," she said, shaking her head. "You ain't like most people, I'll say that. Ain't like most *white* people for sure."

"What you talkin' 'bout?" asked Flora Lee. Her eyes searched Thelma's. Confusion was in them. Guile was not.

Thelma sighed. "Well, you know, it's just . . . most white people, they ain't real friendly to colored, you know? Most white people think they better than us."

And at that, Flora Lee Hodges did the last thing Thelma would have expected. She laughed. It took Thelma by surprise. It confused her. "What?" she asked. "What's so funny?"

Then, the little woman said, "Thelma, I ain't nothin' but poor white trash from the country. My people et dirt. Ain't seen a 'lectric light till I's 10. Ain't seen a indoor privy till they got one down to the church. One thing I do know: I ain't better'n nobody!"

She laughed again. Thelma was surprised to find herself laughing with her. Thelma finally said, "Well, you better than a whole lot of people I could name."

Flora Lee fanned the compliment away. "I know Earl an' his buddies, they believe that, think they better'n you all. I could never understand when they sit around complainin' about you all. Like we was doin' so much better. Always seem to me they just foolin' theyselves. Like they got to have somebody to look down on, make it seem like their lives wasn't the worst, you know? But I couldn't never make myself believe that, 'cause I could too easy look around and see for myself. We livin' in shit and dirt, so poor sometimes we ain't even know how we gon' feed ourselves the next day. How we better'n anybody?"

The eyes searched Thelma again. Thelma shrugged.

"Exactly," said Flora Lee. "Earl my husband and I love him and I follow him anywhere. But just 'cause he want to fool hisself don't mean I got to."

"No," said Thelma. "It sure don't."

Flora Lee brightened. "Anyway," she said, "that ain't what I wanted to talk to you about. I just come to bring you this."

She lifted the grocery bag and held it out to Thelma. Mystified, Thelma opened the bag. What she saw made her laugh. Inside were two boxes of Cheez-Its. She lifted one. "Flora, you ain't had to do this. I told you it was fine."

"Now, now," said Flora Lee, "one thing about us Hodges: we's poor, but we's proud. We pays our debts"—a wicked smile—"when we can afford to."

"Well, thank you," said Thelma.

"You welcome," said Flora Lee. "Now, I got to get back to work. They done made me an electrician's apprentice and I got to go out to that there ship they run down the shipway this mornin' and string the wires."

Flora Lee took a half step, then something seemed to occur to her. She said, "Oh, and you ain't got to worry none 'bout me comin' up on you like that no more. I guess I ain't thought about it when I done it, but I ain't meant to make your friends uncomfortable. You tell 'em I'm sorry and I'll leave y'all alone from now on."

She turned to leave, but Thelma caught her hand. "No," she told her. "You ain't done nothin' to be sorry for. You come talk to me anytime you want to."

There was something heartbreaking in the gratified smile that sprang up in Flora Lee's eyes. Thelma had the distinct sense the little woman had never been . . . *welcomed* before. It seemed an absurd idea and Thelma tried to dismiss it. But Flora Lee's expression confirmed the thought even as Thelma sought to deny it.

Then those eyes changed. They fixed on something beyond Thelma. And the smile in them was replaced by a fear bordering on horror. Thelma turned, thinking she was going to see a ship burning or a crane falling.

Instead, she saw Earl Hodges. He had his garbage can full of brooms and was standing behind Thelma watching them, a lump of tobacco pouched in his gums, his eyes bright with disbelief and menace. Belatedly, Flora Lee yanked her hand from Thelma's as she might have yanked it from hot metal.

His eyes seemed to pin her to the spot. Flora Lee didn't move. She seemed barely breathing. The little man took his time. He regarded his wife for a long moment. Then he turned those eyes on Thelma. After another moment, he spat a long brown stream on the ground, wiped his mouth with his forearm.

Finally, he spoke. "Uh huh," he said.

It was all he said, but Thelma did not miss the malice that lurked inside. And the threat.

"Earl Ray," said Flora Lee again, and a piteous note had entered her voice.

He turned then and walked off. His right leg longer than his left, he rocked up and back with each step. Flora Lee took two steps after him, then stopped, recognizing the futility. She turned to Thelma, arms lifted in a gesture of helplessness.

"Shit," she said.

She went back to work without another word.

Thelma caught up with Ollie Grimes that afternoon as she headed toward the long line for the ferry. The night shift was coming on. Men and women, many with lunch buckets in hand, moved past, chattering. Across the river, you could see one of the ferries setting out from downtown Mobile.

Ollie wasn't in line yet. He was chatting and smoking with two other men, standing beneath the morale posters at the administration building where she had first met him. As she drew near, Thelma heard one of the men say, "He ain't done nothin' but asked for his bag. I swear, I don't know what get into these crackers sometimes," and she knew they were talking about Henry Williams.

"Excuse me, Ollie," she said. "You got a minute?"

At the sight of her, Ollie's grin widened roguishly. He flung his cigarette aside and stood straight, adjusting his collar. "Excuse me, gentlemen, duty calls." The second man poked the third in the side. Thelma sighed. Men could be such boys sometimes.

"I don't know why you got to act like that," she said when they were standing together off to the side.

"Like what?"

"Like *that*," she hissed. She mimicked him in a deep, stupid voice. "Excuse me, gentlemen, duty calls." And she grinned like a fool.

"Oh, is that all?"

"You got people thinkin' we doin' something we shouldn't be doin'."

Ollie affected innocence. "Oh? And what they think we doin'?"

"You know what they think," she said.

"Oh that? Well"—Ollie pretended to give the matter rapt concentration—"if that's the case, maybe we ought to go ahead and do what they think we doin'. If our reputations is already ruined, seem to me we ought to at least get the enjoyment out of it."

Thelma slapped his bicep. The man was incorrigible. "I don't know what I'm gon' do about you," she said.

"So why don't you tell me what it is Ollie can do for you?"

"You know anything about cars?"

He shrugged. "I know a little, I suppose."

"Well, you know, they talkin' 'bout havin' a boycott on account of this man that got shot. Me an' some of the girls was thinkin' maybe we just get off the buses permanently. Get ourselves some nice used car still run good. Only, we don't want to go to no car lot and have them thinkin' they can take advantage of us 'cause we women."

"Say no more," said Ollie. "I'll be glad to help. You an' me can go. I'll tell 'em you my wife and I'm lookin' for somethin' for the little woman and the kiddies."

"You never stop, do you?"

He grinned. "Ain't got no idea what you talkin' 'bout," he said.

"Can we go Saturday? There's a car lot off Davis Street."

"I know the one," he said. "I meet you there about 10."

"Thank you," she said. And then a familiar shape moved in her peripheral vision. "Excuse me a minute," she said. She stepped away. "Flora Lee," she called.

The little white woman was in one of the queues for the ferry. Her head came around at the sound of her name and Thelma gasped. The bruise beneath her left eye was shiny and black and new.

"Oh, my God," said Thelma.

"Oh, this ain't nothin'," Flora Lee assured her, her voice mousy and small. "Walked into a door, is all. It's just a scratch." She attempted a laugh but did not quite pull it off.

"That man hit you? Just for *talkin'* to me?"

"You should probably go on 'bout your business, Thelma."

"You can't let that man keep hittin' you, Flora Lee. It ain't right."

"Earl, he don't mean no harm. Just sometime lose his temper is all. But he always real sweet, after."

"That man ain't got no right to use you as his punchin' bag. None."

"'That man' is her husband. That give me the right to do whatever I feel like." Thelma whirled in surprise. Earl Hodges had come up behind her without a sound.

Thelma stepped back without meaning to. "You go on, get away from here," she said.

Earl Ray didn't bother to dignify the demand with an answer. "Now the thing is," he said, stepping toward her, "why you think you got the right to mix in between a man and his wife? They wouldn't even allow that if you was white. And hell, you a nigger."

Thelma said, "Get out of here. Leave me alone."

Another step. Now he was so close Thelma could smell the Dixie Peach and sweat caked together in his hair. "You need to keep away from her," he said in a low, hard voice. "Leave her alone, y'hear? Stay with your own kind and there won't be no problems. But if you keep stickin' your nose in where it don't belong . . . "

"Thelma? Is everything okay?"

The voice came from behind Thelma. She looked around and saw Ollie and his two friends standing at her back, faces still. There were three of them, and they were all big, much bigger than little Earl Ray Hodges, so she was stunned when she turned back and saw his eyes doing that glittering dance they did, an almost-smile of anticipation curling his lips.

The little fool was actually thinking about it.

"Earl, come on . . . " Flora Lee was pulling on her husband's upper arm.

There was a long, tight moment. Then Earl pointed at Thelma. "You just remember what I told you," he said. "Stay away from her. Mind your own business." He looked to the three men and grinned. "Boys," he said, "we'll finish this another time." And with that, finally, he allowed Flora Lee to lead him away.

He crooked an arm around her neck, bending her head close to his as they walked. If you weren't looking closely, thought Thelma, you might think it was a gesture of affection, but it wasn't.

It was a headlock.

ten

FEELING ALMOST LIKE A CHILD, ARMY PRIVATE LUTHER HAYES pressed his nose against the window as the train clattered over a bridge spanning some river whose name he didn't know. He was struck yet again by a realization that kept taking him by surprise—just how much of the world he had not seen.

He had lived his entire life, every single day of it, within a hundred miles of Mobile, Alabama. Thelma had at least been across the state line once, to Pensacola. Luther hadn't even been that far. His entire world, everything he had known for 28 years, had been Alabama.

Now Alabama was a thousand miles and four weeks behind him. A month ago, he had ridden the train out of Mobile—the first time he had ever been on a train—up through Tennessee, Virginia, Maryland, Pennsylvania, Delaware, and New Jersey, watching in unabashed amazement, scarcely daring to even nap, as mountains, meadows, rivers, streams, and towns he had never heard of before rolled past his window.

Finally, he and a bunch of other new recruits had arrived at Camp Upton on Long Island in New York. It was an old Army processing center in a potato field, where he spent his first two weeks living in a tent. There, the Army had shorn his hair, issued him a uniform, and taught him to march and salute. Gritting his teeth, he had even learned to say, "Sir, yes sir!" when white officers addressed him.

The only thing that had gotten him through all of it was the memory of the white lawyer's promise: if he toughed it out, if he made it through, John Simon would find a way to prosecute the motherfuckers who had killed his parents. He had clung to that promise as his only sanity on days when he would just as soon have punched a white officer in the face and taken the punishment. And he had made it through.

Now, four weeks later, here he was on a train again, the car rattling and swaying down some Virginia valley, en route to a place in Louisiana called Camp Claiborne. They said he was going to learn to drive tanks.

Tanks.

Luther was excited by that idea despite himself.

He pulled his nose off the window as the river retreated behind him and took a deep draw on his cigarette. A man named Jocko Sweeney, who was playing poker in the aisle, looked up from his hand and laughed at him. "First time on a train, Country?"

"Country." This was what they had taken to calling him, all these fellows from Detroit, Philadelphia, Newark—like having lived in the North gave them some knowledge he didn't possess, made them some superior kind of nigger. Even some nigger from Atlanta had taken to calling him this.

The name was a judgment, the way nicknames often are. In this case, it was a presumption of his ignorance, a way of reminding him that he had never been anywhere, never seen or learned anything. Like he needed a nickname to remind him of that.

Luther hated being called "Country," but he had learned to answer to it nevertheless. After all, he reasoned, every man in here answered to something that wasn't his Christian name.

"Second time," he corrected now. "First time was on the way up here."

"Second time." Jocko's eyes rolled like marbles and laughter filled the smoky air. "Excuse me. I stand corrected. Guess you's a world traveler now."

Luther ignored him and went back to staring out the window. If he could put up with saluting some cracker officer and crying, "Sir, yes sir!" without punching him in his fat, white face, what did he care about some smart-aleck, big-city nigger? As far as white folks were concerned, even a big-city nigger was still a nigger just the same. He understood that, even if some of them did not.

"Beg pardon?"

Surprised, Luther glanced around and found himself gazing up at a dark-skinned man with a long chin at the bottom of a long, serious face. His hair was so closely cropped, someone had told Luther with a laugh that the sadistic Army barbers had taken one disgusted look and waved him on. His eyes were lively and intelligent. He had a pipe in hand.

The man's name was—it took Luther a moment to remember this—Franklin Bennett, though everyone called him "Books" for the fact that he was seldom seen without his nose in a book. And sure enough, now that Luther looked, he saw a volume called *The Souls of Black Folk* clutched in Bennett's left hand.

"Do you mind if I join you?" asked Books Bennett, bowing slightly like he and Luther were some kind of British royalty or something. "The fellows are a bit boisterous on the other end of the car."

Luther had no idea why this nigger had to use so many words to ask a simple question. And why was he asking permission in the first place? Hell, it wasn't like Luther owned the damn train. He made an impatient gesture. "Yeah, man, sit down if you want to. It's a free country."

"Well, it isn't, actually," said Books, lowering himself onto the seat next to Luther, "but I take your meaning." He smiled as if satisfied at some private joke and opened his book.

Luther glanced out the window again. The train was moving beneath an endless sky full of shredded clouds. He looked back as Books turned a page, then saw him nod to himself as if in agreement with whatever he had just read. Luther couldn't help himself. "Is that good?" he asked, inclining his head toward the book.

Pity leaked through the other man's expression as he placed an index finger on his page, closed the book, and turned to Luther. "It's great, actually, but not, I am afraid, in the sense that you mean."

Luther knew this nigger was putting him down somehow, but again he couldn't help himself. "What's it about?" he asked.

"It's probably not something that would be of interest to you, Country."

"How you know what interest me?"

Books sighed. "Very well," he said. "*The Souls of Black Folk* is a foundational text of Negro protest, perhaps the most eloquent argument ever propounded for the dignity and humanity of the colored man. It is widely considered the seminal work by the famed Negro scholar William Edward Burghardt Du Bois, a sociologist who is himself widely considered one of the finest intellects the race has ever produced. Indeed, I personally consider him the foremost race man in the country."

It was, Luther knew, a barrage of big words intended to humiliate him, to remind him that he was ignorant. "You ain't got to get smart, nigger," he said. "I just asked you a question is all."

"Perhaps I should move elsewhere," said Books.

Luther shrugged. "Suit yourself," he said.

But Books didn't move. He looked around and saw what Luther had known he would: the only other seat in the car was the one he had left, down there at the other end where Jocko Sweeney and the other men were laughing and dealing cards while debating what made the perfect blow job.

After a moment, Luther said, "I thought you was movin' elsewhere?"

"Look," said Books helplessly, "all I want is to be allowed to read in peace. Do you mind?"

Luther made a suit-yourself gesture. With a sigh, Books lifted his index finger from the page and reopened the brown hardcover. Luther watched him for a moment, then turned away. There was no point saying anything to this nigger, much less trying to be friendly with him. He knew that. Nigger thought he was better than Luther, better than every other nigger on the train. Probably thought he was better than white folks themselves. No point whatsoever in talking to him. Yet once again after a moment, Luther couldn't help himself.

"You know," he said, "they's a reason you ain't had no friends up there at Upton."

This was true. Everyone had remarked upon it. In the time when they weren't being drilled or trained, most of the other men had shot the shit just like they were doing now, playing cards or baseball or just sitting on their bunks talking about Joe Louis or Satchel Paige. By contrast, Books could invariably be found in a corner by himself, the bottom of his face obscured by a book. If you asked him a question about the Brown Bomber, he would say that he didn't care much for what he called "pugilism." If you passed him a deck of playing cards showing girls with ripe pink titties, he sniffed and said something about "lust for white women" being the downfall of the race. It wasn't long before the fellows stopped trying to talk to him or include him in anything.

"Oh," he said now, with a resigned sigh. "Enlighten me."

"It's 'cause everybody thought you's a stuck-up motherfucker," said Luther. "Think you better'n everyone else."

Books's smile was maddening. "Well, they are certainly entitled to their opinions," he said. "But what makes you think I would be at all concerned with their opinions of me? Or, for that matter, with the loss of their companionship, scintillating though it is, I am sure."

Luther was surprised. "You don't care what nobody think about you?" he asked.

Books shrugged. "I don't care what *they* think about me," he corrected. "Or, for that matter, you. But as long as we are talking about the manner in which we are perceived by our fellow soldiers, tell me: Why is it you think these other men have nicknamed you Country?"

Luther swallowed and didn't answer. Books took that as a reply. "So you see," he said, "there really is some advantage in not caring overmuch what others think of you. Now, if you will excuse me, Country, I really would like to return to my reading."

The imperious dismissal stung like a slap. Luther was about to respond, though he had no idea what he would say. Then the opportunity was lost as a sergeant came striding down the aisle. "Close those windows, close those blinds," he barked. "Everybody close the blinds. Move it!"

Mystified, Luther did as he had been told. In a moment, the car was plunged into stifling shadows, the air heavy and hot.

"What's the deal, Sarge?" asked Luther.

The sergeant ignored him. Luther felt the train slowing. He looked a question at Books Bennett, who returned the same confused gaze. Then Books stood.

"Where you goin'?" asked Luther.

"To investigate," said Books.

"Wait for me," said Luther.

He jumped out of his seat to follow, and the two of them made their way to the back of the car. Luther pushed open the door to the platform. Facing them on the platform of the car behind them was a trio of white soldiers who had likewise come out to see what was going on. One of them, a beefy teenager with ruddy cheeks, gave the two Negro soldiers a grin of soft malice.

"Look like they done prepared a little welcomin' committee for you all, snowflake," he told Luther, his voice a husky drawl.

Luther said, "What the hell you talkin' about?"

Books tapped his shoulder and pointed. They were coming into some small country town, its main street sliding into view. The street was crowded with white boys and men standing shoulder to shoulder with squirrel guns and pistols raised toward the train. A few of the smaller boys hefted rocks that bounced lightly off the sides of the railcars. All of them watched the train with a palpable rage, brows knit, eyes tight, weapons at the ready.

"What the hell," breathed Luther.

Books said, "We'd better get inside." But Luther did not move. He felt a red rage washing over him. *Jump off this fucking train*, it snarled. *Jump off the train, charge up the embankment to that street, and rain hell on all those fucking white sons of bitches. Make them drop their pitiful guns and rocks and run for the hills.*

Books made his voice stern. "We'd better get inside," he said again.

It took Luther a moment to return from where he had been. He looked down and was surprised to see that his hands had curled into fists.

"Come on," said Books. Luther nodded numbly, relaxed his hands, and followed the other man back into the car. As soon as the door closed behind them, other men blocked their paths.

"What is it?" Jocko asked. "What you see out there?"

"Yeah! Why we got to put down the shades?"

"The street is full of white men and boys with guns," said Books. His voice was deep and heavy with some emotion barely contained. "Apparently," he said, "white people hereabouts are none too pleased with the idea of Negro soldiers passing through their little hamlet."

"Just 'cause we passing through?" said Jocko.

"Yes."

"Glad we ain't stoppin', then," said Jocko.

"Yes," said Books. "Something to be thankful for."

"I'll be damned," said one of the other men. Something lost and disgusted wandered in his eyes. "An' these the people we supposed to be fightin' for?"

"So it would seem," said Books. "God bless America, fellows. Now if you would be kind enough to let us pass . . . "

The men parted silently, and Luther and Books made their way back to their seats. They did not speak. Books did not pick up his book again. Luther stared into a cauldron of his own fury.

How right he had been. Nigger from the big city. Nigger from a small town. Still a nigger, either way.

The train rolled slowly through the little town for a few more minutes. Finally, Luther felt it pick up speed.

"Y'all can put them blinds back up and open them windows!" The sergeant was passing through again.

Mechanically, Luther did as he had been told. Moments later there was light in the car again, smoky air rushing through the windows. But it didn't matter. The raucous noise, the laughter and shouts that had sent Books fleeing to this end of the car had gone cold. No one was playing cards. No one was debating whether the Philadelphia SPHAS, the powerhouse Jewish basketball team, could handle the Harlem Rens. Luther and Books sat without speaking. Pine forests rushed by Luther's window, unseen. Finally, Books turned toward Luther. "I was wrong," he said quietly, "and I am man enough to admit it."

Luther was confused. "How you mean?" he asked.

"I mean," said Books, "that considering that we are all colored soldiers here and considering the vivid illustration we have just seen of how white people feel about colored soldiers, it probably does not make much sense for us to be bickering among ourselves. And for my part in that, I apologize."

He extended his hand. After a surprised moment, Luther took it. "Yeah," he said. "Same here."

Books watched him with a sly expression. "You were about ready to jump off this train and fight them all yourself, weren't you?"

Luther's laugh was small and tight. "Yeah," he said. "I suppose I was."

"You realize that would have been insane."

"I realize it," said Luther. "*Now* I realize. Ten minutes ago was something else."

"You need to learn to govern your temper, my friend. That is the only way you're going to get through this."

"White people lynched my folks," blurted Luther. "I wasn't nothin' but a boy, but I seen it." He didn't know why he said it. It just seemed to need saying.

"I see." Books was watching him with fresh interest, silent for a moment. "Well," he finally said, "I suppose that explains why you were prepared to throw yourself at them. It still doesn't make it a good idea, though." He softened his words with a smile.

There was a moment. Then Luther said, "Yeah, I know. But sometime, when I be around white people, I just don't think. My sister tell me that all the time. It's like a drum pounding my head till I can't hear nothin' else, can't think nothin' else 'cept how I'm sick and tired of them always puttin' us down, always sayin' whatever they want to us, *doin'* whatever they want to us and don't nobody never make them pay. It's like we ain't nothing, like what we think and feel don't mean shit. I get tired of that, you know? I get tired of bein' treated like a nigger."

Books pondered this for a moment. Then he said, "You know how you asked me a moment ago what that Du Bois book was about?"

"Yeah?"

Books pointed at Luther. "What you just said is what it's about," he said.

Luther shrugged. "Maybe I should read it, then."

"Maybe you should."

"Where you from, Books?"

"Me?" Books brightened. "All over, I suppose. I was born in Harlem, but I spent much of my childhood on the continent."

Luther's confusion must have shown in his eyes. "Europe," said Books. "London, Paris, Antwerp. Father was a painter, though much more appreciated on that side of the world than on this side. He was from the realist school of art, painted in the tradition of Henry Ossawa Tanner, of whom he was quite fond. I grew up following his commissions. Six months here, six months there."

"You ain't had no permanent home? Must have been hard."

A shrug. "Mother had been a schoolteacher before they met and so, luckily, I did not want for education."

"Yeah," said Luther drily. "I can see that."

The joke sailed right over the other man's head. After a moment, Luther said, "So when y'all come back to this side of the world?"

"I came back to go to college. Wilberforce University, class of 1940."

"Where that at?"

"It is in Ohio."

"So, let me get this straight," said Luther. "You done been all over the world, but this gon' be your first trip down South?"

"My father was born in South Carolina. He would never admit it, but I have long suspected that at least part of the reason we spent so much time abroad had nothing whatsoever to do with commissions, as lucrative as they were. I suspect he simply did not want a child of his growing up in the Jim Crow South."

"Can't say I blame him," said Luther. "But he ain't done you no favors."

"I am afraid I do not understand."

"I mean, you ain't got no idea what it's gon' be like for you down there. You ain't got no idea how to get along."

Books stiffened. "I may not have ever set foot on Dixie soil, but I have heard plenty from my father. And I have read a great deal about it."

Luther shook his head. "You done heard and you done read," he said.

"Yes," said Books.

"But you ain't *lived* it," said Luther. "Look, I'm just telling you, be careful down there. Watch your ass."

Books gave him a dubious look. "I tend to be a very quick study."

Luther met his eyes. "You better be," he said.

And the train sped on.

Two days later, Luther and Books stood in a warm, misting rain, their duffels slung over their shoulders, at the entrance to Camp Claiborne. For a few minutes, they simply took it in. Near the front gate stood a collection of ragged shanties sagging against one another. Luther thought the rain might dissolve them into the ground.

"Big Mary's Place" said the crudely hand-painted sign over the dark hole that was the entrance to one joint.

"Pig's Palace" said the sign over the next. A Negro woman, her bright red makeup garish in the gray light of the wet afternoon, stood in that doorway smoking a cigarette, watching the recruits climb off the trucks.

Luther nudged Books. "I think she like you."

Laughing, they trooped into the camp past the sign that said "Welcome to Camp Claiborne." It was illustrated with an image of a white soldier running heroically into battle.

They found the camp to be neatly laid out on a grid of well-paved streets. They passed row after crisp row of freshly painted barracks. They passed a ball field and a servicemen's club. "This won't be so bad," said Books with an approving nod.

Then Luther tapped his shoulder and pointed to something Books had apparently missed. Neatly painted on every one of the barracks, on the entrance to the ball field, on the servicemen's club were the same two words: "Whites Only." He stopped to stare.

Luther paused at his shoulder. "I told you," he said. "Didn't I tell you?"

"Yes," Books admitted. "Yes, you did tell me."

"What you got to do," said Luther, "is you got to teach yourself to see it without seeing it, you know what I mean? 'Cause if you let it hurt you every time you see it, you gon' always be hurt. So you learn to just pass it by."

"That's a terrible way to live," said Books.

"I guess," conceded Luther. "I ain't never knew no other way."

The men regarded one another. Then a white lieutenant came out of one of the barracks and caught them standing there. He glared at them. His expression was filled with all the hatred in the world. Luther shook his head. "Come on," he said, "let's find where our place is."

Following the trickle of colored soldiers, they came to a point where the road crested and then began a descent toward the back of the camp. On the marshy lowland just before the camp surrendered itself to the swamp, there sat a cluster of tents and one-story barracks. The buildings were worn and old, the paint tattered from long years of exposure. Many of the tents were ragged and haphazardly patched. The air carried a pestilent stench. And everywhere they looked, they saw the sign: "Colored."

"Unbelievable." Books breathed this in soft dismay.

"Welcome home," Luther told him.

eleven

THE GUNNY'S ORDER WAS A CRY JUST THINLY HEARD OVER THE crash of the waves and the freight train of blood roaring through George Simon's temples. "Platoon, move! Over the side. Hit those cargo nets! Move! Move! *Move!*"

George moved. He did this without thinking, body reacting automatically, mind a radio station that broadcast only static. Except that every now and then, one bony little thought managed to elbow its way through.

Don't let me mess up. Jesus, don't let me mess up.

Over the side of the transport ship he went, stomach boiling so violently that it was an even bet whether his lavish preinvasion breakfast of steak and eggs would stay where it belonged or end up splattering the helmet of the marine below. The world seemed to seesaw, the ship rolling with the waves, the cargo net leaning out from the hull, the landing craft far below, rising and dropping six, seven, eight feet on the waves, occasionally bouncing itself against the ship. For days, George had suffered recurring daymares in which he mistimed his jump, missed the landing craft completely, and sank into the Pacific under the weight of his gear or got smashed between the two vessels, ending his life as a stain on the side of a Navy ship.

Except that now the moment was here and there was no time to worry about it. Move! Move! *Move!* or get your hand smashed under the boots of the man climbing down behind you. So George's body did what the Marine Corps had drilled it over and over again to do, and he simply watched from somewhere else, marveling at how well it handled itself.

Down the side of the transport his body went, scaling the cargo net. And when the net ended, he jumped without hesitation. A fraction of

a second suspended in midair—*Don't let the boat roll, don't let it roll!*—
and then the deck caught him. With his 165 pounds augmented by 50
pounds of gear, he could not help but land heavily, a painful shock radi-
ating through his knees all the way up to his hips, especially on the right,
where the broken bones had so recently knitted themselves back together.
But George's body ignored this, moving automatically out of the way to
make room as the man behind him leapt unhesitatingly into space.

He found a spot in the front of the boat and hunkered against the
marine in front of him. It turned out to be Jazzman, who turned toward
him with bright eyes and the devil's own sweet grin. "Mornin', Saint," he
said. "Fine day for an invasion, ain't it?"

His real name was Randy Gibson, but he insisted that everyone call
him "Jazzman." He was a skinny white kid from Indiana with freckles and
curly brown hair, but he told anyone who would listen that he was actually
a fiery Negro drummer trapped inside the body of a white boy. "I'm not
what you see, fellas," he always said. The others half believed it, what with
the way he was forever tapping out rhythms on every surface of the ship—
the rack railing, the footlockers, the hatch, the mess trays, it didn't matter.
It was not uncommon for guys to yell at him to cut it out, but it was hard
to stay mad at a guy who was so cheerfully nuts.

"Yeah," George told him. "L-lovely day." Even now, Jazzman's hands
were idly tapping out a slow beat against the gunwale.

From far overhead, there came a sudden, ferocious *crump!* The big
guns were battering the island. "Wow," said Jazzman, his busy hands pausing for a second, "dig that crazy percussion."

Someone else said, "You really got a screw loose, Jazz."

Jazzman grinned. "Well, you know what Satch says. 'You plays how
you is.'"

"I don't even know what that means," the other man said.

Jazzman hunched his shoulders as if to say that anyone who asked the
question was too square to understand the answer.

Above them, the last man took the leap into space and landed safely
on the deck. Marines crouched shoulder to shoulder now beneath the
gunwale. George felt the engine rumbling beneath his feet, and the boat
swung away from the ship, another immediately taking up the vacated
space. They circled, weaving between other landing craft full of other
marines. Finally, the coxswain pointed the bow toward the long, sinuous

coast of Guadalcanal. On the island, a shell burst in a palm tree, raining splinters of bark and palm leaves upon the jungle below. Raising his eyes cautiously above the gunwale, George saw, here and there, fires burning.

"Get your heads down!" barked Lieutenant Colonel Phipps, and George ducked, somehow managing to make himself smaller, pulling into himself like a turtle in a shell. With a lurch, the boat started its rush toward the beach, a shower of salty water splashing back on the huddled marines.

And this was it.

No more fearing it, no more wondering how it would be. George's very nerve endings tingled with a babble of raw emotions—excitement, exhilaration, terror. Terror of dying, yes. Who wouldn't be afraid of that? But more so, terror of not doing his job. He had not admitted this to Mother or Sylvia. He kept his letters to them short and chatty, sharing innocuous anecdotes, responding with appropriate comments to their news and questions—Mother wanting to know if he'd had any involvement in the big battle at Midway, his wife (he was *still* trying to get used to that word) reporting that she had volunteered at a USO canteen. Only in a letter to Thelma Gordy, of all people—a letter he had tossed off as a hasty "you're welcome" to her "thank you"—had he admitted the truth.

"I'm scared of letting any of these fellows down," he confessed. "That's what terrifies me the most."

"You can only do your best," she had replied. "That's all any of us can do."

Jazzman's hands beat faster on the gunwale above him, the sound blurring into something that was no longer a musical rhythm. Rather it was just a clatter of nervous rat-a-tat. And somehow, thought George, that made it the perfect accompaniment to this mad moment of rushing forward toward Japanese guns.

He tugged his helmet lower over his brow. He shifted his weight. He prayed.

Lord, give me the strength to do my duty. And don't let me mess up. Please, don't let me mess up.

"Yes, sir," said Jazzman, speaking to no one but himself, "a real fine day."

And it was, thought George. It was a little after 0900. The sun was hot, the clouds big and puffy. But for the black smoke drifting above them, but for the planes droning overhead in formation, but for this armada of boats rushing toward an enemy shore, it was a flawless day.

"Hey there, Saint. You got a prayer for us?"

Babe Budzinski was at his elbow. Babe had somehow managed to come through the attack at Pearl unscathed. Swifty had not been so lucky. Babe said their friend had dived from the hull of the stricken ship in the same split second that oil in the water below ignited. Babe himself had been a half second behind and had just barely, miraculously, managed to arrest his own leap in time.

"How fuckin' lucky can one sonofabitch be?" Babe had asked George one night over beers, laughing with tears in his eyes. "Why him and not me, you know? I live to be a hundred, I'll never figure that one out."

George wondered what it must have been like for Swifty, hanging in midair for that fatal, eternal instant, knowing he was falling into fire and there was nothing he could do about it. Babe said their friend had been badly burned. Babe said he was horrible to look at.

"K-k-keep your head down," George advised the squat little man now. He smacked him on the helmet. "You'll be all right."

"Roger that," said Babe. His smile was uneasy.

"You boys got nothing to worry about," crowed Tank Sheridan. "Just stay on my ass and I'll get you through. No Jap's gettin' past me."

"Anybody tries to go around that ass better pack a lunch," somebody said. Sheldon Sheridan had been a college linebacker before he dropped out to join the Corps after Pearl. They all laughed at the jibe and Tank joined in obligingly. For a moment, thought George, it was like they were all safely back in their racks, playing cards and swapping lies as the ship plowed through choppy seas under a lowering sky. Then the laughter ended as if by unspoken mutual consent, and he was reminded it was not like that at all.

The silence that followed had weight and dimension. It carried anticipation, fear, whispered reminders of cold mortality. There was something intimate about the silence, something intensely personal. No one looked at the marine next to him. George adjusted his helmet again. He checked his weapon again.

Jazzman's hands continued hammering a tuneless rhythm. George reached up and laid a hand gently on his left wrist. The hands fell silent. Jazzman looked around at him. Randy Gibson's eyes were luminous and large. He looked like what he was, a 17-year-old boy from Indiana.

It amazed George that Jazzman seemed so young to him when he himself was only 20.

It was as he was pondering this that the landing craft shuddered to a stop. With a metallic clank and a dull thump, the ramp at the other end of the boat came down onto the wet sand. "Move out!" the lieutenant yelled. "Come on, girls, you want the Japs to die of old age?"

George clambered to his feet and looked over Babe's head. What he saw dismayed him: a bottleneck of men shuffling down the ramp. Most of the boats were old—they didn't even have ramps yet. But maybe, thought George, surveying the backup of bodies, the men in those boats were the lucky ones—not having ramps meant not having bottlenecks. Babe was too short to see any of this, but he seemed to intuit it just the same, and he spoke a conclusion George had already reached. "Heck with this," he said. "We're sittin' ducks here."

So saying, Babe hoisted himself up on the gunwale and over the side of the boat. George, Jazzman, and a few others followed close behind. George landed heavily in water that swirled up to his knees. He crouched low, rifle at the ready, and moved toward the beach.

He expected to die at any moment. And he wondered morbidly how it was a body could function under the terrible weight of that anticipation. Each second that he found himself alive was a surprise. But death would come in the next second, he was sure.

Would he feel anything? Would it be sudden? Would he even know what had happened? Or would it be like a sudden scene change in the movies so that one second, he was following Babe onto the beach, and the next, with no sense of movement, no sense of time loss or dislocation, he was in the arms of Jesus and everything was over and that would be all right with him?

But somehow, George didn't die in the next second either, or the second after that. Somehow, running in a crouch, rifle ready, senses alive for the merest sight, sound, smell of the enemy, he made it all the way up the beach. Then he stopped, dumbfounded.

He thought his morbid imagination had prepared him for anything he might see when he reached this island. But as it turned out, it hadn't prepared him for what he actually did see.

Which was nothing.

The beach was littered with broken pieces of tropical trees. The suffocating sweetness of cooking vegetation rolled over them from somewhere inland. American warplanes continued to drone overhead.

But the enemy was not there. There were no war cries from the trees, no hail of lead to push themselves through, no glint of steel from the woods, not so much as a footprint in the sand. George struggled to comprehend. Adrenaline coursed through him like white-water rapids. He felt wide open. He felt . . . exposed. And scared. Somehow, the Japanese seemed to terrify him even more in their absence.

Babe came up on George's right. "Where the hell are the Japs?" he whispered. Whispering seemed necessary, somehow.

"Blamed if I know," said George.

"You figure they hightailed it?" The fingers of Jazzman's right hand drummed soundlessly on the stock of the old Springfield bolt-action rifle he had been issued.

George was about to answer when he heard men laughing. He looked toward the sound in confusion. A few men from the 5th Division, who had landed in the first wave, were sitting around in casual disarray a hundred feet up the beach, cackling and pointing.

"What the heck?" said George.

"Hey, what took you so long?" crowed one of them. "We got tired of waitin', so we went ahead and won the war without you."

The Marines had landed without incident. The Japanese were not there.

"You think they've given up the whole island?" asked Jazzman.

"Nah," said Phipps, who had come up on George's left. "They're just shy is all." He eyed the trees suspiciously. "Just want to play a little hide-and-seek." Phipps grinned a hard, eager grin. "Don't worry. We'll smoke the little bastards out."

The 1st Division's objective was said to be a rise the commanders called the "grassy knoll." From that high point, it was said, the Marines could command an excellent view of the airfield the Japanese had built and the Marines had come to seize. And so it was, barely half an hour later, that George and the men of the 1st found themselves formed into squads and pushing cautiously inland from the beach.

It turned out to be a march to nowhere.

They bridged a river somebody said was called the Tenaru. Then they bridged it again. Then they climbed a hill. Then they bridged the river again. Then they crossed a coconut plantation. Then they crossed a field of kunai grass, the tall blades scraping against their hands. Then they bridged the river again.

"How many times are we going to cross this fucking river?" groused a man George didn't know.

"Either this is the crookedest damn river in the world or we are lost," said another man.

"Maybe both," said his friend.

Hearing this, George turned to Babe. "Don't we have maps?" he asked.

"Yeah," said Babe, "but word is, the maps ain't worth shit."

Time passed and they did not cross the river again, and George began to think they had finally put the Tenaru behind them. There was something disheartening about crossing the same water over and over again. It made you feel as if you were making no progress. But finally, they were closing the distance toward the grassy knoll.

More time passed.

The sun had parked itself high overhead, and George was baking in his dungarees under the weight of his gear. He ached for a drink; even the warm, metallic water from the canteen on his belt would have been welcome. But they were under orders to exercise water discipline—allowed to take only tiny sips every couple of hours, then roll that around in the mouth—so the canteen stayed where it was and he licked nervously at the sweat that trickled across his lips. It felt as if the essence of him were leaking out, drop by drop, to slide down his slick skin to oblivion.

"Wouldn't mind seeing that river now," he whispered to Babe.

"You and me both, pal."

"Feels like I'm walking in the devil's armpit," said George.

"Hell of a place, huh?" Babe's head turned as if on a swivel, looking for any sign of movement.

They were walking through a field of kunai grass toward a darkness of trees. *A perfect place for an ambush*, thought George, nervously. But then, he had thought that constantly for hours. "Not my idea of a vacation spot," he replied.

"Keep your minds on your work, fellas." Tank Sheridan spoke without turning around. He was carrying a heavy machine gun over his shoulder with ridiculous ease.

"Oh, I am, I am, believe me." Babe was still craning his neck, still trying to see 360 degrees at once. "But I'm just thinking," he said, "the Japs want this shithole piece of rock so bad, I'd be happy to give it to 'em."

Tank turned. "You know we can't do that. This is"—he affected a voice of portentous solemnity—"a mission of utmost importance."

This was what they had been told when they were briefed the day before. If allowed to become fully operational, the Japanese airfield would give the enemy a base from which to attack ships traveling between the United States and Australia. It would choke off that island continent from resupply and allow the Japanese to invade it at their leisure. So the Marines had to take this airfield. There was no other option.

"Yeah, I know," said Babe. He looked miserable. "A fella can dream though, can't he?"

George's hand came up all at once to slap at a sudden sharp pain in his cheek. It came away smeared with blood and the pieces of a large mosquito. "I'm telling you, this place is a fucking shithole," repeated Babe. He smirked. "Apologies for the language, Saint."

"Yeah," said George absently. He wiped the mess against his fatigues.

"You think they're here, the Japs? The fuckers wouldn't have just given the island up, would they?"

"I d-doubt it. They're out there s-s-somewhere. Maybe watching us right this second."

Babe was still trying to see in every direction. "You think so? God, I swear, I hate those slant-eyed yellow monkeys."

"Come on, now," said George mildly, automatically. "G-Got to love one another like the Good Book says."

It was the kind of thing he always said. It was almost a standing joke. But Babe cocked an eye and spoke with real scorn. "Come on, George. Don't give me that shit. You don't really believe that, do you? Not even you can be that naïve."

The venom of it took George by surprise. He did not immediately respond.

Maybe, he thought, Babe had a point. Maybe it was a stupid thing to say or, at least, a thing in flamboyantly bad taste to say. After all, these particular "children of God" were raping women to death, tossing babies like soccer balls to catch on bayonets, summarily beheading helpless marines. He had seen it for himself on newsreels. And the memory of what he had seen blasted his thoughtless, automatic joke.

What were the gentle admonitions of the Good Book against the corpse of some boy from Arkansas, Oregon, or Kentucky, twitching in the sand on the road to Bataan, blood and gore leaking from the jagged, bony stump where his head had been? How could you not consider the Japanese something other than human—*less* than human—when they could commit atrocities like that with seemingly no more effort than breathing?

Could he really walk through this steamy hell looking for them so he could kill them yet say with a straight face that these animals were God's children, too?

And if he could, what did that make him? What did it make the Japanese born in the good old USA? What about the families he had seen—also on newsreels—looking hurt and bewildered as they were herded out of their homes and piled onto trains because the government had deemed them too dangerous to remain on the West Coast? They were from the same racial stock as the savages now pillaging so much of Asia and the South Pacific.

The proud men in ties and hats walking with heads erect, determined to bear up, the women with glittering eyes and handkerchiefs clutched to their mouths, were they animals, too? What about the little boy, oblivious to war, oblivious to parental agony, walking happily toward the train that was to bear him away from his life, tossing a baseball high and laughing as it plopped into his catcher's mitt? Was he an animal?

George could not figure out what a Christian man should feel.

Babe was looking at him hard, waiting. George tried to joke his indecision away. "Okay," he said, "s-so they're G-God's stepchildren, maybe. His f-foster kids."

Babe gave him a tight nod, satisfied. "Fuckin' A," he said. "Can't always love thy neighbor, pal. Sometimes, you got to hate 'em so's you can kill 'em."

Ahead of them, Tank raised a hand, signaling a stop. George passed the signal back. Then he approached Tank. "What's going on?" he asked.

Tank pointed toward where the trees began. Two officers were crouched there on the ground, jabbing animatedly at a map. It had become a depressingly familiar sight. "You see them trees?" said Tank.

"Yeah. Sure."

"Well, they're not there."

"What do you mean?"

"I mean, I see 'em, too, but apparently they're not there. At least, that's what that map they're jawin' about says. These maps we're usin' are not exactly the last word in reliability, you know what I mean?"

"What you mean," said Babe, coming up to join them, "is that those maps might as well have been drawn by a retarded third grader."

"I think maybe they were," said Tank.

Babe shook his head. "Should've gone to the auto club," he said. "They got good maps."

"Couldn't b-be any worse," said George.

"Ain't that the truth," said Tank. "And meantime, we're sitting ducks for any Jap sniper or patrol that comes along."

"Best n-not to think about it," said George.

"Hard not to," said Tank.

"Snafu," said Babe, slapping at a mosquito.

Tank agreed. "Snafu," he said.

Situation Normal All Fucked Up. Sometimes, George thought it should have been the military's official motto.

They stood there for long minutes, baking in the enervating heat, going nowhere. Finally, the signal was passed, and they moved forward into the trees that were not there.

They traveled single file through a tunnel of green, the landscape rising, the earth soft beneath their boots. George walked hunched over, ready to spring to the ground at the slightest sign of the Japanese. Unknown animals snorted and grunted at them from the darkness. Startled birds jumped into the air, wings flapping furiously, then mocked them from high above. A butterfly as big as a fist went lofting by overhead. George was looking at it when he felt something bounce off his helmet. He spun around just in time to see a rat waddling across a tree branch overhead. "Shit," he hissed.

"We must be in the soup for sure," cracked Babe. "The Saint is using unclean language."

"You men keep it down," hissed Phipps from up ahead, and George was thankful he was spared the need to think up a suitable response. They hacked at the vegetation with machetes, through vines so thick the metal blades took two or three good whacks to get through. Each tree sent out tangled roots as thick around as sewer pipes and you had to step carefully or else go tumbling onto your face into yellow dirt that smelled like dampness and putrefaction.

The jungle was bristling with what was not there. Every long leaf raised high was a saber ready to bite into an unwary neck. In every dark place, one of the emperor's soldiers crouched in ambush, eager to give his life in order to butcher some unsuspecting marine. And it was so damned *hot*. They could not even see the sky, much less the sun, but somehow, the sun could see them. Its fire followed them into the darkness beneath the trees, a moist heat that leached the potency right out of your bones.

"Jesus," whispered George. He found himself panting like a dog. He was half-convinced terror was the only thing keeping him upright.

"Yeah," said Babe.

Jazzman was just ahead of them, carrying the tripod for the water-cooled, .30-caliber machine gun Tank carried slung over his shoulder. His long, lean fingers curled around the metal without tapping it even once. Babe saw George noticing this. "We really are screwed," he said. George managed a laugh.

"Shut the fuck up!" hissed Tank.

They fell silent.

George could not say how long the jungle had held them. Was it one hour, two? Was it more? However many hours it was, the sun had climbed more than halfway across the sky by the time they emerged from the covering of the trees. His mouth hung open. It tasted like dust.

"They got to let us drink soon, don't you think?" Jazzman had slipped back next to George. "I mean a real drink. Not this water discipline bullshit."

"If they don't let us, I might just drink anyway," said Babe, who was on the other side. "Fuckin' officers. How are they going to let us die of thirst when we've got canteens on our belts?"

"Come on now," said George, struggling to grin. "If your thoughts mattered, would you still be a private?"

Babe looked at him. "Well, fuck me," he said.

"Water." Jazzman said this. Whispered it, actually, the way you'd whisper a prayer.

"What are you talking about?" George asked.

Jazzman pointed. It was the river. Somehow, they had reached it yet again. Or if not the Tenaru, some other river. A stream, actually. But did it really matter? Did anyone really care?

It didn't and they did not.

Military discipline broke like glass. Whooping like 10-year-olds at a community pool, the 1st Marines rushed down the bank and into the blessed water. From some distant place, a lieutenant yelled cautions and warnings, but they were wasted words, mere balloon juice. Laughing, George scooped up handfuls of water and buried his face in them. His body was as dry as a cracker. He could feel the water going down, feel it as it slid through his chest, down into his gut. It made his stomach ache. It made his head hurt. He kept drinking anyway.

Jazzman landed on his back in the water, flapping his arms and legs like a child making snow angels, the tripod discarded somewhere. "Hi-de-hi-de-hi-de-hi," he sang out in his best Cab Calloway voice.

"He-de-he-de-he-de-he," a group of them responded. And they all laughed.

It was madness. Perfect madness.

And it was only after he had drunk his fill, only after he was sitting on the riverbank watching Jazzman tap out what he said was a Sonny Greer drum solo on a fallen tree, that it occurred to George to glance up and around and make sure Japanese eyes were not watching them from the trees. They had forgotten the enemy. He couldn't believe it, but they had. And he knew it was only luck—or grace—that the mistake had not been fatal.

Phipps seemed to have reached the same conclusion. "All right, you guys," he barked in a voice of irritation as if he had not, just 30 seconds before, filled his own helmet with water and placed it gleefully on his head, "that's enough. Let's move out."

And they did.

They did not make the grassy knoll that day. The sun fell from the sky like a rock, and they stopped for the night on a ridge. In a shallow, hastily dug foxhole, George ate for the first time since his lavish breakfast, cold rations of crackers and hash from his pack. He had to do it by feel. He had never known such a flawless darkness.

Or a more overpowering silence.

Hours passed. The night deepened. And it became easy, even natural, to wonder: Was the man on his left still there? Had a Jap snuck into their lines and dispatched him with a hand over the mouth and a knife in the throat? Was that Jap even now coming after George?

George tried not to think these things—he knew they were useless—but it was hard. The darkness closed him in. And the jungle around him was alive with the chattering gossip of animals. Things with wings went flapping overhead. Things with feet went scuttling nearby.

No one spoke. Officers fearful of disclosing their positions had given the order, but it was not needed. These men were too exhausted for anything but silence. They were too afraid. And they were too consumed with fearing whatever the darkness held.

George squinted into it, this shapeless, featureless, forever darkness, waiting for some shadow blacker than the others to detach itself, move toward him. But the darkness gave up nothing, guarded its secrets jealously against his intrusions. And the thoughts he was trying hard not to think leapt upon him again with a vengeance. The Japanese might be all around right at that very second, might be close enough to touch, and George would never know until it was too late and knowing didn't matter anymore. He tried not to be terrified, tried not to envision some Japanese soldier taking aim right now, right . . . this . . . very . . . *second*, and with a casual pull of a trigger, erasing George Simon from life forever.

It was as he was thinking this very thought that George heard the crack of rifle fire very near to him.

He jumped, hands going automatically to his chest, feeling for the telltale wetness of his own blood. Had he been shot? Had he drawn to himself the very fate he feared?

But no, there was more gunfire. Somebody had seen something! Somebody had penetrated the impenetrable darkness and spotted the Japs sneaking in! He racked his sidearm and was about to shoot blindly into the shadows when he heard the command.

"Cease fire! Cease fire, damn it!"

It took a moment for everyone to hear. The gunfire petered out. George pressed himself into his earth hole, awaiting answers, wanting answers, wondering what had just happened. Instead, the silence fell again.

It began to rain. He brought out his poncho and huddled beneath it. All around him, he heard men doing the same.

Sleeping was out of the question. But so was staying awake. George sat there stranded somewhere between the two for the balance of the night, frightened of what might happen, yet at the same time, somehow indifferent to it, indifferent to dying, indifferent to his very existence. He felt something closing over his soul, felt some open place in his psyche scabbing over like a skinned knee.

Was he becoming what he had feared he might become? Was it something, as Father had said once, that he needed to become in order to survive? Or maybe he was just tired. Maybe that was all.

He didn't know. He didn't even care.

The rain plopped in great sheets down from the trees. It whispered against his poncho. It dripped heavily from his helmet. He was sitting in it. He was cold, miserable, and wet. And scared. Always scared.

George hated war. He hated every damn thing in the whole damn world.

Morning came.

He supposed he had known that eventually it would, as it always did. But that had seemed a far less certain proposition as he had sat in the silent darkness listening to unseen things scuttling through the jungle.

George was about to haul himself up out of his hole to take the piss he had been holding so long it felt as if his very pelvis had locked when Babe came up. "Come take a look," he said. George would have protested that he needed to pee first, but something in Babe's eyes stilled the words. He climbed up and followed his friend.

"What's it about?" he asked.

"You remember the shooting last night?" asked Babe.

"Of course," said George.

Babe pointed to where a cluster of men had gathered. George ventured a few steps, then stopped at the sight of the body. He was a medical corpsman, lying in the dirt, bloody, dead, a surprised look in his eyes. Next to the body, a couple of marines were digging a grave. The *thunk* of shovels in dirt seemed the only sound in the world.

"Poor bastard." Babe was lighting a cigarette. "Went to take a piss in the night. Couldn't get the password out in time."

"Lilliputian," said George. The Marines used passwords with consonants they thought the Japs wouldn't be able to pronounce. If you heard somebody approach your lines and say, "Rirriputian," you knew it was the enemy. At least, that was the idea. But apparently, the word had also defeated a white man from America. And he had died.

So what was the use of it? What was the use of any of it?

"Yeah," said Babe. "Lilliputian. What the hell is a Lilliputian, anyway?"

George looked at the dead meat that had been a living man just a few hours before—that would still have been a living man but for a stupid fuckup. "It's another w-w-word for s-snafu," he said.

"Yeah," said Babe. He eyed George through a cloud of gray smoke. "What do you think, Saint? You're our resident man of God. You want to say a few words over the dear departed?"

George regarded the dead man again, shook his head. "I've g-got to piss," he said. And he walked away.

They took the airstrip that afternoon. It turned out to be only just barely deserving of the name, a crude runway on a flat plain hacked out of the jungle. The ground was gouged with craters. Trees had fallen. A truck lay on its side, blackened by fire. The Navy had really shellacked this place.

The enemy was nowhere to be seen. Even so, the men stepped cautiously onto this critical piece of Jap real estate.

"So I guess this is what we're f-fighting for?" George said.

Babe smirked. "Yeah. Mission accomplished. Guess we can all go home now?"

"You men shut up." Phipps's voice was frayed with tension.

Small wonder, thought George. Just because you didn't see any Japs didn't mean they didn't see you. He looked to the jungle fringing the airfield, wondering when one of the shadows would resolve itself into a threat. But nothing moved except the marines stealing slowly across the sun-blasted tarmac.

After a moment, they came upon a cluster of tents. Phipps directed a group of men to clear them, George and Babe among them. His rifle slick in his grip, his breathing shallow, George moved toward the first tent. He paused at the opening, looked back to make sure Babe was covering him, crouched low, took a deep breath, and then sprang inside.

No one was there. But someone had been and not so long ago. The man had eaten from the bowl of rice that now lay overturned on the dirt floor. When the order to bug out came, he had probably been reading the pages—personal correspondence, George guessed—that lay nearby in the dirt. He had left his bed neatly made, a pair of boots sticking out from beneath it.

George withdrew from the tent. With his eyes, he indicated that Babe was to cover him again as he moved to the next tent in the line. Babe nodded and they went through it again. George crouched, took a deep breath, sprang inside.

This tent, too, was deserted. Flies circled lazily above a bowl of stewed prunes that sat abandoned on a folding camp table. A scorpion scuttled away under the bed. George picked up a photograph from the floor. An unsmiling Japanese soldier, an unsmiling woman, and an unsmiling toddler on her lap all stared back at him. It seemed odd to think that Jap soldiers had families.

"Nothing here," he told Babe, backing out of the tent.

"I guess they're all gone," said Babe.

"Not all of them." Tank was at the next tent. He waved them over and pointed to the body at his feet.

The dead man lay on his back in a crater just outside the tent, eyes open, staring down eternity. The corpse was mostly intact except that something— probably the force of the same explosion that had dug the crater—had sheared open his left cheek. Beneath his open eye, his teeth and cheekbones were exposed in a terrible parody of a smile that went almost to his ear. The effect was startling. Somehow, the sight of his molars and canines, gruesomely revealed by the ripping of his flesh, made him seem more beast than man. It was as if in his terrible repose, the dead man whispered a reminder of the unutterable truth beneath the soft facade of skin—that for all his pride and pretensions, a man was ultimately just another animal with teeth.

George was contemplating this when, all at once, Tank whipped around the heavy machine gun he had been carrying across his back and smashed the butt of it hard against the dead man's face. He paused, studied what he had done, apparently did not like what he saw, and brought the weapon down again. And again. And again, until the mouth broke, chunks of bone splintering off the jaw, teeth skittering across the ground.

Tank bent to examine his handiwork, picking carefully through the broken teeth like a prospector inspecting the contents of his pan. He lifted one, examined it, flung it away. All at once, he seemed to become aware of George and Babe, staring, dumbfounded.

"Gold," he said.

"B-Beg pardon?" said George.

"Gold," he repeated. "In their fillings. Japs love that stuff. Fellow told me you can make a fortune just collecting teeth from dead Japs." As he spoke, he pulled out his Ka-Bar knife, palmed the dead man's head to hold it steady, and began to saw at the flesh holding what remained of the man's lower jaw.

There was a moment. Then Babe said, "A fortune? Really?" And he knelt down to watch in rapt interest as Tank hacked at the dead man's shattered face.

Transfixed, George watched them both for a moment. It seemed to him that he should be praying, but he had no idea what he should be praying for. He gave up and stepped away, wishing he had not seen what he just saw.

They dug foxholes and camped that night on a ridge overlooking the beach.

There was something dully comforting in looking out to sea and seeing American cruisers on station in the channel. Sitting with his back against a coconut tree, George ate his hash and crackers and swigged warm water from his canteen, savoring the rare luxury of a moment when he did not have to run or do, a moment when he could just be.

The field had, indeed, turned out to be deserted. The Japanese had retreated so quickly that many had left personal effects behind—cigarette lighters, books, clothing, pictures. George was disappointed that he had not been able to lay claim to a sword or a sidearm. He really wanted to come home from war with one or the other. Or a Japanese flag. That would be a nice souvenir, too.

The enemy had also left behind a control tower, an ammo dump, a storehouse of rations—"All the rice you can eat," cracked Jazzman—along with three antiaircraft batteries and assorted vehicles and supplies.

All in all, thought George, swirling the water in his mouth as he had been taught, he was well satisfied with his first combat experience as a marine. It had included no actual combat and the easy capture of the primary objective. Things couldn't get much better than that.

It struck George that he had heard so many lectures about the fierceness of the Japanese soldier, his toughness and resourcefulness, his absolute refusal to surrender, that the enemy had come to seem some nearly invincible superman against whom George's own chances amounted to the proverbial slim and none.

So it did his heart good, it *encouraged* him, to think this formidable enemy had fled in haste rather than face the 1st Marines. Maybe they weren't so fearsome after all.

"Hope they're all this easy," he told Jazzman, who was sitting next to him.

"Nice work if you can get it," said Jazzman. He was contentedly tapping out a slow beat on his mess kit with a pair of abandoned chopsticks.

"What's that mean?"

Jazzman gave him a look. "Billie Holiday," he said, his tone of voice calling George an idiot. And he picked up the beat on the chopsticks and began to sing in his best imitation of Holiday's reedy, plaintive voice.

Holding hands at midnight
'Neath a starry sky,
Nice work if you can get it
And you can get it, if you try . . .

Babe came and planted himself next to them. George had not seen him since morning. He shifted his weight, suddenly uncomfortable, realizing only in that moment that he had been avoiding his friend.

"Fellas," said Babe.

"Evening," said George.

Jazzman nodded, still singing.

"Who's that you're singing, Jazz?"

Jazzman stopped singing. "Billie Holiday," he said.

"That colored singer? Never did like her much. Too mopey."

"You white men have never understood my people," said Jazzman. And he went back to singing.

George said, "You and Tank find any gold in that guy's teeth?"

Babe shook his head. "Nope. Cheap bastard. Fillings all made of lead."

George paused, thinking. When he spoke, he tried to make his voice light. "It didn't bother you, doing that to a corpse?"

"Guy's fuckin' dead. He sure didn't feel it."

"No, I mean—"

Babe cut him off. "I know what you mean," he said. He glared at George, suddenly hostile, and it occurred to George that his friend had been expecting this, had probably come here specifically to get it over with. He turned to George now. "One thing you got to understand: This ain't a church and you ain't no saint, even though we call you that. This is a war. Shit happens in a war. Ugly shit."

"I wasn't trying to—"

Again, Babe cut him off. "Yes, you were," he said. Babe paused. He took a deep breath. "You know what? I like you, George. I really do. You're a good guy. And I know you mean well with all that philosophical malarkey, brotherhood, and God and all. You're just doing what we're all trying to do: figure this thing out, get through it as best we can. But see, here's what you don't get: you're trying to save my soul. Me, I'll be happy if I can just save my ass."

"Why c-can't you save both?"

"Because that's when you get k-k-k-killed, my friend. Face it, George. You're on a fucking island in the asshole of the Pacific Ocean surrounded by a bunch of gooks who would slit your throat as soon as look at you. So you got to do what you got to do to get through it. Sooner you get that, better chance you have of making it home in one piece. And if you don't get it, I'm not so sure how comfortable I am with you watching my ass."

He stared at George. George stared back. Around them, men sat with heads down, studiously eating their meals, playing cards, picking at scabs, studiously not listening. No one made a sound. Babe turned away. He lit a cigarette, blew out the smoke, ran a palm through his hair. He turned back to George. "You know what those yellow fucks did at Bataan, don't you? How they chopped guys' heads off—*our* guys' heads off—for fucking nothing? How they starved them and beat them and buried them alive? You think any of them are sitting out there having . . . moral qualms or pangs of conscience over any of that?"

He waited for an answer. George had none. He was a moral man, a man of God, but on this hot August evening on a ridge overlooking the shores of Guadalcanal, morality seemed a small, impotent thing, and God seemed very far away. George slapped at a mosquito that had landed on his hand. He said nothing. After a moment, Babe stood. "Like I said, George, I got nothin' against you. But you really need to get your head out of your ass."

He walked away.

George sat there a long time, his cheeks flaming. He did not dare to look around, did not dare to face whatever judgment awaited him in the eyes of his fellow marines, who watched him now in pregnant silence. After a moment, sound and movement returned. George still did not move. He looked at Jazzman. Randy had his eyes closed, still singing the Billie Holiday song.

Finally, George retired to his foxhole. Once again, darkness came down like a curtain. George folded his arms over his rifle, found a comfortable position. He slept.

Screams and explosions woke him with a start. George's eyes came open upon a red sky. He grabbed his rifle, poked his head up. "What's going on?" he cried. "What's happening?"

Babe danced by, a shadow limned in red light. "It's the Japs!" he cried happily, the harsh words from just hours ago apparently all forgotten.

"They're getting their asses kicked." Babe pointed out to sea with a hand holding a battle of sake he had liberated from some officer's quarters on the airfield. George climbed out of his foxhole for a better view.

There was a ferocious naval battle underway out in the channel. Ships burned, airplanes wheeled about the sky, great cloud banks of smoke scudded by, tracers trailing scarlet fire arced overhead, and the air pounded with percussive blasts so powerful that they fluttered George's sleeves.

All at once, there came a huge explosion. Some Jap ship had taken a crippling blow. They could feel the heat all the way from where they stood. The men screamed and hooted in triumph. Babe lifted the bottle of sake in his fist. "Fuckin' Japs!" he cried, "take that!"

George, caught up in the instant, felt himself screaming right along. "Yeah! How y'all like them apples, Mr. Hirohito!"

It struck him again how they had built the Japanese up as some kind of supermen. But they weren't supermen at all, were they? These were men who could bleed and die like any other men. George draped an arm over Babe's shoulder. Babe passed him the sake and he took a swig. It tasted like piss. He didn't care. They howled together under the scarlet sky as the Jap ship flamed.

George had never been so proud to be an American.

It was not until morning that he discovered how wrong they all were. The men hiked down to the beach laughing, talking, feeling invincible after the pasting the Japs had taken. And then they stopped, dumb-founded. One man looked at the next man who looked at the next man, each searching the other's face for some answer to the impossible sight they saw. The channel was empty.

The Navy was gone.

The transports and cruisers that had patrolled offshore, the mighty war fleet that had given George such comfort simply by being there had somehow . . . vanished.

"Where's our ships?" asked Tank. His voice was plaintive and con-fused. He sounded somehow betrayed.

It dawned on them in stages. It was not the Japs who had gotten their asses kicked. It was the Navy, *their* Navy.

All those ships whose burning they had cheered . . .

They had just assumed . . .

But they had been watching their own men die. They had been drinking and howling as their own ships lit the horizon with fire.

George swallowed. It hurt.

Now the Navy was gone. Ships sunk or withdrawn . . . did it matter which? No. All that mattered was that they were gone. And the marines were on this godforsaken island alone. Abandoned.

"Boys," said Babe, "we are in the shit."

And it was right as he said it that they heard the drone of planes. George's head whipped around. A formation of fighters was coming in from over the channel. The sun sparkling on their wings rendered them little more than shadows. George squinted his eyes, hoping to see, *needing* to see the blessed reassurance of white stars on their wings. But he did not. Painted on each wing was the hated "red meatball," the rising sun that symbolized the empire of Japan.

"Japs!" he cried.

The planes came in low and fast. They were so close George actually saw a Jap pilot seeing him. Then the machine guns on the Japanese Zeros opened up. There was an angry metallic clatter, starbursts of fire, bullets punching holes in the beach, a line of metal that marched right toward the stranded marines. The men scattered. George wheeled and dove for the ground.

He was in midair when he felt a bolt of fire slice through him.

George crashed awkwardly into the high grass, spouts of dirt kicked up by the Jap machine guns bracketing him. The air was made of the angry buzz of engines and the metallic chatter of guns. Close above him, someone was screaming.

"Doc, get your ass over here! Saint's hit!"

"I'm o-k-kay, I'm o-k-kay." George tried to shout it, but the cacophony above him refused to admit his voice. "I'm okay," he said again, louder, trying to sit up. And that was when a shock of pain ripped through his side and he screwed his eyes shut, snarling with the sudden realization that perhaps he was not okay at all.

The drone of engines was fading, the Jap Zeros banking away. George forced his eyes open. A marine named Tony Burns was cradling his head. And here came the medic on the dead run. His name was Walter Hamm but, inevitably, everyone called him "Doc." He skidded to a stop, hovering over George, his face taut with concern.

"Doc," said George.

"Shut up, Saint. Don't try to talk."

"Doc! How is he?" George recognized Babe's voice, full of fear, calling from some distant place.

"Give me a minute, Babe. Geez, I just got here."

As he spoke, he was tearing at George's dungarees to expose the wound. All at once, he stopped. "Well, I'll be damned," he breathed.

George felt his heart stutter. "What? *What?*"

Doc said, "Don't worry about it. You're going to be fine."

George almost stopped breathing at that because wasn't that what you said to a man when the wound was hopeless? Doc must have read that in George's expression because he grabbed George's face tight between thumb and forefinger. "No, *seriously*," he said, with a wild laugh, "you're going to be okay. Really. Look for yourself."

George stared at Hamm as if unwilling to believe. Then he lifted his head and craned to see. The bullet had torn a shallow, bloody groove across his torso, a crimson line of pain. But not of death. Even he could tell that.

Relief dropped his head heavily. He began to laugh uncontrollably. "I'm okay!" he cried. "I'm okay!"

The medic ripped open a sulfa pack with his teeth and began sprinkling the white powder liberally onto the wound. "I bet your kid brother's hurt himself worse falling off his bike, am I right?" He said this with a giddy laugh, and George realized that he was relieved, too.

Tony Burns said, "Hell, Saint, you're the luckiest sonofabitch I ever knew. Maybe there's something to all that prayer business after all. Somebody up there is sure lookin' out for you. Put in a good word for me next time, would you?"

"A-Ask him yourself," said George. He laughed some more, but laughter turned into a grimace as Doc applied a dressing to the wound, his hands rough and fast and unheeding of pain.

"Thanks, Doc."

"It's going to hurt like a sonofabitch," said Doc, "but you'll be okay."

"I'll bet you thought you had your million-dollar wound," cracked Tony. A million-dollar wound was the wound that sent you back stateside.

Doc said, "More like a $20 wound, I'd say."

"Yeah, but he'll have a really nice scar to show the broads," said Tony. "That's not nothin.'" They all laughed.

Then someone cried out, "They're coming back!"

The words jerked George's gaze to the sky. For just an instant, the distant grinding of engines, the flyspecks on the horizon growing larger froze him solid, and he found himself thinking a silly thought: *It can't be. It's not fair.* He had survived a first strafing by these Jap bastards. It just wasn't right for them to swing around for another try.

Phipps shouted, "Head for the trees! Get into the jungle!" All around him, marines scrambled in response to the cry. George reached to push himself upright, fell back with a grimace, pain lacing his abdomen. And then, just like that, he was moving, sliding backward, his heels digging twin furrows in the sand. Doc and Tony had hooked his armpits and were pulling.

"I'm okay, guys! P-Put me down! I'm okay!"

It was Pearl all over again, someone else about to be killed because he was literally unable to pull his own weight. He did not think he would be able to live with himself if it happened again. The Jap Zeros came beelining in, and he stared again into starbursts of fire from their guns.

"G-Guys!" he called, his voice desperate now, "I'm telling you, just p-put me down. I'll be okay!"

"Saint, would you shut the fuck up!" growled Doc, huffing exertion.

"Will you get a load of this guy," cried Tony Burns. "Thinks he's fuckin' Sergeant York or something!"

They plunged into the trees just as machine gun fire chewed up the kunai grass where George had lain.

You could not run in the jungle. The trees were too close together, the vegetation too dense, the roots too gnarled and thick upon the ground. But somehow, the marines ran anyway, George towing behind Doc and Tony like the caboose on some careening freight train, bumping heavily over the roots and other obstructions in the ground.

When they were deep under the screen of trees, Phipps ordered them to halt. Doc and Tony allowed George to drop into the mud and bent over gratefully, their hands on their knees.

"Stay alert," Phipps whispered. "These woods may be crawling with Japs. For all we know, they're watching us right now."

That got Doc's and Tony's attention. They gazed warily up and around them. "Well, shit," said Tony.

Released at last, George began the task of climbing to his feet. It was not easy, but he waved away helpful hands, determined to do this for himself. He grabbed a low branch on one of the trees and pulled. It made his stomach hurt like hell. He told himself the pain was not there.

It could have been worse, he reminded himself. *It could have been so much worse.*

Babe and Jazzman appeared. "You all right?" Babe's eyes seemed round and luminous in the filtered light of the jungle.

George nodded tiredly. "Just a scratch," he said. "You?"

"I'm okay," said Babe. "Lost some guys back there, though. Logan and Downey."

George nodded. He didn't really know either man. "I saw 'em both go down," continued Babe. "Couple more guys wounded like you. I guess that's what they call 'light casualties.' I guess we should feel lucky, huh?"

"I d-don't feel so lucky," said George.

Jazzman looked at him. "You're luckier than Logan and Downey," he said in a toneless voice.

And this, George had to confess, was certainly true.

The explosion came all at once from all around them—a flash of light and a deep, percussive force more felt than heard. Trees splintered above, shards of wood falling down like rain. George and Babe were knocked off their feet.

"The fuckers are shelling us! Can you believe this shit?" Babe seemed personally affronted.

"We g-got no navy," called George. "We g-got no air cover. What's t-t-to stop them?"

"Where are the other companies?" demanded Babe. "We need to link up."

Another explosion. The ground heaved, rising up beneath them. George hunkered against a tree. He stared up at it warily, afraid the sight of it beginning to topple would be the last thing he ever saw.

Another explosion. Another. All around them men crouched, held their helmets, ducked their heads. There was no cover—nor any way to dig for any in the heavy roots twining together on the ground. There was nothing they could do except take it.

Someone screamed, "All right, already! We get the point!"

Someone else screamed, "Why don't you fight fair, you yellow bastards?"

And Jazzman spoke cheerfully. "Dig that crazy percussion," he said.

Crouching on his knees, hugging a tree trunk with more passion than he'd ever hugged his wife, George whirled around and stared in disbelief. Jazzman was sitting on a large root as casually as a man on a park bench, a blissful smile lighting his face as he tapped on it with the chopsticks he had found at the airfield.

"Jesus, Jazz!" cried Babe, who seemed about to burrow into the trunk of a tree. "Are you nuts? What are you doing?"

Jazzman looked straight at him. "T'ain't what'cha do," he intoned in a voice of utmost seriousness. "It's the way hot'cha do it!"

And here, finally, was one of Jazzman's arcane musical references that George actually understood. He and Sylvia had done the shim sham to that record by Jimmie Lunceford at their prom, a thousand years ago. As the ground lurched beneath him and men screamed futile curses at unseen warships miles offshore, George heard himself begin to sing.

When I was a kid about half past three,
My pop said, "Son, come here to me . . ."

Jazzman grinned a surprised grin and kept on drumming his chopsticks. Babe looked from one to the other as if they had lost their minds. George ignored him, went right on singing in a warbling, terrified tenor even as another blast detonated somewhere far too close. He didn't stammer.

Said things may come, and things may go
But this is one thing you ought to know . . .

And here at the chorus, he heard Babe join in, his voice uncertain and not seeming to believe itself.

Oh t'ain't what'cha do, it's the way hot'cha do it . . .

Several other men joined them now, a reedy chorus of frightened voices.

T'ain't what'cha do, it's the way hot'cha do it
T'ain't what'cha do, it's the way hot'cha do it
That's what gets results.

Another explosion seemed to rip the sky.

George could not remember the next verse. He sang the first one over again, loud as he could. Had the men on the Bataan peninsula done anything like this? Abandoned by their country, no reinforcements, no air support, outgunned and outmanned by the enemy, had they surrendered to this sort of madness long before they ever surrendered to the Japs?

It was not an idle thought. Indeed, George realized, it had lurked at the edge of his consciousness ever since that awful moment the men had emerged on the beach and found the Navy gone. Now, as shells burst all around them, the thought could no longer be ignored or denied.

Would they be forsaken, as the men on Bataan had been? Would the military write them off, desert them as it had those men? And what would become of them then?

George did not want to think like this. It seemed to him somehow disloyal. But he could not shake the thought. He caught Babe's eye, singing, "It's the way hot'cha do it," in impudent, useless defiance of Jap shells, and he knew that his friend was thinking the thought, too.

George thought of a favorite verse from Deuteronomy.

Be strong and of a good courage, fear not, nor be afraid of them: for the Lord, thy God, he it is that doth go with thee, he will not leave thee nor forsake thee.

It did not help.

Oh, God, please.

It did *not* help.

Because with a sickening certainty, George knew he *had* been left. He *had* been forsaken. The realization all but unmanned him. He felt himself at the very lowest point of his life, looking up, beseeching an empty Heaven for mercy.

Please, help. Please.

And it began to rain.

twelve

"Hey, look," said Luther, pointing. "Fresh fish."

Jocko, who was sitting across from Luther, studying his cards with a frown of deep concentration, brought his head up and followed Luther's gaze. Standing at the top of the same rise from which Luther and Books had gotten their first glimpse of Camp Claiborne's Negro section a few months ago stood a cluster of new men, their eyes round, their mouths open.

"Lost children more like," growled Jocko around an unlit cigar, returning his eyes to his cards.

It had become something of a bitter joke to the men of the 761st to watch new men transfer in from points north, where the idea of a colored battalion was taken more seriously. You always saw that same look of shock when they crested the hill and got their first look at the sea of soupy mud, raggedy tents, and worn-out barracks to which they had been consigned.

"You should have more compassion," said Books. "It was not so long ago that you and I were standing in the same spot wearing the same expressions." He was staring at his reflection in a mirror, brushing his hair. Books had a date in town.

"Yeah," said Luther. "I s'pose I should." Still, when the small cluster of men ventured down into the swamp and drew abreast of the tent, he couldn't resist yelling out to them. "That's right, boys. Y'all in the nigger army now. Get used to it."

A smirk hooked Jocko's lip at that, but Books grimaced. He hated that word. Luther ignored him, went back to his own cards. "Them boys don't know yet, but they ain't seen the half of it," he muttered.

Jocko nodded, still studying his cards. "Ain't that the truth," he said.

It wasn't just the condition of the colored section that flummoxed the new men, most of whom had come in from Fort Knox in Kentucky. It was also a training regimen so lackadaisical as to make a joke of the very concept. The new men would watch, appalled and amazed, as their new battalion "trained" by parking their tanks in the field, building fires, and sitting around outside them, swapping lies because they were given nothing else to do.

It wasn't like this up at Fort Knox, the new men would say. At Fort Knox, you marched up Misery Hill under full packs in the broiling Kentucky sun while a drill sergeant screamed at you in language that melted your ears. At Fort Knox, you ran until your lungs spewed fire, and you did push-ups until your arms hung like cooked spaghetti. Most of all, you learned everything there was to know about tanks. You mounted and dismounted a hundred times until doing so was as much second nature as getting out of bed. You climbed down to oil the bogie wheels so they did not freeze up and render the tank immobile. You fired guns and practiced combat maneuvers and learned to extricate a tank from mud. At the end of each grueling day, you cleaned up your tank before you cleaned up yourself.

To which Luther or one of the other men would always respond with a derisive cackle. "Well, son," Luther told one disillusioned young man, "you ain't in Fort Knox no more, you at Camp Claiborne, state of Louisiana, kingdom of Jim Crow."

They laughed, but it wasn't remotely funny, and they knew it. To the contrary, it burrowed in your gut like a worm in an apple, this realization that you were asked to do nothing because you were considered capable of doing nothing.

Some men said, fuck it. Some men said that if the government was willing to pay them $35 a month to sit on their asses, they were happy to accept it. And maybe some of them really meant it—but Luther suspected most of them spoke as he himself secretly did, from an injured bravado that required any man who wanted to call himself a man to find *something* to put a little swagger in his walk, even if it meant he had to lie to himself, even if it meant he had to act as if he liked it this way, as if he were glad to be sitting on his backside instead of training. It was in the moments when a man was no longer shooting the shit with other men, when the world had gone silent and he could no longer pretend not to hear the murmur of his own irresolute thoughts, that he had to face how impotent a "victory" that really was.

"You all think they ever gon' let us fight?" Luther asked as the new men walked away.

"Hell," said Jocko, "got to train us 'fore we can fight."

"I must confess," said Books, now fussing with his tie, "that I am surprised to find you at all eager to fight, Luther. Are you not the one who always says he was blackmailed into this man's army and has no desire to fight for this damnable country?"

"Yeah," said Luther. "I said that. But hell, if I got to be here, seem like they ought to let me do somethin'. That's all I'm sayin'. Man ain't made to just sit around on his ass."

"I agree with you there," Jocko said. "I want to fight for my country."

Luther laughed. "Me, I just want to fight," he said.

"I do share your impatience," said Books. He was turning his chin this way and that in the mirror, looking for razor stubble. "Of course, some of us have been lucky enough to find pleasant diversions to take our minds off the conditions here."

"You mean that girl," said Luther.

Books grinned. "The delightful Andrea, yes."

Lately, she was all he could talk about—Andrea McClintock, a schoolteacher he had met in Alexandria. They'd had three dates and Books was hopelessly smitten.

Alexandria was the biggest town in the area and, at just 20 miles away, also one of the closest. Unfortunately, it was patrolled by mean white MPs and poor white trash spoiling for any excuse to knock a colored man around—especially a colored soldier.

Many of the men had since decided that Alexandria wasn't worth the trouble. But a few had serious girlfriends up there, and like Books, they insisted on going, regardless. Luther and Jocko had told Books repeatedly that it was a bad idea. But he always said he had a right to go anywhere he wanted. Books could be stubborn about his rights.

"She got to be pretty damn delightful all right," rumbled Jocko, apparently deciding to take another shot at dissuading their friend. "You takin' a mighty big risk to chase after her."

"I see it as a risk well worth taking."

"Then you a fool," said Jocko. "You an' all the rest of them cock hounds still runnin' up there in uniform."

Books stiffened. "I am not—"

Jocko held up his hand. "I'm sorry," he said. "I ain't meant it that way. I'm sure she's a decent, respectable girl. I'm just sayin' it ain't safe there. Especially for you, Books. You ain't from down here."

"As I have been reminded on many occasions," said Books in a sour voice. "But while I concede your superior experience in the mores of Jim Crow, I am no fool. I can take care of myself."

"Don't you remember what they told us about the riot?"

It had happened right before the 761st arrived. The word was that many people had been hurt. Some had been shot, some had even died.

"Of course I remember," said Books.

"And?"

"As I have been given to understand it, the disturbance began when some of the fellows objected to an MP's rough handling of a Negro soldier during an arrest."

"Exactly."

"So I shall simply do nothing that might invite arrest."

Jocko threw up both his hands. "I give up," he said. "Go get your ass kicked. See if I care."

"Again, I consider the risk acceptable if it means I get to see my Andrea. Oh, and I recently found out she has a sister, if either of you would like to join us."

Jocko said, "A sister?"

Books adjusted his garrison cap as he spoke. "Delores is not quite as delightful as my Andrea, mind you, but she is fetching in her own right. And I happen to know that she is unattached."

Books looked at Luther. Luther looked at Jocko, who shrugged in response to the unasked question.

"Maybe I can keep him out of trouble," reasoned Luther.

"Sure you can," said Jocko. "And get you a look at this here Delores while you at it."

"Does this mean you accept my invitation?" asked Books.

Luther grinned. "Yeah," he said. "I guess it do."

And so it was, an hour later, that the two men, resplendent in their khaki uniforms, garrison caps sitting just so on their heads, rounded a corner with the McClintock sisters into a Negro neighborhood of clapboard buildings that housed bars, sporting houses, cafes, and theaters. Jazz wafted out from two or three doors, filling the air with a beautiful discord of competing rhythms. They paused to take it all in. Books straightened his tie. Then he offered Andrea his arm. Behind him, Luther offered Delores his own arm, and they followed Books and Andrea into the music and light.

Books had not exaggerated the charms of the McClintock sisters. They were tall and willowy, both with lively eyes and dimpled smiles. But in terms of personality, they could not have been more unalike. Andrea was soft-spoken and shy, exactly the kind of girl Luther would have pictured Books with. By contrast, Delores was the kind of girl he himself liked: brassy, outgoing, and quick to laugh—a gal who knew how to have fun. All at once, Luther's anxieties about coming here felt silly. This was all right, he decided. This would be fun.

Because the girls had rushed home from work to get dressed and hadn't yet had supper, food was the first order of business. The two couples ate at a cafe Delores knew. When they stepped back out into the warm evening, a hot rhythm was spilling out of a nightclub across the street. The foursome wandered in, Books bobbing his head as the band on the tiny bandstand chugged through "Slim Slam Boogie." Marveling that Books even knew that song, Luther claimed a corner table and they all sat and ordered drinks. "Slim Slam Boogie" had become "Walkin' the Boogie" by the time the drinks came.

Books lifted his bourbon glass in a toast. "To two day passes," he said.

"And no tanks," said Luther.

All around them, the night glittered. Hoisting his beer, watching through the haze of cigarette smoke as couples jitterbugged on a dance floor not much bigger than a card table, listening to the shrill music of women's laughter and the baritone bravado of men's lies, Luther felt at home, felt safe among his own. It was how he had always felt drinking in the jukes back in Mobile, the thing Thelma had never quite understood. He knew everyone and they knew him, and if he could sit there long enough, laughing and talking and getting enough alcohol into him, it made the old fear go away. And then, finally, Luther could breathe.

Just as Luther finished his beer, the band went into "Knock Me a Kiss." On impulse, he stood and offered Delores his hand. "May I have this dance?" he asked.

They spun out onto the floor at a smooth and easy pace. Delores proved to be a great dancer, instantly responsive to his merest shift in rhythm or slightest pressure on the small of her back. It was as if they had been dancing together for years.

Luther felt good. He felt better than he had in years.

They danced two more numbers, then returned to the table. There, they found Books pulling on his pipe in that professorial way he had and going on about "the New Negro" and the responsibilities of the modern race man. Andrea McClintock was gazing into his eyes as though the secret to the origins of life might be written there.

Luther laughed. "Damn, Books, you 'bout to talk the woman's ear off. This ain't no lecture hall. This here a juke joint."

"'Books?'" Andrea looked at him, confused. "Franklin, why does he call you that?"

Books's sigh was full of long suffering. "It's a nickname, my dear. Bestowed upon me by my less learned comrades who are eternally mystified that a man would spend his off-hours in the pursuit of knowledge rather than an inside straight. But we all have such nicknames. For instance, the fellows call Luther 'Country' because he hails from the wild woods of Alabama, where electricity and indoor toilets are as yet unknown."

"That ain't true!" Luther protested. He waited a perfect beat, then added, "We know all about electricity!"

Luther's sober-minded friend nearly fell off his chair at that. He bent double, howling with laughter until he began to cough, choking on his own pipe smoke.

"Lord have mercy," said Delores through a chuckle. "I think you like to killed the man, Luther."

"Serve him right," said Luther, still feigning indignation. "Us colored people from the South got to stand up for ourselves when these fancy-pants Northern Negroes get to puttin' us down."

He lifted his glass, and Delores clinked hers with his. It occurred to him that he could learn to like this girl.

"Well, I don't care about all that." Andrea was patting Books's back as he tried to get his coughing under control. "I think you all are mean. What kind of name is that? 'Books.' Just because he likes to read? I mean, really."

Was she serious? Luther didn't know what to say. Fortunately, Books regained his power of speech in time to rescue him.

"It's all right, my darling," he said, still chuckling. "Nicknames are simply part of the rough camaraderie of soldiers. All done to aid our esprit de corps."

"Well," she said, "if you say so."

"Well, now I done seen everything," said Delores. She grabbed her pocketbook. "I got to go to the ladies' room to freshen my makeup. Come on, girl, keep me company."

Luther and Books stood as the two women left the table.

"Well," said Luther, as they passed out of earshot, "don't that beat all?" He sat, lighting a cigarette. "Do this mean I got to call you 'Mr. Bennett' for the duration of the war? Or just when your girlfriend around?"

"Hmm?" Books was not listening. He was still watching after Andrea. A plume of gray smoke drifted from the side of his mouth. It was a moment more before he sat back down.

"I give her credit for one thing," said Luther. "She do stand up for her man, don't she?" He laughed.

It took Books so long to answer that at first Luther wasn't sure he had heard. "Yes," said Books, finally. "She is certainly loyal." There was a distance in his voice. He was still staring in the direction the two women had walked.

Luther watched him a moment, sucking on the cigarette. Then he said, "Of course, only problem is, she done pledged herself to that Joe Louis. You gon' have to fight him for her."

After a moment, Books said, "Yes." Then he turned sharply and said, "Wait. *What* did you say?"

"Just tryin' to see if you was still in there," said Luther.

Books's smile was soft. "Oh," he said. He glanced back in the direction of the ladies' room, then asked in a thoughtful voice. "Luther, how do you suppose it would be if I were to ask that girl to marry me? Do you think she would accept?"

When Luther didn't respond, Books turned to regard him. "Luther?"

Luther was conscious of his mouth hanging open, waiting on instructions from his mind. It took him a moment. Finally, he said, "Marry you? Books, I didn't know ... I didn't think ... "

"I think she is the one, Luther. Now, I anticipate that you will make the sensible objection that we have known each other for only a short time. And you will say that I should wait on this, as there is every expectation that what I feel is merely infatuation and will falter. But I would reply in my defense that I have known infatuation before and it felt nothing like what I feel for Andrea. Besides, in a time of war, can any of us really afford the luxury of waiting? So you see, I have already given your objections due consideration."

Luther smiled. "I s'pose you have," he said.

Books's eyes were serious. "What about her, though? What do you think? Is she not wonderful?"

"Yeah," said Luther. "She somethin' else, all right, way she got you turned around. And if y'all want to get married, I be right happy for you."

"I shall maneuver to get her alone later this evening and pop the question then," said Books, his eyes dancing merrily. "And you, of course, will be my best man."

"Books, I don't know what to say," said Luther.

"Say yes."

"Yes," said Luther. "Yes, man. 'Course I will. I be honored."

They left the nightclub shortly after midnight. It was about a mile to the McClintock home. The streets had quieted, the gaiety of Lee Street fading into an indistinctness behind them. Delores was chattering about something, and every few seconds, Luther would nod or say, "Mmm hmm," in what seemed the right spot, but he wasn't really paying attention. Instead, he was nervously watching Books, who, he could see, was himself nervously pondering the monumental decision he had made.

They were both preoccupied. So they didn't immediately see the white soldier and his date when they opened the screen door of a cafe and stepped onto the sidewalk.

There was no real collision. Books sidestepped nimbly enough to avoid that. But he did brush against the small, dark-haired woman.

"Hey!" barked the man, even as something electric jolted hard through Luther's body. "Watch where you're goin'!"

"I am sorry," said Books automatically, sweeping his garrison cap from his head.

"You damn well better be," said the soldier—a captain, Luther saw—as he looped a proprietary arm around the woman's shoulder. "You damn near knocked my wife down."

And there the matter might have ended, except that Books spoke again. "Entirely my fault, sir," he said with a courtly bow, "and I do apologize. I was paying insufficient attention to directing the course of my own clumsy feet." And he smiled and replaced his garrison cap.

The captain squinted at Books's words, as if convinced some mockery hid within them. Books was extending his elbow to Andrea and didn't notice. Then the white man prodded him with two stiff fingers in the chest, and as Books turned, Luther heard Delores whisper, very softly, "Oh, shit." It summed up his own forebodings quite effectively.

"What the hell did you just say to me?" The white man's eyes were glassy from just enough drink.

Books blinked. "I apologized to you, sir." A nod and a bewildered smile. "And to your wife."

"He done apologized, Cap'n," said Luther, taking a step. "Let's all just be on our way. What do you say?"

The woman said, "Come on, Fred. No need to make a federal case out of it." The man silenced her with a jutting index finger, his eyes never leaving Books.

"I asked you a question," he said.

Books was confused. "I said that I apologize for brushing against your wife. My fault entirely."

The white woman grabbed her husband's arm. "Freddie, he said he's sorry. Come on, let's go."

Her husband ignored her. "Oh," he said, as if just now understanding something that had eluded him before. "You're one of them smart-ass Yankee niggers, ain't you? Been to college and think that make you just as good as a white man, is that it? Hell, you probably think you're *better* than a white man, don't you, nigger?"

At the sound of the hated word, Books's smile shrank and his eyes went cold. "I'm afraid I am not a 'nigger' of any geographical designation, sir," he said, mildly. "There are no niggers."

Now the white man looked confused. "No niggers? What the hell?"

Books touched his garrison cap. "Again," he said, "a thousand pardons for my clumsiness. I shall endeavor to be more careful from now on."

Afterward, it would feel like some evil magic trick. One instant, the white man's eyes were popping like corn. The next instant, the gun was there. It seemed to materialize in the captain's fist out of the night air, appearing so suddenly that at first, Luther didn't even know what it was. Then he did: a nickel-plated Colt .45, gleaming dully in the half-light of a disinterested moon. The white woman gasped. Delores shrieked. Andrea said, "Oh, my Lord. Oh, my Lord."

The white man ignored them. He touched the barrel of the gun to Books's face just beneath his left eye, almost caressing him with it.

"Cap'n, ain't no need for this," said Luther.

The white man ignored that, too. "Say that to me again," he said. "Tell me again how you shall 'endeavor' to watch where you goin'." He cocked his head, as if listening for an answer. Books had angled as far from the Colt as he could. His eyes were moons of sheer terror. He did not respond.

"Come on, nigger," taunted the white man. "Smart-ass Yankee nigger. Say it again."

Books's Adam's apple slid down and up, once. He spoke in a halting voice. "I said that I shall endeavor . . . "

The white man brought the butt of the pistol down hard on his temple, drawing a thin trickle of blood. "Goddamn it!" he spat, "talk like a nigger!"

Books hesitated, still confused. Then he said, "I am afraid I don't comprehend your meaning, sir."

"Books," pleaded Luther, "come on, now. Don't fool around with this man."

"I promise you, I am not fooling with him!" shouted Books. He sounded terrified.

"Mister, please leave him alone," said Luther, hating the pleading sound that had entered his voice, remembering the terror felt by a nine-year-old boy brought eye to eye with Big Floyd Bitters on the worst night of all time and hating that, too. But he put those things aside. "He ain't makin' no fun of you," he cried. "He ain't from down here. He don't know no better. That's just how he talk to everybody!"

The white Army captain did not even look Luther's way. He jabbed the pistol hard against Books's cheek. His voice was a rasp of cool menace. "Well, I ain't everybody and you got one more chance, you uppity shine. *Talk like a nigger.*"

Silently, Luther willed his friend to understand and to obey. Books's terrified eyes found Luther and perhaps they saw this. Something crushed and hurt gazed out at Luther. Luther did not breathe. The street was empty.

Books's voice was a gravel pit. "I'se sorry, boss," he said. "Yassuh, boss, sho' nuff I is. Ain't meant no harm, suh."

To Luther it sounded stilted, like some white man's imitation of a Negro. But it was apparently sufficient for the white captain. He lifted the gun from Books's cheek, pointing the barrel to the sky. He seemed surprised, even a little embarrassed, to find himself with a gun in hand. Luther had the distinct impression of a man who has just awakened from some strange and confusing dream and isn't yet sure what's real and what is not. After a moment, the man tucked the gun back into its holster.

"Can't stand an uppity coon." The white man muttered it, almost as if explaining to himself how all this had happened, how a colored man brushing against his wife had almost become murder. The woman tugged at him. A last bewildered glance around, and then he allowed himself to be pulled away.

Luther watched them go. A shuddering, pent-up breath escaped him when they rounded a corner and disappeared.

So close. It had been so close.

And all of it for nothing. For absolutely nothing.

Then he remembered his friend. Books was still standing there, head tilted back as if the pistol were still on his cheek.

"Books," called Luther. "Franklin."

He came back slowly. Straightened himself. He looked lost. Then Andrea touched his arm. He flinched as if burned and pulled away. "Don't," he said.

"Franklin?"

Confused, she touched him again. He pulled away again. "Don't," he repeated. "Please."

Luther said, "Books, you okay?"

It took Books's eyes a moment to find Luther, a moment more to know him. Then he lowered his head and spoke in a whisper. "I can't," he said.

"You can't what?"

"The girls. See them home, would you? I can't."

"What? No, man. Come on, we do that together, then we catch the bus back to base."

"I can't!" His voice was brittle as a winter twig. "Do you understand?" he asked. His eyes searched Luther's.

Luther was uncertain. "Okay," he said, "if that's the way you want it."

"It is," said Books. "See them safely home. I will wait for you at the depot."

Luther stepped around Books and put a hand on each woman's back.

"Come on, ladies. He want me to walk y'all home. Say he don't feel up to it after . . . you know."

Andrea spun away from him. "Franklin? What's going on? Why won't you walk with us?"

Books smiled an awful smile, and replied softly. "Please, he said. "I just can't do this right now."

He did not wait for an answer. He wheeled around and started walking back the way they had come. In the distance, Luther could just make out the waning lights of Lee Street. Books walked fast. He walked as if he could not wait to be away.

Luther turned back and forced a cheerfulness he did not feel. "Come on, girls," he said, "let's get you home."

thirteen

THE CAR WAS A DARK BLUE 1931 OLDSMOBILE SEDAN. DRIVING it, Thelma sometimes felt as if she should be wearing a sparkly flapper's toque and drinking bathtub gin from a silver flask.

The Olds had certainly seen better days. Patches of rust peeked through the faded paint on the hood, and the fenders curved up over wood-spoke whitewall tires nearly as bald as Gramp. As worn as the car looked, Ollie had assured her when she bought it that the engine was still full of life. And that, he said, was really the only thing that mattered.

Thelma never failed to feel a jolt of pride when she opened the front door to go to work, as she did now, and saw the car sitting in front of the house waiting for her. She pulled on a pair of driving gloves and called back over her shoulder the same thing she always said: "Gramp, I'm gone to work. Don't forget, Mrs. Foster be here with your lunch at noon."

Even though the widow Foster had been doing it for a few months now, the idea of having a woman prepare meals for her and her grandfather when she was perfectly capable of doing so herself still made Thelma feel guilty. Her conscience needled her about it, told her it was an extravagance. But she silenced her conscience by reminding herself that if it was an extravagance, it was one she could well afford. More to the point, she worked 10 hours a day, six days a week, and she was drained when she staggered through the front door every evening.

So it wasn't simply that she could afford it. It was also that she *deserved* it. Or at least, this was what she kept trying to make her troublesome conscience believe.

Thelma was not used to thinking of herself in those terms, as someone who deserved to have a meal cooked for her—indeed, as someone who deserved to have *anything* done for her. But this was a new world. So many things she was not used to had become routine.

Leaning on his cane, Gramp tottered into the front room in response to her call. "Keep tellin' you, I don't need that old heifer cookin' for me. She can't cook worth a damn. Everything she cook taste like boiled socks."

This, too, was something they went through every day. "Now, Gramp, you know better," said Thelma, as she helped him settle in his chair next to the radio. She had left him a glass of water and his pipe and matches right on top of the radio where he could reach them. He pushed irritably at her hands as she fussed with a button on his shirt. She ignored him. "She cook just fine."

"Ain't but one reason Izola Foster hangin' round here and it ain't to steal your money for her so-called cookin'. That ol' biddy lookin' for a husband. She done already buried three and I ain't about to be her next victim."

"Shush, old man. You know don't nobody want you. Now, behave yourself. I see you tonight."

"Thelma, how much longer you gon' have to work at that ship-yard?" A plaintive note had entered his voice. He asked the same thing every morning, and that note—it reminded her of a child beseeching his mother—never failed to sting her. Gramp had never liked her working, even when she was just looking after her white lady's children. But now that her job kept her from home for longer hours and someone else was fixing his meals, that dislike had hardened into an everyday lament.

"Now, Gramp," she said, "you know we done been all through this. If I don't work, how we gon' pay the bills? Besides, I'm building ships for the fightin' men. That's important."

Every day, she had to explain this. It made her wonder if Gramp was just being petulant or if he was getting senile.

The thought filled her with indefinable sorrow. She was not a fool. She knew he was very old and could not live forever. But there had never been a day Roebuck Hayes had not been part of her life. The idea that she might come home some evening and find him gone gnawed at her.

Thelma kissed her grandfather on his bald pate and stroked the back of his neck fondly. "I'll see you tonight, old man," she said.

He grunted in response and reached to turn on the radio. She could hear a news report as she closed the door and walked to the car. They were saying something about a Marine battle on some island called Guadalcanal.

The mention of the Marines made her think of George Simon, and she wondered where he was and if he was all right. She received a letter from her brother nearly every week—a surprising output from a man who had never liked to write letters—and it sounded as if he were taking to tank training really well. But she had not heard from Simon in weeks now.

The very fact of their intermittent correspondence—*What was she doing writing some white man? What was he doing writing to her?*—still felt unreal. No, it felt faintly seditious, like some secret rebellion against the great order of things.

Not that there was any particular substance to their letters. They wrote about the Bible. They wrote about the war. They wrote about their lives. Nothing and everything, they wrote about.

Still, she was surprised to find that she had grown used to it, even grown to depend upon it. Her last two letters had gone unanswered, and she found that she missed hearing from him.

Thelma tried to reassure herself that George was simply too busy to write. Or more likely, she told herself as she worked the stick shift and pulled away from the curb, he simply saw no particular reason to continue writing to some colored girl he hardly knew. And that was fine; she couldn't blame him for that. It would just be nice to know that he was okay.

When they had bought the car, Thelma, Helen, Betty, and Laverne had intended it only as their hedge against a bus boycott, a way of making sure they were all able to get to work if need be. The boycott had never materialized, but the sheer convenience and freedom of the car had proven too seductive to surrender. And they had quickly picked up a fifth passenger. Although he had put no money into buying the car, Ollie Grimes had somehow talked them all into letting him ride to and from work with them in exchange for his performing regular maintenance and any needed repairs.

The girls had talked this over and agreed that it was a good idea—what did they know about oil changes and radiator leaks?—but Thelma knew pragmatism was not the only factor in their decision. The man was good-looking and a charmer, to boot. The other three girls all had crushes on him. And never mind that all three of them were married.

"Ain't nothin' wrong with lookin'," Laverne had said.

Ollie was the first stop on Thelma's morning route. When she turned onto his street, she saw him standing, as usual, outside the boarding house where he lived. His room, he had told them, was tiny—he joked that when he lay on his bed, his feet stuck out the window. But he said he was glad to have his own space, small as it was. Before he had lucked into the boarding house, he'd had only a bed that he rented for eight hours a day, waking up and rolling out just as someone else who worked the night shift was coming in to claim their shared mattress.

"Morning, Miss Thelma," he said, slamming the door behind him.

"Ain't you chipper this mornin'," she said, glancing in her mirror as she wheeled into traffic.

"When you ever seen me I wasn't chipper?" he replied. "Besides, I been lookin' forward to today."

She glanced over at him. "Oh? What's happenin' today?"

"Got a meetin' with the boss man this mornin'," said Ollie. He was lighting a cigarette, and it bobbed in his mouth as he spoke. "Me and some of the other colored mens finally got him to agree to sit down and talk to us."

"Talk about what?"

"We tired of bein' apprentices, that's what." She knew what he meant. The girls had sometimes made the same complaint. Even though the Negroes often performed the same tasks and had the same knowledge as whites, the Negroes—whether electricians, carpenters, or welders—were always officially designated apprentices, a step below their white coworkers in rank, prestige, and income.

Thelma was intrigued despite herself. "So you think you gon' be able to talk them into lettin' some of us have them skilled jobs?"

"We sure mean to try. It ain't right, we doin' the same work them white boys is doin', but ain't gettin' the same pay. They call us apprentices. Hell, I could teach some of them a thing or two 'bout some weldin'."

A shiver of foreboding climbed through Thelma for no reason that she could discern. She said, "You sure you ain't just gon' get in trouble?"

He looked at her. "How we gon' get into trouble askin' for what we s'pose to already have? Ain't Roosevelt put out the order a year ago? Federal government say ain't s'pose to be no more Jim Crow in the war effort. How these Alabama crackers gon' just ignore that?"

Thelma made a sound of derision. "That order, that's just paper, Ollie, you know that. Don't mean nothin' to these white folks down here."

"Don't mean nothin' if we ain't willin' to stand up for it," he corrected. "Can't just let these crackers run all over you and you don't say nothin'. If you do, then you deserve what you get." He paused, a speculative expression on his face as he gazed at her.

Thelma said, "What?"

Ollie favored her with a sudden smile that had sunshine in it. "I swear, Miss Thelma, you just look so pretty first thing in the mornin'."

Thelma looked at him. "You never quit, do you?"

His eyes were round with mock earnestness, his voice weighted with mock seriousness. "Oh no, ma'am," he said. "Ol' Ollie don't never quit till the job is done."

And he gave her his rogue's grin. Thelma just shook her head.

In short order, she picked up Betty, Helen, and Laverne. At each stop, Ollie, as had become his routine, hopped out of the car and held the back door open, doffing his workman's cap and bowing low from the waist. It never failed to make each woman, all of them older than Thelma, titter like a high school girl.

Thelma pointed the car east. The traffic was heavy, but she barely noticed. Traffic was always heavy in Mobile these days. They passed the time chattering about their families, the war, work. Government Street took them into the new Bankhead Tunnel, which carried them under the Mobile River. They emerged moments later on the island, and from there it was a few short minutes to the shipyard.

As was the case every morning, people were streaming from all directions toward the arched sign that said "Alabama Dry Dock and Shipbuilding Company." They came off the ferry. They came out of the parking lot. They came from acres of house trailers parked just outside the gates. People everywhere.

As she locked the car and joined the crowd, Thelma felt the same jolt of pride and purpose she always felt on coming to work—the sense that she was part of something large, a component, however small, however unimpressive, of some great undertaking.

It was as she was thinking this that Thelma spotted Flora Lee Hodges in the crowd. She was about 10 feet to Thelma's right.

It had been weeks since that day when Earl Ray Hodges had leaned so close to Thelma that she could smell his hairdressing and ordered her to stay away from his wife. The two women had not spoken since then. She had seen Flora Lee many times, though—coming to work, leaving work, almost always with Earl Ray somewhere nearby. Sometimes, Flora Lee's fearful eyes caught hers and warned her away. Sometimes, she couldn't see Flora Lee's eyes—the little woman tried to hide her bruises and abrasions behind sunglasses—but Flora Lee would shake her head discreetly when she saw Thelma looking.

She was wearing the sunglasses today, but for some reason, her husband was not with her. As Thelma stared, Flora Lee turned, saw Thelma looking. She didn't shake her head. She didn't do anything. Indeed, Flora Lee's expression was unreadable, as if she hadn't seen Thelma or didn't know her, and that in itself saddened Thelma because Flora Lee was one of those people whose feelings were always written plainly on her face. Then Flora Lee turned away.

Thelma's gait slowed. She wanted to cross through the crowd and speak to her, tell her again that she didn't have to put up with being that man's punching bag. She deserved better.

"Don't you do it." Laverne had seen her looking.

"I'm not," said Thelma.

"You thinkin' about it."

"Yeah, I was," admitted Thelma.

"Well, stop thinkin' about it," Laverne ordered her. "Ain't no good never come from mixin' in white folks' business. Why you want to borrow they troubles? Ain't you got enough of your own?"

"Yeah," said Thelma. The flow of the crowd had already borne Flora Lee away. "I guess I do."

And they walked under the ADDSCO sign into the shipyard.

Ollie, who had been walking ahead of them, turned now and doffed his cap. "Well, ladies," he said through a grand smile, "I guess this where we part company. You all got work to do and me and some of the other fellas, we got a meetin' with the big boss yonder."

He turned back—and stopped.

Thelma followed his gaze and saw what had frozen him. Her hand came involuntarily up to her mouth.

Standing before the entrance to the administration building was a line of hard-faced white men. Some of them had bats. One of them had an axe handle held lazily at his side. They were facing down three colored men. Earl Ray Hodges stood front and center in the line of white men. A crowd of workers, colored and white, had begun to form around them.

"Oh, shit," said Ollie. And he jogged forward.

Thelma brought up the rear as quickly as she could.

"What's goin' on here?" she heard Ollie say.

"We heard you all had a meetin' set with the boss man this mornin'." Earl Ray's voice brimmed with a pleasant malice.

"Who told you that?" demanded one of the men with Ollie.

"Let's just say a little birdie tol' us," said Earl Ray in that same easy voice, menace running through it like an underground river.

"What's it to you even if we do?" asked one of the other colored men. "Ain't none of your business, way I see it."

"Well, shine, we makin' it our business. How 'bout that?" A white man next to Earl Ray Hodges said this.

"Yeah," said Earl Ray. "You want to talk to the boss man, you gon' have to go through us to get there."

"Ain't this some shit," groused one of the colored men.

"No, it ain't shit," said Earl Ray. "It's the livin' truth. You know, everything be fine around here if you niggers just stick to your place. You think we just gon' stand aside and let you all take white men's jobs?"

"What's that to you, Stumpy?"

Ollie's question made the air very still. Earl Ray drew himself up, and sure enough, his eyes suddenly glittered with that hard, menacing light Thelma had seen twice before. "What you say, boy?" All the pleasantness was gone from his voice.

Ollie grinned. Actually grinned. "I said, what is it to you? Ain't nobody tryin' to take your job, is they? You's a fuckin' one-leg janitor, stumpin' round here"—and here he did a lavish imitation of Earl Ray's awkward gait as the colored people in the crowd, and not a few of the white ones, laughed— "pushin' your garbage can. What you care about electricians and welders and shit like that? Ain't you got some trash cans you s'pose to be emptyin'?"

The white men behind him had to snatch Earl Ray out of midair. It took three of them to hold him, and still he managed to swing at Ollie, a wide, looping blow that Ollie simply leaned away from.

"You fuckin' nigger! You fuckin' *nigger*!" Earl Ray's voice had gone high and raspy. His eyes were twin dots of pure fury. "Don't no nigger talk to me like that! You uppity black bastard! You better watch your back, boy! You better watch your back! You done made an enemy out of Earl Ray Hodges, and what you want to go and do that for?"

Ollie regarded the little white man for an amazed moment. Thelma grabbed his arm to pull him away. Ollie looked at her as if he had forgotten who she was. Then he gave Earl Ray a dismissive wave and allowed Thelma to lead him away.

"You're dead, nigger! You hear me? You are *dead!*" Foamy white spittle spewed from Earl Ray Hodges's mouth. The white men holding him traded dubious looks as if this were more than they had bargained for. "I won't forget!" snarled Earl Ray. "Earl Ray Hodges don't *never* forget!"

"Come on," said one of the white men, "you need to calm down."

"We said we's just gon' scare 'em, remember?"

"Don't no nigger talk to Earl Ray Hodges like that!" His voice had become a raw screech.

The white men had to wrestle him away. His feet did not touch the ground.

Thelma and Ollie watched from a slight distance as the crowd drifted apart. "Craziest fuckin' white man I ever seen in my life," whispered Ollie. Then he caught himself. "Excuse my French," he said.

"That ain't no French I ever heard of," said Thelma, attempting a joke.

Ollie just looked at her. He seemed dazed. "Yeah," he said. "I guess not."

Laverne saw them and wandered over. "That one got a screw loose," she told Ollie. "You need to watch your back."

"Yeah," said Ollie, "I think you right."

A couple of the colored men walked up. "Ain't never seen one go off his nut like that before," said the first man.

"So," said the second, "we still meetin' with the big boss man?"

Ollie shook his head. "Can't say I see the point. They done already give us they answer."

"That weren't no answer. That was just a bunch of fool crackers can't stand the idea of niggers gettin' ahead."

Ollie's gaze sharpened. "How they find out about our meetin', Ed? Did you tell 'em? How 'bout you, Gary? You seen any of the security guards around? Usually, they thick as flies on dog shit, ain't they? No, only way them crackers knew to be out there is 'cause the boss man done tol' 'em to be—and he done also told security to look the other way. So far as I'm concerned, we done already got our answer. They say, 'Get back to work, niggers.'"

There was an embarrassed silence as this sank in. After a moment, Ollie said, "So, I guess I'm gon' get back to work." And he walked off.

The rest of them looked from one to the other, each waiting for one of them to have an idea of what should happen next, or to say something that would make sense out of what had happened already. After a moment, Gary and Ed nodded at the two women—"Guess we need to punch in, too," said Gary helplessly—and headed off to work. Finally, Laverne told Thelma, "I see you at lunch," and wandered away.

For a moment, Thelma just stood there alone. Finally, she went off to her locker to get her painting equipment. She had to hurry. The ferry out to the ship would be leaving in a few minutes. Thelma opened the door to the locker room and had just put the key into her padlock when a voice spoke up from behind her.

"You need to tell your friend to be careful." Startled, Thelma whipped around. Flora Lee Hodges was standing there. "Earl Ray, he ain't likely to forget what happened. He might play like he forgot, but he ain't gon' forget."

"Flora Lee."

"And he gon' do somethin'," the little woman said. "You mark my words on that."

She was still wearing the sunglasses. Slowly, without a word, Thelma reached up and pulled them from Flora Lee's face. Flora Lee did not resist. Both her eyes were smudged with bruises, just as Thelma had expected.

"Looks like he's already been doin' somethin'," said Thelma, softly. She handed the glasses to Flora Lee.

"He done got worse since we come down here," said Flora Lee. "Used to be it was just every once in a while, you know, like men sometimes do when they done had too much to drink. But then the war start and the Army won't take him on account of his leg. And we come here and he still can't find no work on account of his leg. Seem like everybody else can— even women can, even colored can—but he can't. And finally, he end up pushin' that trash can 'cause ain't nothin' else for him."

Flora Lee paused, shook her head. "That was a bad thing your friend done, makin' fun of him like that."

"What else he s'pose to do?" asked Thelma, her voice sharp. "He s'pose to just let your husband run all over him and he don't say nothin'?"

Flora Lee held up her hand. "That ain't what I meant," she said. Again, she paused. She seemed so tired. "Earl Ray a proud man. That's what I'm sayin'. I think maybe it's 'cause he not the tallest man or maybe it's 'cause of his leg, he feel like he got to do more, got to make hisself bigger even if it's only in his mind. I think that's what I used to love the most about him before we come here, the fact that he so *proud*. Then I seen how that pride sometime make him do bad things. It ain't gon' let him rest till he make your friend pay. I mean, pay *bad*. You got to tell him that. You got to warn him."

Thelma swallowed. "I will," she promised. "But what about you?"

"Me?"

"Flora Lee, you can't keep lettin' him do this to you."

"He my husband, Thelma."

"Yeah, but that don't give him the right to be beatin' on you whensoever he take a notion. Seem like every time I see you, you got a black eye or you got a cut, or you got bruises. How much longer you gon' let him do that? One of these days, he gon' go too far and he gon' kill you, girl."

"What am I goin' to do, Thelma? Leave my husband? And then what? Where am I supposed to go?"

Thelma surprised herself. "You could stay with me," she said. And then she wondered why she had said such a flatly impossible thing.

Flora Lee's smile brimmed with sweet pity. "I appreciate that. But you know I can't do that, because . . . " And her right hand ticked back and forth between the two of them, between the white woman and the colored woman, invoking all the bizarre laws and customs of Jim Crow that stood sentinel athwart a simple attempt to extend a helping hand from black to white.

Thelma sighed. "Yeah," she said. "I know."

"You sweet to offer," said Flora Lee, still smiling. "You 'bout my only friend, you know that?" And she leaned forward and folded Thelma in a quick embrace. When Flora Lee pulled back, Thelma could see the white woman was as surprised as she was.

Then Flora Lee pulled on her sunglasses. "I ain't got no choice, Thelma. I married him, for better or for worse."

"Yeah," said Thelma, "you sure gettin' the worse now."

"I guess I am." She left without another word.

fourteen

Rice again.

Stinking, goddamn Jap rice. Again.

Sitting with his back against a tree above a sluice of muddy water running through the center of camp, George stared dully at the lump of deathly white mush on his metal tray. Fat, pinkish worms were scattered in the steaming mound. Methodically, he went about picking them out and flicking them away.

"Hey, wait a minute there, Saint," said Tank, as he lowered himself next to George with his own tray. "You're throwin' away all your meat."

Five days ago, seven days ago, 10 or 11 days ago, it had been a funny joke, the kind of dark, defiant humor that gets men through ordeals too trying to be borne otherwise. But George had heard variations of it a hundred times now, and whatever humor had once been in it had long since dried up and blown away. He didn't even look up as he responded in a flat voice. "You're killin' me, Tank. You're absolutely killin' me."

"Too bad you don't smoke," said Tank, exhaling a gray cloud. "Helps to hide the smell."

"Really?" said George. "Hell, that might be a good reason to start."

He parted the mush with his fork, searching through it. Near the bottom of the mound, he found a worm that had escaped his attention. George looped his middle finger and thumb and catapulted the disgusting thing into the trees. Then he began scooping the nauseating paste into his mouth.

He had found it was best just to wolf it down without looking at it, without thinking about it, just get it down and pray your stomach would hold it down. White shit, some of the others called it, and the description was apt for this tasteless, semiliquid slop that was "rice" only in some abstract technical sense that had nothing to do with anything any of them had ever eaten before.

Jazzman stopped by, fingers tapping the stock of his rifle. "Hurry up with that," he said. "Sarge says one of our rifle platoons got hit about three miles from here."

"We're going to provide support?" And even as he asked, something in George realized that he already knew the answer.

Jazzman shook his head. "Sarge wants a patrol to go out and pick up the bodies."

"Damn," said George.

"Yeah," said Jazzman.

George swallowed one last mouthful of the evil mush and tried not to recoil as he felt it slide, frictionless, down his gullet.

He hated this particular duty, going back for the bodies of comrades. He knew it was something sacred, knew it was something men owed to men they had served with, knew it was something he would want done for him, if it ever came down to that, to ensure he was not left to spend forever in some unknown field. He knew this, but still he hated this duty because he hated what he felt when he saw men he had known, faces that had filled his day, reduced to smashed jelly, teeth bared in some awful death grimace, brains open to the sky.

He felt glad it wasn't him.

How long had he been on this island, forsaken of God and man? How long had he lived like this, hunkered on his haunches in the mud like some hound taking a shit, living on fish heads and wormy Jap rice liberated from an enemy storehouse? The calendar said it was less than two weeks, but that told him nothing. Time had no meaning in this place.

At first, Phipps had told them everything would be all right. Phipps had said they just had to hold on to the airfield at all costs. Uncle Sam would not desert them. Uncle Sam *could* not desert them. Yes, they might be expendable—they were just men, easily replaced. But that airfield was not expendable. So yes, Uncle Sam would be back with reinforcements and supplies. All they had to do was hold on.

But then time had piled up, Uncle Sam had not reappeared, Phipps's once clean-shaven face had grown fuzzy like an orange going bad, and he had stopped talking so much.

What was there to say?

Their days had become a routine of listlessness spiked at odd moments by terror. Jap Zeros buzzed them when they ventured from beneath the canopy of the trees. Jap ships pounded them with artillery barrages at all hours, and men hunkered down and called on mama and God to get them through, or else to just make what was coming quick.

And for some men, what was coming came. It came with hit-and-run ambushes during the day. It came at night when some Jap slipped like a shadow into a man's hole and sliced his throat so that he died trying to scream, gurgling on his own blood. It came with a regularity that begat a sense of routine, a numbing familiarity until you were no longer surprised that it came and the thing you felt, the thing you hated feeling as you gazed down upon the smashed body of some fellow you knew vaguely but not too well, was a dull and shameful relief.

After all, it was not you. It was not some buddy of yours.

Yes, it was somebody's buddy, somebody's *son*. And some mother stateside would receive a telegram some weeks from now, bringing the worst news she would ever receive in this life, news that would fell that mother like a blow from a hammer. And that was an awful thing.

But it was not *you*. It was not some buddy of yours.

Somehow, you had survived again. So you went about gathering the pieces of this unlucky bastard and trying to feel deep grief instead of this sick relief that seemed to clot your heart. You dug a hole to rest him in, and you said some words to a God who seemed to need a hearing aid and then you went to get a lump of pasty white shit dumped on your metal plate.

The nights were the worst. Darkness did not steal up on you. No, it dropped down on you like a safe from a high window in some old silent movie.

You did not sleep.

You went on night patrols, probing for an enemy who was probing for you, crouching through a darkness of unseen terrors. And all at once, *contact*! The enemy right there, his gun coming up, your gun coming up—*Lord, let me be fast enough, let me be fast enough*—and *kapow! kapow! kapow!* a frenzied burst of fire, ugly Jap faces seen in staccato bursts of muzzle flash and *Did you get him or did he get you?* and while you're wondering, here come screams in that awful language of theirs and suddenly there are Japs all around and you are firing every which way and everyone is shooting everything and you're too panicked for thinking, too panicked for anything except killing them before they can kill you.

And then it's over and as suddenly as they were there, the Japs are gone or dead and you are alone in the darkness, breathing heavily, and you hear this bass drum pounding heavily right in your ear—*boom! boom! boom!*—and you look frantically around to see where it's coming from and it's a long moment before you realize it's only your heart.

Indeed, the only thing worse than patrolling at night was not patrolling at night.

You sat in your mudhole in the darkness, rain dripping from your helmet, the jungle who-whooing and creaking around you, stomach cramping, needing to take a shit but terrified to go out and do so lest maybe as you're coming back, your tongue gets twisted on some l-filled password—*liberally, lily, lollygag*—and you get shot full of holes by your own guys. So you sat in your mudhole, sphincter clamped against the awful liquid leakage that your shit becomes on a diet of Jap rice and fish heads, and you entered a state of not quite sleep and not quite wakefulness, sitting silent with your own soul, waiting for the telltale scuff of Japanese boots on a tree root, waiting to feel the hand creeping over your throat, the knife biting across your jugular, waiting for the sneak attack exploding out of the jungle, waiting to die horribly, waiting for the dawn.

For George, at least, dawn had continued to come, though he was deeply ambivalent about whether this was really a good thing. But for some contingent of marines lying blasted and cut up in some field a few miles from here, there was no longer any need to be unsure.

George took a swig of water from his canteen, stowed his mess kit, and went to join Jazzman, Babe, and the others.

It took an hour. They found the 12 men in a coconut grove. The mortarmen set up on a ridge overlooking the grove to guard against ambush. George and the rest of the patrol ventured down to retrieve the bodies. They approached gingerly. The Japs were known to booby-trap corpses.

Most of the men had been beheaded, and some of them had been posed, their heads sitting on their own laps, cradled by their own hands. Eleven had also been castrated, their pants down around their ankles, bloody, shredded genitals sticking out from between swollen lips. But the 12th man, the sergeant who had led the patrol, had been neither beheaded nor castrated. He had been gutted like a fish, his intestines pulled out of him, painstakingly unrolled for about 20 feet, and nailed to a tree. His eyes were open.

And that was what did it for George. At the sight of that man, he dropped helplessly to his knees and bent low into the kunai grass. Up came the white shit he had struggled to put down just an hour ago. The vomit splashed the dead man's boots. George heaved until he could heave no more, until he was dry retching. In some distant part of his mind, he noted that a worm lay in the viscous white stuff he had regurgitated. Apparently he had not been thorough enough in picking the damn things out. Tank Sheridan's tired joke came back to him.

Hey, wait a minute there, Saint. You're throwin' away all your meat.

George giggled. He was horrified at the sound, but he couldn't stop himself. He clamped a hand over his mouth, but still the sound seeped through.

Hey, wait a minute there, Saint . . .

"You all right there, George?"

George looked up. Jazzman was standing above him. "It d-don't mean a thing," said George through one last, helpless giggle, "if it ain't got that swing."

"Do wat do wat do wat do wat do wat do wow!" sang Jazzman in response. His usually mobile face was still. His voice was without expression. He extended a hand. "Come on, boy, let's get you to your feet."

George nodded. "Yeah," he mumbled, "sorry." And he accepted Jazzman's hand and stood.

"Nothin' to be sorry about," said Jazzman. "Shit like this, nobody should have to ever see. Ever."

Babe came up. "Well, well, well," he said. "What do we have here?"

Wiping a few flecks of vomit from his mouth with the back of his hand, George followed Babe's gaze. Some Japanese soldiers lay dead in the grass about 10 feet away.

"Looks like our boys got a few licks in," said Babe with a smirk.

"Nice to know they took some of the f-fuckers with them," said George, bitterly.

Babe gave him a look. He had never heard him say "fuckers" before. "Going to have to get you a new nickname, Saint, you keep using language like that." He was smiling an approving smile. Then, without another word, he went forward to investigate. George and Jazzman followed.

They gazed down without feeling on the bullet-riddled corpses of the three enemy soldiers. Then Jazzman bent down and popped loose some buttons from the Jap uniforms. "My sister'll like these," he explained, dropping the buttons into a pocket. "She collects 'em."

Babe glanced back to where the dead Americans were being piled onto stretchers. He stroked his chin. "You know what I'm thinking?" he said.

"What are you thinking?" asked Jazzman.

"I'm thinking one shitty turn deserves another."

Jazzman stared at him uncomprehendingly. Then an awful smile stretched itself across his face.

"W-What are you talking about?" asked George.

In response, Jazzman turned that unsettling smile on him. "He's sayin' what's sauce for the goose is sauce for the gander."

Now George understood. "No," he breathed. "You can't do that."

"The fuck I can't!" snarled Babe and there was sudden venom in his voice that made George recoil. He flung an index finger back toward where other marines were still gathering the pieces of the dead American patrol. "You see that, George? Those are our guys! You see what the Japs did to them? Did you see?"

"Of course I saw," George managed.

"How many times you seen that, George?"

"Too many," said George. "You know that."

"Yeah, I do. And you were right a minute ago. They are fuckers. God-damn vicious, inhuman *fuckers!* They only speak one language, and damn if I'm not ready to speak it right back to them."

As he was saying this, he pulled a knife from a sheath on his belt. It was a long nonregulation weapon, a street-fighting blade with spiked brass knuckles molded into the grip.

George said, "Babe, p-please. You c-can't."

"Really? Why can't I?"

"It's w-wrong, Babe."

A tight grin filled with malice curled Babe's lips. "Look around you, George. It's *all* w-wrong."

"Yeah, it is," admitted George. "But that d-doesn't mean you give in to it."

"You going to tell me again how we're all G-G-G-God's children, Saint? Is that it? We're all God's children, even the bastards who left those men lying back there with their dicks in their mouths? Well, I got to tell you, if those really are God's children, then I don't want to be one. If those are God's children, then to hell with him. And to hell with you, too."

His eyes boiled in their sockets. He stared at George.

George pleaded, "Babe, c'mon."

Babe said, "Don't get in my way, okay? Just stay out of my way."

He turned, fitting the knife onto his right fist. "You comin', Jazz?"

Jazzman regarded George for a long moment, as if thinking. Then he pulled out his knife and went to join Babe. They knelt on either side of the first corpse's head. Babe grabbed a handful of the man's coarse black hair and lifted. To George's horror, the Jap's eyes came open. They were filled with a baleful loathing. The man's hands moved weakly.

Oh, God.

The Jap was alive.

"Babe, look."

Babe did not deign to turn.

"*Look!*" cried George. "He's alive, g-g-goddamn it! That man is alive."

At this, Jazzman looked down at the Jap, then turned to look at George. He shrugged.

Then Babe began sawing into the Jap's neck. The man's eyes flared in sudden pain, his mouth came open soundlessly. After a moment, both closed.

It was not easy. Babe used his Chicago street fighter's knife, Jazzman his Marine-issue knife, and they sawed from opposite directions through skin, muscle, and ligament. Men drifted over to watch. George searched their eyes for some sense that somebody else was appalled, that somebody else saw in this a profane wrongness. He didn't see it. He didn't see disapproval. He didn't see approval, either. All he saw was dull interest. It was not something to approve or disapprove. It was just something you looked at because it was there.

Maybe, thought George, there was something wrong with him, that he couldn't see it that way. Maybe the problem was him.

Jazzman and Babe sawed down to the vertebrae. They pondered the puzzle of it for a few moments, then Jazzman got the idea of pulling the head way back and opening the column of bones wide, exposing the thin spinal cord. Babe applied his knife just beneath where the spine fused to the skull.

All at once, the head lolled to the side, just as if the Jap had taken a sudden interest in something on his left and turned to get a better view. There was a moment. Then Jazzman grabbed the Jap's head by the hair and held it high for everyone to see, held it like a trophy. Jagged shards of vertebrae and tangles of cartilage and ligament trailed from the dead man's neck. Bloody lumps of tissue dripped heavily.

Babe turned now to regard his fellow marines, and his face glowed with triumph. Jazzman grinned. And then he sang.

I've got the world on a string,
Sittin' on a rainbow . . .

The dead Jap's features hung slack as a pillowcase on a bedpost.

fifteen

Babe named it Harvey.

He and Jazzman had patiently boiled and skinned the Jap's head. Then they had cleaned and polished the skull. Now, almost two months later, it sat on a makeshift shelf in their tent, a cigarette clamped in its teeth, grinning down at George. He had come into the tent to take a nap, but as often happened, the sight of the thing arrested him. He stood staring up at it, transfixed.

George was shirtless, his body oiled by a sheen of sweat, his rotting dungarees, tied by a length of rope, hanging on his emaciated frame. He was just getting over a bout of malaria: chills so violent they shook him awake, headaches that felt like someone pushing a railroad spike through the center of his forehead, diarrhea that sent him hurtling from his tent. Rain pattered against the tent, splashing into the soupy marshland that was the main street of their camp. The heat was punishing, and a reek of rotting vegetation and dead flesh coated the back of his throat.

George felt quite certain that he was living in an anteroom of hell. He felt . . . forsaken.

"So, where is your God?"

At first, he thought his thoughts had somehow verbalized themselves without his knowing. Then he turned. Babe was entering the tent, Jazzman behind him.

Babe grinned. "That's what you were thinking, right? Ol' Harvey always puts you in a mood, don't he?"

"Leave him alone," said Jazzman. He took a seat on his cot, the fingers of his right hand drumming restlessly against the frame.

Babe ignored him. "So, what about it? Where is he, your God?"

"I don't know," said George. The admission took something out of him. Something vital as air.

Babe nodded as if pleased. "Now you're learning," he said.

George glanced back up at the skull. Sometimes he woke up in the middle of the night to find it shining in a stray beam of moonlight that entered where the tent flaps did not quite meet. And he would lie there listening to the jungle and wondering who this man was before he became an ornament, a trophy of war. Whose son or father? Whose brother or friend?

"Randy," George heard himself say, "do you believe there's evil in this world?"

Jazzman stopped tapping. "Yeah," he said, "sure I do. Be foolish not to, you seen what we've seen."

George turned, facing his friends. "What about you, Babe? Same question."

"Same answer," said Babe, watching him through narrowed eyes. "Why?"

Looking back up at the Jap skull, George said, "I just wonder sometimes why we always find it so easy to believe in supreme evil but not supreme good. Can't have one without the other, can you?"

"Maybe because we see so damn much of the fuckin' evil," spat Babe.

Jazzman was still considering the question. After a moment, he said, "Wish I had your faith, Saint."

George laughed weakly. "Wish I had it, too," he said.

A silence intervened. George nodded toward the skull and said, "You ever regret doing that?"

"Hell no," said Babe.

"You forget, you talkin' to a colored man," Jazzman said through a sad smile. "My people ain't never had no shortage of regrets."

The tent flap opened, and a corporal poked his head in. "Gear up," he said. "Patrol moves out in five."

George shook his head. It never stopped. Without a word, he threw on his shirt, then hoisted his rifle. He followed his friends into the slop and ooze.

Lieutenant Colonel Phipps led the platoon across the airfield—work crews had finished what the Japanese started and named it Henderson Field, in honor of a Marine aviator killed at Midway—and into the jungle to the west. It was always the same mission: probe for the Japs.

Planes had begun landing at Henderson Field a few weeks back—a welcome jolt to the raggedy marines stranded on Guadalcanal. Shortly after that had come another surprise, even more welcome. Ships had begun sneaking in under cover of darkness to off-load supplies. Now, instead of the stinking Jap rice three times a day, the marines occasionally had stew, corned beef and hash, and other American fare. The men had begun to feel maybe they would not be abandoned after all, like the poor slobs on Bataan had been. Maybe Phipps had been right. The country had to have this airfield and was prepared to fight for it.

But none of that resolved the biggest problem: they needed more bodies on this rock. It wasn't just that every man was walking around in various stages of malaria, diarrhea, or dysentery, wasn't just that a man saw his clothes fall to shreds and his skin rot right off the bone. No, men were wearing out from the *inside*. You saw it in the eyes, in the dead, vacant stare that said the man inside was struggling to hold himself intact, but it was hard, *so* hard, and he was not sure he could make it. Men held on to themselves by their fingertips, the same way a man grasps the ledge high above fatal asphalt. But the fingers were slipping. The ledge was crumbling.

This was something George had felt personally, acutely, ever since Tank Sheridan died. It had happened at night in the thick jungle alongside that crocodile-infested ribbon of green water their lying maps identified as the Tenaru River. A Jap machine gun had carved a third of his skull away. He was dead before he even knew it had happened.

Hours later, when the fighting ceased, George had gazed numbly down on the ruined shell of his friend. Here, finally, was a loss he could not shrug off with shameful relief, grateful that it wasn't him or one of his buddies. Tank *was* his buddy.

And now he was gone. Suddenly. Gruesomely. Gone.

George had wanted to cry ever since, but somehow, the tears were stoppered inside him. He could feel them there, a big, heavy something high in his throat that he could not swallow. They would not fall, but they would not go away.

As it turned out, Tank was one of only a very few friendlies claimed by the battle of the Tenaru—fewer than 50 in all. By contrast, when the fighting was over and sunlight illuminated the field, Jap soldiers lay dead by the hundreds, attended by buzzing clouds of flies. Marines walked among them, hunting souvenirs.

The Japs had thrown themselves at the Marine positions, boiling out of the jungle directly into machine gun fire, rifle fire, and grenade explosions as their tracers gouged red lines in the sky, bathing the jungle in weird crimson light. It had been a bloody, suicidal mess. Eight hundred Japs in all had died, according to the officers—a crushing defeat for the emperor's troops.

Yet it had resolved exactly nothing. Tank was dead, but the Japs kept coming, as relentless as if the battle had never been fought. The Japs kept coming as if spat forth in an endless supply straight from the fires of hell. They harassed the airfield with sniper fire. They sent infiltrators into the Marine lines. They launched suicide attacks.

So the marines had to always be on guard. Which was why George's 20-man rifle platoon now walked in silent single file, arcing west and north of Henderson Field, searching the impenetrable foliage for signs of the enemy. Hearing, seeing, finding, nothing.

Then, all at once, something rustled against the jungle floor just behind them and they all tensed, their heads whipping around toward the sound. An instant later, they released, recognizing the sound as a land crab scuttling sideways through the trees. It amazed George that he now knew the jungle by its sounds.

They were on a ridge overlooking the beach. With hand signals, Phipps indicated they were to rest here a few minutes. George wanted to sit but decided against it. He thought he might not be able to get up again. Instead, he leaned on a tree, unscrewed the cap on his canteen, and took a long drink. His shirt clung wetly to his chest. He wondered if he would have the strength to make it back.

Across the channel, he could just barely make out the gray-green lump of Tulagi Island. The First Marine Raider Battalion had gone ashore there the same day George landed on Guadalcanal. He wondered idly how they were making out. As he was thinking this, an enemy ship passed in the channel between the islands.

George closed his eyes, mopped his wet brow uselessly with his wet forearm, and thought of home. It was October, which meant Nick and Cora were back in school. Nick would have behaved as if he were walking to the electric chair, but Cora would have been eager to go back. She was a real whip, that one. By comparison with this moist inferno near the bottom of the Pacific Ocean, his hometown would be enjoying pleasant, pretty days and comfortable nights. If he was in a good enough mood—and if there were any gas available—Father would probably pile the family into the Packard and take them down to the ice cream shop off Bienville Square. Maybe they'd take their cones down to the water and eat them languidly, watching ships ply the river as the sun drifted down toward twilight.

George wondered idly if Father had made good on his promise to Thelma's brother. He wondered how Luther was adjusting to Army life. And he wondered how Thelma was doing. Trapped here on this island, he hadn't been able to get a letter out—or receive one—since August. He missed hearing from her. George had intended to let their correspondence peter out long before landing here. He'd always felt a vague guilt to find himself writing chatty, earnest letters to another man's widow—a colored man's widow, at that—especially given how hard he had to struggle to find something to say to his own wife. But he couldn't help it. Writing to Thelma always made him feel a little bit—

Japs.

George's eyes flew open. He looked at the men around him, and their wide eyes told him they had heard it, too, voices whispering in the harsh language of the enemy. Cautiously, George looked down. Sure enough, on the sand just below him, a force of 40 or so Japs was moving in the same direction as the marines. Apparently, they had been reconnoitering Henderson Field and were headed back to their own camp.

All eyes swung to Prescott Phipps. Phipps was not a fool. The force below was twice the size of his. Even with the element of surprise and the possession of the high ground, George knew the officer would not like those odds. And he didn't. Phipps made a series of urgent motions indicating they were to remain quiet and let the Japs pass unmolested.

The men nodded their understanding.

And even as they did, there was the crack of a rifle and Phipps keeled over, blood arcing from his temple like water from a drinking fountain.

No one would ever know what it was that alerted the Japs. Did one of them catch movement on the ridge above them? Did one of the Americans make a sound? Did the Japs simply smell them?

It didn't really matter.

All at once, the air was torn by bullets, chewing up trees and leaves and men. The man to George's left went down without a sound. "Fuck!" cried George. He dove to his belly, brought up his rifle, sighted center mass on the first Jap he saw, and fired, then worked the bolt handle to seat a new round and fired again.

But the Japs were relentless. As a child, George had sometimes entertained himself by flooding ant nests, just to watch the way the insects came tumbling up out of the hole, climbing over each other in their frenzy to escape. These Japs reminded him of that. They came churning up the ridge, charging straight into gunfire as if they thought themselves somehow impervious to bullets. Or as if they didn't care. They just came up and took death.

George fired in a fury until his five-round magazine was spent. He threw it aside, no time to reload, yanked out his sidearm, and caught some onrushing Jap in the neck. George wheeled around and caught another Jap in the thigh, dropping him heavily to one knee.

George spun again. But now a Jap was upon him, screaming, "Marine, you die!" And he was thrusting his bayonet, and he was slicing the upper part of George's arm even as George rolled away from the thrust. And it hurt like a sonofabitch, but there was no time for that, so George twisted to the side, scissoring the Jap's legs between his own, and the Jap was falling, going to the ground, bayonet spilling from his hands, and George was on top of the Jap but now the Jap was on top of him, and they were rolling on the jungle floor, grabbing at each other, grappling with each other, locked in their own private war.

"Fuck Eleanor Roosevelt!" cried the Jap.

"Yeah? Well f-f-fuck Hirohito in his ass!" cried George.

And apparently, the Jap understood the general gist of this, because his eyes widened. He got both hands around George's throat and squeezed. George tried to pull the man's hands away, he punched his arms, he writhed and bucked beneath him, but the little Jap was stronger than he looked. His grip was hard and unyielding. George couldn't breathe. The Jap was crushing his Adam's apple.

George's eyes roamed the jungle, casting about hopelessly for rescue, for something or someone that would save him. To his left, Babe was thrusting at some Jap with his street fighter's knife. Two hard jabs in the mouth with the brass knuckles backed the Jap up, then a slashing swing opened his cheek from his ear to his mouth. To George's right, Jazzman was on his feet backed up against a tree, a strange grin on his face as Japs rushed toward him and he shot them with an unhurried, methodical glee.

Neither was in position to help him. No help was coming. He was going to die.

The realization filled George Simon with a desperate new energy. His hands came up fast, and he plunged his right thumb hard into the corner of the Jap's left eye. The man howled. His grip sprang open and he rolled off George, both hands to his face, shrieking to whatever gods Japs embraced. George rolled away, hacking and clutching his throat, but breathing. Lord, breathing. The energy that had jolted him as the Japs came up over the ridge deserted him then like a faithless lover. His head throbbed like heavy machinery.

George was spent. He thought he could happily crouch in that position without moving until the end of time. So exhausted was he that he didn't even start at the sound of a gunshot. He simply looked back without much interest as the Jap he had fought stared down in surprise at a ragged red hole in his chest, dropped the sword he had raised high over George's head, and tumbled forward into the grass. He came to rest with his face not a foot from George's. His eye had gone crimson. It stared through George into infinity.

Babe holstered his sidearm. "Never turn your back on 'em, George," he said. "Only safe Jap is a dead Jap."

It took a moment. "Yeah," George finally managed.

Babe extended a hand. George did not want to take it. He wanted to stay where he was, crouched on the jungle floor, just breathing. It seemed about all he could manage. All he could hope to do. So for a long moment, he just stared at Babe's hand as if he could somehow make it—and all the hated obligations it represented—simply disappear.

Lord, he was empty.

But the hand did not disappear, and George had no choice. He reached up and clasped it. Babe's grip was strong. He pulled George to his feet.

"Come on, Saint," he said. "Let's get back. That's a bad cut you've got on your arm. Doc'll need to stitch you up."

George barely heard him. He looked around. The scene was littered with dead Japs, bodies lying tangled on the jungle floor, on the ridge, down on the sand. And it was littered with dead marines, too.

Babe guessed his thoughts.

"Eight," he said. "We lost eight."

"Where's . . . ?"

And then George's eyes found him. His hands came up. And something in him broke.

Jazzman was against the same tree where George had seen him fighting off Japs. A circle of dead enemy soldiers was at his feet. George counted five. Jazzman's eyes were wide. His throat was torn open.

"Ah, Jazz," said George. He was afraid to say more.

"He fought like a tiger," said Babe. "Last guy I would have expected, but he really held his own and then some. Saved our butts."

"We've got to take him back," said George.

"They'll send another patrol out to retrieve the bodies. You're in no shape."

"No, I'm taking him. I'd hate if the Japs got him, if they . . . "

If they mutilated him like you did one of theirs.

He did not say these words, but something hardened in Babe's gaze as if he had heard them just the same. They regarded each other for a long, still moment. Then George went to Jazz and knelt by him.

The brown eyes had gone dull. His face was smudged with blood and dirt. His restless hands were still.

George hoisted his friend across his shoulders and climbed unsteadily to his feet. Babe was still watching him. Then the survivors lined up single file and began the long journey home.

sixteen

THE CITY WAS DARK.

Its familiar buildings had disappeared, become shadows against the night. Its sidewalks were almost empty of people. There was no leakage of warm light from its homes. Its traffic lights and streetlights were dead, and its cars, their headlights masked by tape, crept slowly through the blackness, trying not to hit each other or anything else.

It was only a practice blackout—wouldn't last more than half an hour—but Thelma could not help feeling uneasy as she guided the old Oldsmobile through town. The darkness was a stark reminder that nothing preordained the fighting would stay "over there," in foreign places with unfamiliar names. For all she knew, enemy bombers might be massed overhead this very instant, searching for the missing lights of Mobile.

The thought made her crane her neck involuntarily, but all she saw above her were stars. Thelma told herself to stop letting her imagination run away with her. Still, she wished she didn't have to be out here in this eerie blackness. She had just dropped the girls off at their homes and wished she were headed to hers.

Instead, she was going to the hospital to see Ollie.

The white men had come for him that morning and caught him alone coming out of the toilet. Thelma had been out on the bay painting a ship when it happened. She had heard about it when she returned to the shipyard.

There were five of them, all wearing masks, and they had dragged him back of the administration building and worked him over good. They had used pipes. When they were done, Ollie Grimes was a broken lump of a man. He might still be lying there, might even have died there, had not one of his friends become concerned and gone looking for him.

Because there was no ambulance willing to transport him, the bosses had allowed a couple of the colored men to load him into a car and take him to a white hospital that maintained a small ward for Negroes in its basement, on the condition they hurry immediately back to work.

By the time Thelma returned to the island and heard what had happened, Ollie had already been taken away and the police were there, two detectives talking to the shipyard manager out in front of the administration building. The manager told the police officers he had no idea who had done this. The cops questioned a few white workers who happened to be standing nearby, and they all said the same thing. Thelma and some of the other colored workers were standing there, too, but the detectives did not deign to talk to them, even after they offered.

"Bastards don't really want to know," a friend of Ollie's had hissed, walking away.

Not that there was any mystery here. From the moment she heard what had happened, Thelma knew who had beaten up Ollie Grimes. Everyone did. And if anyone had any doubts, all they had to do was watch Earl Ray Hodges pushing his trash can around the yard that afternoon with a new swagger in his awkward walk and a satisfied little smirk on his face that said he knew something he was bursting to say and just might, if you only asked. When he saw Thelma going to the colored section of the cafeteria for lunch, he even gave her a spiteful grin.

The sight had made her shiver, and the memory of Flora Lee's warning had hit her like a hammer driving a nail.

Earl Ray, he ain't likely to forget what happened. He might play like he forgot, but he ain't gon' forget. And he gon' do somethin'. You mark my words on that.

Sure enough, he had bided his time, had waited one month, two months, three, and when everyone else had pretty much forgotten all about the confrontation outside of the administration building, when the memory of the spittle-laced threats he made while being dragged off had faded into inconsequence, Earl Ray and his friends had jumped Ollie and beaten him bloody and unconscious.

I should have listened to Flora Lee.

This guilty thought had stung her as she watched the little man push his garbage can. And the sad truth was, Thelma thought she *had* listened, thought she *had* taken Flora Lee's warning seriously at the time, but she realized only now that she had not, not really. She had mentioned it only once to Ollie and told him to be careful, and he had shrugged and said he would, and his friends had promised to watch his back, but then time had passed and their concern had dimmed. All of them had walked past Earl Ray Hodges a hundred times since that day without incident, without his even appearing to notice them, so they had stopped thinking about it. But if what had happened today proved nothing else, it proved Flora Lee knew her husband. They all should have respected that.

I should have respected that.

Thelma parked the Olds. Mobile City Hospital was an indistinct white shape in the shadows of the blackout, a line of three-story white Doric columns like something from an antebellum mansion standing sentinel in front. Thelma hurried to the basement.

She was eager to find out how Ollie was. And also frightened. No one had heard anything since this morning.

It took her a few minutes to locate the little colored ward. She finally found Ollie sitting up on a bed, fully dressed, pulling on his coat with painful deliberateness, a large, square bandage taped to the back of his head. He looked up, surprised at the sound of her, and she saw that one side of his face was swollen and disfigured. His left eye was closed. The bruise was the color and circumference of a plum.

It must have been something in her expression that made him try to smile, but his easy grin hung crookedly on his face, and she saw that he was missing a tooth. "You should see the other guy," he said.

Thelma shook her head. Even after he had been beaten all to pieces, Ollie Grimes was still incorrigible.

"Came to see about you," she told him. "We were all worried."

He shrugged. "Mostly bumps and bruises and this here black eye," he said. "But the doctor say they cracked my melon pretty good."

"What do you mean?"

He pointed. "My skull," he said. "Doctor say they fractured it."

Thelma gasped. "Well then, why you sitting up in bed? Why ain't you lying down?"

He smiled. "'Cause I'm goin' home," he said. "In fact, your timing couldn't be better. I was wonderin' how I was gon' get there."

Thelma was scandalized. "Home? I ain't takin' you home. You need to stop bein' such a stubborn jackass and stay here so the doctors can fix you up."

Some indefinable sorrow crept into his eyes then. "Honey, I ain't the one sayin' I got to go home," he explained in a patient voice. "They is."

"But I don't understand."

"'Course you do," he said. "You just ain't thinkin'. Ain't but so many beds for colored. They got to save what they got for the real serious cases."

"Real serious? You just said you got a skull fracture!"

He shrugged and repeated himself. "Ain't but so many beds," he said. "Now, come on. Doctor done already give me my discharge papers and my prescription. You gon' stand there all night, or you gon' help a man up?"

Still shaking her head, Thelma took his hand as Ollie climbed slowly to his feet. When he got there, he paused a moment, gently swaying like a palm tree in a tropical breeze. He put a hand to his temple, closed his eyes. "Whoo-ee," he said.

"Dizzy?"

He nodded, didn't speak. They stood like that a moment longer. Then he nodded again, opened his eyes—"All right," he said, "let's try it"—and she put her arm around his waist, draped his arm over her shoulder, and led him slowly up the stairs and out the door. She was thankful to see that the city had reappeared, lights marking the hotels and department stores, the streets no longer alien and dark.

"Always knew one day you'd put your arms around me," Ollie said. "Just didn't think I'd have to get my head stove in for it to happen."

She paused, glaring at him in disbelief. "Ollie Grimes, would you just stop? You can't hardly walk, you got a crack in your head, and you *still* tryin' to flirt with me? I swear I ain't never seen a bigger sex fiend in all my life."

His smile then surprised her. It was soft and pitying. "Thelma Gordy," he said, "ain't you figured me out yet?"

"What you mean? Figured what out?"

"I ain't really flirtin' with you, girl."

"Heck you ain't. I know flirtin' when I hear it."

"I ain't," he insisted, and something flickered in his eyes as he added, "Truth is, you ain't my type."

"Not your type?" Thelma was surprised to find herself mildly offended. "What's that supposed to mean?"

"Girl, I'm queer as a three-dollar bill."

That stopped her. She searched his face for some glint of humor in the one good eye, some sign around the mouth of laughter held in abeyance. But his gaze was steady as a headlight upon her.

"You? Queer?"

"Yes, ma'am."

"No you ain't. How you queer? You all the time messin' with me, messin' with the girls. I think you got Laverne half in love with you, and she been married for years."

Another smile. "Can you think of a better way to throw the blood-hounds off the scent?"

And she had to admit, she couldn't. "I'll be damned," she said.

"You really that surprised?" he asked.

"Yes," she said, "I am."

"Well, first day we met, I told you: don't take me too seriously."

"Yes," she said, "but I didn't know ... I didn't think ... " Pause. "Why you tellin' me this?" she asked.

He hunched his shoulders. "I don't rightly know," he admitted. "I trust you, I guess. And you comin' to check on me like this here, that ain't nothin'. That mean somethin'. I ain't got too many friends in this town, Thelma—*real* friends, you know what I mean? You one of 'em and I figure, that bein' the case, oughtn't be no secrets between us."

He paused. Some anxiety tightened his features, and he inclined his head toward her. "It don't change nothin', do it?"

She considered this. After a moment she said, "I guess it don't. It's your life; you the one got to live it. But tell me something: Have you ever tried, you know, bein' with a girl? You might not know what you been missin'."

He flashed her a roguish grin. "Why, honey? Is you offerin'?"

Thelma gaped. Then she laughed. "You the worst man I done ever met," she said.

They moved again toward the car. Ollie grunted and made faces as he settled into the seat, and she understood he was in far more pain than he was letting on.

Thelma stripped the tape from the headlights, then started the car and wheeled it into traffic. "When the doctor say you can go back to work?" she asked.

He made a dismissive sound. "Doctors don't know everything," he told her.

Thelma had been lighting a cigarette. She looked over at him, the match poised. "What he say?" she asked.

"He say I need to take some days off."

"Then that's what you need to do." She rolled down the window, breathed out smoke.

"Hell with that," said Ollie. "You pick me up tomorrow mornin', usual time."

"I ain't doin' no such thing. Did your brains fall out through that crack in your head?"

"You don't pick me up," he told her, "I'm gon' have to get out there and catch the bus. Either way it go, I'm gon' be at that shipyard in the morning when the bell ring. Promise you that."

Thelma regarded him. "Doctor say you need to rest, that's what you ought to do. Why you got to be so damn stubborn, Ollie Grimes?"

"Stubborn ain't got nothin' to do with it," he said.

"Really?" she snapped. "What else is it, then?"

He didn't answer. He looked out the window. She smoked. Waited. Finally, she asked it again, her voice gentler this time. "Ollie, what is it, then?"

Ollie looked at her. "That crazy bastard like to killed me," he said. "Ain't nobody gon' arrest him, 'cause they was all wearin' masks, so I can't swear in court it was him—and that's if they'd let a nigger testify in the first place, which they won't. But it was him. I knowed it even before he hit me, even when I seen 'em comin' toward me, that little sombitch walkin' with that funny walk he got. I told the police about it, but they told me that ain't enough. Told me ain't nothin' they could do."

He looked away and studied the now-congested sidewalks of Mobile. "But Thelma, you and I, we both know that's just they excuse. We both know police wouldn't do nothin' even if them mens wasn't wearin' masks. They would find some kind of reason to let it slide, 'cause he white—even white trash—and I'm a nigger and that's just the way it is. So he gon' get away with it. I know that. Done made my peace with it, best I can."

Thelma brought the car to a stop at a red light, and he turned back toward her. A fierce light danced in his one good eye. "So the onliest thing I can do is let 'em see they ain't broke me. That's the onliest revenge I got against 'em, to walk through that gate on my own two legs when the bell ring tomorrow mornin' and let 'em see—let 'em *all* see—even after what they done, Ollie Grimes still standin'."

His face, usually so mobile and brimming with mischief, was a purple grotesquerie, serious and still. She knew he was waiting to see what she would say. "Queer or not," she told him, "you hard-headed as any man I ever met."

It made him smile. "Thelma," he said as the car moved forward, "that's about the nicest thing you could have said to me."

And the next morning, sure enough, he was on the corner as usual, waiting for her when she drove up. He held himself stiffly erect, his work cap cocked at a sassy angle to cover the bandage on the back of his head. His eye was still a shiny plum.

"Mornin'," he said as he lowered himself into the seat. "You ready to go help Uncle Sam win this here war?"

Thelma ignored the question. "How you feelin', Ollie? And don't you lie to me. You feelin' any better?"

He hunched his shoulders. "A little," he said. "Head still feel like a jackhammer up there. But I ain't so dizzy as I was last night. I be all right."

She was dubious, but she knew arguing would be a waste of breath. So she pulled out from the curb, and they drove without speaking to pick up Helen, Betty, and Laverne.

At each stop, Ollie did as he always did, climbing out of the car to bow low and open the door. At each stop, the women gasped over the ruin of his face and asked him in a solicitous whisper if he was all right, if he might not be better off staying at home a few days. At each stop, he grinned and told them he wasn't a man to let a couple of minor bumps and bruises keep him from putting in a full day's work.

"But Ollie," said Laverne, "can you even see out that eye to work?"

He said, "I can see well enough to know how fine you lookin' this mornin', Miss Laverne."

She giggled like she was 15 years younger than she was and swatted playfully at him. "You such a caution," she said as she got in and he closed the car door behind her.

Ollie winced as he settled back into the front seat. Thelma was the only one who saw.

"We glad you gon' be all right, Ollie," Laverne was saying from the back seat as Thelma steered back into the heavy traffic. "Had us worried."

"You sho' nuff did," said Helen. "You looked a mess when they dragged you out from there."

"Oh, I'll get my good looks back," he said. "You can count on that."

Betty sucked at her teeth. "Them white people," she said. It was all she said, but for the four other people in the car it was enough, more than enough, to encompass an entire universe of feeling.

"Yeah," said Helen.

"Got that right," said Thelma.

Ollie said, "Ain't just white people, though. It's that one in particular, that Earl Ray Hodges. He the one led the group that beat on me. He the one you got to look out for. That's a nasty little sombitch." Ollie swept his hat from his head, held it over his heart, and added, "If you ladies will excuse my indelicate language."

Laverne's lips twisted into a knowing smirk. "Ain't got to excuse no language on account of us, honey. You ain't spoke nothin' but the honest truth."

Thelma parked the Olds in the big lot. They gathered their lunch buckets and walked toward the gate. Ordinarily, it gave Thelma great satisfaction to walk to her job at the beginning of the workday. But satisfaction was absent from her this morning. All she felt was a nibbling apprehension about what would happen when Ollie reported to work.

Already, she saw them seeing him, people stopping as if he were a ghost somehow slipped from its grave to wander among the living. White people stared with stony eyes, black ones gawped with open mouths. Ollie walked with his head high, his gaze fixed on nothing, the four women trailing behind. A slight hitch in his gait, the bandage on his head, and of course, the wreckage of his face testified with mute eloquence to what had happened to him—what white people had done to him.

More people stopped. And as Ollie passed under the arched gate, the crowd parted for him as the Red Sea did for Moses. As Ollie went by him, some colored man Thelma didn't know raised his big, calloused hands and clapped them slowly together. The flat banging of his palms seemed the only sound in the world for a moment. Then a couple other colored men joined him. Then a woman joined in. Then more, then more, then more until there was a wave of ovation louder than the distant hiss of drills or the clanging of metal or the crackle of welders' torches, until all you could hear at the front gate of the shipyard was the sizzle of colored people's hands banging together in honor of Ollie Grimes.

White people watched, some with hostility, some with confusion, some just with disinterest. The Negroes applauded. Then they stamped their feet and cheered, and the thunder of it swelled until it filled up the morning. It was as if Ollie, just by walking into the shipyard, just by showing up to work right on time after what white men had done to him, had made himself the bearer of all their stripes and, more importantly, the embodiment of all their striving, all their defiance, their new resolute refusal to quietly submit to white people's bullying.

How much longer did they expect to keep shoveling shit and Negroes to just take it and grin? Negroes had feelings, had hearts and minds just the same as anybody else. What was wrong with white people that they couldn't see this? It was as this last bitter thought was working its way through her that Thelma saw something that stopped her clapping, that brought her hand to her mouth and sudden tears to her eyes.

Because one white person did not just watch Ollie. One white person was applauding him just as lustily as the Negroes were. It was Flora Lee Hodges.

Thelma had seen the mousy little white woman occasionally around the yard since the day Earl threatened Ollie. They had passed one another without breaking stride, nodded to one another—*Yes, I see you there. Hello*—but they had not spoken. Flora Lee's husband was crazy. Thelma didn't want to get her in trouble with him. She didn't want to have any dealings with him herself. So they had given one another the gift of mutual distance and mutual silence.

But suddenly there Flora Lee stood, front and center in a group of stone-faced white men and women, a smile on her face, one eye ringed with a fading purple bruise from her latest row with Earl Ray, but both eyes tightened by some deep, intentional feeling as she lauded Ollie Grimes.

What was she thinking? Had she lost her mind? Even as she loved Flora Lee for what she was doing, Thelma wanted to tell her to stop it, for God's sake stop it, before it was too late, before he saw. But Flora Lee didn't stop. Indeed, her mouth came open, framing a shrill cheer.

What happened next was fast, but it seemed to Thelma as if it happened in slow motion. Earl Ray appeared in front of his wife. She didn't see him. He yelled something, reared his closed fist back. And a punch she never saw coming landed flush on Flora Lee's left cheek. She reeled sideways from the impact, body out of control, arms flailing, and landed hard on the asphalt.

The applause seemed to stop as suddenly as water from a closed valve. All at once the great shipyard, where work never ceased, where hammers sang and great furnaces thundered all day and all night, seemed to be sheathed in silence so deep Thelma would have sworn she could hear the restless muttering of the waves.

Earl Ray stood over Flora Lee, his eyes bright and hard. "You're applauding for that *nigger*?" His voice rose to a scandalized screech on the last word. "For that *nigger*? What the hell is wrong with you, you fuckin' cow?"

He lifted a foot to kick her, but the white men behind him pulled him back before the blow could land. He seemed not to notice. "What kind of white woman claps for a nigger, Flora Lee? I bet next, you'll be liftin' your skirts for one of 'em, huh? Or maybe you done it already! Is that it, Flora Lee? Is that it?"

For a long moment, she only lay there, stunned, shaking her head, trying to gather herself. Finally, Flora Lee Hodges came slowly to her feet, her hand cupping the latest place Earl Ray had hit her. There was something in her eyes Thelma had never seen there before, something hard and old.

"That's the last time, Earl," she said. Her voice was a raspy scrape, metal raking concrete. "That's the last time you gon' ever hurt me."

Earl Ray's crazy eyes leapt nearly out of their sockets and he tried to get at her, but the men held him fast. "Bitch, you don't talk to me that way!" he snarled. "I'm your husband, you silly bitch! I'm your husband and you goddamn well better respect me!"

She gave him a hard look. Then she turned her back on him and walked over to where Thelma stood. All eyes followed.

When Earl Ray saw this, he tried yet again to leap from the custody of the white men. But their grip on him was sure. "Don't you dare go over to them!" he spat. "You get back here! You hear me, Flora Lee? Get your ass back over here right now, or it's gon' go worse on you!"

She ignored him. Flora Lee said, "Thelma, you remember that offer you made to me that time? Is that still—"

Thelma said, "Yes."

Their eyes locked. Flora Lee smiled. "Thank you," she said. "End of the day, I'll meet you at your locker."

From behind them, Earl Ray laughed. It was a wild, unhinged sound.

"Oh, you done did it now, nigger. Shouldn't never of mixed in white folks' business! I'm gon' get you for this! I'm gon' get both of you! You watch and see if I don't!"

He was looking at Thelma. She felt a coldness climb her spine.

The white men holding Earl Ray bore him off to the janitor's shed to calm down. Flora Lee watched him be taken away, then squeezed Thelma's arm. "Guess I better get to work," she said and hurried away.

Thelma's friends regarded her with dubious eyes. Laverne spoke for them all. "What she talkin' about?" she asked. "What 'offer' you made her?"

Thelma's eyes were on Flora Lee's retreating back. "Told her she needed to leave her husband. Told her if she ain't had nowhere else to go, she could come stay with me." Hearing herself speak it aloud, she knew again how insane it was.

Their eyes widened. "Thelma," demanded Helen, "have you lost your mind? You can't do that!"

"We talk about it at lunch," said Thelma. And she rushed off to her locker even as they were protesting behind her.

Lunchtime came too soon. They took their meals to their table, and the women lost no time telling her there was no way she could take that white woman into her home.

"You ain't thinkin' straight," Laverne said. "Girl, they got laws against that. You want to end up in jail?"

"I got to do somethin'," Thelma said. "You seen what he done this mornin'. Can't just let him keep beatin' on her like that."

"Why not?" demanded Laverne. "That's white people's business. He was right about that much, at least. Let them sort it out."

"She need help," said Thelma, chewing on a tuna sandwich.

"So what?" snapped Laverne. "Ain't your responsibility to help her."

"Yeah, it is," said Thelma. "She my"—and here, she paused, had time to hear in her mind the foolish, impossible word she was about to utter and to marvel at it—"friend."

They looked at her as if she had just claimed dogs spoke to her in Chinese. "She your 'friend'?" Laverne rolled her eyes. Her laughter was a hard sound with no mirth in it. "Lord have mercy, girl, you done lost your mind. That woman is *white*, do you hear me? I'm sure she nice and all, but she can't be no 'friend' to you. Especially with that mad dog husband of hers. Don't you know nothin'?"

Thelma met Laverne's eyes. Her voice was even. "I said she my friend and I'm gon' help her."

Laverne sucked her teeth and looked away as if Thelma were too foolish to bother wasting breath. Helen said, "So how you expect you gon' get your 'friend' home, Thelma? You can't take her in the car."

Thelma swallowed. "Yes I can. Let her hunch down."

Laverne's gaze swung around like a machine gun on a tripod. "Oh, hell no," she said.

"Ride with us?" asked Betty, as if she surely had not heard right.

"Yes," said Thelma, hoping she didn't sound as uneasy as she felt.

"Why ain't you asked us before you decided this?" asked Helen.

"When did I have time?" asked Thelma. "This an emergency."

"Hmph," said Laverne. "White folks' emergency, you mean. Ain't no emergency to me."

Helen put a hand on Laverne's forearm to shush her, but her eyes never left Thelma. "Thelma," she said reasonably, "we all part owners of that car and we got to ride in it, too. Don't you think you should have asked us before makin' that decision by yourself?"

"Yeah," said Thelma, "maybe I should have. But like I say, it was an emergency. Besides, it'll only be the one time. Just to get her out of here safely, get her to my house. Can't have her waitin' on no bus. That husband of hers might see her."

"You puttin' all of us in danger for her," said Helen. And this, thought Thelma guiltily, she could not deny. Worse, she didn't even have the words to explain why she had done it, not even to herself. All she knew was that something had shifted inside her when she saw Flora Lee hooting and applauding for Ollie, this lone white woman in a sea of hostile white people, cheering for Thelma's broken friend. She didn't know if that made Flora Lee brave or just crazy. She didn't know if it mattered.

All she did know was that Flora Lee's courage—or her craziness—had called out to her, demanded something from her in return. And she could not refuse it.

"What if we say no?" Laverne's gaze burned through the smoke of a freshly lit cigarette. "Like Helen say, we part owners of that car. We got some say in how it's used."

Thelma breathed. She lifted her eyes. "Then I guess y'all buy me out and get yourselves another driver."

The other women's eyes grew wide with disbelief. Betty said, "Thelma, you gon' put us down . . . for *her*?"

"Ain't tryin' to put nobody down," said Thelma.

"Hell with puttin' us down," said Laverne. "Like Helen say, she puttin' us in *danger*."

"I guess I am," Thelma conceded. "Ain't got no other choice."

Ollie had been sitting there quietly, listening to them as he idly stirred soup with his spoon. Now he spoke softly. "Seem like to me you all forgettin' somethin'," he said. They turned to him. "Thelma the one in the most danger. And I ain't talkin' about no police officer seein' that white woman in the car. Chances are, we get away with that. It's a risk, yeah, but you all know we probably be all right. But Thelma, she takin' a bigger risk than that."

Helen said, "You talkin' about that husband."

Ollie nodded. "You heard what he said. And he meant it, too. He gon' bide his time, he gon' wait just as good till he think we done forgot. And then he gon' try to hurt Thelma. I'm a livin' witness."

Thelma said, "So what you sayin', Ollie?"

He shrugged. "I'm sayin', if your 'friend' gon' quit and try to find work elsewhere, maybe you ought to do the same. Sell these girls your interest in that there car and find you another job."

Betty covered Thelma's hand with her own. "He might have a point, Thelma," she said.

Helen said, "Make a lot of sense."

Laverne exhaled smoke. Her gaze was flinty. "Hate to see you go," she said, "but it might be for the best."

Thelma looked at them. It was a good argument. She couldn't deny that. And that little man, he terrified her. But still . . .

"I ain't gon' run." She was surprised by her own words. She had no idea where they came from.

Betty said, "Thelma, you ain't thinkin'."

Helen said, "You heard what he said."

"He ain't gon' make me run," said Thelma, her voice growing harder. "I like this job. And you all, you like family to me. This where I belong. If I let him make me run from here, when do I stop?"

She looked around at them. The three women regarded her with taut, unreadable faces. Ollie smiled his broken smile at her. "I swear, Miss Thelma," he said, "you about the stubbornest woman I done ever met."

She returned the smile. "Thank you, Ollie. That's about the nicest thing you could have said to me."

So at day's end, just as she'd said, Flora Lee met Thelma at her locker. She had, she said, already told her supervisor this would be her last day. The supervisor had nodded and replied, "Yes, I heard what happened. I think that's for the best."

"Like it's my fault," said Flora Lee in amazement. "Like *I* done somethin.'"

They walked with Ollie, Laverne, Helen, and Betty. Ollie had asked some of the men he knew to join them, too, just to be on the safe side in case Earl Ray tried something. So Thelma found herself surrounded by a large cordon as she made her way to the parking lot. They all had their eyes out for him, but Earl Ray was not to be seen. In fact, none of them remembered seeing him push his trash can around the shipyard at all that day. Somehow, thought Thelma, his disappearance made him all the more menacing.

"Maybe he got fired," said Betty.

"He ain't got fired," said Thelma. She didn't know how she knew it, but she did.

"Maybe he give up," said Helen.

"Earl Ray don't never give up," Flora Lee said. "He don't never."

They put her in the front seat of the car between Ollie and Thelma and made her scrunch down low so that her pale skin would not show above the dashboard. The last thing they needed was for police to ride by and see five Negroes in a car with a bruised-up white woman.

"This a crazy thing y'all doin,'" one of Ollie's friends said as he closed the car door behind them.

"Tell me somethin' I don't know," Laverne replied sourly. Thelma put the car in gear and wheeled out of her parking space.

They navigated out of the Bankhead Tunnel and into heavy traffic, Thelma's hand sweat-slick upon the steering wheel, eyes flicking nervously left and right, making sure none of the drivers in the other cars were looking too closely. But the other drivers mostly just looked bored, numbed by the now-familiar ordeal of trying to get anywhere in Mobile traffic.

The silence in the car was oppressive. Apparently, it was too much so for Flora Lee, who piped up from the valley between Thelma and Ollie. "Want to thank y'all for helpin' me," she said in her acrid voice.

From the back seat, Laverne snorted. "Don't mention it," she said. "To nobody. Ever."

"I won't," said Flora Lee earnestly. "I know y'all takin' a big risk and I just—"

Betty cut her off. "Flora Lee, how you get mixed up with that character in the first place, you don't mind my askin'?"

"Earl Ray? I done knowed him since I was a girl."

"No," said Betty, "I guess what I mean is, was he always like that?"

"I s'pose maybe he was," said Flora Lee, "but I ain't knowed it at first. He could get real excitable when he thought somebody was puttin' him down on account of his size or his leg. And he was so proud. Like he felt he had to be extra proud 'cause of them handicaps so he was bound an' determined to show you he was good as any man. I s'pose that's why I married him. I liked that pride he had. But it seem like after the war started and the military wouldn't take him on account of that leg, he just ain't knowed how to handle it. That's when he start drinkin' so bad. He never hit me that much before, just once in a blue moon, maybe. But after that, he got real mean and he start hittin' me all the time."

"So what?" Laverne's voice was choked with scorn. "We s'pose to feel sorry for you, is that it?"

"I ain't asked no one to feel—"

Laverne cut her off. "Things are tough all over, honey. We all got problems. Colored people especially got problems, and most of our problems is because of men like your husband."

There was a silence. After a moment, Flora Lee spoke softly. "Yes, I know," she said. "I told Thelma once: I ain't never been able to figure how I was s'pose to be better'n colored people. I ain't nothin' but poor white trash, and I always knowed it. Folks around where I'm from, they always said we was better than, you know . . . you all. But to me, that was just somethin' they said so they could feel like at least they wasn't the worst. At least there was somebody lower'n they was.

"And yeah, Earl Ray talked like that, too, but I never paid it too much mind. Wasn't that much colored around where we from and they mostly stayed off by theyselves. You hardly ever seen 'em, so far as I thought, Earl Ray was just talkin' like everybody else did. But then we come here and this town, it's full of colored, and you seen 'em everywhere, and I think it like to drove Earl Ray plumb crazy. Especially knowin' some of them gettin' jobs he can't get on account of his leg. It showed me for the first time how he really is. I ain't knowed till we come here just how hateful and mean he could be.

"And I just want you to know"—still scrunched down, she turned her head, addressing a back seat she couldn't see—"I'm sorry for what he done. I know that don't help nothin'. I know that don't make it right, especially you all puttin' yourselves out this way. But I am sorry."

Thelma glanced over and caught Ollie's eye, and she knew they were thinking the same thing in that moment: how earnest Flora Lee's regret was. And how useless.

Neither of them spoke. What was there to say? Ollie looked out the window.

In the rearview mirror, Thelma saw Laverne purse her lips. "You sorry," she said in a voice tart as lemons. "Umm hmm. Well, thank you for that."

And again, silence settled heavily on the car.

Laverne was the first stop. She climbed out without a word, slammed the door behind her, and walked toward her house without looking back. Thelma was glad to see her go. Maybe, thought Thelma, she would take some of the silence with her.

Betty was next. "Well," she said uncertainly as she stepped out, "I'll see you all tomorrow, I reckon."

A few minutes later, they were in front of Helen's house. "Well, you all," she said with forced cheer, "I'll see you in the morning." Pause. "Good luck to you, Flora Lee."

"Thank you," said Flora Lee.

Finally, they pulled up in front of Ollie's boarding house. He sat there a moment without touching the door handle. Then he said, "They ain't wrong, you know."

"I know," said Thelma.

"Hell of it is, you ain't, neither."

"I know that, too."

"It's just the way the world is, I s'pose. That's what's wrong."

"Yeah."

He got out of the car, leaned back through the window. "I need you to be careful, okay?"

"I will. See you tomorrow." Ollie waved and went inside.

Flora Lee piped up from below. "I really am sorry, Thelma," she said.

"I know I'm puttin' you out. Maybe you should just drop me at a bus stop. I can go back, talk to Earl."

"Hush up," said Thelma. "Get in the back."

"What you mean?"

"You must be tired of hunchin' down. Get in back and anybody see us will just think you some white lady out drivin' with her maid. Long as they don't look too close, we be okay."

Flora Lee hesitated. "Go on," said Thelma, and Flora Lee obeyed.

"Your friends, they mad with you 'cause of me, ain't they?" she asked, settling into the seat as the car pulled away from the curb.

Thelma sighed. "If you think they mad," she said, "wait till I get you home."

They pulled in front of Thelma's house 20 minutes later. The sun was just sliding from the sky. Porch lights cut meager holes in the gathering gloom. The four little girls who jumped double Dutch in front of the house across the street were wrapping up their rope.

"Hey," Thelma called to them as she stepped out of her car. "Do me a favor. Go get your parents. Knock on the doors of everybody else on the street, tell 'em Miss Thelma need to talk with 'em. Ask if they can come over to my porch."

The girls stood there a moment, confused. Then Flora Lee rose from the car. Their eyes widened, and they scattered in four different directions like startled birds.

"Why you callin' your neighbors?" asked Flora Lee.

"Might as well get it over with all at once," said Thelma.

"Don't mind tellin' you I'm nervous," said Flora Lee, right hand rubbing her left arm as she gazed about her.

"*You* nervous? Why?"

"Ain't never been in a colored house before. Hell, I ain't never been in a colored neighborhood before."

"Yeah, well I ain't never had a white lady in my house before, neither, so I guess we even. Come on."

Thelma led Flora Lee over the plank-board bridge that spanned the open sewer and up to the porch. When she opened the door, Gramp was where he always was, sitting next to the radio, pulling on his pipe. He had been half dozing, but his head came up when he heard her.

"Evenin', Gramp," she said. "Dinner here already?"

"Yeah, that old biddy done brought over some of her damn, uneat-able—" He stopped, cocked his head. "Who that with you?" he asked.

"Gramp, this here is Flora Lee. She work with me. She havin' some trou-ble right now, so she gon' stay with us a little while till she get on her feet."

Flora Lee said, "I'm right pleased to meet you," and extended her hand.

"He blind," said Thelma. "He can't see that hand." Flora Lee dropped it and said again, "I'm glad to meet you."

Gramp said, "She white."

"Yeah," said Thelma, "I know."

"She can't stay here."

"She ain't got nowhere else to go, Gramp."

"She can't stay here," he insisted. "She a white woman and I'm a man, a *colored* man. Thelma, you know better."

"You a hundred years old and you blind, old man. Ain't nobody gon' bother about that."

"If your brother was here—"

"But he ain't here," said Thelma. She couldn't begin to imagine Lu-ther's reaction if she had shown up at the door with some strange white woman in tow.

"Thelma," said Flora Lee, "I don't want to cause no trouble."

"It was always gon' be trouble," said Thelma, "any way we go. Might as well find trouble tryin' to do the right thing as find it any other way."

"Thelma?"

Izola Foster had come up on the lawn, drying her hands on a dish towel. "Little Aggie said you wanted to see me? Somethin' wrong with the meal? What that old man complainin' about this . . . " She stopped when she saw Flora Lee. She gaped, looked again at her neighbor. "Thelma? What's goin' on here?"

"Thelma?" Rafe and his wife were coming up behind Izola Foster. "Ruthie said you needed us?" Then Rafe saw. "Thelma, who's this?" he asked.

"She the reason I asked you to come over," said Thelma. "Just give me a minute, let everybody else get over here so I don't have to say it twice."

She waited in silence for a few awkward moments as the tiny lawn filled with her neighbors. Thelma switched on her porch light and stood next to Flora Lee under its meager illumination. Her heart was chattering.

When they were all there, she said, "Thank you all for comin' over here. This here is Flora Lee Hodges. She work with me over at the shipyard. Her husband been beatin' on her pretty regular—you can see from that bruise on her cheek. He give her that one just this mornin'. She ain't had nowhere else to go. I told her she could come stay with me till she get on her feet. Wanted you all to know who she is if you see her comin' out my door."

There was a silence. Then Izola Foster came meekly forward. She spoke from beneath lowered eyes. "We pleased to make your acquaintance, Miss Flora." Her voice was timid.

"You ain't got to do that," said Thelma, sharply. "You ain't got to call her 'Miss,' and you ain't got to hold your head down when you talk to her. She ain't like the rest of 'em. And I know you all got more to say than 'Pleased to make your acquaintance,' so you might as well come on and say it while you got the chance, 'cause after this, I ain't gon' answer no more questions."

Thelma waited through another beat of silence as they absorbed her words. Then Rafe stepped forward, his hat in his hands. "All right, then," he said. He nodded to Flora Lee. "Meanin' no disrespect to you, ma'am, but Thelma, how you bring this white woman here? That's against the law. What if the police find out?"

"Who gon' tell 'em, Rafe? You?"

He hunched his shoulders. "No, 'course not."

She looked to a woman standing behind him, her arms folded across her chest. "How about you, Katie? You gon' tell 'em?"

"You know better than that," Katie said. "But you still takin' a chance here, Thelma. And you forcin' us to take it with you."

"I know," said Thelma, "and I'm sorry for that. If I had any choice, I wouldn't have."

"Seem like you be the last person to do this, seein' what happened to your folks."

"Yeah, I know," said Thelma.

"You trust this woman?" demanded Katie.

Thelma glanced at Flora Lee. "Yeah," she said, "I s'pose I do." She pointed at Flora Lee's cheek. "You see that there bruise? I told you he give her that this mornin'. You know why he done it? There was a colored man got beat up yesterday at the shipyard. It was Flora Lee's own husband and some of his friends what done it. And that colored man, he come back to work today even though the doctors say he shouldn't because he got a skull fracture, but he wanted her husband to see, wanted all them white folks to see they ain't broke him. When he walk back through the gates, all the colored people, they bust out clappin' for him and cheerin' him. The white folks, they standin' there with they jaws tight, they arms folded, mad as a hive of bees. All except for one, and that was her. She the only one of 'em cheerin' and applaudin' with us, with the colored. That's why her husband hauled off and punched her."

"He punched her?" Izola's face had gone tight with indignation. "You mean, with his fist?"

"Yeah," said Thelma. "I been tellin' her she need to get away from him. But she new in town, she don't know too many of her own kind. So I told her she could come here and we would look after her, help her till she got on her feet. Bible say we s'pose to do that, s'pose to look out for each other. I ain't never seen where it say only look out for them that look like you."

"Why she applaud this colored man," asked a woman in the back, "if she knowed her husband gon' hit her for it?"

"Well," said Thelma, "I think—"

"Beg pardon." Rafe held his hand up. "Can't she talk for herself?"

Thelma looked over at Flora Lee. "Yes," she said, "'course she can." Thelma gestured for Flora Lee to step up.

The little woman swallowed. Her eyes grew large. She came forward, stood next to Thelma.

"Evenin', y'all," she said. Her voice was low and rocky. The ones in back had to strain forward to catch it. "My name, which you done heard already, is Flora Lee Hodges. Uh . . . it used to be Flora Lee Gadsen, but then I went and married Earl Ray Hodges, which I shouldn't never of done, 'cause if I hadn't, I wouldn't be standin' here with no bruise on my cheek tryin' to think what to say to you all."

Someone in the crowd said, "Take your time, honey."

Flora Lee swallowed again. "I don't blame y'all for wonderin' about me. I don't blame y'all for not trustin' me. I done seen the way Earl Ray and some of his friends treat colored and if I was colored, I think maybe I wouldn't trust me myself. And if y'all tell Thelma you don't want me around here, I understand and I won't stay, even if she tell me to. I been standin' here thinkin' about all this from y'all's point of view an' my problem is, I don't know how to prove to you that my heart is different. I can *say* I'm different, but what do that mean? How do you know for sure? You got every right to ask that question and I ain't got no way to answer. All I can say is, 'Trust me,' and that don't make no sense, 'cause why should you trust me an' you don't even know me?"

She paused, wringing her hands. Her eyes glistened. "I don't know why it has to be this way," she said in a frayed voice. "I just don't understand why everything have to be so hard. Earl, he say I'm stupid."

Another pause. She lowered her head. Thelma thought maybe she was finished and opened her own mouth to speak. Then Flora Lee's head came up. "I guess I ain't answered your question yet," she said with a sheepish laugh, addressing herself to the woman in the back, barely visible now in the darkness. "You wanted to know why I cheered. Tell you the truth, I ain't thought about Earl Ray when I done it. It's just, I know Ollie—that's the colored man Thelma told you about—he got beat up bad, *real* bad. Some said he might not make it; that's how bad he was hurt. And then, when I seen him come walkin' through that gate, well . . . I ain't thought about maybe I shouldn't cheer for him 'cause I'm white. I was just happy to see him back, that's all."

There was a silence. It filled a long, uncertain moment. Then Gramp spoke from behind Thelma.

"Well," he said, "y'all can stand out here in the cold runnin' off at the mouth if you want. I'm gon' go in and have my supper, try to force down some of this slop Izola Foster done fixed me." He held a hand out before him. "You welcome to join me if you want, Miss Flora Lee, but I warn you, you gon' need a strong stomach."

People laughed. Flora Lee laughed and wept. She put her hand in his. "Thank you," she said.

"Don't you listen to that old goat, honey," said Izola Foster. "He always complainin' 'bout my cookin', but he always send empty plates back. That ought to tell you somethin'."

She stepped forward into the light, offering her hand. "My name is Izola," she said. Sniffling, still laughing, Flora Lee shook Mrs. Foster's hand. "You ain't got to share his plate," Izola continued. "I made plenty. I go get you a plate of your own." And she trundled off across the street.

As Izola walked away, Thelma gazed out over her tiny yard. Her neighbors had lined up, and one by one, they came up to the porch, the men to touch their caps and nod to the white woman, the women to hug her, all of them to offer her any help she needed, all of them to welcome her to the neighborhood.

Thelma's hand went to her heart. Then it went to her eyes to wipe tears away.

seventeen

JOHN SIMON TURNED A FULL CIRCLE ON THE PLATFORM TO take in his surroundings. To the south, the train track stretched back toward Mobile. To the west, on the far side of the tracks, cotton fields, late-winter dead, unrolled to the horizon. To the north, the faded red caboose of the train that had brought him here shrank steadily away. And to the east, half a mile down a dirt road that curved back from the platform, sat the little collection of dusty, low-slung buildings that constituted the town of Kendrick, Alabama.

His survey of his surroundings having turned up no car for public hire—not that he had expected one in a place like this—John hoisted the valise at his feet and began a resigned walk into town. He was dressed, as usual, as though he expected to argue in court: an expensive double-breasted suit the color of chocolate, his shoes reflecting the meager sunlight like a mirror. Atop his head sat the inevitable Stetson homburg, this one sand-colored with a chocolate band.

John drew curious attention as he entered town. A group of men in weathered overalls sitting on a bench under the awning outside a feed store, a woman in a faded gingham dress yanking a squalling, barefoot toddler behind her, all stopped and stared at him as you would at the sun: brows furrowed, eyes squinting.

To each, John doffed his homburg and smiled courteously. None of them responded and this, too, was as he had thought it might be. White trash living in such degraded conditions could hardly be expected to have a grasp on even basic social conventions.

John had been putting this journey off for a long time. He had known when he struck his bargain with Luther Hayes that a visit to the scene of the crime might be advisable, but he had certainly not looked forward to that distasteful chore.

No, the critical thing had been to resolve Luther's legal predicament so that John's stubborn son would, in turn, give up his refusal to marry Sylvia Osborn. But now, a year later, both those goals having been met, John had decided the time had come to take the measure of the town that haunted his client like a ghost.

Two blocks down the dirt street, he came upon a diner. The flaking letters painted crookedly over the front door identified it as Mel's Place. A metal Coca-Cola sign hung out over the sidewalk. There was another sign, a piece of white cardboard stuck in the screen door. It was as crudely lettered as the one over the door. "White Only" it said. The door gave a loud squeak when John pushed it open.

Mel's Place had eight wooden tables widely scattered on a floor made of yellowed linoleum. Five men and a barefoot boy of about 10 occupied most of them, though apparently none were customers, because none had a plate or utensils. They were just . . . there, passing the time of day. When he stepped in, they all turned as one to stare at him in frank curiosity.

John swept his hat from his head, nodded. No one bothered nodding back. A counter with six empty stools lined up before it ran across the far side of the building. Through the pass-through window in the wall behind it, he could see a cook smoking a cigarette in the kitchen. A woman behind the counter—she had maybe 50 years behind her, lively eyes, and fiery red hair conspicuously devoid of gray—called out to him. "Sit wherever you want, hon. Don't mind this bunch of reprobates."

With a grateful nod, John chose one of the stools at the counter. He put his valise on the floor, set the homburg on the stool next to him, and spent a moment studying a menu that, like the signs at the door, appeared to have been hand-lettered. There was nothing among the restaurant's offerings that he found even remotely appetizing, but John had been traveling all morning and was hungry. Besides, he reasoned, these people would be more apt to help him if he bought a meal.

He ordered Spam and scrambled eggs. The waitress put in the order and poured him a cup of coffee without his asking. He held up a hand and shook his head when she offered him cream and sugar.

"You passing through, hon?" she asked.

John took a sip of the strong, bitter brew. "I have business here," he said.

Her eyebrows rose. She laughed. "Business? *Here?* Hon, I've lived in this town 46 years. Ain't nobody ever had 'business' here. *Ain't* no business here 'cept this place, the thrift store down the street, and a few others like that."

"I meant that I am a lawyer," said John. "I am looking into some matters for a client."

She nodded, impressed. "Really? Wow. What kind of case would bring you to this little wide spot in the road?"

"I am not at liberty to say," said John. He was conscious of eyes boring into his back.

The waitress nodded again. "You just got off the train?"

"Yes," said John. "I came up from Mobile."

She smiled. "That accent ain't from Mobile."

The observation flustered him. Forty-eight years he had been in this country, speaking nothing but English, and still, every once in a while, like some phantom haunting a house, whispers of Hungary turned up in his voice. It embarrassed him. "Nevertheless," he said, hating the tone of stiff dignity that had entered his voice, "I have lived in this country almost my entire life."

She looked at him. "I was just makin' conversation, hon."

He dropped his eyes. "I'm sorry," he said. "I meant no offense."

"That's all right," she said.

"It's Budapest."

"Beg pardon?"

"Budapest. That is the city in Hungary where the accent you hear comes from. We sailed to this country when I was 12."

She looked impressed. "Wish I could say I'd been somewhere else," she said. "I was born and raised right here in Kendrick. Furthest I've ever been is Mobile, and that was just the once." She regarded him for a moment. Then she said, "What's your name, hon?"

"John Simon. Although, it was Johan Simek when I was born."

She gave him a sunny smile and offered her hand. "Doris Orange," she said. "It was Doris Baker when *I* was born, but then I went and married that no-account husband of mine."

John shook her hand, returning her smile. He found himself liking her. And somehow, she seemed . . . *familiar*, too. It tickled the rim of his consciousness, a sense that there was something here he was missing. For the life of him, he could not say what it was.

Doris placed his meal in front of him. He sliced a piece of the salty processed pork, forked up some eggs, chewed thoughtfully. Still, the connection would not come. He decided it was simply his imagination. "Doris," he said, after a moment, "I need to hire someone to drive me about 10 miles out into the country. Is there anyone you would recommend?"

"I reckon Amos Hawley would probably do it," she said. "He's got an old Ford truck he could take you in."

"Wonderful. Where do I find Mr. Hawley?"

In response, she called out, "Hey, Travis!" Behind them, the barefoot boy perked up. "Why don't you go see if you can round up Amos Hawley? This fellow here needs a ride. If you hurry up and don't dawdle, I bet he'll give you a dime!"

The boy was out the door before the echoes of her voice faded. She smiled at John. "Hope you don't mind me volunteerin' your money like that," she said. "Figured it would make him move a little faster. And you look like you could afford it."

John lowered the coffee cup he had been sipping from. "It is not a problem," he said.

The boy was back in less than five minutes, breathing heavily. "He said he'll be right along," he announced. John gave him a quarter, and his eyes widened. "Gee, thanks a lot, Mister."

It was as John was settling his bill that the door opened and a tall, rangy man, his face set in what appeared to be a permanent scowl, stepped into the room. "You the fellow wants the ride?" he asked. His voice sounded as if it could cut rock.

"Yes," said John, climbing down from the stool, dabbing at his mouth with a paper napkin.

"Where to?"

John wished the man had not asked. At least, not until they were in the truck. He had not intended on revealing his destination in a room full of curious eyes, would rather have kept that delicate information to himself a few moments longer. But there was no help for it now. Besides, he was probably being overcautious. "As I understand it," he said, "it's a few miles out of town. It is—or at least, it was—the home of a colored family named Hayes."

As soon as he said it, he knew it was a mistake. A veil slipped over the eyes that had watched him with such interest. He glanced back at Doris Orange and saw that even her open face had turned to stone. Something in her expression pitied him.

Silently, John cursed himself. He knew better. But her friendliness, the way she put a stranger at ease, had caused him to lower his guard. No, it had made him *stupid*.

"What you want to go out there for?" one of the men asked.

"I am doing some legal work for a client," said John. He hoped the vague answer would keep them from pressing him. It didn't.

"What the hell client you got that's interested in that old place?" the same man asked. His voice had curdled like old milk.

"I am not at liberty to discuss my client's affairs," said John. He chased it with a smile, trying to disarm the sudden tension. "You understand," he said.

The man looked as if he were about to challenge John further. Then Amos Hawley spoke up. "You payin'?" he asked in his hard voice.

John put on his homburg. "Is three dollars sufficient?" he asked. It was about enough for a tank of gas, assuming of course, that gas could be found.

"More than," said Hawley. "Get your bag. Let's go."

John felt the touch of their eyes as surely as he would have the touch of their hands as he gathered his valise and followed the stranger out to a boxy old truck of indeterminate color. Hawley climbed behind the wheel, John climbed into the passenger seat, and a moment later, the truck was rattling through the town, kicking up a faint plume of dust.

Doris had been right. There was very little "business" here: the thrift store she had mentioned, a market with wilted-looking fruits on a stand out front, a barbershop, a pool hall, all went sliding by his window in short order. The houses were no more impressive, a series of dilapidated shacks, most of them set back from the street as if hiding from it, obscured by an overgrowth of oak trees and Spanish moss. Minutes later, the truck left Kendrick behind, and they found themselves bumping along between fields of cotton and corn, all of them empty now but soon to see the flurry of spring planting. The ride was rough—John didn't think the old truck even had shock absorbers—each jouncing pass in and over the ruts and bumps of the dirt thoroughfare landing like a punch in the kidney. If Amos Hawley felt any of this, he gave no sign. He leaned over the steering wheel, squinting in hard concentration at the road ahead, saying nothing.

It struck John that the landscape they traveled probably hadn't changed much over the years. The view out his window was likely the same one Mason Hayes had seen on that fateful day he spoke impertinently to Floyd Bitters. For that matter, it was likely the same one Hayes's father had seen when he hoed cotton in this place nearly a hundred years before as the property of some white family. In places such as this, change came slowly.

"There it is, yonder."

Hawley's voice broke John's reverie. The truck had come to a stop, and he found himself staring at what had once probably been a loved and well-maintained home. But those days were long gone, as was the front door. Through the empty frame in which it had stood yawned a blackness that made John Simon shiver involuntarily.

The whole place reeked of abandonment. The roof was losing a long battle against gravity, sagging in over the front room, broken beams showing through missing shingles. The remnants of the chimney were scattered in the yard. The carcass of the Model T still lay on its side, though the tires, headlights, and doors had been scavenged over the years. The fence of the animal pen on the left side of the house where, presumably, the fateful hog had once been kept, was broken in several places. Weeds and overgrown grass marched right up to the porch.

John felt sure he knew the answer to his next question, but he had to ask it anyway. "Has anyone been living here over the past 20 years?"

Hawley shook his head. "Used to get squatters from time to time," he said. "Not so much anymore, since the place has gone to ruin."

"I see," said John. He pondered for a moment. Then he said, "May I look around?"

Hawley shrugged, shut off the engine. "Suit yourself," he said. "I'll wait here."

John climbed down from the truck. He proceeded slowly. It was not that he expected ghosts to come whispering up from the soil. He didn't believe in such things. But this patch of land was sanctified by the obscene things to which it had borne witness. That deserved some respect.

The high grass in the yard where the mob had gathered scraped against his pants like a thousand tiny, beseeching hands. The porch where Floyd Bitters had stood let out a heavy groan as it took John's weight. He poked his head into the rectangle of darkness where the door had been, felt the touch of spiderwebs dragging softly across his brow. He brushed them aside impatiently, stepped into the dead house.

For a moment, he was seized by the impossible sense of having been here before. But the familiarity, he knew, was false, a product of having lived with Luther's story for a year now. The sheer horror of it had stunned him when he first heard it. Over the intervening months, that horror had sunk into him, filtered down like water into the very soil of him. Here was the place—the *home*—Luther said his father had worked so hard to provide for his family. Here was the front room where that family had gathered the night Big Floyd hammered at their door. The furniture was long gone—he supposed the grandfather had taken it when the family fled or it had been stolen in the years since. In the dim light entering through the broken roof, he saw the tatters of what had been cheerful wallpaper the color of butter. It was peeling and dirty. The floor was littered with cigarette ends, beer bottles, scraps of paper, a soiled blanket—evidence of the vagrants who had occasionally used this ruin for shelter.

Here was the kitchen where Annie Hayes had fixed meals for her family, the potbellied stove she had used still sitting there waiting for her, though the stovepipe that had once carried its smoke out through the roof lay in pieces on the floor. Here was the room where the boy Luther and his toddler sister had lain with their grandfather on that evil night. Here was the parents' room, and here was the window where the children had crouched. There, through the window, was the front yard where their parents had been tortured and beaten. And there was the tree where they had been hanged and set aflame. That sturdy branch eight feet off the ground was surely the one the killers had used. The tree was bare here in winter, but it would have been full of leaves rustling in the whoosh of hot air rising from below. Below it, overgrown now with high grass, was the spot where the flaming meat sacks that had once been a man and his wife would have fallen.

John Simon stood there for a time, breathing it in. He took a handkerchief from his breast pocket and dabbed carefully at a mud of sweat and dust that had formed on his brow. "*Istenem*," he said softly.

He had seen enough. He walked back through the little house, emerged gratefully onto the front porch, breathed in a deep lungful of air. Then he breathed again. Not even when he had ripped that rubbery-smelling mask off his face after a mustard gas bombardment in France during the Great War had air ever tasted quite as sweet to him. John walked with a quick step back to the car. He passed the fatal tree without looking at it, climbed back into the truck, and slammed the door.

"We may leave now," he said.

Amos Hawley regarded him. "You know what happened here," he said, after a moment.

It was not a question, but John answered it anyway. "Yes," he said. "I know."

"I seen it, you know," said Hawley. He cranked his truck. The engine grumbled to life, and he put it in gear. "Wish I hadn't," he added.

With a lurch, the truck pulled away from the remnants of Mason Hayes's dream. John had hoped seeing the place would inspire him, but it had not. He had been pondering for a year, and he still had no idea how he was going to leverage a prosecutor into bringing charges against the killers. For the first time, John admitted to himself that he might not be able to find a way.

He knew Luther would be furious if that turned out to be the case. After all, he had only agreed to join the Army and fight for a country he hated on John's promise to seek legal satisfaction. But it wasn't as if the boy would come out of this empty-handed. He still held title to the property as the heir of a man who had died intestate. Not that Luther would ever wish to live here again—but surely he would be able to sell the property to some farmer who would probably knock the house down and clear the land for his crops. Luther would realize a decent profit, although the back taxes and fees owed on the place would probably be substantial. Had the state already taken the property over? John made a mental note to check on that when he got back to his office.

"Look like Big Floyd want to see you."

Once again, Amos Hawley's voice lifted him from the well of his own thoughts. The truck was coming to a stop on the dirt road across from Mel's Place. A few of the men who been sitting around inside when he left now stood out in front, flanking a giant of a man whose stomach flopped over his belt as beer foam does the rim of a stein. One of the men was pointing toward the truck. They had been waiting for him to return.

Mystified, John put three one-dollar bills into Hawley's big hand. "As agreed," he said.

He gathered his bag and reached to open the door. Hawley put a hand on his shoulder, and John looked back. "You want to be careful here," Hawley said.

John gave a curt nod to say that he understood. He cursed himself again for the mistake he had made in the diner. But then he reassured himself. Fine, so this Floyd Bitters was not a man to be trifled with. He was a power in this tiny place, probably *the* power. But John Simon, Esq., was a power in his own right and in a town much larger than this. He was not to be trifled with, either. John climbed down from the truck. The big man met him in the middle of the dirt road. He spoke without offering his hand. "So you're the lawyer," he said. A plug of tobacco swelled his cheek. His teeth were limned in brown.

John doffed his hat politely. "I am John Simon, attorney at law, yes," he said. "And you, I take it, are Mr. Bitters."

"That's right. Most folks hereabouts just call me Big Floyd on account of, well . . . I'm big, and also, I run most everything around here worth running." He spat a brown stream into the dirt, then wiped his mouth with his forearm.

"I see. And what might I do for you, Mr. Bitters?" John was standing in the big man's shade. A small knot of people had formed at Bitters's back. John was dimly aware of Amos Hawley behind him, leaning against his truck, arms folded, watching.

"Well, well. He wants to know what he can do for me," Bitters told the laughing crowd. "That's right neighborly of you, John Simon, attorney at law."

"There is something you wish to talk to me about?" asked John.

"Well, now that you mention it, yeah, there is. What's this I hear about you going out to the old Hayes place? What kind of business you got out there, you don't mind my asking?"

"I had to do some research for a client," said John.

"Oh really? Well, what kind of research was this, exactly?"

"I'm afraid I'm not at liberty to say."

Again Floyd Bitters spoke to the crowd. "Did y'all hear that?" he said through a great, guffawing laugh. "He ain't at liberty to say. Y'all think maybe it'd help any if I said pretty please?"

John smiled indulgently at the bullying fool who towered over him. "Mr. Bitters," he began.

He never saw it coming. The change was instant, the wide smile suddenly a snarl of animal rage. Big Floyd's big hand, hard as a two-by-four, came up all at once, and he slapped John powerfully on the side of the face. It was a blow somehow more humiliating than a sock in the jaw, a blow that said he was a fly, he was an *annoyance*; he wasn't even deserving of being hit like a man.

John was lying on the road in his dapper brown suit before he even knew what had happened. Above him, Floyd Bitters roared, "Who the *hell* do you think you are? You come up here in your fancy suit, stirrin' shit up in my town? *My* town?"

The big man brought his foot up and stomped John hard with his muddy boot. John felt something in his chest snap. The foot came up again, but before it could land, some of the men grabbed Big Floyd and wrestled him back a few feet from where John lay writhing in the dirt.

"Come on, Floyd," one of the men said through a nervous laugh, "he's an old man. He's had enough."

"Calm down, Floyd," said another. "Don't want to kill the man."

"Hell I don't!" Big Floyd shook himself loose like a dog shaking off water. He stood there, chest heaving, pointing down at John. "Where you get off coming up here, riling people up about shit that don't concern you? Shit that happened 20 years ago? You a big-city lawyer, think you'd know better. Think you'd know enough to let sleepin' dogs lie."

John Simon heard this through a haze made up of pain, grime, and sweat. His glasses had flown off. He groped for them uselessly. Then Amos Hawley came up from behind and pulled him to his feet. The other man didn't say anything, just pressed the glasses into John's left hand.

John put them on. Through the dust-smudged lenses, he saw Big Floyd standing there, lips curled in a sneer, chest still rising and falling heavily. "Look at you," he said, and his voice brimmed with contempt. "Big-city lawyer." He spat tobacco, called out over his shoulder. "Where's that Doris said he's from?"

"Some place called Budapest," a voice replied.

"Yeah, that's it. That's a kraut city, ain't it? Hell, you're one'a them our boys is over there fightin' right now."

"Budapest . . . " John had to pause. It hurt to breathe. "Budapest," he began again, "is not in Germany. It is in Hungary."

"Hungary?" Big Floyd's brow creased. "Oh, so you're one'a them bohunks, then. One'a them *hunkies*. Either way you look at it, you ain't nothin' but a damn foreigner come in here stirrin' up trouble over matters that's best forgot."

"I am . . ." Again, John had to pause. He gritted his teeth, drew himself up as best he could. "I am an *American*. I have been in this country since 1895."

Big Floyd came forward, and John flinched involuntarily, his forearm pressed against the pain in his side. The other man's voice was a low simmer of menace. "And I say you're a fuckin' *foreigner*," he said. His laugh was soft and nasty. "You come up here in your fancy suit, pretendin' you're a white man. You ain't no white man. You just look like one."

And here was another blow, in its way, more hurtful than the first. Behind his eyes, 48 years went away, and a 12-year-old boy stepped off a ferry from Ellis Island into the tumult of New York City. The boy's ears filled with cacophony. His eyes were crowded by movement. Great towers stared down with majestic indifference to his very existence, and he felt . . . alien, small, unworthy.

Big Floyd reached a hand behind him without looking, and someone put a little rectangle of paper into it. Big Floyd pressed the rectangle into John's chest. "This is a ticket for tomorrow's train. Make sure you have your ass on it, you hear? You get out of my town and don't you come back. I see you around here again and you're going to think that little tap I just give you was a kiss on the cheek."

"It was always my intention to return home by the morning train. I can buy my own ticket."

The big man pushed the ticket on him again. "Let's just say this is my way of makin' sure," he said. "Take it."

John's hand came up and took the ticket. "It shall be as you say," he said. "I will find a room for the night."

"No."

John was stunned. "What do you mean 'no'?"

"You heard me. No one in this town will rent you a room. No one in this town wants you here." A glance over his shoulder. "Ain't that right, boys?" An obedient chorus of affirmations answered him.

"That's right, Floyd."

"Don't nobody want you here, Mister."

"That's tellin' him, Floyd."

Big Floyd Bitters pointed in the direction of the platform. "Get your ass up there and wait on the platform. Southbound train'll be along tomorrow morning at 8:14."

"I can't . . . you can't be serious."

"Oh, I'm dead serious. You think I'm not serious, why don't you test me?"

"That's inhuman. I will freeze."

"Should of thought about that before you come into *my* town pokin' around in shit you got no business messin' in."

A voice piped up from the crowd. "Floyd, come on, now."

Floyd glared behind him, and the voice fell silent. The massive head came back around, and he leveled his finger at John. "I see you in this town again and well . . . seein' as you're so interested in Mason Hayes, I'll just send you to meet him. That's a promise, from me to you. Now go on, bohunk," he growled, "git."

He said it in the way you would shoo a stray dog. For a long moment, John could only stare, open-mouthed. He could not believe this was happening. And he could not believe it was happening to *him*. So he gaped, waiting for some sign that this was all a joke, all some sort of put-on. This man could not be serious, could not force an entire town to turn him out—*him*, the prosperous lawyer, a pillar of Mobile's legal and business communities. But he saw no such sign. He saw only a few ashamed, averted faces and Floyd Bitters's burning eyes.

John swallowed. Without a word, he turned and began the half-mile walk back up to the train platform. His progress was hobbling and slow, his side stabbing him with each step. He held his left arm pressed hard against his ribs. The depot seemed a hundred miles away.

"Hold on, Mister. I'll give you a ride. Least I can do."

John turned hopefully at the sound of Hawley's voice, saw the rangy man opening the door to his truck. Then Big Floyd said, "No you will *not*, Amos Hawley."

Resistance flared in Hawley's eyes. But only briefly. Only for a moment. Then it was extinguished like a candle flame between moistened fingers. Hawley closed the cab of the old Ford with a slam, crossed his arms, and stood there leaning against his truck, glaring sullenly, impotently at nothing.

With a sigh, John turned back to the endless road and continued his shuffling journey up the hill. It occurred to him about halfway up that he had left his valise and his homburg behind. He had a flickering thought of going back for them, but he knew the idea was foolish. He did not have the strength to go all the way back down there and begin again. And even if he did, he was—and this thought disgraced him, unmanned him, but he knew it to be true—scared to face that big man again.

So he walked, each painful step pulling the platform closer to him by just the tiniest of increments. He walked, humiliation burning like acid low in his gut. He walked, pausing every few minutes just to breathe. He knew they were still watching him. He didn't care. He didn't look back. All he wanted was to reach the platform where he could collapse and be alone with his shame.

He walked.

And was it really less than two hours ago he had descended this hill with a spring in his step, nodding at these same people? It had taken him 10 minutes to get down the hill. It was taking him forever to get back up.

He walked. He thought he might throw up. He thought he might collapse. But he walked. Until finally, he grabbed the bannister and slowly, excruciatingly climbed four steps up to the platform. He staggered around the little ticket booth, leaning against it, and there, like an oasis in the desert, was a wooden bench pushed up against the wall. He dropped onto it, lay back upon it. His heart was hammering, great sheets of sweat drained off him, his ribs answered every stray movement with a stab of pain, and his breathing was fast and shallow. There was not enough air. What had happened to the air?

Something was wrong with him. Something had happened when that insane man stomped his chest. He didn't know what it was. All he knew, with a sudden hard clarity, was that he might not survive it. The realization struck John Simon like a bolt of lightning. He could die. He could die right here, lying reclined on this bench in this godforsaken town.

And it spoke to how drained and wasted he was that this realization did not cause him to sit bolt upright, to charge back into that wretched town demanding help, demanding the simple human decency you would extend without a second thought to the most soiled and wretched tramp. But not to him. Not to the foreigner. Not to the hunky.

It was the same thing they had called him on the Ford assembly line in Detroit 30 years ago, the reason he had never bought a Ford and never would. *What is this strange word?* he had wondered. *What does it mean?* And then, of course, the answer had come.

It means you and me are one step below the micks and one step above the niggers.

It had stunned him. This was not what America was supposed to be. This was not the reason his parents had saved for years and they had all endured two weeks, stuffed elbow to elbow and cheek to cheek in the hot, damp bowels of that ship, crossing the Atlantic. This was not what they had expected when they sailed into the harbor of the mighty city and crowded the railing of the ship for a glimpse of the woman holding high her welcoming torch. In America, it was not supposed to matter where you came from—only where you were headed. In America, you were supposed to be able to go as high and as far as your talent and hard work would take you.

So in the end, that word they called him had only become more fuel for the fire that already burned inside him. He had studied obsessively and worked tirelessly to better himself. He had finished high school, put himself through college and law school, passed the bar, become a lawyer, become a wealthy man. But more than that, he had also made himself a man above all reproach. He had been scrupulously honorable in his business dealings. He had gone to the right church, given to the right charities, made himself admired.

And for what? So that an ignorant, bullying, tobacco-chewing loudmouth who held an entire town in his thrall by the force of his violence could swat him like a fly, could stomp him like a roach, could tell him that he was still just what he had been 48 years ago, when he stood on that dock and gazed up in awe at the mighty spires of New York City. Still just a hunky.

He felt as if he had been blind for almost 50 years. He had fooled himself, allowed himself to believe in a fable. But like Saul in the book of Acts, the scales had fallen from John's eyes. For the first time, he thought with unaccustomed bitterness, he now saw his beloved country as it really was.

Lying there, sipping at the air he could not take in too deeply, John made himself a solemn promise. He would have his revenge. He would, indeed, find a way to see this petty tyrant prosecuted for murder. If he survived.

Without meaning to, John closed his eyes.

It was dark when he opened them again. For a long moment, he did not know where he was or what had happened to him. Then he tried to move, and the pain reminded him.

But he was tired of lying on his back, so he gripped the back of the bench, gritted his teeth, and pulled himself upright, grunting with the exertion.

It was cold. The temperature had dropped. John hugged himself uselessly. His breath hung before him in gray puffs of smoke. A light on the platform had come on. Down the hill behind him, he saw the meager lights from the shacks and shanties of Kendrick, people eating their evening meals or listening to Jack Benny or some such on the radio. More likely, he thought, they would prefer the Grand Ole Opry. Fiddle playing and yodeling were probably more to their taste.

John recognized the bitterness and rage of his own thoughts. He didn't care. Above him, endless stars wheeled slowly across the vast, black expanse of heaven. He had never felt more inexpressibly alone.

He tried to pray. He couldn't. How many years had he sat in that church, listening to the sermons, singing from the hymnal? Had he ever believed? George, he knew, believed effortlessly, believed like breathing. It had always filled John with a kind of awed wonder. In that cold moment, he envied his son.

But then, George was good, good in a way John never had been and never would be. It wasn't that John saw himself as a bad man. Rather, he was just a man, a mostly decent man in his own estimation, but a man who also recognized in himself a share of the selfishness and pride that are to be found in most men.

His son, on the other hand, was an uncommonly *good* man—not a perfect man, no, but certainly a good one, better than his father, better than the usual run of men. Being good had always been important to George. He worked at it, worried about it. Indeed, it was because he was good that he had first stood up to his father and joined the Marines. It was because he was good that he was on the other side of the world even now, just evacuated from Guadalcanal, according to a letter they had received only a few days before.

For that matter, it was because George was good that his father was sitting on this bench in the cold. Alone in the darkness, John allowed himself a sour smile. It occurred to him that someday he would like to meet this Thelma Gordy who was, ultimately, the cause of all his present misery. He would like to see the woman who had inspired his good son to such heights of nobility and sacrifice.

Obviously, George felt some connection with her. It was too bad, thought John, that she was a Negress. Not that it would matter at this point, he supposed. Not after John had sacrificed his son to the foolish dream of being accepted by the likes of Floyd Bitters. *Ach*, what had he done? He had bullied George into a marriage the boy did not want, shackled him to a woman he did not truly love, all to satisfy his own aspirations.

"Sylvia Osborn," he had said with such smug certainty, "was born the right kind of white. Marry her and no one will ever dare to call your children—my grandchildren—'hunky.' No one will ever be able to say they are just a step above the niggers. No one will ever question whether they are American—and white."

Had he ruined George's life?

John wept.

Then he heard the scraping of feet. His heart spiked. Someone was mounting the stairs to the platform. But it was—he checked his watch— 8:32 in the evening. The train would not be along for another 12 hours. What was anyone doing up here at this hour? Was it Bitters, come to finish what he had started?

John tensed. But the figure that appeared from around the ticket booth was not even a man. As she came into the circle of light, John recognized Doris Orange. She was wearing a woolen coat and toting packages he could not quite make out.

"Thought you might want these back," she said. And she placed his valise and his homburg on the bench next to him.

"I . . . thank you," he said in a voice touched by wonder.

"Brung you some other stuff, too." A blanket landed on his lap. A paper sack landed on the blanket. "Sandwiches in there," she said, nodding at the sack. And she placed a thermos on the bench next to him. "Hot coffee," she told him. "Ought to get you through."

"Thank you," he said again. "You are . . . most kind."

"Appreciate if you leave the blanket and the thermos here on the bench when the train comes. I'll pick them up in the morning on the way to work."

"Yes," he said, "I will. Thank—"

She held up her hand, stopping him. "Big Floyd had no call doing what he done," she said, "treating you that way. No call at all. He's a bully, always has been, and everybody around here knows it, but don't nobody have the guts to stand up against him, includin' me. But you? You come up here, re- mindin' people of what happened almost 20 years ago? What did you think they was going to do? How did you think they was going to react?"

John shook his head. "I suppose I didn't think at all," he said.

"Ain't that the damn truth," she said, and there was heat in her voice. "Most people round here, they just been tryin' to *forget* about all that. And here you come, all la-di-da in your fancy suit, just rippin' the scabs off the wounds like it ain't nothin'."

And all at once, he knew why she had seemed so familiar to him. John spoke carefully. "Your name is Orange," he said. He winced with the pain of breathing. "I was told that one of the participants in . . . what happened . . . had that same name. He was a boy."

She lowered her eyes. Her face tightened. "My son Jeffrey," she said. "He was nine. I was there, too. So was my youngest, my daughter Nina. My idiot husband . . . " A pause. She looked away into the darkness on the other side of the tracks. She breathed. "He wanted us to see," she said.

"How awful," said John.

Her eyes came back around. They glittered with some mingling of sorrow, defiance, and tears. "Don't get me wrong," she said. "I don't be- lieve no nigger is equal to me. Never have, never will. And I know they have to be kept in their places, otherwise they'll overrun us. They'll be runnin' things and we'll be the niggers. We can't have that. But . . . "

Another pause. She shook her head. "Floyd ain't had to do what he done. Ain't none of us had to do it. Them poor people, that man and that woman, them babies, they wasn't doin' nothin', they wasn't both- erin' nobody. It wasn't necessary to do what we done. Floyd just wanted to do it, is all. Over a damned hog. He ruined this place when he did that. He ruined us all."

There was a moment. John thought again of how he had come strid- ing into this town, buoyed by his own presumptions. And he thought of how he had left it, how he had slunk from view, slapped down like a bug, brutally dispossessed of those same delusions and presumptions, of the idea that he would ever truly be anything other than the hunky foreigner.

So be it, he thought. *So be it.*

Sitting there on that bench, he reiterated a private vow. No matter how long it took, no matter how much it cost, no matter the lengths to which he had to go, he would see Floyd Bitters pay for all that he had done.

Doris Orange spoke with forced brightness. "Well," she said, buttoning her coat, "I got to go. You should be all right up here now. Don't forget to leave my stuff on the bench. And . . . John . . . " She paused, and he felt her searching for what she was going to say.

"Yes?"

"For your own sake, don't ever come up here again."

She turned to go. "Doris," he called. She looked around. "My name is Johan, remember? Johan Simek."

She looked as if she didn't understand. Then she looked as if she were too weary to care. She simply nodded, and a moment later, he heard her footsteps descending the stairs.

He opened the paper bag. He had not realized until this moment how hungry he was. He unwrapped a sandwich and, with effort, poured a cup of steaming coffee from the thermos.

Johan Simek took a big bite of his sandwich. Spam and cheese. It was the best thing he had ever eaten. Chewing thoughtfully, wincing occasionally from the pain, he leaned back against the bench, ready to wait out the night.

eighteen

GEORGE WILLED HIMSELF TO ABSOLUTE STILLNESS. HE HEARD Japanese troops moving about in the trees on the far side of the field. Then he was running for all he was worth, breath coming shallow and fast. And then he fell heavily into the kunai grass, tripped up by a tree root. Even as he fell, the sky exploded above him, shards of it raining down.

"Come on, Saint! Move your ass!" Lieutenant Colonel Phipps bounded easily over the tree root that had felled George.

When George didn't move, Phipps stopped and turned. "You want to die here? Move it, goddamn you!"

But that wasn't right, was it? Hadn't Prescott Phipps died in a fire-fight on Guadalcanal? George hesitated, but Phipps wasn't having it. "Move your ass, private! That's an order!"

So now George scrambled to his feet, and Phipps smiled at him and patted his shoulder in a manner that was almost tender. "There you go, George," he said, and somehow, Phipps's face was now Father's face. "There you go. Nothing to it."

Then he exploded. A spray of his blood splashed George's face. Chips of his bones nicked George's cheek.

"Come on, Saint! Move your ass!" Lieutenant Colonel Phipps bounded over the tree root that had felled George. "The Japs are coming! The Japs are coming!"

George looked behind and saw them, materializing from the trees. That is, they were not walking out from the trees, but rather, the trees were *producing* them, the Japs somehow appearing out of them. Each had a skull where his face should have been.

"Come on, Saint! You want to die here?" Tank Sheridan rode by on a horse.

But George could not move. He was rooted to the spot. Somehow, he had grown there like a tree. He had been there since the beginning of time, and he always would be. On the Japs came, their skeletal faces locked in vicious grins, bullets whining through the air, the sky exploding and exploding and exploding.

"It don't mean a thing if it ain't got that swing!" Jazzman ran up to him, his face flushed and eager. Somehow, Randy was playing a full set of drums while running and firing back at the Japs behind him. The drums made a harsh, arrhythmic sound, punctuated by a sibilant crashing of the cymbals.

"Jazzman! We got to get out of here!"

"Fine and mellow!" said Jazzman.

"Run!"

"T'ain't what'cha do, it's the way hot'cha do it," said Jazzman.

"Shut up and run!" And somehow, George got first one of his rooted legs and then the other to tear loose from the soil of Guadalcanal. He grabbed Randy's hand—somehow, Randy had a free hand though he was still shooting behind them, still playing drums—and pulled him on through the high grass, stumbling and clumsy like the rusted Tin Man of Oz, the Japs close behind, their skull jaws clicking, the bullets buzzing all around him like angry bees and the sky shattering and falling, lacerated by Jap mortars. Yet they were making it, they were getting away, and then all of a sudden, something lurched—it was as though existence itself changed its posture, moved in its seat to get a better view—and the Japs were gone and the bullets no longer droned past and the sky was just the sky again and the world was silent and you could see that the island, when no one was shooting at you and you were not in terror of your life, was actually a beautiful, peaceful place, and he was so happy, so brimming with joy, so thankful to God and he realized all at once that he still held Jazz's hand tight in his own so he looked back and he looked down and . . .

and . . .

. . . he saw that he was just pulling a piece of Randy Gibson through the kunai, just an arm, a head, and three-quarters of a torso, all of it ripped and shredded and red with blood. Organs and broken bones hung from the ruined chest. One side of Jazzman's face was simply gone, a quarter of his skull cleaved away, yet his brain, when George looked in, was some-how pink and . . . breathing inside. When George looked behind them, he saw that Randy's drum kit lay scattered and broken all over the field. And somehow, that was the worst sight of all.

George wept. "Oh, Randy, I'm so sorry," he said.

Randy looked at him, his ruined face grinning. "You plays how you is," he said. "You plays how you is."

"Hey, you want to pipe down over there?"

Someone else cried, "Tryin' to get some sleep here, for Chrissake!"

Someone was screaming. It was an unmanly shriek, raw with pain.

Only belatedly did George realize that the cries were coming from him. He clamped a hand over his mouth, staring wildly around for Jazzman or, at least, the shredded remains of him that had somehow ani-mated themselves and spoken to him as he was standing in the kunai. But Jazzman wasn't there. George wasn't there. It had been . . .

So real.

A dream.

He sat up, breathing heavily, as reality drifted slowly back into place. The morning sun stabbed his eyes. George screwed them more tightly shut, but it didn't help, so he turned over to escape the light.

Moving was a mistake. Nausea rolled through him like an ocean wave. He leaned over the edge of his bunk, trying to breathe past the queasiness. All at once, his hand leapt to his mouth and with a great, raw "*Hrrrk!*" he filled it with a lumpy, milky mixture that smelled of whiskey and gone-sour meat. The overflow splattered the concrete below. The retching, in turn, freshened the headache thudding through his skull.

Lifting himself slowly from his bunk, George brought his eyes open to survey the mess in his hand. He looked helplessly about for something to wipe it on, considered his own dungarees, settled for a days-old copy of the *Age*, a Melbourne newspaper, lying atop his seabag. His mouth tasted like cotton and vomit.

"Well, well, if it ain't Saint George, back among the living at last. It's a miracle, I tell ya."

Babe was coming back from the showers, toothbrush in hand. He gazed down at George with a thin, contemptuous grin. "Thought we were done for last night when you decided to fight the whole Aussie army by yourself. I like breakin' up a joint as much as the next guy, but that was suicide. Lucky thing that hotel had a back exit, else you'd be waking up in the stockade this mornin', probably with a black eye. My luck, I'd be wakin' up right next to you, even though the only thing I did was try to stop you from gettin' your ass kicked."

The words brought back flimsy memories. A hotel bar. A furious, ruddy-faced Aussie sergeant. Glass shattering. Pandemonium. Running for all he was worth. Laughing wildly.

"He had it coming," grumbled George.

"Hell he did," said Babe. "All he did was say rugby was a tougher game than football. That's a reason to have a friendly argument. It's not a reason to throw a man's beer in his face and call him a kangaroo-fucker. Especially since he wasn't talking to you in the first place. You tryin' to start another riot?"

The marines and the Aussie troops had staged a massive brawl in the streets of Melbourne back in February. "No," said George. "Tell you the truth, I don't remember any of it."

"Maybe that's a sign you should cut back on the hooch."

George bristled. "My mother is nine thousand miles away," he snapped, "and I don't need another one."

"Just lookin' out for you, Saint. That's what buddies are supposed to do, ain't it? Buddies look out for each other, don't they? They back each other up. And they sure as shootin' don't steal from each other. Right, Saint?"

Four months they'd been here and Babe—who usually never held a grudge—was still sour that George had stolen the Jap skull from his seabag and heaved it overboard as the marines were being evacuated from Guadalcanal.

"Stop calling me that," George said, closing his eyes again and holding two fists to his throbbing forehead.

He had never been much of a drinker. A couple of beers, that was his limit. Or at least, it always had been. But it took more than a couple beers to silence the ghosts of Guadalcanal.

It was as if Babe had read his thoughts. "You still havin' those dreams?"

"Don't want to talk about it," said George.

"Wouldn't be like you were the only one."

Babe was trying to sound sympathetic, but George wasn't fooled. "Don't want to talk about it," he repeated.

"Fine. You ain't got to talk to me, buddy boy, but you should probably talk to somebody. Maybe go see the chaplain?"

"Yeah, maybe I will," said George, knowing he wouldn't. The very idea was ridiculous. If he couldn't talk to Babe about it, how could he talk to some priest? How could you begin to make somebody who wasn't there understand what you were going through? What could you say to that person? What could he say to you?

And the last person he felt like talking to was a chaplain. George hadn't been able to get himself into a church since he'd arrived in Australia. He had tried to open his Bible several times but always stopped reading after a couple verses. Something had shifted in him. He didn't know what it was. All he knew was that it seemed like another man in another life who had once been able to open that book and find solace there for all the wounds and transgressions of living. George was no longer that man and this was no longer that life.

I feel like I'm drowning.

He had written that—*confessed* it—in a letter to Thelma Gordy. It was something he couldn't say to his parents or siblings, and Lord knew he couldn't say it to his wife. Upon his return to the world, he had written each of them, brightly assuring them that he was well and having a fine old time of it as the marines recuperated in Melbourne. He had shielded them from the truth.

But somehow, that truth had poured out of him in a letter to a Negro woman he barely knew. He had told her about Guadalcanal and what it had done to him, body and soul. Maybe, he thought, it was the very fact that she *was* a Negro woman—someone he knew but someone who was not close to him, someone who could never be close to him—that made revealing himself to her seem . . . safe.

I feel like I'm drowning, and I don't know what to do.

"So if you won't go see the chaplain," Babe was saying, "how do you plan to spend this fine Saturday? Might not be a good idea for you to go runnin' around the city by yourself. You could run into that big Aussie sergeant again."

"It's a big city. I'll be fine."

"You sure?" Babe was buttoning one of the army jackets the Aussies had donated to replace the soiled and rotting dungarees the marines were wearing when they arrived. On his shoulder was the diamond-shaped unit patch the Corps had issued veterans of Guadalcanal—five stars in the shape of a Southern Cross on a field of blue. In the center was a red "1" with the island's name spelled out vertically down its length. That patch was good for free drinks all over Melbourne, but George hadn't gotten around to sewing his on yet.

"No thanks," said George.

"All right, have it your way. See you later."

And Babe climbed the steps toward what had been the concourse of the Melbourne Cricket Ground. The marines had been billeted in the stands of the stadium, the seats removed and replaced with bunk beds, each with two long and two short legs to fit over the risers. The open side of the stands facing the grassy field had been covered with a plywood wall, but it fell about eight feet short of the roof, a gap that allowed for ventilation. It also allowed the men to be drenched by rain—and stabbed by sunlight.

George rose from his bunk with a grunt. He used the sports section of the *Age* to wipe up the overflow of his vomit, fixed himself a Bromo-Seltzer, drank it down in one long pull, popped four aspirin in his mouth, and went to take a shower. Half an hour later, his red eyes protected by sunglasses from the merciless sun, he boarded a streetcar, taking a seat on a side-facing bench. He had some vague idea of going to see a movie, maybe getting some chow once his stomach settled.

As the streetcar went clattering down the broad, bustling avenue, he leaned his head back against the window and closed his eyes. The aspirin had not been nearly enough to quell the ferocious pounding of his skull.

Even so, George was in a decent mood, all things considered. Four months after his arrival, it still made him almost giddy to go into town. Unless you had spent months in that godforsaken jungle, he thought, you could never really appreciate what it meant to be in civilization, where you could ride a streetcar, go to a dance, have a meal in a restaurant, just as the spirit moved you.

Maybe, he thought, if he were here long enough, he would get used to that again, take it for granted again. Maybe the horror haunting him would become dulled and he would come to feel like a human being again.

Then a child's voice broke through that hope like a rock through a window. "Were you on Guadalcanal, Yank?"

George opened his eyes. Two boys, probably no more than 10 or 12 years old, were leaning forward, staring at him with worshipful intensity. A woman in a hat patted one of them on the back. He was a rust-haired kid with a constellation of freckles on his cheeks. "Peter, leave the man alone," she said.

Peter ignored her. "Were you there?" he insisted.

George nodded. "I was there," he said.

"Did you see any Japs, Yank? Did you kill any Japs?"

"Yeah."

"Tell us about it."

"No."

"Aw, don't be like that, Yank."

"Yeah," the second boy chimed in, "don't be like that, Yank. Tell us what it was like."

George looked to the woman, waiting for her to restrain them, waiting for her to tell them they had no business badgering a stranger who only wanted to be left alone. But the woman, he realized, had admonished her boys only as a perfunctory courtesy. Like them, she was gazing toward him with hungry curiosity.

They wanted stories. They didn't know what they were asking for. Was he some kind of exotic entertainer, there to regale them with tales of heroic derring-do?

It had not been heroic, it had been . . . worse than hell. And he was no fucking entertainer here for their fucking amusement.

They wanted a story? Fine. He would tell them a story.

"We didn't take prisoners," he said. "We had thought we would, but what we didn't understand at first was that the Jap wasn't playing by our rules, the so-called civilized rules. The Jap didn't capture our boys. He slaughtered them even after they surrendered. And he mutilated the corpses. You know, to send a message."

The woman said, "Blimey," and brought her hand to her mouth.

George nodded. "Yeah," he said, "*blimey*. Anyway, this one day, we were sent out to look for a missing patrol. We found them, all right. Found them in a field, all very dead. But that wasn't the worst part. No, the worst part was that the Japs posed the corpses for us. Most of the men had been castrated. Maybe you boys don't know that word. That's when they cut off your penis and your testicles." He made his hands a scissors. "Snip, snip," he said.

"That's enough," the woman said. Her voice was fluttery, and she had her hands over one boy's ears.

George ignored her. "They cut 'em off and they stuffed them into the men's mouths, you see? And then they cut off their heads." George made a slicing motion across his throat. "And so, we found our guys sitting there with their heads on their laps, their dicks in their mouths, their eyes wide open."

"Young man, please . . . " The woman was pleading. Again George ignored her.

"So my friend, Babe, he gets mad at this. We all do. But Babe, he finds this Jap lying in the grass and he's been wounded, but he's not dead." George gave a mirthless chuckle. "Babe wants revenge, so he chops off this guy's head. It's pretty messy business. I mean, it's easy enough cutting through all the muscle and tissue here," said George, touching the wide-eyed boy on the side of the neck. "But soon enough, he hits the bone"— George poked the boy's neck with a stiff finger—"and that takes a little more work . . . "

"Yank . . . "

"He's got to pull the head way back to open up the vertebrae, then he saws it with his knife. But pretty soon, he's through, and the Jap's head pops off, pretty as you please, and old Babe, he has himself a bona fide trophy of war. The rest of us are hoping to collect Jap guns and pins off their uniforms and stuff like that, but Babe, he has himself a Jap's actual *head*. Only thing is, he's got to figure out a way to take the skin off, you see? Otherwise, it's going to start to rot, especially in that jungle heat. So he takes the thing back with him and he plops it in this old fuel drum full of boiling water, trying to loosen up the skin so that he can—"

"That's *enough*, Yank! You've made your bleedin' point."

George looked up and saw a beefy workingman glaring down on him. His cheeks were flushed, and his eyes were filled with horror. The whole streetcar was staring. George would have sworn even the wheels clattering on the tracks had gone silent.

"What kind of sick sod are you," the man demanded, "to tell a story like that to children? They're nothin' but *boys*, man."

George shrugged his indifference. "They asked me," he said. "They shouldn't have asked me."

And he closed his eyes, leaned his head back, and listened to the drumming of his skull as the city flowed around him. He could feel their eyes on him. He told himself he didn't care. He had saved their nation. He had saved their very lives. Who were they to judge him? Just accept the salvation he had provided and be glad for it. And don't ask him any damn questions.

George opened his eyes. The freckled boy was watching him, his eyes awed, frightened, and somehow also abashed.

Stop looking at me like that, kid. It was a stupid question.

But still the boy stared.

George stood up on a sudden impulse, brushed past the mother and her children, and hopped off the still-moving streetcar. Their eyes followed him. He was still well short of his stop, but he could not be on that trolley anymore. He would rather hoof it than sit there across from that damn staring kid.

He crossed to the sidewalk, paused to get his bearings, and then stopped.

He was standing in the shadow of a church. It was a massive edifice, stairs leading up from the sidewalk to three arched doorways. Over the door in the center was a cross, with a statue of a mournful, dying Jesus hanging there. His doleful eyes caught George's.

In another place and time, George knew he would have taken it as a comfort, coming upon this fortress of Heaven in the valley of his doubt. He would have taken it as a sign from the divine, a reminder that whatever comes, God is still nigh.

But here and now, what once might have been a comfort felt only like a taunt, a mocking reminder of something that had once been open to him but now felt closed, felt locked and gone.

"You all right there, son?"

A priest had stopped on the stairs and was looking back at him. Only then did George realize that he was weeping.

He shrugged. "I don't know, Father," he said. "I really don't."

The priest took a step. "Son, why don't you . . . "

George held up a hand to stop him. Then he hurried away, before the priest could ask him any questions.

nineteen

SHE STOOD IN THE BOW OF THE BOAT, WATCHING THE ISLAND approach. It was a warm day in May, and the light spray of river water felt good on her brow. Thelma was sweating beneath the heavy protective gear she had to wear while pressure-spraying zinc chromate and gray paint onto the bulkheads. Glancing back, she saw the brand-new destroyer on which she had spent the morning growing smaller behind her. As always, a sense of accomplishment crowded out any fatigue.

Thelma wondered idly what was in store for "her" latest boat. Was it bound for the Pacific to shell some island held by the Japs? Would it protect a convoy ferrying troops to Great Britain or join the fight to push the Germans out of North Africa? As always, it fascinated Thelma to think something she had touched, some machine that carried her fingerprints and her labor, would go to such far-flung places.

She was the only Negro on this crew, and she stood apart from the other painters, carpenters, and electricians who had worked on the ship. They chattered idly with one another. She kept to herself and did not speak, knowing she would not be welcome. Thelma had never been close with any of them, but until recently, she might have nodded or laughed along with some of the pass-the-time-of-day talk, as the little boat trundled across the waves. But since Ollie's beating, white and colored had hardly spoken to one another in this yard, had said nothing that was not required in the ordinary course of work.

Hand me that wrench.

Tell the electrician he can get in here now.

Go paint the bulkheads on the main deck.

Otherwise, each regarded the other with suspicious eyes and silence.

Sometimes, she overheard white people talking about the colored workers in the yard. She never caught more than snatches of it, but it was more than enough to get the gist. She heard words like "uppity" and "out their places" and "white man's work."

It wasn't just because of what happened to Ollie. The yard had grown tense over the demand that colored workers be allowed access to skilled work. It was a demand that had the muscle and authority of the federal government behind it, but the white men could not have been less impressed.

"No nigger will ever join steel in this yard and I don't care what some Yankee sombitch in Washington says about it!" She had heard one of the white men bray this to the retreating back of an official from the Fair Employment Practices Committee as the government man left a meeting in the administration building. The FEPC official had affected not to hear the angry taunt. The man who yelled it had his back slapped by the men standing with him.

"That's tellin' him, Lou!" one of them had cried, laughing.

Then the one named Lou had turned and seen her looking. He had spat on the ground and fixed her with a hard stare. Thelma had hurried on. Though they had little use for any of their Negro coworkers, white people regarded her with a special bitterness now because they knew that somehow, she and Flora Lee had become friends. Flora Lee, they assumed, was simply not right in the head; this was probably the reason her husband was so hard on her.

But it was for Thelma that they reserved their greatest ire. In presuming to reciprocate Flora Lee's ill-advised friendship, she had upset the established order of things. She had forgotten her place.

A white woman and a colored woman? Friends? Not "friendly," which would have been bad enough, but *friends*? They seemed baffled by the very notion. Not that Thelma blamed them. She was confused by it herself.

Thelma's earliest years had been scarred by white people's murderous cruelties. She knew how things worked. And one of the things she knew was that black and white did not mix. They simply did not. You cooked their meals, you tended their children, you cleaned their houses. And yes, some randy white man with an itch in his pants might occasionally go trolling for a colored woman.

But even then, the limits of the relationship were set in stone. Black people served and serviced white ones. They did not befriend them.

Yet somehow, thought Thelma as the ferryman lined the little boat up with the dock, that was precisely what she had done. Without meaning to, without even knowing she was doing it, she had allowed this white woman to become her friend.

What was it with her and white people all of a sudden? Bad enough she had opened up to one of them about the awful day she lost her baby. Bad enough she was corresponding with him, trying to keep his spirits up after the ordeal he had endured on an island called Guadalcanal. Now she had actually taken one of them into her home and imperiled everyone around her in the process. Luther would be scandalized—and with reason. Where was her loyalty to her own? Where was her loyalty to the mother and father she could just barely recall?

What was she supposed to do, though? They needed her, both of them. Being white, with all the power and advantage that entailed, had not been enough to save them from having to open themselves up to her, a colored woman living on a dirt street. They needed her. Thelma didn't know how to walk away from that. Flora Lee had been at her house for a month now. That first night, after the lawn had cleared of people, after the door had closed and it was just the three of them at the table, had been so . . . awkward. To Thelma, it had felt as if a spotted horse had wandered in and sat down with them for dinner and she and her grandfather were pretending not to notice. Gramp, who customarily filled the dinner conversation with commentary about what he had heard on the news interspersed with inquiries about Thelma's day, complaints about her working, and cantankerous observations on the quality of Izola Foster's cooking, had somehow become someone else. This new Gramp was soft-spoken and solicitous, said things like, "Granddaughter, would you please pass the salt?" or "It's probably time you got an oil change on your car."

He had even smiled at her. Gramp never smiled at anyone.

For her part, Flora Lee had prattled on with a ceaseless nervous energy, talking about the president and the war and life back home and how nice Thelma's neighbors were and how much she appreciated being taken in like this and how she would be no bother at all and how she would get out and look for her new job first thing tomorrow and how she would find her own place just as soon as she was practically able, though she expected that would be difficult since housing was so hard to come by during wartime and she might not be able to get into any of the new federal housing because she was a single woman now and they'd probably want to save that precious space for families, but maybe if she and two or three other women got together, they might be able to find something.

Thelma had listened with wordless wonder to this chattering new Flora Lee and this polite new Gramp. It struck her that each was meeting a version of the other, created and presented in response to this extraordinary circumstance of a white woman eating fried chicken at a colored table. Thelma didn't know how to say this, so she said almost nothing. But she wished Flora Lee would hush up and Gramp would complain about her working.

Finally, the interminable dinner had ended. They had listened to the radio for a while until Thelma sent her grandfather off to bed. Then it had been just her and Flora Lee standing together in the front room.

"Sorry, but I ain't got no room to myself," she had told Flora Lee as she pulled the blanket on the rope across to separate the front room from the kitchen space. "I sleep in here on the floor. I'll get you some blankets, make up a pallet. When you need to bathe, they's an old tub we keep out in the back. You just boil you some water in the kitchen there and let Gramp know so he don't come wanderin' through. He can't see nothin', but . . . you know, it just wouldn't be right, him bein' in there while you washin'. And the privy's out yonder. Take a lantern and watch out for the snakes."

Thelma had been embarrassed by her own words. She had never felt the meagerness of her life quite so keenly as she had at that moment.

Flora Lee had stood there looking around. Then she had shrugged and said, "Just like how it was at home."

Thelma had regarded her for a moment. She hadn't thought of it that way. "Come on," she said. "I got pajamas you can sleep in. Might be a little big for you, but they'll do."

A few minutes later, after they had prepared themselves for bed and were lying head to head in the darkness listening to the night coalesce about them, Flora Lee said, "Thelma, you still awake?"

"Yeah."

"I just wanted you to know how grateful I am for what you done for me."

"You can stop thanking me, Flora Lee."

There was gravity in Flora Lee's voice. "Don't think I'll ever stop thanking you, Thelma," she said.

Crickets chirped. The darkness was complete, except for a streak of moonlight that entered through the window where the curtains did not quite join.

Flora Lee said, "Thelma?"

"Yeah?"

"I just realized: I ain't got nothin' to wear."

"Oh, my goodness. I hadn't thought about that."

"Maybe you could pick up my check for me on Friday? And Saturday, if you don't mind, could you take me to buy some clothes? I suppose I could go back and ask Earl for my clothes, but ... "

Thelma cut her off. "Sure, Flora Lee, I'll take you."

"It's gon' really be somethin'," said Flora Lee, "first time in my life, havin' my own money. Ain't sure I can do it. When I got paid at the shipyard, I used to give that money to Earl and let him handle it."

"You can do it," Thelma assured her. "I been doin' it for years, so I know you can. My brother Luther always give me his money, let me do the bill payin'. He still send most of his money home."

Flora Lee spoke with trepidation. "Is that hard to do, handlin' the money?"

"Well, you learn how to do it and you get used to it. It might throw you at first, but after a while you'll see ain't nothin' to it. And why shouldn't you handle the money? It's yours, ain't it? You the one sweated for it."

"Yeah," said Flora Lee. "It is, ain't it?" She giggled in the darkness at this revelation. It made her sound so young. "I been thinkin' 'bout what I might do, now I'm not with Earl Ray and got a little money of my own. You know what I'd like? I'd like to get me a house all my own, with more'n two, three rooms, an' the privy indoors. That's what I want. You ever think about that? Save your money and maybe rent you one of them nice places up on Gov'ment Street?"

"I can't do that, Flora Lee."

"Why not?"

Thelma sighed, reminded herself that Flora Lee didn't know any better. "'Cause they don't rent them places to colored," she said.

There was an awkward silence. Then Flora Lee spoke in a mortified voice. "Oh. Oh, I'm sorry. I didn't think ... "

"It's all right."

Pause.

"No, it ain't," said Flora Lee.

"It ain't what?"

"It ain't all right. That was a stupid question."

"You just wasn't thinkin', Flora Lee. That's all."

"It ain't fair, you know. Them sayin' you can't have one'a them nice houses 'cause you colored? It ain't fair."

She said this as though the realization would be as new to Thelma as it was to her. It made Thelma smile in the darkness. "I know," she said, "but that's the law."

"Yeah," said Flora Lee, "I guess so. But hell, Mobile ain't the only town in Alabam'. And Alabam' ain't the only state in the country."

"You mean . . . leave?" The idea was so outlandish it gave Thelma an odd, quavery feeling just speaking it.

"Why not?"

"I got Gramp to think of. Who gon' take care of him?"

Flora Lee said, "Thelma, I ain't tryin' to be cruel, but you done told me yourself he over a hundred years old. How much longer you think you gon' have to take care of him? You still young, just like me. I don't know about you, but this war and workin' at this shipyard, they done let me see they's a great big world out there I never knowed nothin' about. And I been thinkin': why shouldn't I go have a look-see for myself? Why shouldn't *you*?"

Thelma groped for an answer. She did not like the unsettled feeling this kind of talk gave her, the way it took her to some unexplored space, untethered from everything she had ever known. "I just can't," she finally said, as much to Flora Lee as to herself.

And something about her own answer had disappointed her. Had she somehow, without even knowing it, become a tree, rooted and immovable, tied to the very soil of Mobile, Alabama? The memory of that thought pushed a private, unintended sigh out of Thelma now as the ferry tied up and she stepped off onto Pinto Island in a crowd of workers. Flora Lee had begun snoring softly a few moments later, but Thelma had lain awake for hours, grappling with her friend's question and her own disappointing answer.

I just can't.

But why couldn't she? Why?

Thelma was so enwrapped in her own thoughts that she did not even notice him at first, waiting there at the dock. And when she did, she stopped short, something electric vibrating through her breastbone.

She had seen Earl Ray Hodges only a few times since the day Flora Lee had left him. Each time, he had stared meaningfully after her, and it had given her a fluttery feeling in the pit of her stomach and made her walk a little faster across the yard.

"You be careful of him," Flora Lee told her, almost every day.

And she always nodded and said she would, but how could she really do that, in a shipyard teeming with so many thousands of people, all going this way and that? In such a crowd, how you could you guard against encountering one man? There was no way. Thelma had resigned herself to the fact that eventually, and no doubt at a time and place of his choosing, their paths would cross. And now, too soon, here he was.

He wasn't the preening rooster of a man he once had been. In just a few weeks without his wife, Earl Ray had changed dramatically. His clothes looked as if he had been sleeping in them. A two-day growth of hair fringed his chin. Gray half-moons cupped his eyes. And those eyes were . . . forlorn.

"What you done with her?" he demanded, without preamble. "You got to tell me, nigger. Bible say you can't come between a man and his wife. What God done put together, don't nobody put asunder. You believe in the Bible, don't you?"

"I don't know where she is," Thelma said, too quickly.

In fact, three nights after moving in, Flora Lee had come home with the triumphant announcement that she had been hired to work in the cafeteria at Brookley Army Airfield, south of town. Earl Ray appraised Thelma now with speculative eyes, and she might have sworn he read this information right off her face. "Uh huh," he said. "Uh huh. Well, I think you lyin' to me, nigger. I think you do know. What do you say to that, huh?"

"I got to go," she said, eyes scanning the shipyard to see who might be taking note of this confrontation over by the ferry docks. But people moved back and forth between the slips and the buildings without paying them any attention.

He must have spied her panic. He held up his hands. "Just hold on a minute," he said. His tone had changed. Something sad, something that in another man's face might have registered as pleading, came into Earl Ray's expression then. "Don't you understand, nigger? She's my wife. I can't be separated from her. I just can't. I need her."

"I can't help you," said Thelma, attempting to step past him.

He grabbed both her shoulders roughly, put his face close to hers. "I *need* her," he repeated in a hiss.

And this much, at least, seemed beyond dispute. It had not occurred to Thelma until that very second that for all his violence and temper, Earl Ray might, in his cramped and hateful way, actually love his wife.

Not that it mattered. "I done told you twice," she said, trying to make her voice firm, "I don't know where she is."

He said, "Please, nigger"—and Thelma wondered for a disbelieving instant if this fool actually thought "nigger" was her given name—"just tell her I forgive her. Will you do that? Tell her she can come home. Tell her . . . " A pause. He bit his lip. Something glistened in his mad eyes. "Tell her I miss her," he said.

"Get away from me," said Thelma. A tremor had entered her voice. "Leave me alone!"

She didn't wait for a response. She wrenched her shoulders free, pushed him off her, then walked away with a quick step. She had to resist an urge to run.

"This ain't over," he called. "She belong with me! Make sure you tell her that, y'hear? She belong with me!"

Thelma would tell Flora Lee no such thing. It would only frighten her and make her fret, and what good would that do? Flora Lee had a new job, had already consulted a lawyer, and had been talking happily about what she was going to do with her life once she was free of Earl Ray. After that first awkward night, life in the little house on Mosby Street had settled back into a recognizable routine—Gramp had stopped smiling so much and was back to complaining about Izola Foster's cooking—and Thelma saw no reason to disrupt that by bringing Earl Ray Hodges back into the picture.

What could anybody do about it, except worry? And what use was that?

Thelma's legs trembled as they carried her away.

She stored her gear in her locker, stood in line at the cafeteria for fried fish and French fries, then took her meal out to the table in the colored section where she and the girls usually ate. To her surprise, no one was there except Laverne, balancing a tray of pork chops and cabbage. "Come on," she said, "we eatin' outside today."

Thelma was mystified. "Why?" she asked, following Laverne to the door.

Laverne shrugged. "Ollie and some of the mens wanted to have a meetin' of the colored workers," she said. "All I know."

The picnic tables out back of the cafeteria were seldom used. They were weather-beaten and paint-stripped. To sit on them was to pick up wood splinters that poked you through your clothing. Most people forgot they were even here. That, Thelma supposed, made them an ideal place to meet if you wanted privacy.

Ollie was standing with one foot on a bench when they approached. He had been in deep consultation with some of the other men, but he looked up at the sound of them.

The signs of the beating were slowly fading. His eye was no longer a plum and the scar on his temple had healed, though it was still visible if you looked closely. Most of the symptoms of the skull fracture had abated, and a doctor had told him the break itself would heal on its own with time. There was still a little stiffness in his walk.

He smiled at them; there was still a hole from where his incisor had been bashed out. "Glad you could make it," he said. "Y'all have a seat." There were about 150 other colored men and women sitting at the tables, waiting.

Thelma and Laverne found a table where Helen and Betty had saved space for them. Thelma lowered herself carefully onto the wood. Sure enough, she felt a splinter pinch her thigh through the rough fabric of her jeans.

Ollie said, "Want to thank you all for comin'. I think most of y'all know me. For those that don't, my name Ollie Grimes. I work metal shop on the day shift." He indicated the three men he had been talking with. "Some of y'all might know these fellas, too. This here Alex Winston. He work night shift in the carpenter shop. That there is J.B. Travers, graveyard shift painter. Lonny Sanford, he work day shift on the cranes."

Each man nodded in turn at the mention of his name. Ollie said, "The four of us, we been meetin' together, talkin' 'bout how we gon' get these white people to give us what we deserve. Don't know 'bout the rest of y'all, but I'm sick and tired of them tellin' me I'm unskilled when I'm the one trained half these white boys workin' over me. I want the recognition I got comin'. Want the money, too. I know I ain't the only one feel that way. Seem to me it's time we do somethin' about it."

Behind Thelma, a man she didn't know spoke up. "But the bosses been meetin' with the FEPC. Maybe we shouldn't rock the boat right now."

Ollie's eyebrows lifted. "Rock the boat? I'm 'bout ready to turn the damn thing over if I don't get what I got comin'."

It brought nervous laughter. The man behind Thelma waited it out, then spoke again. "What I'm sayin' is, ain't it the federal government's place to make sure that happens?"

Ollie snorted his disdain for the suggestion. "Federal government don't seem to be in no hurry to do nothin', do it, Dave? Roosevelt told them two years ago they had to desegregate. Executive Order 8802 been the law of the land since 1941. I don't see these crackers rushin' to obey it, do you? FEPC man come down here to tell them do the right thing and they just laugh in his face. Hell, I had my head busted just for tryin' to get what I'm already s'posed to have. I'm *tired* of waitin'. It's time to make them understand we ain't gon' be patient forever."

"What you got in mind, Ollie?" asked Laverne.

"We havin' these meetin's on all three shifts," said Ollie. "This the first one. We want y'all's okay to tell the bosses we ain't waitin' no more. If we don't get what we s'pose to get, we gon' shut this place down."

A man sitting near the front perked up at that. "Are you talking about a strike?"

Ollie nodded. "Yes," he said. "A work stoppage. Let's see 'em try to slap them ships together without us."

"But Ollie," protested the one called Dave, "we're at war. What you're talking about, it's unpatriotic. It might even be treason. How can we try to shut down production while our boys are risking their necks overseas? They need these boats. This is not a time for us to be turning on one another. We're all supposed to be pulling together."

Like a swarm of bees, a hum of responses rose from the crowd.

"Who the hell are you, to be callin' me a traitor?"

"Maybe he got a point."

"Point, my ass!"

Ollie held up a hand, and when the murmur died, he drilled Dave with his eyes. "Who we s'pose to be pullin' together with, Dave? That's the part I don't understand. Need two mules to pull together. Who pullin' with us? You really think them ofays out there pullin' with us? Is that why I got my skull cracked, 'cause they pullin' with us?"

Thelma looked around then, because she wanted to see this Dave. She was not surprised to find that he was an older man, his hair a frizz of gray flying off in all directions at once, his pecan-colored skin baggy, his eyes just now large and sheepish. "I'm just sayin'," he said, "it's a war. We s'pose to all be together."

"Yeah," Thelma heard herself say, "we s'pose to be. But we ain't, are we?"

Some man she didn't see said, "Who are you to talk, Thelma Gordy? You friends with 'em. What the hell you know about it?"

Out of the corner of her eye, Thelma saw a tiny, satisfied smirk lift the corner of Laverne's mouth. It made Thelma furious. She had not intended to speak at all, had been surprised at her own words. But now that she had spoken, she'd be damned if she would let them cow her.

"I ain't friends with 'them,'" she said. She held up an index finger. "I am friends with *one* of 'them.' She got a name. It's Flora Lee Hodges and only reason we's friends is that I come to see she ain't like the rest of 'em. She a better person than most of them is. Better than some I could name right here, right now." She glared pointedly at Laverne, who held her gaze for a moment, then turned away.

"But you crazy if you think 'cause me and Flora Lee friends, I don't know how white people is. Hell, white people come to my door when I wasn't yet three years old. White people took my mama and my daddy out the house, strung 'em up to a tree and set 'em on fire—me and my brother standin' in the doorway watchin'. I don't need none of y'all to tell me a goddamn thing about how white people is. White people the reason I ain't got a mama nor a daddy and my brother got to drink hisself to sleep every night or else he like to wake up screamin.'"

Ollie said, "Thelma . . ."

She ignored him. "I see how white people treat colored right here in this damn shipyard. Lock us out the best jobs. Tell us we ain't good enough. Hell, when Ollie had his head busted and wouldn't no white ambulance come for him, they sent him to the hospital with Alex there and Lonny. And then they docked them for the time they was off the job. Don't none of y'all tell me I don't know nothin' 'bout white people, 'cause that's a damn lie. I know. Believe me, I know.

"But I tell you somethin' else I know: Ollie right. How the hell you gon' be pullin' together with somebody don't want to pull with you? That don't make no sense. I'm patriotic as anybody. You think I don't want to win this war? My brother, he trainin' on tanks, might get sent overseas any minute. So yeah, I want Uncle Sam to win this here war because someone I care about is out there in harm's way.

"But do that mean I ain't allowed to speak up for myself when white people doin' me wrong? Hell, I believe in standin' up for the country. But country got to stand up for us once in a while too, don't it? Else, what's the point?"

She fell silent all at once, wondering where the unaccustomed cascade of words had come from, suddenly aware of all the eyes on her.

Ollie gave her words space to breathe. Then he said, "I think Thelma done said everything need to be said. We all want to pull together, but it's a two-way street. So I want to see a show of hands. If we go in there and tell them we ready to stop work over this, how many y'all willin' to back us up?"

Thelma's hand went up immediately. Laverne's followed. For an interminable moment, it was just the two of them, their hands waving above the crowd as people interrogated one another with their eyes. Ollie bit his lip.

Then another hand went up. And another. And another.

And another.

Thelma, hand still lifted, glanced behind her. The old man Dave sat there with his arms folded across his chest, staring stonily ahead.

But hands kept going up. After a moment, Ollie took the count. When he was done, he was grinning and there was no need to ask for a vote of the nays. They had voted yes, overwhelmingly. Ollie clapped for the people. And then the people clapped for themselves, awarded themselves an ovation for their own courage. They grinned at each other, amazed at the thing they had done, the step they had taken.

It was a giddy moment. Thelma felt again what she had felt that night a month ago when Flora Lee reminded her there were places in this world other than Mobile, Alabama. She felt untethered. But it didn't terrify her so much now.

"This ain't gon' bring nothin' but trouble," said the voice behind her, and Thelma looked back to see Dave, still sitting there with his forearms barricading his chest. "You mark my words," he said.

Thelma shook her head, laughing. The frightened old fool. He was too used to bowing to white people to stand up for himself and be counted. Thank Heaven the rest of them had more guts than that. Thelma was pleased with herself, pleased with her people, pleased with this blessed moment in time when they had reached a decision to be counted, to act, for once, in their own best interests.

Then she saw him.

Earl Ray Hodges stood about a hundred feet back from the picnic area, leaning on his garbage can, watching them. He saw Thelma seeing him. He raised his index finger, cocked it like a gun, pointed it at her.

And just like that, the sense of being at peace with her world curdled into something cold and sour that sat heavily in the pit of Thelma's stomach. He must have seen this in her eyes because he braided his lips into a malevolent grin. Then Earl Ray Hodges went back to pushing his wheeled trash can across the yard, body rocking up and back in its awkward gait, whistling some idle tune Thelma could not hear.

twenty

FRANKLIN BENNETT APPEARED IN THE TENT ABOUT TWO THAT Sunday afternoon. He had a black eye and a swollen lip. Luther, who had been playing poker with a couple of other men, glanced up but did not speak.

Books stumbled to his cot and fell onto it. After sitting there a moment, he lifted his feet and lay back.

Luther laughed without humor. "You all right there, Books?"

"Not so loud." Books's voice seemed to issue from the bottom of a well.

Luther ignored this. "You must like that there stockade a whole lot," he said. "This your fourth trip in four months, by my count."

One of the other men snickered. Books lay with his right forearm across his eyes. He did not respond.

"And you must really like gettin' your clock cleaned by them white boys." The scuttlebutt was that Books had gotten drunk, gone into the PX for pipe tobacco, and demanded service, even though colored were not allowed in the store. It was said that he had even elbowed some big white sergeant out of the way, slammed his money on the counter, and announced, "I want tobacco, goddamn it!" And then, when the counter girl's eyes widened in surprise, he had said, "What's wrong? Is my money not good enough?"

The white sergeant had beaten him up pretty bad. Then the MPs had thrown him into the stockade. This had become a regular occurrence. It seemed as if all Books did these days was drink and get into trouble. Luther had lost count of how many times his friend had been written up for sassing officers or not doing his work.

"What are you," he asked now, "my mother?"

"Not me," said Luther. "I'm just your pal. But that don't mean I can't say somethin' when I see you fuckin' up."

He turned to the other guys. "Deal me out," he said, laying his cards down. He grabbed a chair, placed it at the head of Books's cot, and sat backward in it. "Books," he said, "you got to stop doin' this to yourself."

"Leave me alone, Luther. I have a terrible headache."

"Ain't surprised you got a headache. You done tried to drink up half of Louisiana, way I hear."

This brought the protective arm down just enough so that Luther could see the skepticism in Books's face. "Let me get this straight," he said. "*You*, an inveterate alcoholic, are lecturing *me* about the evils of too much drink?"

Luther was stung. He'd had his drinking more or less under control since he came here. It had been a struggle, but he had managed. Now he swallowed and forced a rueful smile. "Yeah," he said. "Guess I am. I guess that tell you how bad you behavin', don't it?"

Books gave a snort and lowered his arm back over his eyes. "Go away, Luther. Leave me the hell alone."

Luther's friend had not been the same since that summer night when the white man put a pistol to his cheek and ordered him to "talk like a nigger." Ask him if he wanted to catch a movie and he said no. Ask his opinion of the latest war news and he said he didn't give a damn since "niggers"—he actually used the hated word—would never be allowed to fight.

And he had broken it off with Andrea. Luther knew this not from anything Books had said but because he saw the girl's unopened letters piling up in a cubby next to Books's cot. They had not been back to Alexandria since it had happened. Books had nearly snapped his head off the one time Luther suggested it.

"Why?" he snarled. "Did it amuse you to see me humiliated?"

"No," Luther had protested. "You know that ain't—"

Books did not wait to hear the rest. He had dismissed Luther with an angry wave and walked away.

The other men had learned to avoid him. You got tired of getting cursed at because you made a comment about the weather. And you didn't want to get dragged into some foolishness because you happened to be near him when he decided to act up. So they steered clear of Books and, eventually, just ignored him. They counseled Luther to do the same, but he couldn't help himself. He worried about his friend.

Summer passed into fall. Fall nudged into winter. And nothing really changed.

Their training was still indifferent. White officers came and went like Christmas shoppers through a revolving door at some swanky department store. No one wanted the 761st. No self-respecting white man wanted to find himself stuck here for fear of what it might do to his career. Those white officers who were assigned to the battalion tended to be just out of Officer Candidate School and as green as June grass—but even they arrived already plotting their exits, transfer requests working their way up the chain of command.

It was true that around Christmas a new white officer had arrived who didn't seem in any particular hurry to leave. Paul Bates, a first lieutenant who took over as intelligence and operations officer, was said to be from Los Angeles. Tall, rangy, with a friendly face, he spoke to colored men as if they were men. This was a welcome change from the likes of Executive Officer Charles Wingo, who—if he spoke to you at all—would call you "boy" or "coon."

"He seem like he all right," Luther had observed to Books one night over chow, just trying to get a conversation started.

"If he were all right," Books had replied, "he would not be here, now would he? Trust me: he will be gone soon, just like every other white officer before him."

It wasn't just Books who felt this way. Morale was low for all the men. It rained a lot, pelting downpours that sent rivers of mud rushing through the swamp. No one talked anymore about when they might be allowed to fight. No one believed they ever would. The marines in the South Pacific were being lauded as heroes after taking a Jap island called Guadalcanal. The Army was on the march in North Africa and had the vaunted German General Erwin Rommel on the run. And here sat the 761st, mired in Louisiana mud, watching the war go by. Luther understood Books's frustration. He shared it. But it still troubled him to see the way that frustration was eating at his friend, destroying him, piece by piece.

"You want to catch a movie?" he asked now.

"No," said Books, his forearm still over his eyes.

"You sure? They got a good one."

"I am confined to quarters," he said. "And besides, why should I want to go there so I can sit behind a bunch of white men who are no better than I am?"

"Don't nobody like that!" snapped Luther. "You think any of the rest of us like it? Hell, it's just the way it is."

Books's voice was crusted with ice. "Perhaps it's easier for you to accept that," he said. "After all, you've never known any different."

"Oh? You mean, 'cause I'se just an ignorant hick from the sticks and you done traveled the world?"

Finally, the hand came down. "You said it. I did not."

Luther glared at him. "You think you better than me? Is that it?"

Books didn't respond. "Yeah, I guess it is," said Luther. He was conscious of the other men in the tent staring at them, their cards held suspended. "Well," he said, "I guess you got a right to think that. You done had concrete under your feet your whole life. Me and mine, we still got to go outdoors to take a shit. So yeah, maybe you are better'n us. I tell you one thing about us, though. We don't give up. Life get tough, we don't just roll over and cry about it."

"What the hell is that supposed to mean?"

"What it mean? Mean it's been six months and you still sittin' on your ass feelin' sorry for yourself and makin' everybody else sorry they got to be around you."

Books pondered this with an unreadable face. After a moment, he lay back on his cot. "Please go away, Luther," he said. "Just leave me be."

Luther stared at him. "Fine with me," he said. And he stood up and walked out.

It wasn't as if he didn't understand how Books felt. He felt the same damn way. They all did. They all were bad-tempered and had every reason to be. But did that mean they simply surrendered? Even if you couldn't change a damn thing by bitching about it, shouldn't you keep bitching anyway, just to remind yourself you were a man and how they were treating you wasn't right?

That, Luther realized, was why his friend's sullen, defeated behavior shook him. Because if Books Bennett, who had walked through this mire with such determined dignity, was now running the white flag up the pole, what hope was there for the rest of them? They might as well all surrender, stop slogging around in this Louisiana slime and just accept what white folks said about them.

"Hey, Country, did you hear?"

Jocko Sweeney came tromping toward him, trailed by several other men. His eyes were lit by fire.

"Did I hear what?"

"They done got another one."

Luther did not have to ask what this meant. Another colored soldier fool enough to go into town had been badly beaten. Nobody knew how many men this had happened to, because the Army always refused to investigate.

"How bad he hurt?" he asked Jocko.

"He ain't hurt," said Jocko. "He dead."

At those words, Luther felt his heart give a painful kick in his chest. "*What?* What happened?"

"Don't nobody know. They found him lying on the train tracks. Look like the train come through"—Jocko slid one palm briskly against the other—"cut him in half."

Luther stared. Surely he had not heard right.

"You heard him." One of the men with Jocko said this. "Cut the man in half."

"How he end up on the tracks?" asked Luther. He was still struggling to take this in.

The second man spoke up again. "Army say he was drunk. Say he passed out and fell on the tracks."

"Y'all don't think he did," said Luther.

Jocko shook his head. "Man didn't drink," he said. "Man was a Baptist deacon! He didn't touch the stuff."

And at that, Luther felt a too-familiar fury swimming to the surface of him. Bad enough they forced you into their army. Bad enough that then they would not let you train or fight. Bad enough they missed no chance to insult you. Did they have to kill you, too?

The thought made him dizzy with rage. "Where you all goin'?" he asked. For somehow, he knew they were bound somewhere on a mission to answer this latest outrage.

"Motor pool," said Jocko. "Goin' to grab some'a them tanks and take 'em into that town. We sick of this shit. Time to show them white bastards we ain't to be fucked with no more."

"Well then, what are we waiting for?"

The voice came from behind them. Luther wheeled and was surprised to find Books standing there. There was a moment when all of them simply stared. Then Books repeated it, his voice taut. "I said, 'What in the hell are we waiting for?'"

Jocko gave a tight nod. "Come on, fellas," he said. And Luther and Books joined the small group of men charging toward the motor pool. There, they commandeered six tanks and a half-track. It was easy enough, given that most of the white officers were on leave for the weekend, though a Negro sergeant sputtered angrily and pulled ineffectually at the men as they climbed into the war machines. Luther himself led them single file through the center of camp, down the road toward the front gate, his head sticking up from the turret hatch. He tapped his feet on Books's shoulders to guide him, his driver, down below since the old M-5 Stuart had no radio.

Was it just 10 minutes ago that he had chided Books for doing stupid things? Now here he was, taking a tank into Alexandria with Books driving. It gave Luther a sobering yet strangely giddy sense that the rules no longer applied. Gravity had been cancelled like a radio show and they were all about to go flying off the edge of the world.

But what else could you do? Keep taking it? Let them keep beating and killing you?

Goddamn it, *no*. Enough.

The rumble of the tank made it almost impossible to hear anything else. So Luther could only wonder what the white soldiers on the sidewalk who swiveled their heads, pointed, and stared after them were saying. He imagined they were probably wondering why these colored tankers were going the wrong way. After all, the training field was in the other direction.

But Luther Hayes wasn't going to any training field. He was going to town, and they just might blow that motherfucker off the map before the day was done. Why not? The Army was never going to let them fight Germans or Japs. Those were enemies they were never going to see. So from now on, let them fight the enemy they *could* see: white men.

From somewhere deep in his conscience, the white lawyer told Luther to turn this tank around before he got into trouble and washed out of the Army. If he did this, their deal was over. Floyd Bitters would never go to court. But it couldn't be helped. The lawyer would never understand it, Luther knew. John Simon was a white man, so what would he know about living with white men's insults, their hatred and violence, about putting up with it, turning blind eyes and deaf ears to it until it filled you up and you had no choice but to explode? What did he know about feeling like you simply couldn't take any more?

Then what about Thelma?

That thought almost did stop him. Indeed, he lifted his foot, ready to kick Books in the center of the back, the signal to halt the tank. It was one thing to know he was letting a well-meaning white attorney down. It was another to know that he was letting his sister down, too.

Other than the prospect of seeing Big Floyd Bitters stand trial for murdering his mother and father, Luther's only satisfaction in accepting John Simon's deal had been the knowledge that doing so would make Thelma happy. No longer would he be someone his sister had to put up with out of duty and kinship. Now he would be a soldier. Finally, he would be someone she could take pride in.

But he knew as the tank rumbled toward the main gate, past the nice, neat, new buildings housing and serving white soldiers, there was no way she could be proud of this. There was no way this could bring her anything but pain. He was failing her—yet again. He knew it as surely as he knew his own name. But he could not turn back.

I'm sorry, Thelma.

He lowered the foot he had lifted to signal Books. There would be no stopping.

I'm so sorry.

This *had* to happen. Let the chips fall like rain.

Lost in these thoughts, he almost didn't see the Jeep that had pulled astride his path. Now Luther did kick Books in the center of his back as he signaled to the tanks behind him to stop.

"What is it?" Books asked as the tank shuddered to a halt. Down there, his visibility was limited. But Luther could see just fine.

"It's Bates," he said.

"Oh, hell," said Books. The driver's hatch below Luther opened and Books's head popped out. "Hell," he said again. Paul Bates stood there in front of the Jeep with his hands up. Two of the tanks following Luther moved up, flanking him. The others arranged themselves behind them. Some of the men climbed out onto their turrets to see what was going on. To Luther, Bates seemed far below and very small.

"What's going on here?" he demanded.

"Gon' need you to move aside, sir," said Luther.

"Talk to me," said Bates.

"Nothin' to talk about, sir." This was Jocko Sweeney, atop the tank to Luther's right.

"Try me," said Bates.

"It is very simple, sir. We are sick and tired of being treated as if we are not *men*." Books's voice shook with barely suppressed emotion.

"What do you mean?" asked Bates.

"We are sick and tired of white men presuming their superiority over us, sick and tired of them beating and abusing us while we have no recourse but to take it."

"I still don't follow," said Bates.

Jocko said, "What he mean, sir, is we tired of these goddamn crackers—pardon my French, sir—in these little towns thinkin' they can do whatever they want to us, treat us any kind of way, beat up our men, even *kill* 'em, because we Negroes. Now we have a man dead. Did you hear about that, Colonel? They found him cut in two on the train tracks. And ain't nobody gon' do nothin' about it."

"Let the Army handle it," said Bates.

"The Army?" Indignation sputtered out of Luther at the foolishness of this idea. "The Army ain't gon' do nothin' about it. They never do. Army don't give a damn about us. Can't you see that?"

"If the Army cared about us, sir," said Books, "would we be living in a swamp, spending most of our days lying around doing nothing, because nobody can be bothered to train us? Why should we think the Army would do anything about this?"

"Fine," said Bates. "Then let *me* handle it."

This took Luther by surprise. "You?"

"Yes," said Bates, his voice firm. "Let me go into town and have it out with them. I'll tell them I will not have my men mistreated while they're spending money in that little one-horse shithole." This wrung bitter laughter from some of the men.

Books said, "You would tell them that?" He did not bother hiding his skepticism.

"Yes," said Bates with a crisp nod, "I would."

Books looked up at Luther to see what he thought. Luther looked over at Jocko for the same reason. Jocko said, "We appreciate the thought, but—"

"Look," said Bates, "I know you men are angry. I don't blame you. But what you're talking about doing now is mutiny. That's a court martial offense. The Army could jail you. It could even execute you."

Luther knew this to be true because it had already happened. Gramp had often told him how 13 colored soldiers were hanged at once back in '17 after they stormed into Houston, furious about how that town treated them. So he knew the threat was real. He just didn't know that he gave a damn about it.

Books said, "There are some things worth dying for, sir."

"Nothing is worth dying for," countered Bates, "if you don't have to. What do you say, men? Do we have a deal?"

Luther was dubious and did not mind letting Bates hear it in his voice. "*You* gon' go into town for us," he said.

"I'll put it to you like this," Bates replied evenly. "I'll go in there for you and if I don't get satisfaction, if anything like this ever happens again, I swear, I will lead you into town myself."

Luther stared at the white man so far below. They all did. Could he be serious? Could such an outlandish promise be real? Paul Bates stared back, waiting and unblinking.

Finally, Jocko said, "All right, sir. You always been fair to us. We gon' take you at your word."

He nodded to the other men, who had climbed out of their tanks. In a few moments, the behemoths began to reverse. Luther shot one last look at the white man standing there astride the road, facing down six tanks and a half-track with nothing but an earnest face and a promise.

"The man has guts," he said. "You got to give him that."

"Yes," said Books, "but will he deliver?"

"Ain't but one way to find out, I expect. Come on; let's take her back to the barn. Let's see what the man do."

Bates did as he promised. He went into town. When he returned, he passed the word: the men would have no further problems with the MPs or citizens of Alexandria. Luther and Jocko decided to test this promise. As soon as they could manage to snag passes, they took the bus into town and stepped off in Little Harlem. They went to a couple of jukes. They went into an arcade where the sign said "Can you shoot?" and promised cash prizes. They ate at a rib joint. They chatted up some dames and took them to a movie.

They walked the girls home to their rooming house, retiring to separate corners of the porch to say their good nights. The one girl shook Luther's hand and told him she'd had a swell time, but Jocko came back with her friend's lipstick on his cheek.

"You lucky dog," said Luther as they walked back over to Lee Street.

Books asked them about it the next morning as they were walking to their tank. "Had a good time," said Luther. "Ain't nobody had no problems, that I heard of."

"Yeah," said Jocko around his ever-present cigar, "look like Bates came through like he said he would."

"Maybe you go with us next time?" said Luther.

Books shook his head. A sad smile. "No, fellows," he said, "I'm afraid there's nothing in that town for me anymore. But I am happy to hear that the man kept his word."

"Yeah," said Jocko, "as far as I'm concerned, he an all right guy."

"For a white guy," said Luther, "maybe he is."

A few months later, Bates assumed overall command of the 761st. His first order of business was to call a dress inspection. Luther, Books, and seven hundred other colored men stood at attention, waiting to hear what this latest white boss would have to say. What did he believe? What would he expect of them? Luther did not have long to wait. Bates told the men to stand at ease, then climbed atop a Jeep.

"Gentlemen," he said, "I've always lived with the point of view that the rest of my life is the most important thing in the world. I don't give a damn about what happened before. Let's go from here. And if you're going to go from here, if you're going to make it, we've got to do it together."

It sounded good. This much, Luther had to admit. But so what? White officers *always* sounded good. He was conscious of a stirring in his chest, though, something that suggested maybe this particular white officer meant what he said now, just as he had that day at the gate two months before. Luther strangled that stirring, reminding himself of the danger of putting hope too much on display. It was like leading with your chin in a street fight.

"They say black troops can't fight," said Bates, his voice carrying over the parade grounds. "They say that you *won't* fight. Well, we're proving 'em wrong. You guys are not supposed to be as clean as other people. There's a simple answer to that: make damn sure you're cleaner than anybody else you ever saw in your life, particularly all those white bastards over there." And the white colonel flung his arm, pointing toward the white section of the camp where the buildings were new and you did not tramp through mud to get where you were going. Indeed, it struck Luther that maybe he was pointing toward the whole damn white world.

And now, the stirring that had fluttered in Luther's chest, the dangerous stirring he had thought strangled long ago, seemed somehow to have gotten out, to have gotten loose, because the other men began to look around, each searching the other's eyes for answers to a suddenly urgent question: *Did he mean it? Was this white man for real?*

"I want your uniforms to look better, cleaner than theirs do," continued Bates. "I want your shoes and boots to shine better. I want you to *be* better."

He paused. His eyes surveyed the colored men watching him now with suddenly rapt attention. "Because, gentlemen," he said, "you must get ready. This battalion is going to war."

And the way he said it, you could almost believe it. You really almost could.

Men looked at each other, their eyes asking silent questions.

Sound like he's tellin' the truth, but . . .

Luther did not want to believe the white man's promise. Indeed, he didn't want to give a damn, one way or the other. But he couldn't help it. He did. The realization almost made him laugh. For the first time in his life, and without even knowing it, he had become part of something. And he wanted that something to have meaning. He wanted to fight.

Luther glanced over at Books to see what he thought. But Luther's friend was not looking at him. Franklin Bennett faced forward, his chin lifted, standing at rigid attention. A broad grin split his dark face, and a single tear leaked down his cheek.

twenty-one

HE WAS DREAMING AGAIN. SOMEHOW, HE KNEW THIS.

But somehow, the knowing did not matter, did not soften the terror of lying there breathing, bleeding and exhausted in the tall kunai grass. The sky was peaceful and perfect and blue, the world silent but for the sawing of insects. He turned his head and saw that Jazzman lay next to him, his skull open to the clouds, his face charred like hamburger meat left too long on the grill. Randy grinned and in the deep silence, George could hear the taut, burned skin stretching and crackling.

"Yank." A woman's voice.

"No gal made has got a shade on sweet Georgia Brown," Jazzman sang.

"Yank!" The woman's voice again, more urgent now.

George tried to fight his way up from the dream. But the dream was loath to let him go. It pulled at him like a lover to her bosom, like a devil to his hell.

Grinning maggots with Japanese faces climbed out from Jazzman's brain.

"Yank! Wake up!"

George's eyes flew open. A nurse hovered over him.

"Welcome back, Yank," she said, smiling. "You were dreaming. Must have been a bad one, the way you were carrying on."

She was a vision. Her white nurse's cap was set atop glossy black hair framing an oval face with pillowy red lips and dark, penetrating eyes. It struck him that he could imagine no more welcome sight to awaken to. She made a man want to live. The nurse—her name tag identified her as "Em"—chuckled as if she had read these thoughts. "How are you feeling, Yank?" she asked.

And that's when he remembered: he had been hospitalized for a recurrence of his malaria.

"Better," he heard himself say. His voice was coated with rust.

"Good. That's what we want to hear."

She patted his bicep softly, then moved on to the next man in the ward. George watched her go, instantly in love. But he saw right away that he was hardly the only one.

"Will you marry me?" asked the man in the next bed. He spoke without preamble. She handed him a cup and told him she'd think about it if he brought her back some urine.

With a private smile, George closed his eyes and let sleep pull him down again.

It was his own screaming that woke him up—that and the man in the next bed throwing pillows and yelling for him to pipe down. George sat up, nightshirt soaked, chest heaving. He thought of trying to go back to sleep but feared he might be successful. Instead, he climbed out of bed. He had no real sense of where he was or where he was going. He was simply determined to walk until the knife's edge of the dream had dulled and he felt firmly anchored in waking reality once again.

So George tottered the length of the ward. He pushed through the double door at the end and found himself in a quiet hallway that extended to his left and right and turned corners on either end to some unknown destination. Across the hall was another double door. Impulsively, he pushed through it and found himself standing on a small balcony overlooking the city.

To his sudden embarrassment, he realized he was not alone. Em was standing off to the side. George had trespassed on some private moment.

"I'm sorry," he said. "I didn't know you were out here."

"What are you doing out of bed, Yank?" Her voice sounded as though she was trying to compose herself.

"I couldn't sleep," he said. "I didn't mean to interrupt."

"Another nightmare?" she asked.

His instinct was to lie. What would she think if he told her the truth? That he was a small child, to be scared out of his bed by bogeymen that came for him in his sleep? But in the end, he could not mislead her. "Yes," he heard himself say.

"That happens a lot," she said. "Nothing to be ashamed of. Many blokes just coming back from the fighting have that problem."

"I'll go back," he said. "I'm sorry to intrude."

"It's all right," she told him.

"Are you sure?"

"To tell you the truth, Yank, maybe I could use the company."

"Is something wrong?"

She didn't answer immediately. Then, after a moment she asked in a wistful voice, "Where are you from, Yank? Which one of those united states do you call home?"

"Alabama," he said. He almost laughed at the thought of anyone from his state being called "Yank." "I'm from a town called Mobile. It's in the southern part of the country."

"Tell me about it," she said.

"Not much to tell," he replied. "It's a pretty little town. Kind of slow. We used to have streetcars like you do here, but we replaced them with buses a few years back. The people are friendly. We have this image of ourselves as having what they call old-world Southern charm."

"What kind of work do you do there?"

"Nothing," he said. "I mean, I joined the Marines right out of school."

"Do you have a girlfriend? A wife?"

"No," he said. And the ease of the lie appalled him. Then it made him angry.

Standing here on this balcony, nine thousand miles from home, having survived strafing, bombing, hand-to-hand combat, and two bouts of malaria, George tried to recall the last time he had so much as thought about his wife. He couldn't.

Em lifted an eyebrow. "Handsome bloke like you, I'm surprised."

He said nothing, uncomfortable at having lied so readily and unsure what else to say.

After a pause, she said, "Well, that's too bad."

"How so?"

"It's just sad to think of someone going through this all alone."

"How about you, Em? Is there someone?"

She looked at him. "I'm afraid we're two of a kind, you and I. Alone, I mean."

"Is that why you were out here, you know . . . ?"

There was something arch in her smile. "Well, aren't you the sticky beak!"

"Beg pardon?"

"It means you don't know how to mind your own business."

"I'm sorry."

Pause. "No, I'm the one who should be sorry. I've no reason to be cross with you. It's just . . . my husband . . . it seems he . . . it seems he's found some dolly he fancies more than he does me. Some British girl in London where he's stationed. I got the letter today."

"He's a fool," said George.

Em's smile was heartbreaking. "You're saying that because you think I'm pretty, Yank. But you don't know me. For all you know, he's well shed of me."

"I don't believe that for a minute."

She gave a mirthless little laugh. "Don't you get it, Yank? They assign me to this ward because they want me to flirt with the boys a little and keep their spirits up, remind them of the girls back home and what they're fighting for and all that. And I'm proud to do it, my little contribution to the great war. But it's just my face, Yank. It has nothing to do with who I am."

"I still think he's a fool," said George.

There was a beat. Then she said, "Well, I can't say I disagree with you on that."

They laughed.

George heard himself say, "When I get out of here, let me take you out, show you a good time. It would take your mind off things."

One eyebrow lifted. "Oh? Is that what you're interested in? My mind?"

George stammered helplessly. She laughed again. "I'm sorry, Yank. That was unfair of me."

"It's George," he said.

"I beg your pardon?"

"You keep calling me 'Yank.'"

"I call all the American boys 'Yank,'" she said.

"I know you do. That's why I want you to call me George."

"Very well. George."

"You never answered the question: Would you go out with me?"

She considered it. He felt his heart rise like a balloon in his chest until it became difficult to breathe. Then she broke the balloon. "No," she said. "I thank you, but I can't. Not a good idea to date a patient."

"I won't be one always," insisted George.

"Fine," she said. "Ask me again when you aren't."

And so it was, two weeks later, on a bright, brisk day in April, that George stepped off the streetcar in front of the sprawling white complex of the Royal Melbourne Hospital, where Em would just be finishing a graveyard shift. She had declined to let him meet her at home, even though she lived alone with no parents or roommate to explain herself to. It was as if she was reassured by the impersonality of him knowing her only in relationship to her job, as if she thought it proved this was all just a lark, something to pass the days, with no implication beyond the moment.

George didn't mind this. In fact, he preferred it. He had no illusions about marrying Em and taking her back to Mobile with him once this was all done. He knew she was dating one or two other guys—she had been quite open about this when he asked her out that second time—and this, too, was fine with him. He, too, wanted only the respite of the moment.

He approached her building, but the front door flew open before he could reach it, and she came bolting out and threw her arms around him. Em kissed him—for the first time—on the lips. "Ah, George, what an absolutely bonzer day!"

He pulled back, trying not to feel overwhelmed. "Goodness," he said. "What's got you in such a great mood?"

Her smile was sunshine. "You remember I told you about the hubby? How he took up with some dolly in London?"

"Of course."

She took his arm, and they walked. "Well," she said, "it seems the dolly gave old Fred a roaring case of the clap—and then dumped him. Gave him the old heave-ho, she did." Em laughed. "I just finished reading his letter begging me to take him back."

"Are you going to do it?"

"Hell no," Em said. "I seem to remember a certain handsome Yank telling me Fred was a fool for letting me go. I find that I've come around to his way of thinking. I'm well shed of dear old Fred. But I can't deny that it feels good to have the last laugh." She squeezed his arm. "So, what shall we do today, George? I feel like having a ripper time."

George gazed down at her. Then he kissed her. He thought again of how all he wanted was a respite, and it struck him that this moment—a pretty girl on his arm, a pocketful of pay, and a day stretching ahead of him with no particular thing to do and no particular time frame to do it in—was about as perfect as a man could ask for. It made him wish he could stop time, climb inside this moment, and live in it forever.

"We can do anything you want," he said.

They went to a little amusement park near Port Phillip Bay, where he was soon very glad for the miracle of Bromo-Seltzer. Between the Tilt-A-Whirl, the roller coaster, and the Ferris wheel, he was lifted and dropped, hurled and twirled at high speed in every direction, Em clinging to him as he laughed and screamed with an abandon he had not known for a long time.

There was no war. There had never been a war, much less a hell island where he had seen friends smashed by gunfire and some hapless marine from some hapless patrol sitting in a field with his entrails unrolled like one of those squeaking blow toys from a child's birthday party. There was only this moment. There was only now.

Afterward, they caught a trolley to a pub, where they ordered fish and chips and two beers. The beers came first. George finished his before the meal arrived. He ordered another when it did. The pubs closed at six. He intended to get some drinking done before then.

"Someone's thirsty," said Em.

"Just making up for lost time," he said. "I want to—"

A familiar voice cut him off. "Well, well," said Babe, walking toward them trailing a thin, sullen-eyed brunette half a head taller than he, "I thought this was a classy joint. Looks like they'll let just about anybody in."

He smacked George hard on the back, appraising Em with a practiced leer. "So," he said, addressing George without looking at him, "are you just going to sit there like a lump or are you going to make the introductions?"

Resignation edged George's voice. "Emily Preble, I'd like you to meet Stanley Budzinski. We were on Guadalcanal together. Also at Pearl."

Babe lifted Em's right hand to his lips. "Pleased to meet you, doll," he said, "but only my mother calls me 'Stanley.' Everybody else calls me 'Babe.' And this here"—a head toss, indicating the brunette—"is Lucy."

"Charmed," the woman said.

"Fancy runnin' into you guys here," said Babe. "You mind if we join you?" But he was already squeezing in next to George even as he spoke. Em shot George a look as she scooted over to make room for Babe's friend.

Babe signaled the waitress, ordered two more fish and chips and a couple of beers. "Put all this on my tab," he told her.

"You don't have to do that," said George.

"I insist," said Babe. "My treat."

There was some undefined malice in his smile. And George, who had not eaten since yesterday, who had a basket of hot fish and chips wrapped in grease-stained newspaper right in front of him, found that all at once his appetite had deserted him. He did not want to be there. Em felt the same. He could see it in her eyes. But what could they do?

The woman, Lucy, produced a cigarette and waited expectantly. Babe stretched across the table to light it, then lit one for himself. "So," he said, "tell us about yourself, doll."

"I work at the Royal Melbourne Hospital," said Em. "Or at least, that's what it was called before we lent it to you Yanks. You lot call it the US Army Fourth General Hospital."

Babe gave her a look. "Well you know," he said, "we lot needed some-place to get patched up after getting our asses shot full of holes trying to save you lot down here in kangaroo country."

"Hey!" said George sharply. "She didn't mean it like that and you know it."

Babe's eyes traveled from George back to Em. "I didn't," she assured him. "We lot are very grateful for all the sacrifices you lot have made to keep us safe down here in kanga country."

Babe stared at her another moment. Then his expression softened. He shook his head. "I'm sorry," he said. "Don't know what's wrong with me. Guess I'm just on edge. Still looking for a fight."

The beers came, and he lifted his glass in salute. "I'm drinkin' to you lot here in kanga country—and especially to you, doll. You and a bunch just like you helped to put a lot of my pals back together, especially Saint George here"—he grabbed George's neck in a rough grasp—"and I want to thank you for it."

"Why do you call him that?" asked Em.

"Why do I call him what? 'Saint'?" Babe had taken a long draft from his beer. He wiped a rim of foam from his top lip and laughed. "Ain't it obvious? This here is a man of principle, a bona fide man of God."

He grabbed George's neck again. "That last night at Pearl, me and him and another buddy of ours, Swifty, we're all out that night, havin' a few drinks like we are now and me and Swifty, we get the idea to go over to one of the joyhouses, 'cause that's just the kind of reprobates we are. But George, he won't have none of it. Oh, no. 'You t-t-two g-g-go on and f-f-fornicate and defile yourselves like the s-s-sinners you are,' he says, 'cause you know, he stutters when he gets excited. 'I'm going back to the b-b-boat to p-p-pray.'"

George said, "I never said—" but Babe bulldozed the interruption. "When we were on Guadalcanal and it's terrible and you've got Japs all around and they're trying to kill you and they sure as hell ain't abiding by any Marquess of Queensberry Rules, if you know what I mean, and all the other fellas are saying, 'To hell with it; I've got to do whatever it takes to make sure I come out of this alive' . . . there's old Saint George, and he's more worried about the ethics and the morals of what we're doing than he is about shooting back. Like he's standing in judgment of us or something. Like he thinks he's the goddamn *conscience* of the whole goddamn United States Marine Corps."

He was giving George a hard look when he said, "I tell ya, it was like going into battle with my mother. So yeah, doll, that's why I call him 'Saint.'" And he grinned and grabbed George's neck again.

George had had enough. He shoved Babe's hand away. "Let go of me," he said, the anger boiling out of him.

"What's with you?" Babe's eyes were round in their feigned innocence.

"Don't give me that shit," said George.

"Fellas," said Em, "let's keep it civil."

"Why don't you listen to your girlfriend there, Saint? She's giving good advice."

"Why don't you kiss my ass, *Stanley*?"

Babe fixed George with a cold stare. "He thinks he's better than me because I did something while we were in that jungle, something bad, something that's not in the rule books." He shrugged. "I mutilated an enemy corpse, okay?" Somehow, his voice managed to be defiant but also ashamed, as if he was embarrassed to bring the jungle into this civilized place where music played and the tinkle of women's laughter rode the air.

Babe looked from one woman to the other. He sighed. "George thinks he's better because he would never do what I did. Saint George, man of God? He *couldn't* do what I did."

"That's not it," George said. His anger had disappeared. "Don't you get it? What scares me isn't that I couldn't do what you did. What scares me is that I *could*."

The words hung there.

"God help me, I think I could," repeated George, his voice softened by wonder. "That's what I've come to realize. And that scares the hell out of me. Before all of this, I used to know who I was. At least, I thought I did. But I don't anymore."

Babe gave him a crooked smile, patted his shoulder softly. "Welcome to the fuckin' club," he said.

"Yeah," said George. He drained his glass. "Yeah," he said again.

There was a moment. Then Em said, "George, I'd like to leave."

He looked up. He had almost forgotten she was there. "Sure," he said.

Babe and Lucy slid out to let them go. Babe took Em's hand. "I'm sorry about all this," he said. "You seem like a nice girl."

She smiled at him. "Don't worry about it," she said. "You boys had to endure it. All I have to do is hear you talk about it. Seems to me I'm getting the better of the deal."

Outside, George hailed a cab—a "Sandy McNab," they called them here, for some arcane reason. Em slid in, patted the seat next to her. But George shook his head. "Let's call it a night," he said, and some part of him was hardly able to believe he was saying this. "I'm not feeling well," he added.

She was surprised. "Are you certain?"

"Yeah," he said. "I'm afraid I wouldn't be very good company. Good night, Em."

He closed the door before she could say more. He paid the cabbie, then stood there watching as the car's taillights melted into the twilight traffic. She was a beautiful, desirable woman, and George understood what he had given up declining her invitation, but the knowledge carried no weight.

When he couldn't see the cab anymore, he walked in the opposite direction, hopped a streetcar back to the cricket grounds, and made his way to his bunk. There, he flipped on a lamp and opened his seabag. Two unopened letters from Sylvia sat on top and for a moment, the sight reproached him. He really should have answered her by now. Still, George pushed the letters aside. He dug down until he found what he was really looking for: his last letter from Thelma Gordy.

I feel like I'm drowning, he had written, *and I don't know what to do.*

He felt that drowning sensation again now, after what he had just admitted to Babe . . . what he had just finally admitted to *himself*.

I could have done it.

He remembered the coppery smell of blood, the way he had dropped to his knees to vomit up worm-infested rice at the sight of those men, sitting there posed like that, not just dead but . . . degraded. And then, to come upon that one Jap lying there in the kunai, helpless and alive . . .

I absolutely could have done it.

His hands shook, and his breathing came shallow as he pushed back the envelope flap, reaching in for Thelma's words. He unfolded the pages of her neat script, skimming through the parts where she talked about the labor dispute in the shipyard until he reached the words that, from the first time he read them, had settled him and centered him and reminded him who he was and who he sought to be.

> I think I understand. At least, as well as I can, being a woman who's never been in a war. You want to be a decent man. You want to do what's right. Anybody can see that's real important to you. I could see it that first day you came to my house when you had a duty to do, but you didn't really want to, because you knew it wasn't right. Don't you ever apologize for trying to be a decent man, you hear?

> We need that kind of man, especially since we're in this war where there's nothing decent about it. Before it's over, I think you—maybe all of us—are going to have to give up a lot of things that are important to you, a lot of the good things we try to hold on to. You may have to give up your faith and your hope, George. You may even have to give up your life. But if it's at all possible, you hold on to your decency. You make sure your decency, your *humanity*, is the very last thing you give up. Because without it, I don't think the rest matters too much.

George sat with the letter for a very long time, until his trembling hand stilled and his breathing became deep and even again.

"I don't know if I can," he finally said. He spoke to her. He spoke to empty air. Carefully, George refolded the letter and put it back into its envelope. "I don't know if I can," he said again.

twenty-two

EARL RAY HODGES'S MOOD WAS AS FOUL AS TRASH-FIRE SMOKE
as the ferry full of day-shift workers approached the dock that morning,
but that was nothing new. He had not known a good mood since Flora
Lee left him.

It had been months now, but his fury was still as scalding as on the
very first day.

Bad enough she had done it. Worse, she had done it in public. With the
whole world looking on, she had gone crawling to a nigger—a *nigger!*—and
begged to be taken in. It was a humiliation beyond any he had ever known.
And Earl Ray could not, for the life of him, understand why she had visited
it upon him. He had been a good husband to her, hadn't he? Hadn't he kept
a roof over her head, made sure she had food to eat? Yes, he'd knocked sense
into her head when necessary, but that was no more or less than a husband
was supposed to do, than his own father had done for his own mother.

But had she appreciated him? No, sir, she had not. Five years after
standing before that preacher and promising to love, honor, and obey him
forever, she had thrown him over.

And gone running to that nigger.

That was the part that galled him. That was the part he could not abide.

Even so, and as much as he hated to admit it, he missed her. It wasn't
the sex. That he could replace easily enough with just a few extra visits to
Lizzie Dove, who worked out of an apartment above a Warren Street bar.
He actually preferred fucking Lizzie anyway. She was a professional who
knew how to please a man; you didn't have to tell her every little thing to
do. And she didn't complain if you got a little rough.

But Lizzie Dove didn't make your breakfast. She didn't listen to your complaints or massage the pain in your back and your hips that came from walking on a fucked-up leg. And she surely didn't wash your dirty drawers or iron a sharp crease into your working pants. Earl Ray had always prided himself on looking spiffy when he went out—clothes clean and neatly pressed, pompadour shining with pomade and sitting up there just right. He had always felt that if you were spiffy, it made it harder for people to write you off as just some Alabama hillbilly with a funny walk. If you were spiffy, people had to sit up and take notice. They had to respect you.

But he could not be spiffy with Flora Lee gone. Since she took off on him . . .

(with that nigger!)

. . . he had found himself going about in clothes that were rumpled and soiled. Even his proud pompadour sat indifferently atop his head, unruly strings of hair flying out this way and that.

He missed her taking care of him. He also missed—and he hated admitting this most of all—just having her around, hearing her in the background yammering about whatever it was she yammered about while he was trying to talk to some other fella or just listen to the ball game. All of this had been taken from him by that black nigger cunt. And he had tried to reason with the bitch, hadn't he? He had tried to get her to tell him where she had taken Flora Lee. He had even reminded her what it says in the Bible: what God puts together, no man is supposed to put asunder.

But she had ignored him, put her nose in the air and walked away from him like she was the white man and he was the filthy nigger bitch. Well, that was all right. Earl would make her pay for that. He would get her—and get her good—right when she least expected it. He would have to wait for his opportunity, but that was all right. Uh huh. Earl didn't mind waiting. He was good at it.

What he didn't realize as he stepped off the ferry and headed toward the janitor's shed to begin his workday was that his wait was about to end.

Something felt wrong.

At first, Thelma could not say how she knew this, could not even give the wrongness a name, but she felt it just the same as she locked the old Oldsmobile and walked with Betty, Laverne, Helen, and Ollie toward the front gate. Apparently Ollie felt it, too. His features were wrinkled with faint concern. When he saw her looking, he shrugged and gave a smile that was meant, she supposed, to reassure her. But Thelma wasn't reassured.

"Yard seem awful quiet today," said Betty.

Helen nodded. "You know, now that you mention it, it do at that."

And this, Thelma realized all at once, was what had set her nerves on edge: the absence of sound. As she approached the gate in the usual throng of people coming from the parking lot, she did not hear metal striking metal, welding torches crackling, foremen yelling to get the lead out. She heard nothing. As she passed under the archway into the shipyard, she realized it wasn't just sound that was missing. It was also movement. No forklifts rushed across the yard. No bodies crawled across some incomplete ship like ants on a mound. The great cranes that lifted sections of hull and deck into place stood still as dawn, their loads suspended high above the shipyard.

And white men stood in bunches, talking with soft urgency, gesturing animatedly.

Now other people, colored and white, were noticing it, too. You saw their steps slowing, saw them looking to one another in confusion.

"What's going on?" a white man asked no one in particular.

"Why's everybody standing around?" a white woman asked the same audience.

Again, Thelma looked over at Ollie. He had come to a full stop, his eyes sharp with concern. "I don't like this," he said.

"Yeah," said Thelma, "this is strange."

"No, it ain't just strange," said Ollie, gazing at the still and silent yard ahead. "It's troublesome."

"What you talking about?" asked Thelma.

"Do you remember a few days ago?" he said. "Remember the shipyard give in, said they'd give some of us some of them good jobs?"

Thelma nodded. Of course she remembered. At lunch that day, they had laughed and celebrated and felt light as cream, buoyed by the realization that they had actually managed to make the boss men listen.

Now Ollie said, "Last night 12 colored men worked their first shift as full-fledged welders."

"So soon?" said Thelma.

"Yeah. Shipyard ain't announced it or nothin'. I think the bosses didn't want to make a big deal out of it, get these white folks all riled up. I think they figured if they just showed it was already a done deal, folks wouldn't have no choice but to accept it. But now I'm wonderin' if maybe they figured wrong. And I'm wonderin' where them men are. I hope they okay."

There was something going on. Earl Ray had no idea what it was. But all over the yard, white men stood in tight clusters, talking heatedly. Some had metal pipes in their fists. Some had two-by-fours.

He was trying to make sense of it when he heard his name. "Hey," a man named Jimmy Ross said, "there's Earl Ray Hodges." Jimmy waved him over. "Earl, what are you doin'? Goin' to work? Hell, son, ain't you heard what happened?"

"Ain't heard nothin'. Just got here." Earl Ray joined Jimmy and a group of eight men who stood across from the janitor's shed, talking. "What's goin' on?"

A fat man Earl knew as Gus Puckett drew himself up. "I'll tell you what's goin' on," he said in a voice like stone on stone. "They let the niggers join iron last night. Caved in to the federal government and that goddamn NAACP and promoted 20 of them to full-fledged welders."

"Twenty niggers? You are shittin' me," said Earl Ray.

"Ain't, neither," said Gus Puckett. "I got that straight from Irv Windom, and he works the graveyard shift. Said 20 or 25 niggers was joinin' steel, big as day, laughin' and talkin' about how the federal government helped them push the white man around."

"Goddamn uppity bastards," breathed J.D. Magee. Earl Ray knew J.D. was a good man. He was one of the ones who had helped Earl Ray put the nigger Ollie Grimes in his place.

"Seems to me, the question is, what are we going to do about it?" asked Puckett.

"Is the bastards still here?" asked Magee.

Puckett shook his head. "Worked their shift and went home, the way I hear."

"We can't get 'em?" Magee sounded like a child who has just learned there will be no Christmas.

"'Fraid not," said Puckett, sadly.

Earl Ray was disgusted. "Who gives a fuck?" he shouted. "They's plenty niggers here, ain't they? One nigger's good as another, far as I'm concerned."

And the men grinned and nodded as they realized he was right.

"Are we gon' let them get away with this?" yelled the skinny, near-tooth-less white man from atop a packing crate near the administration build-ing. He raised an axe handle above the crowd as they shouted back at him.

"No!" they cried.

"Hell no!" the man replied. "My daddy rode with Bedford Forrest in the War of Northern Aggression. Him and all them other good men must be turnin' over in their graves at the thought of what has befell this great country—30 niggers taking white men's jobs. So what's next? Today they take our jobs, tomorrow they take our women? How about it, fellas? You want to see one of those big apes putting his paws on your precious daughter, kissing her mouth with those nigger lips? You want to see that?"

A thunder of angry indignation rose from the crowd at the thought of it.

"Hell no!"

"See 'em all in hell first!"

"You mark my words," cried the skinny white man, waving the axe handle around, "that's where we're headed if you and me don't make a stand. Fellas, we have a decision to make. Are we going to take it, or are we going to fight back?"

"Fight! Fight! Fight!" came the cry.

And it was in that moment that the skinny white man caught sight of them, a small group that had been standing about 50 yards back, trans-fixed. He hopped off the box, pushed his way through the crowd.

"What are you lookin' at, coons?"

They snatched their eyes away, but it was too late. The skinny man came stalking toward them. Ollie stood out in front, Thelma, Laverne, Helen, and Betty just behind him. "Ain't lookin' at nothin', boss," he mum-bled, staring at his own shoes.

"Fuck you ain't!" the man cried. "You was starin' at me. You was givin' me the eye, wasn't you, boy?"

"No, sir," said Ollie. "Wasn't givin' you the eye, boss."

"S'pose you think you're good as a white man now, don't you? They let 25 of you niggers join steel in this yard last night, so I expect you think ain't no more difference twixt you an' me, huh?"

Ollie shook his head emphatically. "No, sir, that ain't what I think at all."

"Well, let me tell you what *I* think," said the white man. "I think it's time we showed what happens to uppity coons around these parts. You can tell your federal government that I refuse to live under nigger domination!"

Ollie was still looking at his shoes, so he never saw the axe handle coming. It caught him on the upper arm. He cried out and reflexively shoved the skinny white man back. It was the wrong thing to do. The white man staggered a few steps, arms windmilling, tripped over someone's foot, and landed on his seat in front of the mob. He sprang up like a jack-in-the-box, his eyes enraged, pointing a bony finger at Ollie. "You seen that? That nigger attacked me!"

"We all seen it," one of them growled, a burly man with a two-day growth of beard. He was smacking his palm with a two-by-four. "You niggers just don't know when to quit."

"He hit me!" Ollie protested.

It was a useless cry. Thelma knew it. Probably, Ollie did, too. The big man ignored it. "You think you can take jobs from white men just 'cause there's a war on, don't you? You think you can push us around!"

Thelma's stomach had gone to ice. She tried to make herself small. Some of the other colored men moved to stand next to Ollie, trying to shield the women. Ollie was showing his palms to the white men. "We don't want no trouble," he said.

The big man said, "Well, trouble's what you got, boy." He glanced over his shoulder at the mob building behind him. "Come on. Let's teach 'em a lesson."

The white men came forward, their steps deliberate and slow, their eyes burning with intent. The small knot of colored men and women edged back. Ollie's hands were still up in a gesture of forbiddance. His voice climbed in desperation. "You all get back now! You all leave us alone!"

The big man in front gave a sudden rebel yell that shredded the morning, and the white men charged.

———

"Get back here, nigger, nigger, nigger!"

Earl Ray could not run because of his leg. He had always hated his birth defect, but he had never hated it more than he did in this minute, as some fleet-footed nigger was racing away from him through a metal shop while he tottered along behind as fast as he could—which wasn't very fast at all—unable to catch up, scared he might even fall. The idea that this boy would so easily escape him scorched Earl Ray's considerable pride. He could all but see the nigger laughing at him, telling all the other niggers how he had made a fool of Earl Ray. But nobody laughed at Earl Ray Hodges.

He seized a heavy chain that lay coiled on the floor, whipped it around three times over his head, and then let it fly. It caught the nigger in the back of the head, midstride as he ran for shelter toward one of the slips. The nigger buckled, arms flailing. He crashed hard into a rack of machinist's tools and lay still.

J.D. Magee came puffing up after them just at that second. "Damn, Earl Ray, you got him after all. I thought he was gon' get away from you."

"Hell no," said Earl Ray. "I may not have two good legs, but they ain't made a nigger yet can outfox Earl Ray Hodges."

He walked with unhurried steps to where the nigger lay, facedown. Kneeling, Earl Ray turned over the already unconscious man, grabbed him up by the collar, and punched him. Again, again, again. Then Earl Ray spat on him and stood. He kicked him once in the ribs for good measure. "That's for makin' me run, nigger," he said.

Watching him, J.D. Magee grinned. "This is more fun than a barrel of monkeys, ain't it?"

Earl Ray glanced down at the nigger lying unconscious among the spillage of tools. He laughed. "Hell," he said, "it *is* a barrel of monkeys!"

J.D. laughed with him, poking Earl's side with his elbow. "Guess you right about that," he said. "And by God," he said, pointing out into the yard, "look at them monkeys run!"

Indeed, everywhere you looked, there where white men bearing down with whoops and yells on niggers and niggers running for their lives. Some were running toward the pier to jump into the river. Niggers couldn't swim—everybody knew that—and they flailed in the water and cried out, trying not to drown. Coast Guard boats were rushing in, throwing life preservers and picking them out of the water as fast as they could. Other niggers weren't able to get away, and they simply curled up and held their fists to their heads as swarms of white men and women kicked and punched and spat.

It was pandemonium—an explosion of long-held fury at the eternal uppitiness of damn-fool niggers. And J.D. had been right: God, but this was fun. Indeed, it struck Earl Ray that he had not had a better time since before Flora Lee up and threw him over, running to that nigger bitch for help. The memory kindled a fresh burn in the pit of his stomach, like an acid chewing through him, and all at once he knew what he had to do.

J.D. rapped his chest lightly. "Come on, son," he said. "Let's not miss out on the fun."

Earl Ray shook his head. Less than half an hour ago, he had gotten off the ferry, reminding himself that he didn't mind waiting, that he would get that bitch as soon as the opportunity presented itself. But who would have thought the opportunity would present itself so soon?

"You go on," he told J.D. "I got somethin' to do."

The heavy wrench landed with a crunch on Ollie's left cheekbone and he fell, moaning. Thelma was standing right behind him. She saw the big white man draw back again, flung her hand up, and took the blow on her wrist.

She knew immediately that it was broken. She fell to her knees, crying and cradling it. Ollie was curled on the ground next to her, writhing in pain, the left side of his face streaked with blood.

She found herself crouched in a forest of moving legs, people shoving one another's weight back and forth, wrestling for position, pushing, grunting, cursing, crying, running. And over and over again, she heard the heavy smack of metal and wood against human flesh, heard the terrible crunch of breaking bones, heard people cry out in pain. Through the shifting tangle of legs, she spotted Laverne, running full tilt toward the water. She had no idea where Helen and Betty were. The white people had lost their minds. There was no more elegant explanation for it than that. The simple fact that 12 colored men had been elevated to skilled positions had driven them insane.

Thelma was dizzy with pain. She had to escape, but she couldn't leave

Ollie, who was on his knees just a few feet away, his head in his hands, moaning. She touched his shoulder. "Come on," she said. "We got to get out of here."

His head whipped around and he glared down at her from a perch of hot, angry pain, and she knew that he didn't quite see her.

"It's me, Ollie," she said, keeping her voice calm. "We got to get out of here."

Then he knew her again. The glare softened and he nodded. Thelma gave him her good hand. Her broken wrist screamed with fresh pain, but she ignored it. Bracing one another, they climbed to their feet. Incredibly, the skinny white man was still there, drawing back his axe handle to hit some poor colored man who was cowering against a wall. With a maddened, wordless snarl, Ollie smashed the old man with a right cross that drove him into the wall. He hit headfirst and slid to the ground, unconscious.

Nearby white men noticed. "That nigger decked old Petey!" one of them cried.

"Come here, boy!" thundered another.

And all at once, a half dozen of them had hands on Ollie, were pulling and clawing at him, and for a terrible instant, he disappeared from view in the midst of them. That fragment of time froze Thelma. Should she run? Should she try to help? What should she do?

Then the question resolved itself. Ollie rose out of the middle of the mob, smashing and kicking and shrugging off white men like you'd shrug off a winter coat, his face burning with rage terrible to behold. Ollie Grimes had been seized by a fury bigger and stronger than he was.

It struck Thelma that even she knew this fury. It was the fury found at the end of a fatigue that felt older than rivers and dawns. You got tired of knuckling under to white people. You got tired of looking at your shoes when you spoke to them, tired of going through back doors and balconies, tired of asking permission. You got tired of taking it.

All your life, you swallowed that fury down, hid it in a smile that went no deeper than your lips. But sometimes, sometimes . . .

"Thelma! Run! Head to the water!"

She realized all at once that she had just been standing there, fasci-nated. Now, she ran. With a last roar of exertion, Ollie broke free of the white men and churned after her. Thelma had thought she was running as fast as she could, but he grabbed her wrist—thank God it was the unbroken one—and all at once, she was running even faster, pulled along helplessly through the melee.

They passed the administration building. Absurdly, she glanced back toward the morale posters on the exterior wall. The glass casing surrounding the one supposedly depicting George and Eric at Pearl Harbor had been smashed. She was not surprised.

We're all together now?

It was bullshit, more of a lie than George had thought, maybe more than even Luther had believed.

And if that was the lie, well then, the truth was this terror she was racing through. It was white men, eyes shining with hatred, mouths wide to emit rebel yells. It was Negroes, outnumbered (*always outnumbered!*), running full-out, hoping for sanctuary. It was blood staining tools, pipes, wooden clubs, and white men's fists, and those implements of violence lifted high in hopes of more.

That was truth.

The truth was, there was no "together." There wasn't even a "we." There never had been. And she should have known this, should have learned it as Luther did the night their parents were burned to death while white people not unlike these stood in the glow of the flames and whooped and laughed, watching.

Somehow, she had not figured it out. She had been a fool. That realization opened a bleak fury within her.

But there was no time for that. Thelma ran. It was her and Ollie and a half dozen others. Their goal was a pier running between two slips, extending out into the river. They would run to the end of the pier, and then they would jump. Thelma couldn't swim, but she was too terrified to be frightened. Better the risk of drowning in that water before a boat could pick her up than the certain destruction now yapping and rebel-yelling at her heels. Except that it wasn't only at her heels. Her heart gave a painful kick against the bars of its cage as she glanced to her right and saw them. Four white men were angling toward her to cut the Negroes off at the pier, even as the mob behind her herded them toward it. They would never make it onto the pier, not without fighting their way through those white men.

"Ollie!" she cried.

"I see it!" he yelled back.

Sure enough, the four white men got there first and arrayed themselves before the pier. They grinned, smacking pipes in their hands as they waited for the colored people to realize they had nowhere to go, waited for them to stop.

Ollie didn't stop. He lowered his head, brought his elbow up before his face and charged at them. He caught the white men by surprise. One of them managed to swing his club—the arc carried it harmlessly over Ollie's head—as two of them went down and were trampled. The fourth man wrapped his arms around Ollie, trying to restrain him, but Ollie stiff-armed him and pushed him aside, barely breaking stride as he did so. He pulled Thelma with him and the Negroes were through.

But it had cost them two or three seconds and now the mob was upon them. There was no way they would make it to the water before they were caught.

"Get in there!" Ollie cried. He was pointing her toward a gangplank leading into the hull of a ship under construction. The main deck was not even in place. Essentially, it was a wedge of metal open to the sky.

Thelma turned to protest. "I can't . . . " she began.

But then the mob surged over Ollie and his hand was torn loose from hers and the weight of them carried him to the ground.

"Go!" he cried.

She wheeled and ran up the gangplank, the sounds of the beating that commenced behind her terrible in her ears. It sounded like sledgehammers hitting watermelons, and she knew Ollie and the other men would be at the bottom of it, curled into fetal balls, taking it. There was nothing else they could do.

She expected at any instant to hear footsteps clattering on the gangplank behind her. She didn't. Apparently, the mob was satisfied with the prizes it already had.

Her heart trip-hammering against her breastbone, Thelma plunged into the half-completed ship, away from the sounds of the beating. She found a compartment shielded from overhead view by a partial ceiling. Maybe this would be a mail room on the finished ship. Or a brig. But for now, it was just the place where she would stop and gather herself and try to understand what she should do.

Thelma sank to the floor. And before she knew it, she was sobbing. She reached automatically for a cigarette, but her purse had been torn from her during the melee. Somehow, that made it worse. Thelma lowered her head to her hands and cried. She should have listened to her brother. She had always thought Luther was damaged by what he had seen and could not forget. It occurred to her now that he had actually been *enlightened* by it, stripped of the ability to believe white people could ever be anything except white people. And although that realization had driven him to the bottle, maybe that was better than deluding yourself, living inside a box of lies.

As she had done.

And maybe the biggest lie was calling Flora Lee her friend, taking her into her home like she was just any woman in trouble. Risking everybody else's safety.

But that scrawny little woman could never be a friend, could she? Not really. Not as long as she was white.

Thelma was disgusted with herself. How readily she had embraced the lies, even when people tried to tell her better. How proud she had been of working here. What affirmation it had given her to join herself to the crush of people walking under that archway every morning. How she had embraced that feeling of purpose, of belonging to some great enterprise far larger than herself.

But now she knew better. Those feelings were just more lies. She belonged to nothing. She never had.

Thelma wiped at her eyes. She felt lower than she could ever remember. Then she heard the sound, footsteps scraping metal in an odd, arrhythmic cadence.

And she heard the voice. It whispered a soft, malicious singsong that made her breathing stop.

"Here, nigger, nigger, nigger."

Earl Ray had been lucky. He had seen Thelma and Ollie at the head of a group of niggers running pell-mell toward the pier, but he had known he had no chance to catch up with them. He had almost given up then but had chosen instead to follow along as best he could. He had seen Ollie lower his head and bust through that human blockade like a running back breaking a tackle. Seconds later, he had seen the crowd bury him and a handful of other niggers beneath a tide of human outrage.

And he had also seen Thelma slip away, running up the gangplank into the bowels of this uncompleted ship. He knew others had spied her, too. He had seen them noting her escape, a few of them contemplating whether to go after her. But chasing down the one little woman would deprive them of the pleasure of stomping and beating the five or six full-grown men who had almost eluded them.

They had let her go. There was no contest. But unlike them, Earl Ray had a personal stake in teaching this particular nigger a lesson. And now God had delivered her to him on a golden platter. So he crept forward through the structure, crept around bulkheads and down passageways, his body rocking slowly up and back in the awkward gait that had tormented him since he was a toddler first learning to walk. "Gimp Hodges," they had called him. And "Stumblefoot." And "Clumsy Ray." They had done this until one day, when he was eight, he got sick and tired of it. He had just taken a beating that morning for breaking Pa's favorite pipe (his older brother Gil had actually done it) and when Dewey Coolidge, two years older, six inches taller, 20 pounds heavier, had started in on him as Earl Ray was out sulkily gathering wood for the cookstove—"Well, if it ain't ol' Gimp Hodges. What you doin' there, Gimp? You collectin' wood to make yourself a new leg?"—Earl had flung himself at the startled boy with maddened rage, knocked him down, and beat him till he was unconscious. Beat him for a while after that, too.

The other boys had looked on with wide eyes and slack mouths. When Earl Ray finally stood up off Dewey's chest, breathing heavily, knuckles bloody and scraped, they had each taken an involuntary step back, and thereafter, the word had quickly spread that you didn't mess with Earl Ray Hodges. He had learned something that day that he would never forget: If you want them to respect you, they have to know that you always settle your accounts. They have to know you never let anybody get away with anything, that you will always get them back, no matter what it costs you or how long it takes.

He had taught many people that lesson many times over the years since the day he broke Dewey Coolidge's nose. Now, he was going to teach it again. She was close. He could almost feel her presence.

"Here, nigger, nigger, nigger," he repeated softly, as he moved through a latticework of shadow and light. "Here, nigger, nigger, nigger."

He came upon an unfinished compartment with half a ceiling overhead. He poked his head through the hatch.

And sure enough, there she was, standing in the far corner, pressed against it like she thought she might burrow through the bulkhead. But she wasn't going anywhere. He knew it, and he could see in her eyes that she did, too.

Earl Ray grinned. "Uh huh," he said.

Thelma's blood went still.

Earl Ray Hodges entered the compartment, grinning at her, his eyes dancing. She pushed herself against the bulkhead, the metal horribly solid against her back, rivets pressing into her skin.

"Get out of here!" she cried. "Leave me alone!"

The stupid grin on his face widened. "Can't leave you alone, nigger. You and me got business together. Don't you remember what I promised you?"

Thelma felt hysteria rising in her. "I didn't do anything to you!" she shrieked. "I didn't do anything."

"Fact is, you took my wife away from me. Shouldn't never have got mixed up in white folks' business. Didn't your mammy or your pa never teach you that?" He was right up on her now. They were breathing the same air.

"I'll tell you where she is!" cried Thelma. She was immediately appalled by whatever sudden, awful desperation had made her blurt those words. But Thelma couldn't help herself. Terror was an electric current singing through her blood, rooting her to this spot. She would happily trade Flora Lee's life for her own.

Earl Ray shattered that hope with a single side-to-side motion of his head. "Uh uh, nigger," he said. "Too late for that. That ain't enough no more."

He punched her in the face. Lightning leapt through her eyes. Her good hand came up and was filled with blood. He punched her again. This one snapped her head back against the bulkhead. Blood went everywhere. She hurt. Lord, she hurt.

Earl Ray drew back for another punch. Somehow, she managed to move her head to the side, out of its path. His fist struck the bulkhead with a metallic clang, and he yelped in pain and surprise. Surely, he had broken something. He doubled over, holding his wounded right hand. This was her chance.

Thelma pushed past Earl Ray and made for the hatch.

But it was a hundred miles away. She never had a chance.

He grabbed for her, came up with a fistful of her shirt. "Get back here!" he roared.

Thelma came around swinging both arms wildly. He flinched back, but one blow glanced off his chin. She had used her broken wrist and a shock of pain went tearing through her arm.

Thelma grabbed her left wrist with her right hand, tears streaming down her face. Earl Ray regarded her disgustedly.

"Shouldn't have mixed in white folks' business, nigger," he told her. "This is your own fault."

And, so saying, he grabbed her hair and drove her headfirst into the bulkhead. Thelma caromed off and fell to the deck, just this side of senseless. She lay on her stomach, drooling blood on the hard metal, her body screaming in agony.

She had to get up.

She *had* to get up.

But it was useless. Body and brain had disconnected. Pain had severed the tie.

Oh Lord, so much pain.

And then from behind her, she heard it, the soft whisper of his zipper opening, the sigh of fabric sliding against flesh.

"Please," she whimpered. "Please."

She felt his hands beneath her, opening her belt, opening her pants. She tried to kick at him.

"You better quit it," he said. "Don't make me hit you no more."

And that was when she knew it was over. That was when she knew she was done. The thought of being hit again was more than she could bear. Thelma stopped moving. Her pants came down. Her panties came down. She felt his weight on her back.

He penetrated her. He began to thrust.

The pain was savage and unimaginable. The helplessness was worse, the knowledge that it was happening and she could do nothing about it. She felt herself tear like paper. She felt a moisture between her legs and knew it had to be blood.

But it no longer mattered.

She faded her thoughts to emptiness, willed her eyes to blindness and her ears to deafness, surrendered to what she had no way to fight. She made it so that she no longer was. Earl Ray Hodges did his evil business.

And Thelma Mae Gordy simply went away.

twenty-three

THE LITTLE GIRLS WERE JUMPING DOUBLE DUTCH AND IZOLA Foster was crossing the dirt lane with dinner plates in hand when Flora Lee, walking, turned onto Mosby Street that early evening in May.

She was happy. Her supervisor at the airfield cafeteria had said today that he would be moving her off the cash register and into the accounting department because he liked her attention to detail, the way her cash drawer always tallied just right at the end of the day. Apparently, she was good with numbers. This was something she had never known.

But it wasn't just work. She had consulted a lawyer, and he had promised to file the papers for her divorce as soon as she saved the money to pay his fee.

But it wasn't just that, either. It was the sense that she had found a place to belong. She knew it was strange to think in such a way about a street where hers was the only white face, but it was the truth. She felt at peace here. She felt known and, more importantly, accepted.

It was something she had never felt growing up. Certainly, she had never felt it while living with Earl Ray in that trailer in his mother's yard. Bessie Hodges had always made it clear that she considered no woman good enough for her precious youngest son, least of all Flora Lee. "I hope you appreciate how lucky you are," she had once told her daughter-in-law. She had said this while they were drinking punch and eating cookies in the basement of the church right after the preacher pronounced the couple man and wife.

And in fact, the former Flora Lee Gadsen *had* felt lucky.

She had always known she was not the most beautiful woman in those north Alabama hills. Far from it, with her thin little mouth and her long nose shading it like an awning, with her figure like a 10-year-old boy's.

Worse, folks thought she was slow sometimes because she did not always see things the way everyone else seemed to see them—when she couldn't understand, for instance, why she was naturally superior to the daughters of the colored men who worked in the mines with her daddy and uncles. People got exasperated with her for this. They said she was "contrary."

All of this, she knew. So from an early age, she had resigned herself to the fact that she would never marry, probably never even have a date. And she had told herself she was fine with that. Then Earl Ray Hodges happened along at a church picnic, with his towering pompadour and his brash and cocky manner. He didn't know anyone, but he hadn't been there five minutes before he was slapping men's backs and laughing with them like a politician running for re-election. He had that funny walk, but the thing she soon came to realize about Earl Ray was that he carried himself with so much confidence it almost fixed his leg. After a while, sitting there listening to him joke and tell stories, you pretty nearly forgot about it.

Other girls, much prettier girls, had followed him about the picnic with their eyes, but to Flora Lee's great surprise, when he got up from talking to the men, he had come straight over and sat down next to her, alone on a bench at the edge of the clearing. He had done a magic trick— "How'd you get that there nickel in your ear?" he had asked in mock wonder—and they had talked. He explained that he lived in the next county over and was visiting his auntie, who sang in the church choir. He asked Flora Lee's name and where she was from and what grade she was. And he talked about himself, the plans he had to save enough money to get out of here and go live in some big, fast-moving city like Montgomery where he would work as a mechanic and one day have his own shop. He told her he didn't want to die of the black lung like his daddy, never having gone anywhere, never having seen anything.

She had been listening with only one ear, all too aware of the eyes of the other girls watching them from across the clearing. Finally, she blurted, "What you doin' over here messin' with me? Can't you see all them pretty girls over there makin' eyes at you? Any one of them would just die to have your company."

He gave her a crestfallen look. "Are you sayin' you don't want my company?" he asked.

"Ain't sayin' that at all," she said, eyes down. "Just sayin' they's gals over there a whole mess prettier'n me you could be talkin' to, is all."

To her surprise, he had smiled. "Don't want to talk to them," he said. "Want to talk to you. You want to know why?"

Flora Lee had nodded dumbly, not trusting words.

"Well, you see," he said, "when you get right down to it, I think you an' me, we's a whole lot alike."

"How you reckon that?"

"Well," he said, "you think you ain't so pretty and you feel left out 'cause of that. I expect that's why you picked yourself a seat way back here at the edge of the clearin' where nobody is. Two more steps, and you'd be in the woods. An' me, I got this one leg that's shorter'n t'other, so I walk funny, like I'm gon' tip over any second and I used to feel left out 'cause of that."

She was intrigued despite herself. "Really?"

"Oh yeah."

"But you so . . . *brash*."

He laughed. "I s'pose I am," he said. "But see, I discovered that there is the whole secret. Can't nobody make you feel left out without you helpin' 'em do it, don't you see? And I just decided I ain't gon' help 'em no more."

He regarded her with a frank interest that made her blush. "So what about you, Flora Lee Gadsen?" he finally asked. "Are you done helpin' other people to make you feel bad about your own self?"

He extended his hand as he said it. For a moment, she just looked at it. Then, feeling like she was in some strange dream, Flora Lee took it. "Yeah," she said, "I expect I am."

They stood and he led her to a table right in the center of the picnic. She was barely aware of the other girls talking behind their hands and shooting her looks hot with who-does-she-think-she-is malice. Already, she was in love.

They were married two months later. And he hit her for the first time two weeks after that.

She told herself he didn't mean it. She told herself it was her fault. She told herself it was just something all couples go through. Over the years, she told herself many things, made many excuses, because she was still so besotted with the idea of that brash stranger telling her she didn't have to sit in back of the picnic feeling like nothing. It wasn't until he knocked her down that one last time that she was finally able to see what now seemed glaring and obvious in hindsight: that that cockiness she loved was but the public face of a rage that, though he kept it well hidden, was never far from the surface.

But all of that, she reassured herself as she drew near Thelma's house, was behind her now. Earl Ray was a mistake that belonged to her past, but a wonderfully unknown future now stretched before her. She had come to trust that with a deep and settled certainty.

"Evenin', girls," she called, waving vigorously to the jump rope girls, who called back, "Hey, Miss Flora," without ever missing a beat. She intercepted Izola Foster at the makeshift footbridge over the open trench in front of Thelma's house. Flora Lee was smiling, about to offer to carry the plates for the old woman, when Mrs. Foster spoke without preamble.

"Did you hear what happened?"

Flora Lee was mystified. "What are you talkin' about?" she asked.

Mrs. Foster gestured with her head. "Come on in the house," she said.

Flora Lee did as she was told, following the widow across the footbridge, up the walk, and into the house. The door closed behind her.

Eight minutes later, that door came flying open, and Flora Lee came flying out at just less than a trot. Her thoughts reeled.

A riot over at the shipyard?

Dozens of colored people hurt? Some dead?

And where was Thelma? She should have been home by now.

Flora Lee was barely aware of Mrs. Foster and Gramp coming down the steps behind her. She could not wait on their age and infirmity. One imperative consumed her. She had to find Thelma.

That thought marched her down the street and up to the door of Rafe and Mamie Plunkett. She hammered it urgently. Was hammering it again even as Mamie pulled it open.

"Miss Flora Lee?" She made Flora Lee's name a confused question.

"I need help," said Flora Lee. "Is your husband home?"

Mamie turned and gestured behind her. A moment later, Rafe appeared, wiping his mouth with a paper napkin. "What's wrong?" he asked.

Flora Lee was teetering on the edge of panic, but she forced herself to stay calm. "There was a riot down to the shipyard. Bunch of colored people hurt. And don't nobody know where Thelma is. She ain't come home. She always home before me. So I need you to drive me. We got to go lookin' for her."

Rafe gave her an odd look. "Miss Flora Lee, I can't do that."

And Flora Lee felt the panic overtake her. "What you mean, you can't do that?" she shrieked. "Ain't you heard me? Thelma is *missin'*! Don't you care?"

The odd expression turned sad. "Of course I care, Miss Flora Lee. I done knowed Thelma since she weren't no more'n a little girl. But what I'm sayin' is, *I*"—he stabbed his index finger into his chest—"can't drive *you*." And he pointed at her.

Flora Lee felt herself deflating as the realization of his meaning struck home.

He spoke patiently. "You got any idea what them police do to me—and to you, too—if they caught you in my car?"

"I don't care!" cried Flora Lee.

"You got to care, Miss Flora Lee. And I do, too."

She knew it was the truth, the stupid, inarguable, irrevocable truth. And that made her hate it all the more. Flora Lee felt crushed then by the onerous weight of laws and customs put in force by men she had never met in places she had never been, laws and customs that had nothing to do with who she was or what she felt yet somehow reached all the way down to this front door on Mosby Street to stand between her and going out to look for the person in this world she cared about most.

"She my friend," she heard herself say, helplessly. "She my only friend."

Mamie looked up at her husband. "Honey, what if I go with you? Then it ain't just you in the car with a white woman."

Rafe shook his head. "I don't know," he said.

"You could put me in the trunk, for all I care," said Flora Lee.

Rafe's mouth kinked into a rueful smile. "Yeah," he said, "that's all I need, be found with some white woman in my trunk. Wouldn't have to worry about the police then. Klan get me long time before they would."

"I got to go, too," said a voice from behind and Flora Lee spun around in surprise. She had not realized Gramp had somehow managed to follow her. Izola Foster was behind him. "That's my granddaughter," Gramp said. "I got to help look for her."

Rafe snorted. "How you gon' look for her, old man, an' you can't even see? Far as you know, she could be standin' right here on the porch right now."

Gramp just repeated himself. "I said, that's my granddaughter. If she in trouble, I got to go find her."

And all eyes turned to Rafe Plunkett. He plowed one big hand back through his graying, short-cropped hair. He shook his head. A long groan of resignation escaped him.

"All right," he finally said. "Just let me get my keys."

Five minutes later, they were on the road. Gramp, Rafe, and Mamie rode in the front. Flora Lee rode in back. She directed them to the boarding house where Ollie Grimes lived, and Rafe went in to ask him about Thelma. A moment later, both men came out to the car. At the sight of Ollie, Flora Lee gasped. He was on crutches. His face was covered with purple bruises. He looked as if he had been through a war. And she supposed he had.

"Tell them what you told me, Mr. Grimes," said Rafe.

The shadow of some great reluctance came over Ollie's eyes at the prospect, but he bent down till he was looking in the car window. "Evening, y'all," he said. "My name Ollie Grimes. I work with Thelma. Hey there, Flora Lee," he said, noticing her in the back.

"Never mind all that foolishment," snapped Gramp. "Where my granddaughter? That's all I want to know."

"She at the hospital," said Ollie. "Mobile City Hospital. They got a few beds for colored down in the basement."

"What happened to her?" demanded Gramp.

Again that reluctance ghosted through Ollie's eyes. "I hate to tell you all this," he said.

"Tell us what?" demanded Gramp. "Ain't tol' us a goddamn thing yet, Mister."

Ollie's smile was sad. "She always said you was a feisty one," he said.

Flora Lee realized he was stalling and that made her heart stutter. "Ollie," she said gently, "what is it you ain't tellin' us?"

Ollie heaved a sigh. "I'm the one found her. After they got things settled down, after security pulled them white folks off me, I went lookin' for her. I knew she was hidin' in the belly of this ship so I hobbled on in there an' looked for her. Found her after a few minutes." He fell silent.

Flora Lee prompted him gently. "Ollie . . . "

Ollie grimaced and lowered his eyes. For a moment, there was silence. Then his head came up and he said, "I'm sorry to be the one to tell you all this, but look like somebody got in there after her and he . . . well . . . he violated her."

Flora Lee's hand came to her mouth. Gramp said, "Violated?"

Ollie looked as if he wished he could be anywhere else. "Yes, sir," he said. A sigh, gathering courage. "And not just that. He hurt her, too. I mean, he hurt her bad."

"Violated." Gramp groaned, a sound of agony too pregnant for words.

Mamie Plunkett said, "Oh, my God. Poor Thelma."

Flora Lee was not aware of her own tears. She tapped urgently on the back of the driver's seat and said, "We got to go. We got to go right now." It was all she could do to hold herself there in the car. She felt that if they didn't get moving that very instant, she might get out and run.

Rafe was already behind the wheel. "We goin'," he said in a grim voice. "Just wanted you all to know, so you wouldn't be surprised."

"You all let her know I'm thinkin' about her," said Ollie, straightening up. "Prayin' for her. You come back and let me know how she is, hear?"

But the car was already wheeling away from the curb.

Flora Lee cursed every traffic light that stopped them, every car whose bumper loomed before them, forcing Rafe to brake.

Gramp said, "She got to be all right. That's all they is to it. She got to be all right." He kept repeating it like a prayer.

"Yes," said Mamie. "She got to be." The reassurance in her voice was hollow.

The traffic was unforgiving. It always was. It took them 15 long minutes to reach the hospital. The car had barely stopped moving when Flora Lee sprang from the back seat. She sprinted for the basement door. Rafe was close behind her. Mamie guided Gramp.

Flora Lee went down the stairs, pushed through the doors into the basement—and stopped. Eyes turned toward her, took her in, challenged her, questioned her, or simply noted her presence and waited to see what it meant.

Colored people were everywhere, some sitting on chairs, some sitting on the floor, some just standing against the wall because there was nowhere else for them to put themselves. As far as she could tell, all of them were injured. There were legs in casts and arms in slings, there were patches over eyes and bandages on heads.

Flora Lee had never seen anything like it. "Jesus," she breathed softly, taking a step forward.

"What are you looking for?" A harried nurse had intercepted her. She was a large white woman, wisps of brown hair flying this way and that from beneath her white nurse's cap. "Whites go upstairs," she told Flora Lee without waiting for an answer. "It's colored only down here."

"I'm lookin' for Thelma," said Flora Lee.

"Beg pardon?"

"Thelma Gordy," said Flora Lee. "They told me she was brung in here."

Until this moment, the nurse's eyes had regarded Flora Lee with an impersonal cool. But at the mention of Thelma's name, something in them shifted. "You know Thelma Gordy?" she asked. "How do you know her?"

"Flora Lee?"

At the sound of her name, Flora Lee turned. Thelma's friend Laverne had come up behind the nurse. She was wearing a neck brace, and one side of her face looked as if it had been scraped raw. Laverne, she knew, did not like her.

Flora Lee held up her hands. "Laverne, I don't want no trouble," she said. "I just heard about Thelma. I come to see about her."

Laverne appeared to consider this for a moment. Then she said, "She would want you to be here. Maybe you be able to get her to talk. Doctors can't get her to say a word." She lifted her eyes beyond Flora Lee. "These folks with you?"

Flora Lee turned. Gramp, Rafe, and Mamie were behind her. She had forgotten all about them. "Yeah," she said.

"Can't take but a couple of you back there," the nurse chimed in. "We don't have room for all you all."

Rafe put an arm around Mamie. "We'll wait outside," he said. "You two go see about Thelma. Come back and tell us how she is."

Flora Lee thought it was one of the most generous things anyone had ever done for her. As Rafe himself had said, he had known Thelma far longer than she had. So he had every right to insist on being one of the ones to go and see her. But somehow, he knew Flora Lee *needed* to see Thelma right now, felt as if she might fly apart if she could not reassure herself that her one friend would be all right. Nodding at Rafe and Mamie, hoping they understood the world of feeling she could not speak, Flora Lee took the old blind man's hand. His grip was tight, his palm was sweaty. The white nurse frowned. Flora Lee gave her a level look. "He blind," she snapped. "Now, you gon' take us to her or not?"

The white nurse suddenly looked as if she had eaten something that upset her stomach, but she turned and led them back through the makeshift ward. They followed her the length of the basement to a room at the very end of the floor. Just outside the door, the nurse stopped them. She regarded Flora Lee gravely. "Do you know what happened to her?" she asked.

"Yes," said Flora Lee. "I heard she was beat up bad. And she was . . . she was assaulted."

The nurse nodded in reply. "Just didn't want you to be surprised," she said. "She's not too talkative." Her eyes flickered. "Can't say I blame her, though."

Flora Lee said, "Is anybody called the police?"

"They came," the nurse said. "She wouldn't talk to them, neither." The woman shook her head. Then she pushed open the door and they entered the room.

A train wreck.

That was Flora Lee's immediate thought. Both of Thelma's eyes were blackened. Her face was cut and bruised and so swollen as to seem misshapen. Her left wrist was encased in a plaster cast and held in some pulley contraption that kept it elevated. A big piece of gauze was on her forehead. She lay on the hospital bed, sunken into the pillow, staring at some distant place. Flora Lee wasn't even sure she knew they were there.

From behind, Gramp said, "Is she here? How is she?"

Thelma surprised them by speaking. Her voice was like pebbles rattling on wood, a soft, raspy whisper. "You need to go home, Gramp." She did not look at them.

At the sound of her, the old man pushed past Flora Lee and, with hands lifted, began to grope his way slowly across the unfamiliar space. "Thelma? What you mean, go home? Ain't gon' do no such a thing. You my granddaughter."

Now Thelma turned her head and spoke with more force. "I said, go home, old man." Something in her tone stopped him. "Go home," repeated Thelma, and now her flat gaze fell on Flora Lee for the first time as she added, "Take her with you."

Flora Lee was stunned. The hatred in Thelma's eyes was palpable. And it was hatred of *her*. But what had she done? "Thelma," she said, her voice fluttering like a curtain in an open window, "we just wanted to see you is all. Just wanted to make sure you all right."

"*You* get away from me," said Thelma, and there was heat in her voice.

"Thelma, what's wrong? What I done?"

Thelma's eyes were cauldrons of molten disgust, and they struck Flora Lee with such force that she took an involuntary half step back and brought her hand to her heart. "Thelma?" she said. "I don't understand."

"You don't *understand*?" said Thelma. She stretched and flattened the last syllable, and Flora Lee realized to her horror and embarrassment that her friend was mocking her hill- country accent. "You don't understand? *Of course* you understand. You're the one first told me. I just didn't listen."

"What? What I told you?"

"You told me what would happen."

Flora Lee's mouth flopped open. Thelma's words made no sense. Then all at once they did, and she gasped. "*Earl Ray?*" she asked. "Earl Ray done this?" And she waited and hoped for Thelma's hot eyes to contradict her, to tell her she was wrong.

But those eyes were steady as a surgeon's hand. And they hated her. Oh, God, they despised her absolutely.

Gramp said, "Thelma, what's goin' on? Somebody tell me." He had reached the bed. His hands were fumbling across Thelma's feet.

She ignored him. "You know," she said, and her hot eyes still scorched Flora Lee, "I don't think I ever told you about my brother. His name Luther. And he can't stand you all. You see, white people lynched our parents. Never told you that, neither, but it's true. They set 'em on fire, right there in the front yard when he was nine and I was going on three. I don't remember it, but he remember every detail—can't forget it no matter how he try. And Luther, he always told me you can't trust no crackers. I never paid attention. I wish to God I had, but I thought he was just touched in the head 'cause of what he saw. Now I know he was right. Look what happened to me on account of you white people."

Tears tumbled from Flora Lee's eyes. "No," she said. She shook her head. "No," she repeated. It seemed the only plea left to her, the only language she had for this awful feeling of having her heart gouged out of her chest, word by word, by her only friend. "No," she said. And this time, she was pleading. "Please, no."

Gramp said, "Thelma, why don't you—"

Flora Lee said, "Thelma, please . . . "

"Get out of here!" Thelma's voice had lifted.

Flora Lee took a step back. She said, "I'm sorry, Thelma. I'm so sorry."

"Get out of here!" And now Thelma's voice had risen to an awful shriek. "Get out of here! Get out of here!" Her eyes were bright with hysteria. "Get out of here! Get out of here! Get out of here!" She was crying. "Get out of here! Get out of here!"

The door flew open. The nurse appeared. She assessed the situation with a quick glance. "You two need to go," she said over the sound of Thelma's shrieks.

Flora Lee looked at the woman helplessly. After a moment, she nodded. What else could she do? She took the old man's spindly bicep. "Come on," she said. "Nurse say we got to go."

Thelma's voice had shredded to a wordless cry and the nurse was leaning over her bed, shushing her and preparing some kind of shot. "Ain't nothin' we can do here. She don't want us here." And then she realized that wasn't quite right. "She don't want *me* here," she corrected.

All the way back down the hall, all the way through the waiting area full of broken and bandaged shipyard workers, Gramp kept asking her questions. "What's wrong with her? Why she start yellin' like that? What's that name you said? Who is that?"

Flora Lee didn't answer, but she wasn't ignoring him. The truth was, she barely heard Roebuck Hayes. She hardly knew he was there.

All she knew was that terrible hatred in Thelma's eyes, that awful madness in her voice.

Get out of here! Get out of here! Get out of here!

Flora Lee feared she would hear that for the rest of her life.

She stalked across the basement. The old blind man had to struggle to keep up. Flora Lee led him up the stairs and through the doors. Rafe threw down a cigarette and crushed it out with the toe of his boot when he saw them coming. "Did you see her?" he asked.

"How is she?" asked Mamie.

"She got hysterical," said Gramp, breathless from being pulled across the basement. "Told us to get out. I ain't never seed her like this. She wasn't nothin' like herself. Nurse made us leave, 'cause Thelma wouldn't stop hollerin'. 'Get out of here. Get out of here. Get out of here.' Like she hate us. Like she blame us for what happened."

"Oh, my Lord," said Mamie.

"Maybe she be better after she done had a chance to calm down," said Rafe.

Mamie seized on the hope in his voice. "Yeah," she said, "you probably right. Can't expect her not to be torn up, somethin' like that happen. And the memory still fresh."

Their conversation seemed to be happening in another room. It was a droning sound of which Flora Lee was only vaguely aware, submerged as she was inside her own pain. And all at once, she knew what she had to do. Rafe was saying something about coming back tomorrow. Flora Lee interrupted him. "Would you please see that Gramp get back home?" she asked.

They regarded her strangely. Mamie said, "You ain't goin' back with us?"

Flora Lee said, "No. I done been enough of a burden on you folks already. And I got somethin' I got to do."

Rafe studied her. She read concern in his dark eyes. "Miss Flora Lee," he asked, "are you all right?"

Flora Lee inclined her head toward the building behind her. "Just take care of her," she said. "She gon' need a lot of help."

"What about you, Miss Flora Lee?"

"I be along directly," said Flora Lee, hoping the lie did not sound as transparent as it felt. "Just got to do somethin' first."

She moved away from them before they could question her further, one hand already digging into the front pocket of her work pants, searching for change to ride the bus. The first bus sailed right past the stop, so jammed that people were standing in the stepwell. When the second bus came along 15 minutes later and the front door whisked open, she elbowed her way past a tired-looking man in a battered hat and dirty overalls who said, "Geez, lady, wait your turn, would you?" But she was already on and did not care.

Twenty minutes after that, she stepped off at the end of the line and began to walk. It took her another 20 minutes. She walked past where the streetlights ended. She walked past where the asphalt ended. She walked through trees dripping Spanish moss onto a carpet of wild grass.

The late spring sun was waning in the sky when she came to a cleared space where about a dozen large tents were erected, six or seven trailers were parked, and families were huddled before cook pots on open flames, barefoot, sullen-eyed children looking on hungrily as mothers stirred the evening meal.

When she emerged from the woods, they stared at her as if she were an apparition. "Flora Lee," said a man with a single tooth hanging from the top gum of his grimy mouth. He did not think to keep the surprise out of his voice.

A woman suckling an infant at her breast with her left arm while stirring a cook pot with her right hand said, "Didn't expect to see you again."

Another woman said, "You come back to him, huh?"

Flora Lee ignored the question, nodding toward the last trailer in the row. "He here?" It was the only trailer from which no light emanated, and she was pretty sure she already knew the answer.

"Nope," said the man. "Ain't seed him yet. Tell the truth, since y'all busted up, he don't usually come in till late."

Flora Lee looked at them, her neighbors for most of the time she had been in this city, people whose children she had watched, whose fires she had tended, whose small secrets and sins she had dutifully kept. She seemed to see them as if from some great distance.

"I'm gon' wait for him in the trailer," she said.

"Oooh," the women cooed, their voices rising together in a siren of suggestiveness.

"You go on and do that," one of them said. "He be along directly."

The man with the single tooth—Barney, his name was—leered at her and said, "'Fore y'all get too carried away makin' up, you best remember some of us got to get up and go to work in the mornin'. Don't y'all keep us awake."

Salacious laughter followed Flora Lee up the single step to the trailer door. She tried her key and the door opened. Flora Lee stepped inside and closed it behind her. The small interior was stifling and rank. Flies buzzed about a tower of dishes in the sink. Clothing, his and hers, was strewn about the floor. The little fold-down ironing board was open. One of Earl Ray's shirts lay on it, a scorch mark in the shape of an iron prominent across the sleeve.

She tossed the shirt aside and folded the board back into its spot on the wall. At the far end of the little space, just beyond the sink, was the hard little bed where they had slept. A nightstand, molded into the frame of the trailer, jutted from the wall opposite the sink, narrowing the passageway and giving the sleeping space some vague illusion of privacy.

By now it was dark in the trailer, the sun fully gone, the only light filtering in through the louvered kitchen windows from the two-thirds of a moon that hovered above. But Flora Lee did not need light. She knew this space, its contours as familiar to her as the inside of her own mouth. She pulled open the top drawer of the nightstand and rummaged around for only a moment before she found what she was looking for. Then she closed the drawer and went back to sit on the couch at the table near the front. From outside, she heard meals being dished onto plates, heard children fussing with each other, heard the sharp rapping of wood on wood as somebody triple-jumped somebody else's checkers, and the man who had pulled the feat off hooted in triumph. Insects sang to the night. She closed her eyes and waited.

She had tried. The Lord knew she had tried. She had tried to make the marriage work, living with a mean, impossible man until fear for her very life had driven her away. And she had tried to make her new life work too, had gotten a job, had found friends and a place that felt like home, and had even begun to make plans for herself beyond this war, beyond this place. She had tried. And Earl Ray Hodges had ruined that, too.

From her youngest days, she had been the girl the other girls giggled about when she passed, the one they closed ranks against because to admit her into their circle was to make their circle—indeed, the very idea of circles—meaningless. She had grown used to not having a friend, used to her aloneness, used to whispering her secrets only to God. And then Thelma had come along and changed everything. Maybe she had thought Flora Lee mousy, ugly, and contrary, too, in addition to being white—which, in her world, Flora Lee was starting to understand, would be the worst thing of all. Yet despite that, and at great risk to herself and everyone around her, Thelma had taken Flora Lee in. Even though she had had every good reason not to be, Thelma had been her friend.

And look what had happened. Earl Ray had beaten her. *Raped her*. In so doing, he had taken away the one good thing in Flora Lee's life. And then, almost as if her hatred had conjured him up, she heard him coming.

Flora Lee's eyes came open slowly at the sound of his distinctive gait on the gravel, his voice yodeling some tune she didn't know as he entered the clearing. "Evenin' boys," he called out. His voice sounded jocular—and drunk. "How y'all doin'?"

Some time had passed. She didn't know how long. But she no longer heard the women and the children, so she guessed they were back in their trailers and tents now, the children having bedded down for the night, the women picking up their sewing or some book to read by lamplight. A few men would still be sitting around outside drinking and playing checkers.

She heard Barney cackle in response to Earl Ray's greeting. "How we doin'? We not doin' as good as you, ol' buddy."

"You got that right," slurred Earl Ray. "Fine as frog's hair, that's me."

"No," said Barney with another cackle, "that ain't what I meant a'tall. What I meant is, you got a surprise waitin' for you yonder in that trailer of yours."

"What?" Earl Ray asked. "What surprise?"

"Why don't you go on up there and see for yourself?" Barney said.

There was a moment. Earl Ray would be standing there mystified, trying to figure out if they were putting one over on him, trying to decide if any of this carried some hidden insult to his pride. And then, yes, she heard the scrape of his step on the gravel, felt his weight on the step outside. The trailer door came open.

"Hello?" he called to the darkness. "Who's here?"

"Close the door, Earl," she said. And she scratched a match and lit the kerosene lamp on the table.

"Flora Lee?" he said as light leapt into the room. His voice rose toward hope, and happy disbelief lifted his mouth in a smile as he closed the door behind him. "Is that really you? You come back to me?"

"No, Earl," she said. "I ain't."

His glassy eyes needed a moment to register this, and she took that time to study him. His clothes were sweat-stained and rumpled. She was surprised that a man who took such fastidious pride in his appearance would go out looking like this. Then she realized he had no choice. She was the one who had done his ironing and his washing. And before that, his mother.

"What do you mean, no?" he finally asked, honestly confused.

"Why did you do it, Earl?"

The glassy eyes squinted. "Why'd I do what?"

"She my only friend, Earl. The only one I ever had. Why did you have to take that away from me?"

Earl Ray's mouth puckered. "The nigger," he said. "That's what this is about?"

"Her name is Thelma!" Flora Lee found herself yelling it. "And you ain't had to do that to her."

"She messed with white folks' business!" Now Earl Ray was shouting, too. "She messed with my business. When a nigger do that, she deserve what she get."

"So you raped her. You like to killed her."

A nasty smirk hoisted a corner of Earl Ray's lips. "You best to shut up, Flora Lee, 'fore you piss me off and I go back and finish the job."

Flora Lee brought the pistol up from her lap and pointed it at him. It was a pearl-handled revolver he had inherited from his father. "You ain't finishin' nothin', Earl Ray Hodges. You ain't gon' never touch me nor her again."

Earl Ray's eyes tightened as if he could not make himself believe that he was actually staring down the barrel of his own pistol. Flora Lee's hands trembled. Shooting him had seemed so easy when it was a rage throbbing in her temples like a headache, driving her back to this place with a single-minded determination. But now it was real, now *he* was real, not a hated thought or a despised memory, but a man with shining eyes and sweating brow, facing her from five feet away, and she suddenly realized it wasn't easy at all. She didn't know if she could do this.

He saw. "Just give me the gun, Flora Lee," he said. "Give me the gun and everything will be like it used to be."

She raised the pistol higher in her shaky grip, shook her head no.

He exploded. "Goddamn it, Flora Lee!" he cried, hammering his fist on the table. "I told you to give me the goddamn gun!" And he lunged toward her.

Her index finger made the decision for her, pulling on the trigger. A hard *bang!* filled the tiny space. She had reflexively squeezed her eyes shut. When she opened them again, she saw Earl bringing one hand to a ragged hole in his neck, blood spilling over it. He looked confused. He looked as if this could not be happening.

Then his eyes rolled up and Earl Ray Hodges fell dead across the table.

Flora Lee felt a calmness that surprised her then. She regarded Earl Ray with distant dispassion. From outside, she heard the sounds of commotion, people asking if that was a gunshot, people calling out to her and Earl Ray, wanting to know if they were all right, children crying, men debating whether it was safe to approach the trailer. This, too, Flora Lee regarded with distant dispassion. It had nothing to do with her.

She looked down, surprised to find the gun still in her hand. She placed it on the table next to the dead man's head, then folded her hands and just sat there, thinking nothing, feeling nothing. Flora Lee was still sitting that way 40 minutes later when she first heard the distant wail of the sirens.

twenty-four

ON THE DAY SHE WAS TO RETURN TO WORK, THELMA WOKE UP screaming.

Her eyes came open to find Gramp looming above her, shaking her energetically. "Thelma! Wake up." She heard a mouse skitter across the floor, unnerved by the commotion.

"I'm awake," she said, sitting up. Her mouth was cottony. "I'm awake."

In the darkness of predawn, the old man was little more than a shadow. Even so, she saw the relief that etched itself on his face. "You had that dream again," he informed her uselessly.

"I know, Gramp."

Thelma breathed heavily. Even freshly wakened, rescued from sleep, she could still feel Earl Ray's touch upon her. The terror had become a routine.

"Are you sure you ready for this?" asked the old man. Ollie would be picking her up for work in a few hours. It would be the first time she had been back since.

"I'm sure," she told Gramp. She spoke with confidence she did not feel.

"Thelma, it's only been a few weeks since."

That was the word they used: "since." She refused to allow anyone to finish the sentence, refused to let them speak of what had happened to her, what had been *done* to her. She didn't say it herself, not even in the private recesses of her thoughts. To say it was to make it real.

"Been two months," she corrected.

"Still ain't long enough, bad as you was hurt."

"Doctor say I'm ready. Besides, I can't malinger here forever, old man. We gon' run out of money. We got to eat, don't we?"

"I could get a job," he said.

"Gramp," she said, and then stopped. She had intended to remind him that he was blind and over a century old. Instead, she said, "Thank you for offerin'. But I got to get back sooner or later. Most folks already been back a long time."

This was true.

The shipyard had been in turmoil for a week after the riot, hardly anyone showing up for work, Army and State Guard troops patrolling the city, protecting Pinto Island. The production of ships in one of the nation's most important shipyards had fallen to virtually nothing, right in the midst of a global war. A thousand colored workers had petitioned the federal government for permission to transfer to other plants. The petition had been denied. So, many had simply left the city altogether.

Finally, the shipyard came up with a plan. The local newspaper praised it, the federal government accepted it. It was segregation—the very thing the president had prohibited in Executive Order 8802. But there was a war on, so 8802 was forgotten. The races were separated on the ferry that took workers over to the island. They ate in separate lunchrooms. And the shipyard opened four colored-only shipways where Negroes were allowed to work every job except foreman.

Even at that, the bosses had been reduced to holding mass meetings at the colored YMCA and going so far as to visit individual workers in their homes to coax and beg Negro women and men to return to work. It was a hard sell. Colored people were frightened for their safety. One of the bosses had come to Thelma's home, too, trying to cajole her into coming back to work as soon as possible. But he had taken one look at her and said, "Come back when you're up to it."

"Most folks," Gramp answered her now, "wasn't hurt near as bad as you. Are you sure you ready for this? Are you sure you healed?"

"My wrist is fine," she said.

"Wasn't just talkin' 'bout your wrist," he told her.

For some reason, it made her furious. Not that it took much these days. "Don't need you tryin' to be no mother hen to me, old man," she snapped. "Why don't you just go back there and go to sleep and leave me alone? You worry about you and let me worry about me, all right?"

Her eyes had adjusted somewhat to the darkness, so she could more easily see the hurt that settled into her grandfather's features then. It made her feel guilty, made her want to apologize. But she couldn't think of the words.

"Fine then," he said. And he got up and made his way stiffly to his room.

Thelma lay back down, her hands crossed beneath her head, and watched the ceiling. There was no thought of going back to sleep. Sleep terrified her. Earl Ray Hodges lurked in sleep. But she knew that made no sense. Earl Ray Hodges was dead.

She knew this only because of a cryptic letter that had arrived in her mailbox two weeks after the riot. The return address was the women's jail. When she opened it, a story torn from the newspaper slipped out. The headline: "Woman Held in Husband's Death at Hillbilly Worker Camp." The brief story beneath told how Flora Lee Hodges, 24, had been arrested after police were called to investigate a gunshot at the camp and had found one Earl Ray Hodges, 28, deceased from a gunshot wound. Flora Lee had been taken into custody without incident. There was a note scrawled in the margins of the newspaper. It read, "You ain't got to worry about him bothering you no more."

The note was unsigned but of course Thelma knew who had written it. Thelma didn't know how to feel about it all. There was something frightening, powerful, and somehow . . . intimidating about the idea that Flora Lee had killed her husband. And that she had done it for Thelma. She had told herself she should visit the jail, go see Flora Lee, if only to acknowledge what the little woman had done. Besides, Flora Lee was soon to go on trial. She probably needed a friend. But Thelma simply could not be that friend. Luther had been right. Nothing good came of mixing with those people. The best thing you could do was stay as far away from them as you could get. Wasn't she living proof?

Thelma lay there staring at the ceiling for two hours. When dawn began to burn the shadows from the room, she sighed, threw off her thin blanket, and climbed up from her makeshift bed. She opened the curtain and gazed out upon the new day. The sky was pink at the edges, fading up toward a robin's-egg blue overhead—a beautiful dome for an ugly world. For a moment, Thelma was content simply to watch the waking day unfurl itself from darkness.

Finally, she went to wash up, dress herself, and get breakfast on. She put oatmeal on the table and woke Gramp. They ate in silence. The only sound in the house was the clinking of their spoons against their bowls and the indistinct murmur of war news on the radio.

Then Thelma said, "I ain't had no call to snap at you like that, Gramp. I'm sorry."

"Ain't like that the first time," he said.

"I know," she told him.

"You ain't been yourself ever since."

"I know that, too," she said.

"I'm just worried about you, is all."

"Try not to," she said.

He grunted to say that she had asked him to do the impossible.

From outside came the bleating of the car horn. Thelma glanced over at the clock on the wall. Ollie was right on time. He had been the designated chauffeur since Thelma was hurt. She had a feeling she would never get that job back, and it made her a little sad. She would not miss fighting the morning traffic and making four pickups before driving out to the shipyard. But she would miss being able to go wherever she wished at a moment's notice without walking to a bus stop or asking for someone's help. Just to get behind the wheel and go was a luxury she hated to lose.

A few times during her convalescence, she'd asked Ollie to take her shopping. Shopping had always relaxed her before, but it wasn't the same, knowing he was sitting out in a car waiting for her, reading his paper and, every now and again, maybe glancing impatiently at his watch. Not that he ever complained, not that he ever groused or said he had other things to do, but she knew, all the same.

The horn sounded again and that decided her. She would have to get a car of her own.

"You sure you gon' be all right?" Gramp asked as she pushed away from the table.

"I'm sure," she said. She kissed his smooth forehead. "Be nice to Mrs. Foster," she added as she gathered her purse and went out.

Ollie was waiting for her with the passenger side door open. "Good morning, Thelma," he said.

He didn't grin or joke around with her. That was something he didn't do so much anymore. Thelma nodded at him through a vague sense of loss, remembering all those times she had called him incorrigible. "Morning, Ollie," she said as she slid into the seat.

He closed the door behind her, got behind the wheel, and started the car. They drove in silence for a few minutes. Finally Ollie said, "You lookin' forward to goin' back to work?"

"I don't know," she said. And then she heard herself add in a small voice, "I'm a little scared, to tell you the truth."

She felt, rather than saw, him glance her way. "Why you scared?" he asked.

"I don't know," she said. "I guess, maybe, 'cause it's gon' be the first time I been back there since."

"Yeah," he said with a sigh. "I expect that would be hard. First time in two months."

She turned toward him. "What's it like over there now?" she asked. "White folks still actin' mean?"

He shrugged. "Depend on who you ask, I suppose. Those of us workin' on the colored shipways ain't got much to do with white folks no more. Some of us workin' the unskilled jobs on the other shipways, well . . . " He shrugged again. "They say white folks mad as they ever was before. Maybe madder."

Thelma snorted. "Ain't that some nerve? They done beat the shit out of us, and they the ones mad."

"Yeah," said Ollie. After a moment he said, "So, what do you hear about Flora Lee? How she doin'?"

"I have no idea," lied Thelma. "Can't say I give a damn."

He gave her a look. It angered her. "Somethin' wrong with that, Ollie? You got somethin' you want to say to me?"

Ollie shook his head. "No, ma'am," he said. "Nothin' to say."

Thelma went into her purse for a cigarette and lit it with shaking fingers. She smoked in silence as Ollie wended the old car through the crush of morning traffic. In short order, they picked up Betty, Helen, and Laverne. He got out and held the door for each of them. But there were no grins, no low bows, no touching of his hat. The women did not giggle like high school girls. So much had changed. Everything seemed so different since.

"How you doin', honey?" asked Laverne as she settled into the back seat.

She was the third of the girls to be picked up, which made her the third to ask that question. "I'm fine," said Thelma. She had gotten sick of saying it. She had to remind herself that they were just worried about her. That's what friends were supposed to be.

"You sure you ready for this? You sure you healed up enough?"

"My wrist is fine," said Thelma, and then she silently dared Laverne or any of them to find the nerve to say it wasn't just her wrist they were concerned about. But they had the good sense to say nothing.

After a moment, Betty said, "So, when the last time you saw your white friend?"

They always called her that. Like she didn't have a name. Like being white and Thelma's friend were the only things that defined her. And maybe for them, they were.

"I ain't seen her since," said Thelma in a rigid voice.

"I seen in the paper," continued Betty, "she in jail for killing that husband of hers."

"I guess she finally snapped," cracked Helen. "Can't say I blame her. If I had a husband like that, goin' upside my head all the time, I think I'd have snapped a long time ago." She laughed.

Betty said, "That's how it is, though, with poor white trash. They all the time knifin' each other, shootin' each other, and whatnot. White folk be talkin' 'bout what colored people do, how bad colored people is, they need to look in the mirror sometime."

Thelma stiffened. She was about to say something—she had no idea what—when Laverne beat her to it.

"Y'all need to leave that girl alone," she said, and this was so surprising—*Laverne? Defending Flora Lee?*—that Thelma turned around to look. Laverne was staring out the open window, breathing cigarette smoke into the breeze. "Night they had that riot—same night she shot her husband, I guess it was—that white girl come bustin' in that hospital like the devil hisself was on her tail, sweatin', eyes all wild, demandin' to know what done happened to Thelma." Laverne met Thelma's gaze as she added, "That girl really care about our friend. So maybe we ought to care a little bit more about her."

Her point made, Laverne returned her gaze to the traffic. Thelma turned back, stunned. Of the three girls, Laverne was the one who'd always had the least use for Flora Lee. The fact that even Laverne was standing up for her now made Thelma shift guiltily in her seat, reminded her how she had turned the white woman away that night, screamed at her and told her to get out. And it reminded Thelma, too, how she had spent the two months since then acting as if Flora Lee didn't even exist.

Flora Lee existed, all right. She existed behind bars at the women's jail where she would soon be facing charges for killing her husband for doing the thing Thelma had not been able to speak of, even to Ollie and the girls. But to remember Flora Lee's existence was to remember her own arrogance at allowing that mousy little woman to become her friend. It was to remember how casually she had crossed lines that were not supposed to be crossed, betrayed her real friends to help someone who could never be a friend. Worst of all, remembering Flora Lee was to remember . . . him. It was a circle, one side leading inevitably to the other and back again. To remember Flora Lee was to remember things she could not afford to remember.

So she would remember nothing. She would have no history. This was the first day of her. She was new.

Thelma was glad the conversation—which served only to remind her that she was not new at all—dwindled into silence as the car entered the Bankhead Tunnel. They emerged on Pinto Island moments later and, after a few turns, Ollie found a space in the big lot. The five of them climbed out of the Olds, and they walked toward the gate.

Thelma was not prepared for the rush of emotions that assailed her then. It felt welcomingly familiar walking toward that gate and yet, at the same time, utterly unreal. She had a sense of being outside of herself, as if somehow this was just a scene unfolding on a stage as she sat in the audience and watched herself performing in the role of Thelma Gordy, colored shipyard worker, returning to work for the first time after a long absence. Whatever pride she had once felt at walking toward that arched gate, at being part of that throng of human beings united in a great undertaking had drained out of her. She felt none of that now. In its place was only a greasy anxiousness breaking in slow bubbles in her stomach like the simmering contents of a pot.

Thelma was sweating. She felt her heart chattering in her chest. It was only by an effort of will that she kept herself from running back through the parking lot, back through the tunnel, all the way back to Mosby Street. This was a mistake. She couldn't be here. Earl Ray Hodges was here.

"Thelma?" Ollie squinted in concern. "You all right there?"

"Thelma," said Laverne, "what's wrong, honey?"

Thelma found herself grasping the side of the arched gate. The rough metal felt good in her hands, cool and solid. Real. Somebody was patting her on the back. People were slowing down to stare. It made her angry—this wasn't some damn show—but she couldn't even find the breath to shout at them, tell them to move on, leave her alone. Then her hands were on her knees and she was bent double and with a great, raw sound, she was vomiting onto the pavement. She heaved until she had nothing left to heave. Someone was still patting her back. She didn't know who it was, but she wished whoever it was would stop. Finally, Thelma spat one last gob of mucus onto the pavement. Her mouth tasted like sour oatmeal.

"You okay, girl?" This was Laverne, leaning down toward her.

Thelma nodded. Vomiting had helped.

"Nerves," said Ollie.

"Maybe she ain't ready for all this," said Helen. "Maybe we should take her home."

"No," said Thelma. She stood straight. "No," she said again. "I'm all right. Come on, let's go to work."

She didn't wait for an answer. She walked ahead, and they followed her.

Leaving her things in her locker, Thelma found her old supervisor and reported for duty. She was disappointed to learn that she had not been reassigned to one of the colored shipways, but she didn't complain. She worked her full shift without incident. By the end of the day, she was convinced that what had happened that morning at the gate was only first-day jitters.

But it happened again the very next morning.

As she rose from vomiting, using Ollie's handkerchief to wipe spittle from her lips, a sudden, cold knowing seized her. She barely heard her friends asking if she was okay, scarcely felt the supportive hand on her back.

God, no, she told herself. *God, no. Oh, please, God, no.*

But the horrible knowing would not be denied.

Thelma took off that Friday. She went to her doctor. He did some tests.

The following Wednesday, on the way home from work, Ollie dropped her off to get the results. For long minutes, Thelma waited in a chair in the doctor's office while he examined a patient in the next room.

Her hands worried one another. She read and reread the diplomas and citations on the wall. She tried not to think.

Finally, the door came open and the doctor bustled in. "I'm sorry to keep you waiting," he said in his faintly officious manner, pulling up his desk chair and taking a seat. "Let's not keep you in suspense any longer, shall we? I have your test results right here."

He opened a folder that had been on his desk and adjusted his oval spectacles. For long moments, he did nothing but study whatever it was that was written there. All at once, he looked up and gave a beaming smile she would remember for the rest of her life. And she was not at all surprised by his next words.

"Congratulations, Mrs. Gordy," he said. "You're pregnant."

twenty-five

FLORA LEE HAD LOST WEIGHT. SHE HAD ALWAYS BEEN A SMALL woman, but the figure that sat down now on the opposite side of the visiting room table was downright gaunt. Still, there was a light of real joy in her eyes at the sight of Thelma.

It made Thelma feel worse. Flora Lee was so happy to see her, but she was not happy to see Flora Lee. Seeing Flora Lee made her ache. It was an act of will simply to be in this space with her. Thelma didn't hate her. At least, not anymore.

"You look like you need to get more to eat," she said. It was the first thing out of her mouth.

"What they serve us in here don't encourage too much eatin'," said Flora Lee with a wry smile. "How you been?"

Thelma ignored the question. "I got you an attorney," she said.

"They already give me a free attorney," said Flora Lee.

"This one better," said Thelma. "His name John Simon. He ain't free, but he done agreed to represent you, at least up till trial, and he only gon' charge half his normal rate."

"You ain't had to do that," said Flora Lee.

"You ain't had to do what you done, neither," said Thelma. She was aware that it might sound like a rebuke. Might also sound like gratitude. She supposed it was both.

"Yes I did," said Flora Lee. Her face was solemn.

"Are you sorry you done it?"

Flora Lee did not hesitate. "No," she said. "Even if they put me in the electric chair, I ain't sorry. What Earl Ray done to you was . . . "

"Don't talk about that." Thelma spoke more harshly than she'd intended.

Flora Lee gave her a look and then a slow nod. "I'm just sayin' I ain't sorry, is all. Maybe that's a sin and maybe I'm goin' to hell for it, but I don't care. I can't help how I feel." They sat in a dingy room with 11 other tables just like this one, 11 other people sitting across from 11 other female inmates having 11 other conversations. Except for Thelma, everyone in the room—including the bored-looking guard standing near the door with his arms folded across his skinny chest—was white. The jail maintained hours for colored visitors to visit colored prisoners and white visitors to visit white prisoners, but no one had ever thought to make provisions for a colored visitor to visit a white prisoner. She had seen it in the guard's confused eyes when she presented herself at his gated cage this morning. She could feel it in the questioning of the curious eyes upon her now, but she ignored them.

"Thelma," said Flora Lee, "are you all right? 'Cause it don't seem like you are." It struck Thelma that this was a question she should have been asking Flora Lee—*would have* been asking Flora Lee if all the affection she had once felt for her had not curdled and died.

Thelma shrugged, a sting in the corners of her eyes. "I'm angry," she heard herself say. Her voice was a hissing whisper. "I'm just so goddamn angry all the time."

"You got the right to be angry after what Earl Ray done."

Thelma lifted her eyes. "I'm angry at *all* of you," she said.

It took Flora Lee a moment. Then she sat back. "Oh," she said.

"Yeah," said Thelma.

Another moment. Then Flora Lee said, "Well, I expect you got that right, too."

"I'm pregnant," said Thelma.

It was only the second time she had said the words. The first had been to Gramp. He had felt behind for his chair and collapsed into it, dropping the pipe he had been smoking. "Oh my Lord, child," he had said.

Flora Lee, by contrast, took another long moment. Then her expression slowly collapsed.

"Thelma, no," she said. "Are you sure?"

Thelma nodded. "Went to the doctor, took the test." She was weeping now. Flora Lee put her hand atop Thelma's.

"No touching!" barked the guard at the door.

Flora Lee lifted her hand as if from a hot stove. "I'm so sorry," she said. "I'm so sorry."

"I don't blame you," Thelma managed to say. She felt she owed Flora Lee the kindness of the lie.

But Flora Lee would not accept it. "I don't know why you wouldn't," she said, her own eyes shining. "If it wasn't for me, you wouldn't never of met Earl. And if you had never met Earl . . . " She shrugged her shoulders as if to say the rest of it didn't need speaking.

"I did blame you," Thelma admitted. "That night at the hospital and then, when the doctor told me this . . . I blamed you. I really did. I don't no more. I mean, I guess I kind of do, but I know that don't make any sense, I know it ain't really fair. So I don't. Least, I try not to. But the problem is, when I see you . . . "

"You see him," finished Flora Lee.

Thelma nodded, mashing at her tears with the heel of her palm. "I think that's why I stayed away from here so long. And it's why . . . "

Again, Flora Lee finished the sentence for her. "You ain't comin' back," she said.

And again Thelma nodded, feeling helpless, feeling bereft of language. "I can't," she said.

"Then don't," said Flora Lee. "It's okay."

For some reason, it angered Thelma. "Why you got to be so goddamn understanding?"

People glanced in her direction. The guard's head came up. When the tirade didn't continue, they all looked away.

Flora Lee's smile was soft. "It's all right," she said. "You gon' be all right. Both of us, we gon' be all right."

Thelma made a fatigued sound. The sudden anger had blown through her like a summer storm. She felt wrung out. "I wish I could believe that," she said, "but I can't."

"Can't nobody blame you for feelin' that way, girl," said Flora Lee. "I can't imagine how I'd feel if I was carryin' the baby of somebody who . . . done what Earl Ray done."

"I hate it." Thelma made this confession in a low voice that did not sound like hers. She swallowed, felt fresh tears spring to her eyes. "I hate this baby," she said. "I know that's wrong. Baby ain't never done nothin' to nobody. Baby innocent as anything can be. But I can't help it. I hate it. I hate knowin' some part of that man is growin' inside me. I just feel like I'm the dirt where he planted his seed."

Hearing her own words, Thelma was appalled. "What kind of mother I'm gon' be to this baby, Flora Lee?" she asked, helplessly. "What if it look like him? Every time I see it, it gon' remind me of its daddy. How can you be a mother if you hate your own baby?"

The question hung suspended in a long silence broken only by the sound of Thelma sniffling into a handkerchief and the indistinct murmur of other conversations. A full minute passed.

Then, with a furtive glance to her left and her right, Flora Lee said, very softly, "You ain't got to have it, you know."

Thelma looked up. "What you mean?" she asked. Though of course, she knew.

Flora Lee's brown eyes were steady upon her. "I mean you could get rid of it," she said.

Thelma stared at her. Flora Lee gave a slight nod as if to confirm some unspoken question. "You done already thought about that, I expect," she said.

Thelma said, "Yeah."

Flora Lee said, "Seem like that solve your problem, then. Just promise me you won't try to do it yourself. I done seen gals die who tried to do it theyselves."

Thelma shook her head. "They's a root woman I know about. Her name Mother Suggs. I ain't never met her, but I done heard a lot about her. They say she know how to do them kind of things. They say she done helped a lot of women when they got theyselves in trouble. If I do it, I guess I go to her."

Flora Lee gave another shallow nod. "Well, there you go, then," she said, as if the matter was now settled.

"I done thought about it," admitted Thelma. "Thought about it a lot."

"What's stoppin' you, then?"

"It ain't easy as all that," said Thelma. "It's a *baby*, Flora Lee."

"It's Earl Ray's baby, Thelma."

Thelma sighed. Then she said, "Flora Lee . . . I was pregnant once before."

"You was?"

"Yeah. When I was a teenager. Me and Eric, that's the fella got me pregnant, we got married on account of it. But I lost the baby. My baby was born dead." Thelma paused, dabbing her eyes. "I bled a lot," she said.

"And the doctor, he said afterward that I probably wouldn't never be able to conceive again. So you see, this baby I got inside me, you might say it's kind of a miracle. I mean, I hate it, Lord knows, but it's also a miracle. Can I go to the root woman and ask her to get rid of a miracle?"

Flora Lee pondered this for only a moment. Her nod was decisive. "Yes," she said. "Sure you can."

Thelma was surprised. "I can?"

"You don't love this baby," explained Flora Lee. "Ain't that what you said?"

"I hate it," corrected Thelma.

"Well, you asked the question yourself," said Flora Lee. "How you gon' be a mama to a baby you hate? Child comin' into the world where even his own mama hate him, he better off if he weren't never born at all. Don't you think?"

"So you would get rid of it?" For some reason, Thelma found herself whispering.

"I would," said Flora Lee. "And I wouldn't worry about no miracle, neither. Miracle supposed to be a good thing, ain't it? You carryin' a child by Earl Ray Hodges ain't no miracle. That's a curse. Take it from me. I was married to the bastard five years."

"But it's against the law," said Thelma, weakly.

Flora Lee shrugged. "Who gon' tell the law?" she asked.

The guard called out, "Time's up."

Thelma barely heard him, but Flora Lee stood automatically. She regarded Thelma with a fond smile. "You was the only friend I ever had," she said. "You take care of yourself, hear?"

Thelma looked up helplessly.

And then Flora Lee was gone. For a long moment, Thelma just sat there, unable to move. Other prisoners were filing out, other visitors leaving the room.

She sat there.

You was the only friend I ever had.

It wasn't until the skinny guard was looming over her, staring down expectantly, that Thelma thought to follow the last of the visitors to the door.

She felt buffeted by her own emotions. Thelma was leaving Flora Lee to face alone whatever fate John Simon and the Mobile County district attorney would cobble together for her. But she couldn't help it. Colored and white were not meant to be friends. If Earl Ray Hodges had taught her nothing else, he had certainly taught her that. And even if he hadn't, how could Thelma ever look at Flora Lee the same way when the very sight of her brought back her husband, brought back that awful morning when she had felt his weight pressing her against the deck, brought back the thing that had happened next, that thing she never called by name, that thing so awful and hateful that she'd had to leave her own body to escape it?

What kind of friendship could that be? But still, she and Flora Lee *had* been close once. And how could she have abandoned a woman who considered Thelma her only friend? Not just her only friend now but her only friend *ever*? How cramped and constricted must Flora Lee's life have been up till now that she could say such a thing? So yes, this way was harder, this way caused her pain, but in the end, this way was the only way it could be. Thelma walked out of the jail toward the bus stop and promised herself she would never return.

She did not look back.

But the woman who was no longer her friend had broken some chain inside her, let loose some logjam in her soul.

She did not have to have this baby.

And yes, this was something her mind had already known. But it had not yet whispered that secret to her soul. Flora Lee had bridged the gap for her and now, it was all Thelma could think about.

She did *not* have to have this baby.

It wasn't really a baby anyway, was it? No, it was a thing. It was a tumor. It was Earl Ray Hodges . . .

Here, nigger, nigger, nigger.

. . . having the last laugh from beyond the grave.

But he would not. That thought had hardened into a certainty by the time the bus came and she paid her fare. Thelma barely heard the driver bark at her to get off and reboard in the back. She barely felt the bodies that she squeezed through to find a place to stand. All of her was concentrated on that shining revelation.

She did not have to have this baby.

The decision was hers. And her decision was no.

It took an hour and a bus transfer to bring her back to the little house on Mosby Street. Gramp was sitting in the front room when she opened the door, his pipe clamped in his teeth, listening to a baseball game.

"Afternoon, Gramp," she said.

"You sound like you in a good mood," he said.

The realization made her pause. Then she said, "I suppose I am."

"That's good. Miss Flora Lee doin' fine?"

"Well as can be expected."

"We got anything back there for supper? I'm starvin'."

It was Sunday and Mrs. Foster was at church.

"I'll fix you somethin' in a minute," said Thelma. "Right now, I got to talk to you."

She sat down in the chair on the other side of the radio. He turned expectantly toward the sound of her, and for a moment, she just studied this face she had known all her life. They had always had a special relationship, she and Gramp. He loved Luther and Luther loved him, but Luther had been a prickly boy with a temperament as unpredictable as a March breeze. He brooded a lot and needed time to himself. As a result, Luther had never been especially close to their grandfather—or even to her, now that she thought about it.

But she and Gramp had been another matter. Back when he had not yet lost his sight, they would go on long walks together with no particular destination in mind. The walking itself was the point. She could ask him anything and he would tell her. They talked about slavery and baseball and even where babies come from. She told him her secrets and he even told her his. So it seemed the most natural thing in the world to her that she would share what she had decided.

"I need to tell you somethin'," she said. And she paused, looking for some way to slip easily into what needed to be said. But, she realized, there was none, so she plunged ahead. "I'm not gon' have this baby," she told him.

Puzzlement knotted her grandfather's features, the sightless, rheumy eyes gazing somewhere off to the left of her. "What you mean?" he asked.

"You ever hear of Mother Suggs?"

"Yeah. She a midwife."

"Yes," said Thelma carefully, "she a midwife. She help them that wants a baby to bring it into the world. But she also help them that don't want no baby to get rid of it."

His mouth opened just slightly. Then he said, "You mean, you want to get an abortion?"

"Yes."

"Oh, Thelma."

It was all he said, but the tone of his voice expressed his disappointment more eloquently than a sonnet could have done. She felt an anger that was becoming all too familiar flare beneath her breastbone. It burned her good mood away like tissue paper in a furnace.

"'Oh, Thelma' what?"

"Just . . . " He palmed his bald head with his right hand, exhaled heavily. "Are you sure?"

"Why wouldn't I be sure?" snapped Thelma hotly.

He looked startled at her vehemence. "Thelma, I'm just sayin', you go to one of them old hoodoo women, ain't no tellin' what they do to you. I done knowed 'em to give a girl gunpowder to drink mixed in with whiskey. Or stick a knittin' needle up in there. You could get bad hurt. You could even die. It's a mighty risk you'd be takin', Thelma. You sure you want that?"

"Ain't but one thing I'm sure of, Gramp. I don't want to have that man's baby."

Again his sightless gaze was somewhere to the left of her. "Baby can't be blamed for who it come from, Thelma. Baby don't know nothin' about that."

Anger yanked her to her feet. "But *I'll* know! And I'll hate that goddamn baby just like I hate its goddamn father! I already do! How the hell am I gon' be a proper mother to some goddamn half-white bastard and every time I look at it, it reminds me of . . . reminds me of . . . "

It was no use. She could not make herself go on. Thelma paused, chest heaving, eyes streaming. The old man's face was uncomprehending.

"Thelma," he said, uncertainly.

"Just leave me alone," she told him. "For God's sake, just leave me the hell alone."

And she stormed out of the house, feeling as if its very walls were pressing in upon her. The door rattled in its frame as it slammed behind her.

Outside, she breathed. It felt like the first time she had done so in a week. Thelma sat on the steps. From someone's backyard, a chicken's desperate squawking came to an abrupt end, and she knew the unfortunate bird would end this day as someone's Sunday supper. Across the street, the jump rope girls, Ruthie, Mildred, Vivian, and Aggie, were walking home from church. They would run into their houses and change clothes and within three minutes, she knew, they would be back outside, jumping double Dutch. They waved energetically to her now, four skinny, dark-skinned girls in homemade church dresses. Thelma lifted a desultory hand in response, thinking of how much simpler life would be if all she had to worry about was jumping rope with her friends until the light faded and her mother yelled at her to come in for dinner.

The thought almost made her weep. Thelma was conscious that something was wrong with her. Tears always seemed to be lurking just beneath the surface of her. And when she wasn't sorrowful, she was mad. Lately, she had become so snappish, so easy to anger. When had she ever yelled like that at Gramp before? Not even when she was a teenager and thought she was in love with Eric Gordy and Gramp had tried to keep her from seeing him had she treated her grandfather with such disrespect.

But she couldn't seem to help it. Her moods were so brittle, her temper so hair-trigger. She had the sense that she had lost her very self, like a wrong turn on an unfamiliar road, and she was struggling to get back again. She was glad her brother was not here to see this. But then, if her brother had been here, none of this would have happened. How blithely she had challenged Earl Ray Hodges, how impulsively she had taken Flora Lee into her home, robbing that cruel little man of what, in his crude way, he had actually held dear, wounding his pride in the process. What little thought she had given to how he might take revenge—even after Ollie's terrible beating.

But would she have done it if Luther were here? Luther, who seethed with such fierce hatred of white people that he could not abide their very presence? She probably would have chafed under the restrictions imposed by her brother's presence. But at least she would not be in the situation she found herself in now, pregnant with a hated baby. If Luther were here, she would never have known Flora Lee Hodges beyond nodding to her in the shipyard. She would not have thought of calling some white woman her friend. When Earl Ray slugged his wife for the sin of being thankful, Thelma would have felt bad about it, but she would have known better than to extend her hand to help.

And what was to happen next? Just what did Gramp think she ought to do? Was she supposed to give birth to this little mulatto bastard? And then what? Give it away? Who in the hell would want it? What orphanage would even take it?

Or did he actually expect her to keep it?

How, exactly, would she explain *that* to Luther? What would she say to him when she presented him with his little half-white nephew? How would he ever respect her again? How would she even look him in the eye? Especially if he asked how she had come to have such a child and she was forced to admit it was because she had been . . . because she'd had . . . forced relations with a white man? What would that do to him? Luther was already half-mad with his abhorrence of white people. To come home and find one—even half of one—suckling at his sister's breast would probably drive him completely over the edge. That was another reason it was best just to get rid of the thing.

The sound of the jump rope girls drew her up out of herself. Sure enough, they had come back out on the street, having changed into play-clothes. Aggie and Ruthie were swinging the two ropes, Vivian and Mildred were holding hands in the middle, pigtails bouncing as they jumped. And the girls chanted an old singsong in time to the swing of the ropes.

Oh Mary Mack, Mack, Mack
All dressed in black, black, black
With silver buttons, buttons, buttons
All down her back, back, back

It made Thelma smile to see them. She watched for a few minutes, then got up and went back inside the house. The front room was empty. Apparently, Gramp had gone to his room, the door of which was pointedly closed. In the kitchen, a Wonder Bread bag was open on the table, slices spilling out. Next to it was an open can of Spam; half of its contents had been crudely sliced out by the knife that lay near the can.

Just as he had felt around to find the bread, the Spam, and the knife, Thelma knew her grandfather was perfectly capable of putting those things back where they belonged once he was done with them, blind or not. But she had promised to fix his lunch and instead had yelled and cursed at him. This was his way of getting back at her, of telling her she had not been fair to him. Thelma sighed. Sometimes, Gramp was a hundred-year-old child. She was tempted to leave it all right where she had found it, let the bread turn hard, let the Spam change color. But it was foolish and unpatriotic to waste food with a war on. She didn't even have aluminum foil, which was nearly impossible to get, to wrap the Spam.

Sighing, fighting down an anger that was, she knew, out of proportion to the offense, she closed the bread bag and put it back on top of the ice-box. She dug the remainder of the Spam out of the can, put it on a plate, covered it with another plate and put it inside the icebox. It wouldn't keep for long like that; she would have to cook it in the morning with scrambled eggs. Then she stomped the Spam can flat, opened the back door, and dropped it into the box where they were collecting metals for the war. She tossed the knife into the sink.

Finally, she went back into the front room, fished a cigarette out of her purse, which still lay where she had dropped it when she came in, and sat in her chair next to the radio. The ball game was still playing. She switched over to the news, lit her cigarette, and sat there smoking as she listened.

The announcer told her about reports of mass killings in eastern Poland as the Nazis took over entire villages, slaughtering the peasants who lived in them in order to make room for ethnic Germans to settle there. And he spoke of how a city named Hamburg in Germany had been reduced to rubble by British bombs, with a death toll over three nights that was believed to be near forty thousand.

Sitting there on a Sunday afternoon in her front room in Mobile, the faint sound of little girls chanting "Oh Mary Mack" coming through the thin walls, it was difficult for Thelma to conceive that such a thing was real, that it was happening right now, in the very same world.

Mass killing? How did you even accomplish such a thing? Did you just stand there and shoot unarmed people until you ran out of bullets? How was such a thing possible for human beings to do? And forty thousand people dead? In just three days? How could you even fathom such a number? How could you pretend to comprehend such a slaughter? It gave her an odd, unsettled feeling, as if civilization itself had never been more than a veneer and now the war had stripped it away to show mankind as the brutish animal it really was. The whole world had descended into a chaos of violence, hatred, and killing on a scale impossible for her to understand.

Forty thousand people dead. In just one tiny corner of the war. In just one city. In just three days. Thelma had never done much praying. But sitting there in her front room, listening to the news, she breathed a prayer out loud.

"God, help us all," she said.

———

Thelma was standing on her porch the next morning when Ollie came by to pick her up for work. She climbed in through the door he held for her.

"I'm not going to work today," she told him when he got behind the wheel. He gave her a questioning look. "Tell them I'm sick, would you please? I want you to drop me somewhere else."

The look lingered. Then Ollie said, "Okay." He worked the long gearshift in the floor and pulled away from the curb.

Twenty minutes later, she watched him drive off, leaving her standing on the street in an unfamiliar colored neighborhood that looked much like her own. Same open trenches, same wooden planks making makeshift bridges across, same dirt street, same ramshackle wooden boxes with the same meager lawns half gone over to the dirt. All that was missing were the four little girls jumping rope.

Thelma waited until the Oldsmobile had disappeared into the distance. Then, she crossed one of the plank-board bridges and walked up to one of the houses. Hanging against the door by a black thread was a small claw-shaped object, blackened by age. It took Thelma a moment to recognize it as a chicken foot. She regarded it distantly, pondering what she was about to do. Then she took a breath and made herself knock firmly. The flimsy door shivered in its frame.

It seemed to open instantly, as if the woman behind it had been waiting for her all along. That woman was small and ancient, with mahogany skin and a kind face. Her eyes glinted up at Thelma as if she had just finished laughing at an especially good joke.

"Yes?" she said.

"Are you Mother Suggs?" asked Thelma.

The old woman appraised her with knowing eyes. Then she reached and clasped Thelma's hand in a cool, bony grip. "Come on in, child," she said. Feeling almost as if she was in a daze, Thelma nodded and stepped into the old woman's home. The door closed firmly behind her.

twenty-six

ON THE DAY AFTER CHRISTMAS IN 1943, THE 1ST MARINES went ashore at Cape Gloucester on the island of New Britain. It was the beginning of monsoon season, and it rained as they hit the beach.

And it rained as they set up their bivouac.

And it rained as they set out into the jungle.

Slogging through mud that came halfway up to his knees, George had a bizarre sense that the world was made of water, that it wasn't just rain falling down from the sky on the beleaguered marines, but that it was coming up out of the ground and flying sideways out of the trees, that a whole ocean was being dumped on his head. It seemed impossible that only a day before, he had been stretched out on his rack on the transport ship, listening to Bing Crosby sing a melancholy new song on the radio—"I'll Be Home for Christmas"—and reading letters.

In one, Mother chattered about news from home. Father was working too hard as usual, Nick, who was now 17, was planning to join the Marines as soon as he graduated in the spring, and Cora had blossomed into a beautiful young lady with several eager beaus.

In another letter, Sylvia asked if he still loved her. "I try not to complain," she wrote, "but I cannot fail to notice that I send three letters for every one I receive from you. I understand that you are very busy, but . . ." George had no idea how he would answer her.

But the letter that troubled him the most had come, oddly enough, from Thelma Gordy. He had written to apologize for being so slow to respond to her last letter and to tell her what a comfort her words had been. Her reply, when it reached him, had been terse and cutting.

Dear Private Simon:

You seem to think I've been sitting here waiting for the favor of a letter from you and feeling bad because you didn't write. Well, let me assure you: nothing could be further from the truth.

I only ever wrote you in the first place because you were kind enough to do what you did for my brother. I didn't intend to create some situation where you felt obligated to continue a burdensome correspondence. If that's the way you feel, put your mind at ease. There is no obligation, and if there ever was, I release you from it.

There probably should never have been a correspondence between us in the first place.

You're white and I am colored and it was probably never proper for us to write to one another as we did. What were we thinking? I guess it's the war.

So you needn't worry about writing me back, Private Simon. In fact, I'd prefer if you didn't.

It had stung him, left him feeling as if he had been caught peeking through a window where he had no business and had his wrist slapped accordingly. He had tried to puzzle out what he could have said or done that would have made her so angry. Nothing came to mind. For a long time he had been thinking about what to write her back, her parting shot be damned. Even now, he was still thinking about it and that, he knew, was a mistake. Right now, he needed to be thinking about Japs, and only Japs.

So George made himself dismiss Thelma's puzzling letter from his thoughts and refocus on the task at hand. He walked in a crouch through the wet, his rifle at the ready, his senses alive to every moving shadow, every stray rasp or click from the jungle that pressed against the narrow footpath from either side. The constant rainfall thumping his helmet made it hard to think. A long black snake gave him a start as it went slithering around the trunk of a tree at his approach.

"Goddamn, this shit is crazy!" growled the man behind him in a loud voice. His name, George recalled, was Clark Hardwick, and he was supposed to be an actor from Los Angeles. George thought maybe he had even been in some movie with Jimmy Stewart or somebody. But George wasn't sure and he didn't really want to know. If two years of war had taught him nothing else, it had taught him that it wasn't a good idea to make too many friends. It just made you feel worse when the war took them away.

"Shut up, Hollywood!" Babe snapped from up ahead. "Don't you know there might be Japs around?"

A voice from farther ahead hissed, "All of you pipe down!"

The men set up a defensive perimeter on a high ridge above the footpath. The brass feared the Japs might try to use the trail as an escape route when their airfield was attacked. "Our job," a lieutenant had explained drily, "is to discourage them from doing that."

The men dug foxholes along the top of the ridge, chopping through the heavy underbrush to scoop out the muddy soil below. They set up a gun emplacement for their single machine gun and dug a gun pit behind that. The machine gunners strung a strand of barbed wire around the pit. They pulled pins halfway out of grenades and hung them on the wire like ornaments on some evil Christmas tree. The idea was that any Jap who tried to sneak up on them would jar one of the bombs loose. It would go rolling down the steep embankment into his own men.

Down the hill behind them, maybe 50 yards in from the beach, the marines set up their mortars, facing the green wall of the tropical jungle. This, too, they protected with barbed wire.

And then, there was nothing to do but wait.

And it rained.

And it rained.

And the night came.

And the Japs didn't come all that night.

And the morning came, the unrelieved black burning away to a misty gray.

And it rained.

Once, the rain knocked two of the grenades with their half-exposed pins off the barbed wire, and they went rolling down the hill in the muck. One of the machine gunners crept down after them. He reached for them gently, pushed the pins back in gently. Watching them from his foxhole, George realized that he had stopped breathing. He exhaled.

The smokers griped because they couldn't smoke. Pull out a cigarette and it was soggy and shapeless before you got it to your lips, much less touched it with your Ronson. Some tried to smoke under palm fronds dripping water. Others tried to use their ponchos to shield their Chesterfields and Lucky Strikes from the downpour. Still others tried to curl their bodies around the precious tobacco tube to protect it from the rain long enough to steal a few drags.

Nothing worked.

"I guess the smoking lamp is out, boys!" cracked Donny Hoover from the foxhole on George's right as Stu Leibowitz, the man he was sharing it with, flung his pack toward the jungle after another failed attempt. Donny was a cheerful 18-year-old who hated the smell of cigarette smoke so much that he would leave the area anytime anybody lit up around him.

"Fuck you, Donny!" replied Leibowitz.

They all laughed. Even Donny.

And it rained.

And it rained.

And again the night came.

And again, the Japs did not.

And again the morning came.

And it rained.

And then it stopped. Just as suddenly as if someone had turned off a spigot, the deluge ended. The unfamiliar sun bore down out of a deep blue sky. The men gazed about them in absolute wonder, as if they had forgotten a sky could do anything other than piss on them. And the instant wonder passed, hands went fumbling into pockets and and kits and out came cigarettes, cigars, and even a pipe or two. Out came Ronsons and matchbooks, and within seconds, the ridge was wreathed in the gray-blue smoke of burning tobacco. Leibowitz had somehow got hold of another pack of cigarettes—maybe he carried a spare—and he lit one up and blew a lungful of smoke right in Donny's face. "Cut that out!" he cried. And he sounded so much like Jack Benny that everybody laughed. Even Donny.

"I don't like this," whispered Babe. He and George were sharing a foxhole.

"Don't like what?"

"This," said Babe, gesturing. "Sun comes out, suddenly guys are actin' like it's a church picnic. Even the new guy," he added, nodding over to where Clark Hardwick was standing up high, arms draped around the rim of his foxhole like he was on the couch in his den back home.

"Hey, numb nuts!" yelled Babe. "Get your ass down!" The actor gave him a surly look, but he did as he was told.

"You shouldn't be so hard on 'em," said George.

"Hell I shouldn't. This is just like Guadalcanal. Nothin' happened for a day or two, and then those little fuckers rained all hell down on us."

George considered this. "Yeah, you're right," he admitted.

"Damn right I'm right," said Babe. "We can't let our guard down. They're comin', sure as I'm sittin' here in the mud."

An hour later, black clouds moved in and closed off the sky.

And it rained.

And it rained.

And the night came. And George sat up, staring tensely into the shadows, remembering what Babe had said, remembering Guadalcanal. But the Japs did not attack.

And the morning came.

And it rained.

George lifted his eyes into the wet. His skin was puckered. His stomach rumbled from cold, soupy C-rations. His shirt clung to him like a needy child. His boots were full of water. He was crouched in mud. Soon enough, they would have to climb out and bail water from the foxhole.

Babe looked around warily, his rifle held at the ready. "They're comin'," he said. "I can smell 'em."

And it rained.

And the night came. And George and Babe took turns watching the jungle while the other slept, except that nobody really slept. The most you could hope for was a few minutes in some nether place between wakefulness and slumber where your mind drifted like a leaf in a stream, never quite losing contact with reality, but allowing reality to become less real, less urgent, less there, letting it—

What was that?

George's eyes flew open. His rifle came up.

"Rat," whispered Babe's voice in the darkness beside him.

"Huh?" George had not yet clawed his way back to full awareness.

"Just a rat," repeated Babe's voice in the same whisper. And the shadow of Babe's hand pointed to the shadow of a large rodent, scuttling slowly off over the top of the ridge.

"God," said George, his breathing heavy, his heart banging.

And the wind pushed the trees, whistling through the palm fronds above. And the thunder shook the world. And the jagged bolts of electrical fire threw wild shadows that leapt against the wall of green, gone before they were there.

George stared into the place where the rat had disappeared.

The wind moaned like lost souls. Fire split the sky.

And in that flash of light, a man was suddenly there, a cruel, foreign face staring down on George's position from not five feet away. Panic and terror constricted George Simon's throat just then. To his horror, he heard his mouth say, "Ja-Ja-Ja-Ja," even as his brain screamed, "*Japs! Japs!*"

But though his mouth was frozen, George would be forever thankful that his body suffered from no such impediment. It moved automatically, without conscious command, bringing the rifle up, squeezing the trigger. He saw the surprised look on the man's face as his brains exited through the back of his skull.

"*Japs!*" George finally managed to scream.

But of course, the other marines already knew. They were screaming the same thing. And the night exploded. The shadows turned themselves into Japs, charging the Marine line screaming, "Banzai!" and "Marine, you die!" and taking death as though it were a prize to be cherished, something a man fought to claim. Tracer fire arced overhead, casting a flickering glow on the jungle below. Jap mortars hammered the Marine position, explosions coming so close that George found himself trying to pull his head into his neck like a turtle as broken trees rained down in splinters of wood and palm. American mortars hammered back at the Japs. The machine gun opened up with a metallic chatter.

Next to George, Babe was shooting and screaming. "Come on, you fuckers! Come on, goddamn you!" A mad glee lit his eyes.

George was screaming something, too, though he had no idea what it was. The shadows kept turning themselves into Japs, and he just kept shooting.

And it rained.

Morning came. Once again, the great spigot above turned itself off. Cautiously, the marines lifted themselves from their holes and advanced through a light ground fog to inspect their handiwork. The trees had been denuded by mortars and gunfire. The mucky ground was carpeted with the bodies of the emperor's men, most of them dead, a few of them dying. Some of the marines bayonetted the helpless sufferers. Some refused, preferring to let them linger in their misery.

"I told you so," said Babe, kneeling to rifle the pockets of a dead Jap for souvenirs. "I told you they'd come."

"Never doubted you for a second," said George.

Babe was pulling open the corpse's mouth. He peered closely, looking for gold, then drew back looking disgusted. "Cheap bastard," he said. "Nothing but lead."

Clark Hardwick found a Jap flag one of the enemy soldiers had tucked under his uniform over his breastbone. "Hey, fellas," said Hardwick, standing and unfolding the flag. "Get a load of this fancy handkerchief." And he ostentatiously blew his nose into the enemy banner.

"I hate that guy," whispered Babe.

"Why?" asked George.

Babe shook his head. "Can't say I even know. But I do."

George moved a little ways off from the killing field to stand at the edge of the crest. Babe followed. George found himself looking down at a series of green ridges sloping away over deep ravines wreathed in fog. A footbridge connected this ridge to the nearest one on the east side. It was actually quite beautiful.

"Bet Jazz would've had something crazy to say about all this," said George.

Babe smiled fondly at the mention of their friend. "Yeah," he said, "probably."

"'Don't mean a thing if it ain't got that swing,'" said George.

"'T'ain't what'cha do,'" said Babe. "'It's the way hot'cha do it.' He really liked that one."

"Yeah," said George. "I remember."

"That Crosby tune on the radio yesterday? He wouldn't have approved of that."

George laughed. "Yeah," he said, "you're right. Crosby wasn't really his speed. He liked the colored singers more."

"Well," said Babe, deadpan, "that only makes sense. You remember, those were his people."

George grinned. "Yeah," he said. "He wanted to be colored so bad he could taste it."

"Happy New Year, by the way," said Babe.

"Not yet," said George. "It's only the 30th."

"Really? I guess I lost track out here."

Then a hole appeared in Babe's stomach, and he went down just as he was lighting a cigarette. In the same instant, the crack of rifle fire echoed raggedly across the ridges.

George was stunned. "M-m-m-medic!" he cried. "M-medic!" The cigarette was still in Babe's mouth. Blood pumped from his gut.

George cried out again, more forcefully this time. "*Medic!*"

He was kneeling to comfort his friend when there came another rifle shot and he felt something clang against his helmet and knew that he was hit. George reeled there on the edge of the ridge, trying to hold his balance. Then the muddy soil beneath his feet crumbled away, and he felt himself going backward over the cliff.

For a moment, he was flailing in space. Then the ground hit him like a fist, driving the air from his body, and he tumbled helplessly, rolling with all the control of a boulder down the steep ridge and into the jungle below. George hit a tree stump, but his momentum bounced him over it. He hit a tree and felt one of his ribs snap. He tried to react, tried to reach out for something—anything—that might arrest his fall. But plants and roots tore away in his grasp. Gravity was malicious and inexorable, pulling him down. And then he hit bottom, splashing with a hard shock into a shallow creek running along the jungle floor.

From far away, he heard men crying out, heard more gunshots. He tried to yell. He didn't know if he'd made a sound. He tried to move, but his body had become too heavy for him to lift. His heartbeat thudded ponderously in his own ears, his breathing was ragged, but for some reason, he was not afraid. He knew he should have been. He had been hit, shot in the head, had fallen down the hill and now lay here, helpless and unknown, vulnerable to the enemy.

Afraid? He should be *terrified.*

And he should be scrambling to his feet, screaming for help, for somebody to come and get him. But his body had become as distant and unresponsive as the moon.

Worse, his mind didn't even seem to care. It floated away from him.

Far above, he was vaguely aware, men were still shouting, men were getting shot at, someone was even calling his name. But all that noisy urgency belonged to another world. George felt strangely peaceful lying there, splayed on the jungle floor. He felt oddly . . . accepting.

Darkness appeared at the edges of his vision like some wary jungle animal. George waved it in, welcomed it. He lowered his head, closed his eyes, and the shadows swallowed him down.

Two men were arguing in a harsh language. It took him a moment to recognize it, and when he knew what it was, his heart froze. They were speaking Japanese.

It was only then that George realized he was alive. That shocked him. His head and neck throbbed, and he remembered being shot, remembered falling from the cliff.

George forced his eyes open. He found himself lying facedown in muddy sand on some beach. He could hear the sound of waves somewhere behind him. His arms were pulled behind him, knees bent, hands bound to feet, and a rope looped about his neck in such a way that his slightest attempt to move choked him like two strong hands on his throat. He could not see the men who were arguing, but somehow he knew he was the subject of their dispute.

Then one of the Japs came into view. He saw George seeing him and his eyes became fury. He snarled something in Japanese, lifted his rifle in both hands, drove the butt down on George's head.

And George knew nothing else.

It was night when he came to.

He was still tied like a hog on the way to the barbecue. His face was still pressed against the sand. He spat some of the grit out of his mouth and saw, by the light of the shard of moon overhead, that there was blood in his saliva. There was a pulsing ache inside his skull where the rifle butt had struck him. From behind him, unseen, he could hear the voices of many men talking quietly in Japanese and below that, the restless sound of the Pacific Ocean.

George thought he had known what it was to fear. He thought he had learned it on Guadalcanal, where he had been strafed and bombed and shot at and had clung to a tree like a child to his mommy. But none of that had prepared him for this. George was more terrified than he had ever thought it possible to be.

A bowl was set down in front of his face. When he saw the mushy white paste inside, it was all he could do not to vomit. Rice. Goddamn rice.

A Jap sat down where George could see him, leaning against a boulder. He was a compact man with large ears. He was broad across the chest and powerfully built. If George remembered properly what he had been taught, the insignia on his uniform identified him as a captain.

The man made a gesture toward the bowl. "Eat," he said. "Obviously, I can't untie your hands and give you *hashi*—chopsticks. I'm afraid you'll just have to put your face in it." His English was perfect and without accent.

George glared at him. The Jap tried again. "Eat," he said. "You want to keep up your strength."

"George Alexander Simon," said George crisply, "private, United States Marines. Service number 310115."

The Jap smiled. "Ah yes," he said. "Name, rank, and serial number, is that it?"

"That's it," said George.

"Very well then, George Alexander Simon. I am Makoto Fujikawa, captain, Imperial Army of Japan. Service number 071482."

George regarded Fujikawa warily. Was this Jap making fun of him? Fujikawa took no notice of George staring at him. He lit a cigarette, exhaled smoke, waved idly at some night insect that buzzed about his face. Then he spoke without looking around. "You really should eat, George Alexander Simon."

"No thank you," said George. "Had enough of rice to last me a lifetime."

"*Hai*," said Fujikawa with a tiny smile, "me too."

"You speak good English," said George.

Again the smile. "You mean I speak English well," the Jap corrected.

"Yeah," said George. "How is that?"

"Yale University," said Fujikawa, "class of 1932."

"No shit?" George did not bother masking his surprise. The random fortunes of war would never cease to amaze him. Just a few hours ago, he had bivouacked with one of Jimmy Stewart's costars. Now he was trussed up on a beach talking to a Jap from Yale.

"No shit," replied Fujikawa behind a cloud of cigarette smoke. "I grew up in your country. My father was a diplomat and he was posted there." The smile turned wistful. "I loved America," he said. "I hated to leave."

"Why did you?"

"My father was recalled in '35. I had no way to stay. He's the one who insisted I join the Imperial Army. He saw the war coming even then, and he felt that afterward, those of us who had served would be in position to reap the spoils of victory. We would be important figures in a vast new Japanese empire."

"Is that what you think?" asked George.

Fujikawa's eyes turned sad. "I think Japan is going to lose this war, George Alexander Simon. That's what I think."

Again, George was shocked. "Really?"

Fujikawa nodded. "I don't think my people really appreciate the sheer size of your country or its industrial capacity. If we had any slim chance of winning, it was right after Pearl, with your navy in disarray and your people shocked and disheartened. Maybe then we could have seized your West Coast and forced a negotiated peace. It would have been a long shot, but . . . " Fujikawa finished the sentence by shrugging and spreading his hands.

"But then," he said, "your factories and plants got to work, churning out new ships and planes and guns. Our navy was decimated at Midway Island and, as they say in your country, that was the old ball game. We're just playing out the string, but the conclusion, I suspect, is preordained."

"Then why keep fighting? Why not surrender?"

Fujikawa stubbed out his cigarette, blew out a last stream of smoke. "Have you ever heard of Bushidō?" he asked.

George tried to nod but gagged as the rope drew tight around his throat. Fujikawa, a fresh, unlit cigarette already dangling from the corner of his mouth, reached over and did something to the rope. The result was a slightly increased range of motion.

"Bushidō," Fujikawa was saying, "is Japanese warrior code. It's from the old samurai days. It requires supreme loyalty, fearlessness in battle, and it does not allow surrender. Surrender is the ultimate dishonor, the ultimate shame. Better you should end your own life than subject your family to such disgrace."

"But there's no dishonor in surrendering if you can't win."

"In America, perhaps." Fujikawa lit his cigarette. "In Japan, we see things differently."

"But you said you grew up in America. You have to know that's crazy."

Fujikawa's face turned hard. "I grew up in America, George Alexander Simon, but I am Japanese."

"Fine," said George. "So you're Japanese. But you still grew up in the US. That's got to mean something, too."

Fujikawa repeated himself. "I am *Japanese*," he said.

It made George angry. "Why did you come over here, then? Why are you talking to me?"

Fujikawa didn't answer. After a moment, he said, "Would you like a cigarette?"

George, who didn't smoke, looked at him. Finally, he gave a small nod. Fujikawa produced a cigarette, lit it from his own, and placed it in George's mouth. The Jap cigarette was short and stubby. It tasted like shit.

Fujikawa must have seen this on George's face. "You're right," he said. "It's not exactly Chesterfield. I miss those myself."

George got three or four good, long drags from the cigarette, coughing with each draw. Then he spat the butt into the wet sand.

Fujikawa said, "I'm supposed to be interrogating you. That's why I came over here. As the one who speaks English, the one who knows Americans best, I am supposed to be getting information from you on troop movements and plans."

"But you haven't even tried," said George.

Fujikawa laughed. "You're a private," he said. "What the fuck would you know? Besides, I don't feel like trying to beat information out of you. I've seen enough of that."

"Then what's the point?"

"The point? The point is, we spend some time talking and then I go over there and tell them you've voluntarily confirmed what our intelligence already knows."

"And then they kill me?"

"And then they put you on a ship and take you to a prison camp in Nippon."

"I don't get it. Everybody knows the Japs don't take American prisoners. I mean, we don't either."

"Yes," said Fujikawa. "We've seen your handiwork."

"And we've seen yours," snapped George.

"*Hai*," said Fujikawa. "Neither side has been found wanting for acts of barbarism."

"Then why am I alive?" asked George. "Why are you sending me to this camp of yours?"

Fujikawa smiled. "They think you are the son of a high-ranking American leader. They think holding you will be a great propaganda coup."

"What high-ranking leader?" said George. "My father's a lawyer. Where'd they get the idea he was some government leader?"

"They got it from me. I told them."

"Why?"

Fujikawa took a long, meditative pull on his cigarette, then stubbed it out in the wet stand.

"Why?" asked George again.

Fujikawa sighed, "You shouldn't be alive, George Alexander Simon. You had a bullet glance off your helmet. Something of a miracle, wouldn't you say?"

George nodded.

Fujikawa said, "My second-in-command wanted to use you for bayonet practice. Some of the others wanted to tie you up and bury you up to your neck in the sand and watch you drown as the tide came in. You probably heard us arguing about it before Kenji put your lights out. I told them no. I told them we would deliver you to the prison camp instead."

He gave George a direct look. "I saved your life, George Alexander Simon."

"Why?" asked George, yet again.

Fujikawa had lit yet another of the stubby cigarettes. He waved it toward the sky. George's eyes followed. He found himself gazing upon endless pinpricks of cold white light sprayed across fathomless ebony night.

"You think there's someone up there, keeping watch over us?" Fujikawa asked.

The question surprised him. Was he really lying here in the sand of some remote Pacific island about to discuss theology with a Jap who spoke perfect English, who'd gone to *Yale*? For a fleeting moment, George wondered if he were not hallucinating the whole thing. Maybe he was lying in his rack on the ship, dreaming. Maybe the bullet hadn't ricocheted after all and he was dying.

But the knife's edge of pain in his ribs was too sharp for this to be anything but real. "Yeah," he said. "I do."

"Then what must he think of what he is seeing now?" said Fujikawa. "I'm not just talking about the armies fighting and the bombs exploding. That's impersonal. That's the business of war. No, I wonder what he must think about cutting off a man's dick and shoving it in his mouth while he's still alive, or stabbing out his eyes when he's looking at you. Have you ever considered how much we must hate each other, that we can do such things?"

"Yeah," said George. "I have, actually."

"There's something obscene about that kind of hatred, don't you think?" Fujikawa was watching him closely. "There's something about it that profanes the very idea of God or love or decency or whatever you want to call it. At least, that's what I think."

George said, "I've got a friend who calls me a philosopher. Says I think too much to be a fighting man. He'd get a kick out of you. Under different circumstances, I mean."

Fujikawa sighed out smoke. "I'm not a philosopher. I'm just a man who is tired of it, that's all. I have enough blood on my soul. And that, George Alexander Simon, is 'why.'"

George was silent for a moment, breathing. Then he said, "Thank you."

"Don't thank me," said Fujikawa. His voice was bitter.

They fell into silence then. Heaven pinwheeled slowly above. Waves sighed against the shore. Fujikawa smoked another cigarette.

After about 10 minutes, the Japanese captain spoke softly. "You like baseball, George?"

"Baseball? Yeah, sure."

"I saw Babe Ruth play once. Did you ever see the Babe?"

"No," said George.

Fujikawa gave a sigh. "Oh, he was something else. That day, he had two homers, banged in four runs, and he makes this great, leaping catch that stifles a rally and saves the game. I never saw such a player. It broke my heart when he retired. But I would love to see the Yankees play again someday. That DiMaggio is supposed to be pretty good himself. A 56-game hitting streak. Wow. Can you imagine?"

George felt terror and thankfulness overflowing in him. He swallowed. "I meant it," he said. "Thank you."

"And I meant it too," said Fujikawa. "Don't thank me."

He got to his feet and brushed sand from his uniform. For a moment, he simply stood there on the darkened beach under the sky, facing away from his captive, hands clasped behind his back. Then he said, "You don't understand. What I did was not generous, but selfish. It was for me, not for you."

He turned and looked at George. Whatever he saw in George's eyes rounded his shoulders and lowered his head. "You think I've done you a favor, George Alexander Simon," he said. "Nothing could be further from the truth."

A moment more, he regarded George. Then he squared his shoulders and walked away.

It began to rain.

twenty-seven

THE JAP CAPTAIN'S ENIGMATIC WORDS TROUBLED AND STIRRED
George Simon. He tried to convince himself the man had just been taunting him, but the reassurance felt hollow. In his heart of hearts, George
knew the man had spoken earnestly, and he struggled to conceive of the
kingdom of misery that would justify his enemy's words.

George's dread followed him for the two weeks he spent lying chained
in the reeking hold of a cargo ship. It followed him as he was marched,
manacled, through a Jap city where children, women, and old men spat on
him and threw garbage in his face. This dread was formless and without
weight. But it took on hard substance the moment he was marched into
the camp. He stood there, slowly turning in a full circle, and knew that he
had been abandoned to hell.

It wasn't just the sight of the skeletal prisoners that told him this. It
wasn't just the stench of their sickness or the spectacle of Jap guards swag-
gering imperiously about, occasionally beating a hapless prisoner for no
infraction George could see. No, what struck him more forcefully than all
of this was the palpable *brokenness* of the white men, the way their very
eyes cowered and flinched.

Carrying the paper-thin excuse for a blanket he had been issued and
looking for the hut to which he had been assigned, he found himself walking
past a pair of guards standing upwind of the shithouse, one of them smoking an American cigarette. Four prisoners, scabbed and grimy remnants of
men, regarded the smoking guard with the eager expectation a starving man
might exhibit watching a master chef prepare a sumptuous feast. The guard
with the cigarette pretended no awareness of them, though he darted knowing eyes and a thin, contemptuous grin at the guard next to him.

George's gait slowed, then stopped. Then it happened. Without warning, the guard dropped the cigarette, a third of it still unsmoked, into the mud at his feet. The prisoners pounced for the butt, crashing into each other, tearing at each other, snarling at each other, for the privilege of claiming it from the mud. The two Japs watched, laughing, as the men punched and elbowed one another out of the way, desperate to claim the prize.

George gaped. It was simply impossible that men, *white* men, could act this way, could be reduced to so low and degraded a state. Would this be him in a month? Then one of the contenders rose from the scrum with the butt held triumphantly aloft, like some corrupt mockery of Lady Liberty with her torch. Whereupon the guard gave his friend a nod—*watch this!*—and kicked the prisoner hard, catching him just beneath the sternum. The man folded in pain, and the butt fell back into the mud. Before any of the other men could act, the guard smashed it with the toe of his boot. As he did, he said something harsh to them in Japanese and laughed.

The kicked man writhed in the mud, holding himself. The other men regarded the guards balefully at this denial of a prize fairly won. There was a child's petulance in their faces, the hurt look of a six-year-old who has just learned that the world is not fair. But when the second guard produced a cigarette and, with ostentatious languor, lit it up, the men regarded him with renewed interest, their hope undimmed by the brutal experience of just seconds ago. Even the man who had been kicked rolled to his feet, his forearm pinned to the hurting place, and warily watched the second guard enjoying the cigarette.

"Yeah, that's somethin' else, isn't it?" a voice near George said.

George turned and found himself gazing at a bald, emaciated man about his own height. "Worst thing is, they're our cigarettes. Sent by the Red Cross. Japs like to steal 'em and let us watch them smoke 'em up. They do the same with our food. You're new."

"Yeah," said George.

"Don't get too many new ones in here. The Japs aren't real big on taking prisoners. They must have thought you were special for some reason." He extended his hand. "Andy Grant," he said, "from Bangor, Maine. Come on, I'll give you the grand tour."

The camp was a cluster of wooden huts in the yard of a factory run by a company called Mitsubishi. The factory itself was situated on the harbor in the industrial area of a bustling Jap city. In the distance, green foothills towered above on three sides. Andy took him around and explained how the camp worked. He told him about *tenko*, which was the morning count, and explained how to count off to the Japs' satisfaction—very difficult, since they required the men to do so in Japanese. He taught George that he had to bow to and salute each Jap guard, every time he saw him, and showed him the washhouse, with its cement tub and pot-bellied stove. Andy even showed him how to chew the end of a twig down until it made a passable toothbrush, though of course they had no toothpaste.

"That there is Satan," said Andy, pointing to where a thin guard was strutting across the yard. "He's the head guard. Best advice is to stay the hell away from him. He's a mean fucker. And that one up on the porch"— Andy pointed to a chubby man, short even by Jap standards—"he's the colonel, the man in charge. We call him 'The Watcher,' 'cause that's all he ever does, just watches everything. Nobody's ever figured out his game."

Andy took him to George's hut and helped him get situated. Then he told George how to find another prisoner known only as Quick—"Nobody knows his real name," he said—and explained that Quick, a master scrounger, was the man to see if he needed anything. But, Andy added, "Count your fingers after you shake hands with him. He'd sell his own mother for a pack of Lucky Strikes."

George nodded. He decided he'd give Quick a wide berth. But the scrounger would not be so easy to avoid. Ten days later, Quick sidled up to George as he stood in line waiting for the morning meal and spoke without preamble. "Somebody said they saw you with a Bible the other night," he said.

George was surprised, both that someone had been watching him and that his reading a Bible was news worth reporting. He measured his voice carefully. "Yeah," he said. "So what?"

"'So what' is, that could be worth a lot of money to you, my friend. You know how valuable that thing is?"

Quick was a short, furtive man who spoke out of a mouth filled with what seemed to be too many small teeth. He used the back of his hand to wipe at his nose, which, like his mouth, was always running.

Jake Crossley, a thin, raw-boned pilot who had been shot down over Tokyo, came up to them then and nudged Quick. "So, what do you think is on the menu for breakfast this mornin', Mr. Quick? I'm thinking bacon and eggs, maybe some grits with cheese, nice strong cup of joe."

"Nah," said Quick. "Stack of pancakes with a big pat of fresh butter right on top, and some maple syrup. Or you know what else would be good? An omelet. Had one this time in New Orleans, they stuffed it with crawfish and cheese, hash browns on the side. Oh, man, you talk about good eatin'! What do you think? You want an omelet this morning, George?"

"Don't matter what I want," said George sourly. "What I'm going to get is fucking rice. That's all the fucking Japs know how to cook is fucking rice."

"Wow," said Crossley. "What's with you?"

"Just don't see the point in torturing myself," said George.

"Got to do somethin' to keep from goin' off your nut," protested Crossley.

"Oh, George has already got some help for that," said Quick. "Ain't you heard? He's got the word of the Lord. I'm talking about a Bible. Real, honest-to-goodness Bible."

"Really?" Crossley's eyes widened with new respect.

"Yeah. So what'll you take for it, George? Name your price."

"What? What are you talking about? It's not for sale."

The line edged forward then and, as George had predicted, a dull-eyed prisoner sloshed an ounce of watery rice onto his mess kit and dropped a piece of greening bread on after it, all without ever looking at him.

George moved on and found a table. He was dismayed when Quick sat across from him, while Crossley took a seat at his elbow. Quick said, "Wait a minute there, George. Don't be so fast to turn down the offer. You ain't even heard it yet."

"I don't get it," said George. "Why are you so hot for my Bible?" It was only a pocket-sized New Testament.

Quick grinned at Crossley. "He really is new, ain't he?" He turned the grin on George. "Keep forgetting how new you are."

"Yeah. So I'm new. So what?"

"So, most of the other men, they've been here a long time, that's what. They don't have their Bibles anymore. Means you have kind of a corner on the market."

George shrugged. "Fine. I'd be willing to loan it out, but . . ."

Quick's laugh was a harsh bark. "You still don't get it. It ain't for reading, dummy. It's for smoking!"

"What?"

"Let me explain it to you," said Quick amiably. "You see, there's all kinds of paper, George. And when a man gets his hands on a little tobacco, he'll make a cigarette out of any kind of paper he can get his hands on. He'll use Ernest Hemingway or Herman Melville. He'll use a message pad or a piece of a cement bag. Hell, he'll even use that Jap toilet paper, and that's got more splinters in it than your front porch. Like I say, a man who wants a smoke, he really can't afford to be picky.

"But you know what that man really wants, George? You know what makes him feel almost human again? It's rolling a cigarette out of that Bible paper. It's real thin, you see. It burns even, you get a good drag."

George stared.

"Yeah, I know what you're thinking, George. Sell the Good Book? Rip it up for cigarette paper? That's sacrilege, right?"

"Sacrilege," agreed Crossley.

"But you got to think of the big picture here. I'm offering you one cigarette per chapter. I'm talking real factory cigarettes. There's how many chapters in that there New Testament? You got your Matthew, your Mark, and all those other guys. What do you figure? Fifteen chapters? Maybe 20? Now, I know you don't smoke, so you got no use for cigarettes. But cigarettes is money—and what I'm offering you is a *lot* of money. You could bribe yourself off work details. I know some guards who would bring you shit from outside. How'd you like some fresh meat, George? Or fresh vegetables? I could even get you some toothpaste. We're talking all the comforts of home. So what do you say?"

For a long moment, George just continued to stare through his disbelief. "No," he finally said.

"That's your last word?"

"My last word."

Quick only grinned. "Okay," he said, standing up. "But we'll do business in the end. You'll see."

George watched him go, still disbelieving. He shook his head. Then he forced down the last of the watery rice, shoved the bread in after it, and hustled across the yard to make it to the work truck. He was still hungry, but that was nothing new. He was always hungry now. A little brown

Airedale came yapping at George's heels as he crossed the yard. The dog had shown up the week before, and they had named him Pup. Nobody knew whose he was. Some of the men thought he might belong to one of the secretaries at Mitsubishi. Others thought he might have wandered in from town.

But it didn't matter. George liked having the dog around. Most of the other men did, too. Watching him patrol the yard was a kind of mental vacation, a ticket back to a day when a man was clean, unbroken, and whole. George knelt now and gave the dog a quick scratch behind the ears. "Good boy. How you doin' this morning, boy?" Then he rushed on. Being late for the work detail was not an option.

He gave the mandatory salute and bow to a guard, then climbed into the back of the pickup that would take him and eight other prisoners to the shipyard where they would spend the day driving rivets into some Jap boat. It was hard, repetitive work, but Andy had told him it was by no means the worst duty you could draw. Cleaning the honey hole was the worst, and a crew of officers had been assigned to that until further notice.

It had happened after several of them, citing the Geneva Conventions, refused to do any more slave labor for the Japs. Satan had ordered the officers beaten—the Japs weren't real big on the Geneva Conventions—then got The Watcher to assign them to police the honey hole, i.e., to dip the shit from the benjo pit (*benjo* was the Jap word for "shithouse") and carry it bucket by bucket to the cesspit. None of the enlisted men had been too heartbroken to see their captains and majors reduced to such filthy labor.

The shipyard, by contrast, wasn't nearly so bad. Yes, it was demanding, especially for ill-fed men whose physical strength was eroding like beach sand. But on the other hand, the work gave you the great satisfaction of finding ways to sabotage Jap ships. Andy had taught George how to surreptitiously douse a red-hot rivet with ice-cold water before tossing it into the scuttle for another member of the team to extract and plug into the plating of the hull. They had hopes that this would weaken the metal. They cherished a vision of the ship bursting open while at sea. George suspected it would probably never happen, but the vision itself sustained him.

"I see Mr. Quick is after you," he heard Andy say.

George turned, surprised to see his friend. Andy was climbing carefully into the truck. He had been laid up with dysentery for three days, so debilitated that the Japs had given him a chit excusing him from work.

"Wants my Bible," said George.

"Really?" said Andy. "Must want it for cigarette paper." And the fact that Andy deduced this immediately, that it made complete sense to him, reminded George again that he had fallen through the looking glass into a very different world.

He changed the subject. "What are you doing here?" he asked. "You feeling better?"

"No. But I had a little visit from Satan this morning. He was yelling at me in that pidgin Jap English of his, so I didn't catch the details, but I got the main point, which is that he thinks I've been malingering."

"But you've got a chit. Hell, he's the one signed it."

Andy hunched his shoulders. "Same thing I said. I even showed it to him—which was a mistake. He snatched it from me, ripped it up. Figured I'd better take the hint."

"Bastard," said George. He had to raise his voice to be heard over the sudden cranking of the engine. The truck bed was full. The guard climbed in and closed the gate after him.

"You'll get no argument from me," said Andy.

"You going to be able to work?"

"I guess we'll find out," said Andy as the truck lurched forward.

They reached the shipyard half an hour later. As usual, the guards were bored and did not watch them closely. One was busy flirting with a pretty young secretary in the office; the other two sat on the loading dock having an animated discussion on some subject George could not begin to guess. Right under the guards' noses, George filled a bucket with cold water from a spigot, then followed his team up the bamboo scaffolding that cradled the skeleton of the ship. The lack of attention always inspired fantasies of escape. But they were nothing more than that. Sure, he and Andy might by some miracle be able to overpower the three inattentive guards, but what would be the point? Where would they go? And even if they'd had someplace to go, their height, their words, and their white faces would make getting there impossible. So he put the thought aside and got to work.

Andy fired the first rivet until it glowed red, then tossed it to George, who caught it in the scuttle. With a surreptitious glance around, George poured cold water into the scuttle. Andy grinned as the metal hissed.

"Wish I could be there when the rivets fly off," he said.

"Me too," said George.

He held the scuttle up so the third man in their team could lift the rivet out with long tongs and put it in place. A fourth man would hold the metal plate in place while a fifth man secured the rivet with a rivet gun. There was a certain rhythm to the work, though it was frequently interrupted when Andy had to rush off to the benjo and George had to do both their jobs until he returned.

"Hell of a thing," George said, as Andy came back from one trip to the toilet.

"How's that?" asked Andy.

"Good Southern boy like me coverin' for a damn Yankee named Grant."

Andy laughed.

And so the day passed.

When it was done, they were driven in darkness back to camp. As the truck gate dropped, Andy jumped down, hurriedly bowed to and saluted the three guards, then hustled off toward the benjo. Or at least, he tried. Because Satan came striding up, screaming at them all in Japanese, and he had to stop, bow, salute, and stand to attention. There was a translator among the guards who spoke excellent English, but Satan did not usually bother with him. He preferred to scream at the men in his own language, and somehow, they were expected to just know what he was saying. George had no idea what the man was yelling about. He knew none of the others did, either. It was madness. But then, the whole damn thing was madness.

Misery etched itself on Andy's face as they stood there listening to the incomprehensible tirade, and George realized with horror what was coming if Satan didn't let them go right this very instant—but of course, there was nothing he could do about it. So Satan ranted on and Andy held it as long as he could. Then there came a loud, ripping fart, and George saw his friend's trousers darken.

For a very long moment, the scene was as still as a painting. Andy looked mortified. The other men's grimy faces bore marks of sheer agony as they tried to keep from laughing. Satan's features were at war with themselves, fury fighting disgust. The riding crop came up. Satan slashed Andy twice across the face, then stood on tiptoe to get close to him and yelled something in angry Japanese. Andy did not bring his hand up to where he had been struck. Doing so would have only gotten him hit again. So he stood there, blood trickling down his cheek.

Finally and without warning, Satan spun on his heel, his nose wrinkled with the stench of Andy's dysentery, and stormed off. The other guards followed. It wasn't until the Japs had melted into the night that the pent-up laughter came breaking through. Men were slapping each other on the back. Men were doubled over, hands on knees, helpless before their own hilarity.

"Did you see his face?" cried one.

"Did I? I like to bust a gut from not laughin.'"

"I don't see what's so fuckin' funny," said Andy.

Half an hour later, George had just finished his scoop of listless rice and moldy bread and was about to leave when the chaplain, Father Vince, brought his mess kit and sat across from him. An older man with frizzy, salt-and-pepper hair flying out in all directions, he was said to have once been a priest in Philadelphia.

"Evening, Father," said George.

"Son," said Father Vince, "I wanted to talk to you. I hear that Mr. Quick offered to buy your Bible from you this morning."

George was wary. "Yes," he said, "that's right."

"But you wouldn't sell?"

"No, I wouldn't."

Father Vince shook his head. "Son, I am certain the Lord appreciates your devotion to His word. It is truly admirable. And I can understand your hesitance to sell your Bible, especially knowing the pages are to be torn out and made into cigarettes."

"Yes, Father."

"But son, I just want you to know, it would be no real sin if you were to make that deal with Mr. Quick. The Lord knows your heart, son. And he surely knows that these are trying and extenuating circumstances. You have to remember, son, it's the words that matter. The paper they're written on doesn't mean anything. You have an obligation to do whatever you can to make sure you get out of this alive. And besides that, you have to consider the comfort you might be able to bring to your fellow men. Surely, the Lord would look on you with favor for that."

Father Vince lifted his spoon then, and as he slurped at his rice, George got a good look at the fingers of his right hand. He was not surprised to note that the tips were stained yellow. The other man smiled. The eyes above that smile were hopeful and sad.

George said, "Yes, Father. I'll give it some thought." But he knew that he would not.

As the months passed and winter yielded grudgingly to spring, George's body melted like a candle. He had become a human magic trick, disappearing before his own eyes, his cheeks caving in and his eyes looking terrified in sockets that seemed suddenly too large for them. The change was so dramatic that he began to avoid mirrors and reflective metals. He was always jarred by the sight of himself, always thought, *Who the hell is that?*

They killed Pup in May. George held him down while Andy smashed his head with a rock. They skinned and butchered the little dog and grilled it on a makeshift spit behind the hut, careful not to let anyone see, lest they be forced to share. As they chewed the tough meat, Andy gazed over at him, eyes glistening.

"You know, I've got a little pup of my own back home," he said. "I've always had dogs."

"Don't talk about that," George told him.

But Andy would not stop. Probably couldn't. "Would never have thought of hurting that little dog if I didn't have to," he said. "You know that, don't you?"

"'Course I do," said George. "Me neither."

And then there came a steamy morning in June when things got worse. The men were gathered for tenko. George's gaze was fixed on a mole on the neck of the man in front of him, Daniel Flaherty, who they all called "Danny Boy." Then the mole began to crawl, and two others joined it. George was idly amused to realize they were not moles at all, but fleas. They had been nesting in the hair on the man's back and were wandering about now, just above the neckline of the ill-fitting Jap army uniform he had been issued.

George could not see his face. But George knew he must be in agony, must be dying to scratch. After a moment, sure enough, Danny Boy began hunching his shoulders surreptitiously, trying to roll his neck against the insects without the guards seeing.

George willed him to cut it out. *For God's sake, man, stop.* It was only another few minutes they had to stand there and then tenko would be over and he could scratch to his heart's content. But if the guards saw Danny Boy squirming now, there would be hell to pay, maybe for all of them. George had seen five men beaten once because the guard did not like the way one of them folded his blanket. The other four men didn't even know the guy, much less have anything to do with his damn blanket. George was convinced the Japs were capable of any cruelty you could conceive, and he surely didn't feel like being punished because Danny Boy had an itch.

George flicked his eyes from left to right without moving his head. He was relieved to see that none of the guards were looking this way. Danny Boy had been lucky so far, which meant they all had been lucky. But luck would not hold indefinitely. It never did. Yet still, Danny Boy, the fool, kept hunching his shoulders and rolling his neck, even as the yard echoed with the men counting off in Japanese.

Stop it! Stop it! Stop it!

Anxiously, George moved his eyes again until he was able to make out the colonel's office. As he expected, he saw The Watcher standing there on the porch. He was truly an odd duck. This was the man who set the rules by which they lived. His favor was the margin by which they survived another day, his soft hands juggled their lives and deaths, but all he ever did was look at them. His expression was famously unreadable. You never knew The Watcher's mood, could never say what The Watcher was thinking until The Watcher barked out his decision.

Now, as The Watcher watched impassively, Satan strutted back and forth in front of the men, his riding crop linking his hands behind his back. Satan was unpredictable, too, though far crueler. Sometimes, the prisoners amused themselves by sitting up late into the night fantasizing about how they would someday kill him. They dreamt up extravagant cruelties, rating them on which offered the best combination of excruciating pain and slow death. George favored burying him up to the neck near a nest of fire ants, head held immobile and a trail of sugar running right up into his nostrils. He liked the idea of the evil Jap being helplessly eaten alive, bite by tiny bite.

In that moment, almost as if he knew George's thoughts, Satan glanced over. And Danny Boy—*the fool! the fool!*—chose that instant to make his move. His right hand came up quickly, furtively, raking at the fleas crawling on the back of his neck, and then down. But it was not quick or furtive enough. Satan saw. He came now, screeching even before he got there, pushing men aside as he might have pushed aside cornstalks in a field. And then he was standing before Danny Boy, bellowing up at him in maddened, infuriated Japanese. Even when he was calm, Satan's eyes were predatory and cruel, but when he was angry, as he was now, they seemed to light up from within, to become dark half-moons of fury rising in eclipse against an exploding sun. There was a madness burning hot within.

You could see it now as Satan screamed up at Danny Boy, frothy spittle spraying from his lips. Danny Boy tried to maintain some composure in the face of the tirade, but his attempt at dignity only seemed to make Satan madder. In the middle of a sentence, he abruptly stopped, hauled off, and slugged Flaherty in the gut, the blow doubling the taller American over. Satan's next punch drove Danny Boy to his knees. Satan hit him again. And again. And again. And again. Danny Boy collapsed into the mud. The skin around his eye was torn open. His mouth was a bloody ruin.

Satan glared down at him, chest heaving. Then he barked some order to the guards. Two of them hustled forward and grabbed Danny Boy beneath the arms, lifting him to his feet and dragging him off while the prisoners stood at rigid attention. From the corner of his gaze, George saw them deposit Danny Boy on his knees in front of the colonel's office on a patch of small, sharp stones kept there for that purpose.

Then the guards retrieved a section of telephone pole. It had been cut down to a length of five feet and hooks had been driven into either end to make it easier to handle. Even so, the two guards struggled with the weight as they brought the wooden cylinder to where Danny Boy knelt, dazed. Then they dropped it on his legs, just behind his knees. The weight of it drove Danny Boy's knees down hard upon the stones. Somehow, he restrained himself from crying out. At least, thought George bitterly, the fool had that much sense. He knew better than to make a sound of protest or pain. That would only make it worse.

And at that moment, George went fishing.

It was something you learned to do, a way of escaping the unrelenting degradation and fear. You constructed an elaborate, ongoing fantasy, carefully etching its most minute details in your mind and then, when the reality before you became too onerous to bear, you went into the fantasy to hide. Some men designed their dream homes, deciding what color to paint the hallway and what grade of carpet to choose for the living room. Some men sat in the kitchen with their mother as she prepared their favorite meal. Some men seduced Betty Grable, presenting her with flowers, burying their noses in those shiny platinum curls.

George went fishing. As tears and blood streamed, mingling, down Danny Boy's cheeks, George took a small boat out onto Mobile Bay. The morning glistened. Seabirds arced overhead, occasionally skimming the surface in search of breakfast.

Finally, Daniel Flaherty reached the end of his tether for good sense and self-preservation. He leaned his head back and roared a string of curses at the Japanese, calling them whores' sons and motherless bastards and filthy cocksuckers. Satan, who had been walking away, stopped and turned. And George, knowing what would come next, bent low over his tackle box, choosing a particularly fat and juicy night crawler to bait his hook.

Without looking, Satan reached a hand toward one of the guards. In a second, his hand was clutching the guard's rifle. Satan brought the butt of the thing down with maddened force on Danny Boy's face. Then he drew back and did it again. Then he drew back and did it again. Finally, Satan handed the rifle back, again without looking. He leaned over Danny Boy, whose face no longer resembled a face, and held up two fingers in what felt like a bizarre perversion of Winston Churchill's "V for Victory" sign.

"Two day!" he barked, in English for once. "Two day!"

By which he meant that Danny Boy must kneel on the rocks like that for a day and a night and a day and a night without food, without water, without moving, under penalty of summary execution.

George saw this, but didn't; heard it, but didn't. He was too busy yanking an enormous trout free of the water. It was a beast of a fish, wrestling against the hook with all its considerable might. The sun on its scales wove a beautiful iridescence. He was admiring the fish and thinking of how Mother would prepare it for dinner that night as tenko came mercifully to an end. The formation broke, and George hurried off to stand in line for the morning meal. He was grateful Satan had not visited his wrath for Danny Boy's folly on all of them, and angry with Danny Flaherty for putting them all in that danger in the first place.

Once, George might have whispered an automatic prayer for forgiveness for thinking such thoughts. But he had been here six months, living in this reeking purgatory, and he simply did not care anymore. He was too busy trying to keep himself alive.

He figured he was down at least 40 of the 165 pounds he'd had on his six-foot frame when he'd been in Australia. The rice and bread the Japs served, and the smuggled-in bits of bread and fish on which he spent his Jap scrip and his allotment of Jap cigarettes, were not nearly enough. He was turning into a human skeleton. He was going to starve to death.

Sure enough, as he was thinking those thoughts, here came Quick sidling up to him like the devil came to Jesus in the wilderness, George's own personal tempter. It had become a sort of perverse game between them, a contest of wills.

"Still not interested," said George, as the mushy rice splashed down upon his mess kit.

"Come on," replied Quick, "you can't turn the offer down. You haven't even heard it yet." An ostentatious pause. "Two cigs a chapter. *Two*. Don't tell me you couldn't use the dough."

It was such an insane price that George actually thought about it. He remembered what Father Vince had told him. He had an obligation to do whatever he could to survive. He owed that to the people who loved him. He owed it to himself. Hell, he even owed it to that blind and deaf God.

He glanced at Quick, who was still awaiting his answer. "Yeah, I could use the money," he said, "but not like that."

Quick's face fell, but he recovered quickly. "I suppose it wouldn't help me to raise my price again? Say, two and a half cigs a chapter?"

At that price, George knew Quick probably couldn't even turn a profit. This had become personal for the little scrounger. But George shook his head. "Afraid not," he said, as he sat and began spooning the tasteless Jap gruel into his mouth.

Quick regarded him with consternation. "I don't get you," he said after a moment. "Why won't you sell? I mean, everybody knows you're a religious guy. Hell, I am, too. Did you know that? Bet you didn't. I spent my fair amount of time in the pews. But we ain't home right now and even a religious guy's got to eat. Even a religious guy's got to take care of himself."

George didn't bother correcting the impression that he was "a religious guy," didn't bother saying he had pretty much concluded God had either gone AWOL from his creation or was simply not listening to its pleas. One thing he knew for sure was that God, who had supposedly loved George Simon so much that he sent his son to die for him, was not in this place. Here, there was a very good chance George would have to do his own dying.

"I know," he told Quick.

"You know?" Quick's eyebrows lifted. "Well then, tell me why the holdout, George? Why are you being so stubborn?"

And how to answer? How to find words for what he had hardly been able to explain even to himself? It wasn't faith that had rooted him like some century-old tree. No, faith had run out of him like water through a sieve a long time ago. What rooted George now was faith's remnant: stubbornness.

He remembered the charge Thelma had left him with before abruptly ending their correspondence. He had read her words repeatedly, obsessively, read them until they burrowed into him.

You may have to give up your faith and your hope. You may even have to give up your life. But if it's at all possible, you hold on to your decency. You make sure your decency, your humanity, *is the very last thing you give up. Because without it, I don't think the rest matters too much.*

This was why he could not say yes. This place, this war had taken so much from him. Couldn't he hold on to just one last tiny, useless scrap of the man he once had been?

"I've already given up enough," he said.

"Beg pardon?"

George glanced up, surprised that he had spoken aloud. "Nothing," he said.

"'Nothing,' my ass. You said something about giving up."

"Never mind," said George sharply. "I just don't want to do it. Not for two and a half, not for three and a half. Now go bug somebody else. Leave me alone, will you?"

They stared at each other. Finally, Quick pushed up from the table. "Fine," he said. "But you're one strange fucker, you know that?"

He didn't wait for an answer. George watched him move across the yard, his steps lively with anger. George was guiltily aware of the lump the little Bible made in his breast pocket.

He finished his slop. One of the guards—the prisoners called him "Shitface" because he was so ugly—was beating one of the cooks for giving a prisoner too much food. Somebody was always getting beaten for something. You were just thankful it wasn't you. He walked toward the front gate, passing Danny Boy Flaherty as he did. Flaherty held himself erect, knowing that to allow his body to slump was to invite another beating. His face was red with crusted blood.

George went fishing.

He read his Bible that night. After lights out, he continued reading by the bright light of the moon. He read Matthew. He read Luke. He read Acts. He read it because doing so had always been a normal thing for him, and it remained a piece of himself unsullied by how he lived now. But the familiar words brought no solace. It was only a habit. He wanted it to be more, but it was only that. As he read, George replayed the argument with Quick and wondered if it wasn't true what the other man said, wondered if he were not just being a stubborn, inflexible prig. After all, what good was the book doing him? If they tore it up for cigarette paper, at least it would be helping somebody.

Finally, disgusted, George put the little volume aside. He crossed his arms over his chest and watched the glaring light of the moon climb slowly across the ceiling. He lay atop straw on a shelf of wood nailed into the wall. It contained barely space enough for two, but was occupied by three. You learned to sleep without moving.

George listened to the sounds of the night. The two men next to him snored softly. He heard harsh coughing from all over the room. He heard the scuttling of a rat as it made its way along the floor. He wondered what his family had been told about him. Probably, he had been listed as MIA for a long time. Probably, they now thought he was dead. Probably, that was for the best. He expected it would be true before too long.

George sighed in the darkness. The man next to him smacked his lips as though eating some delicious thing in his sleep. George envied him that escape. He could not sleep. He lay there for an hour. He lay there for two. It was no use. He was exhausted. Spirit and body, exhausted. But he could not sleep.

And all at once, he knew why.

George sat up. He thought about it a moment, told himself he was crazy, but climbed down anyway. He lifted his canteen from a nail on the wall, slipped on the split-toe Jap sandals he had been issued, and ventured out of the hut. He was headed to the benjo. Or at least, he decided, that was what he would say if he chanced upon a guard. The camp was quiet. The dark, angular shadows of the buildings lay elongated on the ground, cut out by the light of the moon. George kept to the darkness as much as he could, stealing furtively across the light only when he had no other option. He crept past the guardhouse and stole over toward The Watcher's house. He slipped silently along the side of the building, rounded cautiously to the front, and came up behind Danny Boy Flaherty.

George knew there would be a guard on the porch above to make sure Danny Boy didn't sneak a few minutes of respite by standing up. But George also knew—or at least, he hoped—the guard would not be terribly alert at this time of the morning. Sure enough, when George chanced a peek, the Jap's rifle was leaning against the wall and the Jap was, too; his chin was on his chest and he was snoring lightly, sound asleep standing up.

George moved in a painful crouch. Danny Boy's body had almost curled over on itself like a question mark, but he was still kneeling on the rocks, the telephone pole holding him in place. George wondered what was keeping him upright. He decided he didn't want to know. He knelt at Danny's side, putting Danny's body between himself and the slumbering guard on the porch above.

"Danny."

George's voice was more suggestion than sound, a barely discernible whisper drowned by the chorus of night insects serenading the trees. Danny Boy did not respond. George tried again. He put his lips next to the other man's ear.

"Danny." The other man stirred uncertainly.

"Shhh." George hissed it, softly as the wind. And then: "Over here, Danny Boy. Over here."

Flaherty's head came around. The wild eyes that beheld George did not know him, did not seem to know anything but panic. For a stricken moment, George was certain Danny Boy was going to cry out. Then all at once his ruined mouth smiled, red with blood, gaping with places where teeth had been, and he said, "George."

"Keep it down," whispered George. He lifted the canteen. "Here."

Danny Boy gave the canteen an uncomprehending stare. He continued to smile vaguely.

"For you," said George.

There was an agonizing moment. Then Danny Boy accepted the canteen. He looked at it as if he had never seen one before, as if he had no idea of its use. There was another moment. Then, with great reverence, he unscrewed the cap. He lifted the canteen to his mouth and drank. He took a long draft, eyes closed in an almost sexual bliss. Above them, the guard grunted in his sleep. George shifted his balance, worried Danny Boy might never stop drinking.

Finally, he did. He handed the canteen back to George. It was noticeably lighter than it had been, the remnants of the water sloshing around on the bottom.

Danny Boy breathed, "God bless you, George Simon."

George nodded. He turned to creep back toward his hut—and froze.

The Watcher was standing there, not 30 feet away. He was alone, dressed for bed in a Western-style robe, though with the split-toe sandals favored by the Japanese. Apparently, he had been out walking. His eyes met George's, but the colonel's placid face, still as midnight, gave nothing away. There was no judgment, there was no anger, there was no approval, there was nothing. George was terrified. He watched the colonel watch him, waiting for the man to holler for the guard or, failing that, do something that would provide George some clue as to what he should do now.

But The Watcher did nothing of the sort. He only watched George watching him. The Watcher did not move a muscle. Nor, as a consequence, did George, except that he swallowed. He couldn't help swallowing, though there was nothing in his throat. And still he crouched there, waiting, though he had no idea what for. A full minute passed. Was George in trouble or not? Was he just some odd specimen of man The Watcher had never seen before? Was he some rare bird in a tree that The Watcher feared to disturb, lest it fly away?

Another minute passed. Should he say something? Should he apologize? Should he explain?

A third minute passed. Tentatively, his eyes still on The Watcher, George put his right foot behind him and took a step back. When The Watcher didn't respond, he did it again. Left foot behind him and a step back. His limbs burned from being so long in a crouch. And still The Watcher did not respond, except that his head turned ever so slightly to follow George's progress. George took another step. And another. Then he was around the corner of the colonel's house and out of sight, and he whirled around and took off running as fast as he could, heedless of light and shadow, careless of who might see.

A few moments later, he pounded into the sleeping hut, his breath coming in ragged gasps. George expected to hear footsteps coming after him, but standing there over the plank that served as his bed, he heard only the coughing of the sleeping men and the singing of the insects outside.

Suddenly exhausted beyond all reason, George climbed onto the straw. The man next to him had spread out in George's absence and George had to push him to make space. The man grumbled in his sleep and slid over—though not far, because there was nowhere to go. George pulled the useless blanket over himself and lay there on his side feeling the heat of the other man's body pressed close against him. He let fatigue overtake him. At the last moment, right before he surrendered to the darkness, he was seized by a nagging thought that he had forgotten something, overlooked something, that something was out of place.

But the darkness was too strong. It pulled him down. George slept.

Reveille came instantly. When he awoke, George remembered the thought that had followed him down into sleep, the sense of some missing thing. All at once, he knew what it was. He jumped down, ran his hands through the straw, and was not at all surprised to come up empty.

His Bible was gone.

An unreasoning fury seized George Simon by the scruff of the neck then. It hurled him out of the hut and into the yard. Quick was standing in front of his own hut with Jake Crossley when George found him.

"You thieving bastard!" he snarled.

Startled, Quick turned, right into George's oncoming fist. He fell like a tree. George straddled him, barely feeling Crossley's arms around his chest. "Get up, you bastard! Get up so I can knock you down again!"

George was not outraged because he had lost the sacred words. No, he was outraged because Quick had violated him, taken away something more fundamental than any book.

Shitface, the guard, had seen what George did. He ran over, yelling something in Japanese. He peeled Crossley off and tossed him aside, then knocked George unceremoniously to the ground.

George had no idea what got into him then. He stared up at the ugly guard. And then he stood and faced him.

Astonished, Shitface said something else in Japanese and knocked George down again. And George stood up again.

His face reddening, Shitface started screaming and hit George again, a harder blow that sent him sprawling. And George shook his head, which by now seemed filled with cotton and sand. Slowly, painfully, he climbed back to his feet. He faced the ugly Jap, silently daring him to do it again.

The prisoners gaped. Even Quick, getting up from where George had decked him, said with alarm, "George, what the hell are you doing?" When a guard knocked you down, you stayed down and averted your eyes. You didn't get back up and glare at him. That was suicidal.

Now Shitface looked confused, unsure how to handle this challenge to his authority. Finally, he yelled something in Japanese, and four more guards rushed over and helped beat George to the ground.

Then, Shitface and one of the other guards grabbed George under the arms and took him out front of The Watcher's office, a crowd of prisoners following. There, the other two guards lifted the heavy pole from Danny Boy's legs. Shitface shoved George down next to Flaherty, whose head hung, insensate. The chunk of wood came down again, this time across both their legs.

Like little stone knives, the decorative rocks cut into George Simon's knees. His skin tore and bled. He howled.

Then, through a watery gray haze, he saw Satan's face come close to his, the two fingers lifted.

George went fishing.

Desperately, he went fishing.

twenty-eight

LUTHER WAS DOWN IN THE BOW GUNNER'S SEAT, OILING THE .50-caliber gun in the cramped interior of the Sherman tank they had nicknamed "Lena Horne," when a head appeared in the open turret hatch far above. "Colonel say, everybody in formation," the man called. He was gone before Luther even knew who he was.

Luther glanced back at Jocko Sweeney, who was above him in the main gunner's seat, refolding a tarpaulin. "What do you think that's about, Sarge?"

Jocko gave a shrug—"No idea," he said—and climbed out the hatch. Luther wiped his hands on a rag and followed. Books had been crouched next to the tank, oiling the bogie wheels. He stood now next to Friendly Sullivan and Arnold Ripson, the other two members of their crew. Books looked up at Jocko and Luther as they clambered out of the tank. "Any idea what this is about?" he asked.

"Ain't but one way to find out," said Jocko.

They followed the drift of men and lined up in a semicircle on a low hill. It was cold, another day of unrelenting rain pounding the fields of northern France into mud. From a distance, you could hear German and American guns hammering at each other. Luther saw Colonel Bates standing down in front of the formation. He looked tense. His second-in-command, Major Wingo, was by his side, talking and gesticulating nonstop. He, too, seemed anxious. The men waited, standing at attention, the rain pattering on their raincoats.

All at once, Luther heard the growl of approaching engines. Several quarter-ton Jeeps roared suddenly into view, parking themselves in defensive positions. They were manned by steely-eyed MPs armed with machine guns. Luther wondered what in the hell this could be. Then another Jeep dashed forward and stopped next to Bates. The three-star general inside jumped out, accepted Bates's salute, and climbed immediately up onto the hood of an armored car. Luther recognized him right away. His eyes widened.

George S. Patton stood with his fists on his hips, the famous ivory-handled pistols holstered on his belt. He wore no raincoat in the cold, pelting downpour. Patton was not a particularly tall man, but his bearing commanded your attention. His eyes were small and steely as he surveyed the assembled tankers for a moment, seeing them and—the entire point, Luther realized—allowing them to see him. He told them to stand at ease.

"Men," he began—Luther was surprised at how high and thin his voice was—"you are the first Negro tankers to ever fight in the American Army. I would never have asked for you if you weren't good. I have nothing but the best in my army. I don't care what color you are, so long as you go up there and kill those kraut sonsabitches!"

Patton paused, allowing his gaze to roam over them. For a moment, there was no sound beyond the raindrops. Then Patton said, "Everyone has their eyes on you and is expecting great things from you. Most of all, your race is looking forward to your success. Don't let them down. And damn you, don't let *me* down!"

With that, he climbed down from the armored car and began talking with some of the men in front. As he talked, he walked about to inspect the tanks. Luther could not hear what was said; he was too far away. But he could not miss the way the men followed close behind Patton, eager for every drop of wisdom from their general's lips.

"Did you hear that?" Books slapped Luther's chest with the back of his hand. "He wanted the best. That's us. That's the 761st. Look out, Hitler—the Black Panthers are coming for you."

It was the new unit nickname the men had chosen. They also had a new unit motto, taken from something Joe Louis said back in '38 when he was asked about his strategy against Max Schmeling, the German who had knocked him out two years before. "I'm going to come out fighting," the Brown Bomber had said.

"Come out fighting" it said on the battalion's new insignia, just below the profile of a snarling ebony panther.

"Guess we're really going to war," Luther said. He had to admit it, Bates had actually come through for them. The men loved him for that. Even Luther did. And Bates seemed to feel the same about them. He was so devoted to the 761st that he had even stayed stateside a few extra days after the unit received its orders so that he might defend one of them, a lieutenant named Jackie Robinson, who had been unfairly court-martialed.

"Looks like it," said Jocko. He was lighting a cigar, puffing on it to get it going good. "Looks that way, indeed."

Wingo was passing by and heard them. "Yeah," he growled, "you coons are going to get your wish, all right. Better hope you don't end up regrettin' it."

Books asked, "What do you mean, Major?"

There was nastiness in Wingo's grin. "I mean, this here is war, boy. Ain't like no Saturday night knife fight in Harlem. This here takes brains and guts . . . *tactics*. You'll see." He moved on without waiting for a response.

Luther heard all of this from a distance, preoccupied with the realization that combat would soon be more than a theoretical possibility. Soon enough, it would be real. He had not been absolutely convinced the 761st would really get to fight. Even after they had traveled to New Jersey for embarkation, he had not been sure. Nor had the long weeks spent in England waiting for orders done much for his confidence. The British people were nice enough, but Luther had soon had a bellyful of Uncle Sam's arrogant cracker soldiers kicking colored soldiers out of pubs, pushing them to the backs of buses, and otherwise trying to enforce the same damn Jim Crow from back home, as if Wimborne, England, were nothing but a suburb of Mobile.

And just like back home, the white boys became furious at any sign of sexual attraction between black men and white women. Luther had not cared to get involved with any of the British girls—it was more trouble than it was worth, it seemed to him, and besides, after a lifetime of looking at his shoes when a white girl passed him by in Mobile, he didn't quite know how to walk up to one in a pub in Wimborne and casually strike up a conversation. Jocko had had no such reservations. He had taken a shine to a pert little blonde named Janet. But their fling lasted only until their second date, when she had asked if she might see his tail.

"I beg your pardon?" he had said, confused. At first, he thought she was referring to his backside. She wasn't.

"Fuckin' honkies done told her we all got tails and swing from the trees like monkeys," Jocko complained that night in the barracks, "and she wanted to see. I tell you, I never been so goddamn mad in all my life."

"You can't blame her," Books had said, mildly.

"Oh, I know," said Jocko. "I know who to blame. Fuckin' honkies. Like we ain't over here fightin' on the same side as they are, riskin' our lives just like them."

"We fight the war to make the world safe for freedom and democracy," said Books, imitating the stentorian tones of the newsreel announcers.

Jocko had given him a weary look. "Yeah," he'd said.

So in the end, Luther had been glad to leave England. They had arrived in France on the same beaches where the great invasion had landed back in June and had driven four hundred miles to this bivouac. They had been sitting here for days, just outside the town of Saint-Nicolas-de-Port, waiting in a constant rain, and again Luther had doubted whether the tankers would really see combat. As far as he was concerned, it was not beyond the Army to keep them waiting here, performing maintenance on idle tanks, until after the treaty was signed. But now Patton himself had come to give them a pep talk, and it looked as if it was really going to happen, because otherwise, why would the great general have driven down from his headquarters in Nancy? As if in confirmation, there came again the faraway thunder of artillery. Luther glanced east, toward the fighting. Then he turned to follow Jocko and the rest of their crew back up the hill to finish servicing Lena Horne. "I'll be goddamned," he said to no one in particular. "We're really going to war."

Luther Hayes's war began five days later on a rain-swept morning before dawn. Four companies of the 761st—Headquarters, Dog, Charlie, and Baker—moved out from the line of departure toward a little farming village. Lena Horne was the second tank in Baker. They crawled all day through the freezing rain, keeping to a sluggish speed limit of four miles an hour to conserve gas. The Red Ball Express, the convoy system ferrying gasoline and other supplies to the front, was stretched beyond capacity, and no one knew when or if they might be resupplied.

Jocko was in command, Books was the driver, and Luther was the gunner. Friendly, a sour-faced Philadelphia minister who insisted on laying hands on the tank every morning to bless it with a long-winded prayer, was the loader. Arnie, a soft-spoken kid from Sandusky, was the backup driver and hull gunner. Arnie claimed to be 20, but Luther strongly suspected he had lied about his age in order to join the Army.

"Boy, you even had your first pussy yet?" Luther had asked him in a British pub once, just to see what would happen. The boy's color had darkened, but he had come back enough. "Ask your mama," he'd said.

The other men had all oohed appreciatively, and Luther had laughed gamely and lifted his glass—he'd had no other choice—but he had not been fooled. If Arnie Ripson was 20, Luther was Joe Louis. Of course, it was too late for that to matter as Lena Horne took them all toward battle, their bodies rocking slightly as the treads transferred every dip in the road straight up through the seats. For the most part they rode in silence, communication reduced to a bare minimum of radio chatter. Not that the thrum and rattle of the tank were conducive to discussion; you could hardly hear yourself think in there. But even if they'd been able to talk, what was there to say? They were doing what defied common sense and simple self-preservation. They were going toward a place where people were shooting. And they were scared, as anyone with a lick of sense would be.

It was really as simple as that.

For Luther, the world was reduced to a narrow periscope view. He saw farm fields sliding past. He saw Colonel Bates in his Jeep driving up and back along the line. He saw the bloated carcasses of dead animals, lying frozen and stiff by the road. He saw German soldiers splayed across the twisted remnants of their war machines.

It was cold. The men breathed gray clouds, and Luther was grateful, for once, for the claustrophobic closeness of the tank. It allowed them to share body heat. In this way, they traveled for a day—a long, slow day. The end of that day brought them to within five miles of the front. The crew of the Lena Horne dismounted in a sodden field where they ate sodden C-rations under a lowering sky. The rain encased everything it touched in thin ice. But having been entombed in their tanks all day, the Black Panthers welcomed even this.

Some of the men asked Friendly to pray, so he did. There was a soft crunch as his knee came down upon the grass, breaking the ice that coated the blades. Friendly praised Jesus and exhorted Heaven for courage and success. Then the men sang "Amazing Grace" and "Precious Lord." They reminded one another to be brave because they were fighting on God's side and that meant they already had the victory. Books, who was an atheist, and Luther, who had lost Jesus the night his parents burned, stood at the fringe of the impromptu church service but not quite away from it.

Jocko noticed them there and sent them to check their equipment. They had checked and double-checked it already, and Luther felt a flash of resentment at the order, but both went without complaint. You could never be too sure of your equipment. And besides, what business did they have listening to other men talk to God?

Luther was about to climb up on the tank when the sound of an approaching engine drew him around. It took him a moment to make it out in the darkness, to separate one shadow from all the rest, but then he recognized it for what it was, a big truck barreling down the road toward them. It had no headlights, only cat's-eye blackout lights that did nothing to illuminate the road ahead. Yet, whoever was behind the wheel was driving like a maniac, plowing through the darkness and freezing rain like it was high noon on an open desert road.

Books was reaching nervously for his submachine gun, what they called the "grease gun" because it sort of looked like one. Luther put a hand on his arm. "Them ours," he said. "Red Ball Express." As the truck grew closer, Luther realized that it was leading a convoy. Four other trucks were stretched out behind. Drawn by the sound, a handful of the other tankers came over from the prayer meeting to see what was going on.

The lead truck came to a stop right next to Lena Horne, slewing sideways a little and kicking up icy mud. The driver pushed open a door pocked with bullet holes and hopped down as the other trucks came to a stop behind him. The butt of a cigarette drooped from his lips, and he threw it into the mud as the rain rendered it useless before addressing himself to the assembled tankers.

"We brought you gasoline," he said.

The men just stared at him in disbelief and he grew annoyed. "You all going to stand there like a lump on a dog's dick, or you going to help me unload this truck?"

Luther couldn't help laughing. "Y'all must be crazy, driving up here at that speed, in the rain, middle of the night. Ain't no tellin' what could have happened to you. Hell, my friend here was fixin' to shoot your ass."

The driver shrugged, unimpressed. "You all need this gas, or you don't?"

"Gasoline?" Colonel Bates stepped forward from the crowd of tankers. The driver saluted and Bates returned the salute. "Did I hear you say you've got gasoline?"

The driver swept his hand toward the other four trucks, whose drivers could be dimly seen in the darkness, dismounting their vehicles and throwing back tarps. "Yes, sir," he said. "We drove it out here from the depot."

Bates said, "What's your name, soldier?"

The handsome soldier grinned. "Pitts, sir," he said. "Leonard G."

Bates said, "Well, good work, Pitts. We'll be very happy to take this gasoline off your hands." He turned to the assembled tankers. "What are you men waiting for? Grab those jerricans and gas up these tanks!"

The order to move came over the radio two hours before dawn the following morning. The crew of the Lena Horne, who had slept in their seats inside the tank all night—or at least, tried to sleep—came instantly awake. Friendly laid hands on the crank that swiveled the gun and bowed his head. "Lord, give us the strength and the courage to do thy will this day," he said. "May our hearts be stout and may our aim be true."

Jocko laughed. "And may we send those kraut bastards straight to hell without so much as scratching our Lena's paint. Amen."

Friendly looked aggrieved—he always did when someone mocked his morning blessing of the tank—and the other men's laughter was lost in the roar of the 33-ton war machine coming to life around them. The cramped space smelled heavily of fuel and men.

The four companies of the 761st rolled east in a column. After a few minutes, a group of tank destroyers and trucks carrying infantry joined them. Bates led the column in his Jeep. Inside Lena Horne, it felt like they were driving into thunder, so heavy and so close was the bombardment of enemy artillery. Luther hunched involuntarily with each explosion. Jocko yelled merrily, "Hell, Hayes, I don't know what you're duckin' for. You should be glad when you hear them explosions. If you can hear it, it means it didn't kill you!"

"Yeah, I guess," Luther yelled back, unconvinced. He glanced down at Arnie. The boy's eyes were large and white in the gloom.

They had gone only a few miles when the column came to a halt. Jocko radioed to see what the holdup was and learned that some French farmer—probably a collaborator with the Germans—had blocked the road with a herd of cattle. Bates was said to have arrested him personally. Some infantrymen cleared the road and the tanks rolled past the bovine roadblock.

The rain slowed. The bombardment ended. Jocko opened the hatch and popped his head out of the turret. Through his sights, Luther could see the faintest hint of the sun on the eastern horizon. The radio crackled continuously, tank crews reaching out to locate one another, encourage one another. Then Wingo's voice broke in. "I want absolute silence!" he screeched, his voice high and fearful. "You boys keep quiet on those radios."

There was a beat. Then over the radio, someone said, "Yo' mama."

"Who was that?" demanded Wingo. "Who said that?"

Inside Lena Horne, even pious Friendly Sullivan laughed himself to tears. But after, the men observed radio silence as they had been told.

The tanks rolled on. Luther yelled up to Jocko, who was still standing with his head and chest poked up out of the turret hatch. "What you see up there, Sarge?"

"It's the colonel," yelled Jocko. "He's standin' by the side of the road on top of his Jeep, directin' traffic like a cop on Michigan Avenue. Cool as a cucumber!" Jocko saluted Bates, then waved for good measure as the tank rolled past him.

Over the radio came the command to assume attack formation. Then a cheerful voice broke in to translate the command into the jive and jazz of big-city streets. "Now looky here, you cats. We got to hit it down the main drag and hep some'a them unhepped cats on the other side. So let's roll on down ol' Seventh Avenue and *knock* 'em, Jack!"

There was a beat. Then the same voice spoke with quiet resolve. "All right, Panthers. Let's come out *fightin'*!"

Inside the Lena Horne, the men were whooping in approval when the explosion came. The blast was close. Luther felt the ground tremble beneath the tank. There came another blast. Jocko was lowering the hatch, getting ready to button up the tank when suddenly, he pushed it open wider, looking behind him. "Uh-oh," he said. "Shit."

Luther, who had been looking through his sights for targets, said, "What is it, Sarge?"

With a heavy sigh, Jocko lowered the hatch and sank into his position. "Colonel was hit," he said. "I saw it. Look like he was shot by some kraut patrol in the trees. I don't know how bad."

"Damn," said Luther. He had come to depend on the white officer's presence. Bates was one of the few white men Luther had ever seen who treated colored men like men.

"Lord, look out for him," said Friendly softly.

"Amen," said Jocko.

"Amen," said Luther, "but who the hell gon' look out for us?"

In that same moment, the voices began crackling out of the radio. "Hard Tack has been hit. I say again: Hard Tack has been hit. It looks pretty bad."

"You know what this means, don't you?" asked Books, turning to look back at Luther and Jocko. His eyes behind the glasses were serious and large. "Wingo is in charge." There was a beat of silence as the men took this in. Finally, Jocko spoke in a low growl. "Put it out your mind, fellas. We got work to do."

Lena Horne rolled forward. German artillery began bursting all around. As he searched for targets, Luther was uncomfortably reflecting on the specifications of the M-4 Sherman tank. Designed for speed over power, its armor was less than four inches thick at its strongest point. American tankers who had taken the M-4 into combat against the krauts in Africa reported that its 75mm shells had little effect on the sloped front end of the heavily armored German Panzers—they literally bounced off—while the 88mm Panzer shells could knock holes in the Sherman big enough to see daylight out the other side. They said your only hope was to flank the Panzer and hit it on the side where the armor was thinner and there was no slope—and what kraut was going to be fool enough to let you do that?

As if that weren't sobering enough, the Shermans also had a habit of exploding on impact. Veterans of the African campaign called the tanks "Ronsons," after the lighter, whose slogan was Lights Every Time. Hearing that, Luther had tried not to think of what it would be like to burn and to know in the few gasping, searing seconds left to him that his weapon was about to become his coffin. He had shared that fear late one night with Books as they were lying in their bunks. But Books had reassured him nothing of the sort could ever happen. "What you mean?" Luther had asked.

"Think about it," Books had said. "We are sitting on top of 75mm shells. In the eventuality you describe, we would be blown to pieces long before we could burn."

Luther had waited for him to laugh. He didn't. Luther had said, "Thanks. You done really put my mind at ease."

Now Books did laugh. "Glad to help," he'd said.

"Hey, Luther, you know, you were right about me that time."

The voice drew Luther out of his reverie. Arnie was yelling from his position down next to Books. His voice was barely audible against the din of explosions and the rattling of the tank and Luther almost hadn't heard it. But he did hear it—the whole tank did—and now Luther looked down to see the boy looking back at him with frightened eyes.

"Right about what?" asked Luther.

"That time in the bar. About . . . never being with a woman."

For a moment, Luther just stared. Then he felt his gaze soften. *How terrified the boy must be*, he thought, *to announce something like that to a tank full of his comrades.* The others pretended not to have heard. Luther was embarrassed for Arnie. He supposed they all were.

He grinned a grin he did not feel. "Well," he said, "I guess we'll have to take care of that, soon as we finish killing these here krauts."

"Both of you clam up!" growled Jocko, pressing his eyes against the telescopic sights. A handheld microphone amplified his voice above the clatter of the tank and the din of the artillery. "Don't know about you all, but I'm sick and tired of sitting out here getting shot at and not shooting back! Driver, stop!"

Books pulled back hard on the levers controlling the left and right treads and the tank slowed to a stop.

"Gunner, come right 15."

Luther spun the crank and the big gun shifted around. "What we aimin' at, Sarge?"

"Sniper in the bell tower." Jocko chewed on an unlit cigar. "One hundred yards. Load the HE. Come on, move it!"

Luther's body took over for his mind, and he felt distantly grateful for the numbing, repetitive practice drills Bates had insisted on while they lingered in Louisiana and, later, Texas, waiting for their chance to get into the war. Luther briskly adjusted the trajectory of the gun according to Jocko's instructions. "One hundred yards," he confirmed.

Friendly yanked open the breach and inserted a shell. He patted Luther's back once to let him know the shell was ready, but Luther had heard the breach close, and he knew. Eyes pressed to the gunsight, he flipped the fire switch and stomped the pedal on the floor. The tank shuddered as the projectile tore out of the big gun toward its target.

For a tense moment, Jocko watched through his sight. Then he scowled. "Shit," he said.

"About 30 yards short, Sarge," announced Arnie.

"I see it," said Jocko. "Gunner—" And then, right in the middle of giving the order, he stopped. They stared at him, awaiting instructions. Instead, Jocko barked a disbelieving laugh.

Luther said, "What is it, Sarge?"

"That son of a bitch, Wingo," said Jocko, still chuckling. "He's running!"

Luther couldn't believe it. "What?"

"I see it," said Arnie, looking through his periscope. "That damn coward! He's turned his Jeep around and he's hightailing it!"

Books laughed. "I would hate to see him at a Harlem knife fight, then."

Jocko said, "Gunner, come up 30. Fire when ready."

Luther made the adjustment. Again they went through the sequence, their movements as synchronized as some Apollo Theater dance team. Friendly opened the breach, ejected the spent shell, inserted a new one, and patted Luther's shoulder. Luther flipped the fire switch, then pushed his foot down on the floor pedal.

He watched. And then the bell tower blew apart, bricks spraying every which way like Fourth of July fireworks trailing sparkles of light. "Scratch one sniper," said Luther as Books, Arnold, and Friendly all whooped in celebration at their first kill.

Jocko's face was still pressed against the telescopic sight. "Books, give me a hard right turn."

"Where we goin', Sarge?" asked Luther. He could feel the adrenaline roaring in his temple.

"Machine gun nest," said Jocko, "sunken road, center of the tree line. Got our infantry pinned down good. Books, I want you to stand in close on these motherfuckers."

"Right, Sarge."

The tank lurched forward. Through his gunsight, Luther saw the Germans coming closer through the futile star-shaped flashes of their machine gun bursts. He couldn't hear them firing, but he heard the bullets clanking harmlessly against Lena's hull, like metal hail. He wondered why the krauts didn't run.

"Close enough," said Jocko. "Luther, I make that about 20 yards dead ahead."

"I can hit it, Sarge." A moment later, there came a great, vast roar and men's bodies went cartwheeling.

"We've got one trying to get away," warned Jocko.

"I got him, Sarge," cried Arnie. He popped open the gunner's hatch. Luther heard a series of short, sharp bursts, and he knew the .50-cal. had done its deadly work.

"Good shootin'," said Jocko. "Okay, next—"

The explosion filled the interior of the tank.

"We got company, Sarge!" cried Arnold, his voice panicky.

"I see him," said Jocko, face pressed to the telescopic sight. "Fuckin' Panzer. Can't let him get the range. Driver, get us out of here."

"Which way?" asked Books, as the tank began to move.

"Any fucking place but here!" cried Jocko.

Lena Horne rolled forward over the machine gun nest and its dead and dying krauts and down onto the sunken road, the men inside bouncing about like toys. Books swung a hard left, and the tank went racing east along the tree line.

"Goddamn it, Books. You're taking us away from our own forces."

"You said," cried Books, "and I quote, 'any fucking place but here!'"

Jocko swore.

Through his gunsight, Luther watched behind them as the enemy tank fired, saw the explosion in the spot where Lena had stood just seconds before. Jocko was listening to the platoon commander on his headphones. The Panzer lumbered down onto the sunken road and gave chase.

"He comin' after us," said Luther.

"I see him," said Jocko. "Books, hard left!"

"Hold on," said Books, and the tank lurched to the left, leaving the sunken road and climbing up the knoll. Through his sights, Luther saw the Panzer mimic the move. The enemy tanker had adopted an angle that would bring him directly across Lena Horne's path. Jocko saw it, too.

"Driver, stop." The tank stopped. Again, the Panzer mimicked Lena Horne's movements. The two behemoths faced one another like gunfighters at high noon on some dusty frontier street. The gun in the Panzer turret was already rising.

"He lining up another shot," warned Luther.

Jocko replied, coolly, "I need you to pop some smoke."

"Roger that," said Luther. He reached to fire the single-shot smoke mortar in the turret. Seconds later, a plume of phosphorous smoke, ghostly white, wiped the other tank from view.

Jocko was still listening to platoon leader commands through his headphones. Luther heard only his sergeant's end of the urgent conversation. "Uh huh. Uh huh. Well, you best tell him to hurry it up, or it ain't gon' be worth the effort."

He picked up the microphone again. "We the bunny in the dog track here. Got to keep him interested."

"He interested," said Luther. "He most definitely interested."

There was another close explosion. The men were bounced in their seats.

"Firing blind," said Luther.

"Are we going to get out of here, Sarge?" asked Books.

"Negative," said Jocko. "We going to show him some leg. Come left. Not too fast."

With a creaking of tread, Lena Horne made the turn. Luther held his breath as the tank crept slowly clear of the blinding fog. He followed the tank's progress through his gunsight. After a moment, he had the Panzer in view. It had not moved. Its front end was wreathed in smoke.

Jocko saw it, too. "Arrogant bastard," he said. "Thinks he can just wait us out. Gunner, light him up. AP shell, 75 yards, zero elevation."

"I hope you know what you doin'," said Luther, bringing the turret around.

"Yeah, I do, too," he heard Jocko whisper.

Luther and Friendly went through the firing sequence. The shell tore free of Lena Horne's 75mm gun and hit the sloped front of the Panzer. Sure enough, it bounced like a rubber ball on concrete.

There was a moment. Then the Panzer turret came around. Luther swallowed down a metallic taste. He thought of Thelma.

And then there was a dull thud and the enemy tank jumped.

The turret of the Panzer lifted with the force of it, landing askew on the body of the tank, the big gun pointing down toward the grass. Fire and black, oily smoke boiled up out of the wreckage. Luther gaped. An American tank crept clear of the smoke. It had managed to flank the

Panzer unseen while the Germans were fixed on the Lena Horne. As Luther watched, two men came staggering out of the torn Panzer. They were wreathed in flame. Arnie reached to push open his hatch so he could get at his machine gun. Books tapped the boy's shoulder and shook his head. "Let them burn," he said.

twenty-nine

It was Sunday morning, the day before Christmas, when the truck pulled into the prison compound. George and Andy stopped and watched with longing eyes as the guards unloaded still more Red Cross packages the prisoners would never see.

"Well," said George, "there they go again." He tugged at his pants, which were constantly threatening to slide off his hips.

"Thieving bastards," said Andy. He sounded resigned.

"So, what are we going to do about it?" asked George. He was sick of being resigned.

Andy laughed. "We could go see The Watcher and ask real nicely if he wouldn't mind giving us our stuff. 'Course, he'd probably just stare at us like we were bugs."

"Why don't we take it?" asked George. "It's ours. They're stealing it from us. Why don't we just steal it back?"

Andy looked at George as if waiting for him to laugh. He didn't. "You're serious," said Andy.

George nodded, realizing that he was.

"But how are we supposed to do that?" asked Andy.

George outlined a simple, impulsive plan. Andy pondered it for a moment. Then he said, "That's crazy." There was a moment. Then Andy hunched his shoulders. "What the hell," he said.

The goods were stored in a back room of the colonel's house. Half an hour later, Andy went to the guard out front and asked to see The Watcher on some trivial matter. Both prisoners knew the colonel had gone into town to bed his mistress. Risking a beating, Andy pretended not to understand when the guard told him The Watcher was unavailable—"No here! No here!"—and shooed him off.

Meanwhile, George wrapped his hand in his shirt, broke the back window, reached around to unlock it, then climbed in and grabbed indiscriminately at the many boxes and packages stacked there with the Red Cross logo on them. He threw a bunch of them out through the window, then climbed back out, scooped them up, and ran, loaded down with so much loot he could hardly carry it all.

He expected at any moment to feel a bullet in the back of his head, wondered if he would even have time to know he had been killed. But the bullet never came. Obviously, it had never occurred to the guards to anticipate that someone might be insane enough to pull a stunt like this. Still, George wasn't fooled by the bullet that never came. He understood himself to be dead, just the same. He struggled to care about this, knew he should. But the truth was, he didn't.

The two friends had a grand time afterward. Hiding behind the benjo, they gorged themselves sick on Hershey's bars and Spam. Andy smoked cigarette after cigarette until he was driven to his knees by his own hacking and coughing. When that passed, he fired up another smoke. When they'd had all they could smoke and eat, they began passing the rest around to other men. They went through the hospital—where men lay groaning or insensate with malaria, beriberi, dysentery, pellagra, dengue fever, and all the other plagues to which flesh is heir in a filthy place where men are kept half-starved—and handed out smokes, chocolate bars, magazines, and tins of sardines. George felt like some prison camp Santa Claus.

The stolen loot also included a bundle of mail, tied together by string. George and Andy had leafed through it, desperately hoping to come across something with either of their names on it. They didn't. But they did recognize the names of a few intended recipients and walked around the camp, pressing long-delayed letters into the hands of startled men. A man with an ulcerated leg wept when George gave him a year-old letter from his mother.

George Simon was the son of a wealthy man. He had grown up in a large house with fine things and always enough money to buy anything he wanted. He had always felt vaguely embarrassed by that. But it occurred to him as he watched the weeping man read his letter from home that nothing he had ever purchased, nothing he had ever owned, held as much value to him as those few pages did to that poor prisoner. But of course, value and worth were calculated differently in a wretched place where you had nothing. A cigarette meant more here than a Cadillac would have. In some part of his mind, George knew that the guards would soon enough be aware of the theft and come looking for the perpetrators. And he knew it was the height of foolishness to walk boldly through camp slipping letters and chocolate bars into men's hands.

But again, try though he did, he simply could not care. It struck him that he had not cared about much of anything for months. Not since the day his Bible had been stolen. Not since he had been forced to kneel in the rock garden next to Danny Boy Flaherty and felt his knees torn to shreds. Somehow, he had done it. Somehow, he had knelt there for the required 48 hours. And when, finally, the Japs had lifted the heavy wooden pole from his legs and allowed two other prisoners to carry him away, George knew that something in him had changed. He knew the Japs had lost their power to make him fear, to make him give a damn about consequences. It wasn't courage he had found. It was submission. Kneeling there beneath that weight, beneath that sun and moon and sun and moon, he had accepted himself as dead, had given himself over to his own inevitable demise. And there was something liberating about that.

In the months since, George had become steadily more daring, more foolhardy. He stole with reckless abandon from shipments that came through the shipyard. He snorted with contempt when Shitface ordered him to hurry up. He neglected to bow before The Watcher's office, took the beating that came, and then repeated the infraction the next day. Some men said he had gone crazy. Some said he had a death wish. He thought both were right. So he made no particular effort to hide what they were doing that Christmas Eve day as he and Andy roamed about the camp giving away the stolen loot. Nor was he especially surprised when Satan and his guards stormed into the mess a couple of hours later and pulled them from the audience of the Christmas show.

The men on the makeshift stage had been in the middle of an obscene version of "The Twelve Days of Christmas," but everyone stopped and turned to look as George and Andy were hauled away. The guards never spoke. Neither did George and Andy. The two Japs threw them, still without a word, into the benjo and pointed for them to climb down into the pit beneath. George didn't even wonder who had ratted them out. He didn't care.

George knew, in a distant, abstract sort of way, that there was something wrong with him, that you were supposed to care about such things. Self-preservation *required* that you care. But a year here had taught him the great secret of life: What you thought didn't matter. What you wanted didn't matter. What you did didn't matter. Even what you prayed didn't matter. So what did it mean to care? What was the point?

George and Andy stood together at attention in the pit. They were directly beneath the toilet seats, and the muck came halfway up to their knees. They were so cold.

"Well," said Andy, "here's another nice mess you've gotten me into."

"I'm sorry, Ollie," whimpered George. They both laughed.

The structure above them rested on bricks, and from where George and Andy stood, their view of the world was constricted to a rectangle. They could see the big mess hut where, just a few minutes before, they had sat in the audience watching the Christmas pageant. George could still make out the sound of the men's voices singing "Joy to the World." At the end of the show, there was supposed to be an ersatz nativity scene where a spectacularly ugly Aussie named Boone appeared as the Virgin Mary. George's sole regret was that he was going to miss that.

From where they stood, Andy and George could also see Satan—or at least, his sandal-clad feet—pacing up and back. He was speaking to them in a voice of patience and reason they had never heard from him, like a teacher instructing wayward pupils. And they could see the feet of the interpreter as he translated Satan's words into English. For whatever reason, Satan apparently wanted this particular speech to be clearly understood.

"You men are not Japanese," the translator was saying in his cultured, manicured English.

Even as George heard this, a fresh sluice of watery shit came raining down. He felt it oozing down his neck and willed himself not to vomit. It was warm and smelled of decay, with a coppery undertone of blood. A furtive voice whispered through the slit above, some prisoner George didn't know saying, "I'm sorry, fellas. I'm sorry. They made me do it. Hang in there."

"If you were Japanese," the cultured voice went on, "you would have spared yourself this disgrace. You would have spared your family this shame. You would have fought until the very end and died honorably in combat. Or you would have killed yourself and your family could have been proud to know you chose death over surrender. Instead, you allowed yourselves to be captured."

Satan stopped talking, paused in his walking, waited for the interpreter to catch up. The interpreter said, "One of you *gaijin* even lied and claimed to be the son of an American senator so that we would spare your miserable life. You are no politician's son, George Simon. We investigated your claim. Your father is a worthless lawyer in a minor town. But you lied and convinced a gullible captain that you were someone important, so badly did you want to live." The interpreter spoke the last word with heavy contempt.

"I never said I was a senator's son," muttered George.

Satan barked something. "Silence, dog," said the interpreter.

"Hell," said Andy, "I'd say I was *Roosevelt's* son if I thought it'd get me out of here. And my family is Republican."

Again, Satan yelled. Again, the interpreter said, "Silence."

Satan took a moment to gather his thoughts. Then he began pacing and speaking again in the same professorial tones.

"You white men," the interpreter said, "have no concept of honor. This is why you will lose the war. It is already happening, did you know that? Los Angeles has fallen. Chicago and St. Louis are no more. Your country lies in ruins; many, many of your people are dead. The emperor's Imperial Army is closing in on your capital city even as we speak and your crippled president is urinating on himself and regretting that he was such a warmonger."

"Goddamn," growled Andy. "Goddamn, goddamn, *goddamn*. It's bad enough we have to stand here. Do we have to listen to this bullshit, too? I swear, George, I'm going to kill this miserable fucker if it's the last thing I do." He began to yell. "You hear me, you slant-eyed bastard? You hear me?"

This time, Satan did not deign to acknowledge the outburst. He continued speaking without a pause. "The American race is a collection of mongrelized barbarians, including black savages not long out of the trees. Yet, you have the audacity to believe all other races are your inferiors and that you can tell us what we may and may not do. Whatever made you think you could give orders to a warrior race that was already many centuries old when Europeans were still learning to make fire? Now see what your impertinence has cost you. Nippon has exposed America before the world for the empty noise that you are, for the decadent fools you have always been."

Now Satan came over, bent his head low so that they could see his face. He held up a finger and pronounced his judgment. "Till morning," the interpreter ended, and both men walked away. With the Jap guard finally, thankfully gone, the only sound was the echo of men's voices. They were singing "It Came upon a Midnight Clear."

"Merry fucking Christmas," said Andy.

"Yeah," said George. "Same to you."

"Teach us to steal from the Japs, eh?"

"Yeah," said George. And he thought of Thelma and what she had written, and how he had clung to it as to a window ledge over a 50-story drop.

You make sure your decency, your humanity, *is the very last thing you give up.*

He had thought once that those words might save him.

But Thelma, he decided, standing there in the pit in the cold, had been wrong. Your humanity is not the last thing you surrender. The last thing you surrender is the belief that your humanity *means* something, that it makes you anything more than just another animal on the earth, rooting around in the mud of your own existence, repetitively eating, fucking, shitting, and then dying at the end. The last thing you surrender is the idea that God gives a damn about you.

Skeletal, covered with bruises, fleabites, and sores, and standing almost up to his knees in muck, his hair slicked to his scalp by the stuff, George knew in that moment that he had made that final surrender. The fact that he was a man, that he was human, that he sought to be decent and moral meant nothing. He was not one of God's elect. God had no elect. George had been stripped of everything—education, wealth, culture, dignity, his race, his country, his faith . . . all of it, gone. He had nothing left but his life, about which he cared very damn little.

From the hut, the men sang "Silent Night," their heavy men's voices lifting the ancient words of holiness and hope like a prayer into the brittle and uncaring sky.

"You okay over there?" Andy asked.

"Yeah," said George.

"You're awful quiet."

"Not a whole lot to say."

"Want you to know, I don't regret what we did. Not a bit."

"Me neither," said George.

"Those men, they needed something to give them hope. And that's what we gave them. Hell, that's what we gave ourselves. Far as I'm concerned, that was a good thing. Especially for Christmas."

"It was a stupid stunt," said George.

"Yeah," said Andy. "But it was a good thing."

Still the men's voices rose from the hut, singing "Silent Night." Still the sky looked down, cold and uncaring.

And out of nowhere, Andy began to recite. "And there were in the same country, shepherds, abiding in the fields, keeping watch over their flocks by night."

George looked over at him in disbelief. Andy met his gaze, his eyes luminous and purposeful in the shadows. "And lo," he went on, the words of Luke echoing off the underside of the Jap shithouse, "the angel of the Lord appeared unto them and the glory of the Lord shone round about them and they were sore afraid."

"Cut it out," said George. The recitation made him uncomfortable.

"Help me," retorted Andy. Without waiting for an answer, he went on. "And the angel said unto them, Fear not: for behold I bring you tidings of great joy, which shall be to all people."

Andy stopped. He fixed George with that same luminous stare. "*Help me*," he said again.

A single tear cut through the muck on Andy's face. And when his Yank friend spoke again, George heard his own voice rise hesitantly in union. "For unto you is born this day in the City of David, a Savior, which is Christ the Lord. And this shall be a sign unto you. Ye shall find the babe wrapped in swaddling clothes, lying in a manger. And suddenly there was, with the angel, a multitude of the heavenly host, praising God and saying, Glory to God in the highest. And on Earth, peace, good will to men."

When they finished, they just looked at each other, their breath puffing out from them in gray clouds. From the hut, George heard uproarious laughter and knew that Boone had just made his entrance as the Virgin Mary.

Andy said, "Amen."

And the night passed.

And the morning came.

The sun still lay below the eastern horizon when George saw the Jap guards go storming through the huts as they always did, heard them kicking and cursing and hitting with rifle butts. A moment later, the men came staggering out to line up for morning tenko.

A guard knelt down, said something in Japanese, and waved Andy and George up out of the pit. They climbed stiffly, slowly, their muscles frozen by cold and by the long night of standing. The guard made a show of covering his nose at the stench of them and gestured for them to walk ahead. George's pants, heavy with muck, would have fallen off his bony hips had he not held them up. He and Andy stumbled toward the formation. Men tried to look at them without looking. Satan was standing there before the assemblage, his eyes the all-too-familiar half-moons of fury, his lips knotted in a knowing smirk. He was wearing some kind of ornamental Jap kimono, a sword scabbarded at his side. The translator was standing with him. The Watcher was watching from the porch of his office, his face unreadable as ever.

As George moved toward his place in the formation, the same guard who had come to get him shouted something in Japanese and pointed, indicating that he and Andy were to stand facing the formation instead. Mystified, George and Andy did as they had been told. The guard said in a tone of command, "*Hizamazuke!*"

George and Andy looked at him. They looked at each other. They had no idea what the Jap was saying.

He repeated it, "*Hizamazuke!*"

He kicked George behind the knee and George went down, even as the interpreter said, helpfully, "Kneel."

Andy knelt beside George. George felt his arms yanked roughly behind him. Then one of the guards tied his hands. He looked over at Andy. The same thing was being done to him. Satan stepped forward and began to strut back and forth, bellowing to the assembled prisoners. The interpreter began to speak a moment later.

"These men stole from the colonel. This means they stole from the emperor of Japan. And that means they stole from *God.*"

Satan turned, looking down on the two men. He spoke and the interpreter said, "Which of you first hatched this blasphemy? Which of you had this idea?"

"I did," said George. He spoke up quickly, for he knew now what was coming and he only wanted to get it over with.

"George!" cried Andy. "Don't!"

George ignored him. "He had nothing to do with it. He was an idiot. I used him. I fooled him into thinking the guards had given me these things and told me to pass them out."

"George, don't!" cried Andy. And then, to the interpreter, "He's lying. Can't you see that? We both did it! We *both* did!"

The interpreter dismissed Andy with a wave. He spoke to Satan. George could tell that none of what Andy said had been shared, because Satan fixed his gaze only upon George and sneered. And even though that was the result he had wanted, it made George angry. "And you know what?" he cried. "I'd do it again if I could. I don't give a fuck what you yellow cocksuckers do. Do you hear me? I don't care what you do!"

As the words were translated, Satan's mad eyes grew madder still, and George felt a distant satisfaction at the knowledge that he had managed to get under the bastard's skin at least once before he died.

It happened too fast. Satan tore the sword free of its scabbard, raised it high, and brought it flashing down. Blood leapt. Andy's body keeled over, and Andy's head fell into the mud, staring up at George with a surprised expression.

It took George a moment to process that this had actually happened. His mind was searching frantically for an out, a recount, a work-around that might somehow make this obscenity not real. But it *was* real, horribly, indisputably, and an instant later, when George's mind finally accepted this, George's mouth screamed. No words, just a scream—just primal hatred, revulsion, red fury ripping out of him. In that moment, Satan leaned close and spoke through a thin smile. George was barely aware of him. He was still screaming, staring at Andy, whose eyes had gone dim. George's tears flowed.

Then the translator leaned down to George's ear and softly, almost solicitously, spoke Satan's words in English. "Do you care now, *gaijin*?" he asked.

Satan did not wait for an answer. With a grunt, he lifted the sword high. Everything that had ever happened to him flashed through George's mind. Everyone he had ever loved was there.

Then The Watcher spoke some harsh command. Satan hesitated. He looked back over his shoulder, and George thought he might disobey whatever he had been told. There was a moment. Then, with a palpable reluctance, Satan nodded and lowered the sword, still stained with Andy's blood. Again the interpreter leaned over. "The colonel said to let you live with it," he said. George gaped. Words seemed to have lost meaning, to have become just a collection of unintelligible sounds.

He bawled without knowing it, bawled like a baby for his friend and for all the things he had surrendered. Satan kicked him and George, his hands still bound, fell sideways into the mud. Behind him, he heard the tenko count begin.

thirty

LUTHER'S EYES POPPED OPEN ALL AT ONCE. FOR A MOMENT, HE wasn't sure what had awakened him. Then he heard the hard clicking of his own teeth.

He was sitting in his gunner's seat in the turret of Lena Horne, his head hunched down, his hands pinned under his armpits, but he might as well have been crouching naked in a freezer for all the good it did. His joints ached with cold. Luther had half a mind to pull out his Ronson and hold the flame against his skin to see if it would burn him. It was— or at least, Luther thought it was—the first day of 1945. Two months of town-by-town, field-by-field fighting had brought the crew of the Lena Horne to this country crossroads, the northbound spoke of which led down into some little Belgian village. German forces controlled it, but the Allies would be massing today to wrest it from them. Lena Horne and two other tanks from Baker Company were guarding this approach to the town until infantry arrived.

Not that Lena would be of much help once the battle ensued. A glancing hit from German artillery the day before had damaged the transmission. But with so many tanks already out of action, both from enemy artillery and mechanical problems, Lena had been towed into position to provide what support she could until reinforcements arrived. Jocko said Heavy Maintenance would be out today to tow them in. Luther was looking forward to it, welcoming even a few hours of respite behind the lines as the tank was repaired.

In those two months of heavy fighting, the 761st had distinguished itself beyond anyone's expectations. White infantrymen who had once balked and complained at following "niggers" into battle had been forced to choke down their words. Many of those same whites now owed their lives to the colored tankers. Some of the Negro men's valor had simply defied belief.

A sergeant named Warren Crecy had climbed out of a tank that was bogged in the mud and under fire from a hidden machine gunner. As bullets screamed off metal and thumped into grass to the left and the right of him, he had calmly hooked up a tow chain so that another tank might pull it free. Another sergeant, Ruben Rivers, had had his leg ripped open by shrapnel from an exploding mine, but refused evacuation or even morphine. A few days later, outgunned and ordered to pull back from an assault on a French commune, he had instead advanced, providing critical cover fire for retreating American infantry. Rivers had been killed.

These and other stories of heroism had crackled from radio to radio, tank to tank, and man to man. Bivouacked in lonely clearings or stretched out in fine houses that lay blasted open to the sky, they swapped tales of what Negroes just like them had done, stories that could not help but stiffen a man's spine and put new pep in his step. And Luther, who had never cared about fighting for his country, found that he was proud to be fighting for, and with, these men.

But goddamn, it was cold. Wearing two pairs of pants and two shirts with three blankets on top and a fur-lined cap pulled down on his head, Luther thought he might as well have been wearing just his underwear. He tugged off a glove and touched his bare fingers to the wall of the turret. He could barely feel it, so numb were his fingers.

Goddamn . . .

To distract himself from how cold he was, Luther started thinking about how hungry he was—though actually, he wasn't hungry so much as he was sick of greasy C-rations, beans and sausage spooned up out of government-issued cans. He wondered if maybe, with some real food in his stomach, he might be better able to bear the cold.

And that was when inspiration struck so hard he sat up straight.

"Sarge?" he said, pulling the glove back on.

"Mmm?" Jocko, arms folded, chin on his chest, sitting in his commander's seat, barely stirred.

"You remember last night, back down the road about a quarter mile, we saw that house where them shells hit? It was near 'bout tore down?"

"Yeah. So?"

"Wasn't no damage to the barn."

"So?"

"Sarge, if there a barn back there, might be hens. If there hens, there might be . . ."

"Eggs." Books, who been crumpled in his driver's seat trying to sleep, sat up all at once. "Fresh eggs," he said, excitedly.

"Might be able to go in the house, liberate us a skillet, come back here, build a fire," continued Luther. "And maybe we ain't got to eat beans out a can for breakfast. What you say, Sarge? It's behind our own lines."

Jocko had been dozing with a cap pulled low over his eyes. He pushed it up now and regarded Luther for a moment. "You really think you might be able to rustle up some eggs, Country?"

"Let him go, Sarge," muttered Friendly, half-asleep. "It's worth a look."

Jocko turned his head fractionally. "Books, you go with him. Be careful. We're supposed to have all the krauts pretty well bottled up in town, but don't run across some stray patrol and get your asses killed."

Luther had grabbed his grease gun and was already pushing open the turret hatch. "Yes sir," he said, grinning as he hauled himself up through the opening and into the crisp air. Luther stopped grinning immediately and wrapped a scarf around his lower face. The cold was like a razor blade on his gums. He climbed down the side of the tank and dropped off into snow that came up to his knees. A moment later, Books joined him. "You'd better be sure about this, Luther," he said, his voice muffled by his own scarf.

"Ain't sure about nothin'," said Luther, "'cept I don't want another can of beans for breakfast if I can help it. Come on."

They set off walking. They had to step high, lifting their legs in almost a sideways motion as they slogged through the snow. In this way, they moved slowly through a landscape of stark blacks and whites, with the exception of an orange flame crackling above a still-burning German armored vehicle Lena Horne had killed the previous day. The blackened, snow-dusted corpse of a kraut soldier lay folded over the side of the open hatch, his legs still down inside the vehicle. The fire and the two men were the only things that moved. It was, Luther thought, almost as if God had sent the snow to blot out signs of human carnage so awful they would have offended his eyes. But those signs were too many. Trees were broken, bowing to the ground at sharp angles, snow piled high on their trunks. Vehicles were upended, metal twisted and mangled. Bodies lay about in various states of dismemberment, partially covered in snow.

"I tell you, Country, if I get out of this alive, I shall be done with war forever." Books spoke out of a deep silence, huffing as he navigated the snow. "Part of me had believed this might be a grand adventure, but now I never want to see war again."

"Make two of us," said Luther.

For a while, it had seemed as if the fighting might be winding down. Then came a surprise German offensive that had opened a bulge in the American lines. The Germans had attacked at a time—the dead of one of the worst winters in memory—and at a place—the densely wooded Ardennes Forest—where they were least expected, and had caught the Allies completely off guard. Now the Americans were scrambling to recover lost ground.

"Did you hear about Bates?" asked Books.

"No. What about him?"

"The scuttlebutt suggests that he is on the mend. He might even return to us before too long."

"Glad to hear that," said Luther. "I ain't never cared too much about no white man's health, but . . . "

"Yes," said Books.

"He a heap better than a lot of 'em. Like Wingo." Luther snorted, stumbling a little as he stepped inadvertently upon the corpse of some soldier buried beneath the snow—enemy or ally, he could not say and did not bother to look. "Wingo," he said again. "All the time talkin' 'bout what cowards colored soldiers gon' be, an' he the first one turn tail."

"I heard some news about what happened to him." Books's eyes were serious above the scarf. "He was evacuated and sent to a hospital. Diagnosed with battle fatigue."

Luther snorted his disbelief. "How he got battle fatigue? That motherfucker ran!"

Books shrugged.

"I be damned," spat Luther. "Don't that beat all? One of us turn tail under fire, you think he find his ass in a hospital?"

"More like the stockade, I would expect."

"Exactly. Cracker bastards. Even when they do wrong, they get treated better'n us. This country never been fair."

"No," said Books. "It has not. But after the war, I do believe that will change some."

"How you figure?"

Books regarded him. "Luther," he said, "in the last two months, I have slept in mud, eaten cold pork and beans from a can, and almost had my ass shot off more times than I can recall, all in service to this ideal they call America. I do not know exactly what will happen after this, but I do know that I have more than earned my piece of that ideal. So I shall never again passively accept the way white people treat us. I would die first. And I suspect I am not the only one who feels that way."

"Yeah," said Luther. "I expect you probably right."

"Things have to change."

"Yeah," said Luther again. He felt exactly as Books did. But at the same time, he couldn't help thinking that his father had probably made a similar speech when he returned from the first war, five years before white men burned him alive.

They lifted their legs over a split-rail fence that lay nearly buried in the snow. They were close to the house now. Luther waved Books down and they crouched behind a wagon. For a few minutes, the two tankers just watched the shattered house, studying the windows to make sure some kraut was not watching them.

"I believe it's deserted," said Books, finally. "What do you think?"

"I believe I want some eggs," said Luther. He stood, still watching the house warily. "Come on."

The two men crept forward, rifles at the ready. The front of the house had been torn open by artillery. A pile of white bricks that had once been a wall stood sentinel in the snow. The two men clambered to the top of the pile and looked inside the structure. It resembled nothing so much as a giant doll's house waiting for some little girl to come and play, the furniture still upright and intact in the rooms. Perfectly normal, thought Luther, except that the front of the place had been sheared away.

"Let's go around to the back," he whispered. For some reason, whispering seemed appropriate. The two men climbed down from the pile of rubble and made their way through the side yard to a back door. Luther tried the knob. It was unlocked. Bringing his weapon up, he stepped cautiously through. The two soldiers found themselves in a large, homey kitchen with walls the color of butter and sunshine. There was a wooden table in the center of the room that was cluttered with papers, bowls, cups, and cookware. Among the jars and cans on a wooden wall shelf was a family photo—a dour-looking old woman, two equally dour younger adults (a woman and a man), and three girls, none older than perhaps 12, facing the camera with irrepressible smiles. He suspected the family had been trying to pack up essential things and leave in an orderly fashion when the war suddenly showed up in their front yard and required them to get a move on.

"I hope they got out before the bombs fell," Books said.

"Yeah," said Luther, setting the photo down. He went to the icebox and pulled it open hopefully, but was disappointed. It was empty except for a wedge of cheese that had gone fuzzy and dark green, and half of an onion that had wilted and come apart. The drip pan beneath was filled with dirty water that once had been ice. Books tried the pantry. It was also empty. He pulled the scarf down from around his mouth and regarded Luther, accusingly. "It does not look promising," he said.

Luther shrugged. "We still got the barn," he said, pulling his own scarf down. "That the main thing." And he reached up and plucked a cast-iron skillet off the table. "We also got somethin' to cook with."

The barn was about 40 feet behind the house, completely intact. Better still, when they stepped into the pungent darkness, guns at the ready, the first thing Luther heard was the clucking of hens. He turned to level a triumphant grin at Books, who was grinning right back. "Pay dirt," he said.

Indeed, it was even better than that. As Luther's eyes adjusted to the gloom, he saw large, brown eyes watching him. There were three cows in all. "Holy shit," he said. "We got milk *and* eggs."

"Forgive me for ever doubting you," said Books.

"I forgive you," said Luther. He put the skillet aside and plucked a couple of pails off a wall shelf. "I'll get to milkin', you go see if any of them hens settin' on any eggs."

Books stopped. "What do you mean?" he asked.

"What you mean, what do I mean?"

"Country, I am from Harlem, New York. The only thing I know about eggs is how to buy them in a carton. This would seem to be more in your area of expertise than in mine."

"You better find you some 'expertise,' city boy, you want to eat. Just open the door to the coop, reach in there, push the bird aside, see if she settin' on any eggs, and pick 'em up."

"Will she . . . allow me to do that?"

"What she gon' do to stop you?"

"She might . . . peck at me or something."

"You done had krauts shootin' at you for two months and you worried about gettin' pecked by a chicken?" Laughing, shaking his head, Luther picked up a couple fistfuls of hay from a bale near the wall and dropped them into one of the buckets to make a cushion. "Here," he said, handing it to Books. "Put 'em in there."

Shifting the sling of the grease gun on his shoulder, Books accepted the pail. His lips were drawn down in an expression so dubious it was almost comical. "Go on," Luther told him, shooing him like a child. As Books retreated to the chicken coops, Luther drew up a three-legged milking stool, placed the other pail beneath one of the cow's udders, pulled off his gloves, rubbed his hands together, and began tugging at the teats with practiced ease. The milk made a hollow sound as it jetted against the metal. Luther even squirted a couple streams of the warm sweetness into his own mouth. It was something he hadn't done since milking had been one of his chores on his parents' farm. The memory of it brought a private smile and he welcomed it.

Behind him, Books was cajoling the agitated hens—"Easy now, girl, easy"—as if they were rabid dogs. Luther laughed again as he paused to light a cigarette. "There you go, city boy. Show them hens who the boss."

When he had finished milking the one cow, Luther went ahead and milked the other two. After the bucket was heavy with milk, he directed the streams into the straw. He hated to waste it, but he had always heard it was painful for a cow if she went too long without being milked.

When he was done, Luther took the bucket over to the chicken coops, where Books was latching the last door. He lifted the bucket full of eggs like a trophy. "We are going to have ourselves a feast," he announced. His expression shone with achievement.

"One more thing," said Luther, lowering the milk pail.

"What?"

Luther's answer was to reach past Books. He opened one of the coops and lifted out a chicken.

"What are you doing?" asked Books.

"Chicken dinner," said Luther. He closed his fist on the bird's head and swung the body around like some ancient warrior with a rock sling. The head came off and the body went flying. It landed heavily in the dirt, wings flapping wildly, then ran in panicked circles for a few seconds before it realized it was dead and lay down.

"Jesus," said Books, appalled.

Luther laughed as he tossed the head aside. In short order, and with the same brutal efficiency, Luther killed two more of the birds. He found an old burlap sack and stuffed them into it along with the skillet, then lifted his pail of milk. "Boys gon' be happy when they see what we brung," he said.

Luther pulled open the door and stepped outside. There, he froze. Something was wrong. He knew that instantly, but it took him a moment to know what it was. Then the realization slammed into him like a truck. He and Books had left two deep ruts in the snow when they entered the barn. Now there were three. The third veered from the kitchen door off to the right.

Luther was turning in that direction when the report of a rifle echoed across the cold and tranquil morning. In the same instant, a fine spray of blood erupted from Books's neck. He grabbed at it, grunted, dropped his eggs in the snow, and fell back against the building.

Luther let the sack and the milk pail fall into the snow, reaching around to bring his gun to bear. He didn't take cover; that would have left Books exposed. Instead, he searched frantically for the shooter. The shot had come from close by, but Luther could not see exactly where. He squinted frantically into the blinding white, desperately aware that every instant of hesitation might be his last instant of life. But he couldn't find the shooter. It was as if the snow itself was firing at them. Luther squinted harder, swept his eyes over the whiteness.

Where you at, you sonofabitch? Where . . . ?

There.

Though Uncle Sam had somehow neglected to do so, the German army had wisely issued winter camouflage uniforms to its men, the white gear rendering them all but invisible against the snow. But there the sniper was, crouched behind a tree 50 feet away. Even as Luther spotted him, the kraut's rifle spat a starburst of fire, and the doorframe six inches from Luther's head splintered.

Luther reacted without conscious thought beyond a disbelieving indignation that this guy had had the nerve to shoot at him. Up came the grease gun and he fired. Two rounds hit the tree. The kraut ducked back. Then, to Luther's great shock, he jumped to his feet and took off running. Or at least, trying to run. The deep snow meant that the best he could manage was an awkward, heavy-legged gallop.

There was no thought of letting him get away. In the first place, Luther was still furious this bastard had taken a shot at him—this was intensely personal in a way no tank duel had ever been. In the second place, if he were allowed to get away, what was to stop the kraut from coming back to try again and maybe even bringing friends?

Luther took off after the enemy sniper, his gait lumbering and slow. Out across the open field they clumped. It occurred to him briefly that the Nazi might be leading him into an ambush, but that seemed unlikely. As near as he could tell, the field was level—no ravine where enemy soldiers might hide—and the tree line was a hundred yards off. Maybe the shooter's buddies were camouflaged, hiding in plain sight as he himself had done, but Luther doubted it. Still, he couldn't figure this kraut's game. Why ambush them, then run off when Luther returned fire? Especially given that he had cover and Luther was standing in the open?

The kraut looked back over his shoulder, saw Luther gaining on him. As difficult as the snow was for Luther, it was harder for the German. The enemy sniper was a small man of slight stature. Where the snow came up to Luther's knees, forcing him to step high and wide to get through it, it came up to the German's stomach, forcing him to breast it, arms high, like a swimmer through an ocean wave. Luther was not surprised when the kraut stumbled. He seemed to panic then. Crouched in the snow, he came around, fumbled with his weapon, tried to bring it up.

Luther had anticipated this. He already had the machine gun up, the stock braced against his bicep, and he pulled the trigger in a smooth, easy motion just as he had been taught. The grease guns were notoriously inaccurate, but Luther was lucky. Even as the weapon bucked in his grip, he saw the enemy jerk like a puppet with the impact of multiple rounds. Then he fell backward into the snow.

Luther stopped. For a moment, he simply stood there, breathing heavily. All at once, he remembered Books. In the surge of adrenaline and fear, he had forgotten his friend. He had to get back to him. But

Luther couldn't turn his back on this kraut without making sure it was safe to do so.

He came forward warily, his finger resting lightly on the trigger just in case the enemy had not been hurt as badly as it seemed. But when Luther got to where the kraut lay in the snow, he took his finger off the trigger and lowered his weapon. There was no doubt. The enemy sniper had a hole in his chest Luther could have put his fist into.

Luther was about to turn and hurry back to Books. But for some reason he would never quite understand, he lingered another moment instead. With the barrel of his rifle, he tipped the sniper's helmet back off his head. He wanted to see this bastard's face, see who it was that had dared take a shot at him.

And he did see. And his mouth fell open.

Dull blue eyes. Corn silk hair. Pimples. The kraut was a boy, his face unlined, his upper lip innocent of even the suggestion of hair. The child could not have been older than 13. Maybe not that old. Luther felt his stomach lurch and was afraid he might be sick. He had killed a *boy*. What was wrong with the krauts that they would send a child out here? Dress him up like a soldier, give him a gun, and send him out to be killed? Yes, Luther had had no choice. If he hadn't shot the boy, there was every chance the boy would have killed him. He might have already killed Books. But still . . .

Luther's shoulders slumped. He felt fatigue settle upon him, was seized with grinding frustration for the eternal foolishness of men. Luther sighed. He wheeled around and went back to see about his friend.

Books was standing, leaning against the barn, grimacing in pain, holding a fistful of slowly reddening snow to his neck. Relief flooded Luther. "You all right?" he asked.

In reply, Books lowered his gloved hand so Luther could see where the bullet had dug a deep red trench in the skin on his neck. Luther gave a low whistle. "You's a lucky man," he said.

Books nodded, then inclined his head toward the field where the boy soldier lay dead. "I saw you get him," he said.

"Yeah," said Luther, and his voice was toneless in his own ears, "I got him. Come on, let's get back."

"Wait," said Books. "Don't forget the food."

Indeed, Luther had forgotten all about it. He hoisted the grease gun onto his back, handed Books the pail with the eggs, and lifted the milk and the sack with the skillet and the dead hens. And they began the hike back to the crossroads.

They walked for long moments in silence. Again, the morning had gone still. Even the crackling fire from the armored vehicle had burned itself out. The only sound in all the world was the crunch of snow as they waded through it and the milk sloshing about in the pail. Luther wondered whether it would be frozen before they could drink it.

All at once, this entire thing seemed a fool's errand. He was tired. He was cold. He had killed a boy. The crossroads came closer. Luther could see the spires of the little town down below. He couldn't even remember its name.

"That kraut who shot you?" he heard himself say. "He was a boy. And I had to kill him."

"What do you mean?"

"I mean he was a *boy*," said Luther. "Younger than Arnie, even. Maybe 13 years old at most. Not even shavin' yet."

"The Germans must be desperate for man power if they are conscripting children now."

"Yeah," said Luther. "Same way I figure it. Hell, somebody need to send Arnie's young ass back to high school 'fore the same thing happen to him. This ain't no place for children."

A moment later, they were standing in front of Lena Horne. Luther placed the pail of milk and the sack with the dead hens and the skillet on the front of the tank near the driver's hatch. "I'm gon' take a piss," he said, tugging off his gloves. "You better tell Jocko to break out the first aid kit an' put somethin' on that scratch 'fore you get an infection."

"Yes, Mother," said Books, waving Luther off as he climbed up on the tank.

Luther was smiling a wan smile as he moved away from the tank toward the trees, already fumbling with his zipper. The unmistakable whine of incoming artillery drew him back around. He saw Books, who was crouched over the turret, glance up toward the sound. Instantly, the shell struck home with a blast that popped the turret right off the tank. And Franklin "Books" Bennett simply came apart. Luther saw this, saw his best friend disintegrate, even as the concussive force of the explosion hammered him down into the snow. Flaming chunks of metal and of men rained down all around him. The heavy cast-iron skillet landed two feet from his disbelieving eyes.

The other tanks came suddenly grumbling to life. He heard turrets moving. The air stank of fuel and exhaust. It stank of men burning. Bullets clanged off metal.

Alone, down in the snow, Luther held his hands to his head and screamed.

thirty-one

THELMA HAD WALKED OUT OF MOTHER SUGGS'S HOUSE, HEARD the door close softly behind her, and for a moment just stood there in the dirt, breathing the morning in and wondering if she had done the right thing. The decision had been difficult, and she knew some of her friends and family would not understand it, perhaps never forgive it. Indeed, she might never forgive herself. But regardless, she told herself, seeking finality, the decision was hers and she had made it. Now she would just have to find a way to live with it.

So it was that, a little over seven months later, on a cold Sunday morning at the end of February, Mother Suggs and Izola Foster midwifed Thelma through six hours of hard labor lying in the back room on Luther's bed, and when it was over she had given birth to a son. She held the squalling, bloody new life to her sweat-shiny breast and knew his name at once.

"You are Adam Mason Hayes," she informed him.

Mason, for her father, dead all these many years at the hands of white men who believed, not unlike this baby's father, that being white men allowed them to stride through colored people's lives with impunity. And Adam for the man in the Bible who was the first, who was new, who came into a world without history. She would try to raise this boy without history because history, she knew, might crush him. It might crush them both. Bad enough he was a bastard, an illegitimate child. Bad enough his birth certificate would show only a blank on the line where his father's name was supposed to go. Bad enough he would carry the mark of his mother's shame his entire life. He didn't need to bear all of that and the truth, too.

No, she thought, let the truth die. Let the truth lie side by side with Earl Ray Hodges in the same unmarked hole.

When the baby had nursed and was quiet, and after Mother Suggs and Mrs. Foster had gotten Thelma cleaned up and presentable, they had allowed Gramp into the room and he had sat on the edge of the bed and they had placed the newborn carefully into his arms. Roebuck Hayes—at least 103 years old by now—had regarded this great-grandson of his with a look of such inexpressible tenderness that if she hadn't known better, Thelma would have sworn he could actually see the tiny, perfect thing that slept unaware in his arms. The juxtaposition of it tugged at her, and she wished she had a camera to preserve the picture—her grandfather, born a slave sometime in the late 1830s or early 1840s, holding a baby who might easily live to see the year 2000 . . . yesterday cradling tomorrow.

Gramp allowed the tips of his long, thin fingers to roam the baby's face. Adam smacked a little as though still suckling in his sleep. When Gramp spoke, his voice was rough like unfinished wood, and she knew that he was struggling with powerful emotions. She also knew what was coming. They had never talked about her decision. Returning to the house that day, she had given him only four curt words—"I changed my mind"—that he had accepted without comment. Now the conversation so long deferred would be spoken at last.

"When you left out of here that day," he said, "I thought you wasn't going to have the baby. I thought that's what you decided."

Mother Suggs looked over at Mrs. Foster. They left the room quietly.

When they had gone, Thelma said, "You're right. I had decided to get rid of it."

"When you come back here, told me you was still pregnant . . . I was shocked."

"I know," she said. "Tell you the truth, I was, too."

"I was glad you changed your mind," he said, "but I always wondered why."

She looked at her grandfather. She looked away. "Day before I went over there," she told him, "you remember, we had that argument. I was sittin' out there by myself listenin' to the war news. I remember they talked about how the Germans wiped out whole villages full of people. Just killed everybody who lived there. And they said how the British bombed some German city. They killed forty thousand people in three days. Think about that, Gramp: forty thousand people in three days."

She paused. She sighed. She regarded him.

"I just got to thinkin'," she said. "Already so much dyin' goin' on in this world right now because of hate. I just didn't want this baby to be another one. I guess that's why."

"I'm glad," said Gramp.

"I know you are," she said. "I can see it all over your face."

"You made the right decision," said Gramp.

"I don't know if I did or not. I hope so. But even if I did, that don't mean it's gon' be easy. What that man done to me . . . " She didn't finish the thought. She couldn't. Silent tears tumbled from her eyes. Gramp shifted the baby to the crook of one arm and reached a gnarled hand across the bed in her direction. Thelma put her hand in his. The old man's grasp was cool and strong. He didn't speak.

When her confinement ended a month later, Thelma went back to the shipyard. For a few dollars more per week, Mrs. Foster agreed to spend days at the house, keeping watch over the baby. Gramp, shockingly, had accepted the arrangement without a murmur of complaint, even though it meant the despised widow would be in the house with him all day, every day. Apparently, thought Thelma, he adored his great-grandson more than he detested—or at least, pretended to detest—his great nemesis from across the street. Indeed, the baby seemed to make the old man young again. He spent hours waggling his fingers in the infant's face, making silly expressions, listening for the cooing or the laughter. He nibbled on the tiny fingers that scraped softly against his face. Thelma had always loved her grandfather, but never in quite the same way she did in those sweet days in the summer and fall of 1944. Her life settled into a routine whose very predictability was a comfort after the upheaval through which she had lived. There was only one problem, one concern that nagged her sometimes in the soft moments before she drifted off to sleep.

She had not yet told Luther.

She knew she had to, but how was she to find language to explain to her brother what had happened to her when she could not even find language to explain it to herself—when even now, a year and a half later, she had not been able to force the terrible word for what Earl Ray Hodges did past her lips? How, then, to tell her brother what this *white man* had done to her when, even on a good day, Luther found white people a pestilence too difficult to bear? And if she had struggled to find a way to love the baby that resulted from that awful thing, how much more difficult would it be for Luther to do so? He would hate his nephew. She was sure of it.

So she wrote him letters full of cheerful banalities that did not come close to revealing the trauma that had upended her life. She told herself she did this out of consideration for her brother, that a man trying to survive a war zone did not need the added distraction of worrying about some awful thing at home that he could do nothing about. But the truth she admitted to herself only in those moments on the edge of sleep when the world grew indistinct around her and the barrier between conscious and subconscious melted and made it all the harder to believe her own lies . . . that truth was something else altogether.

That truth was that she was scared.

So she kept silent, kept sending letters full of cheer and banality to her brother. And the days piled into weeks and the weeks piled into months. And then the months became seasons.

On a too-warm day in March of 1945, Thelma returned from work in an unsettled mood. That day at lunch, Laverne had told them all about a rumor she had overheard from a white girl in the office. The white girl, gossiping with a friend, had confided that the shipyard would soon begin laying off some workers and reducing others to part-time schedules. With the German army teetering on the verge of collapse and the Japs losing on every front, the demand for ships was no longer what it had been at the height of the fighting.

"If they start cuttin' back," Laverne had said, looking at them all meaningfully, "you know who they gon' cut first."

"But what we gon' do if we get cut back?" Helen had asked in a worried voice.

"I don't know," Laverne had said. "At first, my husband didn't like the idea of me workin' a man's job. But I think he done got used to the idea of that extra money comin' in. Be hard to let that go."

"Amen," Betty had said. "Don't know if I could just go back to cleanin' up Miss White Lady's house."

Helen looked at Ollie. "What about you, Ollie?"

Ollie looked up from unwrapping a tuna sandwich and favored them with the dazzling grin that still had Helen, Betty, and Laverne half in love with him. "Oh, I don't know," he had said. "I been thinkin' I might light out for New York City when this is all over."

"New York City?" Laverne was scandalized. "What you gon' go all the way up there for?"

"Well," he said, still grinning, "I just hear there's plenty opportunities up there for a man like me. Think I'd like to give a look-see for myself." And he had winked at Thelma to make sure she understood the meaning buried in his words. Thelma had shaken her head. Even still, the man was hopeless.

"What about you, Thel?" Laverne was watching her through her usual haze of cigarette smoke. "What you gon' do if they let us all go?"

Thelma said, "I . . . " And then she stopped speaking because she realized she had no idea how that sentence ended. The decision wasn't so much about the money. With what Luther sent home from his Army pay and what she was bringing in from the shipyard, money—and it was the first time in her life she had ever been able to say this—wasn't really a problem. She had saved most of what she'd made and if the shipyard cut back her hours or even let her go, she knew she would be okay for a while.

Which meant she was free to decide her future based not on need, but desire. For perhaps the first time in her life, she was faced with a simple question: not what did she have to do, but what did she *want* to do? And in that moment, she realized she had never thought about that— never had to think about it—before. And now that she was, the bigness of it frightened her. There were so many ways to answer the question. How was she to know which was right? What did she want to do?

Thelma almost laughed, so outlandish was the question. She looked at her friends, realized they were waiting for her, and shrugged her shoulders. "I don't know," she began. And then she heard herself say in a speculative voice, "Maybe I'll go back to school. I always wanted to go to college. Maybe I'll do that."

"*College?*" Laverne spoke as if she had never heard the word before.

"You heard her," answered Ollie in a tone of proud affirmation. "College." And he smiled at Thelma. Not the dazzling grin he so often used to tease the other girls, but a more authentic smile full of a gentle fondness. "Me, I think that's a good idea," he said. "You always was smart. And I like the idea of knowin' me a college girl."

Thelma had returned his smile, but all that afternoon, the thought of it had churned within her. What on earth had possessed her to say such a thing? Could she really do that? Could she really just go back to school?

What about Adam and Gramp? What would Luther think? What would she study? And after she had studied, what would she *be*?

These thoughts were tumbling through her when she pushed open the door. She found Gramp in his customary chair next to the radio. An announcer was giving the war news. Mrs. Foster was in the opposite chair, her knitting needles clacking. Adam, chubby and pale with dark, curly hair, was sitting on the floor playing with a ball. She smelled stew from the kitchen. The scene was so homey, it made her smile.

Thelma greeted her grandfather with a kiss on the forehead, said hi to Mrs. Foster, and swept up Adam, who was reaching for her and saying, "Ma-ma."

"You should make that little scamp walk," Mrs. Foster said with a smile.

"I know," said Thelma, guiltily. Adam had just begun to toddle, but still demanded to be carried everywhere. She went into the kitchen and found the day's mail sitting on the table. Bouncing Adam on one knee, she sifted quickly through the bills. On the bottom of the pile was a large envelope with a military return address. She thought it might have something to do with Luther, but when she opened it, she found that the envelope contained only a packet of postmarked letters held together by a string. Thelma recognized her own writing. She undid the string.

The letters were all from her, all unopened, all addressed to George Simon. She had written him a year ago with an abject apology for her letter cutting off their correspondence. She had tried to explain that she had been going through a bad time and that she was sorry for taking it out on him. He had not answered her, but Thelma had continued writing him just the same. She had never quite understood why.

The letters, she supposed, had become a kind of confessional, a kind of diary, a place to confide what she was living through. She never said those things to Gramp, never said them to the girls at work, never even said them to Ollie. But for some reason it felt safe saying them to George. She wrote about Flora Lee, she wrote about the shocking news of her pregnancy, she even wrote the terrible word that described what Earl Ray had done. In a way, the fact that George never answered had made it easier. Indeed, she realized now that at some point, she had come to depend upon his not answering. His response had never been the point. Writing the words, getting them out of her had been.

She had not allowed herself to think too hard about why he never replied. Wartime mail was such an uncertain prospect, after all. Maybe the letters hadn't caught up with him yet. Maybe he was too busy to respond. Maybe he refused to forgive her. Of course, maybe he was dead, though she never allowed herself to think this. After a time, Thelma supposed she had realized, if only subconsciously, that she was deluding herself. But she had continued flinging her letters into the void. And today the void had flung them all back in a bundle thick as a brick, which seemed altogether fitting because the words stamped on each envelope struck her like a rock to the head.

"Missing in Action," they said.

The words seemed to hurt her eyes. She wondered why they surprised her. Hadn't she known? Deep in her heart, buried in her fears, hadn't she known? Poor George Simon. Through it all, he had been such a kind man, such a fundamentally good man.

Stop it. Stop talking about him like he dead. He just missing, is all. That could mean anything in the world.

But what did it actually mean? And how could she find out? Adam touched her face in wonder. "Mama sad?" he said.

And to her surprise, she was crying. For the white marine who had appeared at her door to talk to her about her dead husband three years ago, she was crying. Thelma brushed the tears away impatiently. "No, baby," she told her son, "Mama fine." But she was not. It took her a long time to fall asleep that night.

The following day at work, Thelma found someone to trade shifts with her. The day after that, she caught the bus downtown. She had on a hat and gloves and a white dress with flowers that she wore to church on the rare occasions she went, trying to look as proper and dignified as she could as she ventured into white people's world. She held her purse before her in both hands like a shield and tried not to see the curious stares, the frank way white men and women's eyes interrogated her, wanting to know what she was doing here. Obviously, she wasn't a maid—too well dressed—but what else could she be? Thelma was grateful none of them stopped her to ask. She skirted Bienville Square, where colored people were not allowed to be, and walked into an office building. On the second floor, she found what she was looking for. She had been here only once before, when she needed to hire a lawyer for Flora Lee. Back then, the gold-painted lettering on the opaque glass window of the heavy wooden door had read "John Simon, Esq. and Associates." It had been changed since then. "Johan Simek, Esq. and Associates" it said now. She did not know who that was. She pushed open the door anyway.

People—all of them white—looked up at her entrance, the receptionist sitting behind her desk, the clients waiting in the plush, heavy chairs. Conversations petered out, the clacking of multiple typewriters went silent. Thelma willed herself to calmness. She did not have Luther's hatred of being around white people, but it wasn't something she enjoyed, either.

"Beg pardon," she told the receptionist, speaking as properly as she could, "my name is Thelma Gordy. I would like to see Mr. Simon, please." The receptionist, a middle-aged woman with hair an indeterminate color between brown and gray, regarded her dubiously. She took her time answering. "You mean Mr. Simek," she corrected. "What do you want with him?"

"I'm a client of his," said Thelma, trying to establish that she had both a right and a reason to ask for Mr. Simon. "He helped a friend of mine last year and he's still helping my brother. But what I need to see him about," she added, honestly, "is a personal matter."

Again the receptionist took her time, all the while regarding Thelma skeptically. Finally, she shifted in her chair as if about to return to her typewriter, and Thelma knew that she was about to be dismissed. Then she heard George's father say, "I'll see her, Irma."

He was standing in the hallway just to the right of the receptionist's desk. Apparently, he had been there all along. Now he beckoned Thelma and she went, barely aware of the confused stares that followed after her.

"I apologize for that," he said as they walked down the hallway. "I will have a talk with Irma later."

The apology surprised her. "Thank you," she managed to stammer. Other than Flora Lee and George, when had a white person ever apologized to her before?

"I thank you for seeing me," she said. The hallway was broad and covered with impressive-looking plaques and pictures of important-looking people.

"Well," he said, "you are a client. Or at least, a client once removed. And you did say the matter was personal."

"You changed your name," she said.

A brief and reflective smile flickered beneath his salt-and-pepper moustache. "Actually," he said, "Johan Simek was always my name. I went away from it for a while. Then an event occurred that convinced me it was time to go back."

"Oh," said Thelma, though she didn't really understand.

He led her past other offices and into his own, a spacious room at the end of the hallway, paneled like the lobby in dark, manly woods. His desk was vast and very nearly empty. Only an inkwell, a telephone, a flip-page calendar, a clean glass ashtray, and a sheaf of papers sitting perfectly parallel to the edge of the desk broke the stark barrenness of the polished wood. A small table in an alcove to the right of the desk was filled with family photos, including an image of George in his Marine dress blues that sat front and center. The windows behind the desk overlooked Bien-ville Square.

Simek waved her toward a seat, then situated himself in the high-backed leather chair behind his desk. "What do you hear from Miss Gad-sen?" he asked. Flora Lee had gone back to her maiden name.

"She writes me 'bout once a week," said Thelma. "She seems to be okay, considering."

Flora Lee was at the state prison for women. Initially, the district attorney had sought to prosecute her on a charge of first-degree murder, punishable by death. But the former John Simon had performed what Thelma still considered something of a miracle. He had gathered more than two dozen depositions from people Flora Lee had worked with at the shipyard and among whom she had lived in the makeshift trailer park, all of whom had at some point seen Earl Ray batter his wife. The witness testimony painted a vivid picture of the kind of monster Flora Lee's dead husband had been. When he lunged at her that final time, the lawyer had argued, she had finally had enough. She snapped and shot him. Faced with that evidence, the district attorney had agreed to let her plead guilty to a vastly reduced charge of involuntary manslaughter and to ask for a maximum sentence of two years.

As Flora Lee had related in a letter to Thelma, "Mr. Simon told me the DA was kind enough to not ask what I was doing sitting there with a gun so close to hand in the first place."

"A tragic case," said Simek now, packing a pipe. "Considering the be-havior of that man, she shouldn't have received even as much time as she did, but the district attorney needed at least a few ounces of flesh, if not a pound, and I suppose I can't really blame him. As justified as she was, you can't have a society where people are free to shoot other people to death without paying any price at all. That's a recipe for anarchy. And in any event, she should be out soon. She's still a young woman with her whole life in front of her."

He touched fire to the bowl of the pipe, shook out the match, and took a long draw. He regarded her through the smoke. "So," he said, "you told Irma you had a matter of a personal nature to discuss?"

She clasped her hands atop her knees. "Yes, sir," she said, "though I expect it's more about me than it is about you."

"Oh?"

"Yes, sir. You see, I had been writing your son; that is, we had been writing each other."

He stopped puffing his pipe. An eyebrow arched. "I did not know that," he admitted.

"Yes, sir. It started, I guess, when he went on that tour the War Department sent him on. He started writing me letters and I wrote him back. I guess we became like friends, or something. Pen pals, at least."

"I see," he said. His eyes were piercing.

"I haven't heard from him for over a year. At first I thought he was mad at me for something. Then I thought . . . well, I don't know what I thought. But I kept writing to him anyway."

Mr. Simek held up a hand to stop her. "You kept writing him even though you got no response?"

"Yes," she said.

"For an entire year?"

"Yes," she admitted. "A little more than a year now, actually."

"Why?" he asked.

It was the most obvious question in the world, but it caught her off guard. "I don't know," she stammered. "I guess I just thought . . . I didn't want to believe . . . I kept hoping . . . " She stopped, took a moment to gather herself, finally lifted her shoulders in a little shrug. "I guess it just made me feel better to go on writing him," she said. "That's probably the best way I can explain it."

"I see," said Mr. Simek. A reflective tone had entered his voice. "So what is it I can do for you, Thelma?"

She hesitated, then spoke in a rush. "Two days ago, all my letters came back. They were all stamped 'Missing in Action.' I haven't really been able to sleep since then, for wondering. I'm sorry, I don't mean to impose, but I was hoping you could tell me if you've heard anything else. Is he okay? Have they found him yet?"

A deep sorrow filmed Johan Simek's eyes, and she had her answer before he spoke. He set the bowl of the pipe in the ashtray. "I am sorry to have to be the one who tells you this, Thelma. You obviously hold my son in high regard. He was . . . listed as missing for much of last year, but the military has since designated him as presumed KIA—killed in action."

Thelma gasped. Her right hand flew to her mouth. Her eyes stung. "How . . . ?"

"I have received letters from my son's friends. They say George was shot by a sniper while standing on a cliff on an island called New Britain. Apparently, he fell off the cliff."

"But do they have . . . did they get . . . " She couldn't make herself complete the sentence.

"His body?" Mr. Simek shook his head sadly. "No. Enemy fire was too heavy and they had to pull back. I am assured they did a thorough search once the Japanese were cleared off the island, but George's body was never found."

"But couldn't that mean he's still alive, somewhere?" she asked.

"You don't understand," he said gently. "It was a head wound."

That stopped her, but only for a second. "But even so," she said stubbornly. "Maybe somehow he survived it. Maybe . . . "

She stopped when she saw Mr. Simek's lips curl in a smile freighted by sorrow. "You sound like my wife," he said. "She, too, refuses to accept that our son is gone."

"But maybe the Japanese captured him," Thelma insisted.

Again, Mr. Simek shook his head. "You have no idea how much I would like to believe that, Thelma," he said. "But it is most unlikely the Japanese have George. In the first place, the Red Cross should have notified us if that were true. In the second place, I am given to understand that the nature of the fighting in the Pacific is such that the Japanese . . . " He paused, he breathed. "Well," he said, "they rarely take prisoners. Apparently, our side has the same policy. It is very barbarous out there, I am told. Kill or be killed."

He held up a hand to forestall any more words. "I understand this is difficult for you to accept," he said. "Believe me, it is difficult for me, as well. But I believe there is nothing to be gained by deluding oneself. Eventually, George's body will turn up. Or maybe it won't. Perhaps the jungle has claimed it and he will never be seen again." The thought of it brought a melancholy sigh. His mouth twitched. "Either way," he began, "we must face the truth. My son is . . . "

All at once, his voice snagged. For an instant, Johan Simek looked surprised, and then his face contorted with the pain of forcing the next word loose.

" . . . gone," he said.

With that word, his composure shattered, and Mr. Simek began to cry. He did not weep. He sobbed. "Oh, God," he cried. "Oh, God! My son!" He clamped a hand over his mouth to stifle his own cries, but his agony still escaped him in wordless, anguished groans. His shoulders heaved. Tears flowed over his knuckles.

There was a frozen moment. Thelma stared, amazed, not quite believing, wondering what to do. And then, she did the unthinkable thing that was the only thing she could do. She rose from the plush chair, went around the desk, and took the broken man in her arms. The wealthy white lawyer clung to her like a child to his mother on a scary night. She didn't try to shush him. She didn't say anything. She just held him and let him cry.

It took a while. It took long minutes. The pipe burned, forgotten, in the ashtray. Thelma watched a thin tendril of smoke curl toward the ceiling as she patiently waited the lawyer out. Finally, she felt his shoulders grow firm again. His crying worked its way down to a soft weeping.

After a moment, he said, "I apologize." He murmured against her breast, his voice gravelly with remorse and shame.

"No need," she told him.

A moment passed. He pulled back. He didn't look at her. She sensed that he was too embarrassed. "If you don't mind," he said in the same gravelly voice, "I would very much like to be alone."

She nodded and retrieved her purse. At the door, Thelma paused and looked back. Johan Simek's head was lowered. His gaze, she knew, did not take in the orderly desk, did not see the spacious office, and did not see her. She closed the door softly behind her, walked down the hallway, passed beneath the curious stares in the outer office, went out of the building, waited for her bus, took her seat in the colored section in the back, and went home.

Her heart was a cauldron. She tried to tell herself it was sad the white marine had died—he had been a good man, certainly, maybe even a friend of sorts, but there was no reason for it to affect her beyond that, no reason for her to feel as if the sky had crashed down upon her and the earth had given way beneath her. No reason to feel.

But she *did* feel. And she couldn't make it stop. She stepped off the bus and walked toward home automatically, seeing but not. Thelma realized that she had somehow come to depend on the white marine's being there—miles away, yes, in some far-flung Pacific outpost, but at the same time right *there*, just at the other end of a postal tether. It was why she had continued writing him for a year, even when a pragmatic voice told her she was wasting her time. She had ignored it, continued flinging her secrets and fears out into the void for George to catch, knowing he would help her make sense of them.

And now, pragmatism was having the last word. Her secrets and fears had been flung back to her, once again hers alone to bear. Thelma walked home through a grief that surprised her.

She made the familiar turn onto Mosby Street. It was one of the rare afternoons when the little girls were not out jumping rope. She didn't even hear the cackle of hens from anyone's backyard.

When Thelma reached home, she saw Mrs. Foster standing out front, leaning against the house, arms crossed, head down, as if lost in some private meditation. Then she brought her head up, and Thelma could see that her eyes were glittering. It confused Thelma at first. Was Mrs. Foster crying for George too? Did she even *know* George?

The old woman saw Thelma seeing her. "I'm so sorry," she said. And Thelma's heart gave a sharp, painful kick. She dropped her purse without even knowing she had done so. She had a dream of herself stepping up onto the porch, a vision of herself walking past Izola Foster, pausing at the door, walking in. And seeing.

He had been there before motorcars, airplanes, and emancipation. He had been old when she was born. She was 24 years old now, yet there had never been so much as a day of her life—not one single *day*—he had not inhabited.

He was sitting in his chair next to the radio. An announcer was giving the war news. Thelma reached across and turned the radio off, watched as the light behind the dial went slowly dim. Gramp had died with a faint smile on his face. The baby was asleep in his arms.

thirty-two

Johan Simek was the very image of stillness.

The room was a babble of conversations, husbands and wives earnestly plotting their futures, eager-eyed fathers pleading with sullen-eyed teenagers, brothers laughing loudly at one another's lies. The sound of them eddied about him like a stream around a boulder. He sat alone, waiting in the visitation room, back erect, head up, eyes clear. His dark-blue suit was sharply creased and immaculate; the usual matching homburg sat on the table next to his clasped hands. But though his body was motionless, Johan's thoughts were roiling, and they kept returning to the same conclusion. Somehow, the orderly life he had so painstakingly built for himself had collapsed into a tangle of remorse.

The visit from Thelma Gordy was only the latest example. It was almost two weeks since she had left his office, and Johan still had not gotten over his mortification about what happened. To break down like that, crying like a baby, in the arms of a Negro stranger . . . the thought of it was almost unbearable to him. Yes, he was grieving George. But he would be grieving George the rest of his life. Would every memory or mention of his son cause him to lose self-control, reduce him to helplessness and tears from now until the day he died? What good would he be if he allowed that to happen?

Johan consoled himself, as he had been doing for almost two weeks, that it was only the one lapse, probably destined never to be repeated. Other than that one time, after all, he had done all his weeping in private. So had it been, so would it be.

Besides, it was not simply the mention or memory of George that had so unmanned him. Rather, it was the revelation that George had been writing to her, this unknown Negress, for years, that they'd had some sort of relationship Johan had known nothing about. Standing at his window, watching the woman make her way down the street toward her bus stop, it had been impossible not to wonder what else there was about his son that he had not known. Johan had spent so much time talking to George over the years, so much time lecturing him. He found himself wishing he had spent even a fraction of that time listening to him.

A memory tormented him. Three years ago it was, that day George had come to him, importuning him to help this same woman's brother after the brother refused his induction. Looking over his pipe, Johan had asked his son a question, not out of any serious intent, but only to rattle the boy, only to see what he would say.

"Tell me, George: Are you smitten with this woman? This Negress?"

George had given him an easy smile.

"No. As I said, I simply feel indebted to her husband."

And that had been the end of it.

But sitting there now in the visitation room, Johan wondered, as he had many times since Thelma left his office, if his son had lied to him that day. Lied unknowingly, perhaps, but lied just the same. And if what George said had indeed been a lie, what might have happened if he had told the truth, if George had said to him, "Yes, Father, I am smitten. I have feelings for this woman, this Negress"?

What would Johan have said about that? How would he have felt then? How did he feel about the possibility now? And what, he asked himself impatiently, was the point of speculating over something so outlandish and unlikely? All of it was forever unknowable; he would never be able to ask George about any of these things, so what was the use of pondering what might have been? Bad enough what actually had been. He had bullied his son—the memory of it shamed him deeply—into marrying a girl he did not really care for in order that he, Johan Simek, then calling himself John Simon, might feel more securely *white*.

Sitting there at the table beneath the gaze of the uniformed guard on the catwalk above, Johan allowed himself a tiny smirk.

White.

Floyd Bitters had certainly shown him his error on that score, hadn't he? Bitters had slapped him down like an insect and then, as Johan cringed before him, he had delivered his awful truth.

"You come up here in your fancy suit, pretendin' you're a white man. You ain't no white man. You just look like one."

The recollection made him grind his teeth. Bad enough he'd had to pay the price for his folly. That was only fair. But through him, that price had also been borne by his son—*and* his son's wife—and the guilt that filled him because of it was mountainous. He was not privy to firsthand knowledge about such things, of course. That was far more a woman's province than his. But the scraps of information he had picked up from his wife suggested that the correspondence between George and Sylvia had been infrequent from the very beginning of their marriage and, on George's part, curt almost to the point of rudeness. Eventually, well before George was killed, they had simply stopped writing each other. Johan was given to understand that there had been many tears and much miserable hand-wringing on Sylvia's part, much asking her mother and her moth-er-in-law what she was doing wrong and how she might fix it. Neither woman had an answer.

Then George had gone missing, and they had lived for months with the terrible uncertainty. Sylvia had seemed almost relieved when George was finally declared dead. Four months later—scandalously soon, people said, but by this time, Sylvia did not care—she had married Bailey Win-chester, a boy she had known in high school who had seen action at Anzio. And relations between the Simons and the Osborns had become strained if not downright frosty. Brisk nods, hands lifted in desultory waves as one or the other's car sped past . . . these weak gestures had replaced good-na-tured greetings and drinks at sunset on the veranda. It wasn't even acri-mony. They just no longer knew what to say to one another. Johan wasn't even sure he missed the friendship. In fact, he had been thinking of selling the mansion. With George dead and Nicholas gone to the Marines, did the family really need so much space?

And besides, every time he saw his neighbors, it only reminded him of the encounter with Floyd Bitters and of the folly of trying to make himself white. He had not had words to explain to his family what had happened to him, to make them understand why John Simon had taken the train up to Kendrick one morning but Johan Simek had come limp-ing back, claiming to have fallen off the platform. They had pretended to believe him, for which he was grateful. Indeed, so thankful had he been that he had not pushed it when Lucille, Nick, and Cora—all of them, unlike him, born in this country—had asked dubiously if they would be required to adopt the funny-sounding new name. He had told them no, but even so, Lucille had worried what friends—and strangers too, for that matter—would think of the fact that she and her husband had different surnames.

She had taken to passing it off lightly as a bit of late-life folly on the part of her foreign-born husband. "We're really all Simons," she would explain to some new acquaintance, "but I'm afraid my John has become a little misty-eyed for the old country in his old age. I suppose I should be thankful he hasn't asked the cook to learn to prepare goulash." They would all laugh, and he would smile gamely, knowing that the only thing worse than the humiliation of this lie was the humiliation of the truth.

"Are you Simek?"

Johan looked up. A scrawny young man in a striped prison jumpsuit had come to the table. He had long raven hair that fell in unkempt locks across his forehead. His moustache and chin whiskers were scraggly and thin. The lawyer nodded and waved the man to the seat. "I thank you for seeing me," he said.

The younger man shrugged his narrow shoulders. "Ain't like I get so many visitors they's linin' up outside the door. I mean, my ma comes when she can, but it ain't that often. So what's this about anyway, Mister?"

"What it is about is that I need your help."

The skinny man looked surprised. "My help? What with?"

"I need you as a witness," said Johan.

The prisoner looked surprised. "Witness to what?"

"Twenty years ago, you saw a murder."

"What murder?" The young man's confusion seemed so honest and unfeigned that Johan wondered if he had tracked down the wrong person. Then, in the same instant, realization chased bewilderment from the other man's face, and he turned pale. "Oh," he said. "You mean when that colored couple was lynched."

"Yes."

"You're not with the DA's office."

The man did not make it a question, but Johan answered it anyway. "No," he said. "But I represent an interested party. We are trying to convince the district attorney to prosecute the crime."

The man snorted. "Good luck with that," he said. "Prosecutin' white men for killin' Negroes? In Klan country? Ain't no DA in the world fool enough to take that on."

"Actually," said Johan mildly, "the district attorney has already agreed."

"Really? Huh. Surprised to hear that."

"I don't blame you," said Johan.

Convincing the district attorney had been no simple thing. Because the young prisoner was right: the Ku Klux Klan was a kind of shadow government in Alabama keeping the actual government in check. Its capacity for intimidation—even violence—against those who resisted its power was enough to make sure most officials stayed in line, and Stubbs County District Attorney Horace Mayhew was no exception.

Mayhew was a prematurely balding young man with large, bespectacled eyes that had grown even larger as Johan sat before his desk and explained why he was there. A squeaking ceiling fan had pushed hot air around as he spoke. When Johan was done, Mayhew had sputtered, "You must be out of your mind, Mr. Simek. Me? Prosecute a white man for killing some niggers?"

As he had once explained to Luther, Johan's storied reputation as a lawyer did not rest upon any special ability as a litigator—he had actually tried very few cases—but upon his talents as a negotiator. He had always had an innate ability to horse-trade, to determine the other man's weakness and thus, his price, and to put together some mutually beneficial arrangement. This was how he had gotten Mayhew to agree to prosecute this crime.

What, he had asked himself, *might give the young DA the backbone to do his job?* It had come to him quickly, an answer found in a fortuitous interruption, when Mayhew's assistant came into the meeting to discuss some detail of the next re-election campaign. From listening to their conversation, Johan gleaned that the young prosecutor was facing a tough battle and was not optimistic about his chances.

"How would you like it," he had asked, once the assistant was gone, "if I could get an invitation for you to go to the Justice Department in Washington as a delegate to the President's Conference on Crime Prevention? Perhaps you could even give a presentation. Only a handful of prosecutors from around the country are being invited, so this would be rather a plum for you. It might be rather impressive to the voters as well."

Mayhew's eyes had lit up like Christmas lights. "You could do that?"

"Certainly," Johan had said. "I just need you to promise to prosecute this man, Floyd Bitters. It really is a grisly crime he committed. You should want to have a man like this out of circulation."

"But Floyd Bitters is a county commissioner."

"Oh," Johan had said mildly. "Forgive me. I was unaware that there are separate statutes for county commissioners."

Mayhew had given him a sour look. "This was so many years ago . . . "

"You know as well as I that there is no statute of limitations on murder, Mr. Mayhew. Oh, and did I mention: at the conference there is word the attorney general will chair one of the sessions. And that Mr. Hoover will drop in as well. You would be able to have your picture taken with one or both of them. Wouldn't that be impressive?"

There was no such thing as the President's Conference on Crime Prevention, much less a promise that Attorney General Francis Biddle or FBI Director J. Edgar Hoover would be involved with it. But Johan had an acquaintance on Biddle's staff who owed him a favor, so he was sure something could be arranged. It would cost Johan a pretty penny—likely, he would have to bear the costs for the entire "conference"—but it could be done.

So he had waited through Mayhew's hesitation confidently. "Fine," the DA had finally said with a decisive nod of his head. "I'll do it. I'll prosecute. But you'll have to get me some evidence. This is a small office; I don't have the resources to investigate some 20-year-old lynching. Probably couldn't find anyone willing to do it, anyway."

"But you already have the evidence." Johan had opened his briefcase and placed a postcard on Mayhew's desk. It clearly showed a much younger Floyd Bitters standing in front of a crowd of white men. They were grinning and pointing at two charred heaps that once had been Mason and Annie Hayes. The expressions on their faces reminded Johan of fishermen posing with prize catches. He had tracked the postcard down and purchased it at a significant investment of time and money. But Horace Mayhew had only glanced at it, wrinkled his nose in distaste, and pushed it back across the desk.

"This is not good enough," he had said. "I need a witness."

"A witness? The photograph is your witness."

Mayhew only shook his head. "The photograph shows a group of men and women standing beneath a tree with two blackened piles at their feet. They could be leaves for all the jury knows. No law against burning leaves."

"Leaves?" Johan had pointed an angry finger. "You can see the man's rib cage and there's his forearm. You can see the woman's blackened skull."

The DA gave him a pointed look. "You know as well as I do, Mr. Simek, no jury in Alabama is going to be eager to convict these people. They will seek any excuse to avoid doing so. If you wish to have even the most infinitesimal shot at a guilty verdict—and that's all you'll ever have, by the way, under even the best circumstances—then you need to bring me a witness."

And Johan had sat back in his chair, wondering how in the world he was to accomplish this feat.

"I understand why you would be surprised," he told the prisoner across from him now. "It was not easy to convince him."

"So now you need witnesses," said the man.

"Yes."

"You talked to some other people in the town already."

"Yes."

"So I'm guessin' I'm probably your last resort, on account they all turned you down."

Johan paused. But he could see no point in lying. "Yes," he said.

He had briefly considered going back to canvass the town of Kendrick for someone who would testify against Floyd Bitters but had quickly rejected the idea. In the first place, there was his physical safety to consider. Even if he went there with bodyguards, they would still be alone and outnumbered in a hostile town, vulnerable to whatever Bitters chose to do to them. In the second place, any person who was seen talking to Johan would likely find him or herself marked for intimidation or worse after Johan left town.

So instead, he had chosen to reach out by mail. He had written Doris Orange and Amos Hawley, imploring them to agree to testify. They had both turned him down.

"I couldn't see my way clear," Hawley had written.

"You must be out of your mind," Doris Orange had replied.

Johan had followed up with letters begging them to reconsider.

Hawley had never replied.

Doris Orange had, but when he opened the envelope addressed to him, only the torn-up scraps of his original letter had come fluttering out.

So he had turned to the property tax records and voter rolls for Stubbs County, and had compiled a list of people who had been of age and living in the county 20 years ago. He had written as many of those people as he could locate, making a blind plea: Was there anyone who had seen the crime and was willing to testify about it?

He received very few responses. Most of those who wrote declined to testify or professed to know nothing about the crime. A few berated him for ripping the scabs off old wounds. A few cursed him.

A month after the last of those letters had come back, a letter with no return address had reached him at home. It was postmarked from Kendrick. When he opened it, a .38-caliber bullet had rolled out onto his desk. Lifting it to the light, he had seen that his name was written on one side.

"*Istenem*," he had whispered, lapsing into the Hungarian of his childhood. *My God.*

And that had been enough for him.

Johan Simek was not an especially brave man. And the very clear threat that projectile conveyed, much less the fact that it had reached him in his home, had shaken him, had told him that no matter what promise he had made to Luther Hayes, no matter what promise he had made to himself, it was time to let this crusade go.

And so he had.

And then the woman, Thelma, had come to his office. And something in her, in her straight back and determinedly dignified countenance as she walked to the bus stop, had seemed to demand from him the courage he did not have. And it had occurred to him that there was, in fact, one last witness he had not yet spoken to, one he had forgotten.

Luther himself had mentioned him that day they talked in the city jail, had told how they were playmates as boys, how they used to hunt mudbugs together, and how, on the night of the murder, the other boy raised Mason Hayes's severed finger before the dying man's face. Doris Orange had mentioned him, too, that night on the train platform in Kendrick, complaining how her husband, the boy's father, had taken them all to the lynching. "My idiot husband," she had said. "He wanted us to see."

So Johan had written to the one last witness and asked if he might visit. And Jeffrey Orange had said okay.

Now the young man laughed. "You really are scrapin' the bottom of the barrel," he said, "if you're comin' to me." He lit a cigarette.

"What are you in here for?" asked Johan.

"Car thieving," said Jeffrey, squinting at him through a billow of smoke. "But I figure you already know that."

Johan nodded. This young man was smart. There would be no patronizing him. "Very well then," he said, placing his hands flat on the table, "we shall be straightforward with one another. You saw this crime, the lynching?"

"Yeah, I saw it all right."

"You remember it?"

Jeffrey exhaled. "Every lousy detail."

"Then I ask you to testify. I understand that this is something you might hesitate to do. But I also know that you will be eligible for parole in less than six months. Now, as it happens, I have two very good friends on the parole board and I could—"

Jeffrey cut him off, "I'll do it," he said.

"You'll—you say you'll do it?" Johan stammered, tripping over the momentum of his own words.

Jeffrey shrugged, "Yeah, that's what I said. So I guess you can save the big sales pitch."

Johan tried to cover his surprise. "May I know why?" he asked.

Jeffrey exhaled smoke. "How long did it take you to track me down?" he asked.

"It was not easy," Johan admitted. "My detective went to a library up in Montgomery and searched every phone book in the state with no luck. He contacted the War Department and found nothing there. The Alabama Motor Vehicle Division, the same thing. But we found your birth certificate, and no certificate of death."

"So then you or the dick finally thought to check the prisons and there I was."

"Yes," said Johan. "It explained why we could find no records of you elsewhere."

"When you were looking to see what I was in here for, I assume you saw my record?"

"Yes."

"So then, you know that I've been in and out of places like this since I was 14 years old. More in than out, tell you the truth. Burglary, assault, larceny, and all like that. You ever wonder why?"

The question surprised him. "No."

"No big mystery, really. I drink. And when I drink, I can't hold a job. And I end up doing stupid shit that gets me put back in here."

"Why don't you stop?"

"Ain't that easy. I been a drunk since I was 13, stealing my old man's home brew and replacing what I stole with water. When I drink, it helps me to blot it out. It helps me to forget."

"You mean the lynching."

A nod. "You ever seen a lynching, Mr. Simek?"

Johan stiffened. "No," he said, "I have not."

Jeffrey gave a sidelong glance as he took one last drag from the cigarette and butted it out in a tin ashtray. "Didn't figure you had," he said. "I wouldn't of, neither, 'cept my daddy, he thought it was somethin' we all should see, so he made us come. Well, being in that mob at a lynching is like—it's like you're outside your body watching yourself and all these people you know, your friends and neighbors and whatnot, step outside their own bodies and turn into . . . monsters. I mean, they're hacking people apart and giving out *body parts* as souvenirs, for Christ's sake. My daddy gave me that man's finger like you would give a kid a toy car to play with. And yeah, sure, the man was a nigger and all, but he's still a human being."

Jeffrey paused. He lit another cigarette. Shaking out the match, he said, "You know how you have a dream, Mr. Simek, and you're doing crazy stuff like you're flying or you're 20 feet tall or whatever it is and it seems perfectly normal while you're in it and you don't even question it? And then you wake up and think back on it and you shake your head because it's so damn crazy?"

Johan nodded.

"That's what it was like. It's like you're dreaming, except it's a whole bunch of you doing it, a whole bunch of you having the same dream, and for a few days afterward, it's the only thing people can talk about, they're so excited by what they did. But then, after a few more days, it's like they wake up and it feels like it didn't really happen. You lose the memory of your dreams after a while, right? Well, this is sort of like that, except you don't lose the memory, exactly. It's more like nobody talks about it anymore, like they have this understandin' between 'em, one they ain't got to speak, one they just sort of know. And it says, Okay, we all know this happened, but we're going to pretend like it didn't, and we ain't never gon' say nothin' about it no more."

"I see," said Johan.

Jeffrey looked at him sharply. "Do you? 'Cause I sure as hell don't." He took an angry suck from the cigarette. His fingers trembled. Neither man spoke for a moment. Jeffrey breathed out smoke, held the cigarette up vertically between his thumb and his index finger. He was studying it when he spoke. "I was nine years old," he said. "*Nine years old*. You shouldn't take a kid to no damn lynching. A kid shouldn't see the stuff I seen. I ain't been right since. I ain't been able to forget. Or even to pretend to forget. Maybe some kids could. Me, I wasn't one of them. I can still remember what it smelled like when those people were burning."

He paused. Then he said, "And you know what else? That man and that woman, they was my best friend's parents. Me and their boy Luther, we used to hunt mudbugs together. I been in their house. And what we done to 'em . . . what *I* done . . . it wasn't right and I'm goin' to hell for it. I know that in my heart."

Jeffrey Orange took another violent pull from the cigarette, crushed it out half-smoked, and jumped to his feet. "So, if you want me to testify, Mr. Simek, you ain't got to do no hard sell. Just tell me where and when, okay?"

Johan was stunned. "Thank you," he said.

"Good," said Jeffrey. He reached across and took Johan's hand and grinned as they shook. "'Course, that don't mean shit," he said. "This is still Alabama. That DA ain't got a chance in hell of convictin' nobody."

thirty-three

THE TANK THAT HAD BEEN DUBBED THE "HARLEM STEPPERS" grumbled to a stop on a rise overlooking some unknown Nazi compound. Luther could hear machine gun fire clanging harmlessly off the armor.

Even through the rectangle of it visible to him through the gunsight, Luther could tell the day outside was glorious, the cold of three months before nothing more than a bad memory. The trees were leafing out, the grasses were growing tall, and wildflowers were blooming in riotous colors in the fields below.

In January, when snow had lain thick and white upon the land, it had seemed to Luther as if nature sought to make the world seem innocent of war. Now spring had come, and war was simply an intruder, the verdant meadows strewn with corpses, flowers crushed beneath wrecked war machines, clear blue skies befouled by towers of black smoke. Death crashing a festival of life.

His new sergeant, a mild-mannered Connecticut English teacher named Wesley Clinton, was on the horn. "Yes," he was saying. "Yes, yes."

Then Clinton lowered the microphone and looked over at Luther. "Gunner," he said, "infantry is taking a pounding from those krauts in that shed." He angled his palm to indicate the direction he meant.

"I see 'em," said Luther, peering through his sight.

"Discourage them, would you?" Clinton was lighting a pipe. "Use the HE."

Discourage them, would you?

Luther could not imagine Jocko giving such a prissy order. *Put one up their asses, Country.* That's what Jocko would have said. Then Books would have given him perfect position. Friendly would have had him loaded even before Jocko finished speaking, a synchronicity of motion that made firing the big gun resemble some grim ballet.

By contrast, this new loader—Chuck Allen was his name—gave him a look of cowlike stupidity for half a second as if he had not heard the same order Luther did. Only then did Allen yank open the breach and insert the high-explosive shell.

Damn, Luther missed his old crew. He missed his *friends*.

He tried not to think about it too often. Thinking about it only depressed him, sorrow dropping down on him like an ocean falling out of the sky, submerging him, drowning him. But sometimes, he just couldn't help himself.

"Gunner, come right 30 degrees. Make your range one hundred yards."

"Right 30," repeated Luther, spinning the crank to bring the gun around, "range one hundred yards. Got it."

"Fire," said Clinton in a voice so uninflected he might as well have been ordering a hamburger.

Luther stomped the fire button and watched through the gunsight. Seconds later, the shed the Germans were firing from erupted, planks of wood and pieces of men flying high. "Direct hit," said Luther. Clinton, he had to admit, had one hell of an eye. He often didn't even need to bracket his targets. He blew them to hell on the first shot.

"Good shooting, Sarge," called the driver. Luther could never remember his name.

Clinton was already back on the horn, talking through the microphone, one cup of the headphone held to the right side of his head. "All right," he told the unit commander. "Will do."

He put the headphone down and clicked the mike so that he was now addressing the men inside the tank. "Gentlemen," he said, "it looks like those were the last of the holdouts, so we're going to go down there and see what this place is that the krauts were fighting so desperately to defend. Look alive. Teddy"—this was the driver whose name Luther could never recall—"put us third in line."

"Yes, sir," called Teddy.

And the Harlem Steppers rumbled forward.

"What do you think this place is, Sarge?" asked Allen.

Clinton hunched his shoulders. "Search me," he said. "What do you think, Luther?"

"Don't know," said Luther curtly. He knew they were trying to include him, to make him feel part of their crew in fact as well as in name, but they didn't understand: he didn't *want* to be included. If seeing his best friend disintegrated before his very eyes and the rest of his crew blown to bits in the same instant had taught him nothing else, it had taught him the foolishness of getting too close to anyone in a place where any of them could all too easily be obliterated, wiped from life, any second. Better to keep to yourself. Better to be alone than suffer that again.

When Lena Horne had been hit, he had scrambled up out of the snow and into the wreckage, heedless of artillery exploding around him, bullets whanging off metal to the right and left of him, heedless of the heat of the armor beneath the hands he had already ungloved preparatory to taking a leak, heedless of everything in the world except the one imperative: to get to his friends, to save his friends.

But he needn't have bothered. When he climbed to where the turret had been and looked in, what he saw unmanned him. He stumbled down off the tank and threw himself back into the snow, retching violently. His friends had become a chunky mush of blood and viscera. There was nothing there even to bury. Their remains would have to be hosed out of the tank.

It was not lost on him that he should have died with them. What kind of fucking sense did that make? He was no better than any of those guys—certainly not better than Books, who was smart and capable and deep of mind, and who might have gone on from this war and made something great of himself. So how was it Books Bennett was dead, but Luther Hayes, a drunk who'd had to be rescued from a jail cell even to join this man's army, was still alive and well? And Jocko was gone. And Friendly was gone. And that poor kid Arnie . . .

"Oh, my goodness," said Clinton.

The sergeant's words, spoken with soft incredulity, drew Luther out of the memory. Clinton had been standing up out of the turret hatch. Now the sergeant lowered his head. "Teddy, stop," he said.

"What is it, Sarge?" asked Chuck Allen as the tank came to a halt.

"I'm not sure I know," said Clinton in that same hushed voice. "But . . . my God."

And then, without another word, he climbed out of the tank.

Luther and the other men looked at each other. Then they followed their sergeant.

Luther stood on top of the tank. He felt his mouth fall open. He felt his mind fumble for language. But there were no words.

It was a camp of some sort, barracks arranged in neat rows. And hobbling, shuffling, tottering toward them from every direction came an assemblage of stick men in filthy black-and-white striped prison suits. Maybe some of them were women, too. It was hard to tell. The creatures seemed sexless.

Dazed, Luther dismounted the tank. His mouth was still open.

The creatures swarmed the colored tankers. It was difficult to believe they were even human. Their eyes were like those of small, frightened animals, peering out from the caverns their eye sockets had become. Their mouths were drawn tight against their bony jaws. You could look at them and see where tibia met patella, count their ribs by sight. They were little more than skeletons wearing rags of flesh.

And their eyes gleamed with a madness of joy, an insanity of deliverance at the sight of the colored tankers. They shook clasped hands toward Heaven, they smiled terrible, toothless smiles, they looked up at the Negro soldiers like penitents gazing upon the very throne of God. A woman—at least he thought it was a woman—took Luther's hand and lifted it to her cheek. Her grip was like air. She held his skin to hers, which was papery and thin, almost translucent. Her face contorted into an expression of raw, utter sorrow, and she made groaning sounds that did not seem quite human. It took Luther a moment to realize that she was crying because her eyes remained dry, no water glistened on her cheeks. She had no tears left in her.

And Luther, who had never touched a white woman before, who had never so much as brushed against one in a crowd, who had avoided even that incidental contact with a kind of bone-deep terror accessible only to a Negro man in the Deep South who grew up knowing all too well what messing with a white woman could get you, could only stand there, stricken and dumbfounded, as this woman pressed his hand to her cheek. He was a man who had seen his parents tortured and burned to death before his very eyes at his own front door by white people. It had never occurred to him that their capacity for bestial cruelty was not limited to the woes they inflicted upon Negroes.

But here was the proof, this poor thing whose gender he had to guess, this creature whose age might have been 16, might have been 60, holding his hand in her airy grip, crying without tears.

Luther looked around. The place reeked of death and shit, a stink of putrefaction that surely profaned the very nostrils of God. Naked and emaciated bodies lay stacked in piles exactly like cordwood, only their gaping mouths and sightless eyes attesting to the fact that once they had been human and alive. Flies droned above it all in great black clouds, a few of them occasionally descending to walk in the mouths and eyes of the dead.

At length, the crying woman got hold of herself. Luther gently took back his hand. She gave him a shy, weak smile, touched her feathery hand to his shoulder—some sort of thank-you, he supposed—and wandered slowly away. Luther watched her go, still dazed, still failed by language. And he still struggled to understand. It had never occurred to him, not even in his angriest, most bitter imaginings, that something like this was possible.

How could white people do this to white people?

How could anybody do this to anybody?

"What is this place?" he asked. "Who are these people?"

He was speaking to no one in particular, but a sergeant he did not know answered him. "I spoke to one of 'em who speaks English," he said, a wild anger in his eyes. "Apparently, this is where the krauts sent people who were not part of their master race. He said some of these people are homosexuals or communists. But mainly, it's Jews."

"Jews?" said Luther.

"Yeah," said the sergeant. "I hear they're finding camps like this all over. The krauts work 'em and starve 'em till they die."

"Jesus," said Luther. He felt a scalding fury. "Fuckin' Nazis. Goddamn fuckin' Nazis."

"Some sick sons of bitches, all right," said the sergeant.

Luther wandered forward. It made him uncomfortable the way the creatures stared at him, smiled at him, reached out to touch him. All at once, one of them dropped to his knees, vomiting violently. Above the stricken creature stood Teddy, the driver, his face shrunken to a confused and guilty frown.

Sergeant Clinton came forward. "What did you do, Teddy?"

"Nothin'," protested the driver. "Just give him some chocolate out of my ration is all."

"You can't give 'em nothin'!" A sergeant standing in the turret hatch of the lead tank bellowed this down at them. He was holding a microphone in his left hand and wearing headphones with one cup dangling off his ear. "You hear that, everybody? I know you want to, but command says these people been on starvation rations so long, they can't eat what we eat. It's too rich for 'em."

"Ain't that some shit," said Luther, looking down at the man who had curled in agony at Teddy's feet, chocolate smeared about his mouth. "Poor bastard's too hungry to eat."

The sergeant on top of the tank had his head down, listening to the voice in his ear. Then his gaze came up. "Okay, that's it," he called. "Mount up. We're movin' out."

"Movin' out?" Luther couldn't believe it. "How we gon' move out, Sarge? What about these people?"

"What are you going to do? Cram 'em all in your turret? Command knows where they are now. They're sending help, doctors, some rations they can eat."

Luther accepted this only grudgingly. "I guess so," he said. "Still don't seem right."

"Look at it this way," called the sergeant. "Would you rather stay here and play nursemaid to people you can't help, or would you rather go kill some more krauts?"

Luther glanced back at the prisoners, these wasted remnants of vital human beings. "Ain't no contest," he grumbled and walked back toward his tank.

Five days later, Luther was standing in a corner bakery in the main square of some artillery-blasted little German town. Much of the town had been reduced to a rubble of bricks, houses and shops blown open to the elements, but the bakery, improbably, stood intact. More improbably, the husband and wife proprietors had somehow continued baking. They were watching him now, their faces rigid with some mixture of fear, horror, and haughty, distinctly Teutonic defiance as he stood there, finger on the trigger of a grease gun pointed toward the ceiling, and flipped contemptuously through a display of cookies stacked daintily on a table in the front of the store.

The gun was for show. He didn't consider them a threat, these two old krauts, the woman with her swastika earrings, the man with his little bristle of salt-and-pepper moustache in imitation of Hitler, who glowered down on the room from a framed portrait on the wall. No, Luther fingered the gun only to humiliate them, only to remind them who was now in charge of their fate—him, a big, black *nigger* from Alabama.

He didn't even want the cookies that he pawed through with such contemptuous impunity, occasionally tasting one and throwing the remainder to the floor. Who even knew what black-market substitutes for sugar, eggs, and flour went into the things anyway? No, *hell no*, he didn't want their fucking cookies; he just couldn't stand fucking Nazis, that was all. He just couldn't make himself stop remembering that awful place, that poor creature lifting his hand in her weightless grip, the way his mind had lost language trying to process the realization—no, the *reminder*—that it was possible for people to hate other people enough to treat them like this.

He could not *stand* fucking Nazis.

"Hey, Lu."

He turned and saw Milt Isley, the bow gunner of his new tank crew, striding toward him. They were not such bad guys, Luther had reluctantly decided. They just weren't the crew of the Lena Horne, was all.

"Yeah?"

Milt, an affable Californian with dark skin and a pencil moustache, held up an envelope. "Supply truck just come through," he said. "You got a letter."

And that was good enough news for Luther to finally turn away from taunting the two old Nazis. As a parting shot, he reached to the wall, lifted the portrait of Hitler off its hook, and flung it through the door and into the street with casual scorn. Then he accepted the envelope. It was from Thelma, of course. It was dated from the end of March, so he knew it would not contain any reference to the shocking word of the president's death in April.

That would come in her next letter, he supposed. Luther had been curious to see how his sister responded to the news. He himself had never given Franklin Roosevelt much thought one way or another, so he had been surprised by how bereft the news had left him when Clinton had announced it to the crew. It had felt like someone had taken away the ground beneath your feet or the gravity that tethered you to it, some essential thing that had been there so long that you noticed it only by its absence. Roosevelt had been president for Luther's entire adult life. Now the president was supposed to be some man named Harry Truman. Who the hell was Harry Truman?

"Sarge says we're moving out in 15 minutes," said Milt as Luther stepped out of the bakery, studying the letter.

"All right," he said absently. With a nod, Milt headed back to the tank. Still shaking his head over the idea that this Harry Truman was president now, Luther found an overturned chair sitting on a pile of rubble in the middle of the square. As men went back and forth around him, performing maintenance on tanks, harassing Germans, scavenging businesses and homes for anything valuable, he turned the chair upright, sat down, opened the letter, and began to read.

March 30, 1945

My dear brother:

I have started this letter five times now and each time I have wound up tearing it up and throwing it away. I think the problem is, I keep looking for some way to tell you the things I need to tell you that won't hurt you. There are so many things I need to say to you, some of them things I should have told you a long time ago, but I was too afraid. But I have come to realize that there is no way I can do this without causing you pain. Even though I don't want to, I have to. You have a right to know.

I guess the first bad thing I should tell you is that our grandfather has passed away. Gramp died just a little over a week ago. I just got back from his funeral, in fact. It was a beautiful service. Everyone from our street was there. Mrs. Foster cried and cried, the poor thing. The minister gave a lovely eulogy, talking about how Gramp was born when our people were in chains and lived to see us find freedom and how the old ones never gave up. He said because of that, we can't give up, either.

I know the thought of Gramp's death will grieve you, but keep in mind that he was blessed to live a very long life and that none of us gets to stay here forever. You should be happy to know that he was healthy right up until the end and that he did not suffer. His body just finally gave out on him, is all. I can report to you that he died sitting in his favorite chair, with a smile in his face, holding his great-grandson in his arms.

That's right, Luther, you are an uncle now. I have a son. His name is Adam Mason Hayes and he is 13 months old. He is just beginning to walk and jabber. I will send you a picture in my next letter.

I can imagine what a shock this news will be to you. Or maybe I can't.

I'm sure you will have noticed from the baby's last name that I didn't go and get married behind your back (smile!). So maybe you think your little sister has turned into a woman of loose morals. Well, it's nothing like that, Luther dear. I would give anything in the world not to have to tell you this, but the truth is, your sister was raped.

I have hardly ever said that word or written that word or even <u>thought</u> that word since it happened. I think I felt that if I never used the word, I could fool myself into believing it didn't happen. But it did. And here is the part I truly fear to tell you, the part that has kept me up nights trying to think of a way to break it to you: the man who did it was a white man.

His name was Earl Ray Hodges and his wife was a friend of mine. She was a very good friend, actually, in spite of her being white. Feeling the way you do about white people, I know you will find that difficult to believe, but it is true. In fact, she was such a good friend that when she found out what her husband had done to me, she killed him—shot him dead. So there is no reason for you to be thinking of ways to retaliate for what this man did. That's already been taken care of and he will never trouble anyone but Satan again.

As you might probably guess, there is much more to tell, and I can imagine you have many questions. I will try to answer them as best I can, but I have to beg you to be patient with me and let me tell you these things at my own pace. I hope you understand that none of this is easy for me to talk about.

And yes, I know you will be angry with me for keeping this from you for two years. I feel bad for writing you all those letters filled with gossip about the neighborhood, but never telling you anything about any of this. I hope you can forgive me.

But you have to understand, dear, that I couldn't think of a way to tell you these things. It would be hard enough under any circumstances for a sister to say things like this to a brother, but it was even harder for me, Luther, because like I said, I know how you feel about white people. And I also know you have your reasons. No child should ever have to see what we saw. I'm blessed that I can't really remember it, and I guess you've been cursed that you can't really forget.

I almost didn't have the baby because of that. I went to a woman who was going to help me get rid of it, but at the last second, I changed my mind.

What I realized, Luther, is that, yes, I know what it is to be angry at white people. Lord knows I do, especially after what that man did to me. But I'm not like you. I don't want to have to hate them all just for being white. I know they hate us, most of them. But I don't want to have to hate them back. I don't see how that makes things better. It seems to me there's enough hate going around. It seems to me that's why the whole world is fighting right now.

That's why I started to get rid of the baby, Luther, because I thought I was going to hate it. I didn't think I could find a way to love it, but I did. It wasn't easy; I admit I had to work at it, but I did. I'm hoping you will, too. That's what frightens me most, Luther, the idea that you won't be able to love him. I hope you'll be able to. I hope you'll at least try.

I know I've given you a lot to think about, so I'll let you get to it. I trust this letter finds you safe and in good health. Take care of yourself and Godspeed the day you make it back home safe and all of this is over. I love you, big brother. Please don't ever forget that.

Your sister,

Thelma

When Luther lowered the letter, he could hardly breathe.
He thought . . .
He thought . . .
Hell, he didn't know *what* he thought. His mind tumbled, his heart full to bursting with a calamity of emotions crashing heedlessly into one another like bumper cars at the fair. For the second time in as many weeks, he lost language.
Except for hatred. He thought of hatred. He thought of his parents becoming flame. He thought of that creature in the death camp, touching her skin to his. He thought of the fact that he was apparently now uncle to a half-white bastard nephew conceived in rape.
As he thought these things, he saw the man from the bakery step into the street. He picked up the portrait of Hitler that Luther had flung away. The glass had shattered and cracks fractured the Führer's face. Yet the man held the ruined picture up in both hands and spent a moment regarding it with reverence.
Then the image of him wavered and went gray and Luther realized that he was viewing it through tears.

thirty-four

THE FIRST TIME HE SAW A PLANE, GEORGE THOUGHT HE MUST have been dreaming.

Wrapped in a blanket, he was staggering back from the benjo with Quick, of all people, bracing his arm as he took his tottering, childish steps. His malaria had flared up yet again and it had left him a wreck, body alternately burning then frozen, legs like rubber bands, teeth knocking so uncontrollably he thought they might break. Reality wavered in and out on him like a radio signal that would not hold. George was sure his mind was making a joke at his expense when he heard the drone of a plane. Even so, he looked up just to be sure. And to his surprise, he saw it crossing the sky high above.

He knew it was real because Quick stopped too. In fact, the entire camp paused, guards and prisoners alike bringing their hands up to shade their eyes against the weak sun of early spring. Staggering a little, struggling to keep his balance, George squinted hard, bleary eyes, struggling to bring the aircraft into focus. By God, it looked like an American plane.

Beside him, Quick grinned and he heard men start cheering. George looked closer still. Sure enough, painted on the fuselage, there was a beautiful white five-pointed star.

It *was* an American plane.

George gave a weak cheer—the only kind of which he was capable. For this, Satan ran up from behind and hit him in the back with his truncheon. George fell into the muck. His body throbbed, but even from down there on the ground, he kept his eyes trained on the miracle overhead. Satan hit Quick, too, and he flinched from the blow but otherwise ignored it. Like George, he just kept looking up.

It was the same all over the yard. To their consternation—there was much agitated jabbering and gesturing—the Japs found that, for once, hitting did no good. The scrawny, scabrous men took the hits and went right on cheering, even dancing and shaking joyful fists to the sky. They were impervious in their joy.

So the prisoners craned their necks, watching after the plane until it disappeared over the horizon. By the time it did, the guards had given up hitting. They stood with their truncheons hanging limply by their sides, watching as the American plane went away. When it could no longer be seen, Quick helped George to his feet and led him back to the infirmary. They didn't speak about what they had seen, not at first. Their hearts were too full for that. Each man needed to process for himself what it meant.

Finally, when George was back on the shelf that served as his bed, his useless blanket pulled up over his cadaverous frame, he heard Quick whisper, almost to himself, "Won't be long now. They're comin' for us."

"Hard to believe," said George. "After all this time."

They were silent for a moment. George felt tired and closed his eyes, but he didn't drop off. He had been down for a week and was still surprised that Quick had appointed himself his nursemaid. In fact, the scrounger had sat up nights with him, dosing him with quinine, applying a cold compress to his feverish brow, spooning soup into him that seemed to have in it flakes of actual chicken. At first, George had regarded this with cynicism, then wonder.

Now he opened his eyes, unable to contain the question any longer. "Been wanting to ask you: Why are you doing this?"

Quick looked embarrassed. "What am I doing?" he parried, trying to appear confused.

"You know what I mean," George rasped.

Quick sighed. Then he said, "I don't know. Been asking myself the same thing. I guess maybe I just feel bad about stealing your Bible that time. That thing was worth a lot of money. Figured I owed you one."

"Yeah, but I slugged you for that," said George. Meaning: *we're even.*

"I know you did," said Quick. "I had it comin'. Thing is, I wouldn't never of done nothing like that on the outside, you know. I mean, I ain't no angel, don't get me wrong. But stealing a man's *Bible?* No way. When I did that, I just got to thinking, it's a hell of a thing what this place turns you into. You live like an animal and after a while, you start to think that's what you are."

"Yeah," said George.

"And I guess," said Quick, "I always admired what you and Andy did, stealing our stuff from the colonel like that. Took some balls."

"We were just crazy," said George.

"Maybe," said Quick. "But sometimes, there ain't a whole lot of difference between crazy and brave." Pause. "Too bad about Andy, though."

"Yeah," said George.

He closed his eyes again, felt himself drifting off. His last thought before sleep overtook him was that you never knew about people. You just never knew.

In the following days, as George's strength returned and malaria gave up its latest attempt to kill him, there were more planes and more still, until it became almost a routine sight. Whole fleets of B-29s roamed the skies unmolested, even in bright daylight. The planes flew low and in tight formation and, sometimes, there even came the sound and shudder of distant explosions as American bombs struck home.

At first there were more beatings, too, but as the weeks stretched out and the flights did not end, the Japs' hearts were no longer in it. Some guards even started trying to cozy up to men whose lives they had made hell. The quality of the food improved. Sick men who lingered too many days in the makeshift infirmary discovered they were no longer in danger of being beaten to make them crawl off their sickbeds and go back to work. A few cigarettes, letters, and chocolate bars began to trickle out from the Red Cross stash in back of The Watcher's office. And there were no more mocking taunts about the destruction of Los Angeles and Chicago.

The Japs' silence was a tacit admission that no lie they mouthed could compete with a truth the men could see. The very fact that American planes now patrolled Japanese skies with impunity said more than words about who was winning this war. And if the evidence they saw with their own eyes was not enough, there was also the news the men got from BBC broadcasts on the clandestine homemade radios they'd built into stools and bedposts. According to the BBC, the krauts had already given up. And from the sound of it, the Japs were on the ropes—beaten, but too stupid to know it yet. The war was coming to an end.

George wondered if he would be around to see it. As the year went on, life seemed steadily more unlivable to him. His work detail had changed after Christmas. No longer was he building ships. Now, as punishment for stealing from "God," he was assigned to a mining crew, sinking deep beneath the earth in the mornings to spend his days feebly hacking and shoveling coal in black caverns so low he had to walk in a crouch. He came up out of the earth in the evenings smudged black with coal dust, his saliva gritty on his tongue, his teeth gray. He was worn to a nub of himself by fatigue so all-encompassing he thought he could never be fully rested again.

He told himself to hold on. He told himself the planes overhead meant that rescue couldn't be much longer. He told himself that he owed survival to his mom and dad, and his kid sister and brother. But the words felt like only that: only words. Words could not salve his fatigue. Nor could words stanch his sorrow.

Pretty much every pal he'd had over here, he'd lost. Poor Jazzman, shot and stabbed full of holes by a lousy bunch of Japs on Guadalcanal. Poor Babe, shot through the gut on New Britain. Poor Tank Sheridan, poor Preston Phipps. And poor Andy, beheaded like it was nothing. What was it The Watcher, that unspeakable monster, had said even as Satan's sword trembled above George's own neck? What was the merciless edict he had issued?

Live with it.

Indeed, George hated his own survival. Why him? Why not Andy? Why not Jazzman or Babe? Hell, why not Eric Gordy? There was nothing special about him, nothing that deserved to go on drawing breath while each of those men lost his life so cruelly and suddenly. The more he thought about it, the more he thought God must be mad. So he went down into that grave every morning and dreamed with a longing of the day he would not come up again.

One night, long after spring had bled into summer, George was sleeping on his rack when, as too often happened, one of his dead buddies came to him in his sleep. This time, it was Andy. He knew it was a dream even while he was in it. But the knowing did not make it less horrible to see Andy's eyes looking up at him from the severed head. Instead of growing mercifully dim, as had actually happened, the eyes just kept staring at him. No release, no relief. Just stared, as if in accusation. How could that be anything but a dream, anything but his mind hurling condemnation? Somehow, yes, he did know this, even deep in sleep. In life, Andy would never have condemned him. It was Andy, after all, who had somehow known to reach out for him on that terrible night—Christmas Eve— when he had sojourned on a bleak plain beyond salvation. It was Andy who had encouraged him, knee-deep in shit on a cold night, to clutch on to that damnable green sprig, hope. Andy would not have condemned him. Horrible as the sight of Andy's severed head was, he felt no horror— only a need to make it right. In his sleep, George spoke to the severed head. "Andy," he said, "I'm sorry. Satan should have killed *me*. I was the one mouthing off. Or he should have killed both of us."

The severed head opened its mouth to speak. "George," it began.

And then there was an explosion.

Yanked out of sleep, George bolted upright. At first, he was not sure where or when he was. Then he heard the cheering. He leapt down from the shelf and stumbled through darkness to the doorway of the hut. Outside, prisoners were jumping up and down and screaming themselves hoarse, and it took George a moment to recognize this madness as joy. Then he saw the reason. The Mitsubishi factory had been hit by a bomb, and flames were towering above mangled wood and steel. But somehow, miraculously, the prison compound in the center had been spared. As if by divine will.

George almost allowed himself to believe this. He almost hoped. Almost. But in the end, he did not. When daylight came, the work truck did not arrive to take him to the mine. It turned out the mine had been destroyed in the same strike that hit the Mitsubishi factory. Instead, the guards passed out shovels and mimed orders to dig a pit. The hole was to be six feet deep and 20 feet square. No explanation was offered. No one dared ask for one. Shortly after the men began digging, a group of civilian carpenters began working not far from one edge of the hole. The banging of hammers on wood rang against the morning, counterpointed by the soft whisper of shovels in the soil. After the carpenters had been working for an hour, it became clear the structure they were building was a platform. Confused, George nudged Quick. "What do you suppose that's for?" he asked.

Quick glanced over to where the Jap carpenters sawed and hammered. Then he gave George a look that called him an idiot and spoke in a bitter voice. "What the hell do you think it's for?" he said. "It's a machine gun platform."

It took George a moment to get it. He was standing in his own grave.

Three days later, on the morning of August 9, George awoke to the sound of the guards storming about, yelling, stomping, banging truncheons on the walls and floors. He climbed down from his bunk and followed the other prisoners out into the predawn darkness for morning tenko. He bowed deeply as he passed Satan, hating as he always did the ritualized Jap expression of respect and deference he did not feel.

After breakfast, George joined a crew of prisoners who had been tasked with cleaning up bomb damage in the Mitsubishi factory. He worked there alongside Quick, excavating mangled pieces of furniture and factory equipment. The guards called a 10-minute break at mid-morning. George climbed out of the wreckage, wiping at the sweat that sluiced down his brow. "Let's get some water," he told Quick and they started over to the camp. The sky was clear, the sun pitiless. Then Quick pointed. "Look," he said.

Overhead, a pair of B-29s was flying low, vapor trails streaming off their engines. "Better get to the air-raid shelter," said George. Weeks before, the Japs had reluctantly allowed the men to carve shelters out of the ground to protect themselves from the increasingly frequent American bombings.

Satan was standing before The Watcher's office, a truncheon held behind his back, gazing up contemptuously at the enemy bombers. As George drew abreast of the hated guard, he automatically bowed. Quick did the same, but the gesture was fast and perfunctory and he never took his eyes off the sky. In a sudden blur, the truncheon came out and smashed Quick on the side of the head just above the ear. The blow landed with a sickening crunch that seemed to reverberate and Quick, who never saw it coming, fell heavily.

George stared in stunned disbelief. Quick did not seem to be breathing. Furiously, George rounded on the Jap guard. "What the hell did you do that for?" he demanded.

Satan drew himself up on tiptoe to bring his half-moon eyes closer to George as he sputtered in his infernal Jap gobbledygook. The interpreter ran up behind him helpfully: "He says your friend did not bow deeply enough and you should continue on your way unless you want the same treatment."

George felt dizzy with rage and incomprehension. He could not suck in enough air. Below him on the ground, Quick lay still. Another buddy felled by another lousy, stinking Jap. Satan's half-moon eyes seemed to dance before him in fire and self-righteousness, his lip curled in a sneer. He lifted the truncheon.

And the world turned red. "You dirty motherfucker!" cried George, lunging into a roundhouse punch that dropped Satan on his ass in the mud and sent the weapon flying. For an electric moment, the Jap guard sat stunned, holding up his hands as though he could not believe they were coated with the runny brown filth into which he had stomped so many white men. He was cursing in Japanese when George landed on top of him.

George was distantly aware that he was committing suicide. He did not care. It would be a fair trade, as far as he was concerned. They rolled over and over in the mud, and George Simon surrendered to something bestial within himself, something primal and hateful that had lurked somewhere within him all his life. George snarled in its wordless tongue. Hands reached ineffectually toward them. George, weakened by months of privation, was suddenly too strong to be pulled away. A chorus of voices called out to them, a chaos of words in two different languages. Commands, threats, encouragement—all of it ignored.

The two men rolled one last time. George came out on top. Satan reached for his eyes, trying to gouge them. George bit down hard on two of the Jap's fingers and Satan cried out in sudden pain. The Jap yanked his hand back, and George seized him about the throat, both hands clamping down hard. For the first time, panic came into the man's eyes. The Jap hammered at George's forearms, but George, frenzied, was too strong. Satan's blows weakened. George grinned a mad, mud-flecked grin, ecstatic at the joy of a primal release.

"Look!" someone cried, pointing skyward.

George was barely aware. This lousy, stinking, yellow, son of a bitch, bastard, hateful, motherfucking, goddamn, slant-eyed *Jap* was going to die this day, and George Simon was going to kill him. And that knowledge felt good beyond belief. He felt Satan go limp.

Then a flash of solar fire whited out the world. The light was so intense that George saw his own bones. In the same instant, something thumped twice against the sky. George's grip softened. He looked up. Everybody looked up. Even Satan, coughing and rubbing his throat, looked up.

The air turned to hell, already hot and now, all of a sudden, hotter still. The wind rose, howling. And the sky itself seemed to boil, a towering cloud climbing the firmament toward Heaven. George fell off Satan and sat there mesmerized in the mud, still looking up. Satan whispered something disbelieving in Japanese.

And then the wind rose higher still. And buildings and men were blown away.

George came to covered in blood and half-buried in dirt. He blinked. His eyes ticked back and forth confusedly in their sockets. He had no idea how much time had passed. He had no idea what had happened to him. For a long moment, he just lay there, breathing and being. Just breathing and being were enough. And then, when they no longer were, he grunted and began the long climb to his feet, dirt falling off him in a shower of grit. He found himself standing in a field of nothing. Fires burned over piles of scrap that had once been buildings, vehicles lay gutted and overturned, water spewed into the air from broken pipes, dead bodies lay strewn about. A morning that had been bright and blue was now as gray as if the sun itself had been blotted from existence. He took an uncertain step and his foot struck something. He looked down and it was Satan. The guard lay on his back, half-buried, staring slack-jawed into death. Even now, his eyes were mad.

"George, come on! Let's get the hell out of here!"

He spun dazedly at the sound of his name and saw Quick, one side of his face smeared in blood, waving him forward. All about them, men were scrambling to get away, prisoners and guards alike. George had no idea where they were going. He staggered after Quick.

They ran through a rabble of people with blackened flesh and blind, milky-white eyes, people whose skin hung off them like raggedy clothes so that you could see the tendons and bones below. They ran through a welter of outcry, people trapped beneath debris, screaming for help, wailing over the corpses of children, shrieking in mad incomprehension. They ran through the stink of burning and death. They ran until they reached the water. Then they leapt in and swam. On the far shore of the river, they collapsed in the mud surrounded by other prisoners, by guards, by civilians, by people, all of them breathless, all of them suddenly equal in the simple democracy of still being alive when so many were not.

Wordless, they stared back across the water at the burning charnel house that once had been a bustling city called Nagasaki. George looked at Quick. Quick looked at him. The little scrounger's bloody face was stretched with animal terror.

They didn't speak. They couldn't.

It began to rain and the water was black.

thirty-five

THREE WEEKS LATER.

George stood on the bow of an American hospital ship, staring at the black ruin of Nagasaki. When he and his fellow prisoners had finally located a working radio, they had learned from the BBC that the city had been leveled by something called an "automatic bomb." Or at least, that's how they heard it at first. It wasn't until they managed to catch a second broadcast that George understood that the thing that had saved them was called an "atomic bomb," and that what had landed on Nagasaki had also destroyed a city called Hiroshima. The Japanese had surrendered only after having two of their cities incinerated by this new bomb.

It was five days after the bomb fell that supplies began wafting down from the sky on parachutes into what had been their prison camp. The first crate broke open on impact. It contained Spam. All the Spam in the world. As the days passed, the drops became more frequent. Then they became ridiculous. Two drops a day, three drops a day, four, until it was raining supplies. You had to keep a constant eye on the sky or else risk getting crushed by falling foodstuffs. One man forgot to pay attention. His leg was broken by a crate of canned ham.

"Do not overeat." This was the stern admonition the men found on flyers packed into the crates. It made them laugh. This was a joke, right? How were you supposed to not overeat when you'd been starving on Jap rice and fish heads for one year, two years, or more, and all of a sudden, like manna falling from Heaven, here comes a bounty of chicken and cornflakes and Pet Milk and Cheez-Its and canned pears and grapes and tomato sauce and Wonder Bread and beef stew—good old, all-American food, topped off with real American smokes made from the finest Virginia tobacco? How were you supposed to restrain yourself in the face of that magnificent bounty? Why would you even try?

The men ate. They ate like gluttons. They ate like tomorrow, food would be outlawed. They ate like they were getting paid by the calorie. Men got sick and puked their guts out. Then they came back and ate some more. A couple even died, their weakened bodies unable to take the sudden rush of sugar, fat, and calories. And their friends took them off and buried them and spoke solemnly about the need to show some goddamn restraint, goddamn it.

Then they came back and ate.

Men began to put on weight. They took refuge under makeshift lean-tos when it rained. It was like a camping trip. After a while, some of the airdrops contained clothing and shoes. Some contained tents. The men threw away their rags, drew on the fresh uniforms, erected the tents, and began to feel like men again.

One day, George and Quick ventured into town on foot. What once might have been a busy urban center was now a scar on the earth, block after block after block of barren absence. The ground was carpeted with glass, wood, twisted metal, stone, and the random, fragmented detritus of vanished lives—statuary, hairpins, pipes, picture frames, bicycles, sandals, tatami mats, children's dolls. A car was upended, tires to the sky like a turtle on its back with its stubby legs pawing the air. Bulldozers grumbled about the work of clearing roads. Men with masks over their mouths pulled gnarled black corpses from the rubble and stacked them together. A lone Japanese man rode through the devastation on a bicycle. A US Army Jeep swept past him in the opposite direction, trailing a fantail of dust. Here and there, the remains of a building still somehow stood, poking up from the ruins like a tombstone over a grave.

Standing on the deck of the hospital ship now, George felt the vessel begin moving away from the dock. The ruined city grew smaller. He watched until there was nothing left to see.

Eight days later, the hospital ship passed beneath the Golden Gate Bridge. Men crowded the railings to see the gleaming towers of San Francisco winking in the noonday sun. George wept. He had never seen anything more beautiful. They took him to Letterman Hospital for observation.

He was lying in his bed when a familiar, unexpected face peeked around the partition. The other man's eyes widened, and they spoke the same words simultaneously.

"I thought you were dead!"

"Holy shit," said Babe. He leapt forward, grabbed George's hand, and pumped it like he was trying to draw water. "Holy shit."

"I don't understand," George said, bewildered. "You were shot in the gut." Everybody knew a gutshot was almost always fatal.

"That I was," Babe said. "I guess I'm just too damn mean to die. Or maybe the Big Guy was looking out for me. Truth is, I've got no idea why I survived." Pause. "I think about it a lot, you know?" Something flickered in his eyes, and George knew this was an understatement.

"No point in thinking about it," said George, who had so often thought the same thing. "It just is."

"Yeah," said Babe. "I know. But what about you? I'd have sworn I saw you get it in the head. That's the report I gave."

"I guess the Big Guy was looking out for both of us," George said. "Or just dumb luck, maybe. Helmet saved my life. Bullet ricocheted."

"But you went off the cliff."

"Lost my balance, that's all. Japs found me."

"So we're both just lucky sonsabitches."

It made him think of the Jap captain on that beach, refusing his gratitude.

You think I've done you a favor, George Alexander Simon. Nothing could be further from the truth.

George had not understood what the Jap meant then. He understood it all too well now. He was grateful for the miracle of being alive, but he didn't think he would ever see what he had endured as "lucky." But how to say that? Even to Babe, how to say it?

George just shrugged. "Yeah," he said, "I guess we are."

George wrote home that afternoon. Mother and Father would have received word by now that he was alive, but he knew they would not rest until they heard from him. He even wrote Thelma, just a short note to let her know he was all right. Even though she had said she didn't want to hear from him anymore, he felt he owed her that much. He owed Sylvia a letter, too, but he didn't write it; he still, even after all these months, had no idea what to say to her.

Mother's letter was the first response he received, and it virtually smothered him in love and relief. Reading it, he could all but hear her voice and see her tears. "Oh, George," she wrote, "knowing that you are alive, I feel like I myself have returned from the dead. I have been walking around for the better part of two years in a fog, not dead, but not truly among the living, either. People kept telling me to accept that you were gone, but I could not. A mother's heart knows."

She brought him up to date on his family, bubbling over with gossip and news. Nick had, indeed, joined the Marines and was serving with the occupation forces in Tokyo. Cora had graduated from high school with honors and had finally talked her father into letting her go to college. The letter continued in that vein for a few pages and then, carefully, as if dreading to break what she obviously considered distressing news, Mother told him Sylvia had remarried after he was declared KIA. "Her mourning period was a tad brief, if you ask me," sniffed Mother. "But I wouldn't worry about it if I were you. You're probably better off without her." George laughed aloud at this. His mother didn't know the half of it. The news of Sylvia's remarriage left him almost giddy. It came like oxygen to a drowning man.

As a rule, Father never wrote letters, preferring to send any thoughts or advice he had through Mother. But to George's surprise, this time his father answered him separately in a letter that arrived the following day. "The news that you are alive," he wrote, "is the best I have heard since the day you were born." From George's taciturn father, this constituted a wild emotional outburst. And Father, too, wrote about the end of George's marriage, but Father's tone was starkly different. "As your mother will have no doubt told you, your wife remarried almost as soon as you were declared dead," he wrote. "Your mother is angry about what she regards as Sylvia's unseemly haste, but my response is the same, I suspect, as yours will be: I am relieved. The fact that you are free of her frees me of the guilt of having manipulated you into a marriage you did not want. I only hope that you can forgive me for having put you in that position in the first place."

The words were a revelation. George could not recall his father ever asking forgiveness from anyone, for anything. When he finished the letter, he replaced it thoughtfully in the envelope, pausing to look again at the return address printed there, which had surprised him when he received it. *Johan Simek*. His father had gone back to the name he was given at birth, in the old country. George wondered why, but in his reply, he didn't ask. He simply thanked his father for what he had said and confirmed that he was pleased not to be married anymore. He asked his father to convey to Sylvia and her new husband his best wishes. He made the same request of his mother.

Thelma's letter arrived the same day as Father's. She wrote that she was happy to learn that he was alive, but not at all surprised. "I never believed for a minute that you were dead," she said. "I think I'd have known it somehow if you were." The words thrilled him for reasons he could not quite understand. And she apologized for her last letter. "It was a terrible time in my life," she said, "and I'm afraid I took it out on you, George. You didn't deserve that. I hope you can forgive me."

He wrote back and told her there was nothing to forgive.

With almost two years of back pay in his pocket, George was flush. When he was discharged from the hospital after a week, he and Babe rented a two-bedroom suite in a nice hotel and waited for their orders. While they waited, they dined on lobster and steak, went to movies, and caught shows. Once Babe invited him to a local brothel, but George declined. Babe seemed delighted and relieved that he did.

"Same old George," he said.

But he wasn't the same old George. This much he knew with grim certainty. His sleep was still raddled through with nightmares that awoke him and left him gasping and sweating. And the horrors didn't end when he awoke. He saw Satan's face on every Japanese-American taxi driver, baker, or florist who happened across his path. On the street, he found himself constantly looking around, eyes following some unoffending Japanese man or woman. He wondered why nobody else saw the threat he did.

One evening, George was at a restaurant with Babe when a waiter brought a man at the next table some dish that came with a large side order of white rice. The next thing George knew, he was on his feet, pointing an accusing finger at the man. "You call yourself an American? How can you eat that shit? I ought to knock you right in your chops, you traitor! You dirty bastard!" The man stared at him, uncomprehending. Something about that look of honest befuddlement made George catch himself.

There was a moment. Then he abruptly wheeled around and stormed out. He could feel the touch of a hundred eyes on his back as he pushed through the door, could hear the mutter of confused conversation behind him. Babe found him seconds later, leaning against a lamppost, shivering and soaked with sweat. His friend's eyes asked the obvious question.

"Yeah," George said, "I'll be okay. Japs made us eat that shit, that's all. Every day, every night, fucking rice. Fucking Japs. If I never see a plate of fucking rice again, it'll be too soon."

Babe thought for a moment. Then he said, "How do you feel about a plate of fucking pasta?"

George managed a weak laugh. "Fucking pasta is fine," he said.

Babe slapped his back. "Fine then," he said, "come on. I know a place. Best wop food in town."

thirty-six

FOR LONG MINUTES, LUTHER STOOD BEFORE THE HOUSE, STAR-
ing. Being there felt bizarre, felt as if he had stepped wide awake onto the
stage of his oldest nightmare. It had been 22 years since he had stood at
the window as a nine-year-old boy and watched his parents burn, 22 years
since Gramp had led him and Thelma away.

Now he was here again. And Luther, who did not believe in ghosts,
felt . . . *haunted*.

Behind him, a big black Packard idled softly, the lawyer, his sister with
her baby, and the chauffeur, all waiting for him. Two days ago, when he
and Thelma had sat in the lawyer's office and made plans to drive to Stubbs
County together for the trial, Luther had insisted on stopping here first.
He didn't know why. Thelma had told him it made no sense, served no
purpose, and he knew she was right. But still, he had insisted. He had
needed to come here, to the place where it happened, the place where
all the wrong in his life began. Finally, the lawyer had held up a hand to
silence Thelma's protests and told her Luther was right.

"I went there myself two years ago," he told Luther. "You should,
too, if that is what you want. You should have that right." So it was that
they had set out this morning, hours before the sun, following the tunnel
carved by the big car's headlights down a succession of unlit country lanes
until they wound up here and Luther got out to stand alone in this place
of ghosts. Between his index and middle fingers, a cigarette burned low,
forgotten. When he felt the heat of it, he dropped it absently in the dirt,
ground it out beneath the toe of one shiny black shoe. And kept staring.

Time, he saw, had not been good to the old place. Weather had stripped
the paint. The roof was slowly surrendering to gravity. The door was gone.

It was not what it had been for so long in his memory. Still, he would have known it regardless. There was the patch of dirt where his mother had crawled. There was the porch where the big white man had lifted him high and called him a nigger cub. There was the tree where his parents had been hanged. There was the window where he had watched it all. Even the old car was still here, still lying on its side, though stripped by vandals over the years. This place had been the cradle of all his terrors. Standing there on that brisk morning in early November, Luther realized with a start that he could not remember the last time he'd leapt awake, sweating with some bad dream of what happened here. But on reflection, he decided that made perfect sense. After all, he had new nightmares now. But he also had new hope.

On his first day back, a white Greyhound bus driver had snapped at him, "Hurry up, boy!" as he boarded the bus and Luther had opened his mouth to inform him in no uncertain terms that he was nobody's boy. But another voice had gotten there first.

"What the goddamn hell is wrong with you?" it bellowed. "That's no goddamn boy. Don't you see the uniform? That's a goddamn American *soldier*. And you goddamn well better show some respect, goddamn it!"

Luther had turned and found to his surprise that his defender was a beefy white colonel with blonde hair, his face red as he glared at the shocked driver. And it occurred to him that maybe Books had been right. Maybe the country would change now. Maybe it had no choice.

But the important thing was that Luther himself had changed. He could still feel the feathery touch of that poor creature in that awful camp in Germany, sentenced to die because, though she was white, she was the wrong kind of white. Madness, he thought. Plain and simple, madness.

On the way home, he'd had a few hours in New York City. He had taken a train up to Harlem, found a colored bookstore, and picked out that book that Books had been reading the first time they met, *The Souls of Black Folk* by W. E. B. Du Bois. On impulse, he had asked the man behind the counter to recommend other works he might like to read. He had ended up with a bagful—*The Mis-Education of the Negro* by Carter G. Woodson, *Up from Slavery* by Booker T. Washington, *The Autobiography of an Ex-Colored Man* by James Weldon Johnson, and others—and he had been reading his way through them ever since.

He felt himself transformed by all these new words and observations and ways of framing what it meant to be a Negro. And he knew that whatever it meant now, it could not be the same thing it had meant before he and thousands of other colored men risked—and sometimes, lost—their lives on foreign soil in the service of their country.

Luther gave one last look at the place where a nine-year-old boy had faced his life's defining horror. But, he reminded himself, he was no longer that boy. He was a 31-year-old soldier, a combat veteran, resplendent in his service uniform. He wore his US arm-of-service pin on his upper right lapel, his service stripes and overseas bars on his lower left sleeve. The "ruptured duck" emblem signifying honorable discharge was on his right breast just above the pocket, and the Black Panther patch of the 761st Armored Division was on his upper left sleeve just above the stripes designating him a PFC—private first class—in this man's army.

Luther came to attention. Slowly, and with great feeling, he brought his right hand up, palm rigid, thumb tucked under, and gave a salute to the memory of Mason and Annie Hayes. He held it for a moment, then whipped the hand down. He wheeled around, heel to toe like he was on a parade ground, and walked back to the car.

Thelma was watching him anxiously as he opened the door. "Are you okay, sweetie?" she asked.

He nodded. "Yeah," he said.

The lawyer—"Johan Simek" he called himself now—was sitting on the other side of Thelma. And that, thought Luther with a private smile, was change in and of itself. When had a prominent white lawyer in Alabama ever escorted Negroes in his personal car?

The lawyer tapped the driver on the shoulder. "Let's go, Benjamin," he said. And the car backed out of the lane and returned to the country road. Luther stared out the window as the brown and harvested farm fields flew past. The town, the county seat, was half an hour away. He was lost in his own thoughts and for a moment, didn't realize that Adam was reaching toward him, fascinated by the pins and patches on his uniform. "Come here, boy," said Luther, lifting the toddler from his mother's lap and placing him on his own. The boy fingered the decorations. Luther watched him for a moment, then went back to looking out the window.

Nothing in his life since seeing his parents burned alive had hurt him like the news that some dirty white bastard had raped his only sister, the only family he had in the world. Sitting in that square in that town in Germany, he had cried himself senseless at the thought of it, wept until his fellow tankers grew troubled and came to see about him. When they asked what was wrong, Luther could only lift the letter. Isley, who had delivered it to him, took it and read it aloud to the small knot of men. When he got to the part where Thelma had written, "Your sister was raped," his voice had snagged and he had paused, looking sick.

"Ah, shit, Luther," he said, patting Luther's back heavily. "Ah, shit."

For the first days after he got that letter, Luther had stumbled blindly through his duties, his tank mates watching him with mounting concern. Finally, Sergeant Clinton drew him aside and explained that they understood what he was going through, but he still had to do his job. "The war's almost over," Clinton had said in his soft way, "but that is not the same as being over. You have to buck up, Luther. That's an order."

Luther had nodded and said he understood. What else could he do? He didn't write his sister back immediately. It took him a while to work it out in his mind. At first, the thought of trying to love some half-white baby conceived in rape was too outlandish for him to bear. And he may never have gotten past that point had Thelma's letter not found him while he still had the stink of a death camp in his nostrils.

The sight and smell of all those wretched, tottering creatures, condemned to death—and not just death, but starvation, degradation, and filth along the way, on flimsy charges of creed, religion, and race—had scarred Luther Hayes in a way he thought would probably never heal. And after a few days, it had come to him that his sister was right—indeed, more right than she could ever truly know without being where he had been and seeing what he had seen: there was already too much hatred in the world. Even Luther, who had hated like breathing, who had hated righteously and reverently and with damn good reason, had come to see this.

Look what all that hatred had done. Just look.

He had tried to explain all of this to Thelma when he finally answered her letter. He had written her about what he had seen in the camp, though even as he put the words to paper he was gnawed by the conviction that they were inadequate to the task of making her understand how truly awful it was. But the point, he told her, was that what he had seen made him know he had to do better than hate. The whole damn *world* had to. The alternative was too obscene to contemplate.

And he figured that Adam Mason Hayes was a good place to start.

So yes, he wrote, he would try to love his nephew. He did not know if he could, but he knew that he would try.

"I meant to show you this," Simek was saying to Thelma. He reached into the pocket of his suit, produced a picture, and handed it to her. "This came in the mail yesterday."

"George," she said. There was an unmistakable fondness in her voice that caught Luther by surprise. He glanced over her shoulder at the snapshot. It showed the white marine who had come to their door just before Christmas of 1941 to tell them how Eric had saved his life. He was sitting in a wheelchair. Luther remembered Simon as a callow white boy with a nervous smile. But the thin, unsmiling person who looked out from that picture wasn't a boy at all. Luther recognized that look on his face all too well. He had seen that look on the faces of friends. He had seen that look in his own mirror. It was the look of someone who has seen things he never should have seen, things he will spend the rest of his life trying to forget.

"How is he?" asked Thelma, handing the photo back.

"As well as can be expected, I suppose. He says the doctors are pleased with his progress, at any rate."

"I'm glad to hear that," said Thelma.

"You never gave up on him being alive," Simek said. "You and my wife."

And the look that passed between them then contained something Luther could not quite define. Thelma parried the lawyer's words. "I'm just glad he's coming home," she said.

"Yes," said Simek. "As am I. The happiest moment of my life was when I received the telegram informing me that my boy yet lived. This war has taken so much from all of us. I was thankful that at least it gave me back my son."

The car rolled on in silence. Adam made burbling sounds as he fingered the ruptured duck emblem on Luther's chest. Presently, the town of Stubbs arose on the horizon. They entered it on a residential street of small, weather-cracked shacks pressed too closely together. At the same time, the country lane turned suddenly into bumpy, uneven dirt beneath their wheels. Luther was not at all surprised to see that the toddlers watching from the porch of one of the little houses were all colored.

After a few minutes, the dirt lane turned back into a paved road. It widened out, the ragged bungalows turning into neat little houses with picket fences and Luther saw, again without surprise, that the children and adults watching the passage of the big car were now white. This country missed no chance to express how little it thought of Negroes. He looked over and saw that the lawyer had gone still, his hands resting on the black homburg in his lap, his head up, his eyes staring ahead. Luther tried to emulate what he took as Simek's calm, but couldn't. He felt nervous. This, he reminded himself, was what he had wanted from the night his parents died, what he had bargained with the lawyer for as the price of agreeing to induction into the US Army. It reminded him of the old expression: be careful what you wish for; you might get it.

He was about to get it. He was about to have his reckoning.

Downtown Stubbs, Alabama, was about two blocks long: a tire shop, a couple of restaurants, a thrift store, a druggist, a market, a movie theater, a few storefront lawyers, two churches. At the end of the second block on a street that ran perpendicularly across like the top of a "*T*," stood the only two-story building in town, a shabby, porticoed brick structure with a sign across the top proclaiming it the Stubbs County Courthouse.

A large and restive white crowd milled about in front of the building. There were so many of them that they spilled into the street. Luther was surprised, then realized he shouldn't have been. After all, a county commissioner was going on trial today for killing two Negroes. White people would consider it the most outlandish thing ever, the idea that a powerful public official could be threatened with jail just because of what happened to a couple of niggers over 20 years ago. It would be the best show this side of *Fibber McGee and Molly.* Luther saw heads turning now, people beginning to notice the car as it glided to a stop at the intersection facing the courthouse. His stomach tightened like when Jocko had ordered Lena Horne forward into some strange town, and he could almost smell the krauts all around him.

"Should have left you and the kid at home," Luther told Thelma. She took his hand to reassure him but then, as if to underscore his point, some toothless white woman put her face right up to the window of the big car, shading her eyes with her palm.

"They's niggers inside!" he heard her announce excitedly.

The ripple of anticipation that rose from the crowd chilled Luther's blood. He wished he had his grease gun. He felt vulnerable and exposed.

Simek spoke in a calm, firm voice. "Benjamin, see if there is parking in the rear of the building."

The big Packard moved ahead, even as more people approached, trying to see inside.

"They's a white man in there, too!" someone announced.

"In there with the niggers?" A voice of scandalized disbelief.

The older colored man at the wheel nosed the car ahead through the crowd, and Luther was thankful he didn't stop or pause, just kept moving into the intersection at a slow but steady pace. To stop was to be overrun. Benjamin took a left, then a right up a side street on the west end of the building and another right to bring them up behind it. A few people—children mostly—ran behind the car for a few feet before giving up. Most only followed it with baleful eyes.

To Luther's relief, the crowd in the back of the building was thin and there was, indeed, a parking lot back there. But it was already packed, and when Benjamin turned into it, a uniformed policeman waved him to a stop and motioned for him to crank down the window. He leaned in and told Benjamin, "You can't park here, uncle."

Simek spoke up. "These are the victim's children."

The police officer's eyes went wide at the sight of the white man in the back seat with two Negroes. "What?" he said. He seemed to have momentarily lost all facility for language.

A voice spoke from behind the policeman then. "Let them park, officer. Lord knows I don't want them trying to walk through that crowd out front. Besides, I'd like a word with Mr. Simek there."

The police officer looked behind him, and Luther got a glimpse of a thin, balding white man with an armful of files. His forehead gleamed with sweat. *Sweat.* It was probably 45 degrees out.

"The district attorney," explained Simek. "His name is Horace Mayhew. He is the one prosecuting your case."

The police officer consulted with the DA for a moment. Luther could not make out the words, but the angry tone of the cop's voice was unmistakable. All at once, he wheeled back, jerked his thumb toward a corner of the lot, and spoke in a curt voice. "Double-park it over there," he said. "One of y'all will have to stay with it in case it has to be moved."

They stepped out a moment later, leaving Benjamin behind the wheel. Simek introduced Thelma and Luther to the DA. Mayhew gave them a perfunctory nod, then grabbed Simek's arm. "You see that crowd out front?"

"I saw them," said Simek mildly.

"I never should have let you talk me into this foolishness," said Mayhew, agitation gnawing at his voice.

"But have I not kept my part of the bargain? You will be attending the President's Conference on Crime Prevention. The arrangements have already been made and—"

"Don't give me that crap," snapped Mayhew. "Someone sent a bullet to my office last week, Simek. A *bullet*. With my name on it. My kid is scared to go to school because the other kids pick on him. My wife is scared to pick up the phone for all the death threats. She's talking about leaving me and I don't blame her. Do you know the Klan has put out a wanted poster with my face on it?" Mayhew gave a bitter laugh. "I suppose it's my own fault," he continued. "You suckered me. I agreed to this because I thought going to Washington for that conference of yours would help my career. I was a fool. I have no career now, at least not in Alabama. That's over, but I've accepted it. I'll be lucky to get out of this with my life."

He speared Luther and Thelma with his eyes. "We all will," he said. "Come on."

And so saying, he led them through a side door and up a flight of stairs. They emerged into a crowded hallway. All eyes turned toward them. Luther and his sister followed the lawyer and the DA down a gauntlet of hateful stares. Thelma hugged the baby to her. Even the elaborately bearded and mustachioed 19th-century city founders who watched from portraits on the wall seemed to hate them.

"Nigger soldier."

Someone said this in a soft, raspy whisper of contempt as Luther passed by. Someone else laughed at it. Luther kept his head up and his eyes trained straight ahead. As they approached the courtroom door, a rangy white man in a cheap suit followed by two uniformed prison guards reached for it from the other side. The man hesitated when he caught sight of Luther. Luther paused, too. There was something familiar about this man. Then suddenly, he realized.

"Jeff?" he said.

"Luther?" said the other man.

There was a moment. Luther did not know what to say. The last time he had seen Jeff Orange, Jeff had been a boy—they both had—and Luther's best friend (or so he'd thought) had been holding Mason Hayes's severed finger aloft. Jeff gave an apologetic shrug as if reading Luther's thoughts. He pulled the door open. One of the guards propelled him through it with a shove, then the two of them stepped pointedly in front of Luther, Thelma, and Simek to follow Orange through. One of the guards fixed Luther with a hard glare as he passed.

"Who was that?" asked Thelma as they passed through the door.

"Jeffrey Orange," said Luther. "We played together as boys."

"He is the star witness for the prosecution," said Simek.

Mayhew pointed to a set of stairs leading to a gallery that overlooked the courtroom. A sign on the wall said "Colored."

"You all sit up there," he said.

"I will sit with my clients," Simek informed him.

Mayhew shook his head. "That's for colored only. You have to sit down here."

Simek's jaw jutted forward. "I will sit with my clients," he repeated.

Mayhew shook his head, raised his hands in surrender. "Fine," he said. "Do as you please."

As they watched him walk down to the prosecution table, Simek leaned close to Thelma and Luther. "We should not be separated," he explained.

Luther was pleased by the lawyer's caution. Simek felt the danger, too. They took their seats in the front row of the gallery overlooking a nearly empty courtroom. Mayhew sat below at his table alone, studying documents, occasionally scribbling notes. A bailiff and a court stenographer stood chatting at the railing to the right of the judge's bench. After a few minutes, three white men entered the courtroom, loudly joking, ostentatiously carefree. The man in the middle towered over the other two, a meaty hand on each of their shoulders, face red with laughter. Luther felt his heart kick, for he knew that man immediately. This was the face that had haunted his nights for so many years.

The three took their seats at the defense table. Luther's teeth clamped together, and he had to will himself to remain still. He concentrated on his breathing, on the rhythm of his chest filling and deflating. More than he had ever wanted anything, Luther wanted to be able to take the witness stand, to point his finger at the towering monster and tell the court, tell the world, *There he is, that's the son of a bitch who killed my parents.*

But he could not. He was a Negro. And in Alabama, Negroes did not testify against white men. Thelma turned toward her brother. "Is that him?" she asked.

To Luther's surprise, the answer came from the lawyer, Simek, who sat on the other side of her. "That is Floyd Bitters," he said. "They call him 'Big Floyd.'" He spoke in a soft voice. His eyes watched the big man with an intensity and purpose that caught Luther by surprise. For some reason, Simek hated him, too. In that instant, as if he could feel their eyes upon him, Big Floyd turned and looked up to the gallery. He saw them staring down, and his fleshy face opened in a radiant smile. So much joy beamed from him that you might have thought he was welcoming family at Thanksgiving. Big Floyd lifted one of his big hands in a cheery wave. "Good morning, niggers," he called.

The insult landed like a fist. Luther's breath pushed out of his nostrils in angry gusts. Thelma gripped his wrist hard, knowing what he wanted to do. But Luther willed himself to stillness while Big Floyd laughed. Moments later, the courtroom began to fill. Down below, spectators filed in noisily, chattering, occasionally uttering a sharp bark of laughter. Not a few reached across to the defense table to slap Big Floyd on the back. After a moment, he stood and turned, the better to greet his well-wishers.

By contrast, the colored people filed into the gallery section silently, grimly, women holding their purses in front of them by two hands, men's fingers worrying the battered brims of their hats. They nodded to one another, sat and waited. The jury—all white, all men—was brought into the courtroom a few minutes later. The judge entered promptly as a bell tower clock chimed nine.

And the trial for which Luther had waited more than half his life began.

That first morning was devoted to opening statements. Mayhew promised to show that the defendant had led a mob that committed a gruesome act of murder upon an unoffending Negro couple, robbing two innocent children of their parents. The defense attorney, a rumpled, grandfatherly man named Emmett Wiley, said he would prove Floyd Bitters was the real victim here, a conscientious public servant unfairly slandered by an overzealous prosecutor trying to make his name at the county commissioner's expense.

Mayhew objected to that and the judge, a dour, withered little man behind big, owlish glasses, said, "Keep the blows above the belt, counselor."

Wiley grinned for the benefit of the jurors. "Whatever you say, Your Honor."

Testimony began after lunch. Mayhew called to the stand the now-retired county sheriff, and he established the basic fact of the case: Mason and Annie Hayes were beaten and burned, and died. Under cross-examination by Wiley, the lawman described an investigation which, he said, led him to conclude the murder was the result of a dispute over a card game between Mason Hayes "and some other nigras whose identities we were never able to ascertain."

Card game? Luther's straitlaced father had considered cards to be billboards on the road to hell. Luther rubbed his right fist ceaselessly in the palm of his left hand. On redirect, Mayhew did not bother to hide his incredulity. "So you expect this jury to believe a man and his wife were burned alive over a card game?"

The sheriff gave a laconic shrug. "Well, you seem to think they was burned alive over a hog, Mr. Mayhew," he said, and Mayhew reddened as titters of laughter from the white spectators washed over him. Finally, the judge banged his gavel for order. "All I can tell you," the sheriff continued, "is that there ain't too many forms of devilment I'd put past nigras. Mind you, I'm speakin' as a lawman with 33 years' experience."

And that was the first day. Luther and his sister piled into Simek's big car for the 90-minute journey back to Mobile. White crowds jeered at them and rapped on the hood as the car swung out of the parking lot.

Testimony continued the following morning with Amos Hawley called to the stand. Simek sat up, surprised, as Hawley took his place beside the judge. "I asked him to testify and he refused," he whispered to Luther. "He must have found his courage. Good for him."

Under questioning from Mayhew, Hawley testified how Big Floyd came to his house the night of the lynching and recruited him for what he called "a necktie party."

"He thought that Mason Hayes was too big for his britches," said Hawley. "He said him and some others was goin' out there to teach him some manners."

On cross-examination, the defense attorney got Hawley to admit that

Floyd Bitters had held paper on his farm and had foreclosed on him for nonpayment in 1933.

"It was the Depression," protested Hawley. "Hell, everybody was gettin' foreclosed on. That ain't the reason I come here."

"I'm sure it isn't," said the lawyer, walking away.

That afternoon, Jeffrey Orange took the stand. He testified to having played with Luther Hayes as a child. He gave a recitation of his criminal record. Finally the DA said, "Now, let us talk about August 28, 1923."

For the next two hours, Mayhew led Orange through the events of that evening in painstaking, excruciating detail. Orange spoke of the knock on the door one night when he and his sister were about to say their prayers and of the man who invited their father to help "teach an uppity nigger a lesson." He spoke of how his father not only assented eagerly but also dragged him, his sister, and their mother to the Hayes place, promising them a "real good time." He spoke of seeing the colored man and his wife beaten, then strung up to the tree and set afire. He spoke of how his father gave him the man's finger as a souvenir.

Luther listened, transfixed. Thelma wept quietly, the baby asleep on her lap. The lawyer's face was unreadable.

"Is the man who came to your door that night, the one who led this lynching, in this courtroom today?"

"He sure is," said Jeff Orange.

"Please point him out."

"There he is right there. Sittin' with them two lawyers at the defense table."

A ripple of sound moved through the courtroom. Mayhew said, "Let the record show that the witness has identified the defendant, Floyd Eugene Bitters."

Finally, Mayhew produced a blown-up version of the postcard showing the lynching party clustered around its handiwork, grinning for the camera. He placed it on an easel in front of the courtroom. Luther saw faces wrinkle with distaste. Beside him, Thelma was still weeping. He patted her hand absently, absorbed in the drama unfolding below.

"Now," said Mayhew, "can you tell the court what this is?"

Orange nodded. "That is a picture of all of us gathered that night outside of the Hayes place. Somebody made a postcard out of it. My daddy bought a bunch of 'em and sent 'em out to friends."

"I see," said Mayhew. "And can you identify any of the persons in the photograph?"

"That's me, down front," said Orange, "the little fella with the big grin. That's my mother behind me, my father is third man to the right of me. There's Oscar King. He was a farmer. There's Ross Haig. He was the teacher at the white school. There's Millicent Jefferson; her daughter and my sister was best friends till they moved away."

"What about the defendant? Do you see him in the picture?"

"Oh, yes, sir," said Orange, pointing to a large man who towered over the others, his face opened in a broad smile. "That's him standing in the center, right between the two bodies. He's got a cigar and he's smiling that big smile."

"You're sure?"

"Yes, sir, I'm sure. I'd know him anywhere. That's Big Floyd, all right."

"Thank you," said Mayhew. And then, to the judge: "The prosecution offers this photo into evidence as Exhibit 1."

The judge nodded. "Exhibit 1 is admitted."

Mayhew said, "I have no more questions for this witness." He took his seat.

The defense attorney rose slowly, scratching his head as if confused. "You say you're sure that's my client?"

"Yes, sir."

"Even though it's been 22 years and you were just a boy of nine at the time?"

"Yes, sir."

"Even though, by your very dramatic testimony, it must have been a terribly traumatic night for you? I mean, for a little boy to see such things . . . ?"

Mayhew rose. "The question has been asked and answered, Your Honor."

The judge gestured for Wiley to hurry up. Wiley plucked the blown-up photo from the easel and set it next to the DA's table where the jury could not see it. "Very well," he said. "It's been a long day, Mr. Orange, and I won't keep you. Just a couple of things I want to clear up in my own mind. You say you were a playmate of the little nigra boy who lost his daddy."

"Luther Hayes. Yes, sir."

"So you were friends?"

"Yes, I guess you could say."

"Good friends?"

"I suppose so. We was only boys."

"But you *were* friends. With the nigra?"

Mayhew stood. "Objection. Again, Your Honor: asked and answered."

Wiley raised a hand. "I'll move on, Your Honor." He smiled at Orange. "Could you tell the court again what your current address is?"

Mayhew jumped to his feet. "Objection," he said. "Relevance."

Wiley said, "Goes to credibility, Your Honor. The witness, by his own admission, has a record of larceny and other crimes."

The judge took only a second. "I'll allow it," he said.

Mayhew sank back into his seat. Wiley grinned. "Now, Mr. Orange, would you please tell the jury what is your present address?"

Orange jutted his chin. "Atmore Prison Farm," he said. "Atmore, Alabama."

The attorney nodded and his grin broadened. "Well. I'll let you go," he said, "as I'm sure you're eager to get back there. No further questions, Your Honor."

The prosecution rested. The following morning, the defense began its case. To Luther's disappointment, Floyd Bitters never took the stand. Instead, Wiley called three witnesses, who each testified to having been with Big Floyd on the night of the killing. One said he had been playing gin rummy with him. A retired waitress from one of the local restaurants swore she had served him coffee and pie. A third said there was no way Big Floyd could have gone all the way down to Kendrick to participate in some lynching when he had seen him late that same night, working in his office.

When Mayhew challenged them, demanding to know how they could remember with such specificity the details of a night 22 years in the past, they all gave variations of the same reply. The reason they remembered that night in such detail was precisely because of the Hayes murders.

"It was just such a gruesome thing to hear," said the waitress piously. "That's why I've never forgotten that night."

"What kind of pie did you serve the commissioner that night?" asked Mayhew. His voice was leaden with sarcasm.

The waitress didn't miss a beat. "Rhubarb," she said.

By the time the jury was instructed and sent out to deliberate, it was almost five thirty. "I know it's been a long day, gentlemen," said the judge apologetically, "but I'd appreciate if you could get a little work done tonight and then we'll pick it up again in the morning."

And Luther, Thelma, and Simek went outside to wait. The trial would probably recess within the hour, Simek told them as he lit his pipe. The jurors would be sent home and he and they would drive back down to Mobile one last time and then return in the morning to await the verdict.

Luther nodded. It was dark outside, the air moist with the threat of rain. The streetlights had come on. Standing out there in the parking lot felt good after being shut up in that courtroom all day. Luther and Thelma were leaning against the Packard smoking cigarettes and Mayhew was complaining to Simek about how he would have to leave Alabama after this and start fresh somewhere new when word came that the jury had returned a verdict. Stunned, Luther checked his watch. It was 6:17. The jury had not spent even an hour deliberating. He caught Simek looking at him and he knew. If he'd any doubt in the world, any hope, it was gone. He *knew*.

Back into the courthouse. Back up to the gallery.

The judge: "Have you reached a verdict?"

The jury foreman: "We have, Your Honor."

"In the case of the People v. Floyd Eugene Bitters, how say you?"

Minutes later, Luther pushed his way out of the courtroom with the sound of white people's joy still ringing in his ears. His eyes burned with the image of Floyd Bitters, mobbed by well-wishers, a thicket of hands straining toward him to be shaken or to pat his back in hearty congratulations. At the next table, Horace Mayhew had somberly gathered up his papers and thrown them into his briefcase.

Luther trotted down the stairs and emerged back into the blessed cool. He felt as if he could not get away from this place fast enough. Some young white punk with greasy hair came at him from the right, grabbing two fistfuls of his tunic. "Hey, boy," he said, "lookin' real spiffy there. How's a nigger get a uniform like that?" A short, rodent-faced boy with him laughed. Luther barely broke stride. He shoved the punk roughly off him, wrapped a protective arm around his sister, and kept moving.

Stumbling, the white boy yelled after him in an affronted voice. "Hey, nigger, who do you think you are? Hey, nigger! I'm talking to you!"

"We need to get out of here," said Simek, shepherding Luther and his sister toward the car. Little Adam watched with wide eyes over his mother's shoulder as Thelma leaned into the vehicle.

"Yeah, that's a right good idea, nigger lover!" yelled the white boy. "Get your niggers out of here if you know what's good for you."

Simek whirled, his cheeks flushed. A furious torrent of words erupted from him. "*Ti kis fattyúk!*" he cried, shaking his fist. "*Ti kurafik! Takarodjatok kifelé! Takarodjatok innen, és hagyjatok minket békén!*"

Surprised by the outburst from this always-controlled white man, Luther wrapped a restraining arm around Simek's waist. "Come on," he said. "We got to go."

With a final pugnacious glare at the two punks, Johan Simek allowed himself to be guided toward the car. Luther got in after him.

"What was all that?" Luther asked as the door closed behind them.

"I was uncomplimentary about their mothers," said Simek. And then, to the old man in the front seat, "Benjamin, let's go."

The Packard swung in a wide arc that forced the two punks, still standing there with mouths agape, to jump back. The car dove for the street with enough speed to rock the passengers in the back seat. A left, a left, a right, and they were back on the road out of town. Luther looked behind him. He was not surprised to see two carloads of white men following them, arms sticking out of windows banging the sides of their cars like you would a horse's flanks. He could even dimly hear the shrieks and war whoops.

"We got company," he said, wishing again that he had his grease gun.

"Oh, God," said Thelma, turning to look.

"I see 'em," the old man behind the wheel said grimly.

And the car leapt forward with a sudden force that pressed the passengers back into their seats. The pursuing vehicles tried to stay with them, but they were no match for the Packard's eight roaring cylinders and its 160 galloping horses. By the time the big car was jouncing over the rough dirt ruts of the colored neighborhood, its pursuers were nowhere to be seen.

Simek glanced behind him. "You can slow down, Benjamin," he said. "The hooligans are gone."

"Yes, sir," said the chauffeur. And he eased up on the gas, but only fractionally.

They rode for a few minutes in silence, the night-darkened country fields flying by. Finally, Simek spoke. "I am truly sorry for that," he said. "That trial was a farce. And that verdict . . . " He made a sound of disgust.

Luther shrugged. "This still Alabama," he said. His words carried an acceptance he did not feel.

"Well," said Simek, "there is, at least, a moral victory in all of this. When has a man like Bitters ever had to stand to account for crimes against Negroes? That's something, I think."

Luther shook his head. "It ain't enough," he said.

"Luther!" Thelma was scandalized. "Don't be that way. Mr. Simek did his best."

"I know he did," said Luther. "And I ain't mad at you, Mr. Simek. You kept your end of the bargain. But ain't no way even you could make a jury of 12 Alabama crackers—pardon my language—do right by no dead Negroes."

"No," said Simek with grim resignation. "I suppose there is not."

"All I'm sayin' is, moral victories ain't won the war. Took more than that. Took fighting. Took real victories. And that's what colored people going to need. No more moral victories. Real victories."

"And how will these victories be won?" asked Simek.

Luther grimaced. "Been studying on that," he said. "Ain't figured it out yet, but I will. I ain't fought my way across Europe just to come back here and go back to being somebody's nigger."

"I see," said Simek. He paused thoughtfully. Then he said, "You will do me a favor, Luther?"

"What's that?"

"When you do figure it out, let me know what you intend to do. I would like to help in any way I can."

thirty-seven

It was on December 20 that their orders finally came through. They were to go home. It was all over. With any kind of luck, they might even be home for Christmas.

That afternoon, hopeful, George and Babe took a cab to the Greyhound terminal. That hope died when George stepped out of the vehicle. He saw to his dismay that every sailor, soldier, and marine in the San Francisco Bay area had apparently had the same idea as he and Babe. The line for the ticket counter stretched out the door and down Mission Street. So they waited.

And they waited.

"You ever think about Jazz?" Babe asked this after they had spent an hour moving 20 feet forward.

"All the time."

"You know, I got his records."

"Really?"

"Took 'em out of his seabag, yeah. You remember how guys were when somebody died. Spend 30 seconds in mourning and then go raiding his bag to see how much of his stuff they could snatch. I didn't care so much if they got his razor blades or his socks, but his records . . . "

"Jazz loved his music."

"He sure did. That's why I thought maybe I'd take his records home to his folks. Thought maybe they'd like to have 'em. He was from Indianapolis and that's only a few hours south of Chicago. I was thinking I might drop 'em off on my way home. Be a nice Christmas gift for his family, you know?"

"Yeah."

"I was going to ask if you wanted to come with me," said Babe, "seein' as he was your pal, too." He sighed as he glanced at the interminable line stretching ahead of them. "But I'm guessing I'll have to put it off. I got a feeling we'll be lucky if we can get our own asses home."

It was another hour before they finally reached the ticket booth. A gray-haired woman in cat-eye glasses gave George the news he had dreaded but expected. The earliest he could get a bus to Mobile was January 3. And she couldn't get him to Pensacola, New Orleans, Montgomery, or any other town that was reasonably close.

George felt himself getting desperate. "You think I might have better luck on the train?" he asked.

The woman hunched her shoulders. "I couldn't say, hon, but I doubt it. From what I hear, the trains are just as bad as the buses right now. Lot of people trying to get home for Christmas."

Babe leaned around from behind George. "What about Chicago, doll? You got anything going there?"

She consulted a schedule on a clipboard, hunched her shoulders again. "Chicago's worse than Mobile," she said. "January 5 is the earliest I can get you there."

Babe's grin was almost maniacal. "What about Indianapolis?"

Her head went down to the schedule again. When it came up, she said, "Actually, I could route you boys to Indianapolis. Your first bus leaves in 45 minutes, though."

Babe rapped George's arm. "Don't you see?" he said. "It's kismet. We're meant to go see Jazz's folks together, 'cause we were his best buds. And you never know: maybe you'll have better luck getting a bus from there. Or if you don't, my Uncle Lou can drive down from Chicago and pick us up and you can spend Christmas with me and my folks. I know it won't be the same as being at home, but it sure beats being in a hotel room. What do you say, George?"

What could he say? They bought two tickets.

It took three days to reach Indianapolis. They had to change buses twice. The roads and highways moved at a pace that would embarrass a reasonably athletic snail. Finally, with a wheeze and a sigh, the Greyhound came to a stop beneath a sign that said "Welcome to Indianapolis."

It wasn't until they had gotten off the bus, claimed their bags, and were ready to go see Jazz's folks that Babe and George realized the obvious:

they had no idea where their friend had lived. There followed half an hour of feeding nickels into a pay telephone and calling every Randy, Randolph, Randall, and R. Gibson in the Indianapolis phone book—without success. Babe hung up on the last number and gave a sheepish shrug to indicate that it had been another bust. His tie was askew. The butt of a cigarette hung defeatedly from his lips.

Then, as if suddenly zapped by a cattle prod, Babe sat up straight. He snapped his fingers, dove into the seabag at his feet, and produced Jazzman's 78s. He pulled one of the discs out of its cover and pointed triumphantly. Sure enough, right there on the label, Jazz had written, in his flowing hand, his name and address.

"Too bad you didn't remember that half an hour ago," grumbled George.

Half an hour later, their cab pulled to a stop before a neatly tended wood-frame house. What the two men saw as they peered through the window made them gape in surprise. The father and son untying a Douglas fir from the top of the Ford in the driveway across the street were Negroes. The woman walking home bundled up against the chill with a bag of groceries cradled in her arms was a Negro. The four little girls in winter coats jumping rope on the sidewalk, heedless of the occasional flake of snow floating down upon them, were Negroes.

Babe turned to the driver. "You sure this is the right address?" he asked.

"It's the address you gave me, Mac," the man replied.

Babe looked at George. "What do you think?"

George hunched his shoulders. "You know how much Jazz loved colored music," he said.

"Yeah. But enough to move to a colored neighborhood? That's carryin' love kind of far, don't you think?"

"Maybe. But you know, Jazz was different."

"I suppose," said Babe. He addressed the driver. "Wait for us, pal."

"Sure, but I've got to keep the meter running."

"No problem," said Babe as he stepped out of the car, clutching Jazzman's records to his chest. "We won't be but a moment."

The whole street paused as the two white marines came into view. The woman with the groceries slowed her pace. The father with the Christmas tree stood with one gloved hand plunged deep into its branches but made no move to lift it. The jump rope stopped slapping the pavement in rhythmic time. Babe stage-whispered to George as they made their way up the walk, "They're starin' at us, ain't they?"

George glanced over his shoulder and met the eyes of the woman with the groceries. She immediately became deeply fascinated with the barely there flurries of snow.

"Like a three-headed cat," said George.

They walked beneath the crisp colors of an American flag overhanging the porch. Attached to the front window was another banner—a gold star in a rectangle of white surrounded by a field of red. It symbolized the loss this family had endured. George and Babe removed their hats and regarded the placard silently for a moment. Then Babe knocked on the door. It opened a few moments later upon a handsome older woman, drying her hands on an apron. She had gray hair and a smile warm enough to melt butter. She was a Negro. "Yes?" she said, expectantly.

Babe said, "Beg pardon. We'd like to see the lady of the house, please."

The friendly face stiffened. She drew herself up and spoke with a great, affronted dignity. "I am she," she said.

"There must be some mistake," said Babe, helplessly.

"You think I don't know if I am the lady of my own house?" she asked.

Babe's mouth opened, but it produced no immediate sound. George rescued him. "Beg pardon, ma'am," he said, "my friend didn't mean it like that. This is Stan and my name is George. We served in the Pacific with a guy named Randy Gibson, who gave this as his address. But you see, Randy was white."

Something soft came into her eyes at the mention of the name. "Randy was my son," she said.

This time, it was Babe who had to rescue George from a stunned silence. "But Randy was *white*," he insisted, as if perhaps she had not heard it the first time.

"No," she said, and the affronted dignity had given way to a proud grief, "he wasn't. But after Pearl Harbor, when Randy learned that he had to be white in order to defend his country, that's what he pretended to be."

And now, as both men stood dumbfounded, she looked past them. "Is that your cab?" she asked.

"Yes, ma'am," Babe managed to say.

"Why don't you send him on and you two can have Sunday dinner with us?"

Babe said, "Thank you, ma'am, but we were just going to drop off some of Randy's things and then get on back to the Greyhound terminal to see if we can get a bus home. George here is trying to get down to Mobile and I'm going to Chicago."

"Nonsense," said the woman in a voice that did not brook dispute. "You boys just got back from the Pacific. I'm sure you can't even remember the last time you had a good home-cooked meal. And you were friends with my *son*. You'll have dinner with us and afterward, my husband, Edgar, will take you down to the Greyhound. You," she told Babe, "send the taxi on its way."

Babe looked at George, George looked at Babe. Wordlessly, Babe transferred Jazzman's records to George and went out to tell the cabbie he was no longer needed. George stepped inside. He found himself in a homey living room pleasantly cluttered with framed photos, a Christmas tree strewn with tinsel in one corner. Jazz, handsome in his dress uniform, watched the room from a spot in the center of the mantel.

Arrayed around him were images of people George took to be his sisters and brothers and other kin. The Gibson family, he saw, was a human rainbow, a congregation of ivories and ebonies, tans and reds. George lifted a photo of an impish-eyed man regarding the camera as if trying to decide whether to smile or laugh outright. He could have been Jazz, except that he was older and his skin color, though pale, was identifiably Negro.

The woman came up next to him. "That's Edgar," she said. "That's Randy's father."

"Yeah," said George, "I can tell."

"I know you're wondering," she said, "so I'll tell you: Edgar's father was white. His mother was a maid who worked for the family and, well, you know . . . " Her voice trailed off as if nothing more needed to be said. At that moment, the man from the picture came ambling down the stairs. He wore wire-frame glasses and was nattily dressed in a vest and tie with dark slacks. George was struck again by his resemblance to his son.

"Ida," he said with a tentative smile, "whom do we have here?"

The woman made the introductions, even as Babe struggled through the door, bearing the two seabags. As George took the older man's hand, he heard himself laughing.

Jazzman's parents regarded him with mild confusion. George held up his other hand. "I'm sorry," he said through his chuckles. "I'm just remembering something Jazzman used to always say."

The man cocked an eyebrow. "Jazzman?"

"That's what we used to call Randy, on account of he loved jazz so much. In fact"—remembering the 78s, George transferred them to Jazzman's father, who took them wonderingly and flipped slowly through them with eyes that had turned gentle and reminiscent—"that's the reason we looked you all up, to bring these back to you."

"I see," said the woman, "but what was it Randy said that made you laugh?"

"He used to tell us all the time that he was colored," George laughed. "You remember that?"

"Oh yeah," said Babe, and now he was laughing too. "He said it all the time. 'You white men don't understand my people.' He used to always say that."

This made George laugh harder. He wiped a tear from his eye. "We thought he was kidding!"

"Kidding, hell," said Babe almost helpless with amusement. "We thought he was half-crazy!"

This made Jazz's mother smile and his father laugh out loud. "That sounds like something Randy would have done," the man said. "He loved to joke around."

"Yeah, but this joke was on us," said George. "He was telling us the truth the whole time and we didn't even know it. Right to our faces, he was telling us the truth." He sniffled up the last of his laughter, looked across the room at Babe. "What do you think, Private Budzinski? I think he got us good."

"In more ways than one," said Babe. He chuckled again, shook his head. Then his gaze grew serious. "But you know something?" he said. "I think he was makin' a point, too, even if he was the only one who knew it. Jazz was one of the best marines I ever knew. He shouldn't have had to pretend he was white to serve his country."

"Amen," said George reflectively.

Edgar Gibson nodded, his eyes moist. "Amen," he said. He didn't seem to trust himself with more words just then. None of them seemed to know what else to say. Finally, Jazzman's mother clapped her hands as if breaking a spell. "Why don't you men make yourselves at home?" she said. "I have to see to my dinner."

George had spent the last few months eating in the finest restaurants San Francisco had to offer. But the meal he had that Sunday afternoon in the Gibson home was the best he could remember. It was simple food, well prepared and plenty of it: pork chops, cabbage, macaroni and cheese, mashed potatoes and gravy, yams, and thankfully, not a grain of rice. But it wasn't just the food that made the meal memorable. Jazz had three older sisters and they came by for Sunday dinner with their husbands and children. He also had two younger brothers, rambunctious boys who were soon roughhousing about with their young nieces and nephews, necessitating several stern warnings from their parents and grandparents that Santa Claus tended to bypass the homes of naughty boys. Once or twice, one of the fathers had to gesture toward his belt to restore peace. The three husbands were veterans, too—all Army, so there was a banter of friendly interservice rivalry with the two outnumbered marines.

The family's dining table was large, though not large enough to accommodate so many people. But George and Babe were given seats of honor, and those family members who couldn't find places at the table stationed folding chairs at the edge of the room or ate standing in doorways just to hear the conversation. To uproarious laughter, Babe and George talked about Jazzman's habit of using every available surface as a drum or breaking the tension with words of wisdom from Duke Ellington or Jimmie Lunceford.

As Jazzman's records played on a phonograph in the background, the family told stories about him. It turned out he had, indeed, been a talented drummer, though never in Harlem as he had claimed. He had wanted to go, planned to go, but then Pearl Harbor happened and everything changed. "My son," said Edgar Randall Gibson, Sr., in a proud, quiet voice, "felt he had to do his bit." Beside him, his wife nodded.

It was dark, the lights on the tree winking off and on, when the party broke up and Edgar drove the two marines to the Greyhound station. He shook their hands with feeling as they stood together beside the car. "Thank you," he said, cold smoke leaking from his mouth. "You brought Randy home to us and that was the best Christmas gift you could have given."

"It was an honor, sir," said George. "Your son was a great guy."

The older man's eyes turned reflective. He gave a short, sharp nod and got back in the car. Probably, thought George, he didn't want them to see him weep.

"Good people," said Babe, as they hoisted their seabags and watched the man drive away.

"Yeah," said George.

"Wasn't that something about Jazz? Being colored, I mean? Would you have ever guessed?"

"Not in a million years."

They only had to wait an hour to reach the ticket window. Babe was able to catch the last seat on a bus bound for Chicago, though it wouldn't leave until six in the morning. He resigned himself to sacking out in the depot. George was not so lucky. "Sorry, hon," said the woman behind the counter. "There's a bus leaving for Mobile in 10 minutes, but it's full."

"There's no way you can get me on it?" George asked. "I'll ride in the luggage rack." He was only half joking.

She gave an apologetic smile. "Sorry," she said.

"Yeah."

"Look," said Babe as George turned away from the counter, "why don't I cash in my ticket? I'll call my Uncle Lou and he can come get the both of us. Like I said, you're welcome to spend Christmas with my folks and me."

George didn't want to accept. Babe was his friend and George was sure his family were good people. But he had not been home for three years and he had lived in hell for the last two. And damn it, he wanted to be home. *His* home. You were supposed to be *home* at Christmas.

But what choice did he have? George sighed. "Sure, Babe," he said, hoping he did not sound as defeated as he felt. "Thanks."

And that was when an older man with owlish glasses and a professorial moustache approached them. "Excuse me?" he said.

"Yes?" said George.

"I'm sorry; I could not help but overhear. You're the one trying to get to Mobile?"

"Yes, sir, that's me."

"Then I want you to have this," said the man and he placed a rectangular piece of paper into George's hand.

George gaped at it in surprise. It was a ticket for the bus that was, at that moment, boarding for Mobile.

"What is this?" asked George, stupidly.

The man smiled. "It's a ticket for that bus out there."

"I know that," said George. "What I mean is, I can't take this. This is yours."

"You can take it, and you will," said the man firmly.

"But it's your own ticket," insisted George.

"Son, I can delay my trip. It doesn't matter to me. But you're a serviceman trying to get home for Christmas. That's far more important than my travels. You and all those other gallant men, you saved the whole world. You should at least be able to enjoy the first Christmas of peace at home."

"But I can't—"

Babe cut him off. "George," he hissed, "don't insult the man. Take the ticket."

A voice on the loudspeaker said, "Last call for Louisville, Kentucky; Nashville, Tennessee; and Huntsville, Birmingham, Montgomery, and Mobile, Alabama."

George said again, "I can't—"

The man said, "*Please* take the ticket, son. It would make me very proud if you did."

George dropped his seabag, reached for his wallet. "At least, let me pay you."

The man's eyes widened, horrified at the thought. "No," he said. He held up his hands and backed away. Safely beyond the reach of George's money, he paused. "Don't miss the bus, son," he said. "Merry Christmas." And he walked away.

"Wow," said George. "Wow." He stared after the man for a long moment. Babe broke the trance.

"'Wow' nothing. You'd better move your ass, George, or you're going to miss the bus!" And sure enough, George saw, through the glass doors of the depot, the bus idling in its bay, the driver standing there accepting a ticket from a lone passenger. All the others were apparently aboard.

George hoisted his seabag and reached out his hand. Babe took it. "Babe," said George, and then he stopped, because he didn't know what else to say.

Babe smiled. "I know, buddy," he said. His voice was husky. "Me, too."

And that was enough. Or at least, it would have to be. The driver was turning to board his bus. George nodded to his friend, wheeled about, and hustled out to the bay, calling out to the driver. He stowed his seabag in the luggage compartment beneath the bus, climbed on, and made his way to the only available seat—a window in the back directly in front of the toilet. He took it gladly.

Babe came out and waved. George waved back. Then the bus door closed with a hiss. George leaned back in his seat and watched as Indianapolis slid away.

The trip was a blur of bus stations and traffic jams, intermittent snow and good-natured crowds. Servicemen were everywhere. They filled the lobbies of the bus stations. They crowded the counters of the coffee shops. They stood in line at the taxi stands, some holding teddy bears as large as small children, others hoisting brightly wrapped packages. Office buildings were festooned with floodlit signs. "Welcome Home" they said. At every stop, volunteers served coffee and doughnuts to men in uniform. Holiday lights made cheery little holes in the darkness. And everywhere George traveled, all through that long, crowded night, people seemed to be in a good mood. They smiled easily and laughed often. They tipped their hats and allowed the other guy to go first.

He reached Mobile 17 hours after he started out from Indianapolis. It was two o'clock in the afternoon on Christmas Eve. George thumbed through a newspaper in the back of the cab on the way home. He found it full of advertisements that weren't selling anything. Stores and banks and auto dealerships had taken out space just to speak of gratitude, just to offer prayers, just to say Merry Christmas.

George's keys had been sent home with the rest of his effects when the military declared him KIA, so he had to knock at the door. Benjamin answered. The old man's eyes widened in surprise, then filled with tears. When Mother called from the west parlor to ask who was at the door, Benjamin couldn't respond, so she came to investigate for herself. She shrieked when she saw him standing there, and this brought the whole family running. Even Nick was there, having managed to wangle leave from Tokyo. It took a full five minutes for George to disentangle himself from Mother, and when he did, the front of his shirt was as damp from tears as if he had just come in out of the rain. Then the rest of his family had their turns. Father shook his hand solemnly, his lips pursed, his eyes glistening. Nick slapped his back; the hero-worshipping little brother George remembered had grown a foot and now carried himself with a marine's unmistakable bearing. Cora flung her arms around his neck and kissed his cheek repeatedly. She had become a young woman. She was even wearing lipstick now. *Lipstick!* And was that a promise ring on her finger? What boy had given her that?

"Why didn't you tell us you were coming home?" asked Mother, finally regaining her composure.

"I didn't know if I was going to be able to make it," explained George, "and I didn't want you all getting excited for nothing. Traffic all over the country is murder."

They retired to the west parlor. Alice brought a tray of pastries and tea. She kissed George's cheek as she left the room. "So happy to have you back," she said. As the sun made its long, slow fall, they talked excitedly, bringing one another up to date on their lives. George felt almost as if he were awake inside a dream, walking knowingly through something that was not real and could not be. Except that it was. He had to remind himself of that every few minutes.

It *was* real. It was.

After a couple of hours, Cora begged Mother to play Christmas carols the way she always had on Christmas Eve when they were children and the family gathered around and sang together as they had for as long as George could remember. And Father sang off-key as he always did, and his children made the same jokes about it that they always made. Except that this time, George paid attention to it, caught himself in the act of enjoying it. He had lived this moment a hundred times, but he knew the very familiarity of it was a sacrament.

Probably, he realized with a start, this was the last time it would ever be like this, just the five of them, all together for Christmas. Cora was going away to school and would probably be getting married to whomever had put that ring on her finger. Nick would be going wherever the Marines told him to go.

And him? What would he be doing?

George had no idea.

After another hour, Benjamin tapped Cora and told her she had a call and she flounced from the room to take it. Mother excused herself to go check something in the kitchen. George took that opportunity to slip out the front door and stand beneath the portico. Darkness had pulled itself halfway across the sky. In the distance, streetlights were beginning to wink on. There was a slight crispness in the air. George breathed it gratefully.

After a moment, the door opened behind him. "Am I interrupting?" asked Father, coming to stand beside him. He was packing tobacco into his pipe.

"No," said George. "I was just thinking."

"I would imagine it's all a bit overwhelming," said Father.

"It is."

A silent moment passed.

George said, "I'm sorry things didn't go the way you wanted with that lynching case." Father had written him about the acquittal of Floyd Bitters.

"I am, too," said Father. "But some good may come of it yet. Luther Hayes and I are collaborating to push for anti-lynching legislation. I want to see if we can get hearings before Congress."

"Collaborating?"

"I'll do the lobbying, of course. But I want *him* to tell the story. He can do it in such a way that they will have no choice but to listen."

"I see," said George.

His surprise must have shown, because Father smiled. "I agree, it's not the sort of thing you would expect me to be involved with. But I suppose I've changed some these last few years."

"We all have," said George.

"You know, his sister never gave up on you being alive."

"Thelma?"

Father nodded. "Even when I did, she—and your mother, of course—never did. She simply would not accept it."

George felt something kick him hard inside his chest. He ignored it. "Father, tell me something." His father, who was touching flame to the bowl of his pipe, lifted his eyebrows in response. "Johan Simek? Why did you go back to using that name?"

Father exhaled a stream of smoke. His smile was meditative. "You know, I have been asked that many times, including by your mother, and I usually make a joke of it or say that I just began feeling sentimental. But you, I will tell the truth. When I went up to Kendrick to investigate what I might be able to do for Luther, that Floyd Bitters beat me up pretty good."

Whatever he saw on George's face caused Father to nod. "Yes," he said.

"I was talking to a waitress at the local diner and a touch of my accent, that accent I had worked so hard to lose, somehow came through. She asked where I was born and I told her. She or one of the men loitering in the diner must have relayed it to Bitters. I went out to see the house where the lynching took place and he was waiting for me when I returned and he knocked me down. He stomped my chest and broke my ribs. I will never forget what that man said to me, George. He said, 'You come up here in your fancy suit, pretending you're a white man. You are not a white man. You just look like one.'"

Johan Simek turned toward his son. "I stood there with blood and dirt on my face, barely able to breathe. I heard him say this, and George, all I could think of was you. It was as if a light went on in my head. I had always hated it so much when they called us 'bohunks' and 'hunkies.' I had worked so hard to become a white man in America. I had wanted it so badly that I would even manipulate my own son into a loveless marriage. And lying there at the feet of that man, hearing him tell me I was only pretending to be white, I suppose I had a revelation. And I asked myself: What is white, really, and why did I need it so much? Why was it not enough simply to be a man, and good? So I decided that is what I will henceforth strive to be. Just a man, and good."

Father's eyes were shining. George didn't know what to say. Father put his pipe in his mouth and turned away. From inside the house, George heard Mother start playing the piano again. He looked through the beveled glass in one of the panels flanking the door and could make out the shadows of his brother and sister standing before the giant Christmas tree. Its lights had been turned on, their glow rendered soft and indistinct by the prismatic window. Cora and Nick were singing "Joy to the World."

A year ago, standing knee-deep in muck beneath the benjo, this moment had been a thing too absurdly wonderful to dream. It was what he had striven for, strained toward, all the miles from San Francisco to here. It was the whole world. It was everything he wanted.

And it wasn't enough.

The realization stunned him. It wasn't nearly enough.

"Father," he heard himself say, "I have to go."

Father beheld him with an expression that contained no surprise. Then Father nodded. "I'll tell your mother you'll be back after a while," he said.

George nodded back, barely hearing. He went back through the house, down the hallway separating west parlor from east, through the kitchen where Alice was stirring a pot and Benjamin was sitting at the table. He ignored their surprised glances and went out into the garage. The keys to the little car he had received for a graduation gift, the one he had almost never driven, were right where they should have been, on a peg just inside the garage door, as if waiting for him. The car itself was freshly waxed, and when he started it up, he found that it had a full tank of gas.

Thank you, Benjamin.

Five minutes later, George Simon was driving through the city of his birth. Trees and homes were festooned with lights. Walkers were few. Traffic was thin. The city was quiet. *How still we see thee lie*, he thought, randomly. *The hopes and fears of all the years . . .*

He steered east and south across the city, drove until the houses were smaller, the streets dark and unpaved, the lights of Christmas few or none. And he parked in front of the house he had first come to four Christmases ago when his hip was smashed and he was still a simple man who lived by simple beliefs in a much simpler world.

George walked up to the front door. He had no idea what he was doing. He only knew that he had to do it. George paused, took a deep breath, knocked.

A moment later, the door opened. Luther was standing there. He wore a tank top undershirt, and a cigarette drooped from his lips.

George held up his hands. "I don't want to fight with you," he said.

Luther's expression might have been a smile. "We ain't got nothin' to fight about," he said. And then he called his sister's name.

She appeared a moment later, drying her hands on a dish towel. She was wearing an apron and sweating. Her dark hair had been gathered in a haphazard ponytail, from which half of it seemed to have escaped.

She was beautiful.

"George," she said, surprised.

"Hi," he said.

"I didn't know you were back."

"I just got back today. Listen . . . I know this is . . . I mean . . . " He had to pause because his throat had become painfully dry. He coughed. "What I mean to say is, would you like to go for a ride with me?"

George died a thousand times in the two seconds that she paused. Finally, she said, "Okay. Just let me get my coat."

She closed the door. After a few minutes, she opened it again. She was bundled for the light chill. She had tamed the ponytail. And in her arms she was carrying a toddler, a pale-skinned little boy, almost swallowed up in his coat.

George heard Luther speak from inside the house. "I can watch him if you want," he said.

Thelma glanced back at her brother. "No. I'll take him with me," she said.

"Are you sure?" called Luther's voice.

She was looking at George now, her gaze steady and direct. "I'm sure," she said. And she closed the door behind her. The boy snuggled against his mother and regarded the stranger curiously. "Who's this?" asked George.

"This is my son," said Thelma.

George's heart stuttered. "Your son?"

A nod. "His name is Adam. He's almost two." And then, to the boy: "Adam, this is my friend, Mr. George. Can you say hi?"

The boy stared with solemn eyes that did not blink. He said nothing.

George swallowed. "You're married now?"

She paused, looking up at him. "No," she said. "I was . . . assaulted." She covered the boy's ear. "Adam was the result."

"Jesus," said George. "How . . . what . . . ?"

"I know," she said. "It's a lot to take in. And I'll tell you all about it, I promise. But not tonight, all right? It's Christmas Eve."

It took a moment. Then he nodded. "Yes," he said, "of course."

They walked to the car, and he held the door for her. He slid in behind the steering wheel, cranked the engine. Then he turned to her, stricken all over again by the awful weight of what she had said. He spoke hesitantly. "But Thelma, are you . . . okay?"

She considered the question for a moment. Then she said, as if the realization and the words had come to her at the same time, "Yes, I am. I really am."

George nodded. He pulled away. They drove the dark streets in silence. He still had no idea what he was doing, nor any clue how to do it. He tried to think of what to say, but his mind was fresh snow. He glanced over and saw that the boy was still watching him. He had his mother's eyes.

After a moment, Thelma said, "So what are you going to do, now that you're back?"

George shrugged. "I don't know," he said.

But just then, he did know.

"Maybe the seminary," he said. "That was my goal before the war and I put it aside. But I think that's what I'd like to do."

"You'd make a good preacher," she said.

"I don't know about that," he told her. "I lost my faith for a while there. With everything I was going through, it was kind of hard to see the hand of God. I didn't know if I believed in Him anymore."

"So what changed your mind?"

He considered this a moment. Then he said, "I saw so much evil while I was over there. I saw so much hate. And I *felt* so much hate. You almost had to feel hate in order to survive. It just seems to me that where there is so much hate, there has to be a corresponding love—there *has* to be, even if sometimes we can't see it or make sense of it." He hunched his shoulders. "At least, that's what I think."

She regarded him for a moment, then looked forward as they drove. "Yes, you'll be a good preacher," she said.

George felt himself blushing. "What about you?" he asked. "What are you going to do?"

"I'm going to school," she said, "with the money I've saved."

"Really? What are you going to—"

She cut him off. "Law," she said. "I'm applying to college and when I get my degree, your father has promised to help me find a good colored law school."

For a moment, he was flabbergasted beyond speech. A woman? As a lawyer?

"What do you think?" she asked. Her voice was carefully neutral.

"I think . . . " He paused, glanced over at her. The tone of her voice belied the earnestness in her eyes. "I think that's wonderful," he said. "I think it's great."

And she smiled.

George drove without a conscious destination in mind. After a moment, he realized that his aimlessness had brought him to Bienville Square. And that seemed appropriate. The stores were closing up, a few last-minute shoppers were rushing to their cars. The trees were bright with lights.

He pulled up to the curb. "Let's take a walk," he said.

"George, I can't. You know I can't."

It took him a moment to understand exactly what she meant, and when he did, it made him furious at the whole misbegotten world. "Yes you can," he said in a firm voice. "The hell with them."

He got out of the car and came around to open her door. He offered his hand, but she didn't take it. She hesitated. Then she climbed out on her own, struggling a little under the toddler's weight. They stood there a moment, taking it all in. And then they walked into the Square beneath a canopy of white Christmas lights. George led her to a bench facing a department store window across the street. The display showed a train endlessly looping a track to the delight of a mannequin boy in an engineer's hat. Next to him, his mannequin sister cuddled a doll with pink skin and curly blonde ringlets. Above the window hung a metal sign depicting a rosy-cheeked Santa Claus drinking Coca-Cola. George's heart was full, but once again, his mind had gone empty. There was so much he needed to say, but he did not know the words. His mouth felt rusted shut like the metal man in *The Wizard of Oz.*

"What's she doing here?"

George looked up. A portly white man glowered down on them, a finger pointing to Thelma like dog shit on a sidewalk. George saw Thelma lower her head.

Fury yanked him to his feet. He put his nose a half inch from the other man's and yelled in his face. "What's she doing here? What are *you* doing here? She's a human being and she's taking the air in a public park, that's what she's doing! If you don't like it, you can go to hell. You think I just spent three years fighting the Japanese master race so I could come home and have to fight the white cracker master race?"

"George . . . "

Thelma called from somewhere behind him, but her voice was small against the thunder in his head. George grabbed the stunned man by the collar.

"People like you make me sick!" he cried. "There's a whole world out there, full of all different kinds of people, and most of 'em, they just want the same thing anybody else wants. But people like you just can't see it. You're too busy staring down at your own bullshit lives, your bullshit hate! You need to look up sometimes. Goddamn it, just look *up* for a change!"

"George . . . " It was Thelma again. She had his arm and was tugging it. George glared at the portly man, whose eyes had gone wide in a face that was slack and pale. George shoved him back. The man stumbled. Then he gathered himself and walked away at a quick step, glancing over his shoulder once to make sure George wasn't following. George scowled after him, his chest heaving. Finally, he allowed Thelma to lead him back to the bench and they sat. They didn't speak. George was conscious of Thelma and her son staring at him. He gazed down as if the mysteries of the universe might be locked in the pavement at his feet. He had never felt like such a fool. He tried to think of how he could extricate himself from this moment with whatever remained of his dignity.

Then, a sound of childish delight. "Look." George lifted his eyes. Thelma's son had just noticed the window display. He was pointing a chubby finger and his whole face was alive with excitement.

"That's a choo choo," Thelma told him in a cooing voice. "You want to see the choo choo?"

She was speaking to the boy, but her eyes were on George, luminous and filled with some question he could not define. But he nodded just the same. "Let's go see the choo choo," he said. And they crossed the empty street to the department store window. There, they stood for a long time, framed together in the light from the window, the little boy laughing, transfixed.

All around them, the world had gone still. Nothing moved, except the train continuing its endless loop and the Santa Claus sign creaking gently in the breeze.

acknowledgments

VIRTUALLY EVERY BOOK IS MADE UP OF OTHER BOOKS—NOT TO mention films, institutions, and people—that lent the author expertise, inspiration, or some other assistance. That is truer of this book than of any other I've ever written. From conception to publication, so much went into this novel that I couldn't begin to tell you. But I'm here to give it the old-school try, just the same.

Bear with me, then, as I give credit where it is due and also point out a few of the places where history and this piece of historical fiction diverge.

I will begin with David Alsobrook and Scotty Kirkland, who were, at the time I was researching this book, the director and the curator, respectively, of the History Museum of Mobile. Both men were more than generous with their time and knowledge. Thanks to them, I left Mobile with a copy of the government-produced short documentary *War Town*, about Mobile during World War II. They also assembled for me a trove of documents and clippings, including a 1972 master's thesis by one Boyte Austin Preswell, which proved invaluable in painting a picture of African-American life in Mobile during the war.

While in Mobile, I drove over to Pinto Island, where ADDSCO used to be, though little sign of it remains. The riot there is a matter of historical fact, though it's heavily fictionalized here. I also took the opportunity to visit the USS *Alabama* memorial park to tour the old warship.

Speaking of ships: *Trapped at Pearl Harbor: Escape from Battleship Oklahoma* by Stephen Bower Young was my bible when constructing the opening chapter of this book. The attack on George's unnamed ship and the experiences of the men trapped in steering aft are based on what happened in real life aboard the *Oklahoma*, as recounted in meticulous detail by Young.

And from the "small world" department: after I had tried without success to reach the author to ask him to clear up some technical details, I was happily surprised to discover that he was a high school classmate of a guy named Andre Anderson, with whom I went to college. I'm indebted to Andre for making the introduction and to Young for graciously answering my questions.

Another friend, John Dolen, enlisted an Australia-born friend of his, Dennis DeRome, to help me nail down some questions about Aussie slang.

Dr. S. J. Rao patiently answered my grisly questions about how to saw off a human head.

Lauren Pearson Riley of the American Academy of Orthopaedic Surgeons connected me with Dr. Scott Gordon, who enthusiastically helped me devise a medically acceptable way for a fit young marine like George to end up with a hip fracture.

Rev. R. Joaquin Willis and my brother-in-law, Rev. Robert Davis, helped me think through George's struggles with his loss of faith.

My portrait of the 761st Tank Battalion is mostly based on three books: *Brothers in Arms: The Epic Story of the 761st Tank Battalion, WWII's Forgotten Heroes* by Kareem Abdul-Jabbar and Anthony Walton; *The Black Panthers: A Story of Race, War, and Courage* by Gina M. DiNicolo; and *Patton's Panthers: The African-American 761st Tank Battalion in World War II* by Charles W. Sasser. Colonel Paul Bates was a real man. So was Charles Wingo, the Negro-hating major who fled from battle. The attempted mutiny led by Luther and Books is loosely based on an actual episode recounted by Abdul-Jabbar and Walton.

And here I should also note that the Panthers' liberation of a concentration camp is a matter of some historical dispute. Some say it never happened. Indeed, DiNicolo writes that "no evidence of interaction with a concentration camp appears in the primary-source material" used for her book.

On the other hand, Abdul-Jabbar and Walton, along with Sasser, describe elements of the 761st's liberation of concentration camps in their books. And in the 1992 documentary *Liberators: Fighting on Two Fronts in World War II*, aging tankers and aging concentration camp survivors also recall the day the 761st set suffering Jews free.

Here's my bottom line: this is a work of historical fiction, not history. I needed the liberation to happen, so it did.

The prison camp at Nagasaki was real, though as described by at least one survivor, the conditions there were relatively—repeat: *relatively*— humane in comparison with those at other camps. Which left me with a dilemma. I needed the camp where George is interned to be at Nagasaki so that it could be in the path of the atomic bomb. But having been mesmerized and appalled by the hell that historian Gavan Daws describes in his book *Prisoners of the Japanese: POWs of World War II in the Pacific*, I didn't want to give a false impression of what the typical POW endured.

So for the record, the actual prison camp at Nagasaki may or may not have been as bad as the one depicted in this book. But the average camp was much, much worse. A rereading of *Unbroken: A World War II Story of Survival, Resilience and Redemption*, Laura Hillenbrand's riveting recounting of the life of former POW Louis Zamperini, was also useful in this regard. If you haven't read that book, you should.

You might also want to pick up *Christmas 1945: The Story of the Greatest Celebration in American History* by Matthew Litt, a vibrant and joyous depiction of that first Christmas of peace. It will make you smile.

Here are some of the other books I leaned on in crafting this book:

Guadalcanal by Richard B. Frank

An Illustrated Encyclopedia of Uniforms of World War II by Jonathan North and Jeremy Black

Mobile: The New History of Alabama's First City edited by Michael V. R. Thomason

Forth to the Mighty Conflict: Alabama and World War II by Allen Cronenberg

Nazi Prisoners of War in America by Arnold Krammer

Battleship Oklahoma BB-37 by Jeff Phister, with Thomas Hone and Paul Goodyear

The Road to Victory: The Untold Story of Race and World War II's Red Ball Express by David P. Colley

Hit Hard by David J. Williams

The 761st "Black Panther" Tank Battalion in World War II by Joe Wilson, Jr.

Cassell's Dictionary of Slang by Jonathon Green

Australian Slang: A Dictionary by David Tuffley
The Essential Lingo Dictionary of Australian Words and Phrases by
    John Miller
Panther vs. Sherman: Battle of the Bulge 1944 by Steven J. Zaloga
*Hiroshima Diary: The Journal of a Japanese Physician, August 6–
    September 30, 1945* by Michihiko Hachiya, MD
World War II Day by Day by DK Publishing
Pearl Harbor Christmas: A World at War, December 1941 by Stanley
    Weintraub
Helmet for My Pillow: From Parris Island to the Pacific by Robert
    Leckie
With the Old Breed: At Peleliu and Okinawa by E. B. Sledge
*Voices of the Pacific: Untold Stories from the Marine Heroes of World
    War II* by Adam Makos, with Marcus Brotherton
A Doctor's War by Aidan MacCarthy
First into Nagasaki by George Weller
"The Good War" by Studs Terkel
Day of Infamy by Walter Lord
Severed: A History of Heads Lost and Heads Found by Frances Larson
Hiroshima by John Hersey
*Prisoner of Japan: A Personal War Diary, Singapore, Siam and
    Burma, 1941–1945* by Sir Harold Atcherley
The Caine Mutiny by Herman Wouk (I read Wouk's novel to get a
    sense of shipboard life from a writer who had lived it.)
At Dawn We Slept: The Untold Story of Pearl Harbor by Gordon W.
    Prange
Double Victory: A Multicultural History of America in World War II
    by Ronald Takaki
Women of the Homefront by Pauline E. Parker
*Our Mothers' War: American Women at Home and at the Front
    During World War II* by Emily Yellin

I watched a few movies and television series, too, both documentaries and fictionalized accounts. They included *Fury*; *The Pacific*; *Band of Brothers*; *Tora! Tora! Tora!*; *The War*; *Birth of Victory*; and *Battlefield: "Guadalcanal."*

I am also indebted to Kelly and Cheryl Harris (my cousin and his wife, both lawyers, who helped me craft the courtroom scenes and did some research into Alabama law); Paul Taylor of the Communication and Outreach Division, Naval History and Heritage Command; Chuck Melson, chief historian, United States Marine Corps; Paul J. Weber, deputy director, History Division, Library of the Marine Corps University in Quantico, Virginia; Megan Lewis of the United States Holocaust Memorial Museum in Washington, DC; Douglas E. McIntosh, a history professor who answered my panicked online all-call for anyone with military expertise who might be able to assure me that I wasn't making a complete botch of this; Chris Graham of the American Veterans Center; Patrick K. O'Donnell, an author on military history who gave me some pointers for the tank battle depicted here; the National Museum of the Marine Corps in Triangle, Virginia; the AAF Tank Museum in Danville, Virginia; the National WWII Museum in New Orleans; American Language Services, which provided the Hungarian and Japanese translations; the Library of Congress, where I sat in the periodicals reading room immersed in old issues of the *Mobile Register*, and then trucked over to the map room where the staff helped me get a sense of Honolulu circa 1941.

Finally, to the home team.

I thank Judi Smith for her eagle-eyed proofreading and policing of extraneous commas, which is especially remarkable given that she had to read some of the more gruesome passages of this book through the fingers covering her eyes.

I thank my longtime agent, Janell Walden Agyeman, as always, for her quiet grace and ability to remain centered and optimistic, even when crazy is breaking out all around.

I thank my editor, Doug Seibold, who did a yeoman's work on this one, pushing me to sharpen characterizations, clarify motivations, and streamline plot.

I thank my wife, Marilyn, for the fact that she couldn't even look at me for two days after she read what happens to Thelma—"How could you do that to my girl?"—in the bottom of the unfinished ship. Her being ticked off at me was a high compliment and a needed assurance that I was building something here that had emotional heft and dimension.

I also thank my wife for eventually forgiving me. And for loving me as I have loved her through five kids, 13 grandkids, and 37 years of matrimony.

For all of them, for all of this, and for all of you, I thank God.

about the author

LEONARD PITTS, JR., is the author of the novels *Grant Park*, *Freeman*, and *Before I Forget*, as well as two works of nonfiction. He is a nationally syndicated columnist for the *Miami Herald* and the winner of the 2004 Pulitzer Prize for Commentary, in addition to many other awards. Born and raised in Southern California, Pitts now lives in suburban Washington, DC.

reading group guide

This is a discussion guide for *The Last Thing You Surrender* by Leonard Pitts, Jr. It includes suggested discussion questions, which may help spark new and interesting conversations in your reading group.

1. Thelma and George, despite their many differences, find that they have a natural ease in talking to and confiding in one another. Why is it easier for them to talk to each other than to their family members?

2. In discussing Babe's actions against the Japanese soldiers' corpses (page 290), George explains, "What scares me isn't that I couldn't do what you did. What scares me is that I *could*." Do we all carry the capacity for cruelty? Do you find Babe to be a sympathetic character? Why or why not?

3. Pick a chapter that stands out to you. What elements make it memorable?

4. On page 408, Books explains how much he has endured in the war "all in service to this ideal they call America. I do not know exactly what will happen after this, but I do know that I have more than earned my piece of that ideal." If Books were alive today, would he be satisfied with his piece of the American "ideal"?

5. After killing Earl Ray, Flora Lee sits and waits for the police. Why does she not try to flee?

6. On page 245, the narrator says, "George was good, good in a way John never had been and never would be. It wasn't that John saw himself

as a bad man. Rather, he was just a man, a mostly decent man in his own estimation, but a man who also recognized in himself a share of selfishness and pride that are to be found in most men." What is the difference between a good man and a decent man? By the end of the story, does George's father become the type of man he wants to be? Why or why not?

7. Who, if anyone, is the moral authority in the Hayes family?

8. Thelma names her child Adam, after "the man in the Bible who was the first, who was new, who came into a world without history. She would try to raise this boy without history because history, she knew, might crush him. It might crush them both" (page 416). Give examples of other characters who are haunted by their history.

9. Thelma and Flora Lee's friendship is complicated and dangerous for both women. Discuss the ways their struggles are the same and the ways they are different.

10. The book's portrait of the 761st Tank Battalion is based on real events and real people. Had you heard of the Black Panthers before reading this book? Why do so many portrayals of World War II focus solely on the contributions of white soldiers?

11. Explore the book's main themes—morality, humanity, discrimination, survival—in the context of today's world, rather than World War II. What has changed? What has stayed the same?

12. Andy and George take enormous risks to carry out theft, sabotage, and other acts of defiance. What benefit do they derive from defiance that is worth risking so much?

13. Describe the character of Franklin "Books" Bennett at the beginning of the war and at the end of the war. How do his ideals change, and why?

14. Many characters struggle with their own identities and the identities of others. Discuss the differences in the ways Earl Ray Hodges, Johan Simek, and Randy "Jazzman" Gibson view the question of identity in America.

15. Nearly every character undergoes profound changes during the war. Who changes the most, and in what ways? The least?

16. When Makoto Fujikawa sends George to the POW camp instead of killing him, he says, "What I did was not generous, but selfish. It was for me, not for you" (page 359). What does Fujikawa gain from it?

17. On page 498, while reflecting on the war, George says, "I saw so much evil while I was over there. I saw so much hate. And I *felt* so much hate. You almost had to feel hate in order to survive. It just seems to me that where there is so much hate, there has to be a corresponding love—there *has* to be, even if sometimes we can't see it or make sense of it." Do you agree?

18. This book contains scenes of great violence and cruelty, usually inflicted by one group of people against another. What do you think the author sees as the common element that allows one group of people to be so violent and cruel toward another group?

19. Discuss the similarities in what Thelma, Luther, and George endure during the war, despite their disparate settings.

20. In a letter to George on page 291, Thelma writes, "You may have to give up your faith and your hope, George. You may even have to give up your life. But if it's at all possible, you hold on to your decency. You make sure your decency, your *humanity*, is the very last thing you give up. Because without it, I don't think the rest matters too much." By the war's end, which characters have managed to hold on to their humanity?